THE MAIDEN'S WAR

Tyler Weaver

Copyright © 2019 by Tyler Weaver

First trade paperback edition July 2019

Cover art by Bekarys Zhabagin

ISBN 978-1-7330341-2-8 (Trade paperback)
ISBN 978-1-7330341-1-1 (eBook)

Published by the Royal War Ministry Press
Email: rwmpress@gmail.com

The book is published with print-on-demand technology and that little line of numbers used to track printings within a single edition is unnecessary. The more you know!

To my father, Brian Weaver

Who gave me what was both the best and the worst idea I have ever had

Table of Contents

Chapter 1 – A Knight Takes His Leave – 1
Chapter 2 – A Fine Spring Day – 6
Chapter 3 – Council of War – 13
Chapter 4 – Charlie Company – 20
Chapter 5 – Royal Presence – 29
Chapter 6 – The Road from Jade Falls – 38
Chapter 7 – Tea With a Princess – 50
Chapter 8 – Forged Steel – 57
Chapter 9 – 9:15 to Drakenburg – 66
Chapter 10 – The Prince and the Private – 73
Chapter 11 – The Ravine at Fire Ridge – 80
Chapter 12 – The War in Drakenburg – 90
Chapter 13 – A Very Big War – 99
Chapter 14 – Certain Victory – 105
Chapter 15 – Whispers in the Mist – 114
Chapter 16 – The Lone Horseman – 121
Chapter 17 – Battlefields at a Distance – 130
Chapter 18 – Steel and Moonlight – 139
Chapter 19 – A Visitor by Darkness – 153
Chapter 20 – Wasps Under a Blue Sky – 160
Chapter 21 – Flag of Victory – 167
Chapter 22 – Commanding General – 185
Chapter 23 – Masked Intentions – 196
Chapter 24 – An Eventful Patrol – 210
Chapter 25 – A Chance Encounter – 228
Chapter 26 – Point of No Return – 239
Chapter 27 – The Day of Battle – 250
Chapter 28 – The Burning Ridge – 263
Chapter 29 – The Royal Oath – 277
Chapter 30 – Fix Bayonets – 284
Chapter 31 – An Eye for the Battlefield – 296
Chapter 32 – By Fire and Steel – 305
Chapter 33 – The Knight and the Dragon – 320
Chapter 34 – By Deeds Alone – 339
Chapter 35 – The Message and the Messenger – 358
Chapter 36 – The Kingdom's Spear – 375
Chapter 37 – The Last Trench – 388
Chapter 38 – The Reaper's Scythe – 395
Chapter 39 – The Bloody Roses – 403
Chapter 40 – The Black Knights – 416
Chapter 41 – The Long-Haired Dragoon – 427
Chapter 42 – Heir to the Throne – 442
Chapter 43 – The Rattlesnake Regiment – 452
Chapter 44 – Supreme Commander – 466
Epilogue – 475

Postscript - 480

Chapter 1

A Knight Takes His Leave

Light streamed through the fencing hall's tall windows. Cool air, still tinged with a hint of frost from the winter, wafted through the enormous room and brought with it the many scents of spring and the song of the birds that seemed to have taken up roost on every tree of the palace grounds. The cold had led her to perch herself on one of the windowsills facing the morning sun while she waited.

Waiting was unusual. Her brother was never late. Ever. If he couldn't make it he would tell her beforehand. Had something happened? She was about to hop down and go in search of him when the doors at the front of the hall opened and he strode in.

Her eyes widened. Something *had* happened. He wasn't dressed for a fencing lesson, he was in uniform. He looked ready to go gallop off to the Empire and start cutting down dragoons by the squadron. He looked around the room, saw her sitting in the window and hurried towards her. She pushed off from the ledge and ran to meet him.

"Arilin!" He called to her, "I'm sorry I'm late!"

She skidded to a stop in front of him, "Adrian! What's going on?"

He crouched a little like he usually did when he was talking to her privately. It wasn't her fault she barely came up to his chest. "Raven Wing fortress is under attack. We're mobilizing."

That explained the uniform. Now that they were face-to-face she felt a chill run through her. She'd never seen her brother looking so worried. Or so obviously trying to hide it from his beloved little sister. "You're... you're going?" She managed, hesitantly, "It's so sudden..."

Adrian smiled at the sight of Arilin chewing her lip, and he patted her shoulder, "It's not like the Empire makes a habit of giving us notice. That's just how war is, Arilin. We have to deal as best we can."

She replied indignantly, "I don't see what *we've* ever done to the Empire that's made them so angry at us."

He chuckled, "That's the first funny thing I've heard all morning." He smiled, "Maybe when this is done you can go over there and talk some sense into them."

She smiled, "I wish you didn't have to go. Or that I could go with you."

Adrian's face hardened and he stood. She found herself looking at the middle of his polished breastplate and took a step back as he said, "Trust me, you don't. War is awful, and the Empire is very, very good at it. To tell you the truth, Arilin, I'm worried enough about myself." He went on, softly, "The thought of you out there terrifies me."

She sighed, "I just want to *do* something. And I'm worried for you."

Adrian smiled, "I'll be alright. We'll be home by Christmas, just watch."

Arilin pouted, "I still want to go. You went with Father to the March-lands when *you* were my age."

Adrian shook his head, "An experience I would not wish to put you through." He cut off her objection, "And not because you're a girl, or because you're young. A lot of what I saw, *nobody* should go through."

"I *understand* it's all very awful, but I don't see how I can lead this country if I know nothing of war or the army." Arilin looked up at him defiantly, "One day you're going to be king and I'll need to help you however I can."

Adrian gave her a stern look for a couple seconds before he snorted and softened. Chuckling, he reached out to tousle her hair, "You're a fierce one, milady. I think I'll just marry you off to the Stahlbergs – with your attitude you'd be running their country in no time and I could sit back and enjoy my peace and quiet here."

Arilin pouted harder, "You are too mean."

He teased her, "Archduke Francis seems *nice*. I mean, he was making eyes at you at that ball last year."

"Yes, and if I wanted to go to church every day I'd be interested in him too." She shot back.

Adrian winced, "Ouch." He went on, "Anyway, I owe you a fencing lesson. I need to get my blood flowing again after being in meetings all morning." He walked with her over to the rack of training weapons on the wall, "A whole lot of making easy decisions unnecessarily complicated. Field Marshal White still hasn't decided whether this is a real attack or some kind of elaborate feint. He didn't want to order mobilization, you know."

Arilin took a steel foil off the wall, one of the smaller ones. For a grown man it would simulate the kind of sword worn to a party, a lighter and smaller version of a service weapon. For her it was about the right size. She gave it a couple of practice swings and a thrust and then looked over at Adrian, "But he went along anyways?"

Adrian reached to the top of the rack and took off the longest and heaviest sword he could, essentially a blunt version of the cuirassier's saber he had slung from his belt. Arilin looked at it warily – even blunt, she had no doubt he could easily kill somebody with it. He wiggled it back and forth to warm up his wrist, "Yes. Admiral Kensington was practically standing on the table he wanted to get the fleet to sea so badly, and he brought White around." He noticed her look, "I need some practice with my actual sword, Arilin. I hope you don't mind."

"Of course not." They tied on fencing helmets, walked to the middle of the floor and took up positions. The princess brought her weapon to her face, blade vertical in the swordsman's salute. "On your guard."

Adrian came to the same position, "Defend yourself!"

Arilin stepped forward into the middle guard, and Adrian sprang forward from the salute into a vicious backhand cut before her right foot had come out halfway. She reversed herself, stepping back diagonally as Adrian's sword hissed by an inch from her chest, shuffled forward and stabbed at him. Adrian quickly spun his sword, knocking hers harmlessly aside as it came back and tapping her sharply on the forehead on the forward stroke.

Arilin recovered herself and objected, "Your hit, but no fair. You surprised me."

Adrian shrugged, "I told you to defend yourself. War isn't fair, you know."

"Fine," Arilin stepped away and leveled her sword, "Again."

Adrian leveled his own sword, took a quick step in and was upon her. In one spiraling movement he knocked her sword aside, lunged forward and slashed down at her shoulder. Arilin brought her sword around to block, felt an incredible shock and then Adrian poking her in the ribs with his sword's point. She looked at her hand, surprised that she had kept hold of her weapon.

"Ow. Your hit," Arilin winced. Her hand had gone numb. She gingerly took her sword's blade with her left and shook out her right hand.

"I was trying to disarm you. You have a stronger grip than I thought." Adrian flexed his wrist around again, drawing a circle in the air with his sword's point, "Never try to block something like this–" He wiggled his sword for emphasis, "With something as light as your sword. You're going to lose, especially if you're fighting a Mask."

The feeling had come back to her hand, and Arilin seized the hilt again and got back on guard. Warily, she said, "On your guard."

"Then attack me." Adrian dropped his point into the lower guard, hovering it around the level of his knees. Arilin obligingly lunged forward, and Adrian slapped her sword aside and rapped her hard on the wrist.

Her hand was stinging, "Your hit." Normally Adrian used a lighter sword when training with her. He also went much easier. She got the feeling that he was using something close to his actual skill now. She asked, "Don't the Imperials use two-handed swords? I think that would slow them down."

She couldn't see his eyes, but she got the feeling that Adrian was giving her a very serious look behind his mask, "You'd be wrong. The swords the Masks use have very long hilts compared to what we're used to, but the blade is actually somewhat shorter." He brought his sword back up into the guard, "What they lose in reach, they make up for in speed and power. They will engage, get close and kill you. To win against them you cannot fight on their terms."

Arilin got back on guard. *Avoid fighting on their terms. Avoid fighting on Adrian's terms.* He had incredible reach thanks to his height and his long sword. He had so much power in his slashes she literally couldn't block them. And he was fast, probably a little faster than her. It was the only thing she could fight him on. As he flashed forward again, sword hissing through the air, Arilin flexed her knees and waited a heart-stopping instant for her brother to commit to his attack.

She backed away from his first slash, feeling the wind from his sword as it sliced by inches from her face and stepped back in, thrusting at Adrian's exposed sword arm. He turned his hand-guard to deflect her point, but he parried her down rather than up and her sword came back on line. Arilin drove forward with her left foot, stabbing at his ribs as she felt something hard slam into the side of the head.

Stars danced in front of Arilin's eyes as she staggered aside. She'd tried to duck under his return stroke. Apparently she hadn't quite made it. When the world stopped spinning she realized that Adrian was looking at her, concerned, "Are you all right, Arilin? I think I hit you a little harder than necessary, I apologize."

Arilin took a deep breath, "Yes... I'm fine. Thanks. Your hit."

Adrian shrugged, "A fine counter. If you'd been faster you would have had me." He nodded, "Very, very good, little sister. I'm having a hard time taking it easy on you."

Arilin felt herself blushing beneath her mask, "Ah... thank you!"

Adrian drew his sword back up. "One more pass. On your guard."

Stepping back and shaking off the rest of the fog in front of her eyes, Arilin raised her sword again, "On yours."

Adrian shuffled forward ever so slightly, crossed swords with her and gently pushed her point aside. In a flash, Arilin circled her sword under his, brought her back leg forward and leapt at him. Adrian quickly pushed her thrust aside, spun around and grabbed the back of her collar as she flew past him. She jerked to an abrupt halt and thrashed helplessly, her feet a good foot off the ground as he picked her up.

She heard him saying, "A fleche? Good fighting spirit, at least. Get faster and I'll start getting worried." Adrian set her back on the ground, spun her around and whacked her softly on the top of the head with his sword, "Ha. My hit."

Arilin was grateful for the fencing mask – it at least concealed how red she was getting. Adrian was undoing his own mask, and she realized the lesson was over. She looked up at him, "Do you really have to go now?"

Adrian knelt down in front of her again, "Yes, I'm sorry. Duty is duty. Here, let me help you with your mask." He stood up again and reached for her head.

She brushed his hands aside, "I can do it myself, you know." Pulling her mask off, she said, "Promise to write me?"

Adrian bowed his head, "As often as I can. Just don't give our father trouble." He chuckled, "Or your mother, for that matter."

"I wouldn't dream of it. Just make sure *you* come back." She suddenly had an idea, "Here, take this." Arilin pulled loose the ribbon that had been securing her hair. Freed from its confines, her hair flowed across her back in a jumble of golden tresses, and she shook her head to settle it as she held out the ribbon to Adrian.

He took it from her. It was thick, stiff pink silk fringed with lace, the kind of ribbon a princess would wear. Adrian smiled, "A lady's favor?"

Arilin was blushing again, "Just make sure you bring it back."

Adrian nodded, "Of course. I promise."

And with that he was gone.

Chapter 2

A Fine Spring Day

A breath of cool spring air blew through the classroom, ruffling students' books and sending a few cherry petals dancing through the air. A girl sitting by the open windows closed her eyes and breathed in, enjoying the peaceful scents of spring.

"Sophia Rose!" She opened her eyes. So much for peace and quiet, "You've been looking out the window this entire class. Considering that you *obviously* know the material so well, why don't you summarize today's lesson for us all?"

Sophia looked at the teacher, shrugged and stood up at her desk. "Okay." She looked around the classroom. Not a lot of help. "We were going over the history of the Empire, right?"

Mrs. Renton looked at her, exasperated, "Yes, of course we were. Have you heard a single word I've said for the past half an hour?"

Sophia sighed, "Actually, no. But I did do the reading last night."

Her teacher gave her a hard look, and then sighed herself, "Well, I don't suppose I can blame you with what's been going on recently. Well, go on, out with it."

Sophia cleared her throat and started, "During the Great Uprising against the Elves fifteen hundred years ago, a human sorcerer drew upon dark magic, giving up his face and binding his soul to a mask. This gave him incredible power and immortality, but also warped his mind and turned him completely evil."

She went on, "After the Elves were defeated, he laid claim to land beyond the Night River in the far east of the continent and crowned himself the Faceless King. Because he had no face, he forced those under his rule to wear masks like he did, which is why it is called the Empire of Masks." Sophia grimaced at the thought, "The Empire expanded to the west until it ran into our own Kingdom one thousand years ago.

"We fought the Empire for five hundred years, but they eventually took the city of Drakenburg to break through the Shield Mountains and besiege the Capital itself. During the siege, the Imperial Black Knights kidnapped the King's daughter, Angelique." The classroom muttering and snickering at her expense had stopped, "He offered her hand in marriage to any knight who could rescue her."

She was getting to the good part, "A squire, Maximilian Wehrherz, took up the challenge and pursued the Black Knights back to Draken-burg. With a few companions he stormed the citadel, defeated the Face-less King, rescued Princess Angelique and married her after their return. This made him heir to the throne and he became King Maximilian the First, founder of the Wehrherz Dynasty that rules us to this day."

Mrs. Renton raised an eyebrow, "And in the Empire?"

She wasn't getting a break here. Sophia cleared her throat again and went on, "After the Faceless King was defeated, the Empire fell into a civil war which ended when Vai Najai defeated the other Imperial lords and crowned herself Empress." Sophia felt a chill run down her back just talking about the Dark Empress, "Vai continued to attack us-"

Mrs. Renton cut her off, "Okay, that's enough. Good job. You may sit down. And I wish the rest of you paid as much attention to your school-work as Miss Rose." Sophia felt a dozen glares directed her way as the teacher turned back to address the board, drawing a crude map of the western part of the continent on it with chalk, "Now, class, the traditional story is that Maximilian and his Companions essentially charged out of the High City and defeated everything in their path for hundreds of kilo-meters," She drew a dotted line from the Capital to the city of Drakenburg square in the middle of the Great Pass through the Shield Mountains, "Until they kicked down the door to the Faceless King's throne room, killed him, untied Angelique and walked back out while the Imperials were distracted by the death of their God-Emperor."

She picked up a yardstick and slapped the board with it for empha-sis, "Mr. Gravesend, there is an obvious problem with this story. What is it?" She was looking at another student who also seemed to have not been paying very close attention earlier. Sophia wondered if she had a list somewhere.

Tony stood up, hastily steadying his chair as it threatened to tip over, "Uh... that's a long way and the Masks are pretty good at fighting?"

"Exactly. You may sit down." Mrs. Renton sighed, "In the last few years we have been able to examine Imperial accounts of the period directly, and while they are self-serving to say the least particularly with regard to their near-*worship* of Vai Najai, they have made a few things clear." She looked back at Sophia, "When Miss Rose said that civil war broke out in the Empire *following* the Faceless King's death, well, that's what is in your history books. However, Imperial sources all state that Vai was leading her army against the Capital when she rebelled against the Faceless King. Maximilian likely exploited the chaos of the ongoing civil war to get into the fortress of Drakenburg and attack and kill the Faceless King."

"The fact that Vai Najai, or as the Imperials call her 'Lady Vai', crowned herself Empress in Drakenburg incidentally explains the centrality of that city to Imperial propaganda. They talk about reclaiming that city a lot more than they do, say, destroying the Kingdom. Fortunately for us all," Mrs. Renton smiled thinly, "They're a *long* way from doing either right now."

She went on, "Now, class, your assignment for to..." She trailed off as the muffled sounds of a conversation in the hallway drifted in. From her seat at the other side of the classroom Sophia couldn't make out the words, but she heard the principal talking with someone with a deep, commanding voice who wasn't bothering to keep quiet in the hallway. This other person also seemed to be in a hurry.

In fact, this other person sounded a lot like her *father*. A few of the students closer to the door turned to look at her nervously, as did Mrs. Renton. Sophia felt her stomach curdle as the door opened and her father strode in, followed nervously by the principal. She could see why he was nervous. Her father had a side-job that occasionally made him the most influential man in town.

John Rose, all six feet and two inches of him, ducked his head and swung his shoulder to get his slung rifle under the classroom's low door frame. Heavy boots thudded solidly on the wood floor. His presence expanded to fill the room as his eyes swept the class, settling first on Sophia, then on Tony, whose attention had been wandering for the same reason hers had been, and finally on Mrs. Renton. He nodded politely and started, "Ma'am, I'm sorry to disrupt your class, but I need a couple of your students."

She looked up at the towering figure in Royal Army blue and replied nervously, "Ah... Mr. Rose, right? T-They're not in trouble, are they?"

Her father chuckled, "Not unless they decide to desert. And I'm not too worried about one of them." Sophia exchanged looks with Tony and pushed her chair back in anticipation as her father looked back at the class, "Private Gravesend! Private Rose!"

They both leapt to their feet, "Yes, First Sergeant!"

"We've got our orders. The company marches for Southbend tonight." He paused, looking between both of them seriously, "Get yourselves home, get ready and say your goodbyes. We're mustering at the armory at sixteen hundred. That's..." He glanced at his watch, "Two hours and thirty-eight minutes from now. Get moving."

They replied in unison, "Yes, First Sergeant!"

Mrs. Renton looked at them, eyebrows raised, "I didn't know you two had joined the Army."

Tony collected his bag and said, "Yeah... we've both been in since last summer."

"Well, ah... that's... very commendable of you!" She bowed her head, "Thank you for serving."

Sophia, painfully aware of the stares of the entire class boring into her, smiled nervously as she picked her bag up off the side of her desk, "Ah, thank you..."

As though a switch had been flipped, the rest of the class jumped up and flooded around them, "Yeah, thanks!" "That's great!" "You two are awesome!" "Take care of yourselves!" "Kill a Mask for me!" "I wish I was going with you!"

Blushing, Sophia was eventually able to extricate herself from the appreciative hubbub and backed out the door, her father following them out. She heard Mrs. Renton calling for order as he closed the door behind them. He pulled a list of names out of his pocket, read down it and turned to the principal, who was still hovering nearby. Nodding politely, he said, "Thank you, that's everyone, we'll see ourselves out." Her father gestured to Tony and patted her on the back for emphasis.

The principal muttered something darkly and stalked off down the hall away from them. Sophia looked after him, then up at her father questioningly, "What's he so mad about?"

Her father put a hand on her shoulder, turned her around and ushered them out. The polite façade fell from his face as he growled, "I never saw that coming. He didn't want to let me pull you and the others out. I had to threaten to arrest him for interfering with mobilization during wartime."

Sophia's eyes widened, "Oh, my... you didn't..."

Her father squeezed her shoulder reassuringly, "Don't worry, I just implied it and he got my message. Either way, I think I've probably worn out my welcome with the faculty for a little while." They walked out the front doors into bright sunlight and cool air, and the blooming cherry trees out front took the edge off the atmosphere. He looked at his watch again and stopped as they reached the front gate, "Alright, like I said, you two go home and get ready. Sophie, help your mother close up shop while you're at it. She'll be coming out to see us off."

"Will do, First Sergeant." "I'll do it, Dad." They replied simultaneously.

Her father chuckled, "Come on, Sophie... I guess it can't be helped.

See you both in two hours." He turned and walked off down the side-walk towards the armory, adjusting his rifle as he went. Sophia and Tony turned the other way and started walking home.

He gave her a sideways glance, "Isn't interfering with mobilization ba-sically the same as treason?"

Sophia laughed nervously, "Yeah... it is." Trying not to think too much about that one, she changed the subject, "Are your parents going to be okay with you leaving?"

Tony shrugged eloquently, "I talked to them about it this morning when the word about Raven Wing started going around. They'll be al-right." He sounded dubious. He went on, "I'm just worried about my little sister."

Sophia smiled, "What, she's a crybaby?"

Tony laughed, "No, the opposite. She told me this morning that she hopes I shoot a Mask in the head and all his brains come flying out."

She snickered, "I can see how she'd be a problem."

"And your mom? It'll be hard on her running the bakery alone."

It was Sophia's turn to shrug, "It's not the first time she's done it. Dad's gone to war before and she's been alright. And she had me to take care of me too."

"Well, say hi to her for me." They'd reached his turn, and he waved and walked off towards his house. Sophia continued on and eventually stopped in front of the sign for the Rose Bakery. She looked at the script with the red floral border, admiring her handiwork until she realized she was procrastinating. With a sigh, she pushed in the swinging door and walked inside.

"*Sophia!*" The bell on the door hadn't even stopped ringing and her mother had already wrapped her arms around her. "How are you? Did John come and get you? I can't believe this is happening again..."

Sophia hugged her mother back and rested a cheek against her hair. The couple of patrons in the shop gave them understanding looks, and Sophia understood why. Her mother was *shaking*. She must have been crying. Sophia abruptly realized that the cheerful woman she remem-bered from the last time her father was called up had been putting on a façade for her sake. "Mom, I'm alright. Dad came and picked me up a little while ago." She patted her back, "How are *you*?"

Her mother pulled back a little and looked up at her, "Oh, it's been *awful*, after you left for school we heard the news and a little while ago

Josh Thorn came around with orders for you and John and he left and I don't even know what to do with myself..."

Sophia gave her mother a final squeeze and extricated herself gingerly, telling her, "First, we're going to close up the shop. I think business is over for the day."

Her mother blinked at her, "Yes... I suppose it is."

Sophia smiled, "Then I need to put my uniform on and go in." She looked down at herself, self-consciously brushed her pleated skirt and made a correction, "My *other* uniform. And we'll go down to the armory together."

Sophia looked up at the couple of late customers who were getting an exclusive look into the Rose family's private affairs and announced, "Alright, we're closing early today because of the war. Please finish up. We'll have extra day-old goods tomorrow, half off!"

They shooed out the customers in record time and Sophia reconciled the receipts for the day while her mother swept out the shop. The bread business was pretty constant as a rule, but with news of the war it seemed like most people were making do with whatever they had stashed away from yesterday rather than buying their stock. Sophia sighed at the thought of the lost money, finished the ledger and went upstairs to her room, glancing at herself in the mirror as she walked in. With her short brown hair and bright blue eyes she looked like a tall, tomboyish schoolgirl.

Opening her closet, Sophia pushed her dresses aside and pulled out her uniforms, tossing them onto her neatly-made bed. Two pairs of heavy leather boots came out of her shoe rack, and she pulled a leather-brimmed Royal Army field cap from among her hats on the overhead shelf. A military rucksack came out from under the bed. She reached under it again and pulled out a box with the rest of her Army gear and her knives. Looking over the semi-organized chaos, she shook her head and got packing. Her extra clothing went into the rucksack, and she folded and rolled her wool military blanket and cinched it neatly down on top. After she finished, Sophia looked at the last uniform left on the bed, then down at herself and sighed. It was time to get changed.

Sophia sat down on her bed, kicked her shoes off, took off her heavy knee-socks and pulled the scarf out from under her school uniform's sailor collar, then pulled her blouse off over her head. Standing up, she unbuttoned her skirt and let it fall around her ankles. Lacy underwear was inappropriate for the battlefield, and she sadly tossed her bra and panties into the clothes hamper after everything else. She replaced them with a pair of tight but otherwise excessively practical shorts and a very sturdy sports bra that would hold her heavy breasts in place no matter how many Masks she was fighting. Tucking her dog tags into her cleavage, she felt the cool metal warm to her body and turned to her actual uniform.

She pulled on the light blue undershirt and heavy wool socks, stepped into the dark blue pants, threaded her knife onto the belt and pulled it secure around her hips. Pulling on the heavy ankle-boots, she tightened the laces, tied them off and tucked them in, then picked up two rolls of black wool cloth off her bed and set to work wrapping them around her calves. A couple minutes later she finished tying off her puttees under her knees and stood up, flexing her legs to try out the fit. Sophia smiled as nothing shifted or loosened, then picked up her jacket.

The Royal Army service jacket was simple and practical, dark blue with deep cuffs and four pockets on the chest and hips. Hers had the single chevrons of a private across the shoulders and, she noted with a twinge of pride, white collar patches showing the infantry's crossed rifles with numbers for the Second Battalion of the Twenty-Fourth Infantry Regiment. She shrugged into it easily, worked the buttons, closed the standing collar and looked at herself in the mirror.

A soldier looked back at her.

Sophia grinned, picked up her equipment and went downstairs. She had a war to fight.

Chapter 3

Council of War

Arilin glared up at the guard. He looked back down at her steadily. Exasperated, she said, "Let me through!"

He shifted a little, "Sorry, ma'am, but only authorized personnel are allowed in. I have strict orders."

Arilin put a hand on her chest self-importantly, "Being a *princess*, I would expect that I am *authorized*."

He cleared his throat, "General Staff personnel, general officers, Prince Adrian and His Majesty *only*. Everyone else requires an escort." He looked up and behind her as sharp footsteps came up the hall and braced to attention, "Ma'am, coming in?"

A cool voice sounded behind her, "Yes, thank you, sergeant... is something the matter?" Arilin turned to see a tall woman in a Royal Army uniform looking at them quizzically. She didn't need to see the stars on her shoulder boards to know who it was – there was only one Patricia MacMahon.

Arilin cut the guard off, "Yes, I was just trying to get in and see how the war is going."

Patricia smiled, a little skeptically, "Shouldn't you be in school at this hour, milady? I understand your enthusiasm, but still..."

"So many people had family leaving that they let us out early." Arilin pouted for effect, "I just want to see Father..."

Patricia winced, "Alright, milady, you can put that pout of yours away." Straightening up, she looked at the guard, "She's with me, sergeant. Although," She looked at Arilin, "I can't guarantee it will be very entertaining though. Most of these meetings are *dreary*."

The man opened the door for them as Arilin said, "That's fine, I..."

"What do you mean you would have the First and Second Corps retreat? You fool, we'd *lose the Marchlands!*" A chubby general was standing up, shouting across the War Room's enormous round table at the top of his lungs. Arilin recognized him as General Albrecht, commander of the Tenth Corps. His white dress uniform made his face look even redder as he went on, "Need I remind you how many men *died* over that place in the last war? For all we know this Imperial attack is a feint intended to make *people like you* panic and tell our men to run like *cowards*."

A much skinnier, balding general on the other side of the table shrugged theatrically, the gesture making his monocle glint in the light from the room's enormous windows, "I suppose you'd prefer they surrender like *heroes* in a month after the Empire mops them up?" He gestured to the maps strewn across the table, "You can believe what you like about flank positions, Richard, but at this rate the war will be decided west of the Dark Forest." To her surprise, Arilin didn't recognize him.

Arilin's eyes fell on her father, seated with his back to the windows, as he turned and spoke to a man sitting to his right. The man stood and the room instantly quieted, "General Albrecht, General Haas is correct. If we leave those two corps in position we will lose the Marchlands and two hundred thousand men. If we pull them out, we only lose the Marchlands." Field Marshal White's voice boomed over the suddenly-quiet room.

Albrecht nodded, but replied quickly, "Sir, we should have them *immediately* reinforce Raven Wing. They could seal the Imperial beachhead-"

White growled, "Impossible. First and Second Corps will retreat *immediately*." He looked down at the King and said, "My lord, I presume you have no problem with that?"

William IV rubbed the bridge of his nose tiredly, looked back and said, "Given the circumstances, Lawrence, no, I don't. Please proceed." His eyes drifted across the room, then snapped quickly back as he noticed the newcomers. Standing abruptly, he said, "Arilin! What are you doing here?"

Complete silence. Every eye in the room turned to look at her. Taking a deep breath to steady herself, Arilin smiled, bobbed a curtsey and said, "Father! I wanted to see for myself how the war effort was going." She raised her eyes innocently, "I hope I'm not being a burden to you..."

He gave her a stern look for a second, then snorted, "Alright, Arilin, you can drop the doe eyes. Just don't make yourself a nuisance, understand?" He sat back down and cleared his throat, "Go on, gentlemen."

Conversation gradually built back up. Noticing a free seat at the table next to the monocled general, Patricia walked up with Arilin in tow, and then hesitated before she sat down. Arilin looked up at her and asked, "What's wrong?"

Patricia looked back at her and smiled slightly, "You should probably take it, milady."

Arilin bowed her head, "You're the general. I'll sit on your lap."

Patricia gave her a look, "Don't be too cute, milady. People will notice." Arilin pouted at her, and she rolled her eyes and stalked off to get herself a chair as the princess reluctantly sat down.

The man sitting next to her smirked into his whitening beard and chuckled, then looked back down at a stack of what looked like intelligence reports and a small map of the Night River estuary. Arilin noticed that he'd drawn a series of curves and circles over Raven Wing Fortress. Patricia, returning with her own seat on her other side, glared at him and said, "What, exactly, is so funny?"

The man turned to look at them and smiled, "Sorry, Patricia, but you two are *adorable*." He pushed his chair back a little and turned to his other side, saying, "Isn't that right, Ziggy?"

Arilin recognized the new man, who laughed and leaned his lanky frame back in his chair, "Absolutely, but..." Siegfried Reinhardt trailed off as Arilin glared at him, then winked at her and went on apologetically, "I'm staying out of this one or I'll hear about it from my girls later."

The general chuckled again and said, "Oh, right, little fingers and all. I wouldn't want to get you in trouble with your kids."

Patricia, reddening, glared at him and growled, "Don't you have a corps to command, *Walter*?"

Walter Haas stroked his neatly-trimmed beard and replied, "Yes, but it's much more entertaining watching you two." He smirked mischievously and went on, "Anyway, Lady MacMahon, I didn't know you were old enough to be *babysitting* just yet."

Patricia flushed all the way back to her ears and sputtered, "Why, you..."

Her tirade was cut off before it could get properly started by someone announcing, "Attention please! New dispatch from Raven Wing!" The room quieted as a mildly-overweight colonel walked up to the table and read, "Imperial forces have crossed north of fortress, believe to be in corps strength. Naval gunfire extremely intense. Forts Two and Three stormed, Fort One exploded, fighting ongoing at Forts Four and Five. All remaining forts suppressed." Noticing Haas studying his map intently, Arilin reached a hand out and slid it over so she could get a better look. Haas glared at her for a moment, then leaned over and went back to studying it as the colonel went on, "Imperial forces attacking south towards the city center. Casualties catastrophic. Estimate can hold out for twelve hours." The man paused, his voice cracking, "God save the King."

Field Marshal White stood up again, angrily, "Twelve hours? Raven Wing should last *for a month*." He glared at the unfortunate colonel, "Tell General Martineau that his 'estimate' is *unacceptable*. Once he masters his *fear* he will *immediately* counter-attack and restore control of the detached forts, then hold until relieved." His eyes were ice and death, "I want that message telegraphed to him in five minutes."

The colonel replied, shakily, "Also... sir... General Martineau has fallen, Colonel Desmond has assumed command-"

White looked at his watch and snarled, "*Four minutes and forty seconds.*"

The man fled and White straightened his coat and sank back into his chair. Haas steepled his hands in front of his face and stared at the table grimly as the room slowly grew louder. Siegfried got up and walked over to stand between them so he could get a better look at the map. He said, sadly, "Peter? I can't believe it. He was a good man."

The color had drained out of Patricia's face as she replied, "Isn't his wife there with him?"

Siegfried replied, "Yes, she is. My wife writes her sometimes. He and I were lieutenants together, you know."

Haas grunted, "Damn it." Looking up at him, he went on, "I'm sorry about that, Ziggy."

Siegfried shrugged, "He wanted command of Raven Wing. Said it would be good for that third star. Nothing we can do about it now."

Arilin looked at the map again and traced out the arc of the five forts that had come under attack. Set some distance away from the city itself, they ran in an arc from directly north of Raven Wing to the edge of the bay to the east, each a couple kilometers apart, and more forts circled to the west until they butted up against the banks of the Moon River southwest of the city where it flowed into the Night River. Arilin noticed that Haas had crossed out several more forts located farther up the coast and drawn rough range fans reaching over from the Imperial side of the bay, more than twenty kilometers away. She tapped the map and asked Patricia, "Why are these forts crossed out? Aren't they coastal guns?"

Patricia looked where she was pointing, furrowed her brow and said, "They are, but I don't know why..." She looked at the other two generals, "I'm assuming this has something to do with the Black Fleet?"

Haas chuckled morbidly, "They're related, but no. The coastal forts weren't destroyed by the Imperial Navy."

Arilin looked at the range fans again. They were very long and ran back onto land, over a series of railway tracks set back from the shore. She ventured, "Railway guns?"

Haas looked at her, surprised, "Yes, actually." He tapped the destroyed forts for emphasis, "I'd been saying for *years* that those naval forts, the ones we *designed* to keep the Imperials from getting their navy into Night Bay, were in range of modern railway guns fired from the Imperial side of the bay." He shrugged, "But what do I know, I just served in the artillery for twenty years."

Siegfried finished the thought for them, "And with those forts destroyed the Empire anchored about thirty battleships off Raven Wing. That's more than three hundred heavy guns alone, plus secondary batteries, *plus* their army's siege guns."

Patricia paled noticeably at the thought of the heaviest artillery bombardment in history cratering the city of Raven Wing into a new branch of the Moon River, "My God... I'm surprised they've held out this long."

Haas jerked his head at the Field Marshal, who was distracted talking with the King and muttered, "Try telling him. He's been getting worse and worse all morning." He went on philosophically, "There is something to be said for being willing to receive bad news. And," He looked straight at Arilin, "As you'll soon find out if you stick around here, young lady, war's not all parades and fancy uniforms. Although come to think of it," He teased, "Lady MacMahon knows more about those than most of us."

Patricia squawked, "Hey..."

He shrugged, obviously enjoying himself, "Please, milady, you should be proud of your record with the Valkyrie Knights. In fact, I've heard they're even thinking of actually deploying them with the Capital Corps this time around."

Arilin looked at Patricia and asked, "You were with them?" The pink-jacketed 14th Hussar Regiment was the only all-female unit in the Army. It also had another well-known nickname: the Finishing School. Whether it was for unmanageable young ladies or future Army wives depended on who you asked. Arilin supposed it was probably a little of both.

Exasperated, Patricia replied, "Yes, I commanded them a couple years back. And," She glared at Haas, "Turned them into a fighting unit." Laying a hand on her chest, she puffed up with pride, "We showed the Red Brigades a thing or two."

He chuckled, "Well, I'd be happy to see them charging *my* guns any day." Siegfried, who had been struggling to maintain a straight face during the exchange, started coughing suddenly.

Arilin changed the subject before Patricia had time to challenge Haas to a duel, "Ah, so, why did the Imperials attack at Raven Wing? It's awfully far north..."

Siegfried looked at the fulminating Patricia and quickly bent down between her and Haas, "Ah, well, milady, if you look here you'll see there are several rail lines supplying our fortresses on the west side of Night Bay, some of them almost along the shore." He pointed them out on the map.

Arilin leaned forward, "Oh, I see. They can just march west from there and not have to worry about transportation. It's probably even faster than it is from the Marchlands."

Haas cut in, "And they obviously have enough transport ships, if reports are anything to go by." Patricia grunted noncommittally and looked out the windows away from him and Siegfried.

Throughout all this Arilin had noticed Admiral Kensington, commander of the Northern Fleet, sitting on her father's left, writing what looked like a lengthy letter and occasionally talking to members of the naval staff. A messenger came in, handed him a small sheet of paper and quickly left. Kensington read the note quickly, then stood and knocked on the table, "My lord, gentlemen, if I could have your attention!"

Her father remarked as the room quieted, "I think you have it whether we like it or not. What do you have there?"

Kensington said gravely, "I have just been informed that the battle line is prepared to sail within the hour." Looking at the King, he said, "My lord, I intend to bring the Black Fleet to battle and, once engaged, to smash them once and for all. Do you have anything before I depart for the fleet?"

William stood and shook his hand, "You know what you're doing, Admiral. Good luck and God speed."

Kensington nodded and said, "Thank you, sir." With that he spun on his heel and hurried out the door, closely followed by his aides. He almost ran into the fat colonel from earlier on the way out. Arilin could see him start making a remark and think better of it when he saw the man's face. He was shaking so badly Arilin could see it from her seat at the table.

The colonel started, "Ge-ge-gentlemen, attention p-please!" The hubbub of conversation, which had risen as the admiral left, immediately died now. Arilin got the feeling it wasn't so much out of respect for the messenger as dread for whatever had scared him so badly.

Field Marshal White said, "Well, out with it!"

The man said, "Sir, I-I, I mean we... we have received another message from Raven Wing..."

White rolled his eyes, "Of course, and...?"

The colonel shook like a leaf as he tried to read the message, "I, I... oh, my, I'm sorry..."

Haas grunted, heaved himself up and walked over to the poor man before White exploded. Taking the paper, he adjusted his monocle and read through it quickly once, then again. Then he read through it a third time and shook his head sadly.

White said drily, "We're all waiting, Walter."

Haas tipped his head in acknowledgement, "Gentlemen, the message reads, 'Pleased to inform His Majesty that we have accomplished all tasks directed previously. Forts One through Five are secure as well as the city center. We have received the surrender of the enemy commander.'"

Her father stood, saying, "Well, this is wonderful news..." He trailed off at the look on Haas' face.

He went on, "Sir, it goes on as follows. 'Long live the Emperor.'" He paused and said gravely, "Raven Wing has fallen."

Silence, then shouting. Arilin started to blush at the language being used and Patricia said, "Milady, I think it's time you went home." Reddening a little herself, she added, "Why don't I escort you? Someone should tell the Queen..."

Arilin rose and said shakily, "I... I think I'd like that, thank you."

Siegfried and Haas gave them an understanding looks as they left.

Chapter 4

Charlie Company

"Sophie!" Her mother met her as she came down the stairs, "You look, ah..."

Sophia looked down at herself and remarked, "It's not my cutest outfit."

Her mother smiled, reached out and straightened her uniform's collar, "No, Sophie, I was going to say how you looked *so* much like your father." Seeing the expression on Sophia's face, she corrected herself, "Ah... if he was a cute girl. And much younger."

Sophia doubled over laughing. When she'd recovered enough to breathe again she managed, "I'll take that as a compliment, I guess. You *did* marry the guy."

Her mother looked indignant, "Yes, and it was the best decision I ever made, and I got you out of it."

Sophia put down her backpack and hugged her. Her mother didn't seem to want to let her go, but Sophia patted her on the back and said softly, "Come on, Mom, we need to get going." She stepped away reluctantly, and Sophia put her hands on her shoulders and said, "Mom, don't worry. Dad and I will come home. I'll carry him back myself if I have to."

Her mother hugged her again, saying, "I know, but I'm so afraid of *losing* you two..."

It sank in to Sophia this was the third time her mother had seen her loved ones go to war. Today could very well be the last time she'd see her husband or her daughter alive. *It can't get any easier to say goodbye*, she thought, and she embraced her back until she was willing to let her go. Eventually her mother stepped back, sniffling, and Sophia picked up her bag and said, "Come on, Mom, let's get going."

"Oh," Her mother said, brightening, "Your friend came by while you were changing to pick you up. You two go together – I'll finish up here and go see you off afterwards."

"Really, Mom? You're sure you don't want to walk with me?" Sophia asked, surprised.

"Oh, yes, I'll let you two go together. No need to hang around intruding on things." Her mother said mischievously.

Sophia said, "Alright, Mom, if you say so..."

Her mother leaned in and whispered to her as she ushered her into the front room, "And he's *super* cute."

"Mom!" Sophia squawked, "Come on..."

Tony was wandering around the couple of tables they had set up in the front of the shop, pretending to examine their display cases. He turned at the sound of them walking in and grinned nervously, "Sophia! And, uh, Mrs. Rose, how are you?"

Sophia smiled a little awkwardly and said, "Uh, Tony, thanks... I wasn't really expecting you, sorry."

Tony rubbed the back of his head anxiously, "Well, I got changed fast so I figured I'd pick you up."

Her mother cut in, teasing, "Ooh, how bold of you."

They both squawked, "Hey!"

Her mother laughed. It sounded a little hollow. Shooing them out the door, she said, "You two... you two take care of yourselves!" Sophia heard her voice cracking.

The spring air outside started cooling the blush off her face as Tony asked, "Is she doing okay?"

"Mom?" Sophia shook her head a little, "No, not at all, but she'll be alright. How's your family?"

He sighed, "My mom and Beth-" His little sister, "-both think I'm going to die. Dad's dealing with them."

They started walking, the ridges of the cobblestones dull under their boots. Sophia looked at him sidelong and cracked, "I'm having a hard time picturing Beth crying over you."

He chuckled, "Like I said, *she thinks I'm going to die.* I don't think I've *ever* seen her that happy."

"Now that's the Bethany Gravesend we both know and love." Sophia remarked, "How do you even deal with her?"

Tony said, "Oh, you get used to her after a while. She's actually pretty funny."

"What'd she actually say?" She asked.

Tony imitated her voice, "She said, 'I hope you get your head chopped off, and I'm taking your room.' *Totally* deadpan. Dad *lost it.* In fact, he's probably still yelling at her right now."

Sophia snorted, "That *is* actually kind of funny. What'd you tell her?"

He chuckled, "I told her I would *haunt* her for the rest of her life."

She shook her head, "You're nuts." Getting an idea, she went on, "You should write to her. I think she just wants more attention from you. She'll probably get really lovey-dovey in a couple months."

He raised an eyebrow, "You think? I can give it a shot... although the thought of Nice Beth is kind of scary." They were coming up on their turn by the school, and heard excited conversation around the corner. Turning, they ran into a crowd of students who had just gotten out clustered around a man in Royal Army uniform. Sophia recognized him as another student, Jack Mulligan. He was a year ahead of her and Tony and was as good with girls as he was with a soccer ball. As far as Sophia cared, this meant he showed off a lot while making the easy goals.

Girls love a uniform, though, she thought. He was holding forth with his admirers, "Oh, don't worry, I'll chase those Masks back where they came from. I'll send you all postcards from the Black Citadel!" He noticed the two of them and paused, "And my two, ah, comrades over there are going to help me."

Sophia looked at him levelly, "Come on, Jack, we've got to get going."

He sighed, brushed his hair back from his forehead theatrically and said, "Yes, duty calls..." Tony chuckled at the look on his face as he realized he didn't have an audience any more. Sophia was too busy dealing with them to notice.

"Wow, Sophia, you're so brave!" "And handsome!" Giggles all around, "You're like a knight in shining armor!"

Sophia stammered, "I... ah... thanks, everyone, I guess..."

Somebody said, "It's your chance, now or never!" Sophia looked over to see a younger, mousy-looking girl getting pushed to the front of the group. She thought she recognized her from... where exactly? Now that she thought about it, she'd seen her sneaking glances at her for the whole last year. Sophia opened her mouth to say something and the girl leaned in, tilted her head up and kissed her full on the lips.

Sophia's mind went blank for a moment as she stiffened like a board. Getting ahold of herself, she relaxed a little, put her hands on the girl's shoulders and gently pushed her back a little. The girl's lips left hers reluctantly, and as she pulled back Sophia ventured, "Hi?"

Sophia didn't think she'd ever seen anyone blushing that hard in her life. The girl chirped, "Hi," turned and fled through the gaggle of now-screaming schoolgirls, who all promptly ran off after her. Sophia hesitantly looked over at her two companions. Jack looked indignant.

Tony was shaking with laughter.

"Hey Jack," Tony chortled a few times, "Hey Jack, she's got you beat. Sophie, if we had a *camera*, the look on your face right now, oh my God..."

Sophia didn't need a mirror to tell her she was as red as the other girl had been. Sighing, she said, "Come on, I... I wasn't expecting that!"

Tony smiled slyly, "But it sure looks like you *enjoyed* it."

She glared at him, "She's a *girl*."

He was just getting rolling, "So I bet if I kissed Jack here he'd get all doe-eyed like you are? We're both *dudes* and all." He looked at Jack and grinned evilly.

Jack blanched, "Okay, you two, let's get going. We do have a war to fight, you know." He started walking briskly in the direction of the armory, calling back over his shoulder, "The Masks aren't going to defeat themselves!"

They eventually made it the rest of the way to the company armory without any more run-ins with secret admirers, although Jack made a few comments about wishing random girls would kiss him while Tony mercilessly teased Sophia about it. A crowd was gathering by the open front gate, held back from spilling into their parade field by a couple of guards. A murmur went up as they were noticed, and the crowd parted to let them through. Sophia heard more than a few admiring comments about them from the women in the crowd, and they didn't all seem to be directed at the boys.

Sophia recognized the guards, both older reservists who had no problem telling people to keep out of the armory. They smiled as they approached and one said, "Good to see you three. Go on inside, most of the company's here now."

They were about to go in when another, louder murmur went up from the crowd. Sophia felt people moving aside behind her, and the guards lifted their rifles and snapped them vertical in salute. The three of them quickly turned around and saluted the arriving officer.

Lieutenant Thorn saluted them back and they relaxed, the guards dropping their rifle butts back down to the pavement. He smiled at the three of them, "Hello, you three," before turning to the guards, "How much of the company has reported by now?"

The talkative guard from earlier said, "About three quarters, sir. The First Sergeant has the list."

Thorn nodded, pleased, "Is Captain Jaeger here yet?"

The man shook his head, "No, sir, I haven't seen him all day. The First Sergeant sent a man to go get him about an hour ago."

Thorn raised an eyebrow and asked, "Who's in charge here then?"

"The First Sergeant, sir." The man saw the look on Thorn's face and went on, "Ah, Lieutenant Stahl is the officer in charge, I mean, sir."

He signed in relief, "Whew. I thought I was going to have to take command."

The other guard piped up, "We wouldn't want that, sir."

Thorn gave him a dirty look, then turned to Sophia and her friends, "Alright, you three come with me. No sense standing around out here." Hiking up his backpack, he entered followed by the three of them. Walking up the long flagstone walkway bisecting the parade field towards the armory's front entrance, Sophia spotted her father talking to a couple of soldiers leading a horse team and wagon around the front of the building. Drawing closer, she saw that it was their water tank wagon, and she guessed what her father was saying before they got close enough to hear him.

John Rose stepped up onto the wagon as the horses came to a halt and popped open the top cover with a dubious look on his face, saying, "You're *sure* this was cleaned out properly? You did it yourselves?" He gave them a hard look, "Last time we went out this had dead mice floating in it." He noticed the approaching group, straightened up and saluted, "Afternoon sir. And you, Sophie."

Thorn returned the salute quickly and asked, "How many are we still missing, First Sergeant?"

Evidently satisfied with the state of their tank wagon, he closed the top hatch, jumped down and replied, "With you four in, nineteen including the commander. And they've got half an hour."

"Have you seen Stahl around here anywhere?" Thorn asked.

"Yeah, he's inside. Regiment's been contacting us directly asking for information. I guess nobody's heard from Battalion all day." Her father grimaced, "The usual garbage. It's not like we're getting on a train tonight."

Thorn raised his eyebrows, "Oh... I'd better get in there and help him. Uh, see you."

"Take care of yourself, sir." Thorn turned and hurried up the steps and her father turned to them, saying confidentially, "I don't envy him his job. If I had to deal with higher that much I'd go crazy." He looked them up and down critically, "You all look alright. Better than some of the men I've seen today. Dog tags and ID cards?"

He was quickly presented with three sets of dog tags and Royal Army identification cards. He nodded and said, "Very good. Gravesend, Mulligan, go draw your weapons. So-, ahem, Miss Rose, stay here for a second, I've got something for you."

The boys said, "Yes, First Sergeant," nodded goodbyes at her and left quickly. You didn't linger around John Rose when he wanted you to take off. Sophia asked, "What is it, Dad?"

He smiled, put a hand on her shoulder and said, "Sophie, I've been thinking about doing something for a while but I've been holding back because it would look like I was favoring you." He gave her shoulder a squeeze, "But with the war on, I need someone I can really trust to do this for me."

Sophia was pretty sure she knew what he was talking about, but she asked anyways, "What do you need me to do, Dad?"

He smiled, "Go get the guidon out of my office. You're carrying it from now on. And put it on my spear, not the normal staff. I told you how to break down the shaft on that, right?"

Sophia felt herself warm with pride, "I just have to take the pins out, right?"

He nodded, "Yeah, it's really simple. Now go on."

Sophia said, "Thanks, Dad," turned and hurried up the stairs herself.

Avoiding the scrum in front of the arms room and the supply room on the ground floor, she turned and went up the stairs to the offices. A clerk manning a desk at the top of the stairs stopped her, "Afternoon, Sophie. What's your business up here?"

She replied, "First Sergeant told me to get the guidon out of his office. I think we're having formation soon."

The man gave her a critical look, then shrugged, "If it was anyone else I'd send them back, but I don't think you'd steal your own father's guidon."

Sophia looked at him, shocked, "Who'd steal a guidon in *wartime*?" Stealing another company's colors was a common prank when the battalion or the regiment was together, but that was during training exercises. Who would be so deranged as to do something like that when the Kingdom was at war? And more to the point, who was going to do it when they only had one company in town?

He shook his head, "I've heard of it happening. Anyways, come in."

Walking in, she dodged a few clerks digging through paperwork and walked into her father's open office. Papers lay scattered around his desk and some banal tasks from last month's training exercise were still written on the chalkboard on the wall next to much more important ones he'd obviously written this morning. She noticed he'd had time to check off, 'Get kids out of school' as completed.

She got the company guidon out of its usual resting place in the corner and looked at the wall behind the desk. Her father's NCO sword had been strapped to his hip earlier and was missing from its usual place, but above its empty spot on the wall his spear was very much present. Setting the guidon across one of the chairs in the office, she went behind his desk and carefully lifted it up. From lethal blade, sharp enough to need its own scabbard, to the black-lacquered shaft and wicked butt-spike it was a good eight feet long.

Sophia saw the pins to break it down into more manageable sections and with some effort managed to loosen and pull the ones holding the top section free. Unscrewing their regulation guidon's decorative spearhead, she pulled the company flag free and slid it onto the spear's top section. She carefully tied the flag in place and tucked the loose ends back into the tube of fabric around the spear's shaft, put the spear back together, pulled the scabbard off the lethal blade and stepped back to admire her handiwork.

It looked *badass*.

Sophia grinned and put the scabbard back on so she wouldn't accidentally stab anyone on the way out. As it was she almost ran into Captain Jaeger as she stepped out of the office. He glanced at her, took a long look at the spear she was carrying, chuckled and asked, "Taking that out to your father?"

Sophia nodded, "Yes, sir. He told me to change out the guidon."

Jaeger smiled, "He's been saying recently if we went to war he was using that spear of his, and you were going to carry it. Well, formation's in fifteen minutes. Get going."

"Yes, sir!" Sophia walked downstairs and promptly ran into Tony, who handed her rifle to her. She took it with her free hand, smiled and said, "You got my rifle for me? Thanks."

Tony shrugged, "I figured your father was going to keep you busy for a while." He took a long look at the spear she was holding, "Is that the spear out of his office?"

Sophia nodded, "Yep. We're using this for a guidon from now on."

He said, "That thing scares the hell out of me. You're carrying it, right?" Sophia nodded, and he went on, "Congratulations. Now come on, we need to get to formation. You especially."

Sophia slung her rifle over her back and followed him out. The company was milling around on the parade field, separating itself into platoons under the watchful eye of her father, who caught her eye and waved for her to come over as she came down the steps. She hurried out to meet him in front of the formation and handed him the spear as she arrived. He looked it over, inspected the flag's attachment to the shaft, nodded and gave it back to her. "Looks good," he said, "Unsheathe the blade before we fall in. You know where to stand, right?"

She said, "Yeah," and stepped back and to the left of him. Sophia uncovered the gleaming blade with a quick tug, tucked the scabbard into her belt, shook out the company flag and planted the buttspike in the ground next to her right foot. That being done she went to parade rest, slanting her weapon forward with her right hand, moving her left foot aside to open her stance and putting her left hand into the small of her back.

The breeze stirred the company flag in the wind. Embroidered in black on white cloth were a "C," a "2," and a "24," surrounding the Infantry's crossed rifles. Charlie Company, 2nd Battalion of the 24th Infantry Regiment of the Royal Army. That was their unit and these were their colors

She could hear the company finishing sorting itself out behind her. Her father took a look at his watch, adjusted his position minutely, came to attention and shouted, "Company!"

She heard the platoon sergeants shout, "Platoon!" behind her.

Her father shouted, "Fall in!" An instant later there was a single enormous footstep as one hundred and forty people came to attention at once, Sophia included. Her father shouted again, "Report!" and she heard the platoon sergeants reel off their numbers, the banal accountability taking stark importance with the reality that war was upon them. They were missing two men, both of them out of town. By their standards it was amazing. Usually ten or twenty guys would find excuses to avoid drills.

Satisfied, her father shouted, "At ease!" Another enormous footstep sounded as they collectively loosened their stances, Sophia letting the spear slant forward again. He looked towards the very rear of the formation and said, "Sir, the company is formed!"

She heard Captain Jaeger shout back, "You can fill them in, First Sergeant. I just got here."

Her father said, "Yes, sir," shook himself out and stepped forward a couple paces so he was almost standing beside her. He started, "Gentlemen, when we got our mobilization orders this morning all we knew was that the Empire was moving on Raven Wing in a big way. Unfortunately, we just heard from Regiment that the fortress has fallen." A collective murmur went up. Raven Wing was well known as the strongest fortress in the Kingdom. Her father went on after letting it sink in for a bit, "This is *not* the first time the Empire has gone through our fortifications like they weren't even there. I was *in* the Salient when the last war kicked off."

The fortresses of the Salient on the east side of the Night River had previously been known as the strongest in the Kingdom, supposedly able to hold off the entire Imperial Army indefinitely. Fifteen years ago the Masks had torn them apart in a week and overran most of the Eastern Marches before the Army mobilized and drove them back over the Night River. The Salient itself was still in Imperial hands, and the Marchlands War still gave the Royal Army's soldiers chills.

Her father was going on, "I don't think I need to tell you that we're dealing with serious people here. But," He paused for effect, "The Masks *can* be beaten. *We* beat them last time. We did. And we'll beat them *this time*. You are all capable of it. I *know* you are. *You* know you are. And I'm damn proud of every last one of you." Her father looked across the formation, "I haven't been proud of every unit I've served with, but it's an honor going to war with you today. Now let me hear you."

He stepped back to his original position and shouted, "Company!"

"Platoon!"

"*Attention!*"

They thundered, "*By Fire and Steel!*"

Her father smiled, nodded and said, "We step off for Southbend at eighteen hundred. Fall out."

Sophia picked up her spear, stepped back and spun around. She needed to get ready.

Chapter 5

Royal Presence

Arilin strode out the front entrance of the War Ministry and down the building's imposing front steps, white granite burning orange as the sun sank out over the Grand Harbor to the west. Looking across the sky from the sunset she saw the sharp, bright point of the false sun, chasing the true one closely at this time of year, then the great gleaming sickles of three of the five moons directly overhead. If she'd had the time she could have started picking out planets, but this was no time for stargazing no matter how interesting the night sky was.

A couple of soldiers trailed after her apologetically. The duty officer has been quite disturbed when she showed up unescorted earlier and had promised to give her some guards going home. Never mind that her home was literally on the other side of a heavily-guarded street. She supposed that they could never be too careful in wartime. Guards sprang to attention as she walked across the stretch of deserted pavement between the War Ministry and the Royal Palace's grand rear gate, and a sergeant hurried over as she approached, asking, "Going in, milady?"

She nodded and said, "Yes, thank you." Turning, she told her escorts, "You can go back now. Thank you for walking me over." They saluted and hurried back across the street as the sergeant opened the gate's sally port for her, and Arilin walked through onto the Palace grounds.

Looking at it on a map the Palace resembled an enormous "H", with a considerably truncated top and extended bottom embracing a grand plaza. The actual Residence, where the Royal Family and their personal servants resided, stretched across the fourth and fifth floors of the central rung directly over the Throne Room on the first floor. Even coming in from the rear the building's sheer size was intimidating. The long walk up the plaza from the south was nothing less than overwhelming.

It was however Arilin's home and she knew how to get from the parts designed to overawe foreign diplomats to the part she actually lived in very quickly. The guards posted at the throne room's rear entrance jumped to and let her in without question. She noticed a large group of guardsmen milling around the room's gigantic front entrance and, curiosity piqued, walked over. As she approached she heard a steady murmuring through the walls and saw that the guards had closed the heavy steel shutters that protected the room's ground floor windows.

The lieutenant in charge of the detail noticed her approaching and shouted, "Platoon, attention!" The soldiers froze in mid-mill as he said,

"Good evening, milady. What can we do for you?"

Arilin looked at the group and said, "You can all relax." They shook themselves out and went on talking quietly as she asked him, "What's going on here?"

The young man self-consciously straightened his white uniform jacket and replied, "Well, milady, a crowd's been gathering outside since a couple hours ago. They're waiting on the King to make a statement on the war." He added helpfully, "A lot of ministers have been coming and going from upstairs."

"Why?" She wondered, "It's not like Father is there. He's still at the War Ministry."

The lieutenant shrugged and was about to reply when she heard a familiar voice behind her, "They all feel that they absolutely must speak to him at this... critical hour, yet have yet to muster the courage to go across the street and face the Field Marshal to get to him." Mr. Drake, their butler, gave her a slight bow as she turned, "I think they find imposing on your mother's hospitality much easier, milady."

Arilin imagined Field Marshal White personally throwing the War Minister out of a window and snickered, "I wonder why." She asked him, "What brings you down here?"

Drake gave her one of his sphinx-like smiles through his bushy moustache, "Oh, just checking on the troops, milady. Old habit, I'm afraid." He looked at the lieutenant and said, "Speaking of, sir, two of your men don't have any cartridges and *you* need to polish your boots again."

The man looked at Drake blankly for a moment, then at his boots, then at his soldiers. He said, "Really? I polished them this morning."

Drake nodded slightly, "And that, sir, is the problem. It is now the evening and the polish is smudged. You need to do it after lunch as well. Now see to your men." Arilin stifled a laugh as the lieutenant turned and began barking at his soldiers to show him their ammunition, and Drake turned to her, "Now, milady, your mother has been *very* worried about you, so if you'd please come upstairs with me."

"Sure." She walked towards one of the side doors with him, "You could have sent someone for me, you know. I told Abby I'd be at the War Ministry after I got back from school."

Drake said, "Your mother *also* didn't want to send anyone. You know how she is."

Arilin sighed, "Oh, I do."

"Just please have some consideration for her, milady." He admonished, "She is not comfortable handling affairs of state and the ministers have been weighing on her mind."

They started climbing the grand staircase just off the throne room, and Arilin replied, "I don't understand why she felt she had to even receive them. It's not like they want advice on making soufflés. She *can* tell them no."

Drake chuckled, "I have half a mind to see them out myself if they insist on staying much longer."

Arilin smiled as they reached the top of the staircase, made a turn and started climbing a much more normal-sized one into the Residence proper, "I think I'll save you the trouble and throw them out myself." She changed the subject, "How's Beatrice?"

He gave her that smile again and replied, "She's just fine, milady, although she's pretending to be ill right now so your mother has an excuse to be a poor hostess to the ministers."

Arilin raised an eyebrow, "And I'm guessing Mom thinks she's genuinely sick again?"

He said philosophically, "What is it, to deceive your enemies you must first deceive your friends? *I'm* not going to tell her."

One of the maids was coming down and she stepped aside and curtsied to the two of them on the fourth-floor landing, her white dress and apron shining against the dark wallpaper. They both nodded back to her and started up the final flight of steps. Mindful of listening ears, Arilin looked sidelong at her butler and said conspiratorially, "Thanks, Jack. I think Mom's better off in the dark sometimes."

Drake snorted drily and said before he opened the final door, "Ready to deal with the government, milady?"

Arilin shook herself, looked up at him and said, "Yeah. Let's go."

He opened the door and they stepped out into the hallway. Arilin heard excited conversation coming down the hall from the parlor. Before she went to deal with the politicians, however, she needed to see her mother and her sister. Arilin turned the other way, walked past the library and opened the heavy wooden door into the sitting room.

Her mother had her sister laid out on one of the couches and had pulled a chair over so she could sit by her side. Beatrice had a blanket pulled over her slender form and from what Arilin could see was fast asleep. Her mother didn't seem to notice them at first, but looked over as the door started to swing back closed and jumped a little as she saw

Arilin. She started to gather her dress to stand, but Arilin quickly walked over and she settled back in her seat, saying softly, "Arilin... I'm so happy to see you."

Arilin leaned over and hugged her, "You too, Mom. How's BB?"

Her mother looked at Beatrice worriedly, "She said she wasn't feeling well, so I had her lay down." Beatrice stirred a little in her sleep, shifting her silver-blonde hair on the pillow, and her mother sighed, "She's sick so much, I really worry about her."

Arilin squeezed her mother's shoulder reassuringly, "Don't worry, Mom. I'm sure Beatrice is fine. I bet she's just tired from all the excitement today." She leaned over and nudged Beatrice, ignoring her mother's murmur of protest, "Hey, BB, I'm back." Beatrice stirred, mumbled something and slowly opened her eyes as Arilin asked, "How are you feeling?"

With her pale skin and silvery hair, Beatrice's bright red eyes always stood out. Arilin had them too, just a shade darker. They called it the Stigmata. Everyone immediately in line for the throne had it apparently back to King Maximilian himself. Beatrice blinked the sand out of her eyes and said sleepily, "Just fine." She looked over at her mother's worried face and said, "I think I just needed to lie down."

Arilin ruffled her hair, "You shouldn't scare Mom like that, BB. She's really worried about you."

Beatrice tried half-heartedly to escape, "Aw, come on, Lin, I really *was* feeling faint."

Arilin ruffled her hair some more, "Yeah, sleepy more like it. Come on, I need some help."

Beatrice gathered the blanket around her and sat up, drawing her legs under her. Arilin smoothed her skirt out and sat down next to her in the space she'd opened, saying, "I don't think Dad's getting back from the War Ministry any time soon and I think I should say something to the people outside."

Beatrice furrowed her brow and thought, "Yes. You should just be confident." She thought some more and nodded, "Talk about Raven Wing. They'll want to know."

Arilin asked, "What about mobilization?"

Beatrice said, "Mention it, but remember it's boring." She gave Arilin a look, "I know you want to."

Arilin pouted, "Aw..." Their mother was starting to laugh softly and they both looked over at her.

She finished chuckling, wiped her eyes and said, "I don't know where you two *get* it. I'm always so proud of you..."

"Thanks, Mom," they choroused. Beatrice pointed at Arilin as she remembered something, "Oh, Arilin. There are strikes going on right now. Appeal to the unions to get back to work."

Arilin raised her eyebrows, "It's a High City crowd out there, BB. I don't think they're that influential."

Beatrice shook her head, "And journalists. Whatever you say will be in all the papers tomorrow."

Arilin blushed, "Really? You think?"

Beatrice grinned, "A cute princess calms the public while her father and brother are riding off to war? They'll reprint the *whole thing*."

Arilin ruffled her hair again, "Maybe *you* should do it for me, BB."

She gave her a dirty look for her trouble, "No way."

Arilin got up and asked her mother, "Is there something around here I can stand on, Mom? Safely?"

Her mother furrowed her brow, "Well, there should be something... ah!" Her mother's gaze shifted up and behind Arilin, "Abby, that would be great. Thank you."

Arilin turned to see Abigail Montrose, her mother's lady's maid. The woman was carrying a footstool from the library, and she said, "I think this will do perfectly, milady."

Now that she thought about it, Abby had been standing in the room *the entire time* and she hadn't even noticed her. She always noticed the other maids – it's not like you could miss the white uniforms. Even people conditioned to look past servants tended to notice them. Abby just had a way of completely suppressing her own presence so you looked past her. Arilin resolved to ask her about it sometime. With that in mind she said, "Thanks, Abby," turned and walked back out and down the hall towards their parlor.

The harsh thrum of male conversation ground into something she could understand as she approached the parlor's open door. The war, how it was going terribly, when the King would show up, why he had no consideration for the Assembly, so on and so forth. Some of it was borderline treasonous. She hesitated just outside for a second, took a deep breath and strode in.

"Good evening, gentlemen." She announced loudly. Conversation ground to a halt as she went on, "Why are you visiting us tonight? I would think you would need to see to your jobs, but if there's anything I can do for you..."

The youngest of the men in the room must have been three times her age. The Prime Minister was pushing five times it, and he registered the jab and looked over at her dismissively, "We're here to see your father, Princess." He sniffed, "We in the Assembly have gone all day without the slightest word from the King, and with the war we all have matters of the utmost urgency to discuss with him."

Arilin narrowed her eyes, "My father has matters of *greater* urgency to discuss with the Army. I doubt if he's going to be back from the War Ministry any time soon, and that he'll be in any mood to speak to you when he returns." His eyes flashed but Arilin went on, gesturing to the open glass doors that were letting chill night air drift into the room, "I don't suppose you've been using *my* balcony to speak to the crowd from?"

The Prime Minister visibly choked back anger and replied, "In the King's *absence* I thought it good to make a few remarks to the people, yes." The Minister of Labor chuckled rudely, she wasn't sure at whose expense. The man was a socialist and she was pretty sure he liked his own coalition's Prime Minister only slightly more than her father, if that.

Arilin looked back at him levelly, "I'd have thought it would make more sense for you to speak from the Assembly steps." She shrugged, "Anyways, I'll talk to them and you can all get back to your jobs afterwards."

The War Minister spoke up, "Princess, I really must speak to the King about the mobilization..."

Arilin shrugged and said blandly, "He's across the street in the War Ministry. I'm sure he and the Field Marshal would welcome your presence in the War Room."

At the mention of Field Marshal White the man visibly shrank. He said, "It's not of utmost urgency, I'll, ah, see if I can catch him later."

Abby had ghosted past her and set up the stool out on the balcony. Arilin nodded slightly to the ministers and said, "Now, gentlemen, if you'll accompany me outside, I'd like to show the people that the Assembly and the Crown are united in this dark hour." Arilin made a shooing motion with her hands and the politicians grudgingly stood up, stretched and walked out onto the balcony. As they emerged she heard the crowd grow quiet with anticipation.

Abby had come back inside, and Arilin self-consciously ran her fingers through her hair and asked her, "How do I look?"

The maid laughed gently and said, "Nervous, milady?" She reached over and brushed some imperceptible dust off Arilin's shoulders, "You *look* perfect. Now go make history."

"Thanks, Abby." Arilin turned, walked out onto the balcony and stepped up onto the stool in front of the railing, raising her above the ministers. The oceanic murmur of the crowd slipped into dead silence as they caught sight of her. And the crowd could only be described as oceanic. The people of the High City and the Capital below had come to the Palace square by the thousands, filling the vast space with a sea of humanity craning their necks to look at her. Waiting for her to say something.

Arilin extended an arm, waved slowly, put on a friendly smile and shouted, "Hello everybody!"

They went *nuts*. A wall of noise reached up from below and smashed into and over her, drowning her in cheers and whistles. She saw guards, islands of white in the sea of color below, struggling to keep the crowd from surging into the palace itself as it shifted excitedly. Arilin kept resolutely smiling, waved a few more times and then motioned for them to quiet down. In a few seconds the noise dropped off enough that she could speak again.

She put her hands on the railing, leaned forward earnestly and said, "Good evening to you too!" She gave the laughter from that one a few seconds to die down, then went on, "Even as I speak, my father is at the War Ministry with Field Marshal White and his generals, preparing a counterattack to throw the Empire back. I can say right now that mobilization is already in full motion, and the Army will soon be on the march!"

The crowd roared with approval, surging against the guards again. Arilin let it die back down and then went on, "My brother Adrian has already departed for the front with his regiment. And if you've looked over the harbor recently, you'll know the Northern Fleet has sailed for battle. I have complete faith in our fighting men to smash the Empire on land and drive the Black Fleet from the seas!"

Arilin paused and the crowd roared again. As the noise died back down she heard someone scream, "I love you, milady!" from below. Arilin smiled and waved in his general direction to a ripple of laughter.

She said, "But! I would be lying now if I told you this will be an easy battle. As I am sure most of you have heard already, Raven Wing Fortress has *already* fallen to the enemy and they are even now crossing the Night River." The people let up a distressed murmur. She went on, "Our soldiers at Raven Wing did everything they could today. They fought like lions against the Empire's assault. *No one* could have done better."

The crowd rumbled uneasily. The Army should never have played up the impregnability of Raven Wing so highly. Arilin kept going, "I do not need to remind you that the Imperials have a record of being stronger than we think they are." More rumbles from the crowd. She motioned for quiet and plowed ahead, "But! But! *We* have a record of victory! And with your help, *we will win!*"

The crowd erupted, thousands of people howling for blood. Arilin fought to keep from wincing at the noise. She felt sorry for the guards down in the midst of it all. Waiting until the noise subsided enough for her to think, she waved for quiet and went on as the crowd subsided, "Dark days are ahead for us all, though. The battle will be very hard! We must all stand together against the Empire, or we could fall!" Arilin pointed at random people in the crowd, "I need you! And you! And you! And *all* of you," she added with a sweep of her finger, "To do everything you can to win the war!"

"If you are a reservist, hurry to your unit! If you are not, the Army and the Navy are recruiting!" A laugh rippled up. There would be lines around the block to join the military tomorrow. "If you cannot fight, the Red Cross will need donations and volunteers in the days ahead." She gestured to the men standing behind her, "If you are in the *Assembly*, I urge you to put aside party and coalition, government and opposition, and stand together with the Crown against the Empire. And if the Assembly raises your taxes to fund the war, please, pay them!"

She got another laugh out of that one. Her father never missed a chance to remind his subjects who was actually responsible for taxation in this country. She forged on, "If you are a businessman, the government will be buying. Please make sure your business is worth the government's money!" Arilin remembered Beatrice's advice and went on, "And if you are a worker on strike, or thinking of striking, please return to your job. I urge employers to deal honestly with their workers' demands and resolve their disputes quickly like patriots."

The crowd murmured uneasily. The High City wasn't traditionally a hotbed of socialism. She ignored it and pressed ahead, "All of us, from my father on down, are in this war together. And if we *stand* together, my people, my friends, *we will win.*" Feeling the tension drain out of her, Arilin let out her breath, waved again and shouted, "God bless all of you! God save the King!"

"*God save the King! God save the King!*" The crowd chanted deafeningly in reply. Arilin was raising her hand to wave again when a pair of strong hands grabbed her under her armpits, lifted her off her stool and placed her gently on the floor. Arilin turned, surprised, to see her father standing there. He patted her shoulder and smiled.

Before she could say anything he turned to the crowd, stepped forward and put a hand on the railing commandingly. She could almost feel his presence filling the square as the noise of the crowd died suddenly. He leaned forward and said, in an almost conversational tone that somehow managed to carry to the back of the crowd, "My daughter is a *jewel*. I bet all you parents out there are jealous right now." He chuckled, drawing a laugh out of the crowd before he said, "I have nothing to add. God bless you, and have a good night."

The King spun on his heel, took her by the shoulders and shooed her through the open door back inside while the crowd was still standing there in shock. As the crowd roared like an avalanche outside, he smiled at her broadly and squeezed her shoulder as they walked. When they could hear again he asked, "So, any word on dinner?"

Arilin said, "No, sorry, Dad. I should have asked Mom earlier, she probably knows."

He chuckled, "Don't worry about it. I am hungry, though."

Arilin looked up at him and grinned, "Yeah." She said, "Me too."

They both laughed.

Chapter 6

The Road from Jade Falls

Sophia watched from a distance as her parents shared a farewell kiss at the foot of the armory's stairs. Her father said something to her mother and she replied tearily. Sophia read his lips as he told her mother he loved her and reluctantly tore himself away. A hundred similar farewells had taken place in the past hour as the sun sank and the moons brightened overhead. Sophia had thought her mother would never let go of her. But the last of them ended as the First Sergeant walked away from his wife, the officers checked their watches and the company's soldiers shouldered their packs without being told. The time for romantic goodbyes was over. It was time to march.

Sophia shouldered her own pack, tightened the straps and settled the frame onto her back. It didn't weigh much to pick up, but she knew from experience that it would turn into an anchor a few miles down the road and she was careful to adjust it properly. Even with her short time in the Army she'd seen soldiers bleeding out of open sores on their backs after long marches. And this wasn't any training march, over in a day. This was a war, and the Empire was a long way away.

Her father stepped to his position a little to her right, called the company to attention and gave the fateful command, "Right face! Column left and guide out the gate, march!" Packs and rifles turned a sharp parade-ground spin into an awkward shuffle, and the lead platoon awkwardly wheeled about and headed for the gate. Sophia hurried to get in front of them with the guidon and found herself walking next to Lieutenant Thorn as Captain Jaeger trotted out the gate before them on his horse.

Jade Falls had turned out to see them off. In front of them Jaeger drew his sword and ceremoniously saluted the mayor, who had stationed himself on the nearest street corner, to wild cheers from the crowd. Thorn hastily drew his own, a little awkwardly with all the equipment he was carrying, called for eyes right and saluted the man as they marched past. As Sophia swung her spear down to horizontal in salute she suspected that their portly mayor had never gotten this much official recognition before in his life.

Thorn turned his head, yelled, "Ready-front!" and returned his sword to its scabbard. Looking over at her as she stiffly rotated the guidon back to vertical, he said, "You can relax, Miss Rose. We've got a *long* way to go tonight."

Sophia looked at him, smiled and said, "Thanks, sir." She shifted her spear to a more natural slanted carry and followed after him, enjoying the supportive crowd in the dying sunlight. The whole town was out on the streets and it seemed like every other person had a flag, turning the sidewalks into a whirling sea of blue and gold in the twilight. She saw most of her friends from school and some of her teachers, cheering and clapping them on.

A brass band assembled in a side-street struck up a spirited rendition of "Blue Banners" as they marched by, and Sophia laughed out loud in surprise. Thorn looked over and she saw that he was grinning broadly as he said, "You can't mind this kind of sendoff."

Sophia smiled back, a little embarrassed for all the attention they were getting, "I don't, sir."

Thorn replied, "I don't either, Miss Rose." He winked at her, "I just hope we get the same reception coming back!"

Sophia laughed, "So do I!" She remembered seven years ago, waiting with her mother for the company to march home from the last war. They'd celebrated all night, went to bed, gotten back up and kept on all the next day after her father and his men had finally marched into town late in the day, dusty and gaunt. A few men had died, but aside from some teary moments it hadn't really affected the party. But that had been the last war.

When Sophia joined the Army, her father had finally told her about the war before that one. The Marchlands War had broken out when her father was a young sergeant at the Dragon's Jaw Fortress, newly married with a wife and a baby daughter to take care of. It had earned the name as the very tip of the Salient, a vast fortified area the Kingdom had held onto jutting into the heart of the Old Empire beyond the Night River. Her father had tumbled out of bed one night as the enemy's siege cannons opened fire and shells rained from the sky like meteors, and he'd killed two Imperial infiltrators by the time he reached his post. Then the Masks themselves came, just shapes in the fire and darkness, pressing closer and closer. And that had just been the first hour. Out of a company of a hundred and twenty men, fewer than thirty made it out alive.

They were marching against those Masks. Sophia felt a chill run down her spine at the thought. But it all seemed so unreal, so abstract. She couldn't imagine all her friends, all her fellow soldiers, just *dying* like that, and she felt the weight of the thought lift off her as the crowd cheered them along. She even caught a fleeting glimpse of the girl who had kissed her earlier, disappearing red-faced into the crowd a moment after she saw her. Sophia smiled, embarrassed at the thought. The girl *was* really cute but while forbidden schoolgirl romance was all very *dreamy*, she was ultimately into *boys*. There were going to be some awkward conversations when she got back.

Thorn looked over and asked, "What are *you* blushing over?"

It was showing on her face. Sophia replied hurriedly, "Ah, nothing, sir!"

He teased her, "What, just saw your *crush*?"

She shook her head quickly, "No, no, of course not, come on, sir!"

Thorn snickered, "Come on, tell me, who is it?"

Sophia said, "Not telling! No sir!"

He laughed, "You're no fun."

The crowd thinned out with the buildings, although groups of people were still standing by the road cheering them on for a good mile out of town. Things finally quieted down as they clattered over the bridge over the creek north of town where the last group of well-wishers had stationed themselves, the trees closed in overhead and they found themselves walking through the nocturnal peace and quiet of the Fairy Forest. They walked on in silence for another half an hour, the dark road lit only by moonlight filtering through the leafy canopy. Sophia felt her pack growing heavier and her boots rubbing at vulnerable spots in her feet, and she was relieved to hear her father calling for a halt as they emerged into a moonlit clearing.

The company shuffled to the side of the road and dropped their packs, letting up a collective groan of relief. Feeling strangely light without the weight on her back, Sophia felt the night's chill seeping through her sweaty uniform as she planted the guidon in the ground, sat down on her pack and unlaced her boots. Her father came around as she was rubbing foot powder into her feet.

He crouched down next to her and asked, "How are you holding up?"

She looked over and grinned, "Couple of hot spots on my feet. How's the rest of the company?"

He grunted, "Worse off than you. Couple of stragglers."

Sophia looked around at the night meaningfully and asked, "So... when are we stopping tonight?"

Her father looked at his watch, "If we want to make Southbend tomorrow, *late*."

She sighed. Southbend was a day and a half's march from Jade Falls, and they'd stepped off at sunset. She'd had a sinking feeling they were going to be up all night when they left. She replied, "Can we at least sleep in tomorrow before we leave?"

Her father laughed and patted her back, "I'll think about it."

He got up, exchanged words with Lieutenant Thorn as to when they would start again and how they needed to march like there was a war on. Then he walked back down the line to check on the rest of the company. Soon enough Thorn shouted for the platoon to get ready and Sophia laced her boots back up, re-did her puttees, collected her pack and guidon and got back on the road.

As they stepped off Thorn called for the combat road march formation, and the platoon obligingly spread out along the sides of the road as they went. Sophia turned around for a few paces and saw the entire company splitting down the middle and spreading themselves out, dense blocks of soldiers marching down the middle of the road turning to loose files along the edges. Captain Jaeger turned in the saddle at the commotion, shrugged, and kept riding out ahead of the company. They were a *long* way from the Empire, but Sophia supposed that it was never too soon to start getting ready for combat. She tightened her grip on the guidon and stepped out after Thorn.

They walked on like that for what seemed like an eternity as the false sun set, the night darkened and the moons rose in the sky. They passed through Lantern Woods, the sleepy village north of Jade Falls, made two more stops and each time the soldiers filed back onto the road more reluctantly. Sophia felt herself nodding as they walked on in silence, and her pack seemed to get heavier and heavier. Looking over at Lieutenant Thorn, she could see that he was feeling the effects as well. They hadn't marched a long way, but it was very late and they had all risen early for a normal day, had the shock of the news and frantically prepared to march in a haze of adrenaline. Hours on the road under a heavy pack took all the romance and excitement out of war.

Her father finally called for a fourth halt as they came to another clearing in the forest. Moonlight had a way of changing how things looked, but Sophia was pretty sure it was the same place the company had stopped for the night returning from their last training exercise in Southbend. Sophia planted the guidon, sat down on her pack and closed her eyes as her father walked up the road past her. She heard him conferring with the commander for a second and felt someone prodding her shoulder.

"Sophie? Sophie? Come on, wake up." She opened her eyes and saw Jack and Tony looking down at her.

She said, "Uh... was I asleep there?"

They both laughed. Tony said, "Yeah, Sergeant Cross sent us to go find you. We're camped over there with the platoon." He pointed off further up the clearing, where Sophia saw a group of soldiers slowly putting tents together. The company had spread around the clearing looking for convenient places to sleep. Red-faced, Sophia got up, recovered her equipment and walked over to the platoon's area with her two companions.

Sergeant Cross looked up from rolling out his ground sheet as they walked up. He worked in forestry ordinarily and he looked every part the strapping lumberjack. Sophia was a very tall woman and he loomed most of a head over her as he stood. He said, "Rose! We've been looking for you. Where did you two find her?"

Jack said, obnoxiously helpful, "She was sitting on her pack back there sleeping, sergeant."

Tony shot him a murderous look as Cross chuckled and said, "Gotcha, she was talking to the First Sergeant. Mulligan, you really need to cover for your buddies more." He looked at her, "Rose, you and Gravesend are together, right? Go pitch your tent, chow's coming around in a few minutes."

Tony and Sophia chorused, "Yes, sergeant," and walked off to find where Tony had dropped his pack. Jack moodily walked back over to his area with the rest of the machine gun team and went back to putting his tent together. As Sophia planted the guidon again and dropped her pack, Tony said, "You know, I *was* going to cover for you."

Sophia laughed and said, "Thanks." Tony already had his ground sheet out, and they had their shelter halves buttoned together and their tent most of the way up in a few minutes. They were working on staking it out correctly when Sergeant Cross came back around.

Cross knelt down, pointed back towards the far side of the clearing where the company's wagons were pulled up and the horses staked out, and said, "Chow's ready. Get yourselves over and get some food." They saw a line of soldiers forming at the company's cook wagon, moonlight glinting off steel mess kits.

Sophia said, "Gotcha, sergeant... uh, our tent isn't quite ready though."

Cross looked at the current state of their work and said, "Eh, I'll give you two a couple minutes to get that thing standing. Two minutes." He glared at them while they finished putting their tent together in record time and then shooed them along towards the mess line. As they walked over Sophia noticed her father, Lieutenant Thorn and Sergeant Falcon, her platoon sergeant, ceremoniously standing around watching soldiers go through the line. Cross looked over at Falcon as they walked up and said, "Last three from me, boss."

Falcon said, "Thanks." Sophia saw him look over at her father and Thorn and say, "First is up. Go get in line, sir, I want to talk to the first sergeant here." Thorn looked at him, shrugged, and got in line. Her father and Falcon walked off towards the forest, talking softly.

The Army's cooking wagons were technical marvels able to prepare hot food for soldiers on move, and the company's cooking section had outdone themselves on this first night of the war. Sophia and Tony were handed a loaf of bread to share and got generous portions of stew dispensed into their mess kits, along with a scoop of some sort of sweet-smelling dessert thing. Sophia identified it as the Royal Army's attempt at apple cobbler, then took a look at the bread, raised an eyebrow and asked the cooks, "Made a supply run before you left, huh?"

Corporal Harris, in charge of the company's three-man cooking operation, admitted, "Well, it was available. Would you rather have crackers?" He gestured to his wagon, "This cannot make enough bread for a hundred people, Sophia."

The oven was a little small for the task, to be fair. Sophia laughed and said, "No, no, of course not. Thanks for the food."

As they left to find somewhere to eat, Tony said, "That's your bakery's bread, right?"

Sophia said, "Yep. Can't complain about the Army's business." They found an unoccupied spot to lean against a supply wagon and ate with the quiet enthusiasm of the very hungry and exhausted. They finished quickly, made the walk back to the cooking wagon to clean their mess kits and feeling sleep weighing on their heads finally walked back to their tent.

They brushed teeth, washed faces, armpits and groins and changed out of sweat-soaked underclothing. Sophia sheepishly disappeared into the tent for the last two. Sergeant Cross, who barely seemed to be feeling the effects of the day, came around to tell them they didn't need to worry about guard duty. They thanked him and Tony crawled inside as Sophia broke down the guidon. He had already rolled himself in his blanket and fallen asleep by the time she made it in herself.

Sophia didn't last much longer.

* * *

The bugler was doing an enthusiastic but not particularly competent rendition of Reveille.

Sophia groggily opened her eyes in the tent's grayish darkness and saw Tony shift a little and then obviously go back to sleep as the bugler finished. She could see him, which meant it must be getting light outside. They *had* slept in. She untangled an arm from her blanket, prodded him and whispered, "Hey, Tony, wake up."

Tony didn't respond so Sophia grabbed his shoulder, shook him and said, much louder, "Hey, Tony, time to get up."

He shook himself, looked over at her blankly and said, "Guhuh? Nandishwakesheup? Unnh..." He cleared his throat, blinked a few times and said, "I... really need to pee." He quickly untangled himself, felt around for his boots and started putting them on. And now that he'd mentioned it, Sophia realized that she also had a desperately full bladder. She quickly grabbed her rifle and found her own boots.

Sophia got out of the woods to see their camp coming to life in the morning's gray light, soldiers shuffling through the morning dew stretching and starting to tear down tents. She walked up on Tony sitting on his backpack halfway through shaving, looked him over and said, "I don't envy you."

Tony shrugged, took another stroke with his razor and said, "I don't envy *you*. The cooks have coffee ready if you want some."

Sophia yawned widely and said, "Yeah, I do. Any word on breakfast? Or when we march out?"

Tony said, "Nothing but rumors. I heard we step at nine."

Sophia did some mental math, "So we'll hit Southbend by three or four."

Tony replied, "We'll be up all night cleaning the barracks anyways."

She sighed. The prospect of cleaning their barracks at Southbend from top to bottom after marching all day in the sun wasn't pleasant. But that was the Army way of doing things. Sophia shrugged and said, "It can't be helped. I'm going to get some coffee, you want some?"

Tony gestured with his steaming canteen cup, oily and sludged with shaving debris, "I'll get some later."

Sophia grimaced, collected her mess kit and walked over towards the cook wagon. The cooks had apparently been hard at work since well before the rest of the company got up, because they were finishing breakfast as she arrived. She was first in line and she got back to her tent with a helping of dubious Army eggs, dubious Army bacon and some slightly stale bread.

Military scrambled eggs varied in quality from "alright" to "vomit thickened with corn starch" determined largely by how vindictive the cooks were feeling that day. Today's eggs were "okay" mostly because they were still hot when she started eating. She quickly finished, cleaned her mess kit and got to work breaking down their tent. Between her and Tony the job was done in a matter of minutes, and Sophia put the guidon back together and sat down on her backpack to wait for the word to move.

It was a fine, cool spring morning. The sun climbed through the clear sky, a gentle wind shifted her hair and birds called cheerily from the forest. Sophia and Tony talked, and Jack tired of his machine gun team's company and joined them after a while. They were the only high-school students in the platoon, and whatever their differences in normal life it drove them together in camp.

Sophia, Tony and Jack were all under Sergeant Cross in First Squad, of Charlie Company's First Platoon. Their squad had thirteen soldiers with three teams of four, plus Cross himself leading it. Two of those teams were armed with rifles, and their job in combat was to close with and assault the enemy under the covering fire of the third team's machine gun. First Platoon was supposed to have four squads, but given that the company was a reserve unit and terminally under-strength it could only muster three and an extra machine gun. Sophia and Tony were both riflemen. While Jack *had* a rifle his main job was to carry extra ammunition and spare barrels for the machine gun, and he wasn't particularly happy about the extra weight.

Eventually the order came down to move out and the company shouldered packs and got back on the road. Sophia took up her usual place next to Lieutenant Thorn at the head of the column as they marched back into the cool darkness of the shaded road, and the miles ground by beneath her feet. On the western edge of the Fairy Forest villages and fields took bites out of the forest like holes in Swiss cheese, and they had passed through a couple villages and back into the forest's shade when Sophia started hearing a soft, distinctive squeaking off to their right.

She turned to Thorn, who was staring determinedly down the road in front of them, and said, "Sir, I think someone's coming up on us on the right. I hear wagons."

Thorn looked over at her blankly, then off to his right. Turning back to her he said, "I don't see anything... are you sure?"

Sophia nodded, "Yeah, definitely wagons." A horse whinnied off through the trees as she finished, "Hear that sir?"

Thorn shook his head as though to clear it and said, "Yeah, barely..." He looked over at her appraisingly, "You have *really* good hearing, Rose. You said you heard wagons?"

She nodded, "Yeah. Lots of them."

Thorn turned and called for the commander, and Captain Jaeger quickly rode up. They explained the situation and he galloped off ahead to see what was going on. As he disappeared around a turn up ahead, Sophia asked Thorn, "Sir, what was that for?"

He pulled a folded map out of his bag and pointed to a spot on it, "We're about here, and there's an intersection up ahead. The *last* thing I want is for us to get stuck behind a bunch of wagons on the road and have to march through their dust."

Sophia replied, "Oh, I see, sir." They walked around the turn themselves and Sophia saw that Thorn had been correct. A little ways ahead, Captain Jaeger was having an animated discussion with another mounted officer. As they got closer she started seeing horses and wagons through the trees, lots of them. The wagons didn't look like normal supply wagons, either. Some of them looked like boxy wooden cases on wheels. Others were slender, dark gray and sinister. Sophia realized they were field guns propped up on their limbers for travel. They had walked across an artillery battery.

Captain Jaeger won the argument with the battery's commander over who would be first on the road when Sophia and Thorn marched past the intersection to nasty looks from the waiting artillerymen. Thorn saluted sarcastically as they went by, and Sophia laughed. She said, "Very nice of them to wait for us, sir."

Thorn looked over at her slyly, "I think Captain Jaeger didn't want to look at them the rest of the way to Southbend."

They marched on uneventfully for another hour as the forest thinned and the fields got larger before they went through another village and her father called a halt for lunch in the local square. The artillerymen seemed to have pulled their wagon train off before they hit the village, probably so they'd have an open space to deal with their horses in. Sophia shrugged off her pack and sat down gratefully, loosening her boots to let air circulate around sweat-soaked feet. Thorn plopped down next to her, took a deep breath and shook his head.

Sophia asked him, "Doing alright, sir?"

He looked over at her, "Yeah, fine. This marching is killing my feet."

She asked, "Tried two pairs of socks? And I think the medics have powder and wraps and... stuff. Sir." She pointed at the company medics trying their best to hide out behind a supply wagon. As they watched she saw her father walk over, tell them to do their jobs and send them hurrying over to the platoons to make sure his soldiers still had skin on their feet. Sophia and Thorn shared a laugh.

Thorn said, "Your father sure is something, isn't he?"

Sophia replied, "He's my dad. I guess I'm used to him?"

Thorn chuckled, "You'll have to let the rest of us in on your secret."

They heard a voice behind them, "Lieutenant Thorn, there you are! You really must join us for lunch."

They twisted to see Captain Jaeger and Lieutenant Stahl. Sophia started to stand, but Jaeger waved her back down. Thorn replied, "Sorry, sir, I really need to get my feet looked at."

"Oh?" Jaeger frowned, "You need to make sure you take care of yourself, Thorn. In that case Stahl, I'm sure there's a café around here somewhere, let's go find it." The two officers turned and walked off.

Sophia took her boots and socks off and let her feet dry out while the medics came around. They gave her feet a cursory glance before they set to work putting Thorn's back together. He had some purple spots on them that should have been white, and as they set to work on his blood blisters Sophia supposed that he probably didn't do a whole lot of long-distance walking at his job at the bank.

Lunch consisted of a different recipe of Army stew and a thick slice of fresh bread from the local bakery. Sophia was pretty sure they used pork instead of beef this time around, and the ratio of green vegetables to potatoes had gone way up. Sophia filled her mess kit and ate quickly with her friends, speculating on how much longer they'd be on the road and how much work they'd have to do once they got to their barracks. They were about four miles from Southbend, and at the rate they were going that would be another two hours before they hit the town. It was already well past noon, and Sophia doubted they'd finish moving in before nightfall. As she was making the point she noticed Thorn eating with her father and probably having the exact same discussion with him.

After they'd been halted for an hour the other officers reappeared and they got back on the road, Thorn walking a little gingerly under the weight of his pack. As they left the village Sophia saw wispy smoke rising to their north, and soon the trees in the distance had been replaced by the city itself stretching out to embrace them. The area around Southbend was flat and forested enough that it was impossible to get a good look at the city

before actually walking into it, and they quickly found themselves marching through its southern suburbs through a growing crowd of civilians.

Sophia unsheathed her guidon's spearhead and raised the flag high,
to cheers from the crowd. Flags started appearing, and they walked the
last mile to the barracks through a street lined with Royal blue and gold,
cheered on by an enthusiastic crowd. Sophia saw a few photographers
snapping away as they went by, and she turned to Thorn and raised her
voice over the noise, "Sir, you think we'll make the papers tomorrow?"

He grinned and waved to the crowd, "I hope so! Just keep smiling!"

They sighted the high wall around their barracks after a few more
minutes, and the imposing main gate topped with the regiment's coat of
arms showing its coiled rattlesnake quickly came into view. The soldiers
on guard swung it open to let them in. Captain Jaeger rode his horse in
first, noticed somebody important to his left and quickly turned to salute.
Thorn did the same as he walked in, and Sophia dropped her guidon in
salute at the group of men sitting just inside on horseback. She couldn't
see their rank from her angle, but the one front and center looked pretty
old and distinguished under the shadow of his cap. She guessed he was
Colonel Paget, the regimental commander.

Sophia and Thorn walked up a couple of long steps, through an archway cut into the long building in front of them and into the regimental quad. The unit's drill field was surrounded by four large rectangu-
lar buildings, three barracks for the battalions and the one furthest back
with considerably nicer quarters for those officers who didn't have houses
in town and offices for the regimental staff. Soldiers were leaning out of
the first battalion's barracks to watch them come in, but the second and
third battalion buildings, housing units drawn from out of Southbend
itself, seemed deserted. Sophia realized they were the first company to
arrive from out of town.

The long file of soldiers snaked onto the drill field and her father
shouted them into a formation. Sophia found herself once again front
and center next to him as he said, "Alright! We're here! Whose feet hurt?"

Sophia heard a general disgruntled murmur from the company behind her. Her father laughed and went on, "Join the club! Now, the faster
this barracks gets cleaned the faster you can eat dinner and bed down for
the night. I'll be coming through at..." He looked at his watch, "Nineteen
hundred. That's three hours. And I *will* have a white glove. Company!"

The platoon sergeants shouted, "Platoon!"

"Fall out!" She heard her comrades take a step back, spin on their collective heels and start crowding into the barracks, grumbling about white

glove inspections in wartime. As she turned to leave her father asked her, "Sophia, how're you holding up?"

She turned to look at him, "Just fine, Dad. Thanks."

He smiled and patted her on the shoulder, "You'd better go help your friends. Those barracks are going to be dusty as hell."

She looked at him and raised an eyebrow, "You're *really* going through with a white glove?"

He smiled slyly, "We're a little far from the Empire to be dropping the standard, even if it is wartime."

Sophia deflated, "Alright, Dad. I'll tell them you mean business."

He patted her on the shoulder again, "That's my girl. Thanks, Sophie."

Sophia turned and sighed. Her father had a *point*, but it didn't change the fact those barracks didn't get lived in a whole lot, they were dusty as hell, and when First Sergeant Rose said "white gloves" he wasn't joking. She had a *lot* of work to do.

Chapter 7

Tea With a Princess

Patricia MacMahon leaned against the railing and watched the storm come in.

It had built up over the great Northern Ocean, pressure systems colliding over the icy sea a thousand miles north of the Empire and spiraling westwards. Now it was poised to finally make landfall and break over the Capital itself. Its miles-high thunderhead had already turned the northern sky black, and Patricia could feel a cold wind starting to shift against her face.

There was probably some divine irony there. War breaks out on a fine spring morning and two days later, as the casualty lists come in and the war fever dampens, a storm blows in to set the mood. Patricia smiled a little at the thought. Maybe the weather was a good sign. Most of the disasters she'd seen had happened under a clear sky.

In any event she had a good place to watch it from. Her office on the north side of the War Ministry had an amazing view out over the Capital. She could go out on her balcony and look almost straight down into the Lower City that stretched from the cliff-face below out to surround Sapphire Bay miles away and far downhill. As the stiffening wind cleared haze from the air she could see, far in the distance, a destroyer squadron scurrying through the headlands seeking shelter from the storm. She didn't envy Admiral Kensington. He was probably dead in the middle of it right now with the battle fleet.

Someone opened the French door behind her, and she heard her aide's distinctive soft knock on the sill. "Milady?" Lieutenant Gable said, "Ah, Princess Arilin's here for tea."

Patricia pulled herself away from her thoughts, turned and smiled, "Thank you, Vanessa. Everything is set properly?"

The younger woman fidgeted, "Ah, yes, ma'am, I checked it myself."

Patricia nodded, "Then I'm sure it's fine." She walked past her and back into her office, noting with some satisfaction that her table was set properly for tea. Vanessa didn't exactly inspire confidence to talk to, but she was smart and diligent and Patricia could trust her to do sensitive things like handle visiting members of the Royal Family. She asked, "Princess Arilin is waiting outside, right?"

Vanessa chirped, "Ah, yes, ma'am. I, ah, told her to wait there while I, uh, got you..."

Patricia smiled again, "Relax, you did just fine. You can take a couple hours off, come back at seventeen hundred and I'll tell you if I had any commitments come up tonight or if we can both go home for once."

Vanessa said, "Thank you, ma'am."

Patricia opened the door to the outer office to see Arilin sitting on the couch and leafing through one of the magazines she kept out there. She'd at least changed out of her school uniform before coming over. Noticing her, the girl set down the copy of *Equestrian Weekly* and quickly got to her feet. Patricia spread her uniform's skirt in a curtsey and greeted her, "Milady, I've been expecting you. Please come in."

Arilin curtseyed back, "Thank you, General." She followed Patricia inside, and Vanessa ducked out and shut the door behind her as they sat down.

Patricia turned on the lights, brightening the room as the day darkened outside. She said, "I tried to anticipate what you'd like for tea, milady. I hope it's to your liking."

Arilin smiled and sat down, "It is, thank you!"

Patricia smiled and took a seat herself, "Thank my aide. Vanessa set the whole thing up, I just gave her some pointers."

Arilin asked, "She was the one who left just now?"

Patricia nodded, "She came up here from the Fourteenth a couple of months ago. She's a big improvement over her predecessor, too, although it took a couple weeks to get her to talk to me normally."

The princess observed, "She seems kind of shy."

Patricia said, "She's just really quiet. Colonel Bennett down at the regiment barely knew what to do with her." She shrugged, "I had the opposite problem. My first commander thought I was crazy." She changed the subject, "Now, milady, how about some tea?"

Arilin nodded, "Of course, thank you, General." She looked at Patricia and fidgeted a little as she poured her a cup, "Ah, do you mind if I call you Patricia? General is so... harsh."

Patricia burst out laughing, narrowly avoiding spilling tea all over the table as she poured her own cup, "No, of course not! And," She thought for a second, "It is kind of harsh for this kind of thing. But I have *one* condition."

Arilin sighed, relieved, "Thanks... but what's your condition?"

Patricia smiled mischievously, "Do you mind if I call you Arilin, milday?"

Arilin nodded, "Not at all, Patricia." She asked, "Now, how is it that you have a whole tea setup in here? I've seen Field Marshal White's office, and he sure doesn't have anything like it."

Sighing, Patricia said, "I have to entertain a lot of ladies here. Any time someone important wearing a dress walks into this building they usually end up in my office."

Arilin took a sip of the aromatic tea and thought for a moment, "That seems strange. I mean... it's not your job, so why?"

"Arilin, on a good day maybe half of what I do is actually related to my job *per se*." Patricia smiled, "*Somebody* needs to deal with Lady Strathclyde when she comes barging in here trying to get the Army to sponsor her daughter's debutante ball."

Arilin laughed and, recovering, said, "Really? I think I *know* her daughter."

Her smile got a little sly, "I told her 'no' five different ways and she left an hour ago in a huff."

"Well, it serves her right." Arilin furrowed her brow, "But, Patricia, what *is* your actual job?"

Patricia shrugged helplessly, "Beats me." Seeing the look on Arilin's face, she snickered and said, "I'm actually the deputy chief of staff for strategic plans, which means I make sure a bunch of colonels who work for me spend their time figuring out what the Army needs to look like ten years from now instead of *golfing*." Arilin laughed, and Patricia smiled and went on, "Right now I've got them down to only playing on Fridays, and I make them send me a memo afterwards detailing what they figured out on the course."

The princess sipped at her tea some more, hesitated and ventured, "That sounds, ah... nice."

Taking a long swig of tea, Patricia sighed and said, "Yeah, it's kind of a joke. But, when they moved me up here last year everyone in the shop spent *all* their time golfing and nobody actually worked, so it's really a big improvement. And this is an important job." She pointed at the pile of papers on her desk, "The reason the Empire could sail their fleet up to Raven Wing is because when they expanded the fortifications after the Marchlands War they didn't build any new coastal gun emplacements. We had this enormous fortress that couldn't defend itself adequately from the sea. Somebody in *this* shop should have figured that out."

Arilin's eyes widened, "Oh." She finished off her cup of tea and went on, "So, what are you doing now, with the war?"

Patricia picked up the teapot and refilled Arilin's cup. A thick whorl of steam rose from the elegant china as the room darkened noticeably and the first drops of rain pattered against the window. Setting it back down meditatively on its plate, Patricia replied, "Very little, actually. White pulled my entire department to work for him yesterday standing up the field army. He did not see fit to pull *me*."

Arilin asked, "The 'Army of Drakenburg' they're talking about?"

She smiled halfheartedly, "Yeah." She gestured at the stack of papers on her desk, "I've been helping out the intelligence guys in the meantime, but, well, I've read a hundred dispatches today and most of them contradict each other. We're still losing."

The princess narrowed her eyes and asked, "Why aren't you going east with White? You should be up to command a division. I think you'd be an obvious choice."

Patricia felt her eyebrows rising in surprise. It wasn't every schoolgirl who could connect the dots on Army politics. And now that she thought about it, why was Arilin in her office, anyways? Was she here for girl talk or was she after something? And if she was smart enough to ask the question, she was smart enough to understand the real answer. Patricia replied, carefully, "Arilin, how much do you know about getting a command in the Army?"

Arilin furrowed her brow, "Well, if you're at a certain rank and you're competent you should get a chance to command a unit that corresponds with your rank. You're a rising star in the Army, so I don't understand why they wouldn't give you a division..." She hesitated for a moment, "I mean *I've* seen what you did with the Fourteenth."

Patricia leaned back in her seat, crossed her legs and smiled, "Arilin, does this look like the office of a *rising star* in the Army?" The rain drummed louder on the window as the question sank in.

The princess sipped her tea, looked around the room searchingly, looked back at Patricia and said, "No." She paused for a second and went on, "But in that case, how can you be the first lady two-star in the Army's history and one of the youngest if you're *not*?"

Patricia said, "Easy. I was... promoted out of responsibility."

The girl sitting across from her narrowed her eyes, "How does that work?"

"There is no regulation that states this, but it is an unwritten rule that in order to get a command you must first have commanded at the next lower level." Arilin nodded and Patricia went on, "And the Army is a very male club. If ladies like you and I want to *fight*, we are expected to serve in the light cavalry. It would be unheard-of for a woman to serve in the cuirassiers, let alone have authority over them. Remember that every cavalry brigade in the Army has a *heavy regiment*."

Patricia saw the light come on across the table as Arilin said, "They didn't want to let you command a *brigade!* And..." Arilin trailed off, hesitant.

She encouraged the girl, "Go on. You're halfway there."

The princess narrowed her eyes, "But you must have demanded it based on your record, and they wouldn't be able to stonewall a duchess forever, so they... promoted you?"

Patricia nodded, "Exactly. I got into the history books as the first lady major general... and I'll never lead soldiers in combat again." She sighed, "If my father were still alive he would have put a stop to it, but regardless I'd feel pathetic asking him to help me out with my career as a *general*."

Arilin's red eyes flashed, and she set her teacup down with an angry click, "That's *terrible!* I should talk to my father about it. He *signed* the orders."

Patricia made a calming motion, "And start a battle with Field Marshal White? He was behind the whole thing. I'm not even sure if your father could win that one."

"It's still not fair." Arilin grit her teeth, "You deserve better from the Army."

Patricia smiled, "Thanks. I hope you remember that if you become Queen one day. And..." She felt herself blushing, "Thanks for letting me vent. I don't have a lot of confidantes."

Arilin turned red herself, "Ah... thanks, any time."

Conversation paused for a minute as Patricia refilled their teacups. As Arilin helped herself to one of the butter cookies Vanessa had set out, Patricia took a sip of tea and asked, "So, Arilin, why did you ask to see me today?" She smiled disarmingly, "I'm sure there are plenty of more interesting things for you to do on a day like this."

Arilin sipped her tea nervously, looked at Patricia and said, "I've been thinking I should do more to help."

Patricia leaned forward on the table, folding her hands in front of her, "Oh? I think you've done more than enough already. After your speech the other day I don't think there's a worker still on strike in the Kingdom."

"Thanks," Arilin said nervously, "So, last night I asked my father if I could accompany the Army to the front." Patricia's expression became flat and unreadable as she went on, "He said yes, *if* I could find someone to take responsibility for me." Arilin looked her straight in the eyes, "Will you do it?"

Patricia sighed, shook her head to clear it and glared at the girl, "You're a little young for the battlefield."

Arilin glared back, "I don't see how much trouble I could get up to around headquarters. And anyway, Adrian was younger."

Patricia snorted, "Yes, and it was the height of irresponsibility to have him running around the Marchlands at the time. I don't know *what* your grandfather was thinking."

Arilin said, "I'm not exactly planning on getting into swordfights with any dragoons. I just want to learn about the Army at war."

Patricia replied coldly, "The Army at war is pretty awful, Arilin. On my first patrol we got into a fight with the Masks and one of my troopers took a slash. To this *day* I can still see his horse trotting back up with the lower half of his body still in the saddle. And then we had to go *find* the upper half."

Arilin gritted her teeth, "I understand that. But I still have a duty as a member of the royal family to defend this country as best I can. I might be Queen one day."

Patricia gave her a hard look. Escorting Princess Arilin would get her a free ticket to go forward with the Army, be part of the war and make friends in the royal family. It would certainly help to rejuvenate her career. And it was obvious that Arilin would go on to do great things in the future. Her request was really an incredible honor. On the other hand, the girl was *thirteen*. No matter how canny she was, Arilin was a child and deserved all the protection the adults of the world could give her.

Arilin said, "Please?"

Damn it, Patricia thought, *I am a terrible person*. Sighing, she said, "I'll speak to your father."

The princess's eyes got wide, "Wow. Thank you."

Patricia growled at her, "No guarantees."

Arilin fingered her teacup nervously, "No, of course not. Uh... do you need an appointment with him?"

Patricia leaned back and pinched the bridge of her nose, feeling a headache coming on, "Yes, actually, I do, but I'll talk to your butler about it. I'll be over around seventeen thirty. Can you tell him I'm coming please?"

Arilin chirped, "Sure."

Patricia shook her head and looked at Arilin again, "Do you have any other bombshells for me today?"

The princess smiled a little, "Just that one."

She sighed and said, "Thanks. Would you mind if I asked you to head home? I need to think."

Arilin shook her head, said, "Not at all," and finished off her teacup.

They stood, and Patricia saw her to the door. Before Arilin left Patricia said knowingly, "Bathroom's five doors down the hall on the right."

Arilin blushed, "Thanks."

She smiled, "You drank a lot of tea."

The guards Arilin had left in the outer office jumped to their feet as she walked out, and Patricia shut the door behind the girl. Going back to her desk, she sat down and buried her head in her hands. What had she just *agreed* to? Was the King actually okay with this, or was this some scheme Arilin was working? And, assuming everything was actually alright, how was she going to actually do this?

Patricia massaged her temples. There was no way she could go with the Army headquarters. The less time she or the princess spent around Field Marshal White the better, and it would be too far forward for true safety. That meant they needed to accompany a trail corps, one that would stay out of action but still have a clear idea what was going on. Many of the corps commanders were White's men, though, and would see them as a nuisance at best.

Many, but by no means all. She hated the thought, but there was one man who fit the bill perfectly. He was in charge of Ninth Corps, which was far to the rear of the order of march and wouldn't leave for another few days. Although he was an unpleasant, patronizing horse's ass, he was smart and would actually explain things if you asked him to. His chief of staff was a family man with daughters Arilin's age. She had enough history with him to ask for what amounted to a favor. And he had his own problems with the Field Marshal.

Patricia sighed heavily and got to her feet. She needed to go talk to Walter Haas.

Chapter 8

Forged Steel

Someone gently shook her shoulder and said, "Come on, Rose, time to get up."

Sophia opened her eyes, groaned and sat up in bed. The lights were on in her platoon's bay and she could see soldiers climbing down from bunk beds and milling around groggily getting ready. Outside the windows all she could see was a slate-gray fog. She looked over to see Sergeant Cross standing by her bedside already in uniform and said, "Unh... what time is it?"

He scowled and said, "Six-ten. Formation for bayonet practice at six-thirty."

Sophia sighed. So much for sleeping in after staying up half of last night cleaning the place. She was beginning to think her father had a thing against sleep, "Thanks for getting me up, sergeant."

Cross shrugged, "Eh, you kids all need to be woken up. At least you *get* up. I had to drop your friend Gravesend on the floor and kick him just now."

Sophia looked past him to see Tony stumbling around like a zombie and chuckled. She also saw more than she really wanted to of some guys further down the room and replied, "Uh, sarge, I need to get changed, so can you...?"

"Oh, yeah, sorry," Sergeant Cross turned and went to go deal with someone else, and Sophia got out of bed and pulled the screen she had around her bunk for privacy closed. She liked most of the guys in the platoon, but not enough to change in front of them when she had an alternative.

Twenty minutes later, as the Kingdom's blue-and-yellow flag hit the top of the flagpole and the last notes of the bugle call died away her father faced about and told Charlie Company to drop their salutes and form a semicircle. As they pressed in around him he hefted his training rifle with its padded tip and started, "Good morning, Charlie! This morning we'll be working on bayonet drill. Any questions so far?"

She heard Jack pipe up in the back, "I thought we were running."

Her father smirked, "You are. Run a lap around the quad, Mulligan." Jack cursed and slowly started away from the group. Her father shouted after him, "Sprint! Rifle over your head, private!"

As Jack completed his orbit of the parade field her father went on, "We'll do drills first, then move on to free practice. Sophia and I will be demonstrating. Everyone pair up, get into a circle, take five minutes to stretch out and we'll begin." The company dispersed into a circle around them and her father looked over at her, "Sorry it's not our usual morning routine, Sophie."

She shrugged, "I need a break every now and then, Dad."

He chuckled, "I guess you deserve one after yesterday. Don't spread this around too much, but you guys did a great job on the barracks last night."

High praise from a first sergeant. And she'd thought he'd cut them some slack by only telling them to go back and clean harder once. She replied, "Really? Thanks... I thought you were going easy on us."

He smiled slyly, "Me? Ease up? In *wartime*?" He settled his mask on and leveled his training rifle, "Girl, I'm going to have to knock some sense into that thick skull of yours."

It was on now. Sophia tied on her own mask, readied her weapon and jibed, "Bring it, pops."

Her father floated forward and his bayonet went through the space her throat had occupied a split-second earlier. Sophia crouched aside and sprang forward, stabbing at his chest as he drew his arms in, knocking her thrust aside with his buttstock. She took another step and drove her weight into him as their rifles crossed. He stepped back and she bounced away, cleared her rifle, dug her feet in and lunged low at his groin.

Something hit her in the chest hard enough to lift her off her feet. Even with the rigid bayonet-fencing plastron it felt like she'd actually been stabbed in the chest as she staggered back. Instinctively dropping back into her half-crouch, Sophia flipped her bayonet level only to see her father rubbing at the side of his hip. He looked over at her and said, "Trying to cripple me this early in the morning, Sophie?"

She shrugged, "I thought you wanted to fight. And anyways, Dad," she rubbed at her ribs, "You got me pretty good there."

Her father chuckled, "Yeah, you got some air. Just take it easy during the free practice." His serious look was obvious even through the mask's grille, "If you try that stuff with some of these guys out here we're going to have a body on our hands."

Sophia sighed, "Yes, Dad." She didn't blame him for being nervous about her, as annoying as it was. Last time they'd done company bayonet practice she'd flattened Lieutenant Stahl, although in her defense he *had* told her to not go easy on him.

Her father called the company to order and they got down to business. Her father started off as the ring of soldiers drew closer and quieted, "Does anyone here know how many casualties the bayonet produces in battle?"

Someone spoke up, "One in twenty, First Sergeant?"

He chuckled, "Good guess, but it's not even that much. In the Marchlands fewer than one in every *one hundred* casualties, from us or the Masks were from bladed weapons, bayonets or swords. More men froze to death than had Imperial bayonets stuck in them. That being said," He paused, "Why are we here today?"

One of her squadmates, Edward Bellamy, ventured sarcastically, "Because bayonet practice doesn't cost the Army money like ammunition does?"

Her father glared at the miscreant, "No. Do pushups." Edward sighed, got down and started pushing as he asked again, "Any other guesses?"

Tony spoke up, "Uh... because we have to fight the enemy face-to-face sometimes?"

Her father nodded, "Exactly. Our *job* in the infantry is to *attack* the enemy and *take* their positions from them. And you can't do that with artillery, or by shooting at them from half a kilometer away like we'll be doing on the range later today. You do that face-to-face, with bayonets." He gave it a moment to sink in, "If you don't know what you're doing and you come around a corner in a trench and there's a dragoon swinging a sword at you, you're going to *die*. And I've seen it happen." He looked at her and went on, "That being said, let's get started. Sophia, we'll demonstrate the throat thrust first."

There were three targets in bayonet fighting as far as her father cared. They were the throat, to be attacked with a two-handed thrust, the heart, to be attacked with a two-handed thrust, and the groin, to be attacked with a two-handed thrust. Everything else built off those three basic techniques. The Army's bayonet masters would disagree with him, but Charlie Company had won the divisional competition eight times in the last ten years and people had long since stopped complaining about his non-doctrinal techniques.

They practiced techniques. They practiced counters to those techniques. And then they squared off and fought. Her father started them off one against one and it built from there. By the time they got to all-out, platoon-versus-platoon war the fog had burned off and they'd attracted an audience. Sophia's head spun with exhaustion by the time they finally called it quits, but she collected the guidon and filed into the barracks after her comrades grinning with adrenaline-soaked happiness.

And that was just the start of the day. Sergeant Falcon caught Sophia and Tony about an hour later as they were leaving the battalion chow hall and told them to get their rifles and link up with Cross to get ready to shoot later that afternoon. They trooped upstairs and found their squad lying on the tile floors on their side of the bay, sighting in their rifles. Off to the side, Jack and the rest of the machine gun crew were finishing putting their gun back together.

Sergeant Cross noticed them as they came in, "Tony, Sophia! Come over here, we're doing coin drills."

They walked over, and as Sophia sat down to get started she noticed the machine gunners trying to cycle their weapon. "Trying" was the correct term, because the action was just sliding back and forth as they worked the charging handle. She looked at Sergeant Cross, "What's going on with them?"

He leaned in and whispered to her, "I stole their recoil spring out last night and I'm waiting for them to figure it out."

She whispered back, "Wow, mean."

He smirked, "They'll get it eventually. It's kind of a big part." He looked at the two of them sternly, "Now you two get to work."

Sophia knew there were four things she needed to pay attention to if she wanted to shoot something – or some*body*, like an Imperial soldier trying to do the same to her – and have any chance of hitting it. Two of them were easy. She had to actually put the sights on target, which was difficult to screw up, and anyone could look at her and tell her that her body position was bad. Breathing was tricky, but it was also simple to fix – all she needed to do was not breathe in or out when she was pulling the trigger.

Pulling the trigger was the hard part. If she jerked the trigger, or put too much pressure to one side or the other as she squeezed her rifle would drift off-line of the target as she fired and she'd miss. She had to pull straight back, *hard*, because the Royal Army's R02/10 rifle had a stiff trigger to discourage jumpy soldiers from accidentally shooting their friends in combat, and keep her rifle on target as she fired.

Hence the coin drill. Sophia lay down on the floor, settled her weapon into her shoulder, worked the bolt to cock the weapon and sighted in intently at nothing in particular while Tony gently balanced a penny on her rifle's barrel. As he lifted his hand away she settled her breathing and gently squeezed the trigger.

Tink. Tony picked up the penny and gingerly balanced it back on her rifle, and she tried again. *Tink.* It took her five or six more tries before she got it right and the penny wobbled, but didn't fall off. Sergeant Cross looked over at her approvingly, "Good job, Miss Rose. Now if you two both do it ten times in a row you can take off."

Sophia grinned, "Sure thing, Sergeant." She had Tony reset the coin and fired again.

Tink.

It was going to be a *long* couple hours until lunch.

* * *

The company formed back up after lunch, weapons in hand and ammunition pouches heavy with rounds, and stepped off to march the two miles to the rifle range. As they snaked the formation around and back out of the quad Sophia noticed that Lieutenant Thorn was looking sour, and she realized she hadn't seen him since breakfast. She asked, "Something bothering you, sir?"

Thorn smiled half-heartedly, "Regiment came running down here looking for Captain Jaeger for this meeting, and Stahl didn't want to go so I got stuck with it. *This,*" He gestured at the troops behind him with his head, "Is a break for me."

Sophia furrowed her eyebrows, "You know, I haven't seen the commander since... last night?"

Thorn shrugged, "I think Colonel Paget took them all out drinking last night or something. The ones that were there all looked *real* hungover." He noticed the look she was giving him, "Hey, it wasn't my idea. *I* was *here* last night."

"Sir," Sophia said, "Please don't ever change."

Thorn laughed. Without packs it was an easy walk to the range and they made good time. About halfway there they passed Bravo Company coming in, and they roared a greeting at the tired soldiers as they marched by. Bravo gave them a half-hearted cheer and trudged onwards. Coming down from north of the city they had farther to march from their armory than Charlie did, and they looked worse for it.

Another few minutes of walking got them to the regimental firing range on Southbend's eastern outskirts, and her father took charge and got the company to work setting up targets. Lieutenant Stahl stood in for the commander to give the Army's mandatory briefing on not shooting your own feet off and they started shooting. With the war on the soldiers took it more seriously than they usually did, and the entire company zeroed rifles and machine guns, shot for qualification and had burned off the last of their ammunition taking potshots at the eight hundred-meter targets by the time the sun outlined the Shield Mountains to the west in a blazing sunset.

They marched home by moonlight as the bright point of the false sun sank before them, and arrived at the barracks as it dropped below the mountains and the sky noticeably darkened overhead. Her father must have called in some favors with the cooks, because they'd kept the chow hall open for them and they were able to file straight in for dinner. Full and tired from the long day, Sophia turned in her rifle to the company armorer and headed upstairs for bed.

She was sitting on her bed unwrapping her puttees when Sergeant Cross came by again. Looking down at her, he said, "Hey, the trash needs to get taken out. Grab Gravesend and get it between you two."

"Sure thing, sergeant," She finished stripping off her puttees, rubbed at her calves as they decompressed, stood up and called over to her friend, "Hey, Tony! We've got the garbage tonight, come on."

Tony looked up from the letter he was writing and said, "Really? Give me a second to put my boots back on."

"Alright," Sophia said, walking over, "Who're you writing? Your cute little sister?"

Tony snorted as he tightened his bootlaces, "I'd hardly call her cute."

Sophia smirked, "She is, and you didn't answer the question."

Tony glared at her, "And I'm not going to."

"You know, I bet she's just *pining* for love from her dear brother..." Sophia trailed off suggestively, then changed the subject, "Are you done yet? We've got to go here."

Tony finished tying off his boots and stood up, "I am now. Come on."

They collected the garbage, headed downstairs and out into the cool night. There were a couple of soldiers standing around smoking and there were still plenty of lights on in the headquarters building, but otherwise the night was quiet. The arc lamps that could light up the quad at night hadn't even been turned on, and they walked down the sidewalk heading out back passing in and out of the shadow of the trees lining the parade field.

Sophia pointed at the headquarters as they approached, "What do you suppose they're doing in there this late?"

Tony shrugged, "Train schedules? We've got to get east somehow."

Sophia said, "You know how sometimes we get stuff to do that doesn't make any sense, but we have to figure it out anyways?" Tony nodded and she went on, "From talking to Thorn, I think it's that way all the way up."

Tony laughed as they passed into the headquarters building's shadow, "So they're trying to figure out stuff from Division that makes literally no sense?"

Sophia imagined a bunch of distinguished officers standing around puzzling out bizarre orders, and laughed. She replied, "It *does* make the Army make a lot more sense, now that I think about it."

They walked out the back gate, greeted the guards there and turned to walk down the back street behind the barracks. Garbage was actually dumped in an alley to the side of the compound to be picked up in the morning. As they came close to the turn, Tony started up again, "Hey, Sophie, how long do you think this war's-"

Sophia noticed a scruffy-looking kid leaning against the far wall of the alley as they drew closer. His head was turned to talk to somebody further down, and he didn't notice them for a couple seconds. He turned his head back towards them and froze, eyes widening. Sophia stopped in her tracks and Tony bumped into her, saying, "Hey, what's going..."

The kid yelled, "Guys, *run!*" He bolted down the street as Sophia and Tony dropped their bags of trash and ran into the alley. Garbage was everywhere, a gang of little kids was milling around in surprise and one older, taller boy with jet-black hair was stuffing some papers into a knapsack. Sophia locked eyes with him, he smirked and she launched herself at him as he turned and ran.

Sophia burst through the pack of fleeing children, dug deep and raced after the boy. He was *fast*, and they'd run the full length of the alley by the time she was close enough to lunge for him. He must have felt her coming on and leapt aside at the last minute. Sophia fell, rolled, came up and saw something flash towards her out of the boy's outstretched hand. She twisted aside the throwing knife – knives, *three* of them – gouged chunks out of the brick wall behind her.

Who is this kid? She pulled her fighting knife out and started forward again, but her momentum was gone and the boy was already across the street. He vanished into the shadow of the next alley and Sophia realized he was as good as in the Empire for all the hope she had of chasing him

down. His young conspirators, on the other hand, were all trapped between her and Tony. Sophia sighed, sheathed her knife, did an about-face
and put on her evilest grin. Kids scared easy, and she was *angry*.

About three minutes later the duty sergeant and a couple armed soldiers rushed out the back gate to investigate all the screaming and crying that had suddenly erupted and found Sophia and Tony herding eight
shaking, pale-faced juvenile delinquents out of the alley. Tony smiled
to see the reinforcements and called out, "Sergeant! We've caught some
spies!"

The man looked at him, puzzled, "These are street kids."

Sophia handed him some grimy papers, "Street kids who were being
paid to go through our trash for stuff like *this*."

The sergeant glanced at the papers, did a double-take and looked
through them carefully. "My God," he said, ruffling through the papers,
"Personnel reports... intel teletypes, briefing minutes, train schedules..."
He gave her an uneasy look, "I think we need to start burning this stuff."

Sophia frowned, "Their leader got away with a lot of papers. And..."
She hesitated, "It sounds crazy, but I think he was a Black Cloak. He
looked like a kid, though."

The man gave her a look, and the two soldiers with him exchanged
nervous glances. "As in, an *Imperial intelligence* Black Cloak? What
makes you say that?"

Sophia rubbed the back of her neck nervously and replied, "He...
threw a bunch of knives at me while he was running away." She produced
a throwing knife she'd recovered.

He shrugged, "Good enough for me. Can you give a description?"
Sophia nodded and he turned and spoke to one of his soldiers, "Hey, go
get Major Matheson and tell him what's going on. The Colonel's going to
want to hear about this. And we'll need to call the police... have him do
that." Noticing the nervous looks Tony and Sophia were giving him, he
said reassuringly, "Don't worry, you two, Matheson's just the duty officer
tonight. He'll want to talk to you two, but he's nice."

One of the children whimpered, "Sir, can we go home, please?"

Tony said, sternly, "Maybe... it depends on how cooperative you are
with the sergeant here, isn't that right, Sophia?" Sophia snickered and the
children shrank away from her fearfully.

The sergeant crossed his arms and nodded theatrically, "Yes, indeed,
I'll need your utmost cooperation if you expect *leniency*. You two, please
go up to the duty office with my man. I'll take over here." He gave them a

serious look, "Good work out there."

"Thanks, sergeant." They chorused. After they went upstairs and told their story to an increasingly-disturbed Major Matheson, however, Sophia started to get the feeling it was going to be a *long* night.

Chapter 9

9:15 to Drakenburg

Walter Haas pulled out his monocle and polished it with a handkerchief as he looked sidelong at his companion. Lady MacMahon was fidgeting and checking her watch every ten seconds as she looked down the street. He tucked his monocle into his breast pocket and reassured her, "You know, milady, it's only eight. When did you tell the princess to arrive?"

She looked at him nervously, "Ah... eight-fifteen?" She bit her lip and went on, "I'm just worried about Arilin. I mean, maybe the King had second thoughts. Maybe *she* had second thoughts. Maybe she's been in a carriage accident or something."

Walter raised an eyebrow, "Arilin? You two *are* pretty close." He snorted at her dirty look, "Calm down, milady. Princess Arilin does not strike me as someone who shows up late. I'm just surprised the King agreed to this."

Lady MacMahon laughed nervously, "I haven't been that scared talking to somebody for a *while*." She smiled, "Thanks for helping me out. It really means a lot."

Walter chuckled and went on, "I could barely believe you when you came by earlier."

Patricia smiled sheepishly, "I was having a hard time believing *myself*." She went on, her eyes brightening, "Just like old times."

Walter glanced at the stars on her collar and raised an eyebrow as he replied, "I'll say." Before she could reply he jerked his head at Siegfried extricating himself from his wife and daughters over by the railway station's main entrance, "Just between us, milady, Ziggy mopes when there aren't any women around. If you two can keep him happy you'll have more than returned the favor."

She laughed at the sight, "I feel sorry for him. He's got such a cute family, don't you think?"

"I don't think I'm qualified to comment." Walter replied drily, "Cute isn't really my specialty."

She actually pouted at him. *God, she's about five minutes older than the princess*, he thought, *How does this girl keep getting promoted?* As she was about to reply he noticed a block of red-jacketed horsemen turning the corner down the street, and he nodded in their direction and interrupted, "I think that's the princess, milady."

Lady MacMahon turned around, saw the princess's carriage as it turned the corner between two formations of escorting cavalrymen and visibly relaxed. Looking at her watch, she remarked, "Wow... ten minutes early. I just hope she doesn't have too much baggage."

Walter replied, "Reminds me of this lieutenant I once knew."

She gave him a half-hearted glare, "I *thought* I was traveling light, you know."

"Yes, that's what worried me at the time." He rolled his eyes theatrically, "Was the *piano* really necessary?"

She tossed her hair dismissively, "I play. And it's not like it was a concert grand."

Walter snorted and shook his head as the princess's carriage glided to a halt in front of them. Several of the cavalrymen dismounted and set to work unloading two sizable trunks from the rear of the vehicle while another one set a portable step beneath the door and opened it ceremoniously. The two generals bowed as Princess Arilin climbed out and alighted on the cobblestones. Lady MacMahon greeted her, "Milady! How was the ride down?"

Arilin replied, "Better than usual. And... General Haas?" They straightened up as Arilin nodded at him, "You honor me, sir. I'm sure you have other duties."

Walter chuckled, "I can attend to them later, milady."

Lady MacMahon pointed at the two trunks being carried into the station between pairs of straining guardsmen, "Is that all of your luggage? There isn't more on the way?"

The princess colored a little, "Ah, yes... I hope it isn't too much. Mom was kind of insistent."

Walter gave MacMahon a meaningful glance and she flushed a little herself, "Um, no. That's... great!"

A businesslike woman climbed out of the carriage behind the princess. Seeing the two generals, she made an effort to be unobtrusive that failed as MacMahon turned to her and asked, "And who might you be, miss?"

The woman curtsied deeply and replied, "Rebecca Stone, ma'am. Lady Arilin required a servant for this trip, and I volunteered to go."

MacMahon probed further, "What brought that on?"

Rebecca shrugged, "I didn't have much of a choice, ma'am." She explained, "I served as an Army nurse in the Jihadist War, so I'm familiar with the territory. None of the other girls are."

Lady MacMahon smiled, "That's great. We'll have to talk later." She nodded over her shoulder, "We have a carriage prepared for the princess, if you would like to see to it." Thus dismissed, Rebecca hurried off past them towards the station, and the princess and the two generals began walking after her at a more measured pace.

The King Maximilian Railway Terminal was one of the Kingdom's showpieces, the gateway to the High City and the Royal government. It looked the part, looming far above them in stately magnificence as they walked into its grand hall. Harried-looking soldiers had replaced the usual flow of government workers, turning the entire platform into a patchy sea of blue uniforms as the IX Corps staff bustled about getting itself ready to depart.

Spying four red jackets climbing out of the train, Walter leaned over to Lady MacMahon and muttered, "Two trunks? I'm starting to like this girl already."

She whispered back, "What are we going to use that extra boxcar for now?"

Walter smirked, "Still got that piano?"

"Go to hell, Walter." She gave him a half-hearted glare.

He raised his eyebrows, "Walter, huh? If we're on a first-name basis now, milady," He stroked his beard and looked Patricia up and down, "Hm. What do you think about Trixie?"

Patricia looked at him, twitched, spun on her heel and stormed off after Arilin. Walter snorted and let them go. Taking his monocle from his pocket, he rubbed it again with his handkerchief and screwed it into his eye. The princess had been right. He did have other duties to attend to, not the least of which was that they were scheduled to leave in an hour and at this rate they'd be lucky to make it in three.

* * *

The princess's red dress, white blouse and golden hair stood out like fire amidst all the blue uniforms as Patricia hurried to catch up the princess. Arilin gave her a sly smile as they stepped up into the train and remarked, "You two get along well."

Patricia snorted dismissively and said, "Are you talking about the same General Haas I know?" She wove through a group of soldiers what looked like carrying electrical equipment forward and led Arilin towards their accommodations at the rear of the train.

They stepped through the vestibule and into a lounge car full of military clerks trying to make an office's worth of clutter fit into a railcar a tenth its size. Someone saw the princess and called the car to attention, people falling over themselves as they scrambled upright. Patricia waved them back to work as Arilin replied, "He doesn't seem to have a problem doing you favors. I don't think he's doing this for *my* sake." The soldiers made a show of going back to their business while sneaking glances at the princess, and she asked, "Are they really going to do this in *every* car we go into?"

"Yes, unfortunately. We'll put something out later if it's annoying you. And..." She looked Arilin up and down appraisingly. The princess looked back with her piercing red eyes. Patricia sighed. Arilin was sharper than most adults and she would figure it out eventually. Glancing around at the soldiers surrounding them, Patricia went on, "I think we should get somewhere more private before I tell you about my relationship with General Haas, if you could call it that."

Arilin smiled and took her arm, "I'd love to hear all about it. Lead on, milady." Patricia shook her head. She could only imagine what the princess was going to be like in a few years. She felt sorry for the King. Conducting Arilin back to their railcar, she waved a dozen cars full of soldiers back to work as they leapt to attention for the princess. By the time General Haas' aide pulled the vestibule door aside and let them through into their own car it was even starting to wear on her.

Vanessa and Rebecca curtsied and greeted them as they walked through the door and into the coach's large sitting area. There was already a steaming pot of tea prepared and sitting on the table for them, and Patricia smiled and said, "Thank you, Vanessa. You two seem to have hit it off already."

Vanessa replied, "Becky was just telling me about her time in the service, ma'am."

Patricia said, "She told me she served in the Jihadist War earlier. I'd love to hear about it myself sometime." She pursed her lips for a second, "But I have something to talk to Princess Arilin about. Could you two please give us some privacy?"

Rebecca said, "Of course, milady," and quickly ushered herself and Vanessa out. Patricia pulled out a chair and sank into it gratefully. She pinched the bridge of her nose as Arilin sat down and poured herself some tea. She didn't want the girl getting the wrong idea.

Patricia started off, "Arilin, let me ask you a question. Do you think all military officers get along with each other?"

Arilin cocked her head to the side quizzically, "No, of course not. You've told me so yourself."

"Exactly," Patricia said, "The Army is a gigantic organization. There are over a thousand generals. Factional fighting comes with the territory." She reached up and rubbed one of her shoulder boards reflexively, then went on, "You could say that General Haas and I are in the same faction, as is Siegfried and many of the people around here."

Arilin leaned forward and smiled, "Oh? I wouldn't think of you two as like-minded."

Patricia laughed, "No, we're certainly not!" She went on, "I don't think you could find two generals with less in common than us, honestly. But we do share one thing. Neither of us particularly cares for Lawrence White."

Arilin raised an eyebrow, "The Field Marshal? I'd have thought Haas would get along with him. He seems prickly enough, and I'm assuming they came up together."

"You'd think, right? Now, there are a few things going on between them. For starters, White is junior to Haas but got promoted past him because he had all the right connections, but that's just a personal thing." She shrugged and went on, "I resent White playing games with my career and I *really* don't care for him personally, but I can say that about a lot of people."

Arilin gave her a look, "I'm assuming there's something more going on?"

Patricia leaned forward, resting her elbows on the table and pressing her fingers together as she said, "Field Marshal White thinks that if we hit the Empire hard and fast they'll collapse. You saw how he acted when Raven Wing fell. You should have heard the harangue he gave all of us after your father had left for the night." She scowled, "As far as White cares the Imperial Army is still a gang of rebels defying Royal authority. He holds the Empire in *contempt*."

Patricia went on, "*We* don't. General Haas has spent most of his career fighting the Imperials. I spent my time as a lieutenant in his brigade at Dragon's Jaw Fortress, and that was enough for me." She shook her head, "They are a *terrifying* enemy. Arilin, Raven Wing wasn't a fluke, not any more than the Quadrilateral was in the last war. The Empire is *that* good."

Arilin nodded, "I see." She gave her another one of her sly smiles, "So, wait, you were in his brigade as a lieutenant? Wouldn't that make him...?"

She hung her head and sighed. She shouldn't have let that detail slip. Looking up, Patricia said, "Yes, at one point Second Lieutenant MacMahon reported for duty to Brigadier General Haas. He still gives me grief over it." She pinched her nose again and leaned back in her chair, "And while we may be friends, milady, there is no way I'm going to tell you my lieutenant stories just yet."

The princess smirked, "Oh? I'll have to ask him then."

Patricia glared at her, "Don't you *dare*."

Arilin was giving her an award-winning pout when somebody knocked on the door. They turned as it opened and Siegfried stuck his head in, saying, "I hope I'm not interrupting anything."

The princess shrugged, "Just girl talk. Boys, mostly. You can come in."

He stepped in and set a stack of messages on the table between them, explaining, "Word travels fast. We just got a telegram from Prince Adrian for you, milady," He nodded at Arilin, "And ten invitations from Drakenburg society over the next week. I was wondering if either of you was interested."

Arilin pulled out the message from her brother, popped it open and started reading it voraciously. Patricia picked up the rest of the messages and looked through them, saying, "Don't these people know there's a war going on?"

Siegfried said, "All the more reason to throw a ball in support of the troops, I suppose."

"I wish they'd do it in peacetime. I'd be more inclined to attend." Patricia remarked, then gave Siegfried a quizzical look, "Wait, Siegfried, do *you* want to go?"

He looked at the ceiling innocently and said, "Well, if your ladyships felt like attending a ball, of course you'd require a male escort for protocol's sake." Siegfried sighed theatrically, "The sacrifices I make for King and Country, they really are *so* much to bear."

Patricia laughed and said, "Well, I suppose we don't want to burn ourselves out too early. And some of these look like A-list parties." She looked across at Arilin, who was folding the telegram and sticking it into a pocket, "What do you think, milady?"

The princess gave her a blank look, "Huh?"

They both laughed. Patricia replied, "You didn't hear a single word we just said, did you, milady?"

Arilin blushed deeply. It made her about three times cuter. Stammering, she ventured, "Uh, b-ball invitations right?"

"Yes, but," Patricia teased her, "What did the prince write that's gotten you so red?"

Arilin looked at the floor and replied, "Uh... he's going through Southbend with his regiment. And, uh, love, you know."

She chuckled. It would be cruel to tease the poor girl further, so she let her off the hook, "What do you think about going to the Lord Mayor of Drakenburg's ball this evening with Siegfried and me? He's been kind enough to send us an invitation, and we should arrive in plenty of time."

The princess thought for a moment and replied, "I've met the Lord Mayor a few times. He seemed alright to me." She shrugged and looked at Siegfried, "Sure. I assume you'd be escorting us, milord?"

"Of course, milady." He gave her a short bow, "It would be my pleasure."

Arilin looked between Patricia and Siegfried, then stood abruptly, "Then it's decided. Siegfried, do you have a moment?"

He nodded, "Of course, milady, what is it?"

Arilin jerked her head at the door, and he followed her outside and shut the door behind them. Patricia watched them leave, surprised. Wondering absently what scheme the princess was hatching, she poured herself some lukewarm tea and took a sip. Even cold, it was heavenly. She made a mental note to ask Rebecca how she did it, leaned back in her chair and stretched her arms over her head. They hadn't even left the Capital and already Arilin was proving herself a handful.

Patricia was startled from her thoughts by the shriek of the train's whistle. A few moments later the carriage lurched and she saw the station start to move past the window. Next stop Drakenburg. Fortunately, she'd packed a ball gown.

Chapter 10

The Prince and the Private

"Alright, Charlie, up and at 'em!" The inside of her eyelids brightened as the lights snapped on, and Sophia groaned and turned her head aside. It was earlier than usual this morning. Had to be. Raising a hand to shield her eyes, she slowly sat up in bed and listened to the rest of the company coming awake for a minute. Sighing, she eventually peeled back the sheets and swung her legs out of bed, feeling the chill of the tile floor seep into the soles of her feet.

She had padded over to her footlocker and started pulling out a fresh fatigue uniform when she heard Sergeant Cross announce to the squad, "Good news and bad news, guys. Which do you want first?"

Sophia called out, "Good news!"

Sergeant Cross chuckled, "The good news is that Tony got up on his own this morning. Congratulations, Tony! Also, no PT." Her squad sarcastically applauded and he went on, "Bad news is we're going to be in formation for an inspection by someone important at eight, so I'll be inspecting you all at seven. Service dress with rifles and bayonets, no web gear. Spit-polish *everything*."

Jack spoke up, "Any idea who this guy is, sarge?"

She could hear Cross shrugging, "Somebody important enough to have the Sergeant Major climbing the walls this morning, according to the First Sergeant. And speaking of screwed up," His tone got sterner, "Clean this place up while you're at it. For all I know this guy is going to walk through the barracks, and this place is a mess. I've got... four fifty-five right now, so you all have two hours to get ready."

"Yes, sergeant," they chorused tiredly. Sophia sat down on her bed and sighed. This meant that she had two hours to clean herself up, spit-polish her boots, shine every last brass button and pin on her uniform, buff the guidon's spearhead and her bayonet, get the dirt and grease out of her rifle's stock and *then* clean the barracks. They needed all day. Unfortunately they didn't have that, and Sophia quickly finished pulling on her fatigues, slid her curtain aside and headed for the bathroom to wash up.

Two hours and thirty minutes later Sophia was standing at parade rest while her father, Sergeant Cross and Sergeant Falcon stared intently at her left collar from about a foot away. Her father gently reached a white-gloved hand up and pulled the top of her crossed-rifles pin away from her white collar patch to get a better look at it. He glanced over at Falcon and said, "Does this look discolored to you? Right there on the edge?"

Falcon leaned in and squinted, "Yeah, it looks like she didn't rub the polish off completely."

Cross weighed in sourly, "Trick of the light."

Her father snickered, "Sore loser more like it. Five marks, pay up." Cross rolled his eyes, pulled a bill out of his pocket and handed it to him. Her father jibed him, "Your fault for betting me I couldn't find something screwed up with my own daughter's uniform."

"Can I relax now, Dad?" Sophia asked.

He patted her on the shoulder and smiled, "Yeah, go ahead, Sophie. You did great. Now," He leaned in and murmured to her, "If you could teach your friend Mulligan there how to shine his damn boots sometime I'd *really* appreciate it."

Sophia looked over his shoulder at Jack inelegantly rubbing at one of his boots and whispered back, "Is this before or after I teach him how to shoot?"

They both laughed. Cross and Falcon exchanged quizzical looks as her father turned around and told them, "You guys pass. There's only so much they can expect out of us on three hours' notice." He peeled his white glove off ceremoniously and went on, "Have your people downstairs in ten minutes. And make sure they're hydrated, nobody here's had breakfast yet and somebody's going to pass out in formation at this rate."

Sophia slung her rifle over her back, picked up the guidon and trooped downstairs with the company, joining the rest of the battalion spilling out of their barracks and into the quad. Captain Jaeger was already waiting for them in front of their assigned spot on the parade field, pacing back and forth nervously. Her father went up and spoke to him briefly and he relaxed a little as Sophia walked up with her spear. She gave him the color-bearer's salute with her left arm across her chest and asked, "Sir, where do you want me?"

Jaeger waved his right hand near his head, which Sophia was gathering passed for a salute among particularly harried officers, and pointed to a spot on the grass, "Right there, Miss Rose." She walked over to the place he'd indicated, and he looked between her and the assembling company and said, "Ah... take a step right." Sophia obligingly sidled over, and he looked again and corrected himself, "Left about a half-step, I think." She moved back in the other direction and he nodded, stepped into his position to her right and watched the company fall in behind her.

Off to her left she saw the battalion commander, Colonel Thompson, walking out to his position in front of the unit with the color party in tow. He made his own adjustment, pointed out where he wanted the flag-bearers to stand and let them sort themselves out. The Kingdom's flag, with its blue sky and twin suns and the white, black and gold battalion colors stirred gently as a breeze shifted through the quad and their bearers fell into line.

Across the parade field Sophia saw Third Battalion milling into position, a mass of blue-uniformed soldiers fringed with gleaming bayonets and spiked with battle flags. Off to her right in front of headquarters First Battalion was solidifying its ranks, and over Jaeger's shoulder she could see a tall, lanky man on horseback riding out into position in the center of the quad trailed by the regiment's colors. The color bearers behind him found their positions without help as Colonel Paget looked around, surveying his command. He looked at his watch one final time, then came upright in the saddle and shouted, "Regiment!"

The three battalion commanders echoed back, "Battalion!"

"Attention!" Colonel Paget shouted. Sophia pulled her guidon erect as the regiment braced to attention with a dull thud of thousands of boots on grass. And they waited. Sophia bent her knees a little to keep her blood circulating and appreciated the faint wind stirring through the quad. She felt sorry for the soldiers behind her, surrounded by other men on all sides and slowly feeling the air around them turn hot and stagnant. The colonel's horse shifted about nervously, and she saw him pull on the reins a couple times to steady it.

Faintly, Sophia heard the clatter of hooves on stone. She shifted her eyes to the left to see a man on a powerful white horse lead a group of horsemen out of the quad's arched entryway. They expertly guided their horses down the long stone steps to the parade field as Colonel Paget rode forward to greet them. The colonel saluted smartly and the man at the head of the group returned it with a quick almost-wave. Sophia got the sense that whoever this man was, he returned enough salutes that he found it tiresome.

As Colonel Paget turned his horse to ride beside him and they set off down the line of troops across from her, Sophia observed the man. Even seated in the saddle and on a tall horse, he was *gigantic*, easily taller than the colonel and with immensely broad shoulders. He wore the gray uniform jacket, red pants and jackboots of the Kingdom's elite heavy cavalry, and Sophia supposed that he felt no need to wear the heavy armor and helmet while inspecting someone else. The cap he was wearing struggled to contain his curly blonde hair, and he looked immensely at ease as he surveyed the assembled troops and chatted with the visibly-nervous Paget.

Also, he looked *young*. Despite his dignified air, he didn't look that much older than Lieutenant Thorn. How was he *possibly* this important? He certainly wasn't a general, or an important politician, and Sophia hoped the colonel wouldn't put the whole regiment in ranks to impress some young noble. But he was apparently here in some official function, and he was young and very important. And he was tall and blonde and handsome. In fact, she thought, he looked a little like Prince Adrian, the Kingdom's most eligible bachelor and heartthrob to millions.

Oh my God, she thought, *He's Prince Adrian*. She was thankful she'd unlocked her knees earlier, because she felt like fainting. She took a couple deep breaths to steady her nerves as Adrian, his entourage and Paget turned at the corner of the quad and started riding across the front of First Battalion. Now that he was closer she could see he was carefully looking over the assembled troops, occasionally pointing something out to Paget. He paused for a couple minutes and had a muted conversation with First Battalion's commander, then rode onwards and out of her line of sight.

Sophia felt her heart beating faster and faster as seconds dragged into minutes. To their right, Delta Company's commander called his men to salute. She could hear hooves stepping closer and closer and murmured conversation among the riders as the royal group drew closer. Delta dropped their salutes and Captain Jaeger hoarsely called, "Present arms!"

As if in a dream, Sophia hoisted the guidon and swung it horizontal, letting the company flag hang open as the spearhead glinted lethally in the morning sunlight. Off to her side, she saw Jaeger salute with his sword, holding his position as that big white horse stepped into her field of view again. Thanks to her cap's brim she couldn't even see the prince himself from the waist up, just his hips and obviously muscular legs on that gigantic horse. He rode in front of her, close enough she could have reached out and poked him with her spear had she wanted to.

Sophia saw Adrian shift in the saddle a little as he pulled on the reins and stopped directly in front of her. The seconds crawled by, Sophia's heart thundering in her ears. Adrian shifted his weight forward a little, rose in the saddle and swung his leg over. His attendants murmured in alarm as he stepped down from his horse, spun on the ball of his foot, strode past her spear's point and stopped in front of her, maybe two feet away. He was so tall she was looking straight at his chest. She could hear him breathing. She could see the tiny Royal Army crests in the blackened buttons of his uniform. She could smell his cologne, and it was *amazing*.

Prince Adrian crouched suddenly and his face dropped into view, all of a foot away. The tale about the Royal Family having red eyes was completely true. His eyes were red as a demon's, and they were staring into her soul. They narrowed slightly, and he cocked his head and looked down at her chest for a moment. At her breasts, actually. Sophia felt herself start blushing as he looked back up and said, slowly and deliberately, "Miss Rose... you are the first woman I have ever seen in the Infantry."

Sophia realized belatedly that he'd actually been looking at the nametape on her chest. She was somehow disappointed he hadn't been checking her out. But what was she supposed to say to that? She swallowed hard and replied, "There's not many of us, my lord."

He snorted, "I'll say." Adrian straightened back up, his head zooming out of sight. Crossing his arms in front of her face, he went on, "How's your route march time?"

Sophia replied levelly, "I carried a machine gun fifteen kilometers yesterday, my lord." She added quickly, "We didn't keep time, but I kept up."

"Oh?" Adrian sounded interested. He went on, "Can you shoot?"

Of course she could. What was he getting at? She said, "I qualified last week, my lord."

"Hrm," She could hear him frown, "Can you *fight?*"

Sophia felt the corner of her mouth twitch up, "Battalion bayonet champion, my lord."

"Not regimental?" He questioned.

Sophia looked up at him, smirked and said, "We haven't had the tournament yet, sir."

Prince Adrian looked down at her sternly for a second before his hard-edged features softened as he chuckled. Reaching a hand out and patting her on the shoulder, he said, "Keep it up, Miss Rose. I'm sure I'll see you again."

Adrian's hand felt like warm, living steel. Sophia felt herself blushing deeply as she replied, "Yes... yes, my lord!" Adrian smiled, spun on his heel and quickly remounted his horse. He gave it a tap with his heel and set off down the line, taking his companions with him in a buzz of conversation.

As they moved off, Sophia heard Captain Jaeger call hoarsely, "O-O-Order... arms..." She quickly spun the guidon back to vertical, planted it in the ground, stepped aside and caught him as he fainted. Lieutenant Stahl and her father quickly ran up from behind the formation, and her father

helped her with Jaeger as Stahl pulled a man out of ranks for the guidon and stepped into the commander's place. They got under his arms
and hustled him back under the shade of the trees behind the company,
where a couple bored-looking medics were tending to a dozen or so of
men who had passed out standing in formation. Sophia didn't recognize
any of them.

One of the medics woke up a little, got up and rushed over to help
them with Jaeger. After they set him down and the medic started examining him her father remarked, "You know, Sophia, I thought we were doing
really well."

Sophia looked at him questioningly, and he went on, "We hadn't had
any fall-outs from the company, and down goes the *commander*. The
Sergeant Major's going to *kill* me."

Sophia laughed nervously and said, "You're not worried about the
Prince talking to me?"

Her father patted her on the back and said, "He looked a lot happier
afterwards, so I'm guessing he liked what he heard?"

Sophia smiled slyly, "I told him the reason I wasn't regimental bayonet
champion was because we hadn't had the competition yet."

Her father snorted, "Hey, missy, if you want to be the *real* champ
you've got to beat the *old* champ, and you're about a thousand years too
early for that."

She smirked, "So, Dad, does that mean next time I kick your ass I get
the All-Army title too?"

They both laughed.

* * *

Sophia was playing cards on her bunk with Tony and Jack that night
a few minutes before lights-out when her father walked into the bay. She
noticed him and looked up as someone closer to him down the bay asked,
"Hey, Top, what's going on?"

Her father scowled, "Night court. Every day I thank God that you all
keep out of trouble." He paused, "So don't go starting trouble now that I've
let you know that."

Sophia raised an eyebrow. Nobody in the company had done anything
dumb enough to warrant military justice lately that she knew about. Jack
asked the question she was thinking, "What happened?"

Her father glared at him, "It wasn't in the company. Beyond that, trust
me, you don't want to know." He cleared his throat theatrically, "Also, I

have some good news and some bad news for you all."

A burly, weatherbeaten soldier sitting on a bunk a little further down the bay said, "Good news first, boss."

Her father shrugged, "Sure thing, Janssen." Allen Janssen was their squad's machine gunner and Jack's boss. Her father went on, "The Army Post finally got its act together. The mail's coming up in a few minutes."

The platoon burst out in sarcastic applause. Nobody had gotten mail since mobilization, and people were beginning to complain. Sophia was anxious to hear from her mother, and she'd seen Tony writing a few letters to his sister since they'd arrived at Southbend. She wondered if the mail had worked better in the other direction and if so whether she'd bothered to write back.

Her father went on, "All right, now for the bad news." He pulled a piece of paper out of his pocket and said, "The Army Rail Service has *also* finally gotten its act together. Regiment got our orders about an hour ago."

The excited chatter about the mail died instantly. Her father let the tense silence gather for a moment and then announced, "We leave for the front at twenty-two hundred tomorrow night." Sophia swallowed hard and shared glances with Tony and Jack. This was it.

Charlie Company was going to war.

Chapter 11

The Ravine at Fire Ridge

"I'll see you later, Lucky." June Anjanou rubbed his horse's neck and passed his reins to a waiting dragoon, already holding seven or eight other horses. Lucky snorted at him sadly as he was led away, and June reluctantly turned and went to go find his platoon. The leaves had just emerged on the trees in the last couple weeks, and the morning's dappled sunlight played and shifted around the forest floor as he wove through groups of soldiers preparing for the day's mission.

He quickly spotted the newly-familiar silhouettes of his non-commissioned officers through the woods. They were huddled together in conversation, and as he approached he saw that the platoon was lying out on the ground around them cleaning their weapons. June stepped over one of his machine-gunners as he walked closer, and they heard his murmured apology to the man and turned. As he approached, Sergeant Amira Khan asked, "Sir? What can we do for you?" His platoon sergeant's tone was flat, testing him.

June looked between the sergeants, then from side to side to encompass the platoon. He asked her, "When will we be ready to move out?"

Imperial war-masks were flat and featureless, two narrow eye-holes and a slit for breathing. They turned an Imperial soldier into an anonymous blank designed to terrify the Emperor's enemies. June could sense Khan's eyes narrowing regardless as she replied, "In enough time for us to step off, sir."

June crossed his arms and said, "Alright. Then do you have a plan for this reconnaissance you're particularly attached to, sergeant?"

Khan said, "Of course, sir, I was just going over responsibilities with the squad leaders now. First and Second Squad will handle the mission and Third will man our patrol base."

June cocked his head a little and replied, "I meant *where* we're going."

"Ah..." Khan and the other sergeants looked between each other before she replied, "Uh, no, sir, we haven't gotten that far yet."

June nodded and said, "That's fine." Unbuckling his map bag, he produced a map of the Fire Ridge area and turned to show it to his sergeants. As they looked over his shoulder, he pointed to a couple inked dots on the map, "We're here right now. And I want to look at this area here." He pointed to an area several kilometers to their west, where a small stream flowing from the Dragonspine Mountains to the south had turned to the east and eaten a ravine out of the rising terrain of Fire Ridge.

Sergeant Itogawa, First Squad's leader, spoke up, "Why there, sir?"

June said, "Why not? If the Royals have it guarded, we'll find out. And if they don't, it should lead us into their rear area. Seems like the best place for a reconnaissance for me." He looked at Itogawa and went on, "I'll go with First Squad to investigate down the length of the ravine. Second squad will check out the area around its mouth, and Third Squad will hold down our base. How does that sound?"

The NCOs murmured, and Khan looked at the map and thought for a minute before replying, "Sounds good to me, sir. Hayate, can you get us there?"

Itogawa examined the map closely, stroked the chin of his mask for a minute and said, "Yeah, looks like five kilometers at... two-sixty degrees or so? We'll follow the side of the hill and then drop down."

June nodded, "Alright." Looking at his watch, he turned to Khan and said, "The commander wants us out of here in thirty minutes. Can you get the platoon up and ready to go?"

Khan replied, "Ah, of course, sir. I'll get right on it." June could sense that his soft tone was winning the woman over. She quickly sent the other sergeants packing and went to go get the platoon up and ready. June ran a hand through his long, black hair and sat down on a convenient rock to examine the map some more while his sergeants did their work. As if to emphasize his thoughts an artillery battery started up in the distance, hurling shells at the Royal Army troops dug in further up the ridge.

A month ago, June had been a cadet at the Imperial Military Academy in Lady Vai City, studying for the statistics finals and working on his paper on the effects of the Kingdom's decision to abandon the Gold Standard after the Marchlands War. The finals had been postponed and the paper abandoned on his desk when word came down they were going to war. The next morning June was commissioned with ten thousand other cadets on the Academy's parade field. Two days later he was riding with the Fifth Dragoons through the scorched moonscape that had once been Raven Wing Fortress. And just yesterday, Colonel Vann had come to see him while he was working with the regimental staff. She'd told him that he was making himself too indispensable and that he needed to get on his horse, ride down to First Squadron and take over a platoon.

And thus here he was. Fire Ridge was a long, rocky spur that cut north from the Dragonspine Mountains that ran east to west across the continent, almost a small mountain range itself. It dominated the terrain for a hundred miles and the Royal Army had taken advantage of the obvious defensive position and dug in on it. The Imperials had to either march around on the coastal plain to the north, lose a week and with it all of their momentum or try to break straight through. The correct choice was obvious, and the Fifth Dragoons had been sent far up the ridge to its forested south end to find a way into the rear of the Royal defenses. A frontal assault up the ridge would take days of fighting. Infiltration would collapse the Royal line in a matter of hours.

Staring at his map, June realized that he wasn't going to make much more sense out of contour lines than he already had and got up to go make sure his platoon was actually ready for combat. Sergeant Khan seemed to be a reasonably capable person, but he was basing his evaluation of her off of five conversations and the fact that all of his soldiers appeared to have water and ammunition.

They started marching twenty minutes later, the forest quickly closing in and forcing them into single file as they moved generally uphill. After June reckoned they'd walked most of a kilometer, he tapped Itogawa on the shoulder and they turned and started following the ridge's slope around. The dragoons marched silently for about an hour, June feeling his pack getting steadily heavier as he plowed through the loose earth and old leaves underfoot.

June eventually signaled for a halt and the dragoons flopped down gratefully. Sitting on his pack, he drank some water and listened to the shelling, which had grown into a general exchange of fire as they'd walked. Sound traveled strangely in the hills sometimes, but he thought he could get a pretty good idea of where they were from it. By now the booming Imperial guns were well behind them to the east and he could hear the pops of exploding shells about level with them to the north. He supposed that was the Royal front line on the cleared farmland further down Fire Ridge itself. Mixed in with the popping shells were cracking Royal Army field guns and the occasional booms of heavier howitzers firing back at the Imperial batteries.

Sergeant Khan found her way up to him and they conferred for a moment with Itogawa. After a couple minutes of discussion they decided that they needed to start dropping back down, and June reluctantly climbed to his feet, shouldered his pack and signaled for his platoon to get going. They walked downhill diagonally across the slope for what seemed like an eternity, the platoon gradually spreading out as the forest thinned, and after another hour of walking in the green-dappled sunlight June spied a dense and distinctive stand of beech trees and made a hand signal towards it.

The platoon angled towards the stand of trees and the front two squads fell in on line to clear it. They swept through the trees, found nothing unusual, collapsed back in and dropped packs. June conferred with his sergeants for a moment to finalize the plan. After he finished talking, Khan told him, "Sir, take care out there. You'll be a long way from help." She looked over at Itogawa, "Same goes for you, Hayate. *Try* to keep our new lieutenant alive."

June felt himself flushing. What was he supposed to *say* to something like that? Cocking his head, he stroked at his hair for a second and replied, "Sure... sergeant. Just try to keep hidden back here." He looked at Khan pointedly, "And I don't want to come back and find you all asleep."

Khan chuckled, "Sure thing, sir. Now get going, we don't have all day."

Second Squad set off first, breaking into two teams and heading off in opposite directions to check the high ground on either side of the ravine's entrance. June waited a few minutes, then set off with Itogawa and the rest of First Squad. The ground rapidly rose on either side of them as they walked into the ravine, turning from steep hillside to sheer rock cliffs rising a hundred feet or so above the forested valley floor. The slot slowly grew narrower as they went along, and they eventually crossed over a small stream flowing in its bottom and hugged the north face for concealment. As the ravine narrowed further, June hoped the Royal Army was only patrolling the north side, as enemies on the other side of the ravine wall would have an easy shot at them.

They had been walking uphill the entire time, and June sighed with relief as he saw the cliff walls start to level off, a short waterfall appearing in the distance at the head of the ravine. June motioned the squad down and they crept forward cautiously, bent over their rifles and searching for blue Royal Army jackets. June motioned to Itogawa to bring the squad after him as he cautiously slithered up the sloping ground near the waterfall, crawled over the ravine's lip and got behind a large, convenient tree. The rest of the squad came up behind him, one by one.

June could see nothing but trees, a deep green forest stretching ahead of them. He motioned Itogawa over, and as the man stole towards him an earth-shattering crack split the air. June curled himself into the tree as the series of bangs reverberated through the forest. Itogawa quickly rushed over on hands and knees and said, "What the hell was that?"

June furrowed his eyebrows behind his mask and said, "Hm... hold on a minute." They waited motionless, barely breathing, for a minute before another series of hammer-blow cracks rang through the trees. They looked at each other and June said, "Royal heavy artillery. And it's *close*."

The sergeant patted him on the shoulder, "Well done, sir. Let's find out more."

June nodded, "Yes. I'm with... Miss Lai, right?"

Itogawa said, "Yes, sir." He looked at June, then at the waterfall behind them, "Release point here?"

June nodded again, "Yes." They'd worked out the plan ahead of time, and it went like clockwork. Two dragoons stayed behind to guard the release point, and the other eight of them paired off and fanned out to reconnoiter the area. One pair dropped back into the ravine and crossed to the other side to ensure it was clear of Royal troops, while the other three investigated to the north. June found himself creeping forward with a dark-haired girl with "Lai" written on the nametape on her breast.

The artillery thundered again as they moved forward, almost on hands and knees. June took advantage of the noise this time to dart forward up the gentle slope, the sound drowning out his movement. He curled himself into a large tree's roots and looked out to his right as Lai rushed forward herself. Nothing. Lai dropped down beside him as June looked left and froze. Noticing him, she started to look herself and June pushed her to the ground with his free arm.

"Sir?" Lai whispered "What-" June pushed harder and she shut up as he slowly dropped into the hollow of the roots with her. Through the trees they could hear the crunch of marching feet on gravel. Hundreds of them, coming closer. June gestured with his head, and they both squeezed tighter into the roots as the Royal soldiers marched nearer.

Pressed close together, June could feel Lai trembling and hear her short, raspy breaths. He wrapped his arms around her reassuringly, and she buried her face in his chest and slowly grew still as the enemy footsteps almost reached them and then passed by, the Royal soldiers seemingly close enough to touch. From their perspective further downhill, the road had been perfectly concealed as a cut in the hillside. June hadn't noticed it until he had actually stuck his head above the road surface and seen Royal troops marching straight at him.

After an eternity the company finally marched past, their footsteps disappearing in the distance. June patted Lai on the back and she sheepishly extricated herself from his embrace. Slowly picking up his rifle, June thumbed off the safety and slid around the roots carefully, scanning in case the Royal troops had noticed them and left someone behind to search. He saw nothing, carefully looked both ways on the road and whispered at Lai, "We're clear. Follow me."

As Lai slowly moved around behind him, June thumbed his rifle back on safe and darted across the trail. He plunged through the brush on the far side, turned and motioned her across. It was another eternity before she made it herself and they were on the move again, quickly this time. Getting some distance from the road, June slowed down and took stock of the situation. Lai looked shaken up, and June asked softly, "Lai, are you doing alright?"

She stammered back, "Y-y-yes, sir. Just a little... shaken up. I-I've never been that close to the enemy."

June smiled behind his mask, "That makes two of us. Tell me, what's your first name?"

She took a deep breath, visibly calmed down a little and said, "Anastasia, sir."

June said, "Alright, Anastasia. Let's go find those guns." Right on cue the battery fired another salvo, so loud it seemed almost on top of them. Anastasia started moving, but June held up his hand to stop her and listened intently. Very faint, he heard gunners shouting fire commands from over the next rise. June felt himself grin predatorily he said, "I think we just did. Come on."

The pair crawled to the top of the slope in front of them and June again cautiously poked his head over the top to see the forest open up into farmland, with a Royal Army gun battery drawn up on line dead in front of them. June guessed it was no more than a hundred meters away, and he could clearly hear the gunners shouting back and forth as he motioned Anastasia up next to him. As they watched the Royal soldiers rammed rounds, loaded powder and fired another deafening volley. Noticing a couple of the gunners making a game out of throwing the gigantic brass spent cartridge cases and trying to get them to land upright, June thought to himself that they didn't seem to too worried about fighting the Empire.

Their fire mission complete, the gun crews dispersed a little and June could see past the battery as the cloud of gun smoke cleared. The entire area was a swarm of Royal Army activity. What looked like an infantry company was marching forward on a road beyond the guns in front of him, and more guns were laid out beyond them. Further beyond that, maybe a couple kilometers away, was a small village. June carefully took out his binoculars and was able to see riders moving back and forth from it in all directions, probably messengers.

June motioned for Anastasia to stay put and moved a few feet back down the slope and out of eyesight of the Royal troops. Rolling onto his back, he quietly produced his map and took a couple minutes to mark out what he'd seen on it. He tugged on Anastasia's leg and after she pushed herself back down towards him motioned for her to follow him. It was time to leave.

They wordlessly crept back down towards road they'd crossed earlier, which stood out clearly through the forest from above it. Their caution paid off when Anastasia spotted blue-jacketed soldiers through the trees and they again took cover, this time at a safe distance. They watched thirty or forty more Royal soldiers march by and darted across the road behind them after they'd moved off out of sight. After they were across the road June and Anastasia hurried back to the release point, June finding the waterfall easily.

The dragoons guarding the point waved them through, and June skidded down the slope behind them to find the other dragoons waiting for them. Sergeant Itogawa looked up at him and remarked, "Good to see you, sir, I was getting worried." June reached the bottom and sat down near him, and he went on, "So, find anything?"

June smirked behind his mask, "Just their artillery and division headquarters." He produced his map and pointed them out, "Here and here. You?"

Itogawa nodded, "Good work, sir." He produced his own map and pointed some things out to June, "There's some more guns setting up over here, and after I worked around them I saw what looked like an infantry battalion moving up to the north." He gestured to the other dragoons, "Marin's team saw a couple large Royal patrols out to the south side of the ravine, twenty or thirty soldiers. Tarai found some infantry camped out on her side." Corporals Marin and Tarai threw the sergeant mock salutes when he called them out.

June said, "Excellent. Let's get out of here." He looked at Itogawa, "I hate to backtrack, but I don't want to hit one of those patrols. We'll use the ravine."

Itogawa nodded again, and they quickly got the squad up and moving. Splashing across the river, they hugged the steep south side of the ravine and started quickly making their way back. As the cut narrowed and the rushing of the stream covered their rustling footsteps, June started to relax a little and sternly caught himself. *You're not out of the woods yet*, he thought.

A moment later June heard faint rustling on top of the cliff and instinctively grabbed the man in front of him and pulled him into the shelter of the undercut cliff side. The rest of the squad, behind him, flattened themselves to the rock a moment later. June fought the urge to look up as the rustling went on directly overhead for what seemed like an eternity. His heart leapt in his chest as he heard from far above, "See anything? I thought I heard something moving down there."

Another voice replied, "No, nothing. Probably a deer."

The first man laughed, "I wish. I'd shoot it. Come on, let's go."

The vegetation above them rustled again and the Royal soldiers were gone. June waited a minute as his breathing slowed, then silently motioned the squad out of hiding and got them moving again. The rest of the return march to the patrol base was uneventful, although June felt like he was going to choke on his heart every time the wind picked up and started rustling trees.

June spotted the familiar stand of trees marking their patrol base and waved slowly to attract the attention of the sentries. A green form detached itself the shadowed ground in response, waved back and gestured them in. June and his companions walked in to find the rest of the platoon there and Sergeant Khan waiting for them. She gave June a sour look and said, "I hope you found something good, sir. You're late."

June glared at the woman for a moment before he realized she'd been *worried* about him. That wasn't too bad. June shrugged and replied, "Their artillery, their headquarters, an infantry regiment, a route into their rear area... sorry we took a while coming in, sergeant."

Khan chuckled softly, "I like it. Ready to get back to the company, sir?"

His legs were starting to feel sore and the prospect of putting his pack back on and marching all the way back to the company was depressing. He could only run on adrenaline for so long, and he felt exhausted after the day's scares. But it couldn't be helped. Sighing, June said, "Yes, unfortunately. Let's go."

The platoon shrugged into their packs and headed back towards the company, by a mercifully more direct route this time. Even so, June walked through the perimeter and tiredly counted his men back through in the ghostly light of the false sun. June let his sergeants take care of the platoon and went to hunt down his commander to make his report. Dragoons traveled light, and June quickly located the one tent the troop had that was big enough to stand up in and stuck his head inside.

Captain Marsten and First Sergeant looked up from their card game at the disturbance. Marsten gave him a hard look for a moment before he recognized him and said, "Oh, June. I didn't realize your platoon was back."

June stepped inside and closed the tent flap behind him, saying, "We just got in, sir." The two older men had removed their masks, and June pulled out a camp stool and tiredly removed his helmet and unbuckled the straps holding his war mask in place. The tent's warm, stuffy air caressed his bare face as he set his mask aside, stretched and ran a hand through his hair, feeling it shift damply down his back.

Marsten observed, "You look like you've had a rough day, lieutenant." He pulled a card out of his hand sarcastically and put it on the table, "Seen this guy out there?"

June picked it up and chuckled. The Imperial Army had issued every soldier a deck of cards immediately before the campaign featuring line-drawing portraits and thumbnail biographies of important people in the Royal government and military. By now every soldier in the Imperial Western Area Army could identify every divisional and above commander in the Army of Drakenburg, the entire Royal Family and most of the Cabinet on sight. And depending on their inclinations most of them were in love with the strapping Prince Adrian or the adorable Princess Arilin. If she was half as cute in person as the artist had made her out as, in a few years she'd be causing traffic accidents by walking down the street.

The card June picked up was unfortunately neither of them. Field Marshal Lawrence White, Ace of Spades, stared back at him briefly before June put the card back on the table and said, "No, but I might have found the four of diamonds or something."

Marsten raised an eyebrow, "Oh, really?" He set his cards down, motioned to the First Sergeant that the game was over, and turned to June, "Now you have my attention. How about you make your report?"

June nodded and said, "My pleasure." Taking out his map, he spread it out on the table and went on, "Now, if you'll look here, sir..."

About two hours later, June was happily sitting on his pack and working his way through a hot dinner when Captain Marsten appeared with a familiar person in tow. June quickly set down his mess kit and made to stand, but Colonel Vann waved him back down. Her ice-blonde hair seemed to float like a halo around the dark wedge of her war mask as she said, "You can stay off your feet, June. You'll need them later."

June looked up at her and asked, "Ah, ma'am?"

He could sense her smiling, "I was very impressed with the report I got from your commander just now." She paused for a second before asking, "Do you think you can find your way back there at night?"

June asked, "Do I have a choice?"

The two officers laughed, and Vann said, "No." She went on, "The Army is attacking at dawn to seize the ridge, and the regiment is infiltrating on your route tonight. I need you to lead us in."

June could feel the motivation leaking out of his body. Didn't anyone in the Army *sleep*? Still, he supposed, they weren't going to win the war without a few rough nights. Stifling a sigh, he looked up at the colonel and said, "Will do, ma'am. When's the briefing?"

Marsten looked at his watch and said, "Fifteen minutes. Eat fast."

The pair walked off, leaving June to his thoughts. June glumly picked his mess kit back up and started shoveling food into his mouth. He needed it after a long day, and tomorrow was going to be much longer.

Chapter 12

The War in Drakenburg

Arilin felt Rebecca secure her braided hair up behind her head with a long hairpin. Satisfied, the woman stepped back and said, "That should do it. What do you think, milady?"

Arilin looked up from her book into the mirror and saw a young lady prepared for the ball, with her golden hair done up in braids and makeup accentuating her piercing red eyes. Her gown, modestly cut for a girl of her age, was a vivid emerald green. Standing and smoothing her skirts with gloved hands, Arilin smiled and replied, "I'm very happy, Becky. I couldn't ask for more."

Rebecca gave her a short bow and said, "Thank you very much, milady. Now, if you'll excuse me, I think I need to assist Lieutenant Gable."

Arilin giggled at the thought of Vanessa struggling to get Patricia into a ball gown and said, "I'm guessing she's not as good at this as you are?"

Rebecca smiled slightly, "No, but by the time this war is over I'll make a fine maid out of her." Turning, she walked out the door into the sitting room of the suite Arilin was sharing with Patricia, opened the door to Patricia's bedroom and disappeared inside. Arilin followed her out, and though the Grand Monarch Hotel was a classy establishment and solidly built she could still faintly hear Becky reproaching Vanessa through the closed door.

Arilin sat down, leaned back as much as was possible in her corset and went back to reading. After ten minutes or so and a few more muted exchanges in Patricia's room someone rapped on the door twice, firmly. Getting up, Arilin went to the door, looked through the peephole, giggled and eagerly pulled it open.

Walter Haas, resplendent in his shining white gala uniform, bowed and said, "Milady, I understand you and Lady MacMahon require an escort to the ball tonight."

Careful now, Arilin, she thought. Curtseying, she replied, "It would be an honor, sir." They both straightened up, and Arilin gestured for him to come in and asked, "I thought General Reinhardt would be accompanying us tonight... we spoke to him earlier about it."

Walter unclipped his sword from his belt and sat down with a sigh, "He came to me about an hour ago and said that he had come down with the stomach flu that's been going around lately." He looked at her carefully and went on, "I'd wash my hands frequently if I were you. It's a nasty illness."

Well played, Siegfried. Arilin covered her mouth with her hands to cover her smirk and said, "Oh, my. I hope he feels better soon." Getting her expression under control, she went on, "Thank you very much for covering for him."

Walter snorted, "Taking two cute girls to the ball is hardly an imposition. I'm not *that* stiff." Spying the book on the table, he changed the subject abruptly, "*The Dark Empress*? That's a bit grim for a girl your age, don't you think?"

Arilin replied, "The war's pretty grim, too, you know."

Walter chuckled, "Well, if you're into history, milady, you're welcome to borrow my copy of *The Fall of the Faceless King*. I brought it along, actually."

"Didn't that come out a couple years ago?" Arilin asked, "I remember reading that historians were angry about it."

"Of course they were," Walter snorted, "You'd be too if you were an academic and someone came along and proved that your research was garbage. And," he smirked, "I'm quoted in it, so of course I'm a fan."

Arilin was about to press him further when the door to Patricia's room opened and she strode out, saying, "Sorry to keep you waiting, mila..." She saw Walter and trailed off abruptly, then said, "Ah, Walter, uh... I was expecting Siegfried..."

Walter stood up and bowed slightly, "He's unwell, and asked me to take his place. I hope you're not displeased, milady?"

Arilin noticed Patricia starting to turn red as she replied, "Er... certainly not! I'm just surprised, is all."

Walter smiled slyly, "What, that I'd pass up a chance to go to a ball with two beautiful girls?"

Patricia got redder and replied, "Well, I thought you'd be with the staff..."

Walter laughed gruffly, "The staff, milady, needs a break and as a good commander I'm obliged to give them one. I think they're drinking out the hotel bar as we speak. Now," He offered them his arms, "If both of you are ready, we have dancing to do."

Arilin leapt up and quickly seized Walter's left elbow. Patricia looked between them for a second, then stepped in and hesitantly slipped her arm around his right. Arilin snuck a few glances at her as he walked them downstairs and to their waiting carriage and saw that she was blushing deeply the whole way. Patricia climbed in with obvious relief, and Arilin piled in after and squeezed in beside her. Walter climbed in after her and sat down across from them as the carriage started moving forward, bumping across the rough cobblestones of the old city.

Patricia didn't seem to be in any mood for conversation, so Arilin asked Walter, "So, how did you end up being quoted in a history book?" She smirked and teased him, "Beyond having known Maximilian, I mean."

Even in the carriage's darkness she could see Walter wince, "Ouch. I'm not *that* old, milady." He went on, "But to answer your question, I've spent an awful lot of time in and around the Empire. Even if the people there weren't that friendly, I got to know a few things about them over the years. You know, I even went into the crypt of the Faceless King once."

Arilin leaned forward eagerly, "Really? What's that?"

Walter pulled out his monocle, polished it theatrically and set in back in before he went on, "Well, milady, if you go into the dungeons under the Black Citadel in Lady Vai City, *all* the way down to the deepest, darkest vault, you'll find a steel-plated door with five huge iron bars across it. Each of those bars must have weighed a hundred kilos." He paused, obviously enjoying himself, "We opened the first door, walked into a corridor cut into the rock maybe fifty meters and came to another one just like it. So we got the bars off it, pushed it in, and what did we find?"

Arilin, on the edge of her seat, said, "The crypt?"

Walter chuckled and shook his head. As he continued, Arilin realized that Patricia was holding onto her arm harder than was really necessary, "No, milady, we found *stairs*. A spiral staircase, cut into the black rock, going down into complete darkness. I was there with a couple of friends, and after we'd walked down for a couple minutes we started seeing Elven characters, first a few, then more, then the walls, the floor, the ceiling were *covered* with them. And I don't read much Elvish, but it was pretty clear they were all part of a spell." Walter leaned back in his seat and went on, "At this point my friends had enough, and they turned back. I kept on going down, *alone.*"

Patricia abruptly put an arm around Arilin's waist and pulled her close to her. Arilin could feel her shivering as she said, "W-Walter, a-are you sure this is appropriate for the princess?"

He smirked, "She seems to be enjoying it, milady." Arilin nodded enthusiastically and he went on, "After a few more minutes the stairs just ended at another steel door, this one covered in spell-characters. And this one's locking bars had been broken and piled against the wall. It looked like they'd been smashed with a sledgehammer. So I pushed in the door to the final chamber." Patricia was shaking as Walter leaned forward in his seat, his voice dropping to a low growl, "And I *felt* it."

Arilin leaned forward a little against Patricia's tight hold on her, and Walter went on, "Milady, don't ever let anyone tell you otherwise. Evil is *real*. I *felt* it standing there." He paused and went on, "The last room looked like a bowl. The floor sloped inwards towards a hole in the middle of the floor, maybe half a meter wide. At one point there had been this stone plug in it, but someone or some*thing* had pulled it out and set it aside. It must have weighed half a ton." Walter trailed off for a moment and went on, softly, "And the worst part was the Elven characters. They were on every surface in the room, but it was like they had *melted* together. It looked... insane, it's the only way I can describe it."

Patricia yelped, and Arilin said, "Walter, this is *much* too scary. Would you mind finishing the story for me later, in private?"

Walter actually laughed and said, "Of course, milady. Are you doing alright, Trixie?"

Patricia replied shakily, "No... no thanks to you I'm not."

Arilin opened her purse, "I think I have smelling salts in here if you need them."

"Milady!" Patricia squawked, "I-I'm fine, I'm just no good with... horror, is all."

Walter shrugged, "Well, I'm *very sorry* then. I wish you'd told me sooner, milady." They could see the carriage pass under an impressive gate out the window, and the clack of the horses' hooves slowed. Soon the carriage stopped under a brightly-lit portico before an enormous, arched entryway, and a footman decorously opened the door and bowed.

Climbing out first, Walter helped Arilin and then a pale Patricia out of the carriage. Arilin grinned as she noticed Patricia quickly take hold of his arm after he finished helping her down, and turned away quickly so they wouldn't notice. Walter said a few words to the driver, and the carriage moved out as they made their way to the grand entrance.

Another manservant met them at the doorway, bowed slightly and said to Walter, "Good evening, sir. May I have your names, please?"

He replied, "I am General Walter Haas, this is the Lady General Patricia MacMahon, and," He gestured at Arilin with his free hand, "The young lady needs no introduction." Arilin looked at the servant and gave him a nod.

The man looked at her for a couple seconds, then paled and bowed deeply, saying, "Your grace! We are honored by your presence." He straightened up and turned back to Walter, "Sir, if you would please follow me, we will take care of you three straightaway."

Walter replied, "Certainly," and they followed the man into the wide entry hall. Servants appeared, took their jackets and vanished just as quickly as they walked towards the double doors leading into the grand hall. The manservant rushed ahead and spoke to another, larger man standing by the inner doorway as they approached, and he bowed deeply as they walked by.

The three of them stepped into the ballroom, and Arilin heard the big servant swell himself up and announce them in a stentorian voice, "Ladies and Gentlemen!" He paused for effect, "Princess Arilin, Lady MacMahon the Duchess of Sevara, and General Haas."

The hubbub of conversation in the room died instantly at the mention of her name. Even the orchestra stopped playing. The silence lasted long enough for Arilin to hear her two companions start whispering sarcastically to each other. Finally, through the press of guests of the far side of the room, Arilin saw a violinist shrug and start playing again. With that the noise returned, louder and shriller than before. Fortunately the ball guests were too cultured to all rush them at once, but Arilin noticed a general drift beginning in her direction as they walked further into the ballroom.

Walter, standing head and shoulders above Arilin, looked out over the crowd and remarked, "Milady, it looks like the Lord Mayor's coming over with his, ah... entourage."

Arilin looked up at him and asked, "Notice anyone else important?"

He shrugged, "Not with my eyes at this distance."

Arilin smiled, "Then I suppose we should be sociable."

The Lord Mayor soon arrived with a group of men and women in tow, sweat beading on his balding forehead from the exertion of hurrying across the immense ballroom. A rotund man, he bowed ponderously and smiled as Arilin curtseyed back, saying, "Milady, we're honored indeed to have you tonight. I hope everything is to your liking?"

Arilin replied, "It is, although," she paused politely, "We just arrived. But I'm pleased to see you again."

His smile broadened, "I'm glad you remembered, milady. You certainly were radiant at the Midwinter Ball last year. I presume you remember my dear wife?" He turned and indicated a sizable woman standing next to him, her corset obviously struggling to contain her figure.

"Lady Gertrude, I presume? I remember everyone I meet." Arilin nodded politely, "It's part of the job."

The woman chortled, "Oh ho! I'm honored, milady! But," She furrowed her eyebrows, "The job! That's an awfully negative way of putting it... although I could see why you'd think that way, dear." A few of the other women surrounding them made sympathetic noises as her husband shot her a nervous glance.

Arilin raised her eyebrows innocently and asked, "Why would that be, ma'am? It's just a figure of speech."

She replied, "Of course it is, dear, but a *job* is something you, well, that you take on. And I can see how you'd think that way, my dear, with your mother and all." She pursed her lips, "The King is *such* an honorable man, doing right by her."

The Lord Mayor plucked at his wife's sleeve nervously as Arilin widened her eyes and asked, "What do you mean, ma'am, by doing right by her?"

Lady Gertrude came back, "Well, of course, by marrying her and, oh my, *legitimizing* you two girls. That caused quite a stir around here, you know."

Arilin cocked her head and asked, as the Lord Mayor started sputtering, "Why's that, ma'am?"

Gertrude laughed, "Why, my dear, that's simply *unheard of.* My God, the old queen was barely-"

"My lord, your wife is *very drunk.*" Walter cut her off brusquely, "She should retire *immediately.*"

The woman gasped and glared at him, flushing with anger. Arilin fancied that she heard her corset creak with the strain. Walter held her gaze for a second, then very deliberately turned his glare on her husband. The two men stared at each other for a moment, Walter's eyes narrowing a hair as the Lord Mayor turned white. Gertrude had opened her mouth to start again when the Mayor visibly set his jaw, seized his wife's arm and pulled her away, ignoring her objections. His entourage dispersed a little in dismay and didn't follow as they walked out of the circle.

Patricia was shaking with barely-contained laughter as Walter guided them towards the dance floor. She finally calmed down enough to say, "Wow, Arilin, you really had her going there, didn't you?"

Arilin gave her a sly look, "I don't know *what* you're talking about. I was just making conversation."

Walter patted her on the shoulder gently with his free hand, "Don't overdo it, milady." Arilin sighed heavily and he went on, "I understand you, believe me. Don't take it so personally."

Arilin shook her head, "I just hate how people talk about my parents. It's awful. I don't know how my mother deals with it."

Patricia said, "Arilin, there are a lot of people who didn't agree with the Legitimation and who never will. They're not a majority." She chuckled, "It's pretty hard to hate you and your sister. Now," She looked up significantly at Walter, "I want to *dance*. And by the way you've been looking around, I take it you have a partner in mind for Arilin?"

He snorted, "Of course. You know him yourself, milady." He pointed to a handsome man in gala uniform threading his way through the crowd towards them, "It wouldn't be a party without the cuirassiers."

The man arrived and bowed gracefully, "Your ladyships, sir, it's a pleasure seeing you tonight."

Patricia said, "Jenssen! I didn't know you were in town."

He straightened up and smiled, "Just got in yesterday with the squadron. They put me in charge of Two-Eight just last month, you know." He paused and tapped the major's rank marks on his collar, "Although that promotion hasn't caught up with me yet. I think this guy has something to do with it." He pointed at Walter.

The older man snorted, "Yes, Eric, I had your orders incinerated last week."

Jenssen laughed, "Sounds like you. Let me guess, they've been sitting on White's desk since January?"

Walter replied drolly, "Last I checked they were actually with his assistant vice chief of staff."

Jenssen rolled his eyes, leaned in and muttered something, too soft for Arilin to hear. The three officers laughed before Jenssen turned to Arilin and extended a hand, "But enough politics. Milady, would you like to dance?"

Arilin reached out, took his hand and said, "Yes, ah... is Eric okay?"

He smiled broadly, "Of course, milady." The music stopped and he led her out onto the dance floor. Arilin heard a few approving murmurs from the onlookers as they walked out. The music swelled up again and he slipped an arm around her waist and started waltzing her gracefully around the floor. Eric was a fine dancer, and she almost felt like she was floating as he spun her around in his arms.

After a little while she looked up at him and remarked, "You're very good at this, Eric."

Smiling, he said, "I'm dancing with a princess. Of course I'm on my best game. And you're a fine dancer yourself, milady."

He was really very handsome. Arilin felt herself blushing as she looked up into his bright blue eyes, "Ah, thank you."

He looked over to the side for a moment, and Arilin followed his gaze as he said, "But what I want to know is how you arranged *that*." Across the floor Walter was twirling Patricia around, a little stiffly, but she looked like she was enjoying it. Eric looked back at her, "How'd you get *General Haas* out of his office and set him up on a *date?* Not to mention Lady MacMahon. I couldn't believe my eyes when I saw those two."

Arilin gave him a sly smile, "I did have a little inside help."

"Oh?" He raised his eyebrows, "I don't suppose a certain General Reinhardt had *anything* to do with this?"

Arilin shrugged a little in his embrace, "A lady never reveals her secrets. Or her conspirators."

Eric looked at the couple again, then back at Arilin, "Whatever you two are doing, keep it up."

Arilin smiled, "My pleasure." The music wound down, and Eric managed to spin them to a halt next to Walter and Patricia. Arilin let go of him a little reluctantly and curtseyed. Eric bowed back gallantly.

Turning to Walter, Eric asked, "Care to switch, sir?"

Walter nodded and took Arilin's hand as the music started back up, saying, "Milady, I'm a little rusty, but I hope you'll indulge an old warhorse like me."

Arilin looked up – way up – at him, smiled and said, "I'd love to." With that, Walter put a strong arm around her waist and they stepped off. She hadn't been too far off in her assessment earlier. Between his height and his being out of practice, it was a little like dancing with a bear. Still, Walter managed to avoid stepping on her feet. Arilin supposed that, given the circumstances, that was all right.

* * *

Patricia stroked Arilin's hair gently as their carriage bounced over the cobblestones back to their hotel. Exhausted from dancing late into the night, the girl had started nodding as soon as they'd climbed in. Patricia had pulled her over on her side and pillowed her head in her lap, and Arilin was fast asleep in seconds. She looked over at the carriage's other occupant and said, softly, "Thank you for coming out tonight, Walter."

He inclined his head slightly, "Thank you for having me, milady." He shrugged out of his overcoat quietly and laid it over Arilin to ward off the evening cold. Sitting back in his seat, he went on, "Although I fear this will be our last pleasant night for a while."

"Oh?" Patricia raised her eyebrows questioningly, "News from the front I haven't heard yet?"

Walter scowled, "More like news I'm expecting to hear. The last report I saw had them trying to set up a defense on Fire Ridge. I think they're going to get attacked at dawn."

Patricia asked, "Do you think they'll hold?"

He shook his head, "No. How long they hold on is going to make the difference whether the Empire gets to Grenville or we stop them short of the city."

"Grenville?" Patricia said, "That's, what, three hundred kilometers from Fire Ridge? You're serious?"

Walter nodded, "The Empire has a lot at stake here. They'll move fast."

Patricia looked down at the sleeping girl in her lap. She looked so peaceful, like she didn't have a care in the world. Sighing, she looked back up and said, "For our sakes, I hope they don't get that far."

He shrugged, "That makes two of us."

They passed the rest of the carriage ride to the hotel in silence, as rain began to sheet down onto the city and beat at the windows. As the horses clopped to a halt in front of the entrance a doorman hurried out into the wet night and opened the carriage door for them, and Patricia made to wake up Arilin for the walk inside. Walter put out a hand to stop her and shook his head. As Patricia watched he gently reached over, cradled the princess in his arms and picked her up. Arilin didn't so much as stir as they walked inside and back to their rooms.

Chapter 13

A Very Big War

Sophia had expected the regiment's deployment to be more dramatic. She'd expected a ceremony, speeches and cheering crowds as they marched to the railway station with flags flying and the band playing. As things actually turned out, they finally finished the thousand and one things they absolutely needed to do prior to departing all of half an hour before the battalion was scheduled to step off. Shuffling into the harsh light of the quad's arc lamps with the rest of Charlie Company, Sophia dropped her pack and sat down against it, sighing in relief as the load came off her feet.

A little while later someone poked her in the ribs, and she came to and looked up to see her father prodding her with his foot. He smiled and said, "You were out pretty hard there."

Sophia shook herself and looked up at him, asking, "Time to go, Dad?"

He said, "You could say that. Get the guidon out, please."

Sophia nodded, "Will do." Getting to her feet, she pulled the spear out of her pack's straps and quickly assembled the pieces, noticing the company starting to get to its feet and shuffle into formation as she did. She walked out and took her place next to her father in front of the block of soldiers, and a couple minutes later the sergeant major strode out in front of the long battalion formation, called them all to attention and got them marching out.

As the long formation snaked around the quad towards the arched entryway Sophia could see the regimental staff and the soldiers of First Battalion still scurrying around getting ready to march out after them. Third Battalion's barracks stood empty. Each troop train could only hold a single battalion with its equipment, and they had marched out hours ago. By now they were probably already on a train headed east.

Sophia watched the ranks ahead of her rise up the long steps out of the quad and disappear through the entryway, the quad silent but for the ragged thudding of eight hundred soldiers marching in step. She climbed the steps herself, passed under the entryway, caught a glimpse of Alpha Company turning right out of the gate towards the railway station and just as quickly descended the other side and buried herself in the mass of marching soldiers again.

Charlie made the turn and marched on towards the railway station. It was too late at night for marching songs, so they went in silence but for the crashing footfalls on the Southbend cobblestones. Somehow they all knew how to keep in time. Blue uniforms burned black by the harsh streetlights, packs creaking on their backs, blonde rifle-stocks glinting as they bounced on slings, Second Battalion marched to war through a gathering fog that wet Sophia's face and made the battalion's colors out in front of Alpha Company look like they were flying in the Spirit World.

A few curious citizens stuck their heads out of upper-story windows as they went by, probably woken up by the racket from Third Battalion going by earlier. Otherwise the streets were deserted. Sophia heard a few shouts of encouragement from overhead, but she suspected most of the town was trying to sleep. After the turnout in Jade Falls it felt wrong. Sophia rolled her eyes at the Southbenders' lack of patriotism and marched on.

The road sloped down gently and Sophia smelled the river before she saw it. The battalion took another right to march down the waterfront and she looked to her left to see the Serpent River, wreathed with fog through the warehouses and jetties along the banks. Ahead of them the lights of the railway bridge shone through the fog, and past those in the distance she could see the lights of the new road bridge, faint points of light burning dimly in a sea of cloud.

The battalion took another right in front of the railway station's long platform, marched down the length of the structure and halted. The sergeant major gave them a left face and, when they had rearranged themselves and dressed the formation to his liking, gave the command to fall out. The soldiers quickly surged up onto the platform, dropped packs, sat down against them and made to go back to sleep. Sophia even saw Lieutenant Thorn stretching himself out on one of the platform benches.

"Looking for a place, Sophie?" Sophia turned to see her father standing behind her. He always did have a way of being able to sneak up on her. He went on, "Better get to it, the good spots are filling up."

Sophia asked, "What's keeping *you* up, Dad?"

He shrugged, "I'd like to say the welfare of my soldiers, but," He went on, rolling his eyes, "The sergeant major wants to have another meeting with me and my five best friends. Probably over those two idiots who fell out of Alpha while we were walking here."

Sophia said, "Collective punishment?"

Her father reached out, plucked her hat off of her head, ruffled her hair and jammed it back on down over her eyes. As she protested and straightened her cap he replied, "It wouldn't be the Army without it. Get some rest and I'll wake you up when the train gets here."

Sophia nodded sheepishly as her father turned and walked away down the platform, navigating around soldiers sprawled on the concrete. Farther down she could see the sergeant major waving his arms around in front of a group of NCOs trying their best to pretend to be chastened. Snickering, Sophia dropped her bag next to Lieutenant Thorn's bench, lay down against it and closed her eyes.

A familiar prod in the ribs woke her some time later. Opening her eyes, Sophia saw the train slowly rolling into the station as soldiers began climbing to their feet around her. She heard her father's voice from overhead, "Wake up, Sophie, time to go."

Sophia looked up at him blearily and said, "Sure, Dad." Shaking herself, she slowly got to her feet and picked up her pack, noticing that Thorn had gotten up in the meantime. She saw him walking around the platform kicking the rest of the platoon awake. As the train finally screeched to a halt her father got the company organized into a human chain to load their packs and supplies into the baggage cars, and with that finished they went to lend a hand to get the horses and wagons loaded. By some minor miracle nobody was seriously injured by a panicked animal or mishandled field kitchen.

After about an hour of work Sophia finally climbed into her platoon's passenger car. Sitting down on one of the hard wooden benches next to Tony, she managed to stay awake long enough to answer to her name at the roll call before she put her head on his shoulder and went back to sleep.

When she awoke next the car had brightened a little, dim gray light starting to seep through the windows. Lifting herself off of Tony, Sophia winced at the crick in her neck and the leaden feeling in her bottom, and gingerly stood in the aisle and stretched herself. Looking out the window she could see black tree trunks, standing still in a dark forest just starting to lighten with the morning's light. For whatever reason they must have pulled off and stopped.

Curious, Sophia walked down the aisle to the door on the other side, stepping carefully over sleeping soldiers and a couple of machine guns, and quietly eased the door open. The cool morning air was a relief on her skin from the car's stagnant atmosphere. Realizing how awful the car actually smelled, Sophia rolled her eyes and slid the door all the way open. The only real cure for that smell was bathing, but fresh air wouldn't hurt.

Sophia heard a steam whistle from further down the tracks and stuck her head out to try to make out the train that was overtaking them. Unfortunately the tracks curved behind the siding they were pulled off on and she could only hear another blast on the whistle, then a slow and steady clattering that built as the train approached. She thought it sounded a little deeper and heavier than what she would have expected from a normal train.

The heavy chug and clatter of the oncoming train built slowly until it was loud enough for some of the soldiers behind her to start stirring, then built to a roar as the train came around the bend and into sight. Sophia gasped as she saw the train's cargo swing into view behind the locomotive and fuel cars and she instinctively pulled her head back inside as a gigantic railway gun rushed past behind the thundering engine. It looked like something that belonged on a battleship at sea, and she noticed a smug-looking crewmember wave at her from one of the trailing passenger carriages as he shot past.

The noise had woken pretty much everyone else up, and someone in the back of the car complained, "Come on, Sophie, shut the door, we're trying to sleep here."

Sophia sat down next to the door as their train blasted its whistle and started to grind forward on the tracks again. Snorting, she replied, "As if anyone could sleep with the smell in here. Open some windows."

After some heated argument most of the platoon came over to Sophia's side that the carriage did in fact stink like death and her fellow soldiers eventually opened the windows. That made the rest of the ride considerably more pleasant. Sophia spent the rest of the morning and into the afternoon talking with her friends and playing cards as the train sped through the lush countryside. Gradually the dense trees and jagged hillsides of the Fairy Forest thinned and turned to rolling farmland as they passed into the great central plains of the New Kingdom, sweeping north to the ocean and east to the Marchlands and the Empire. The shadows were long on the ground and the western horizon a sea of fire when they rolled slowly through a fort built across the railway line and Sergeant Falcon came back to tell them to get ready to unload.

The train didn't stop long at the outlying fort. After a couple minutes it ground forward again and they proceeded slowly for another half hour until the train ducked into a tunnel that rose from the ground, emerged briefly into light only to speed through a second tunnel passing through a gigantic wall that had appeared out of nowhere. As they passed into sunlight for a second time and the middle of a built-up town, Sophia realized that they'd gone through the glacis and sunken defensive wall of a major fortress. Looking out the window behind them she could see parapets studded with stubby, old-looking guns.

The train moved slowly through the town before finally arriving at the station and braking to a halt with a short screech. Sergeant Falcon walked back into the carriage and yelled, "Alright everybody, we're here! Move out and assemble on the platform with the company." He paused for effect, "Welcome to Wolf Rock Fortress!"

Sophia thought about that for a moment as she got up, collected her rifle and the guidon, and stepped out into the warm afternoon. Wolf Rock was a long way from Southbend, but it was even longer to the Marchlands. She was thinking about asking her father how long they'd be staying at the fortress when she saw the second thing that day that took her breath away.

She thought they were clouds at first, glinting in the sky to the south. The others noticed Sophia looking at them, and soon all of Charlie Company was looking on in wonder. They had a good view down Wolf Rock's main boulevard to the south, and beyond the studded gun positions of the fortress wall a silver oval was rising to catch the sun's dying light. It looked like a toy at this distance, but it must have been gigantic. Beyond it, rising into the sky to the east, Sophia saw two more shining ovals, then another one far in the distance, catching the sun at a great altitude.

Sophia had never seen an airship before. She even noticed her father taking time to appreciate the spectacle of the Airship Corps taking to the skies. The great ships rose majestically into the sky, tiny propellers barely visible at the distance carrying them east towards the war. As she watched she noticed a couple dark specks rise over the battlements after the airship, winging their way past it before turning off to sweep north around the fortress, and Sophia's breath caught in her throat again as the fighters' wings caught the golden sunlight against the darkening eastern sky. After a minute or so of gawking at the sight a Railway Service officer approached and told them they had forty-two minutes to get off his platform before he told the train to depart with or without their equipment, and they reluctantly set to unloading the train.

A liaison officer eventually appeared to take them to their billets, and the battalion formed up and marched off through Wolf Rock's bustling streets. It seemed like half the people there were in uniform, many of them from units and even branches of the service she couldn't identify. A squadron of hussars in brilliant uniforms clattered down the road past them, imperiously pushing the normal traffic of carriages and other soldiers on horseback to the side. They had to stop and wait for a battery of enormous howitzers to cross an intersection in front of them, guns so large they had been broken down and the barrel and carriage each needed eight horses. By the time they finally arrived at their barracks, a nondescript series of blocky buildings on a back street, Sophia's head was spinning.

Sophia had always thought of Charlie Company as the Army, a small group of people, all of whom she knew personally, who occasionally marched out of Jade Falls to fight the King's enemies. Even the 24th Infantry Regiment was hardly a faceless organization. Southbend was a large town and Sophia had been there many times and seen other members of the regiment out and about. The concept of the division, the corps, the Army itself, had all been abstractions to her. Seeing it all up close, she realized for the first time what a small cog they all were in the Kingdom's war machine.

Throwing her pack down next to her bunk and watching a cloud of dust rise as it hit the floor, Sophia also realized how late they were going to be up. This was a transit barracks and she doubted her father cared too much about making it extremely neat, but she doubted it was really safe to be breathing the air. As she and Tony started opening windows, she wondered absently when the part of the war that didn't involve sweeping and mopping would begin.

Chapter 14

Certain Victory

Sunlight flooded into the room and Arilin stirred in her sleep. Slowly opening her eyes, she rolled onto her back in the unfamiliar bed and propped herself up on her elbows as the night's cobwebs slowly cleared from her mind. The last thing she remembered was climbing into the carriage with Walter and Patricia, putting her head in Patricia's lap and closing her eyes. Arilin lifted the sheets to examine herself and realized that this meant that they had carried her inside, undressed her and – she felt her hair to confirm it – bathed her, put her in pajamas and put her to bed. And judging by the sun rising over the mountains surrounding Drakenburg it was already mid-morning. She knew she was a deep sleeper but still, how tired had she *been?*

This was a little embarrassing. Still, they had been out late last night. Arilin took some solace in the thought of Patricia snoring away herself, climbed out of bed and padded into the bathroom she shared with the lady general. The shower was still wet, so she couldn't be that far behind her. As she pulled her clothes off and stepped into the hot stream she thought about Walter feeling the effects of the night and giggled. He'd probably gotten up at whatever ungodly hour he normally did, scowled and carried on as though nothing had happened.

After a couple minutes in the shower she heard a hesitant knock on the door and Becky called out, "Milady? Do you need any help in there?"

Arilin paused from working shampoo into her long hair and replied, "No, I'm alright... could you lay out some clothes for me?"

"Of course, milady! Just call if you need anything, please!" Becky said from the other side of the door.

Arilin went back to working the fragrant-smelling goop into her thick hair. How helpless did Rebecca think she was? She didn't need to be washed like a child. Although, thinking about it, Arilin realized that Becky had actually spent most of her time prior to this helping to take care of Beatrice. And Beatrice let her servants spoil her. Arilin rolled her eyes and resolved to have a talk with her sister when she got back.

Emerging from the bathroom a little while later, Arilin discovered an outfit laid out on the bed and Becky standing by, corset in hand. It was a little too cute for her tastes, but she couldn't bring herself to complain. Discarding her towels, she stepped into her panties, pulled her chemise over her head and took the corset from Becky as she approached helpfully. She was fastening the stiff metal busk up her front when Becky started, "Ah, milady, let me help you with that."

Arilin reached behind herself for the laces and replied, "I can dress myself, Becky." Pulling them tight, she sighed as she felt the corset tighten snug around her body. She went on, "I don't suppose *you* have someone help you with your corset in the morning?"

Becky cocked her head, "No, but... you're a princess. And you didn't complain last night."

"That's because it was a *ball gown*." Arilin gestured at the considerably simpler dress on the bed, "This is much easier."

Arilin sat to put on her stockings, and Becky suddenly laughed out loud. She quickly covered her mouth with her hand as Arilin looked at her and explained herself, "I apologize, milady... I just realized how Miss Montrose can keep up with you and your mother while there are five of us taking care of Lady Beatrice."

Arilin laughed, "Just between us, Abby's getting sick of it." She looked Becky up and down, "How would you like to keep working for me when this is all over?"

Her words sank in, and Becky thought for a few seconds before stepping back and bowing gratefully, "I would be honored, milady." She gave her a small smile, "Although I'd have to ask your mother."

Arilin stood up, pulled her dress on and smiled, "Great. Now let's get downstairs, I'm starving."

Getting off the elevator downstairs, they headed for the hotel restaurant and discovered Vanessa sitting at a table by the windows reading a book. As they approached Arilin was able to make out the title, *War* by General Steinwitz. Patricia was nowhere to be found. Totally absorbed, Vanessa finally looked up as Arilin and Rebecca sat down at the table and leapt up, saying, "Milady! I'm sorry! Er, ah, what can I do for you?"

Arilin giggled and replied, "Relax. You can start by eating breakfast with me." She went on, "Also, where's Patricia?"

Vanessa gingerly sat back down and shrugged, "General Reinhardt came by a few minutes ago and grabbed her. I guess they wanted her opinion on something. She told me I was free until we leave for the hospital later on. So," She gestured with her book, "Here I am."

"Oh, right, the hospital." Arilin suddenly remembered that, along with the invitation to the ball last night, she and Patricia had decided to visit the Drakenburg Central Military Hospital later on that morning. She looked at the clock quickly, realized she had a couple hours to spare and relaxed. A waiter quickly appeared to take their order and they were eating in record time.

Arilin pushed the remains of her breakfast away, stood, stretched and asked Vanessa where the staff was working and where she could presumably find Patricia. Vanessa pointed her in the right direction and, she told Becky she was also free until they visited the hospital and went to find out how the war was going. Finding the IX Corps staff wasn't hard. Arilin spotted a messenger who looked like he was going in the right direction and followed him into one of the hotel's smaller ballrooms. Walking in, she found that the staff had turned it into a fairly impressive war room given the circumstances.

Siegfried called out as she walked in, "Attention! The morning operational update is beginning! Those of you not involved, *keep it down!*" He noticed the princess and went on, softer, "Also, good morning, milady. You're just in time." Most of the room turned to look at her and then quickly went back to their business. The word about leaping to attention whenever she walked in seemed to have gotten around.

Patricia, sitting at the central, U-shaped conference table, gestured at one of the clerks as she approached and the man quickly hurried up with a seat. Arilin found herself sitting between Patricia and Siegfried as he sat back down. On the Siegfried's other side, Walter looked over and gave her a nod as she sat down before returning to the papers in front of him. She saw another two-star on Walter's other side she didn't know at all, who she supposed was one of the divisional commanders. The rest of the table was filled with officers she recognized as being part of the staff.

Walter rapped the table with his knuckles sharply, and the side conversations died down. Adjusting his monocle slightly, he looked up from the papers and said, "Let's begin with the big picture, last 24 hours. How are we looking at Fire Ridge?"

A one-star sitting close to the head of the table stood. Arilin noticed that his nametag read "Stiles" as he said, "Sir, we believe the defense is collapsing. The Army of the Marchlands will probably be retreating within hours."

Walter scowled and leaned forward on his elbows, "I know that much already. How'd your people come to that conclusion?"

General Stiles explained, "Reporting from Fire Ridge has been very contradictory. Some reports say the defense is holding, others that the rear area is being overrun. We believe the Imperials infiltrated a significant force through the line last night and are rolling up the position."

Walter nodded, "Thank you, Richard. Looks like we'll be fighting in

Grenville." His gaze shifted to a naval officer seated far down the table, "Now, Commander Steiner, I believe you have some fairly important news from the battle fleet." He looked around the table to emphasize his words, "Let's not forget Raven Wing, gentlemen." He looked at Arilin and Patricia, "And ladies. If the fleet comes through our job will become immensely easier."

Steiner stood and straightened his blue-black uniform. Clearing his throat, he started, "Gentlemen, last night the First and Second Battlecruiser Divisions fought an action with what we believe was the vanguard of the Black Fleet. We lost *Goliath, Gladiator, Mercury* and *Vengeance*," A commotion went around the room at the announcement. Arilin felt queasy herself. She'd visited the *Gladiator*. He went on, "As well as several smaller warships. We believe the Empire lost at least three battlecruisers."

Arilin did some quick mental math and paled. The fleet was in the far north, where the water was icy and would suck the life out of a man in minutes. Most of the men on those ships were dead. And each of those battlecruisers had more than a thousand men on board. The Kingdom had lost five thousand or more sailors in a couple of hours. She shared an uneasy glance with Patricia as Walter interjected, "How do you know that?"

Steiner replied, "Two large Imperial warships suffered massive propellant fires during the battle and we chased down and sank the *Nephilara* at daybreak." He cleared his throat and went on, "The Imperial ships pressed through our formation and headed towards the fleet's main body, probably trying to verify its position. They should engage them shortly. We're still trying to pin down the rest of the Black Fleet."

Walter nodded, "Thank you, Commander. We all wish Admiral Kensington the best of luck." He grunted and went on, "Now, for our own corps, I know the 30th Division has already closed on Gyrburg, so if I could get an update on the cavalry brigade..."

As Walter went back and forth with the staff on minutiae of moving a hundred thousand soldiers to the other side of the Kingdom, Siegfried leaned over and whispered, "So, how did last night go?"

Arilin whispered back, *"Perfectly."*

He smiled and replied, "Excellent. We need to keep this up, milady."

Walter kept the briefing in hand and it wound down and concluded quickly enough. After it broke up Arilin and Patricia both stood and stretched with their arms overhead, then looked at each other, froze, and laughed. Patricia ventured, "Great minds think alike?" Arilin nodded, and she looked at her watch and went on, "I think it's about time we headed out, milady."

Leaving the war room, they collected Becky and Vanessa, piled into one of the military automobiles the corps staff kept on call and told the driver to get them to the Central Military Hospital. He got the engine going with a clatter and plume of black smoke, and they bumped out over the cobblestones across town. Arilin looked down from admiring the mountains surrounding the town through the car's open top to see Patricia looking pale across from her, and she asked, "Are you feeling all right?"

The woman shook her head, "Not really, but I'll be fine when we get there." She paused, "I don't really like cars. The exhaust makes me sick."

Arilin replied, "You should have said something! We could have taken a carriage. Or ridden." She looked around appreciatively again, "In fact, I probably wouldn't mind walking."

Patricia chuckled, "This would be a nice town to walk through. We should do that later, milady."

Arilin smiled, "Certainly!" The car bumped along in relative silence for a few more minutes, broken only by the engine's guttural growl as the driver negotiated some particularly steep streets. He finally turned sharply and pulled up before an imposing wrought-iron gate with a sentry standing guard on either side. They recognized the passengers, leapt to attention and quickly swung the gate open so they could pull inside.

The Drakenburg Central Military Hospital was a tall structure set far back in its compound, surrounded by a small park for the benefit of the patients and staff. Trees shaded the long drive to the front doors, and the scent of grass and spring flowers replaced the harsh smell of the city outside as they drove in. The driver deposited them out front and pulled around behind the building to wait for their return.

The hospital's commander and his aide were waiting for them. He approached and saluted as they walked up, saying, "Good morning, your ladyships. It's a pleasure having you visit today."

Patricia returned his salute and replied, "The pleasure is all ours. It's the least my lady and I can do."

He smiled, looked nervously at Arilin and replied, "Of course. I'd be honored to show you around."

Arilin smiled pleasantly and said, "Then let's begin." She looked at the man, thought for a second, then turned to Rebecca and asked, "Becky, you used to be a nurse. Who should I visit first?"

Rebecca replied without missing a beat, ticking them off on her fingers, "Amputees, disfigurement cases, the paralyzed, the seriously ill with non-contagious diseases, the burn ward... we should probably stay away from the psych cases." She cocked her head and asked, "Have there been any gas casualties yet? We definitely need to see them."

The commander grimaced and said, "Milady, I do have a few wards picked out as particularly suitable, especially for a girl of your age. I'm sure the residents would be disappointed if you didn't visit them."

Arilin smiled and bowed her head, "I appreciate your concern for my sake, but I'm here for those who would benefit most from Royal attention. So," She paused and looked back up at him, "Let's start with your amputees."

The man looked at Patricia for help. She shrugged. Finally he growled, "Just don't blame me later, young lady."

Arilin glared at him, "I don't scare easily. Now let's go."

He reluctantly ushered them inside and into an elevator and pressed the key for the sixth floor. The doors opened and an awful smell rolled into the elevator, the harsh tang of disinfectant lying over stinking rot. Arilin heard a man moaning in pain off down one of the corridors. They stepped out of the elevator and the commander said, "Welcome to the burn ward." As he led them through the halls he explained, "The Empire's been using white phosphorous shells with their artillery lately. They set fire to whatever they hit and phosphor particles produce extremely deep, severe burns. Not as immediately *lethal* as shrapnel, I suppose, but," He led them into a ward full of heavily-bandaged patients hooked up to clusters of IV bags. A few of them looked blearily in their direction as he continued, "Needless to say, *extremely* painful."

A few hours later an extremely pale Arilin gratefully sank into a chair in the rehabilitation ward's staff room. Vanessa looked like she was on the verge of tears as she collapsed into the seat next to her, and even Patricia looked unusually grim. Totally unaffected, Rebecca produced a fan and started fanning the two younger girls as she told Patricia, "I think we should call it a day, milady." Arilin overheard her as she leaned in closer and muttered, "The princess is fine, but if we see another bad case your aide is going to faint."

Patricia snorted and said, "I agree." She turned to Arilin, "Milady, I think it's time we headed back."

Arilin shook her head to clear it and replied, "Yes... I think this is enough for today." Standing, she stretched herself as Becky helped Vanessa to her feet. Accompanied by the commander, they were headed back towards the elevator when they saw an armed guard standing outside one of the floor's few private rooms. As they approached Arilin asked, "Who's in there?" She looked up at the commander and went on, "Someone important?"

He snorted dismissively, "No, actually, and you are *not* going in there."

Arilin looked at him and raised an eyebrow, "Oh, really? Is it contagious?"

"Ah, no, milady... wait!" Arilin walked past the surprised guard, opened the door and walked in. Patricia followed her into the small room a moment later, shushing the man as she went. Arilin barely heard her as the room's occupant looked up from her game of Solitaire and locked eyes with her.

The girl's surly expression melted after a second, dark eyes widening as she looked between the two of them. Straightening up from where she was propped up in bed, she swallowed hard and said, "Ah, m-milady, what..." Her eyes narrowed as she seemed to collect her thoughts, "What's the occasion?"

Arilin smoothed her skirt as she sat down on the foot of the bed. Looking over at the girl, she smiled disarmingly and replied, "I'm visiting patients." She went on, "They didn't tell me there were Imperials here." The girl blushed and looked down at the tray with its playing cards in her lap, and Arilin asked, "How'd you get hurt?"

The girl looked back up at her sheepishly. Sighing, she replied, "My, uh, horse got hit. It fell on my leg." Arilin looked down and started up guiltily, and the girl laughed, "My right leg, milady." She pointed to the lump under the sheets closer to the wall, unnaturally bulky with a heavy cast, "No worries."

"Oh," Arilin settled back down, relieved. Leaning in closer to the dragoon, she noticed something and picked up a playing card from the tray. Examining it, she raised an eyebrow and turned to Patricia, "This is pretty good, actually."

Patricia took it from her and chuckled, "I'll say. I'm the Queen of Diamonds, huh?" The girl's cards featured flattering line art of practically every important person in the Royal government and military. The Royal crest with 'KNOW YOUR ENEMY' over it was printed on their backs.

"Here you are, milady." The girl handed her the Ace of Hearts, and Arilin blushed as she realized half the Imperial Army was probably in love with her by now.

Laughing, Arilin looked up at Patricia and asked, "Do you have a pen, by any chance?"

The lady general smiled and replied, "I do, in fact."

They both signed their cards and gave them back to the girl, and she replied, "Wow, thanks!" Chuckling, she went on, "Well, I guess I can't complain. I got to meet you two, and I got to Drakenburg early."

Patricia gave her a hard look, "*Early*, you say?"

"Well, yes, milady." The dragoon smiled awkwardly.

Arilin felt a chill work its way through the room as Patricia's glare burned into the girl. Finally, the lady general replied coldly, "Your friends have a *long* way to go, young lady. But. We're pleased to have met you. Get well." She gave Arilin a look that brooked no disobedience, "Milady, it's time for us to leave."

As they walked out of the hospital a few minutes later Arilin remarked, "She didn't seem too awful." They climbed into the car and she went on, "*Irreverent*, maybe."

Patricia chuckled, "Milady, it's not often you get the chance to fight genuinely awful people." She gave her a thin smile, "Jihadists, maybe. The adults. Towards the end a lot of them were kids not much older than you. But take the mask off an Imperial and they're as normal as we are."

Arilin thought for a moment and said, "Sure, I guess I understand... but why are we still at war then?"

The lady general's smile broadened. She said, "Allow me to quote Emperor Sai when I asked him that same question." Arilin felt her eyes widening as she went on, "He told me, 'You people destroyed my country when I was twelve years old and I have fought my entire life to reclaim it. The Empire of Masks will not be whole until Drakenburg is restored, and it will not be safe until the High City *burns*.'"

Arilin closed her jaw with a force of will and said, "You've *met* Sai?"

Patricia shrugged, "When I came into the Army any Imperial prisoners we took were shot. When we decided we were going to clean up our act someone had to take a message to the Emperor and ask him to reciprocate." She smiled sheepishly, "I was young, stupid, and most importantly my father was too prominent for them to kill me out of hand, so I volunteered."

"My God." Arilin thought for a second and then asked, "What did Walter say?"

Looking warily at the other two women in the car, Patricia leaned across and whispered to Arilin, "He patted me on the head and told me about the painting he keeps in his private study." Her smile got very sly,

"But you'll have to get *that* story out of him yourself."

They arrived back at the hotel to find the mood had darkened considerably. Shortly after they'd left the telegraph had lit up with news from the fleet. Details were sketchy and confused, but it was clear they were locked in a death struggle with the Black Fleet. Admiral Kensington was dead, lost with the *Vanguard* and fifteen hundred men. They'd lost a dozen other battleships with it and the Empire had taken at least as much punishment. Night had fallen over the ocean, a storm was blowing in and any sane admiral would have retreated to lick his wounds.

The Imperials kept coming on and the telegraph kept chattering late into the night. Princess Arilin, pale and withdrawn, had no appetite for dinner and Patricia took her upstairs and put her to bed early. She ran into Walter coming back down. He asked, "The princess?"

"Asleep. She passed right out." She replied, "She'll be fine in the morning. That girl's tough."

Walter chuckled, "Reminds me of someone I know." He pulled a cigar from his breast pocket, "I'm going for a smoke. Care to join me, milady?"

"You know I don't smoke, but..." Patricia gave him a half-hearted smile, "If you've got some whiskey, I could use a drink."

Walter offered her his arm, "That shouldn't be a problem."

Chapter 15

Whispers in the Mist

The rain came down in sheets and the forest sang with it. Every leaf shook and fluttered in the storm, thick droplets pattering down on the soldiers riding far below. June closed his eyes and enjoyed it for a second, the cascade of sound, the smell of new growth and decay, Lucky's powerful muscles between his legs. If he'd had a bath in the month of May it really would have been a nice ride even with the war going on. As things stood the damp was making him itch worse than usual and even Lucky thought he smelled terrible.

The forest thinned and June waved for the platoon to spread out. The dragoons quickly spread off the road into a loose wedge as the rain washed over them. June felt it starting to soak through his gaiters and into his boots and on a whim he unstrapped his helmet and took it off, tucking it under his arm as he untied his braid and worked his stiff hair loose with his fingers. His hair came free and fell across his back in a greasy, dirty mass all the way down to his saddle. June worked the water into it with his free hand and it got a little looser.

"I like your idea, sir." June looked over to see Anastasia taking her own helmet off and shaking her hair out. Looking around, half the platoon was doing it. Sergeant Khan gave him a dirty look from her position to the rear, clear even through her mask. June rolled his eyes, held up his hand for a halt and went back to washing his hair. No point in keeping riding when nobody was looking for the enemy.

I should have joined the Navy, he thought idly, *although on second thought, maybe not.* He chuckled to himself as he thought of the letter he'd gotten a couple days ago from his old friend, Samantha Gage. The good news was that she'd survived the Battle of the Diamond Shoals, unlike more of the Black Fleet than he really cared to think about. The bad news was that she couldn't go into further details about what had happened because she'd been fished out of the water with hypothermia and about a pound of metal embedded in her by a particularly dreamy Royal Navy lieutenant named Felix. The cold water had kept her from bleeding out.

Sam was the only woman on the HMS *Defiance* right now and they'd posted three married petty officers to keep the suitors at bay, although she sounded like she wouldn't mind seeing more of this Felix guy. June rolled his eyes at the thought, tied his hair into a ponytail, put his helmet back on and waved his platoon forward. They could shower in Drakenburg.

If his reckoning was correct they were about a day's march southeast of Grenville. Every now and then he could hear faint rumbling to the north from the ongoing artillery duel on the city's outskirts, but they hadn't seen a single Royal soldier this far out yet. Hopefully they were around the Royal Army's right flank and they wouldn't get into a serious fight on this patrol. June doubted he was that lucky.

June perked up his senses as they crested a rise and the rain abruptly lessened to a misting drizzle. If the weather had been clearer he probably could have seen Grenville's church spires from the top. As things stood all he saw was gray mist, half-grown wheat and the dragoons spread out behind him. There was probably a farmhouse around here somewhere, but he couldn't see it. After pausing for a moment, June waved the platoon on and they rode slowly into the valley.

June felt his stomach dropping as the ground behind them and the mist only seemed to thicken. Without the drumming of the rain the whole world was tomb-silent and in the cocooning mist even small sounds seemed magnified. The soft creaking of June's saddle was like nails on a chalkboard and the thud of Lucky's hooves on the dirt road sounded like gunshots. June could hear his breathing, could hear his heartbeat throbbing in his ears. He could hear a faint clinking sound from further downhill and voices whispering out of the fog.

Very slowly, June pulled Lucky to a halt and raised his hand. Corporal Marin had stopped just ahead of him, and he turned to look at June and wordlessly pointed downhill. June nudged his horse up alongside him and whispered, "Are you hearing that?"

Marin nodded, "Yes, sir. Digging in at the bottom of the hill, maybe?"

June beckoned Anastasia over and she weighed in, "I hear it too, sir... do you think they can hear us?"

June shook his head and said, "No. Now spread out." Riding up a little to the very front of the formation, he turned and theatrically held his finger to his mask's lips, twisting in his saddle so the entire platoon could see him. When he was satisfied they weren't going to be making any battle cries, he slowly drew his sword and held it overhead. A thicket of glinting blades appeared, stretching back into the mist. Marin drew his pistol instead and June imagined him rolling his eyes behind his mask.

Lowering his sword, June started down the shallow hill. He heard his platoon follow him in a cascade of soft hoofbeats. And he heard the whispers grow louder. They resolved into voices. Someone called loudly for sandbags and another voice replied that they were getting some. A deeper, scratchier voice told them to hurry up, they didn't have all day.

A voice came out of the fog, very distinct, "Hey, do you hear that?"

Someone else replied, "Sounds like... horses?" June saw a dark shape in the gray sea as the man called out, "Hey! Identify yourselves!"

June kicked Lucky, raised his sword and screamed, *"For Lady Vai!"* His platoon charged after him as his horse exploded forward, shrieking like demons. A couple of gunshots broke the mist as June slashed down on the sentry in front of him, felt his sword bite bone and come free as he charged past. June charged on blindly for seconds that felt like hours. People seemed to be shouting all around him, more wild gunshots ringing out as he tried to will the mist out of existence so he could see his enemy.

And then the mist boiled with shapes, with Royal soldiers standing in half-scraped foxholes, men in dark uniforms throwing down shovels and scrambling for their weapons. Bullets tore the air, cracking as they snapped by. A horse crashed to the ground and someone screamed behind him. June raised his sword, kicked Lucky again and smashed into the infantry like a meteor. His first, underhand stroke caught a man's back as he ducked and June brought his sword up, around and down into another soldier's head. Directly in front of him a Royal soldier raised his rifle to fend off an expected slash, and quick as lightning June pulled his sword back and stabbed him as he charged by.

Someone fired a long burst on a machine-gun, far to his left. They must have come in on this unit's flank, rather than dead center. Looking behind him for a moment, June saw most of First and Second Squad behind him and off to his right. Third Squad was fighting in a whirl of blades just left of where he'd come through, and he noticed Sergeant Khan helpfully bringing up the rear with the machine gun squad. And the ground was littered with dark lumps where they'd charged through.

June swallowed hard, pushed the carnage to the back of his mind and hauled on the reins. As Lucky came around he screamed over the battle, "First and Second, line on me! Wheel left!" He pointed at Khan with his sword and shouted, "Get the machine guns set up here!"

Sergeant Khan raised her sword in acknowledgement and shouted back at him, "Got it, sir! We'll cover you! Go!"

June kicked Lucky again and charged off down the Royal defensive line, the two squads swinging in behind him. Royal soldiers appeared out of the swirling mist in groups, sergeants screaming to get them on line, to fix bayonets. More gunfire rang out, June saw Sergeant Itogawa fall from his horse beside him and then they were upon the infantry again, scattering the men like screaming tenpins.

The mist lifted slightly as they thundered on and June saw a group of men spilling from a small tent with a company guidon planted outside, and more dark shapes boiling further away in the mist down the line beyond them. The officers drawing their swords didn't concern June quite so much as the infantry squad that came out with them, bayonets fixed, machine gunner sprawling into the dirt.

June looked to his left and his right, pointed his sword down the defense line and shouted, *"Keep going! I have the CP!"*

Corporal Marin gave him a dubious look in the instant he had, but he raised his pistol and shouted, *"Follow me!"* as June hauled Lucky out of line and swung behind the charging dragoons. The infantry raised their rifles and started shooting at his men as they charged past them. They didn't notice him coming straight for them. By the time heads turned in his direction, mouths opening to shout a warning, it was too late.

Lucky crashed through them, scattering the infantry aside as June's sword flashed and bit like a steel viper. Soldiers toppled as the horse charged free and June leapt from the saddle, turning in the air to land on his feet, his momentum driving him back into a crouch as his boots bit into the wet ground. Lunging forward, he slashed a bayonet thrust aside and came up with his sword under the man's arms and cutting. He stepped through and pivoted left as his sword came free, snapping it into another man's neck as he stepped back. June spun, sidestepped a bayonet thrust and continued the cut into another attacker's side. Pushing him aside as he toppled, he darted into the rest of the men before him, sword shrieking through the air as he struck again and again.

A few seconds later he deflected a sword-thrust from one of the officers, slashed the man's arm open with the same motion, kicked him to the ground and marched over him towards the last soldier still standing in front of him. The man just stood there, arms slack at his sides, sword-point digging into the ground. June walked up to him and put his sword-point at his throat, snarling, "I'll assume you surrender. And," switching his sword to his left hand, he drew his pistol and aimed it at the machine-gun team he'd missed coming in, "How about telling them to surrender too before I *shoot* them?"

The man jerked like he'd been shocked, dropped his sword and raised his hands. Looking at him for a moment, June noticed that he was an older lieutenant. Probably a family man. He looked back at the machine gunners and exhaled slightly as he saw them slowly raising their hands. June nodded at a clear spot on the ground and said, very deliberately, "Drop whatever weapons you have right there, *slowly*. And then," He jerked his head at the twitching, moaning bodies behind him, "Tend to your friends."

The Royal soldiers did as he'd told them, shaking as they pulled three of their companions from the carnage, slipping on grass slicked with rain and blood. The rest were beyond helping. June holstered his pistol and pulled out a handkerchief to wipe his sword clean, noting absently that the gunfire had died down and all he could hear was voices. His dragoons were screaming at prisoners up and down the line, dark shapes galloping around on horseback in the fog as they herded their charges like cattle. Underneath that a chorus of injured men cried out pitifully. It sounded, he thought, like hell.

June felt warm liquid flowing down his left arm as he wiped at his sword. He looked down and saw his handkerchief was bright red, soaked and dripping with blood. It had run down his gloved hand and under his sleeve and was probably staining his uniform. June looked at his arm, expecting to see a black streak growing on the heavy green cloth.

His arms were completely black, sodden with liquid warmer than the cold rain from earlier. June looked at his chest and saw his uniform coat and load-bearing harness were smeared and spattered with blood. He touched his face and felt his fingers slip on the smooth metal of his mask, saw them come back wet and darkened. He was *covered* in blood. June took another look at the prisoners, saw how they shook as they tried to put tourniquets on limbs slashed to the bone, saw their eyes widen with terror as they snuck glances at him.

A dragoon galloped up, leading a flashy black horse with four white hooves and no rider. June recognized Anastasia leading Lucky and smiled despite himself as he walked over. She dismounted and greeted him, "Sir, good to... my God, sir, you're... and this, uh..." She looked at the carnage, then at him, and shrugged helplessly.

June shook his head and said, "It's not mine. Them, on the other hand..." He sheathed his sword slowly and pointed at the small group of prisoners as they worked on their wounded, "Watch them while I go sort the platoon out."

Anastasia said, "Yes, sir," and drew her pistol dramatically, a pointless gesture considering how broken the men looked. June climbed into the saddle and nudged Lucky forward. On a whim he yanked the defeated company's guidon out of the ground as he rode by and went to go find someone who knew what exactly was going on.

June spotted a horseman riding about purposefully in the mist and nudged Lucky after him. Sergeant Ghaznavi of Second Squad, generally known as Ghaz, looked over at his approach and reined his horse in. As June approached and he got a better look at him, he said, "Sir! Are you hurt?" June shook his head and he went on, "Well done then."

His blood-soaked uniform was making his skin crawl. June scowled under his mask and said, "It wasn't a fair fight." Changing the subject, he went on, "How's your squad? And do you know anything about the others?"

Ghaz replied, "My squad's fine, no casualties. Everyone besides Hayate in First is okay, too. He's..." he choked up a little, then steadied himself and went on, "He's dead. Headshot."

June narrowed his eyes and spat, "Damn. He was right beside me. And Third?"

Ghaz hesitated for a moment, then said, "Kovacs is dead, and Gil's as good as. Everyone else is wounded, more or less. They should all be able to ride back."

One whole squad down and two more good men dead. Plus God knew how many prisoners, most of them probably wounded. June asked, "Got a count of the prisoners?"

The sergeant must have read his concern. He replied, "Sixty-five so far. Maybe forty can march." He cocked his head and asked, "By the way, sir, do you know where Sergeant Khan is? I haven't seen her anywhere."

June chuckled grimly, pointed off in the fog in her rough direction and said, "She's got the machine guns over that way somewhere." He thought for a moment, then said, "Go get her and have her bring the guns up here. Tell her I'm putting her in charge of getting the wounded and the prisoners back to the rear. She'll keep the machine gunners for guards."

Ghaz shook his head, "She's not going to like that, sir."

June nodded, "I know, but I don't have a choice. Now get going."

The man saluted and rode off into the mist, and June turned and headed off towards what sounded like the prisoners and the rest of his platoon. Marin and Tarai had taken charge of the situation, separated the healthy prisoners from the wounded and prodded the Royal medics into action. June pulled Lucky up next to Marin and asked, "You've heard about Sergeant Itogawa?"

The man nodded angrily and waved his pistol at the huddle of Royal soldiers, "I didn't need to. I saw it myself." He paused and spat, "Royal bastards."

June reached out, set his hand on his shoulder and squeezed it, "Calm down, corporal. I need you to take over the squad. For Hayate."

Marin looked over at him for a couple seconds, then gritted, "Yes, sir.

Will do."

June nodded and let go of his shoulder, "Good man." Turning to the knot of prisoners, June hefted their guidon and rode closer. Even the defiant-looking ones deflated once they got a good look at him, and the group shrank away as he approached. June slowly looked across them, picked out the man that looked the most terrified, waited a moment for effect and pointed, "*You*. I want to talk to you."

The prisoners practically evaporated around the man – boy, actually, he looked about sixteen – leaving him standing alone. June looked to the side and waved his hand, and a dragoon on foot seized him and dragged him along as June turned and rode out of earshot of the rest of the prisoners.

The boy, and the other two prisoners June talked to as Sergeant Khan sorted the situation out, was pathetically eager to please. The information didn't make June any happier. The company was part of the advance guard of the Royal Army's Fifth Corps, just arrived out of Wolf Rock. They'd been told they were going to hold Grenville at all costs.

Another shiver worked its way up June's spine as he got his two remaining squads back into formation to press west. He'd probably just started the Battle of Grenville and half his platoon was down already.

Chapter 16

The Lone Horseman

The motion of the train changed and jolted Sophia from her sleep. Normally the train felt very solid on the rails, but now it felt like it was almost floating, swaying slowly up and down. She opened her eyes slowly in the boxcar's gray darkness and realized it was early morning. Turning her head to the side to look out the open sliding doors, she saw the guardrail of a railway bridge and a wall of deep gray fog beyond.

Somebody was pressing into her other side and she turned her head back to see Tony's face from about three inches away. He must have rolled over in his sleep. He *better* have rolled over in his sleep, because if he had decided to roll over on top of her in the night and put an arm around her chest on the assumption she'd be alright with it later, she'd, well... she thought for a second and drew a blank. She pushed him off and sat up. Either she had a thing for him or, she thought as she looked around at the sleeping soldiers piled on the boxcar's plank floor, her standards had declined dramatically in the last few weeks. She looked back at Tony, with his curly hair cut off short in the Army's style, freckles and sunburn finally turning into a tan, and decided it might be both.

The train came off the bridge and back onto solid ground, and Sophia scooted herself back to sit with her back against the wall as they rolled onwards. A few houses and a railway station raced past in the fog before the boxcar darkened and trees appeared beside the tracks, trunks marching back to disappear into the mist. She felt her head slowly clear as the ghostly scenery flowed by, and soon her thoughts turned to the river they'd just gone over. If it was the Great Steel River flowing through Grenville they were almost at the front. She pulled her rifle into her lap and felt its familiar form nervously. She might be firing it at the Imperials in a few hours. The romantic glow in her chest turned to ice at the thought.

They rolled onwards for another hour or so as the fog slowly lifted and misting rain started drifting through the open doors. The soldiers around her started groaning and sitting up as the boxcar brightened. Soon enough even Tony thrashed his way back to the land of the living and pushed himself back up against the wall next to her.

She looked over at him and said, "Good morning, sleepyhead. How do you *ever* get up back home?"

He glanced back and gave her a sly smile, "Beth wakes me up." He ran his hands through his hair, grimaced and went on, "Usually by kicking me."

Sophia raised an eyebrow, "If she actually hated you she'd avoid you. Speaking of her, any progress?"

Tony chuckled, "Yeah. She sent some drawings of how she'll remodel my room after I get killed. Even had a little shrine to me."

She laughed, "At least she's writing back."

He replied, "I can't complain, I guess." He changed the subject, "You wouldn't happen to know where we are, would you?"

"East of Grenville, I think." Sophia replied, "Surprised we can't hear the..." She trailed off and looked at Tony intently, "Did you hear that?"

He raised his eyebrows, "What... artillery?"

"Shhh, yes, listen," Sophia said, then paused for a few seconds. Over the clatter of the train on the rails she heard a dull thumping sound, surprisingly loud. She looked around, surprised nobody else had noticed it before turning back to Tony, "Yeah... sounds close, too."

He shook his head and smiled sheepishly, "I can't hear anything over this Train, Sophie. How do you *do* that, anyways?"

She shrugged, "I listen, I guess?" She gave him another look, "We should be stopping soon."

On Tony's other side Corporal Janssen had been listening in on their conversation. His bored expression perked up as Sophia spoke and he announced to the car in general, "Hey, the little lady says we're at the front!"

A wave of nervous laughter swept over the soldiers. On the far side of the car, Sergeant Falcon asked loudly, "Heard the artillery, Miss Rose?" She nodded and he went on, "I wish I was young again and hadn't stood next to so many machine guns!" The older men laughed and he went on, "Alright, everyone, secure your gear. We might have to unload in a hurry."

They fell to repacking rucksacks, buckling on harnesses and retrieving weapons. A couple minutes later, as Sophia was tightening her own load-bearing belt on, the train braked hard. She fought to keep her balance and Tony quickly reached out, grabbed her harness and pulled her back upright. He quickly let go and stammered, "S-sorry, I just..."

Sophia cocked her head and said, "Why... oh." He'd basically just groped her. She snorted, "No problem." She finished putting the belt on, grabbed her rifle and rucksack and got up on one knee as the train slowed quickly. Tony, struggling with his own equipment, finally got himself together and kneeling next to her as a station's platform appeared beside the car.

The station moved past for a few seconds until the train squealed to a halt. Sergeant Falcon stood and shouted, "Alright, everyone out! Move!" They stood as one and flooded onto the platform, making a tired-looking Rail Service officer stumble backwards to avoid them.

The man recovered his dignity and remarked, "I wish everyone that came through here moved like that. Although..." He looked past them to a very empty platform as they heard most of the battalion stumbling around trying to put equipment on inside their rail cars, "Your friends need some work. 2-24 Infantry, I presume?"

Sergeant Falcon replied, "Yes, sir, that's us."

The officer snorted, "The 77th Regiment seems to have misplaced their third battalion." He rolled his eyes, "I was hoping you were them. In any event, excuse me, but this train isn't going to unload itself."

The man walked off towards the rear of the train as soldiers started milling onto the platform. Sophia noticed her father, looking more rumpled than usual, barking at the rest of the company to hurry up. Hearing a familiar voice behind her, she turned to see Lieutenant Thorn had appeared and was talking to Falcon. Thorn gestured to a map in his hand and Falcon shrugged, turned and called for the platoon to gather round. Thorn was about to start talking when a string of loud cracks tore through the air, very close. The whole company cowered for a moment before Sophia's father called out, "That was outgoing! Get back to work!"

Thorn straightened back up, cleared his throat and said, "Alright, everyone. The plan's not changed much since we left. Charlie's going up on the right of the battalion and we're leading them in. We'll follow Bravo once they step off," He gestured to the soldiers preparing to move out on the platform in front of them, "And split off outside of town. I've got a road picked out." He paused for a moment, looked around the platoon and went on, "The 25th Regiment has some companies thrown out front to screen us, so don't go thinking anyone you see with a rifle is a Mask. We're going to go forward and link up with them. Questions, anyone?"

Jack spoke up in the back, "What then, sir?"

Before Thorn could reply Sergeant Falcon cut him off, "Then we're going to go kill some Masks!"

Sophia chuckled grimly with the rest of the platoon. The artillery fired another salvo, as if to drive the point home. Janssen raised his hand in the back as the noise died down and Thorn pointed at him in acknowledgement. The big man asked, "Sir, do you want us to load?"

Thorn looked surprised for a second at the question. Then he gave a short nod and said, "Yeah. This is the front. Lock and load."

Sophia unslung her rifle, grasped the bolt's cold, round knob, turned it and opened the action. Opening one of her ammunition pouches she pulled out a long ten-round stripper clip, stuck it into the guide on her rifle's receiver and pushed the cartridges into the magazine with her thumb. The long, thin brass clip was left standing above her rifle like an empty twig in winter. Gritting her teeth, Sophia drove the bolt forward and the clip popped free. The platoon's spent clips made an icy sound as they bounced on the concrete platform. Sophia thought they sounded like evil wind chimes.

The battalion's first two companies eventually got themselves together and marched off the platform. Charlie Company followed them through the town's streets, the misting rain making the cobbles under their feet slick and treacherous. Sophia noticed a few curious faces looking out of windows and doorways, but otherwise the town may as well have been deserted. She felt a chill work up her spine.

Nobody cheered them on as they marched out of town and into the open countryside beyond. Looking to the side Sophia saw the artillery battery from earlier drawn up in a field just off the road. The wet-looking artillerymen clustered around the guns watched them march by with dull curiosity. Shortly afterwards Thorn pointed out the road they were taking to her, and Sophia led the company as they slowly snaked away from the rest of the battalion.

They marched on in silence for another hour as the rain slowly let up and the clouds lifted. Most of the farms along the road looked abandoned, barns standing open and empty. The quiet was only broken when one particularly drunken farmer came out on his porch to wave an old-looking rifle and shout incoherently in their direction. A woman quickly came out and pulled him back inside.

The road passed through a row of trees planted for a windbreak many years ago and grown massive with age. After she passed underneath Sophia looked to her left and saw Bravo Company across the fields, shrunken to dots with the distance. She thought she could even make out some of Alpha even farther away. Back to her front the road slowly slanted down the other side of the hill they were on, and Sophia's eyes widened as she saw two figures in blue hurrying up it towards her. Thorn had been walking right behind her the whole time, and she turned and told him, "Hey, sir, looks like our guys up ahead."

Thorn stepped up next to her as she pointed at the two men in the distance. Squinting a little, he said, "Yeah, it does." He looked harder, then remarked, "Is it just me, or do they not have rifles?"

"No, they don't." She gave him a sideways look, "And why are they running?"

He returned her glance, "Don't know." Holding up a hand to stop the platoon, he told her, "Let's go see what's going on. I don't like this."

Sophia nodded and followed him forward as the platoon stopped behind them, soldiers stepping off the road and kneeling to make smaller targets. She could imagine her father squinting forward and trying to figure out what was going on up front. As they walked forward the two figures coming up the road in front of them quickly resolved into a pair of soaked solders shambling along in a half-run. Their eyes were wide as they stopped in front of them and Sophia saw them shaking with something more than exhaustion as they gasped for breath.

Sophia and Thorn shared another glance. She thought he looked a little strained himself as he led off, "Who are you two with? What happened?"

"*Dragoons.*" Sophia felt an icy knife twist in her heart as the soldier went on, "Hu-hundreds of them, there must have been. They, they j-just hit us."

His comrade joined in, "They came out of the fog and hit the company. I think we were the only ones that escaped... we were off watching the rear."

The first one came back, "W-we thought we needed to warn you."

Sophia and Thorn exchanged another, longer glance. She shook her head, very gently. Thorn grimaced, turned back to the two men and said, "I have a couple more questions for you. First, are you two with the 77th Regiment?"

The second man spoke up, "Yes, sir, why?"

Thorn nodded, "Very good. Also, where are your weapons?" Sophia drew her bayonet and latched it onto her rifle as though to prove his point. Thorn saw her move, nodded and turned back to the pair.

The first one stammered, "Uh... we-we were on a detail, we left them with the company."

Thorn's eyes narrowed, "Right. Well, I believe your unit was attacked. But," He paused for a moment and growled, "You two are cowards and deserters, and you're coming with me. Sophia, you too. Guard the prisoners." The two men recoiled at the announcement and he glanced at her and added, "I wouldn't mess with her if I were you. She's knocked men twice your size out cold."

Sophia snorted, hefted her bayonet and gestured with it. The deserters visibly deflated and tamely came along as they marched them back through the column. Her father quickly met them and, after they explained things, collared the two men and dragged them off to the rear of the column. They heard him calling for a detail to guard prisoners as he went.

Thorn sent Sophia back to the front of the company while he went to go discuss events with the commander. After a few minutes he came back gritting his teeth and Sophia asked him, "Are you doing alright, sir?"

Thorn shook his head, "Yeah, I'm fine. But," He leaned in close to her and spoke softly, "You'd think Jaeger would care more that we could get attacked any minute."

She thought for a minute. Since they'd marched out of Jade Falls, Sophia had only seen Captain Jaeger a handful of times. He hadn't even walked through the barracks once. She didn't even know where Thorn had gone in the column to find him. It wasn't a pleasant thought, and she didn't know what to say in reply. Finally, after Thorn had leaned back out, she said, "I'm not worried, sir. We've got everyone else."

He smiled and said, "I like your thinking. Now let's get going." Thorn waved for the company to move out again and they continued on their way. Sophia, nervous at the thought of whatever had befallen the unit in front of them, walked more slowly than usual and Thorn didn't object.

Another half-hour passed as they slowly made their way into the valley and lost sight of the rest of the battalion off to their left. Trees rose up around them again, breaking up the farmland with scattered forest. Sophia found herself straining her eyes to see into the wooded depths as the road snaked through them, and after they passed through a particularly dark patch she said to Thorn, "Hey, sir, I'm starting to worry about getting ambushed here."

He gave her a serious look, "You think they'd attack us here?"

She glanced back at him, "It's a good area for it, I think. I can barely see off the..." Sophia trailed off. The road in front of them ran off through a broad swath of farmland and curved off around a small hill. There was another band of forest at its base, but the top was clear. A person could stand up there and probably see the entire countryside around them. And there was *something* on top of it. Sophia squinted and changed the subject abruptly, "Do you see that?"

Thorn followed her gaze, "What... there? Maybe?" He held up a hand to stop the column and produced his binoculars. Focusing them on the distant hill, he said, "Yeah, there's someone up there on a horse." He handed the binoculars to her, "Take a look yourself."

Sophia took them and brought them up to her eyes. After a little fiddling the distant figure came into focus, although it was still too small to make out any detail. It looked like someone wearing dark clothing, on top of a dark horse, looking out across the countryside. She said, "Yeah, I see him... can't make out any details though. Think it's a dragoon, sir?"

She heard Thorn shrug, "Could be one of ours. I've heard the hussars are always off riding around doing their own thing. Might not even be from our corps. But..." He trailed off skeptically.

The overcast day had brightened steadily as they marched, and patches of blue sky showed through the clouds. Through the binoculars Sophia saw a patch of sunlight moving the right direction and said, "Wait a second..." The light swept up the hill as she saw the trees at its base ripple and shimmer in a sudden gust of wind.

She saw the figure's long hair catch the wind and flow out like a banner, saw him (her?) raise a hand to brush it back from his face. In the sudden bright sunlight she saw he was wearing a green jacket and had brown leggings laced up to his thighs. Sophia made out the rifle in a scabbard at his knee and the bulging military saddlebags. Lowering the binoculars, she looked at Thorn and said, "Sir... he's wearing green and has three feet of hair."

Thorn set his jaw and said levelly, "Damn it."

Sophia quickly raised the binoculars again. The dragoon wasn't looking out across the landscape any more. He was so far away she had a hard time telling, but the chill working its way up her spine was clear. The profile of his head was even, his hair streaming out from behind him. He was looking back at *her*. From more than a kilometer away, he held her gaze for a couple seconds before dismissively turning his horse around and vanishing behind the hill. A little shaken, Sophia lowered the binoculars and handed them back to Thorn, saying, "He... they... know we're here sir. We should get moving."

Thorn nodded and made a few hand signals. The platoon started moving forward again, squads spilling off the road into a formation like an enormous arrowhead. Sophia heard Thorn and Falcon talking behind her as they slowly moved forward and shortly afterwards she heard the footsteps of a runner heading back to warn the rest of the company. Sophia realized she was an easy target in the road herself, jumped the ditch and pressed on towards the Imperial position through a half-grown hayfield.

They'd gone maybe three or four hundred meters across the fields towards the hill when something hissed over her head. A couple seconds later a whole swarm passed overhead, lower and closer. She heard them thudding into the ground behind her and realized they were bullets as she heard distant, cracking gunfire.

That was all the encouragement Sophia needed to throw herself to the ground as another Imperial machine gun opened up, sending bullets slashing through the air around her. Kicking herself forward into a firing position, she brought her rifle to her shoulder, thumbed off the safety on the rear of the bolt and lined up the sights.

Someone was shouting behind her. More Imperial bullets sliced through the air like singing wasps. Her finger curled into the trigger guard and Sophia felt the fine serrations of her rifle's trigger on her fingertip as she pulled it to the rear. It moved smoothly for an instant, stopped and then gave way as she increased the pressure.

Her rifle kicked against her shoulder and Sophia worked the bolt and fired again. Heaving herself to her feet, she ran a few paces forward and threw herself down again. To her left and right, other soldiers were firing, running forward, shouting. She heard her squad's machine gun shriek to life behind her as she brought her rifle back to her shoulder. Off to the side another machine gun fired a long burst as she worked her rifle's bolt and fired again.

Thorn was shouting behind her and she imagined her father bellowing at the rest of the company farther to the rear. Spread out. Get into formation. Keep moving. It was just like training, Charlie Company rushing through the fields outside of Jade Falls, just with more ammunition. As she thought that, Tony flopped to the ground next to her and Sophia felt the adrenaline haze lift from her mind. They were in combat, yes. They'd trained for it. And she couldn't think of a bunch of people she'd rather be shot at with than Charlie Company.

Tony was shaking, eyes wide as he looked over at her. Sophia reached over, patted him on the shoulder and shouted over the gunfire, "Are you alright?" It seemed to snap him out of whatever state he was in. Swallowing hard, he nodded and she yelled, "Great! Now cover me!"

Sophia held her breath as another wasps' nest of Imperial bullets hissed overhead, then rolled aside, got up and ran again as Tony fired past her. After a few steps she dived to the ground again and fired while Tony came up next to her. To her left and right the whole platoon was doing the same thing, rushing and firing in turns. After they'd gone a couple hundred meters Sophia heard the rest of the company's machine guns shriek to life behind them and the Imperial fire started dying off.

A few minutes later Sophia made the final lunge into the woodline at the base of the hill, crashing through the brush bayonet-first. No Imperials leapt up for her to stab. Panting, she dropped into the hollow of a tree's roots and poked her head out cautiously, looking for telltale movement in the leafy darkness. Nothing. Cautiously climbing over the roots, she stepped directly into a pile of shell casings and spun, expecting to see a masked soldier lunging for her. She only saw a muddy, ashen and panting Lieutenant Thorn stumbling up after her.

Thorn dropped down on the other side of the tree and gasped, "What... what's going on, Rose?"

Sophia, feeling naked on the wrong side of cover, dropped to the ground and said, "I think this was one of their machine gun positions. Shell casings right there. And..." She trailed off as she realized the wet leaves she'd thrown herself down in were too sticky for water. She went on, feeling a little queasy, "It's... it's covered in blood back here, sir."

Thorn stuck his head over to look at the scene himself and said, "Yeah, looks like it." Dropping back down, he called over to her, "See any Masks from your side?"

Very chivalrous, she thought. Still, she dutifully poked her head out of her shallow scrape in the ground and scanned the forest as it sloped gently uphill. Rolling on her side, she said, "No, sir."

Thorn sighed with relief and said, "Alright, we're... we're consolidating here. Push out a little more so we can set up a perimeter."

Sophia replied, "Sure." She paused for a second and added, "Sir, can we keep the rushes to *less* than a kilometer next time?"

Thorn gave a gasping laugh, "Yeah. We're not doing this again. Ever. I promise."

Sophia rolled to her knees, brushed the bloody leaves off her uniform and wearily walked deeper into the forest. Finding a convenient fallen tree to hide behind, she settled down and listened to the rest of the platoon filling in the perimeter behind her. Nobody seemed to have been killed or even hurt. She had an uneasy feeling that wouldn't be the case next time. And there was that long-haired dragoon. She felt the hair on the back of her neck stand up as she thought about locking eyes with him from a kilometer away. She couldn't imagine what he would be like up close.

But Sophia got the feeling she would find out soon.

Chapter 17

Battlefields at a Distance

Patricia, panting, raised her free hand in surrender as she said, "That's enough for me, milady." Tiredly pulling off her fencing mask, she asked, "Who's been *teaching* you?"

"My brother, mostly," Arilin tried and failed to keep the smugness out of her voice. She'd asked Patricia for some fencing practice that morning and ended up spending the last half-hour chasing her around the back lawn of V Corps' Wolf Rock headquarters. At the risk of sounding insufferable, she added as she pulled her mask off, "Sorry... I should have gone easy on you."

Patricia threw back her head and laughed. Recovering, she walked over and tousled the princess's hair, chuckling, "I did not expect to hear that from you when I agreed to take this job."

"Hey..." Arilin half-heartedly attempted to fend off Patricia's hand, "I'm not useless, you know."

Patricia kept on rubbing the girl's head as she replied, "Oh, I know that now, you little demon." Crouching down a little to even out their height, she went on, "Really, I owe you an apology. I should have gotten you a proper instructor instead of trying to fight you myself." She smiled, "I'm no master with a sword, as I'm sure you know by now."

Arilin replied, blushing, "That's... that's fine, thank you. But..." She thought for a moment, then went on, "If you aren't that good with a sword, how did you fight?"

Patricia straightened up and raised her eyebrows questioningly, "What, on the battlefield?" Her attitude changed suddenly and she smirked, "I use pistols."

"Oh." Arilin cocked her head, "I just assumed..." she gestured with her sword to finish the thought.

The older woman smiled grimly, "You don't sword-fight dragoons, milady. They're *very* good." She thought for a second, snorted and went on, "Of course they have guns too, but it's more even." Looking carefully at Arilin she asked, "Say, have you ever shot before?"

The princess blinked and said, "No, actually."

Patricia's smile broadened, "Want to?"

Arilin nodded, "Sure!"

A few minutes later they had returned to their quarters on the other side of the parade field, where Lady Kunst had been kind enough to accommodate them while her husband was at the front commanding V Corps. Patricia retrieved a heavy, locked box from her luggage and set it on her desk. Laying the day's newspaper down to catch any oil, she opened the box and started pulling guns out.

Patricia quickly laid two pistols side-by-side on the desk. The first was once an elegant Army service pistol, now gouged and worn with what must have been years of use. Arilin felt her stomach clench as she realized some of the scratches on it were so long and deep they must have come from sword blades. The second... Arilin cocked her head and gave Patricia a dubious look. The thing looked like a double-barreled artillery piece with a handgrip.

The woman laughed and picked it up, "*This* is a Lancaster Pistol. They were popular a long time ago, mostly in a more *practical* size. Less to go wrong than a revolver." She gave Arilin a wicked grin as she broke the action, barrels large enough to accommodate her thumbs swinging open for loading, "Walter used to have one just like this. He'd use it to break in the new lieutenants." She chuckled, "I fired both barrels and asked him where I could get one for *myself*."

Arilin raised an eyebrow skeptically, "Why?"

Patricia shrugged, "At the time, because it was fun. Now," She snapped the action closed and set it back down on the table, "It's my hunting back-up. This will stop anything in the Kingdom in its tracks."

"You hunt?" Arilin asked.

"Yes, milady." Patricia snorted, "Although I don't know what got into me, thinking I'd have time to on this trip. Still, I'd love to take you out sometime." Picking up the old, worn pistol, she racked the action to clear it and handed it to the princess. It was heavier than she expected. Arilin felt the faint, worn checkering on the grips and ran her fingers over the gun's scarred metal as Patricia said, "Are you familiar with the Luger, milady?"

Arilin cocked her head as she thought of the wicked-looking pistols the Army used, replying, "Yes, I think. This *is* one, right?"

The lady general smiled and replied, "Yes and no. I've had this one since the Marchlands, since before it was actually adopted by the Army. Our standard pistols at the time were so clunky they'd actually issue you two or three just so you didn't have to try to reload them in combat." She snorted at the memory, "*This* has never once let me down."

"Wow." Arilin tried working the action on the weapon herself. It was smooth as butter. With a new appreciation for the weapon Arilin carefully set it down and asked, "So... where do you want to start?"

Patricia laughed, "The Luger should fit you, but I'm not done yet." Reaching into a slit in the side of her uniform's skirt she produced a little pistol, barely larger than her palm, "Bet you didn't realize I had this on me, did you?"

Arilin's eyes widened in surprise, "I was wondering what that slit was for."

Patricia smiled broadly and lifted her skirt to her waist. She had a small leather holster strapped to her right thigh, over the top of her stocking. The princess blushed and she dropped her skirt back and, smoothing it, said, "Usually I keep it in my purse, but I'm not taking any chances with you around." Arilin reached out to take it, but Patricia pulled back and said, "Not so fast, milady. Before you start shooting, you need to learn a few things."

About an hour and a long lecture on firearms safety later, Arilin stepped up to the firing line at the pistol range that occupied part of the basement of the V Corps headquarters building. Carefully sliding the magazine into her pistol, she racked the slide, flicked off the safety, lined up the sights on the target down her lane and pulled the trigger. The gun kicked sharply in her hands as it recoiled. Patricia patted her on the shoulder and told her to keep shooting, and Arilin finished off the rest of the magazine before setting the gun down.

Patricia pulled the overhead line to bring their target back in so they could inspect it and laughed at the results, "Well, at least you winged him. Once." Arilin gave her an aggrieved look and she smiled and patted her shoulder encouragingly, "Milady, you're better than I was when I started. This isn't easy."

The V Corps staff officers were mostly used to her presence at this point and too polite to crowd around and gawk openly, but Arilin noticed all of the lanes next to them fill up as she as Patricia shot over the next hour, and there was a lot of craning of heads and whispered commentary whenever they reeled their target back in to look at it. Hopefully most of it was positive. By the time Patricia's bundle of ammunition finally ran out her wrist was very sore, but she was actually hitting the target silhouette with most of her rounds.

They packed up and ran into General Haas on the stairs back up. He smiled slightly and greeted them, "Good morning, my ladies. I heard you two were shooting downstairs and decided to see for myself."

Patricia smiled apologetically, "We actually just finished. Ran out of ammunition. But Arilin shot very well. She's better than I was at her age."

Arilin sighed, crestfallen, "Thanks, I guess."

Walter chuckled, "Cheer up, milady. I'm sure Lady MacMahon will have you shooting like a hussar in no time." He paused, gave Patricia a look and smirked, "Now, I'm not sure if that's a *good* thing."

Patricia rolled her eyes at him, and Walter snickered and changed the subject, "I was also wondering if you two would like to have lunch with me. Ziggy's off sorting out the cavalry brigade, and," Walter growled, "I'm not in the mood to hold court with the rest of the staff."

Patricia hesitated for a moment, giving Arilin a chance to chirp, "Of course!" The older woman gave her a weak look, which Arilin ignored as she said, "We'd love to. Where were you thinking of?"

Walter replied, "There's this café out on the Promenade I've taken a liking to." Arilin could have sworn his eyes twinkled as he mentioned, "I noticed they have gelato."

Patricia perked up instantly, tried to hide it, saw Arilin looking at her and sighed. Falling into step beside Walter, she looked over and asked him, "Do they have strawberry?"

Walter looked back at her, "Yep. And I think they swirl it with vanilla and put fresh fruit on top." He chuckled, "You're drooling, Trixie."

"What?" Patricia wiped her mouth with her sleeve, realized he'd been teasing her and actually *pouted* at him. Arilin fought to keep from laughing as she said, "Hmph. It *better* be good."

Looking between the two of them, Arilin barely suppressed a gleeful giggle. Her little plan with Siegfried was working out better than she could have imagined. Together, they walked out the headquarters building's back door, across a couple tree-lined streets hosting tasteful brick administrative buildings and emerged onto the broad, shaded lane of the Wolf Rock Promenade. A number of other soldiers out and about starting the lunch rush saluted the two generals as they walked along. Walter quickly led them to their destination, a small café that was already starting to fill with diners.

They secured a table and got their food in record time. Patricia remarked, "I don't think they serve a lot of generals here. If we were back in the High City we'd still be in line."

Walter looked at Arilin and chuckled, "Or royalty." He changed the subject, "Speaking of royalty, I'm thankful you didn't decide to teach Arilin with your hand cannon, Trixie. I know you give that thing to lieutenants without warning them."

Raising an eyebrow at him, Patricia replied, "I got it from you, you know. I'm just paying it forward. Plus," She snorted, "I didn't want to destroy the range."

Chuckling, Walter replied, "Yes, but I warned you about my howdah pistol before I let you fire it. Because you *asked* to. Although," He looked back at her and went on, "It didn't seem to bother you that much at the time."

"I have strong wrists, I guess," Patricia shrugged, then smiled, "Now that I think about it, we did some pretty crazy stuff back at Dragon's Jaw. I can't believe I was like that *myself*."

Walter actually laughed. Recovering, he turned to Arilin and said, "You know, milady, once I actually caught Lady MacMahon here riding around the fortress with no fewer than *eight* pistols on her." Patricia reddened and buried her face in her hands as he went on, "She was supposed to have *three*." He turned back to the lady general and said, "Was that the second or third time we gave you the award?"

Patricia weakly held up two fingers and said, "Gelato or no, this is too much, Walter."

"Oh, I'm just getting started. What were those all for?" Walter counted on his fingers, "The first was for the piano you showed up with, the second was for the eight pistols, the third was for, what, putting makeup on while on patrol?"

She gave him a weak glare and said, "I looked awful. And we were about to go through a town. And I was only powdering my nose."

He shrugged, "Quibbling. Let's see... then we had the ice cream incident and the billeting incident. And," He smirked, "After the Great Ammunition Migration we just decided to make you a lifetime achievement award holder and name it after you." He turned to Arilin, "We renamed it the Patricia MacMahon Excellence in Military Leadership Award."

Patricia sat back in her chair and gave him an indignant look, "I had *nothing* to do with that, you know."

Walter shrugged, "I knew that at the time, but... I decided to give it to you anyways." He looked at Arilin and smiled slyly, "All of Patricia's misdeeds as a lieutenant were funny and harmless. People actually got charged over the last one though, so it's not like I could give it to someone facing a court-martial."

Arilin was laughing uncontrollably. Slowly recovering, she asked, "What's the *award*?"

Patricia laughed herself and said, "Every Army unit has an award they give out to whoever's done the dumbest thing recently. It's like a medal for idiocy. We had, what, that old bent shell extractor?" Walter nodded and she went on, "I had to carry that thing around to every function we had for the better part of a year."

The gelato came out and Patricia retreated into a little strawberry-and-vanilla existence. Casting a dubious glance at their blissful companion, Walter asked, "So, Arilin, any word from your brother?"

Arilin tried her own gelato. It was actually pretty good. She let it melt and spread creamily around her mouth before replying, "Yes, actually. He just got to Grenville with his regiment. Apparently Field Marshal White's going to set up headquarters there." She frowned for a moment, "He wants to get into combat, but he doesn't think White's going to commit him and his men any time soon."

"I wouldn't hold my breath if I were him." Walter said, "I suspect he's the operational reserve right now. The Lawrence White I know isn't the type to make that kind of commitment until he's certain of victory. Probably explains why it took him so long to get married."

Arilin giggled, "Really? I like his wife, you know."

Walter gave her a slight smile, "His philosophy has its points. He chose well." He paused and went on, "Any word on what he's thinking or the mood around headquarters? I hate to say this, but your brother probably has a better idea of what's going through White's mind than any of us corps commanders do. He isn't very communicative."

The princess thought for a moment and said, "Yes... he did mention that White was very eager to get into battle. That's why he's pushed the headquarters all the way up into Grenville. Apparently everyone up there can't wait to get into the fight."

The general chuckled, popped his monocle out and started polishing it on his coat, "Sounds like White. And again, that is a valid thing for him to do in these circumstances. But... well, milady, how would *you* defeat the Imperial Army right now?"

Arilin looked around nervously and said, "Me? Really?"

Walter nodded encouragingly, "Yes, you. Queen Arilin, in command of her army. Why are we fighting this battle? And what would be the best way to bring about that end?"

The princess cocked her head and thought for a few seconds. Then she took a bite of ice cream and thought for a few more. Swallowing, she finally said, "We should aim to destroy the Imperial Army. If their forces are defeated, retaking the Marchlands will be easy." Narrowing her eyes, she went on, "And in that case... we should hit them with overwhelming force and crush them."

"We will make a general out of you yet, milady." Walter nodded and leaned forward, elbows on the table as he spoke, "Now, if we want to strike with overwhelming force, *where should we fight?*"

Arilin furrowed her brow and thought for a few seconds more. Noticing the exchange, Patricia tore herself away from her gelato, wiped her mouth sheepishly and joined Walter in looking at Arilin. Finally the princess said, "We should fight as far west as possible. That will give us time to mass our troops."

Walter chuckled and leaned back in his seat. Noticing that Patricia had rejoined them, he looked over at her and said, "My lady, I don't know what you've been teaching her, but keep it up." He returned his gaze to Arilin and said, "I agree with your analysis. So, why do you think Field Marshal White is rushing to fight a battle in front of Grenville right now, to the point of committing the Army piecemeal?"

Recalling her earlier conversation with Patricia, Arilin said, "He's too aggressive and has contempt for the Empire?"

Walter laughed and gave Patricia a look. Still chuckling, he said, "Lady MacMahon, you and I need to have a serious talk about who you're sharing our mutual opinion of Lawrence White with." She reddened a little and he turned back to Arilin, "It's partly that, partly he doesn't want the bad press from losing Grenville, and partly that's what circumstances forced us to do in the last war. It worked that time, somehow, and I'll tell you it was *very* good for his career."

Arilin felt a chill on the back of her neck, and it wasn't her melting gelato. She felt herself blushing as she said, "So he's risking the Army in battle now recklessly? I... I should tell my father." She stopped suddenly and sighed, "As though he needs another thing to worry about."

Patricia pushed her finished ice cream away, leaned forward in her seat and asked, "What's wrong, milady?" She and Walter exchanged glances, and she went on, "Now that I think about it, we hardly hear anything about what's going on in the Capital these days."

The princess shook her head, "You wouldn't like it. The fleet, what's left of it, got back from Diamond Shoals a few days ago and that started it." She grit her teeth for a moment and continued, "News of the battle was bad, but then sailors started coming ashore and talking to the press. And the fleet looked *bad*... the *Guardian* rolled over and sank, right as they were towing it into the harbor." She went on as Patricia paled, "The communists came out and took advantage of the whole thing. Right now the Capital is about to boil over."

Walter scowled, "Just what we need, another one of their revolutions. I was hoping we'd seen the last of them three years ago." He gave Arilin a serious look, "I have no idea how your father tolerates their socialist friends in the legislature, honestly."

"They keep getting elected. I don't think banning them would do any good at this point." Arilin smiled weakly, "I mean, the legislature's in complete chaos right now, but that's pretty much normal. Father doesn't sound too worried about *them*." The two generals laughed, and she sighed and went on, "He doesn't sound too worried about *Uncle*, either."

Patricia raised an eyebrow, "Alphonse is back in the Capital?" She shared a glance with Walter and went on, her eyes narrowing slightly, "He picked quite the time to reappear. Helping with the war effort, I presume?"

The princess shrugged, "Father trusts him."

Patricia gave her a hard-edged look, "Do you?"

Arilin remembered eyes like frozen rubies sweeping across her and Beatrice, two little girls newly arrived at the Palace, and cold fingers worked their way up her spine. Shaking her head, she replied, "No... but I've only met him *once*."

Walter chuckled and remarked, "I don't envy your father."

Trying to lighten the mood, Patricia asked, "Heard anything from Lady Beatrice recently? How's she?"

Arilin frowned and said, "She's doing well... but her last letter, well... it was scary."

They both leaned forward, concerned. Patricia narrowed her eyes and asked, "What do you mean by *scary?*"

"She said that food prices in the west are going to start spiking soon because the war is keeping farmers from harvesting properly in the east of the country." Arilin sighed, "Beatrice said she'd brought it up with Father and he'd kind of ignored her, so she wanted *me* to write to him about it."

Patricia paled. Walter's eyes narrowed as he said, "If I recall correctly, Princess Beatrice is *ten*. And that... is a remarkably astute economic observation." He raised an eyebrow, "Is there something going on with her that isn't public knowledge?"

Arilin laughed, leaned back in her seat and said, "Yeah, I guess we have kept that pretty much under wraps." She paused, thought how to phrase it and went on, "Beatrice is *very, very* smart. She can read High Elvish faster than I can read *period*. She'll read one of their chronicles like you or I would read a novel. But," She shrugged, "BB's my little sister, and otherwise she's pretty normal."

Laughing weakly, Patricia said, "She sounds like quite the handful."

Arilin sighed, "Tell me about it. She's been getting into the grimoires lately. I'm worried she's going to get herself cursed or something."

Walter chuckled and said, "Well, it seems we all have problems." Scraping back his chair and standing, he looked at Arilin and continued, "Marching armies around the map is an easy exercise, milady. It gets hard when they're real units full of soldiers who get tired and have to be fed. So with that in mind," He nodded at both of them, "Would you two care to join me with the staff after this? This corps isn't going to get itself to Grenville."

They both stood. Patricia nodded gratefully as Arilin said, "We would be honored, sir."

Chapter 18

Steel and Moonlight

"Here, Sophie, have some coffee. I made enough for both of us." Sophia could hear the faint crackling of Tony's camp stove over the crickets around them. The trees they were under threw long, ghostly shadows under the False Sun's dying light as it sank behind them, and three of the moons blazed high overhead in the dark, clear sky.

"Sure, thanks. Uh..." Fishing around her load-bearing harness for a few seconds, she found her canteen cup and passed it back to her friend. She heard pouring behind her before Tony tapped her shoulder and she reached back, gingerly feeling for the hot metal mug before taking it around the rim to keep from burning herself. Sophia felt the coffee's harsh smell bringing her back to life as she set it on a flat patch at the edge of their foxhole.

Tony remarked, "You know, you don't have to watch for the enemy every single second." She heard him sip his own coffee and go on, "You can at least look back from time to time."

She rolled over and glared at him, "I don't want to *die*, Tony." He visibly recoiled, and Sophia could see him shaking a little as he set his cup down. *He's terrified... and he's trying to act brave,* she thought. Softening, she went on, "I'm just nervous... there *are* dragoons out there."

Tony exhaled softly, got to his knees and propped himself up on the hole's edge, looking out towards where they supposed the enemy was. She rolled back over and joined him, and he looked over and quietly asked, "How many do you suppose we were fighting today? I think there was a good company out there at least."

Sophia snorted, gave him another look and said, "Ten or twenty maybe?"

She looked back out at the rolling field in front of them as Tony said incredulously, "Ten or twenty? Are you serious? We were in it *all day*. We probably killed more than that."

Sophia shrugged a little and replied, "Maybe... but we never got hit with more than one machine gun."

"Huh." Tony thought for a second then shrugged himself, "I can see that, I guess." His stomach growled audibly and he asked, "Do you know when dinner's coming around?"

Snorting, Sophia replied, "If my father has anything to do with it, soon." Her own stomach rumbled and she felt herself reddening in the ghostly light, "I'm hungry too!" Her ears perked up as she said it and she raised a hand to shush Tony's reply. Someone was moving, very quietly, close to them. Either they were about to get jumped by dragoons, or more likely...

Sophia rolled over and said, "Hi, Dad."

Her father, standing maybe five feet behind their foxhole, snickered and said, "You're getting a lot harder to sneak up on, Sophie." He walked forward and crouched down next to them, "I've gotten into half the company's foxholes without them noticing so far tonight."

She smirked, "What about the other half?"

He shrugged, "Well, I pulled your friend Jack *out* of his before he woke up. And I haven't gotten to the rest of the company yet." Tony and Sophia both laughed quietly. Her father noticed the coffee, looked at her friend and said, "Thanks for taking care of Sophia for me, Tony. Are *you* holding up yourself?"

Tony looked at his feet and replied, "Uh, yes, I guess..." Sophia noticed his fingers tightening on his rifle as he said it.

Her father smiled and said, "First battles aren't easy for anyone. I know what you're going through."

Tony looked up at him and asked, "Does... does this get any easier, First Sergeant?"

"No, it doesn't." Her father chuckled, "You get braver, though."

Tony sighed, "Thanks, I guess." He changed the subject abruptly, "Ah, do you know when food is coming around? We're both starving."

Her father said, "A few minutes, I think. The cooks were finishing up when I started my rounds." They both sighed with relief, and he smiled and stood up, "Alright, you two carry on. *Someone* in this company needs to keep watch. And," He added, "Don't count on getting too much sleep tonight. Your platoon is doing a patrol later."

They both groaned in unison. Sophia said, "Really?"

"Yep." He smirked in the moonlight, "We can sleep *after* we win the war."

Sophia sighed and said, "Sure, Dad."

He walked off down the line, and a few minutes later a couple cooks made their way up with the evening's stew and bread. Sergeant Cross found them while they were halfway through dinner and told them they were going on patrol and the briefing was in thirty minutes at the company's command post, and a few minutes later some soldiers from third platoon showed up to take over their foxhole. They finished eating, collected their equipment and walked back through the woods to what passed for the company's headquarters.

Sophia quickly spotted the two boxy tents in the woods and the skeletal shapes of wagons behind them. They walked into the one that didn't have the Red Cross on it to find Lieutenant Stahl writing something by lamplight at a field desk. He looked up irately and said, "Patrol brief? Josh took over the medics' tent. And can you tell your little buddies that too? You're the fifth group that's been in here and I'm starting to get pissed off."

Sophia stepped back a little and apologized, "Ah, sorry, sir. We'll leave."

"Wait." Stahl asked pointedly, "Have either of you seen the commander recently?"

They looked at each other, "No, sir," Sophia said, "We haven't seen him since this morning."

Stahl rolled his eyes, "*Great.*" He turned his attention back to his report and made a dismissive motion with his pen, "Thanks, now get out of my tent."

They retreated and walked over to the medical tent to find the cots pushed to the walls, the medics standing angrily in a corner and half of First Platoon crowded into it. Lieutenant Thorn noticed them as they walked in and said, "Ah, Miss Rose! Come up here, I need you to see the route." Sophia pushed her way through the press of soldiers to the front of the tent, where Thorn had a map spread over the medics' table. Looking at the route he had marked out, it didn't seem too bad. They'd be finished by midnight. Assuming they didn't get into another fight.

Sophia shivered at the thought of fighting dragoons in the dark with just the platoon. As she looked around nervously to see if anyone had noticed she heard more soldiers filing into the tent and Thorn asked, "Is that everyone, Sergeant Falcon?"

The platoon sergeant had followed the men in. From the back, he said, "Yes, sir, unless someone's slipped under the sides in the last few minutes." He paused and went on, "Listen up, everyone! The lieutenant's going to bring us up to speed on the mission tonight, which I'm sure you're all *thrilled* to be on. I sure am." A nervous chuckle went around the tent as he pushed his way forward, "NCOs up front so you can actually see something. The rest of you better listen up." He emerged next to Thorn up front, glanced at Sophia and finished his speech, "I don't need to tell you what we're up against. We've been fighting them all day. We're going out tonight to find them and *kill* them."

Soldiers murmured approvingly as the sergeants and corporals pushed their way forward. Sergeant Cross gave Sophia an approving nod as he saw her, and she spotted the three team leaders crowding in around him as he stepped forward, bulky Corporal Janssen, Vinson's slender form and the short Corporal Slaughter, leader of their third team. He belied his name by giving her a reassuring smile. Behind them she caught a glimpse of Tony standing on his tiptoes trying to see something, Jack standing next to him with a sour look on his face and Edward looking bored as ever.

Looking around further, Sophia saw more faces she recognized in the other teams and squads. A warm glow blossomed in her heart at the thought of her friends, and she smiled to herself as Thorn cleared his throat and began to speak. "Alright, men! And, uh, Miss Rose." She nodded graciously, "This is the briefing for tonight's patrol! As you know, we've been fighting dragoons all day..."

Thorn went on and on, looking at his notes at he talked. Their mission, routes, rally points, formations, contingencies, passwords. Any rattling equipment was to be secured and bayonets darkened with soot. Feeling her head spinning with all the information, Sophia fished for her notebook and wrote down the important parts. The plan was simple enough: move forward from their lines using the cover of darkness, locate the enemy and if possible kill them at close quarters. If there were too many, dig in and hold out until reinforcements arrived. Apparently the other battalions were sending out their own patrols, and if that wasn't enough the regiment would attack again at daybreak.

Sophia wrote down the map coordinates for their objective. If they didn't run into dragoons before then, they were to occupy a prominent farm located on a ridge about five kilometers forward of their current position and defend the area. That would serve to screen the rest of the battalion come the morning and let them move up unimpeded. She felt the warm glow in her stomach turn to ice at the odds of getting that far without a battle.

Thorn eventually finished and told the squads to get ready. Sophia turned to leave herself, but he put a hand on her shoulder to stop her. She turned and he asked, "How're *you* feeling, Rose?"

Sophia cocked her head, thought for a moment and replied, "I... kind of wish I was back in Jade Falls."

"Don't we all," He snorted, "We'll just have to get through this together." Raising an eyebrow, he went on, "You've got the route, right?"

She said, "Across the field, follow the edge of the forest until we hit the trail, take it to the river and uh... go uphill from there?" She furrowed her brow at the look on Thorn's face, "It's not like we're just going to walk a compass heading, sir."

The lieutenant chuckled nervously and said, "I'm sure we'll get there somehow."

The platoon gathered again at the front line about half an hour later. The rising moons lit the sky like a celestial chandelier, bright moonlight streaming through the canopy overhead to spatter the forest floor with spots of milky light. Crouching at the head of the long, snaking file of soldiers, Sophia noticed her father speaking intently with Thorn and Falcon off to the side. Her father eventually nodded and the group approached her.

Sophia and her father exchanged nods, and he asked, "Ready to head out, Sophia?"

She nodded, feeling her hands involuntarily tightening on her rifle, "Yep."

He turned to look at Thorn and said, "Alright, sir. They're all yours. Move out." He clapped Sophia on the shoulder and said, "Now you take care of your lieutenant, Sophie. *One.*"

Thorn raised his arm and waved the platoon forward. Stepping forward into the dappled half-darkness, Sophia heard her father pat him on the shoulder and count, "*Two.*" Then Vinson, behind him, "*Three.*" And Tony, "*Four.*" Edward, "*Five.*" Sergeant Cross, "*Six.*" And then she stepped into the full blaze of moonlight and her father's soft counting faded from her consciousness.

She had always thought of the soft moonlight as a comforting thing, lighting the path in a dark night so she could walk safely. Sophia felt the instincts of her childhood melt as she walked into the ghostly light, her skin crawling as she imagined a thousand Imperial machine-gunners staring down their sights at her from across the fields. She walked a few paces, then a few more, and they held their fire. Conscious of Thorn standing a few feet behind her, she took a deep breath and started walking.

A chill breeze ruffled the knee-high grass as she went along and the dew-wetted fields shimmered in the light. In other circumstances it would have been beautiful. Passing through the field, they plunged into another dense forest and Sophia turned to keep the woodline off to her right. After what seemed like an eternity of walking through the light-speckled darkness, Sophia spotted a lightening in the darkness ahead of her and pushed through some brush to emerge onto a rutted trail.

Sophia held up her hand to halt the platoon and knelt at the trail's edge, carefully peering down the cut in both directions. She heard Thorn move up from behind her after a few seconds, and he knelt beside her and asked, "What do you see, Rose?"

"Nothing." She sighed, "Yet. Let's go, sir." She climbed to her feet and turned off down the trail to her left, hearing Thorn motion the rest of the platoon back into motion behind her. It wasn't much more than a cart track roughly cut through the woods, not even wide enough to do more than create the occasional break in the canopy overhead, but it was much easier than stumbling over roots and underbrush in the forest. Sophia was able to pick up the pace, and after a little while she heard a river bubbling in front of her as the forest petered out into a broad swath of bright moonlight.

Thorn walked up next to her as she stopped, and she looked over at him. He snorted and asked softly, "See a bridge?"

Sophia shook her head and replied, "No, sir." She sighed, "I hate getting my feet wet."

Thorn looked at their boots and whispered back, "With this dew, I'm not sure how they could get wetter regardless. Now stay here for a minute, I'm going to bring the other squads up." He stepped off behind her and Sophia heard him talking softly to Sergeant Cross. The rest of the squad moved up around her as he walked farther back. A couple of minutes later the rest of the platoon had come on line and Thorn was back beside her.

Machine guns clicked and rattled around her as the platoon's gunners set up to fire, and she heard Cross and Thorn talking softly behind her again. Sophia gathered enough to know her squad would be first across the river, and they'd have to make the way safe for the rest of the platoon to cross. They'd practiced similar maneuvers back in Jade Falls, but the thought of Imperial soldiers opening fire on them when they were waist-deep in water and couldn't so much as duck made Sophia feel the hand of death closing around her throat. Looking to her side she could see Tony's face, white in the pale moonlight. His eyes were wide as he looked back at her.

Cross knelt next to her, got the squad's attention with a wave, poked her in the back and said, "We're going. Stay cool." Sophia nodded, stood up and walked into the light. With her eyes fixed on the other side she walked down the gentle, muddy slope into the ford, stepped into the river and started walking. Cold water scythed through her boots as she awkwardly stepped across large river-stones. The current pulled at her knees, then her thighs as she got to mid-river, lifting her rifle clear of the water as she struggled ahead. Fortunately the river flowed slowly enough she could keep her balance and she made it across without falling.

Sophia moved as quickly as she could to the other bank and lunged up the shallow slope when her feet came free of the water, plunging through the brush and back into the cover of the trees. Behind her she heard the rest of her squad doing the same thing, and they spread out into a rough semicircle in the dappled darkness. An owl hooted disinterestedly in the distance. Nobody shot at them. Sophia sighed with relief as Sergeant Cross waved the squad forward, and a few minutes later Thorn was standing behind her again and they were back on their way.

The trail twisted off to the north soon after the crossing, and Sophia reluctantly took them back into the forest proper, angling the platoon off towards the south as the ground rose gently. Gradually she became aware of a brightening in the forest ahead and she started to feel uneasy. It was as though something was ever so slightly off up ahead. She raised a hand to halt the platoon and turning to Thorn, asked, "Sir, do you mind if we take a minute here?"

The lieutenant looked at his watch, then shrugged and whispered back, "We've got all night. What's wrong?"

Sophia looked back at him and said, "I don't know... I just want to listen for a minute." Kneeling, she took her hat off, brushed her hair back behind her ears, closed her eyes and *listened*. She heard the soldiers behind her, Thorn's breathing and the rustling of leaves as he crouched. She heard trees rustling softly in the cool breeze. She heard the chirping of the night's insects all around her. She heard the owl again, hooting self-importantly off ahead of them. Something small scampered through the underbrush off to her side. A dog howled faintly, far in the distance. Artillery rumbled faintly off to the north near Grenville.

And then she heard it, so faint she thought at first her ears were playing tricks on her. Thorn shifted and started to say something next to her, and she held up her hand to forestall him as the sound grew louder for a moment. It sounded like... scratching? Digging? But mixed with a few muffled yips and growls, and the wet sound of things being dragged. Whatever it was, it didn't sound human and it was out in the field ahead of them. Opening her eyes, Sophia looked over at Thorn and said, "Sir, there's something going on up ahead. Animals digging, maybe?"

Thorn narrowed his eyes and said, "Digging? Let's go take a look. Lead on, Rose."

Sophia put her hat back on, picked up her rifle and started creeping forward. She heard Thorn making hand signals behind her and the platoon started spreading out to either side as they advanced. By the time she reached the woodline and could actually look out beyond it they were in a huge wedge, ready to fight any Imperials they found beyond it.

Crouching at the edge of the forest, the moonlight in the fields beyond was so bright it almost dazzled Sophia as she first looked out. Giving her eyes a moment to adjust to the sudden light, Sophia looked uphill to her left and saw the farm they were aiming for clear in the distance, maybe still a kilometer away up the long slope beside a road that shone white in the moonlight as it twisted down into the valley. Then she turned her head to look downhill and gasped.

Low, dark shapes prowled around the middle of the fields off to her right, not far away at all, digging at a long line of black scars in the earth. Their eyes shone in the moonlight, occasionally jerking and dancing as they snapped at each other. Sophia saw a sudden frenzied burst of activity as the dogs pulled something out of a hole, something long and black and larger than they were, a pale face rolling to the side to stare at them with sightless eyes.

Sophia felt her stomach curdle as the soldiers around her murmured. Someone vomited loudly off to her side, and she looked to see Janssen of all people heaving his guts out, Jack patting him on the back reassuringly. On her other side Tony made a noise like he was about to join the burly lumberjack. Thorn snorted angrily behind her and said, "Damn. I guess those two were telling the truth about being attacked."

Turning her head to see him, Sophia asked, "You... do you think that's their unit, sir?"

Thorn, pale, set his jaw and replied, "Yeah. The masks must have buried them in their foxholes. You can see their line there." Sophia looked out at the scene again and noticed the dark scars in the earth were laid out into what looked like a defensive line. He went on grimly, "Not deep enough, obviously."

She looked back at him and asked, "Sir, should we go take care of them? Although..." Sophia looked back at the farm further uphill, a neat white farmhouse and barn. She could feel her skin crawling as she looked at, imagining that long-haired dragoon from the morning staring back at her. She went on, "It might blow our cover."

The lieutenant sighed, "We have a mission. I'm not risking anyone on account of the dead." He paused and went on softly, "Whoever did this is out there right now. Let's go *find* them."

Sophia nodded, "Yes, sir." Backing into the shadows, she stood and walked away into the forest. The rest of the platoon drew away reluctantly behind her. They were of course reluctant to abandon dead comrades to the animals but, she thought, if they abandoned the mission to see to them properly they might end up joining them instead. Sophia shivered at the cold thought, but she kept walking. Soon enough the ground beneath her feet grew level, and as they drew near the edge of the woods she could see the dark bulk of the farm's outbuildings through the trees close ahead.

Her feeling of unease hadn't faded as she crouched behind a tree near the edge of the forest, painfully aware she might be watched by invisible eyes from the house's dark windows. Almost unconsciously, Sophia drew her bayonet and locked it to her rifle with a click that sounded much louder than it really was. The soot-darkened blade's bright edge shone as a bright line in the moonlight, and Sophia felt her breathing grow steady as she hefted her rifle.

To her side Sophia heard another soft click as Tony fixed his bayonet, then another and another, spreading out to her sides as the platoon followed their example. Lieutenant Thorn hissed with what she supposed was displeasure at all the noise, but she heard his sword rattle as he popped it free in its scabbard and seated it again. She realized he didn't have a bayonet for his rifle, but she supposed that sword of his was just as good in a fight.

She heard Thorn make another hand gesture behind her, and he backed off into the woods for a couple minutes to speak to the squad leaders, who came over as stealthily as they could. After a couple minutes Sergeant Cross appeared and whispered the plan to her before moving off down the line to get the rest of the squad up to speed. When Thorn gave the signal to move out, First Squad, Sophia's, would move up and storm the barn in front of them, then cover Second Squad as they moved on their right and stormed the house. Thorn would be with them. Third Squad would cover them both from off to their left.

After a couple more minutes Cross came back and laid down beside her, looking off to their right for the signal. It came and he poked her in the side, muttering, "Okay, let's go. *Move.*"

Sophia reluctantly emerged from behind her tree, crept forward to the edge of the forest with Sergeant Cross at her shoulder, dropped to the ground and slithered under a board fence at the edge of the paddock, leapt to her feet and rushed towards the barn. Cross outpaced her a little, making it to the wall beside the barn door first, and she ducked behind him. She heard Tony, Vinson and Edward run up behind her a moment before the other team ran up and took position on the far side of the door, the machine-gunners running past them and flopping down at the building's corner, Jenssen setting the heavy gun against his shoulder as Jack crouched next to him and pulled fresh ammunition from a bag.

Cross reached out with his free hand, grabbed the barn door's bolt, rotated it and pulled it free with a horrid squeak. Flicking his rifle off safe, he swung the door out a little and rotated his body into the barn, bayonet first. Sophia ducked in after him and crept forward slowly on his left as they advanced slowly down a double row of stalls, the rough wood barely visible in the windowless building.

The barn was cold and silent, smelling only of stale straw and dust. Whatever animals had once been housed there were long gone. Their soft footsteps on the dirt floor were the loudest sound to be heard as they slowly walked forward, bayonets stabbing into the darkness ahead, where Sophia could see a thin crack of moonlight open around the front door as it shuddered in the wind. Near the far door the line of stalls ended and the barn opened out into a sort of antechamber, and even at this close distance she could barely make out the outlines of tools on the far wall. Her sense of creeping dread was back, overwhelming, gnawing at the back of her skull as she moved ever farther down the dark corridor.

A black shape lunged at her with an inhuman shriek, blade flashing as it loomed out of the darkness. Sophia bent her knees, lunged and felt her bayonet punch deep into the mass in front of her as its sword glanced harmlessly aside. It reeled back, fell, tried to rise and Sophia lunged again. Her bayonet caught the dragoon under its mask as a gunshot shattered the darkness, incredibly loud and close. She pulled her rifle free as another dragoon fell on the other side of the hall, Cross working his rifle's bolt automatically behind her.

Sophia looked from side to side quickly. She saw nothing, just tools, dirt, straw and two dying dragoons gurgling and twitching in the darkness. And *nothing happened*. For a few seconds she just stood there in shock. This was supposed to be the part where everything exploded into chaos and shooting and screaming. Turning a little, she looked at Cross and said, "Uh, Sergeant?"

Cross looked at her blankly for a moment, then shook his head and shouted, "*Contact!* Two dragoons-" *Then* a machine-gun shrieked to life, almost right in front of them. Sophia found herself on the floor as bullets smacked through the side of the barn and the platoon's machine-guns roared off to their left. Whatever Cross was saying was lost in the hammering chaos. Sophia crawled forward as another Royal machine-gun roared to life just to her right, wincing at the noise as she pushed the barn door open with her bayonet and rolled into a firing position.

There wasn't much for her to do. She could see the platoon's machine-guns shredding the house's first floor, white clapboards pimpling with bullet holes and buckling under the assault. The fire lifted for a moment and Sophia could hear Thorn blowing his whistle, giving the signal to shift fire. A moment later the dark shapes of Second Squad darted across the lawn towards the house, Thorn's drawn sword almost glowing in the moonlight.

There was a flash in one of the upstairs windows and Sophia heard a high-pitched gunshot as one of the running soldiers fell. More gunshots rang out, incredibly fast, as she adjusted her aim on the upstairs window and fired. Cross, beside her, saw where she was shooting and joined in, and she felt Tony slide in on her other side and fire as well. They stopped after a few rounds and as the noise died down she could hear Thorn shouting commands. Dark shapes moved against the white farmhouse, a soldier kicked in the door and another man threw a grenade, its long-handled shape silhouetted for an instant before it disappeared inside.

The soldiers outside fell to the ground, someone shouted faintly and the house lit up from the inside for an instant, windows blazing hellfire. The squad leapt back to their feet and charged in, shouting, Thorn in their midst. For a moment they could hear Thorn and the others, loud and excited as they moved into the house. Then a soldier shouted, muffled inside the house but clear even through the ringing in her ears, "*Dragoon!*" And then someone *screamed*.

Gunshots lit the house as Sophia saw something long, bright and *curved* flashing through the windows, fast as a viper. The one scream became two, three, four, shrieking with pain, heavy weights thudding to the floor. *Oh, my,* Sophia pushed herself to her knees unconsciously, *God help us,* got her feet under her and lunged forward. Sergeant Cross yelled something behind her that she barely heard as the farmhouse loomed before her, the dragoon's murderous sword glinting through the windows one last time as she leapt into the entryway.

The door from the mudroom into the house proper had been kicked ajar and dark shapes - some of them too small to be whole bodies - littered the floor beyond. As she flew through the door she saw two figures at the far end of the room, Thorn falling backwards, his sword's broken blade glinting in the light as it spun away. Long hair billowing behind him like a cape, the dragoon raised his sword to strike the killing blow and for an instant the brutal, curved blade hung frozen in the moonlight.

Sophia leapt at him, her bayonet reaching out. Time seemed to stand still as he turned his head slightly, and even in the darkness she could feel his gaze boring into her. She saw his weight shift back slightly as he pivoted to face her, his sword's icy blade narrowing as he brought it around. Sophia took one last step forward and *lunged*.

The dragoon slashed and knocked her attack aside, sparks flying as his sword bit into her rifle. Their weapons locked for an instant as they spun together, Sophia skidding to a halt in front of Thorn as the dragoon stepped past her. Flexing her knees, she brought her rifle around, started to lunge again and turned the movement into a desperate parry as his sword flashed at her again. Her rifle shuddered in her hands she staggered backwards and his sword reached for her again, slashing *up* at her exposed ribs. She brought her rifle down and felt his sword bite through the stock as she blocked. She wrenched her rifle down and stabbed at him as he stepped back, sword arcing around again.

Sophia's rifle bucked in her hands again and she watched her bayonet spin through the air as her rifle passed through the space the dragoon had been standing in. He spun aside and drew back for an instant, sword flaming white as it foreshortened. She saw the brutally curved tip, the bone-white metal with its ghostly patterning running down to the small, circular guard. She saw the dark, spidery stains of her comrades' blood streaking the blade and speckled shadows in the metal where others had before them. And she saw dark shapes moving behind him as he lunged.

Sophia twisted away and fell. The dragoon stood over her for an instant, sword rising, then turned and leapt away. Two gunshots lit the room a moment later, the bullets cracking over Sophia as she lay on the floor. She heard Tony say, "Did we get him?"

Sergeant Cross replied as he worked his rifle's bolt, "No, I don't think so... Sophia! Are you alright?"

Pushing herself up on her elbows, Sophia replied, "Yeah, but he's still in here! Be careful!" She noticed Thorn starting to get to his feet and rolled upright herself, hefting her rifle. She hoped it still worked. She heard him drop his sword's useless hilt on the floor and a soft pop as he unsnapped his holster's flap and drew his pistol. Looking over at him for a moment, she saw his mouth open to speak as something small and heavy skipped off the floor between them, bounced off the wall and spun away, hissing.

Sophia got a good look at it as it rolled across the floor, knurled surface reflecting the moonlight. Thorn's eyes got big as she screamed, "*Grenade!*" and rushed at him, knocking him off his feet. He fell beneath her as the room exploded behind them, shrapnel seething overhead and the blast tearing at her body.

Her ears rang and her world spun as Thorn pushed her body aside and raised his pistol to aim at the doorway. Sophia lay beside him for one, two, five, ten seconds as Cross and Tony slowly advanced with their rifles raised to cover the opening. She sensed more soldiers entering the house and fanning out behind them and as Thorn climbed to his feet Cross and Tony ducked through the door into the house's kitchen, quickly followed by a few others.

There were no gunshots or screams. Sophia pushed herself against the wall as Vinson stepped out of the kitchen and said something to Thorn. Through the ringing in her ears she heard Thorn reply, "-er to Third Squad and have them move up alongside the house." The lieutenant shot a glance at the carnage on the other side of the room and went on, "And for God's sake get the medics in here. *Now!*"

Vinson stiffened up and hurried off the way he had come in, stepping gingerly over the bodies and wounded men lying all over the floor. Thorn crouched next to her and asked, "Miss Rose, are *you* hurt?"

Sophia shook her head and regretted it instantly as pain seared in her brain. Grimacing, she replied, "I... I think I'm okay, sir. Just," She groaned as the pain rolled back over her for a moment, "My head kind of hurts, sir."

Thorn patted her on the shoulder and said, "You saved my life today, Rose. *Twice.*" He smiled and went on, "But I think you have a concussion. Just stay there and I'll have the medics look at you as soon as they can."

Sophia nodded gingerly and mumbled, "Yes, sir. Will do."

The medics quickly arrived and started patching up the survivors from Second Squad, a couple of men who'd been lucky enough to lose limbs instead of their lives. Jack came in a moment later with the machine gun, the other two members of the gun team behind him carrying a familiar, bulky form between them. They laid out Allen Janssen on the floor with the rest of the wounded and one of the medics rushed over, checked his pulse, checked his eyes, fussed with him for a few seconds and then shook his head.

Jack set the machine-gun on the floor, crouched down and seized the medic by the collar, hauling him half-upright as he shouted in the man's face, "*Damnit!* The hell do you mean he's dead? You're wrong! Check him again!" The medic looked away, and Jack's two companions quickly stepped in and pulled him off the man. Jack pushed them away after a moment, shook himself violently and picked up the machine-gun, growling, "You... you'll check him again if you know what's good for you." He looked at the other two gunners and said, "Come on. We... need to set up."

The three gunners disappeared into the kitchen, and after poking at Janssen for a minute the medic shrugged, grabbed his arms and dragged him off to the side with the rest of the dead. His grim task complete, the medic noticed her sitting against the wall and walked over, kneeling next to her. Sophia asked, "Janssen's really dead?"

The medic nodded, "Yeah. Took five or six bullets. Even if I'd been right there I couldn't have done anything." He paused, shook his head at her dubious look and said, "You *know* I live down the street from him."

Sophia said, "Yeah... sorry. It's just... ugh..." Her head was hurting again.

"Got your bell rung, huh?" The medic took out a light, shone it in her eyes, asked her a few questions she struggled to answer and finally said, "Yeah, you're concussed. Here, let me help you." Putting a hand around her back, he helped her to stand, walked her over to the far corner of the room, stripped her equipment off, had her sit and started unbuttoning her jacket. She gave him another look and he rolled his eyes and said, "Oh, *come on.* You need something to use as a pillow."

Sophia blinked, "Oh. Sorry."

The medic chuckled, finished pulling her jacket off, wadded it up and eased her head down on top of it. Looking down at her as he stood, he said, "Now just go to sleep. Your brain needs to rest. Doctor's orders."

Sophia chuckled, "Sure, doc." She closed her eyes, and a couple minutes later felt someone put a blanket over her.

Chapter 19

A Visitor by Darkness

Patricia MacMahon leaned against the wooden railing surrounding General Kunst's back deck and watched the fireflies glowing in the park behind Generals' Row. Beyond the trees and grass Wolf Rock's old fortress wall loomed against the dark sky, battlements and guns jutting like the teeth of a great, ragged saw. She saw a sentry faintly silhouetted against the bright night sky as he walked his walltop patrol in the distance. In an earlier age she supposed the sight would have been intimidating, the unassailable wall and rows of cannons poised to blast apart any invader. Nowadays she just found it charmingly antiquated.

Speaking of charmingly antiquated, she thought as the wind shifted and she caught a whiff of Walter Haas' acrid cigar. Glancing disapprovingly at the older man, she said, "Walter, have you ever considered smoking something that smells less *awful?*"

"My lady, this is authentic Malakar tobacco," Walter replied, blowing a smoke ring for emphasis, "And it smells *heavenly.*"

Patricia rolled her eyes, "Remind me to stay away from your heaven." She took a swig of brandy out of her flask and went on, "It smells like *feet*."

He shrugged, "You don't have to stay out here, you know. I'm just being considerate to Arilin."

She sighed, "Well, I can't exactly drink during a piano recital, either."

On cue, another ripple of notes sounded faintly inside the house. Arilin and the Young Lord Kunst had started another song. They'd been playing piano duets for the last hour and judging by how hard the princess was struggling to keep up with the boy, Patricia saw him having a short and unhappy Army career forced upon him by his father before settling into life as a concert pianist. Lady Kunst had practically been *salivating*. Patricia thought drily that the boy might have a shot if he was as quick with a sword as he was on the keys.

Walter gave her a look of his own, "You don't *have* to be drinking, you know."

Patricia shot back combatively, "I always drink after dinner!" Walter raised an eyebrow and she softened, "Sorry. That... came out wrong." Looking down at her almost-empty flask, she self-consciously slid it into a pocket and sighed. She was probably drunker than she realized.

Stubbing out his cigar in a convenient ashtray, Walter turned to her and said, "Patricia, I've known you for nineteen years now. I don't remember you drinking this much before."

She chuckled, "Twenty-three, actually." Walter raised his eyebrows questioningly, and she went on, "We met at the Royal Christmas Ball in, what, '99 I think?"

He thought for a moment, then nodded and said, "Oh, yes, I remember! You were with your father."

Patricia gave him a sly look, "I recall being rather angry with you at the time. Daddy was introducing me to about every officer in the room, and after an hour of being fawned over by handsome men in uniform you ignored me completely and had this incredibly *boring* conversation with him about artillery pieces."

"Daddy?" Walter teased her. She felt herself redden as he chuckled, "Now that I remember, you *did* look kind of annoyed." He went on, "I was trying to avoid being *improper* with a young lady, but I apologize for being rude instead."

She looked at him and smiled, "I got over it. And..." She felt her blush deepening and hoped it wasn't noticeable in the darkness, "Thank you, even if I didn't appreciate it at the time."

Walter pressed her, "You're avoiding my question, though, Patricia."

Looking away, Patricia turned and leaned back against the railing, resting her elbows on the worn wood as she looked into the house's soft lights. Looking back at him sidelong, she remarked, "We also haven't exactly spent this much time together before, at least in present circumstances."

Walter slid in beside her and said, "*Still* avoiding me, Trixie." He gave her a warm look, "You *can* talk to me, you know."

Patricia sighed heavily. What choice did she have? Finally she said, gesturing, "It's... it's all *this*. I'm babysitting a princess because my career is finished. And don't get me wrong, Arilin's great. I feel like she's the daughter I never had. But," She sighed again, "She's the daughter I *never had*." She smiled sadly and looked up at her companion, "You probably think I'm being emotional, I bet."

"Yes, actually." Walter reached out behind her, slid his arm around her shoulders and drew her close to him. He smelled faintly of cigars and stale sweat, and Patricia realized she didn't mind too much. He went on, "That doesn't mean it's a bad thing."

She grasped his arm and held on to it for a moment, "Thanks, Walter. For everything."

He chuckled, "No, thank *you*. You may not realize it, but right now you and Arilin are the two bright spots for me in a pretty depressing war."

Patricia blushed, hoping he wasn't looking at her, "Ah... how so?"

She felt him snicker, "Well, no soldier has ever complained about beautiful women around camp. But if you're talking about the *war*, let me ask you this." He paused and went on philosophically, "Today we heard the Empire is *apparently* retreating from Grenville. After fighting for less than a week. We are of course in full pursuit." He snorted and looked down at her, "So, my lady, what *kind* of trap do you think Lawrence White is walking the army into?"

She looked back up at him, grateful for the change of pace, and replied, "I almost don't want to think about it too much."

He withdrew his arm, patted her on the back and stepped away a little, smiling sadly, "That makes two of us." He went on, "I retire next year. I wonder how much of the Kingdom will be left for me to retire *to*."

Patricia was about to reply when a shadow appeared in the frosted glass of the house's rear door. It opened to reveal Rebecca, a concerned look on her face. The princess's maid said, "Milady, there's a visitor here for you."

Patricia, surprised, turned to her and raised her eyebrows questioningly, "At this hour? Who is it?"

Rebecca replied, "It's a Colonel Jenssen, milady. He was quite insistent about speaking to you."

"Jenssen?" Patricia gave Walter a worried look, "I hope everything is all right."

He raised his eyebrows, "As do I. Shall we go see him together, milady?"

She shrugged, "May as well. This is probably going to be as much your problem as mine."

The two of them followed Rebecca back into the house. As they walked through hallways ringing with a cheery piano duet they passed the parlor and got a glimpse of Arilin determinedly trying to keep up with the young lord's effortless skill on the piano. Lady Kunst, rapt with the scene of her son and the princess playing side-by-side, didn't even notice them as they walked by. Patricia smiled and commented to her companion, "I bet I know what *she's* thinking."

He snorted, "We can all dream, milady. She has more reason to than most of us."

"Isn't that the truth." They approached the waiting room close to the front door, and Patricia came back to the task at hand. Rebecca ushered them into the room and Eric Jenssen looked up as they entered. He saw Walter and leapt to his feet, surprise written on his fine features.

"Sir!" He said, looking between them, "I didn't, ah, realize you were here. I apologize if I'm intruding."

"Nonsense." Walter said, "I'm just here socially. Lady Kunst invited me to dinner." *Third time this week*, Patricia thought sarcastically as he went on, gesturing to include her, "I understand you have something private to discuss with milady?"

Eric stammered, "W-well, yes, sir, I do."

Walter raised his eyebrows, "Now, while it may be a matter for discretion, is it a private matter between you and Lady MacMahon, or is this something I am eventually going to have to hear about?"

Eric hesitated, looking between them, and Patricia said, "You don't have to be worried. I trust Walter with my life." She paused and added, "And if this is Army business I'd probably just take it to him anyways."

Eric said, "If... if you say so, ma'am. I'm just... not sure how much of this is actually Army business."

Walter snorted contemptuously and said, "Then it's probably *entirely* Army business. There are few truly personal matters among soldiers. Now let's hear it."

"Gentlemen," Patricia interjected, "Perhaps we should go somewhere more private first?"

Looking around, Walter grunted and said, "You're right. The study?" Patricia nodded, and they walked back through the house to General Kunst's private office. The door was unlocked and Walter ushered them in, turned on the lights and settled himself behind the man's massive desk. Patricia looked at the seating arrangements for a second, then chuckled and perched to one side on the desk itself.

She felt Walter give her a stern look from behind, but he said nothing and she started off, "So. Eric. What is it exactly you're here about so late in the evening?"

The younger man cleared his throat nervously and started, "Ma'am, I've become increasingly... concerned about some of the talk going around the brigade."

Patricia leaned forward a little, "Oh? How so?"

Eric avoided her gaze, "Most of it is just people blowing off steam. We don't always speak well of people behind their backs. And, well, I'm sure you know that when men speak in private sometimes we are... indelicate."

She rolled her eyes, "Don't I know." She looked back at him and went on, "But I get the feeling this goes beyond that?"

He sighed and finally looked back at her, "Yes. Earlier this evening General Chapman invited us all to have a few drinks with him. And I mean a *few*. He got quite drunk."

Walter snorted, "That explains a few things." He paused for a second, then said, "But please, go on."

"I had a bad feeling about the whole affair, so I didn't have too much. Eventually someone mentioned the princess and that set Chapman off." Patricia raised her eyebrows and Eric went on, "He said the princess was a foolish child playing at war."

She chuckled, "A couple months ago I probably would have agreed with him. But he kept talking, I bet?"

Eric snorted grimly and said, "Yes, ma'am. He said a few things about you afterwards that were... extremely rude. Scandalously so, if you get my drift. And they didn't just involve you, he included *you*, sir," he nodded to Walter, "And a few other people who weren't present up to and including the King. He said that he was personally uninvolved although... not because you didn't *try* to involve him at one point."

"*Why that...*" Patricia hissed, reddening, "How *dare* him? I'll *ki-*"

Walter grunted behind her, cutting her off, "Dueling is illegal, milady, although I understand your feelings. That being said, Eric, if what you're saying about Chapman is true that's pretty ripe stuff coming from a man whom I know has a mistress." Through the blood pounding in her head she heard him open his jacket, carefully remove a cigar, go to light it and then stop suddenly. He snapped his lighter back closed and tapped his unlit cigar on the table contemplatively, "The problem is, of course, *if* what you're saying is true."

Patricia twisted around and glared at him, "I *doubt* he'd lie to us."

Walter gave her a level look back and replied, "Oh, as do I. But what will happen if I stand the rest of the cavalry brigade's commanders on my carpet and they all deny it? It's happened before, and my investigation would end there." He grunted, "Truth be told I've been looking for an excuse to get rid of Chapman. His brigade has not been performing and I – and Siegfried – have spent far too much time dealing with their failures."

Eric flushed and said, "I... I apologize for any failings on our part, sir."

Walter rolled his eyes, "They're not *your* failures or those of your men, Jenssen. They mostly have to do with General Chapman's inexplicably casual attitude towards logistics, which has absolutely infected his staff. I swear it's as though he has never seen a rail schedule before. But I digress."

"So what do you propose we do about it?" Patricia asked, "We can't just let things stand like this!"

He gave her a cunning half-smile, "Why bother investigating if we can just get Chapman to *confess*?"

"I... think I see where you're going with this." Patricia narrowed her eyes.

"I thought you would." Steepling his fingers, Walter leaned forward on his desk and turned his attention to Eric, "That's quite enough though, Colonel Jenssen. Milady and I will handle things from here. Congratulations on the promotion, by the way. I'm surprised to see it went through this quickly."

Eric looked surprised for a second, saying, "Oh, ah, thank you, sir. The orders came down about a week after we met at the Lord Mayor's ball, actually."

"I think I know a young lady who may have been responsible." Patricia laughed, "I can just see her writing her father over you."

"Quite." Eric smiled and bowed slightly, "Then I will take my leave. Good night, sir, ma'am, and please give my regards to the princess."

Patricia nodded, "Of course. Good night, Eric." The man turned and left, and as the door shut softly behind him she turned back to Walter and said, "Speaking of a certain young lady, I'm guessing whatever plan you're cooking up will require her cooperation?"

He gave her that same sly smile, "Of course, milady. I need you two to bait the trap."

"And you'll slam the jaws shut?" She gave him a predatory smile back, "*My pleasure.* So how do you want to start the hunt?"

Walter chuckled, "Sometimes, milady, Arilin can get a little annoying. She's a kid, and I know she can't help it." He paused for a moment, "But do you think you could get her to be... *especially* annoying? I know a certain general who is going to get told, at about ten tomorrow morning, that he needs to come teach the princess about the proud history of the cuirassiers. Because, you know," He gave her a look, "*Clearly* you know nothing about the subject."

Patricia laughed, "Oh, don't worry. I'll talk to her. She'll be *absolutely obnoxious.*"

Walter's eyes twinkled, "I don't expect that will be too hard for her." Standing, he went on, "Now, milady, *I* need my rest, and I suspect you and the princess do as well. We have a battle to fight tomorrow."

She smoothed her skirt as she stood and replied, smiling, "A polite little battle over tea and cakes?"

"Better than one with bullets and shells, milady." He gave her a grim smile back, "We'll have plenty of *that* soon enough."

Chapter 20

Wasps Under a Blue Sky

June blinked, felt himself nod and startled awake. Shaking himself, he dropped back into the tangle of tree roots he was using as cover and prodded his companion. Anastasia woke up after a moment, rubbed her eyes and looked at him questioningly. He said, "Can you keep watch for a while? I need to go walk the line."

She raised an eyebrow and said, "Falling asleep, sir?"

He chuckled, "Yeah. That too." Sighing, he added, "I... didn't get a lot of sleep last night."

"I don't blame you, sir." She shivered, even though the morning was increasingly warm. She didn't need to say anything more. They'd both been lucky to escape with their lives, and they'd left three men behind. Sergeant Ghaznavi had been shredded moments after he'd fired his machine gun and June had no idea what had happened to the two men who had been keeping watch in the barn. Given the Royal soldiers that had come pouring out of it he didn't have much hope they were alive.

He and Anastasia had barely made it out themselves. She'd had to jump off the house's rear roof and run for it, and he'd almost been skewered. Somebody in the Royal Army knew how to use a bayonet. And he could have sworn that Royal soldier was a woman. It wasn't her frame, tall but too slender for a man. It was the blue eyes flaming in the moonlight as she leapt at him, heedless of the death all around her. June shook his head to dispel the thought, thanked Anastasia and set off down the ragged line of what was left of his platoon. The odds of him dying in single combat were a lot lower than from gunfire or artillery, and he had more than enough of those to worry about.

It didn't take long for him to walk the line. Including himself he was down to ten soldiers, eight of them scattered into four different sets of tree roots, scrapes and crags coming out of the rocky ground, looking out across the rolling fields and forest to the west. The other two were taking care of their horses some ways off to the rear. With the gentle summer sunlight sifting down onto them from the forest canopy and painting the scene in front of them in cheery green and gold, it made for a very peaceful scene.

June knew it was a lie. There were thousands of Royal soldiers massing just out of sight, at least a regiment's worth. When they advanced they were going to simply roll over his squad and sweep it away. The only thing he could do was try to drag the fight out as long as possible. Hearing a whistle behind him, he turned to see Corporal Marin hurriedly gesturing to him. June rushed over and laid down next to the man as he shook the soldier sleeping next to him awake.

"Sir, they're coming." Marin nodded downrange, and June followed his gaze to see a small dark dot cautiously emerge from the forest opposite them. A few moments later more followed it, until ten or so Royal soldiers had emerged and started picking their way downhill. Hearing Marin adjusting the sights on his machine gun, June looked over at the man and shook his head.

The corporal raised his eyebrows questioningly and June explained, "They're just scouts. They *want* us to shoot at them." Marin shrugged and set his machine-gun back down, barrel slanting upwards where it was supported by the gun's bipod. June patted him on the shoulder and said, "Wait for my signal. *I'll* fire first."

June quickly walked up and down the line again, reassuring his dragoons and repeating his instructions, before settling back in next to Anastasia. She looked over at him, then out at the few blue dots walking through the fields in front of them. Finally, she asked, "Sir, are you *sure* this is a good idea?"

June chuckled nervously, "No. But we're going with it."

"That's comforting to hear... wait. *Look.*" June followed her gaze to see more Royal soldiers starting to move out of the forest and down into the valley in front of them. They were a little more bunched together, moving a little faster than the scouts as they tried to keep in their loose formation. And they just *kept coming*, dozens of them spreading across the distant landscape. Looking to either side, June saw more Royal soldiers breaking cover far on either side of them, spreading across the landscape like a gigantic ink blot.

June sighed, brushed his long hair out of his face and hefted his rifle, working the lever set underneath the stock to chamber a round. It was time. Raising his voice to reach his soldiers, he shouted, "*Enemy main body! Eight hundred meters! Machine guns, one magazine and displace! Fire on my mark!*" Flicking off his rifle's safety, he leveled his sights on a group of enemy soldiers just emerging into the fields, exhaled and slowly pulled the trigger. His rifle cracked and thudded at his shoulder. He racked the lever quickly, sighted and fired again as the rest of his squad opened fire around him.

The dark specks across the fields in front of him disappeared as hundreds of men dove for cover. And then, between the staccato cracking of their gunfire, June heard something small and fast hiss by overhead. Then he heard another and another, the first drops of a thunderstorm. As the enemy fire thickened his gun teams finished their magazines and one by one, pulled their weapons down out of the line of fire, picked them up and ran for their next position. He heard Tarai finish first, then Marin, then the last team, Privates Sagara and Han. June looked to see the two dragoons running behind him hunched over against the rain of bullets, Han carrying the heavy gun cradled in his arms.

Slapping Anastasia on the back, June shouted, "It's time! Let's go!" She looked back at him blankly, so June grabbed the back of her load-bearing harness and pulled her out of her position, yelling, "*Move! With me!*" Understanding flashed through her eyes and she sprang to her feet and took off running after the last team. June rolled upright himself and followed on her heels as the rain of bullets around them turned into a slapping, tearing hail. Splinters of wood and shot-off branches rained down on them as they rushed through the undergrowth, up a slight slope. A little farther on the ground would fall off and they would be back into cover.

Someone screamed ahead of them, and June thought he recognized Han's voice. They ran up to find Sagara dragging him by the back of his harness into the meager cover of a tangle of tree roots, his machine-gun forgotten where it had fallen. June scooped up the weapon on the way by and crouched by the fallen man to see blood starting to pour out of his lower leg as Sagara fumbled with a tourniquet.

A shell whistled overhead and exploded a ways behind them, and June looked between his two unwounded soldiers and said, "We don't have time for this. Both of you, get him back to the horses. Sagara, you take him back to the rear once you're there. It shouldn't be too hard to find the regiment once you get moving east." He pulled the machine-gun's magazine out, saw that Han had reloaded his weapon and said, "I'll cover you from here. Move!"

Slinging his rifle over his back to get it out of the way, June rolled to one knee, rocked the machine-gun's magazine back into place and started firing as the two privates picked Han up behind him and rushed him away. After he fired his first burst he heard another gun shriek to life off to his right, probably Tarai's. Marin opened fire a few seconds later as June got up and, cursing every ounce of metal in the damn boat-anchor machine gun he was carrying, ran for the rest of his squad and the safety of the back side of the hill.

He didn't have far to go, and soon the enemy bullets were whistling harmlessly overhead instead through the air right in front of him. Moving on a little ways farther he saw Marin's gun team, sliding downslope

a little as they pulled out of their firing position, and looking a little farther he saw Tarai setting her machine gun back up. Marin saw him as he
rushed up and asked, "Sir, Han's hit? How bad is it?"

June shook his head, "Not bad, but I hope we can get him back to
Regiment in time."

The corporal scowled at him, "It would help if we knew exactly where
they *are*, sir."

June narrowed his eyes, "There's nothing I can do about that right
now."

"We could *all* retreat, sir." Marin gestured angrily, "There's not much
of the platoon *left*."

June sighed. He had a point. Given their casualties and the soldiers
he'd lost to take care of them, he was down to five dragoons including
himself facing what he was pretty sure was an entire Royal division. Another shell thudded down in front of them as if to punctuate the thought.
That being said, June looked back up at Marin, "I don't like this either,
but we have our orders. We'll delay them as long as we can, then head for
the horses."

The corporal shook his head, muttered, "Yes, sir," and headed off
across the slope to his next firing position, June following along behind
as the rain of bullets overhead thickened. The slope offered them good
protection, though, and they gradually moved down it from position to
position for the next few minutes as Royal bullets splintered the trees
overhead and shells crashed down off to their left. June eventually realized his little force with their three machine guns was so small their
enemies didn't have any good idea where exactly they were.

June was setting his gun up across the ruins of what looked like an
old stone wall near the bottom of the ridge when he heard a cry off to his
side and turned to see Tarai jerking away from her wrecked machine-gun.
Even from the distance he could see the shredded receiver from a Royal bullet. Someone out there was either extraordinarily lucky or, June
thought as he looked downslope and felt his heart freeze, *extraordinarily
close*. Pushing his shoulder into the buttstock, June brought the muzzle
down and emptied the weapon at a group of Royal soldiers swarming up
the hillside maybe fifty meters away. They were so close he could hear
someone screaming as he dropped back to reload.

Marin must have realized what was happening, because he swung his
gun onto their attackers and fired. An enemy machine-gun thundered
to life, incredibly close, and June rolled over and swung himself back up
to see bullets walking uphill into Marin's position from a Royal gun crew

he could see clearly downslope. They were so close they'd had to traverse their weapon over to fire at Marin and had exposed themselves to him as they shifted. June dropped his sights onto the group of men, pulled the trigger and the enemy gun abruptly fell silent.

A bullet snapped a couple inches past his ear and June hurriedly dropped back beneath the crest of the hill. Royal soldiers were shouting to each other, incredibly close, commands to fix bayonets and prepare to assault. June dropped his machine gun and was reaching for his sword when someone on the other side of the hill shouted, *"Grenade! Move!"*

Looking over, June saw Tarai and her companion pull pins on their second grenades and hurl them over the hill. The air hissed with shrapnel as the bombs exploded and June thought dimly that Tarai had probably had a better plan than him as far as defending their position. Picking his gun back up, he shouted, "Bound back! Move!"

Tarai got the message and fell back down the hill, quickly followed by Marin. June waited as long as he dared, heaved himself up and ran down himself, Marin firing a burst past him as he went. The enemy stayed on their side of the hill and June felt the tension running out of him as they bounded backwards into the forest, then turned and ran for the horses. They came into a particularly thick stand of trees after a short while and June, panting under the weight of his machine gun, called a halt. He realized he was shaking as he knelt on the soft forest floor and tried to steady himself as the two corporals dropped down beside him.

"What's the plan, sir?" Tarai asked, "We're about out of ammunition... not to mention my gun."

Marin said, "We need to get out of here. We're all going to die if this keeps up." He gave June a look and added, "Sir."

June snorted grimly and handed her his machine gun, "Here you go. We've got more ammo with the horses." He looked back at Marin, "We'll ride back a couple kilometers and set up again. I don't think we're done just yet."

Marin shook his head disbelievingly, "Seriously, sir? We're not going to be able to keep this up."

Narrowing his eyes, June replied, "We've done alright so far. I don't see any reason to give up now."

The man snorted, "Besides the whole Royal division attacking us?"

"They haven't won yet." June chuckled, then looked back at him, "And we're not going to let them."

Marin started to say something, but Tarai cut him off, "No, sir, they haven't." She glared at the other man and said, "Calm down, Doug. You know our orders as well as anyone else here."

"That doesn't mean I have to like them." Marin spat, "We do have some latitude here."

June looked between them, then cut Tarai off before she could reply, "Yes, we do. This is my call to keep fighting. Like I said, we're *not done yet.*"

Marin sighed, "Whatever you say sir. Let's get moving at least."

They picked up and quickly headed through the forest to where they'd left the horses earlier, and emerged into an isolated field to find their horses, Anastasia, and the two dragoons they'd left there earlier as guards. Visibly exhausted, Anastasia picked herself up off the ground and went to greet them. June asked her, "How's Han doing?"

She shook her head tiredly and said, "He's doing alright... they left just a couple minutes ago. I felt like I was going to die myself carrying him all the way over here."

June said, relieved, "Thank you. Now mount up, we're heading out ourselves."

Tarai added, "We almost got overrun. They're not that far behind us right now."

Anastasia's eyes widened, and she rushed over to tell the other dragoons to get ready to move. They listened to her for a few seconds, then started frantically throwing their equipment on and loading their horses. June and the others set to and within a couple minutes they were riding east. The bright late-morning sun blazed down on them out of a clear blue sky sky as they emerged into open country and rode down into a broad, shallow valley, the red roofs of a town emerging amidst the scattered forest and pastures that spread out before them.

June started to look for the way they had taken coming in a few days ago, bypassing the town to avoid any angry civilians still in residence, but as his eye wandered across the buildings he noticed something. Holding up his hand to stop the group, he pulled out his binoculars and focused them on the distant village square. They'd avoided the place to begin with because he'd seen a Royal flag flying defiantly in the center of town.

June smiled. Fluttering in the breeze, a black and red Imperial flag had replaced the blue and gold Royal banner. Looking closer, he thought he saw a few green-uniformed soldiers in the streets as well. Turning to his companions, he said, "Looks like we found the rest of the Army. Let's go."

They ran into an Imperial roadblock after about a mile and June told the commander where they were coming from and that there was a Royal division heading straight for them. The woman hurried off to her field telephone station, had a short conversation and came back quickly, saying, "So you're June Anjanou? We've been hearing all about you lately."

June chuckled and rubbed the back of his neck, "Uh, thanks, I guess. Can we get through? I really need to report."

She replied, "No problem. Colonel Vann will be waiting for you at the town hall. It's right in the main square, can't miss it." She smirked and added, "And don't worry about the defenses here. I think you all were actually in the middle of our screen line. We've been wondering who was doing all the shooting for the last couple hours."

June laughed, thanked her, and rode onwards. They passed by several defensive positions on the way in, and inside the town itself dragoons were hurriedly sandbagging windows and building barricades in the streets. Colonel Vann and Sergeant Khan were waiting for him on top of the steps leading up to the town hall, and June dismounted and hurried up. Saluting, he said, "Ma'am, Lieutenant Anjanou, reporting back in."

The colonel laughed, saluted him back and said, "The lost dragoon finally returns. Someday you and I need to have a talk about *interpreting orders*." Still chuckling, she stepped forward, clipped something onto his collar and said, "Good job out there. Here's your Citation for Valor. The general actually signed off just this morning."

A Citation for Valor? What? He just stood there and replied, dumbly, "Uh... ma'am?"

"Oh, *now* you're speechless." Vann went on, "Your platoon captured over a hundred prisoners and if all the wounded dragoons you've been sending back are to be believed, you've been fighting half the Royal Army by yourselves for the last few days. I'd be remiss if I *didn't* give you a medal. Now, that being said," She gave his platoon sergeant a sidelong glance and whispered, "Sergeant Khan here actually *kind of* wants to kill you, so if I were you I'd try to butter her up a little after we're done here."

June looked over at Khan. She glared back at him. Swallowing, he turned back to the regimental commander and whispered back, "Yeah, I think I'll do that." He cleared his throat and said, louder, "Uh, I owe you a report, ma'am."

Vann nodded, "Of course. Let's go inside." She turned and led him into the heavy stone building. As he stepped inside, a wave of thuds rattled the windowpanes and shells shrieked overhead. June recognized it as the regiment's horse artillery, firing west.

Chapter 21

Flag of Victory

Sophia stirred and slowly opened her eyes in the dim light, filtering onto her through what looked like a white sheet a few inches in front of her face. Blinking, she pushed the blanket covering her down and rolled onto her back, looking up to see a dark shape looming low overhead with legs planted on either side of her head. *What in the... oh,* she thought, *someone put a table over me while I was sleeping.* Looking down at herself, she noticed a cardboard sign on top of her blanket and reached down to examine it. It read, 'Concussion casualty, do not disturb'. That explained things.

The floor squeaked as someone walked up to the table and picked something up off it. Sophia heard pouring liquid before a man said, "Damn, it's cold again." She heard him take another drink and go on, "Eh, I've had worse. Hey, have we gotten word yet from Division about that food we asked for?"

Someone on the other side of the room replied, "No, sir."

The man took a step away and said, "Well, get on the radio and call them again. And if that doesn't work we'll send someone. Colonel Paget is going to kill me if we run out of rations tonight." Sophia thought she recognized his voice from somewhere, but she couldn't quite place it. Shaking her head, she felt for her rifle and found it wedged between her body and the wall. Peeling back the blanket and extricating herself from the table's legs, she gingerly lifted the tablecloth and crawled out from underneath it.

The lieutenant across the room was opening his mouth to reply when she emerged. He stared at her for a moment, then leapt up so quickly his chair clattered to the ground behind him, saying, "Ah, sir! B-behind you!" There were a couple other soldiers besides him in the room, and they froze and stared at her. The clerk in the corner looked up from her typing and stopped suddenly, the hammering sound of her typewriter fading away. Sophia could have heard a pin drop, and she smiled nervously.

Major Matheson turned, looked at her and raised an eyebrow. Looking back at his shocked subordinates, he chuckled and said, "Did I forget to tell you all she was sleeping under there? Sorry. I forgot the night shift set this place up." The female soldier in the corner shrugged and went back to her typing, and on that the rest of them slowly went back to their work. Looking back at her he said, "Good morning, sleeping beauty. Y'know, I thought I recognized you from somewhere."

Sophia tilted her head to one side, thought for a moment and said, "Oh. You were on duty that night. Uh, sir."

He gave her a look, "Do you have *any* idea how much pain you put me through? The boss was out of his mind when I told him. Plus *you* try explaining to the police that you've caught an Imperial spy ring entirely made up of ten-year-olds."

Thinking back on the short fight in the alley beside their barracks, Sophia laughed, "What'd you end up doing with them, sir?"

Matheson rolled his eyes, "They were all local kids. We gave them back to their parents eventually. As far as I know the police never caught that one you said got away. Your supposed Black Cloak." He paused and went on, "Even with those throwing knives you showed me, I still have a hard time imagining them employing children."

Sophia looked back at him, 'He couldn't have been older than twelve or thirteen, sir. And you don't just learn to fight like that anywhere."

Matheson sighed and took a sip of his lukewarm coffee, "Yeah. Anyways, you need to get back to your unit." He thought for a moment, "Actually, they should be around here somewhere. C Company, Second Battalion right?"

Sophia nodded, "Yes, sir."

"Yeah, they're in reserve right now. Should be a couple kilometers down the road with Regimental headquarters." He snorted, "Your First Sergeant was *not* happy about leaving you here with us when we took this place over, you know."

Sophia blushed and fidgeted, "Well, he *is* my father."

"Really?" He laughed, "That's understandable. And I can't say I blame him after the fight you guys had for this place." He grimaced, "There's still bloodstains all over the parlor. I haven't seen something like that since Khorfan."

She remembered screams, bodies strewn on the floor and a sword burning in the cold moonlight, and she shivered uncontrollably. *That long-haired dragoon,* she thought. Hesitantly, she said, "Sir, do you know anything about a dragoon with really long, black hair? I've seen him a couple times now. He was the one who did all... that."

Matheson furrowed his eyebrows, "I can't say I... wait, no. I do. Hey, someone bring me that intel report on important enemy personnel. Yeah, that one." A soldier came over and handed him a sheaf of papers, and he paged through them quickly. Finding what he was looking for, he pulled it out and read off, "About five foot eleven, slim, black hair to his waist, sound about right?"

Sophia raised her eyebrows, "Yeah, it does, sir. Who is it?"

"June Anjanou." He smirked, "Name ring any bells?"

Sophia cocked her head again and said, "Anjanou... isn't he an Imperial general or something? But he'd be older. And not out this far. Unless...?"

The major nodded, "Yeah. You're thinking of General Slade Anjanou. We think he's in command of the invasion force." He paused, "June's his son."

"Oh." *June Anjanou.* It was a name, at least. It made him a little less scary. Sophia replied, "Thanks, sir."

He shook his head, "No, thank you. This is important information." He smiled and patted her on the shoulder, "Now, Miss Rose, you need to get back to your unit."

"Yes, sir." Sophia collected her equipment from under the table and headed out, trying to avoid looking at the blood all over the parlor. It was hard. There was some on the *ceiling.* Shouldering her pack, she started off down the road, following the general flow of messengers going back and forth on horseback. She could hear gunfire faintly up ahead and occasionally a wave of thuds as an artillery battery fired. She shivered again, though the sun was hot. It sounded like a hell of a battle was brewing.

After a couple kilometers Sophia came over a rise and noticed a large farmhouse with a number of wagons parked near it. A group of soldiers was working to set up what she realized was a radio antenna between two trees in the yard, and as she watched a messenger galloped up from the direction of the front, dismounted and went inside. That, she guessed, was Regimental headquarters. And just past it, in the irrigation ditches that crisscrossed the fields, she spotted the occasional blue uniform. Charlie Company was down in cover, but occasionally someone would get up and she could see them at a distance. She smiled and set off towards them.

The fields were shot through with farm paths, and Sophia made quick progress. When she drew near the company a sentry stood up from behind one of the ditches and near the road and challenged her, "Halt! Who goes th... oh, Sophia." Jack turned around and shouted, "Hey, everyone, Sophia's back!"

About half the company popped up in the blanket of wheat to look at her. Sophia recognized her father as he stood up and hurried in her direction. She smiled and rushed to meet him. He wrapped his arms around her and picked her, pack and all, up in a bear hug as they met. She gasped for air a little, but he put her down before too long. Stepping back a little, she looked up at him and said, "Hi, Dad, uh... sorry you had to leave me." She rubbed her head sheepishly, "I must have been out like a light."

"You were out cold. The medics didn't want to wake you up." He stepped beside her and patted her on the shoulder, "Now, when I was your age I would have gotten kicked in the ribs anyways, but it's a whole new army these days I guess."

She smiled at his ribbing, "Aw, come on, Dad."

He looked over at her and cracked a half-smile, "On the other hand, I don't remember half the Marchlands because I got blown up too many times, so I'm not complaining. Come on, let's get you back to your platoon." He started guiding her in what she presumed was the right direction, "I know a lieutenant who's pretty grateful to you for saving his life last night. Twice apparently."

Sophia set he jaw grimly, "He was about the only one I saved." She sighed, "I wish I'd gone in there first, not after most of Second Squad, well..."

"Look at me, Sophie." Surprised, she stopped and looked over at her father. He turned around, looked her in the eyes and said, "I know how it feels. Trust me, I do. Those are seven more men, good men with families, dead on my watch, and I'll have to answer for it when we get back home. But you can't let it get to you or you'll crack and then you'll be next." He pushed her hat down over her blurring eyes, "Now don't you go crying on me, Sophie. I have enough problems to deal with."

She quickly wiped her tears away and sniffed, "Yeah... thanks, Dad."

Lieutenant Thorn had noticed them coming over and met them with Sergeant Falcon. The two men looked grim, and her father quickly pulled Falcon off to have a private conversation with him. Thorn coughed and said, "Ah, good to see you again, Miss Rose. Thanks for, uh, saving my life last night. I really thought I was done for a moment."

Sophia shrugged, "Sorry I couldn't do more, sir."

Thorn snorted, "You and me both, Rose."

Remembering her earlier talk with Major Matheson, Sophia said, "Oh, by the way, sir, I found out who he is. That dragoon with the long hair. Regiment has a file on him."

He raised an eyebrow, "That would have been good to know a couple days ago. Who is he?"

She said, "June Anjanou. Son of General Anjanou, apparently."

"Great." Thorn said sarcastically, "Maybe he and Prince Adrian can fight it out. Actually..." He gave her an inquisitive look, "Think you could beat him with that spear of yours?"

Sophia furrowed her brow as she thought for a moment. June was a powerful fighter and so fast she'd barely been able to even defend herself. But a bayoneted rifle was a slow, short and clumsy weapon compared to a real spear. Looking back up at Thorn, she answered, "Maybe, sir. He's *good.*"

"I'll keep that in mind if we see him again." Thorn jerked his head at a section of the platoon's line, "Now get back to your squad. Sergeant Cross has been bothering me all day about you."

Sophia nodded, "Yes, sir."

Cross, Tony and the rest of her friends were glad to see her back and she slipped off her pack and sat down on the edge of their dry irrigation ditch, grateful to take a load off her feet. Artillery thundered off to either side occasionally and she could see an occasional ambulance or supply wagon going to and from the front line, which she guessed was on the other side of a long, low wooded ridge a ways in front of them. Waves of gunfire popped steadily in the distance, and she turned to Tony and asked, "Has it been like this all morning?"

Sitting beside her, Tony shook his head and replied, "No. There was a little shooting earlier, but this started up right before you got here."

Sophia saw smoke and dirt spray into the air up on the ridgeline, and a couple treetops slowly toppled out of sight. A few seconds later the thudding of artillery shells washed over them. Looking back at him nervously, she said, "I don't think that was ours."

He shook his head, "I don't either." They both looked into the ditch simultaneously and he said nervously, "Uh, why don't we...?"

"Yeah, let's." Sophia replied, as they both climbed into the shallow trench. They didn't have much of a view from it, but as the gunfire on the far side of the hill suddenly built in ferocity Sophia was grateful for the little protection it provided. After a few minutes and another volley of enemy shells digging up the ridgeline, she got out her entrenching tool and started digging.

The battle in front of them built all afternoon as they scraped a foxhole out of the side of the ditch. A steady stream of messengers on horseback and ambulances full of wounded men rolled down the road past headquarters, and their own artillery batteries hammered away steadily. Thorn came around and filled them in after a couple hours, pointing things out on his map as he did. Apparently the Imperials were dug into a town, Lorenvale, on the far side of the ridge in force and the regiment was trying to force them out. The gunfire did soften a little as the day wore on and the regiment pressed closer towards the town, but given the number of green Imperial tracers she saw ricocheting over the ridge as the sky darkened she didn't care much for their prospects.

The False Sun had set and they were eating dinner by the ghostly light of the moons when Sophia heard a commotion over towards Regimental headquarters. Looking over, she recognized Thorn, Lieutenant Stahl and her father talking to a tall, thin man she didn't recognize. He was wearing a sword, so she supposed he was an officer from Regiment. The man unfolded a map and pointed out several things on it as the other three huddled around him. They talked on for several more minutes before they came to some kind of agreement, exchanged salutes and broke up. Thorn headed back to the platoon, whistled, and spoke to the sergeants as they gathered around him.

Sergeant Cross came around a little later and gathered the squad. As they huddled around him he said, "We're being committed. Apparently the rest of the battalion has managed to break into the town, but they're bogged down and need our help. We're to pass through A Co and take the town square and City Hall. The higher-ups think the Masks are using it as a headquarters and they'll pull out if we take it." He looked around, "How's everyone on ammo? Water? Rations?" The squad murmured and nodded affirmatively and Cross went on, "Everyone hit the ammo wagon after we break here. They should have enough grenades for two per, and everyone take a belt for the machine gun." He paused, looked at his team leaders and said, "Vinson, Slaughter, both of you get sledgehammers from supply. They have some in their wagon for wire pickets, and we'll need them." He glanced at his watch, then went on grimly, "This is an urban fight we're going into. It's going to be rough. We're moving out in half an hour, so get to it."

The squad murmured again, stood and started filing over towards the supply wagons. Sophia went to follow them, but Cross grabbed her arm and said, "No, I've got something else for you, Rose." He pulled two grenades off his harness, handed them to her and said, "Here. Don't bother with getting ammo. Lieutenant Thorn needs to get you up to speed on our route, go see him."

Taking the bombs and clipping them to her own harness, Sophia said, "Yes, Sergeant," and went to go find her lieutenant. She quickly spotted Thorn talking to the new officer towards the center of their company's perimeter, and they both looked at her as they approached. Thorn smiled and said, "Ah, Miss Rose!" Turning to his companion, he said, "Sir, this is Sophia Rose. She's one of my best soldiers, and she'll be leading us in tonight."

"Oh? I've heard a great deal about you, Miss Rose." The man nodded slightly, his gaunt features reminding her more than a little of a skeleton, "Captain Cauldwell. I'm taking over for *Jaeger*, as of an hour ago." He almost spat the man's name.

"What happened to him, sir?" Sophia asked, "We've all been wondering."

The new commander glared at her icily, "He has been... invalidated."

Sophia raised her eyebrows, "Ah, yes, sir." Cauldwell clearly had little time for privates. She'd have to get the story out of her father later. She asked Thorn, "Sir, Sergeant Cross said you had the route?"

Thorn looked at her for a moment, then shook his head quickly and said, "Oh, yes, I do. Let me show you here..." They would take the road over the ridge until they got out of the forest, then cut through the outskirts to link in with their battalion. Apparently Second Battalion headquarters was set up in a school on the western edge of the town, and they would get better direction from there. As Thorn finished explaining things she saw that soldiers had started shrugging packs on and getting into formation for movement, and they headed over to get ready to move together.

Charlie Company marched out quickly, got onto the main road and spread way out as a precaution against artillery fire, though they hadn't seen any Imperial shells for a couple hours. As the sky darkened Sophia had noticed an orange glow over the ridge in front of them, but she didn't realize how odd it was until they were most of the way up the hill and she saw strange clouds in the clear night sky. It almost looked like they were coming up from the town.

As they crested the ridge and looked down on Lorenvale, Sophia saw the town was on fire. Many buildings billowed flames into the air and others poured smoke from gutted shells. Streams of red Royal Army and green Imperial tracers danced back and forth occasionally, tracing out the front line in bursts of sharp light. As she watched a string of shells crashed down near what looked like a square in the middle of the town, a couple hitting an imposing building that fronted onto it. She supposed that was probably the town hall. Looking nearer, she saw a bulky building through the trees on the western edge of town that matched what Thorn had told her earlier, and she waved the company off the road and set off towards it.

It took them about half an hour of jumping fences, trudging through fields and filing through more than a few back yards before they came up on the school. Thorn put a hand on her shoulder to stop her, waved the company to ground and went to get Captain Cauldwell. He came back a couple minutes later and the three of them went forward, working their way through the grounds. Examining the building carefully as they advanced, Sophia saw the side towards them was scarred by artillery fire and pimpled with what looked like thousands of tiny pocks gouged out of the concrete. Bullet holes. The Empire had fought for this place.

She also saw a dark shadow move in one of the ground floor windows. As they got closer she picked up a rock, looked at Thorn and Cauldwell and threw it inside where she had seen movement. They flattened themselves to the ground, and a few moments later a voice called out, "Flash!"

Captain Cauldwell said loudly, "Lightning."

"Hey." The sentry stood from his hiding place, his uniform a dark smudge against the gray interior, "Charlie Company?"

The three of them stood. Thorn said, "Yeah. Is this battalion?"

"Yeah," The man replied, "They're expecting you upstairs. Come in."

Cauldwell told Thorn to go back and keep the company in place and took her in with him. The damage on the inside was as bad as the outside. The walls were gouged with bullet holes and what Sophia was beginning to recognize as sprays of shrapnel from grenades, and everywhere shattered glass crunched underfoot. More than a few long, smeared bloodstains stretched along the floor.

Sophia heard the low growl of an electrical generator ahead and, as they turned a corner, saw a group of medics sitting on the floor outside a harshly-lit room. Their uniforms dark with blood, they barely looked up to acknowledge them as they passed. Caldwell didn't even bother to look at them, and Sophia swallowed hard and hurried to keep up with his rapid pace. Climbing a flight of stairs and turning around, they saw another lit room with a soldier standing guard outside. After a brief exchange the man let them in.

The battalion staff had rearranged the classroom to their liking, pushing desks together to form tables and hanging ponchos across the windows to keep light from leaking outside. The blackboard was covered in figures keeping track of various aspects of the battle. Sophia immediately noticed that the battalion had taken one hundred and fifty-nine casualties of whom forty were dead, one hundred and two evacuated and the remainder presumably still downstairs. That amounted to more of the battalion than she wanted to think about. Also they were out of hot rations. Remembering Major Matheson's predicament, Sophia chuckled and Cauldwell gave her a stern look.

Seeing the new arrivals, the officer on duty had jumped up and re-treated to the next room. After a moment a major she vaguely recognized emerged, scowling as he buttoned his jacket. He looked at her compan-ion and said, "You're Cauldwell? Welcome to Second Battalion. I've been waiting on you."

"My pleasure, sir." Cauldwell replied. Grimacing, he went on, "I'm sorry about Colonel Thompson."

The major snorted, "Nothing you could have done about it. We'll all feel his loss." *The commander?* Sophia drew her breath in sharply and both men looked at her. The major raised an eyebrow and said, "Although it looks like your soldiers haven't been informed yet. You should probably tell them at some point."

"Yes, sir." The captain paused and went on, "I've been told we're to attack and get the battalion moving again. What's our objective here ex-actly?"

"Let me show you." The major walked over to a map set up on four desks pushed together and started pointing things out. It looked like a municipal map of the town of Lorenvale itself, not a large-scale military map that would have only showed the town as a small smudge of build-ings in a vast countryside. She saw that someone had marked out the front line on it as he started, "We made it a good way into the city earlier today before Alpha got beat up to the point they had to stop. Bravo's still in fighting condition, they're just dug in over here," He pointed to the northern side of town, "Waiting on you to relieve Alpha. Once you get in position they'll attack with you." He pointed out an Imperial position just forward of the front line, "Alpha got cut up trying to take this strongpoint. You'll need to take it, then push forward through the town square. Once they lose the center of town Regiment thinks the Masks are going to pull out."

Cauldwell said, "Their position is precarious, sir. First and Third Bat-talions are several kilometers forward of here already."

"Let's hope so." Sophia finally got a good look at the man's name tag. It read, 'Clark'. He scowled and went on, "I can't see any problem in their logic, but the Masks are always full of surprises. Questions?" Cauldwell shook his head, and Clark went on, "Alright. I'll have a runner guide you in to Alpha's positions. Can you attack at zero-one hundred?"

Cauldwell looked at his watch, "Can do, sir." Satisfied, Clark nodded and called for a runner to take Charlie Company forward. A few minutes later Sophia was following the man through a residential side-street that hadn't been damaged too badly in the fighting, the rest of the company behind her. She saw a few curtains furtively drawn aside, but beyond that the houses were dark and silent. Heading towards the center of town, they cut through a few yards and a park before a row of battle-scarred multi-story buildings rose in front of them. The runner flashed a signal with his flashlight, and a red light blinked back in reply from a second-floor window.

They crossed the street and Sophia climbed through a shattered storefront to get into the buildings. Mannequins dressed in cheery summer fashions were tossed to all sides and clothing covered the floor in absolute chaos. Sophia snorted at the thought of making off with a dress and headed for the back of the store. Finding a set of stairs, she crept up to the next floor and peeked into a darkened hallway, lit only by a little moonlight coming from a couple open doors farther down. She noticed a shadowy figure pressed against the wall near the open doors and, raising her rifle, said, "Flash."

The figure moved. She could see it raise a rifle and look from side to side before it said in hushed tones, "Thunder." Sophia pushed the door the rest of the way open with her rifle and stepped into the hall, and the figure turned to look at her. The soldier asked, "Charlie Company? That was your signal just now?"

Sophia nodded, even though it was dark and she realized the man probably couldn't see it, "That's us." Turning, she spoke back into the stairwell, "Sir, they're up here."

Lieutenant Thorn emerged from the shadows behind her and said, "Thanks, Rose." Squinting to make out the soldier down the hall, he said, "Who's in charge up here?"

The man replied, "Lieutenant Curtiss. I'll take you to him." He pulled open a door on the far side of the hall and disappeared inside, Sophia and Thorn after him. As they stepped into the entryway the stench of gunpowder and burnt oil washed over them. Candlelight flickered from what looked like a kitchen to the side, and Sophia and Thorn stepped in to find a young man wearing lieutenant's rank slumped over the kitchen table, asleep.

Thorn prodded him and Curtiss jerked awake, teetering in his chair. Sophia quickly put a hand out and grabbed his jacket to keep him from falling backwards, and suppressed a chuckle as she saw his frankly ridiculous blonde moustache. He settled his chair back on the floor and shook himself as he looked up at them, saying, "Wha... what, who are you?" He looked between them and ventured, "Charlie Company?"

Sophia said, "That's us."

Thorn looked at his watch and added, "We're attacking in half an hour. Are you guys ready to support us?"

Curtiss looked at them blankly for a second, then abruptly stood and said, "Uh, yes, we will be, give me a minute..." Rushing past them, they heard him shaking soldiers awake deeper in the apartment. Haggard-looking men from Alpha Company soon started rushing past them out the door.

Sophia turned to Thorn and commented, "Sir, I'm just a *little* scared right now."

He chuckled, "You and me both, Rose." He gave her a half-smile, "You need to get back to your squad. Can you send the squad leaders and Sergeant Falcon up here when you go back downstairs?"

She laughed and said, "Yes, sir. Let's do this." Stepping by him, she walked out the door and headed back downstairs. The rest of the platoon was cautiously setting up in the shops fronting on what was left of the far side of the building. Most of the façade had crumpled into the street, and the building across the way looked to be in even worse condition. Much of the brick frontage had been shattered by shellfire and explosives, leaving a honeycomb of rooms open to the air over a pile of rubble. Sending the sergeants on their way, she found Tony cautiously peeking around the counter of what looked like it had once been a coffeehouse and sat down beside him.

Looking over, she asked, "See any Imperials?"

Tony pulled his head back and whispered, "No... I think there's a couple bodies in the street, though."

She raised an eyebrow, "Ours or theirs?"

He shifted uncomfortably, "Probably ours."

Sophia shivered and let Tony get back to watching the far building. After a few minutes Sergeant Cross came around and explained the plan to them. In a few minutes the battalion's mortars were going to start hitting the building across the street, then shift back and work with the artillery to keep any Imperial reinforcements at bay. When the fire shifted they would launch their assault. If they ran into resistance they couldn't handle they were to go around it and let Third Platoon, following behind them, mop it up. Second Platoon would be off to their left to plug the gap between them and Bravo Company.

Jack and the rest of the machine-gun team crept up behind them and started getting ready. Eventually he replaced Tony at the edge of the bar, gun resting beside him. The rest of the squad crept into position in the blasted-out coffeehouse as the minutes dragged on, hiding behind whatever scraps of furniture they could. Sophia self-consciously drew her bayonet and locked it to her rifle as slowly and quietly as possible. After a few seconds the rest of the squad followed suit, the clicks painfully loud in the silence.

Something whistled low overhead and cracked in the street outside. Shrapnel hissed through the air and tore at the walls, and Sophia and Tony flattened themselves to the floor. Another mortar bomb, then another, then a whole storm of them tore at the street and the far building, filling the air with fragments and dust. Burning, glowing fragments rained in the street outside, pouring thick smoke. Sophia smelled reeking phosphorous as the bombardment went on and on, seconds turning into hours. Someone screamed upstairs and called for a medic.

And then the shrapnel stopped churning the air as the bombs fell a little farther away. Sophia leapt to her feet even as Cross shouted, "Move, now!" Leaping the bar, she rushed for the street as machine guns erupted overhead and Jack hauled his gun up and started firing behind her, painfully close. Bullets tore at the far building as she dashed across the street and ducked into the little cover the rubble pile at its base provided. And then despite everything Imperial machine guns screamed inside, green tracers snapping by inches over her head.

Sophia rolled as Tony dove into the pile of bricks beside her, heard another burst of gunfire and saw a flaming green tracer punch through Corporal Vinson's chest. As he staggered she looked back and saw the inside of the coffeehouse flaming green as Imperial rounds searched for Jack and his team. Unclipping a grenade from her belt, she frantically screwed the safety cap off the bottom of the handle, yanked the arming ball, rolled to her knees and hurled it into the building. Tony threw his own a second later and they both dropped and grabbed each other as the air overhead shattered.

She was on her feet at once and darted into the building. Red tracers flared beside her and something sparked and exploded to her right. Somebody screamed. An Imperial gun shrieked on her left, incredibly close, and she saw the loophole in the wall they were firing from. She also saw a door in the rear of the store and a plan came together in her mind. Tony was somehow still with her and she stepped aside, shouting, "*Tony! Kick the door!*"

Tony smashed the door open with a furious blow from his foot and she was inside, pivoting left, bayonet coming up and through a dragoon as he rose, twisting, coming out and forward again into the gunner's side as

she fired another burst. The woman thrashed as she died, hand clench-
ing on the gun's trigger. It fired the rest of its magazine out of control as
Sophia spun to see a dragoon disappearing through the rear exit as Tony
came through the door. She shoved him out of the way and made it to
the door in time to see the man making a run for it through the alley. She
leveled her rifle only for him to duck aside and disappear.

Somebody nudged her in the ribs and she turned to see Sergeant Cross
and the rest of the squad behind her. A scared-looking Jack staggered out
of the door behind everyone else, alone. Sophia absently hoped the other
two men on his team were alright as Cross said, "Damn. Good work, Rose.
Now follow me." Waving them forward, he stepped into the alley and
moved off to the right, the same way the dragoon had gone. Sophia hurried to catch up, the rush of adrenaline wearing off and her senses coming
back to her as they went. Every crack of a shell out in the town square
just past the next row of buildings and every burst of gunfire and grenade
explosion off behind them seemed magnified, distinct somehow. Sophia
realized she was shaking, swallowed hard, and pressed on after Cross.

Catching up to him, she asked, "Hey, Sergeant, is Vinson alright? I
saw him get hit."

Cross held up a hand and they stopped. She followed his gaze and
saw a door half-open a few meters to their front. Leveling his rifle, Cross
said, "I hope so. The medics have him." He blinked, looked at her and
then back down his rifle. Not looking at her, he went on, "And that leaves
me down a team leader. Looks like I'm going to have to put you in charge."

Sophia inhaled sharply. *Me? A team leader? Are you kidding me?
But,* she thought, *it's not like there's anyone else.* And the middle of a bat-
tle was not the place to have a discussion about her leadership abilities.
Exhaling slowly, she said, "Okay. What now?"

He gave her a sidelong look, "Now we hit this building. Check the
door for booby-traps."

They crept up on the door and Sophia carefully approached, sweeping
the room inside with her rifle as she walked closer. Nothing. She poked
her bayonet through the frame and swept it from top to bottom, then
nudged the door further open. Nothing. Stepping inside, she found herself in a hallway beside what looked like a café's kitchen. Cross walked at
her shoulder as they advanced, rifles sweeping to create a crossfire in the
hall for anyone who emerged. As they got further in she heard the rear
team break off into the kitchen, and she thought she heard Lieutenant
Thorn shouting out in the alley behind them.

They emerged into the café's large dining area as another wave of shells crashed down, painfully close in the square outside now. A piece of shrapnel hissed through the air and gouged plaster from the wall overhead as she pressed herself against one of the low café partitions for cover. Sophia heard something hiss above her, looked up and saw a small object drop at her from the café's open second floor. It hit the ground and bounced as Sophia dove away screaming, "*Grenade!*"

It went off just as she managed to get around one of the flimsy partitions. Shrapnel and splinters filled the air overhead, but as her ears rang she rolled to her feet, flipped off her rifle's safety and fired. She got three or four shots off before Jack realized what was happening from back in the corridor and started shooting into the ceiling with his machine gun. Sophia darted for the stairs as Cross pitched a grenade up, flattened herself on them as it went off and then sprinted forward, shouting for Jack to cease fire.

Through the cloud of dust Sophia saw the dragoons had smashed a hole through the wall into the next building. As she was digesting the implications of that the room flashed green and down below Cross shouted for the squad to take cover. She looked down to see Jack slam his machine gun down on top of a table and return fire, filling the café with the harsh light of his gun's muzzle flash. Looking over, she saw the fire was coming from the town hall and she quickly ran back downstairs, heedless of the gunfire, to talk to Cross.

Lieutenant Thorn had appeared, looking a little shaken, and as they ducked into one of the side dining rooms out of the line of fire. Sophia started, "Sir, they've got mouse-holes smashed out upstairs. If we try to find this one guy we'll be here all night."

Cross added, "We're not making it across the square into that fire. We need to flank them."

Most of First and, she supposed, Third Squad had poured into the café by then and the new machine-gunner let off a long burst. Sophia saw a painting fall off the wall. Thorn winced and shouted, "*Yes!*" Looking at her, he went on, "Can you get us there, Rose?"

"Yes, sir!" she replied.

He nodded, "Alright! We'll leave Third Squad here until the other platoons can come up and support us. Looks like it's down to us for now, Sergeant."

Cross smiled grimly, nodded, and they went to pull their soldiers off the firing line. In the smoke and chaos Sophia had to physically pull Tony and Edward away before they realized what was going on. She led them back out with Thorn and the rest of the squad close behind, emerged into the alleyway and got moving. She heard the rest of the squad hurrying to keep up as the firefight raged on behind them.

Sophia took them down dark alleyways and deserted streets, skirting around the town square as the battle behind them built. Their machine guns built to a constant roar behind them, tracers turning every glimpse they got of the square into a seething hellscape. Ricochets spun overhead and more shells crashed down, painfully close, as they crept through the last alley and finally saw the rear of the building.

Tracers lit the scene an eerie, flickering red as they bounced across the street and spun overhead, and Sophia gave Thorn a look as she said, "Sir, we need them to shift fire before we can move."

He chuckled, "I've got that covered. Mulligan!" Jack pushed his way up to the front of the column, and Thorn said, "Set up here and cover us. We'll cross the street to the left and assault from the side of the building. The company will shift fire on your tracers." He looked back at Sophia, "Your team first. Cover the rest of us after you get set up."

Jack flopped into the prone and set his machine gun on its bipod, laying out a coil of ammunition beside the weapon as Sophia, Tony and Edward crouched behind him, out of sight of the building. Lieutenant Thorn looked at them, nodded and counted down, "Three, two, one, *go!*"

The gun roared and the three of them sprinted for the other side of the street. A bullet cracked by them and Sophia saw the stream of fire from the machine gun rake up the side of the building and through a second-floor window as they ran. Then she ducked into a shop entryway with her companions hot on her heels. Gunfire flashed in the distance down the street and a couple green tracers flashed by, and Sophia rolled onto the sidewalk, shouldered her rifle and fired back.

Sophia pushed herself forward and ran to the next entryway as more bullets popped by, a couple green tracers flashing down the street. Across the street she saw Thorn and the other team spill out of their hiding place and find cover on their side to return fire. She was starting to get worried about their situation when the burning firestorm around the city hall in front of them seemed to lift and move farther away as a string of shells burst in the air farther down the street, filling the air with smoke and shrapnel.

Seeing their chance, Sophia waved to Thorn and he and the other team rushed to her side of the street. They quickly ducked into the alley beside the town hall and found a side entrance. The door was locked when Sophia tested it, but Corporal Slaughter quickly smashed the lock with his sledgehammer. They pressed against the wall as Sergeant Cross stood to the side and knocked the door open with his rifle butt, and an instant later an Imperial grenade went off inside. Smoke poured from the doorway, and she saw Cross pull the igniter on one of his own grenades and throw it into the open door. *Three* separate explosions hammered at them from just inside, and Cross looked over at her and his mouth moved as he hefted his rifle.

Sophia nodded grimly, shouldered her weapon and followed him into the stinking smoke pouring out of the building. Hopefully that was all of the booby traps. Dim orange light guttered through the inky hallway as they entered, footsteps soft on the carpeting. They advanced a short way and found the door at the far end blown off its hinges by a blown booby trap, the light pouring into the hallway from a fire in the lobby.

Her hearing had mostly recovered and she heard someone shouting, "*Come on! Move! That won't have slowed them down for long!*" Sophia crouched beside the doorway, stuck her rifle out and tried to scan the lobby beyond. The guttering fire and the ornate furniture painted dancing shadows on the walls. Maybe she saw movement. Maybe she didn't. After a second Cross tapped her on the shoulder and she got up and carefully moved into the room. The rest of the squad fanned out behind her as they slowly swept through the lobby towards the rear of the building.

Behind her, Cross said, "Sophia, take your team and come with me. We'll sweep this floor. Slaughter, take the se-"

A familiar small, round object bounced out of a doorway on the left rear of the lobby with an evil hiss. Sophia interrupted the sergeant as she dove behind a convenient desk, "*Grenade!*" It went off a couple seconds later, shrapnel hissing through the air overhead. Climbing to one knee, she fired into the doorway as two people threw grenades back and ducked back into cover as they went off. Rolling back upright, she rushed for the doorway, crouched and pivoted into firing position. Nothing.

Just behind her Tony asked, "Want another grenade in there?"

He had followed her, apparently. Not looking up, she said, "Yeah. Do it." She heard him yank the igniter on a grenade, step around her and throw it into the hallway beyond. They both flattened themselves against the wall as it went off. Sophia was just starting to get up when another, much larger blast knocked her back to the floor. Plaster rained from the ceiling and she thought she heard the building's façade collapsing.

Carefully climbing to her feet, Sophia looked in the doorway to see a mass of debris blocking the hallway. She thought she saw moonlight shining through the smoke, and she felt the hair on the back of her neck as she looked at the damage. The Empire wasn't screwing around. That bomb had been powerful enough to kill anyone caught in that hallway when it went off.

Behind them, Cross was saying, "-ing, we'll clear this floor. Slaughter, get your guys upstairs. And for God's sake watch where you're stepping." Thorn went upstairs with the other team and Sophia shook herself, found Edward hiding behind a column and went through the rest of the ground floor with Sergeant Cross. They found a couple bloody drag marks, medical litter and some empty ammunition boxes and shell casings around the sandbagged fighting positions the Imperials had built on the ground floor. She heard a few shouts upstairs. Apparently there was a body up there.

By the time they finished the sweep and headed upstairs to join the other team Sophia's adrenaline rush had worn off and exhaustion was starting to grip at the back of her mind. She saw another bloody drag mark from the rear windows into one of the offices, sighed and went to pull guard at a window until the rest of the platoon came up. Captain Cauldwell appeared after a while as she started noticing Royal soldiers moving through the streets below, walked through their position, took a look inside the office with the dead Imperial and left.

Speaking of dead Imperials, she had killed two people earlier that night. Sophia shuddered as she realized she hadn't even thought about them since then. She'd just turned and run after Cross. She doubted the woman had even known what was happening. She'd still been firing her machine-gun as she had bayoneted her, in and out through the side, both lungs and probably her heart. She wondered if it had been painful. Looking at her still-fixed bayonet she saw it was striped black with dried blood. Shaking a little, she unclipped it from her rifle, wet her handkerchief and cleaned the blade.

Sophia was staring at her bloodstained handkerchief when she heard her father behind her, "Doing alright, Sophia?"

"Yeah..." She shook her head. He could tell she was lying, "No, not really."

He snorted and patted her on the head, "Let me rephrase that. Doing well enough to keep going?"

She looked up at him and gave him a half-smile, "Yeah. I'm okay."

He chuckled sadly, "I think we're all about there tonight. Have you heard about Falcon?"

She looked up at him in surprise, "No, I hadn't... although I haven't seen him all night I guess."

"He's dead. Lucky, random shot." He sighed heavily, "Probably didn't even feel it."

"Damn... what about Vinson?" She asked, "I saw him get hit."

Her father raised his eyebrows, "Now that man has the Devil's own luck. I've *never* seen someone get shot in the chest five times and not die. He'll probably be back with us in a couple months." He thought for a moment, "And in your squad... oh, yeah, Blake got shot in the ass. I got a laugh out of him and his buddy coming by earlier. My God was he screaming and moaning. Thought for sure he was dead."

Blake was one of the assistant machine-gunners. That explained where Jack's entire team had gone. Sophia started laughing nervously at the thought. As she recovered her father went on, "I heard you're filling Vinson's place now?"

She looked back up at him, surprised, "Yeah. I mean... you don't want to keep me there, do you?"

He snorted, "You sell yourself short, Sophie. We're out of corporals anyways, and Cross and Slaughter are both moving up." He patted her on the head again, "And speaking of being a leader, you need to go walk your line. Your friend Tony is racked out on the floor in the next room. We *are* still in the middle of a battle here."

Sophia stood up quickly, "Oh, ah, thanks, Dad. I'll go wake him up." Her father had disappeared by the time she got back from rousting Tony, and the rest of the night dragged on. Every now and then she'd hear a gunshot or a burst from a machine gun, most of them Royal. By the time the sun rose Lorenvale was back in the King's hands and dazed-looking civilians had begun emerging from hiding. The town flagpole had been blasted down in the fighting, so they draped the Royal flag from the town hall's balcony as the sun rose and called it good enough.

By that afternoon they were on the march again. To the north the Empire had broken off the battle for Grenville and begun retreating. The Army of Drakenburg was in full pursuit, them with it.

Chapter 22

Commanding General

The day was already starting to heat up as Arilin walked up the back stairs to the Kunst residence, damp from her morning fencing practice. Opening the door for her, Patricia noticed the princess's new instructor throw her a salute as he packed up to leave. He looked only slightly better-off than the girl. Smiling and saluting him back, she ushered Arilin inside and handed her a damp towel.

"Thank you." Arilin looked up at her after she wiped her face and asked, "This is a bit unusual though. Is something happening? Not to be rude, but I was expecting Becky."

Patricia smiled, "Becky's helping to set up a little morning tea. We have a special guest with us today, milady."

Arilin perked up, "Oh? Who?"

"General Chapman. I think you know who he is?" Patricia asked.

Thinking for a moment, Arilin replied, "Commander of the cavalry brigade, right?" She looked at her suspiciously, "What's the occasion?"

Patricia sighed, "I owe you an apology in advance, milady. I'm going to ask you to get involved in a little scheme Walter and I cooked up."

The princess gave her a sly smile, "Does this have something to do with that visitor you two saw last night and didn't tell Mrs. Kunst or me about?"

God, it's hard to keep this girl in the dark. Patricia chuckled and said, "Yes, actually. Can you help us out, milady?"

"Of course!" Arilin said eagerly, "What do you need?"

Patricia smiled predatorily, "I need you to drive Chapman *absolutely crazy*. Think you can do that for me?" She chuckled, reached over and ruffled the girl's hair, "Ask him a bunch of dumb questions. I *know* you hold back with me."

Clearly enjoying being petted, Arilin half-heartedly tried to fend her off, "Oh, come on," Giving her a quizzical look from under her hand, she asked, "What has he ever done to deserve this?"

Patricia replied, "Two things, really." She let the girl go and counted on her fingers, "One, he's done an awful job with the cavalry brigade. Ziggy has spent more time dealing with *them* than he has doing his actual job, and at that point we start wondering why Chapman still has *his* job." She flicked up her other finger, "And two, I assume you remember Eric Jenssen?"

The princess perked up immediately, "Yes, I do!"

Smiling apologetically, Patricia went on, "Well, he visited us last night." Arilin looked crestfallen, and she went on quickly, "Sorry, sorry, but it wasn't an appropriate or particularly pleasant occasion. He worked for me a few years back, and we're still quite good friends." Grimacing, she went on, "It seems that Chapman has been getting drunk lately and saying, well," She coughed, "Unkind things about you and me. And Walter. And your father for that matter."

The girl cocked her head, "What's he saying that's so awful?"

Patricia turned a little red, "It calls for discretion, milady."

The princess thought for a moment. Then she furrowed her eyebrows and thought some more. *Oh God, she's connecting the dots*, Patricia thought as Arilin's eyes suddenly widened and the girl blushed deeper than she had ever seen her. Stammering, she finally replied, "Y-y-yes, I suppose it does." Arilin swallowed hard and said, "I-I'll help. B-but what are we trying to get out of this?"

"I'm trying to get the man *fired*, milady. We make him angry, Walter stops by 'coincidentally' and he says something improper about us to him afterwards. Disrespect to a superior officer *and* a member of the royal family is grounds for relief." Patricia shooed her towards the stairs, "Now go take your bath. You're all sweaty."

Arilin came back down about an hour later, still looking a little red. Patricia was speaking to Vanessa and they looked up as she came down the stairs. Patricia smiled. Usually a severe dresser, Arilin had put on a delightfully cute outfit for the occasion. Seeing them as she alighted, Arilin came over and asked, "When can we expect Chapman?"

Pulling out her pocket watch and giving it a glance, Patricia replied, "In about an hour. Now go run along, milady. I think I saw Thomas around here and I'm sure he'd be happy for your company." The younger Kunst had poked his head in a few minutes earlier looking for Arilin, "I'm not going to subject you to another lecture on Steinwitz this early in the morning."

Arilin smiled and hurried off to look for the boy. Turning back to her aide, Patricia said, "Now, where was I? Oh, right. Steinwitz is a great starting point on strategy, and I'm actually very surprised you've read him." She went on sheepishly, "I actually didn't until I was a major. However. His views on tactics were colored by the technology and military practices of the day. He himself only used examples from his own lifetime or shortly before it."

Vanessa raised her eyebrows questioningly, "Like when he talks about the value of reconnaissance?"

She nodded, "Yes, actually. In his day they'd send the cavalry out, try to find the whole enemy army marching along in a mass and call it a failure if it was anything less. When armies started fighting in divisions spread across the countryside this became impossible, so Steinwitz dismissed the value of detailed reconnaissance." Vanessa nodded, and Patricia went on, "These days our ability to analyze information brought in by scouts is much greater, and we look for *specific* things that would confirm what the enemy is doing based on what we know about how they fight."

"Like their engineering equipment, milady?" Vanessa asked.

"Yes," Patricia smiled, "Even the Empire won't haul out their pontoons unless they're planning to cross a river." She thought for a moment, chuckled and went on, "*Usually.* But even Steinwitz himself would admit his view on the issue is very wrong these days."

Vanessa replied, "That *had* been troubling me, milady. I didn't like... having the entire point of the hussars just dismissed like that."

Patricia looked at her for a moment, then threw back her head and laughed. Recovering, she said, "Sorry, sorry. I just admire your, ah, cavalry spirit." She chuckled, "Reminds me of when I was younger." She went on, "Do you know what the biggest thing I got out of Clausewitz was?"

Vanessa gave her a small smile and asked, "What's that, milady?"

She snorted, "Anyone who talks about war in the ancient world as though it's still relevant in this day and age is a blowhard."

Vanessa laughed. Patricia looked up, surprised. She'd never heard the girl do that before. Smiling, her aide said, "Milady, my degree's in Elven history."

Patricia replied, "Well, have you used it yet?"

Her aide looked at the ceiling innocently, "Alaranna the Flame's admonition to the young knight is with me constantly."

Tolerate your elders when they confound you, for they are as mortal as you are. "Huh," Patricia said, "I suppose I walked right into that one. Although I would refer you to her instructions to her captains before the Battle of the Starlight Gate."

Vanessa bowed her head, "Touché, milady."

She winked, "I've read my share of the classics too. Now go get cleaned up, Chapman will be here soon."

General Chapman arrived eight minutes late to tea. Becky ushered him onto the veranda where they were sitting and disappeared inside soundlessly as Mrs. Kunst rose to greet him. Vanessa started to push her chair back, but Patricia glared at her and tapped her finger on the glass table. Swallowing hard, she stopped and looked over at Arilin. The princess just smiled politely and said, "General Chapman, thank you for finding the time to visit us."

He gave her a strained smile and replied, "Of course, milady. Anything for the royal family." He carefully slid his muscular frame into a dainty chair and smoothed the front of his white dress uniform, "I trust your brother is well?"

"Yes." Arilin replied, "Last I heard he was up around Grenville. I..." She hesitated, wringing her hands, "Worry with him so close to the front."

Chapman chuckled and leaned back in his seat, "Don't worry too much, my lady. Prince Adrian is in fine hands up there with the Field Marshal."

The princess sighed, "Thank you. I try not to think about it too much. It's just, well..." She looked at Patricia, then back at Chapman as she went on, "I've heard in the past the cuirassiers have charged and, well, with the cannons and machine-guns the Empire has these days that it has turned out badly."

"Oh, my lady?" He glared at Patricia for a moment, "When did you *ever* hear of that? You should be careful about what you believe, and from whom." He waggled his finger at her, "The heavy cavalry, milady, has saved the Army on many a day."

"Oh?" Arilin asked innocently, "I'm always hearing about the hussars from General MacMahon," She nodded politely at Patricia, "But I never hear anything about the cuirassiers. Even my brother complains about having nothing to do while the infantry is doing the fighting up front."

Chapman closed his eyes for a moment. Patricia was pretty sure he was fighting to keep from rolling them. Clearing his throat, he said, "Well, my dear, I'm sure that the Field Marshal is waiting for the correct moment to commit your brother's regiment. It's exactly the same as the knights of Maximillian's day. He would wait until the perfect moment and," he snapped his fingers, "He'd order the charge and they'd sweep the enemy before them."

"How would he know?" Arilin took a sip of tea and went on, "I mean, it's not as though he can just stand on top of a nice hill like King Maximillian would have. I suppose he'd get blown off by artillery."

Patricia tried and failed to stifle a laugh as Chapman reddened. He glared at her and she replied, "I'm sorry, I've been teaching her all about the Army and she really is just *fascinated*." She steepled her hands, leaned forward a little and went on, "Of course, war is so *complicated* these days. I have such trouble explaining things to her, although," She smiled, "Arilin seems to be learning fast. I'm sure she'll be in the regiment in no time."

"The Fourteenth?" He chuckled, "I'm sure she'll have a *thrilling* time around the Capital. Parades, balls, handsome young men in uniform..." He let it hang for a moment before going on, smiling, "It's an *ideal* finishing school for adventurous young ladies like her."

"Oh, absolutely." Patricia took a sip of tea, turned to her aide and asked, "Vanessa, I think you'd know this. What was the last charge the Valkyrie Knights made as a regiment?"

Vanessa thought for a moment and answered, "The Battle of the Dockyards?" She cocked her head and went on quizzically, "Didn't you *lead* it, milady?"

Chuckling, Patricia took a sip of tea and replied demurely, "Part of it, anyways. After we pushed in I was really just riding around directing traffic." She looked over at Chapman and went on, "I recall you came around eventually to help out."

The man gave a strained laugh, "It was my pleasure rescuing you fine ladies from a few thugs."

"I guess there were a few left when you got there... still, I appreciated it. My sword-arm was getting tired." Patricia smiled sweetly, "I haven't fought like that since the Marchlands. And I suppose we needed some help carrying all those red flags back."

"Oh, I remember that!" Arilin broke in, "I was watching when you came back to the Palace afterwards."

"Your father sure looked shocked." The lady general chuckled grimly, "Only battle I've ever fought in my dress uniform. God, were we a sight."

Arilin opened her mouth to reply, but Mrs. Kunst cut her off, "Enough of *that*, young lady." Giving the princess a stern look, she brightened and turned to Chapman, "Please, sir, you haven't even tried your tea. It's quite good."

Chapman grunted, picked up his teacup and sipped at it experimentally. Raising his eyebrow, he tuned to Mrs. Kunst and said, "My regards, madam. This is excellent."

The woman smiled and replied, "Why, thank you. Although you should give your regards to Miss Rebecca. She made it."

"The maid from earlier?" Chapman grinned, "I have half a mind to poach her from you. In fact I probably still would if this tea was *awful*."

Arilin snickered, "She's one of mine, and I don't think you'd succeed at any rate." Changing the subject abruptly, she went on, "What do you think about women serving in the heavy cavalry, by the way?"

Chapman snorted, "Considering there aren't any, milady, I think very little about it."

Patricia took a sip of tea and replied, "Perhaps you should start. I understand Arilin's going to ask her father about the matter." She nodded at Vanessa, "For Lieutenant Gable here for instance, it would benefit her career if she could serve with the cuirassiers. This isn't like the old days where you could just stay in the regiment forever." She steepled her fingers again, "I'm all for the idea, myself."

"Well I certainly wouldn't support it. Neither would the Field Marshal." Chapman rolled his eyes, "Heaven help us if you give the King an idea that would just blow up like that, milady."

"Oh?" Arilin raised an eyebrow, "Why do you think it's such a bad idea?"

"The cuirassiers, milady, are *big men* on *big horses*." Chapman cast a look around the table, "All due respect to present company, but I doubt there are any women out there who could bear the weight of our armor and fight as well as *any* of my men."

Arilin asked, "Didn't the Fourteenth Regiment wear armor in the old days? They're called the Valkyrie *Knights* for a reason."

Patricia smiled, "We did! In fact we've got old suits all over headquarters. I should take you there sometime, milady, I think you'd enjoy it."

Chapman shrugged, "Well, those were the old days. The idea didn't catch on, *clearly*." Looking at his watch, he grunted and said, "And look at the time. My apologies, your ladyships," He bowed his head slightly, "But I really must be going. I have some pressing business to attend to." He stood to leave, "Good day."

"Oh! You're sure you can't stay longer?" Arilin asked, "You've barely touched your tea... I hope we haven't inconvenienced you."

Chapman grimaced, "Of *course* not, milady, but I have a pressing appointment with General Haas and I really must be going. Good luck with your studies, I am sure Lady MacMahon is an able *teacher*."

Patricia took a sip of tea, raised an eyebrow and remarked, "Lady *General* last I checked, David."

Chapman gave her a short bow, "Of course. How thoughtless of me, *milady*. Now please excuse me." The man turned on his heel and made to walk back into the house as they heard a door open behind them. Patricia turned to see Chapman almost run into Walter as he stepped out onto the veranda. Stepping backwards quickly, the man exclaimed, "Oh! Well, hello, sir. I was just on my way to see you, actually."

"Oh, were you?" Walter checked his watch and chuckled, "That's very convenient for both of us. I may as well speak to you while I'm here." Nodding in their direction, he said, "I apologize, your ladyships, I have something quite urgent to discuss with General Chapman here. Please carry on without me." He gave Chapman a thin smile, "Come on, we can use the office."

Walter ushered Chapman inside, and she heard him say as the door closed, "So they've been drag-"

Patricia took a demure sip of tea and gave Arilin a look. Arilin looked back at her and asked, "So, do you think that was good enough?"

"I *do*, actually." Patricia smirked and looked over at her aide, "What do you think, Vanessa?"

The lieutenant shrugged, "He seemed quite angry to me, milady."

"Yes he did." Bowing her head to Lady Kunst, who was looking increasingly confused, Patricia went on, "I apologize for involving you in a little scheme of mine, ma'am. If I can do anything to make it up to you, please let me know."

The older woman laughed, "Oh, please! I've been in a few Army intrigues myself." Smiling, she leaned forward and said conspiratorially, "You know, there's a register in the kitchen. If you listen at it you can hear everything happening in the office clear as day."

Raising an eyebrow, Patricia said, "Oh, really?" She steepled her fingers slowly, "I don't suppose I could impose on your ladyship to, ah... show us this register?"

A couple minutes later Patricia and Arilin had shooed out the servants and pressed their ears to an air return in the kitchen as Vanessa looked on, failing to conceal her amusement. Patricia didn't care. Lady Kunst has been right. She could hear *everything*, and it was getting good.

"I can't believe you let those two just impose on you like that, sir. MacMahon at least has *rank* on me. Tell them you're busy with the corps." Chapman went on, "Those two... if I'd stayed any longer I would have said something sharp."

"Oh, really?" They heard a glass clink and Walter went on, "Care for a drink?"

"I need one after that. Thanks." There was a pause before Chapman said, "Aah, that's good. I don't suppose General Kunst knows you're raiding his stash?"

Walter chuckled, "I'll buy him a new bottle after we win the war."

"Good enough." Chapman laughed, "I had to tell them I had an appointment with you to get out. I was worried you were going to blow my cover there."

"You? Never. Although that would be the earliest you've ever shown up for anything, Dave." Walter remarked, "So they were driving you crazy, eh?"

They could hear the pause as Chapman took another drink, "God, yes. I'm not sure who is worse, the princess or *her ladyship*. How did you *ever* put up with that girl?"

"Which one?" Walter laughed. Arilin started, narrowed her eyes and looked across at Patricia for a moment. She supposed the princess had never thought of her as a girl before. Patricia held a finger to her lips to silence her as Walter replied, more seriously, "It took an immense amount of patience and effort on my part."

Chapman laughed, "Patience and effort, eh, sir?" He paused for a moment and went on, "You could put it *that* way, I suppose. Although," She could almost hear his sneer, "She's gotten a lot of patience and effort from a lot of men in her career."

There was a pause before Walter said, "How so? I rather think she's had a rough time of it."

"Heh, you could say that too. She's had one hell of a *rough* time." Chapman chuckled, "Every time I look at her and her two damn stars I just feel my blood boil. There's only *one* reason she's that rank and we both know it, sir." He paused, "And don't even get me started on that *child*."

Walter replied, almost too casually, "The princess? What about her?"

"She's a... well, I have no idea how you tolerate her." Chapman growled, "Really, if I had to deal with her down at the brigade I would go insane."

"I just think of it as an investment in the future of the nation." Walter said philosophically, "That girl's going to lead the Army into battle one day whether any of us like it or not."

"You think?" Chapman chuckled, "I'm sure that's what *she* thinks. I think she's a convenient royal suitor away from a one-way ticket *out* of this country. Maybe she should be practicing her *etiquette*."

"Perhaps." Walter paused for a moment. Patricia could almost see him take his monocle out and polish it absently. Eventually he went on, "But discussing the benefits of marriage alliances is not why I asked to speak to you, David. You see, a little while ago they broke up the Guards Cavalry Division to send to the front. I asked for a regiment. And last week I learned that I was getting one."

Patricia felt her eyes narrowing as Chapman brightened up, "Really? The brigade is getting upgraded? Why, *thank* you, sir!"

"Yes, but this in itself gave me a new headache." Walter chuckled, "One which you've just helped me resolve."

Chapman asked, "How so, sir?"

"We're getting the *Fourteenth Hussars*." Patricia felt her heart skip a beat. She was sure Walter was giving the man an extremely level look as he went on, "And considering you just called their former commander a *whore*, I think this makes you entirely unqualified to lead the new division. I've got your new orders right here. The Remount Service needs a new deputy chief."

There was an extremely long pause. Finally Chapman snarled, "I never thought you'd fall for someone like *her*, sir. I *assure* you, I will take this matter up with the Field Marshal. Not to mention, I am the only person *available* to take command."

"Oh, is that so?" Walter actually snickered. Patricia felt the blood draining out of her face as he went on, "There happens to be an *exceptionally* qualified major general at this headquarters ready to take command right now."

Chapman spat, "You have to be *kidding* me, sir."

"Not at all. Patricia MacMahon is getting your job. I've got her orders from the King in my pocket." Arilin was giving her a very strange look. Patricia felt the breath catch in her throat as he went on, "And if you really want to go take it up with the Field Marshal, I remind you that you've been slandering a superior officer and a member of the royal family to anyone who will listen, including me, for weeks now. Don't expect to get very far."

Chapman pleaded, "Sir, I've known you for ten years. I can't believe you're doing this to me."

"I've known Patricia for *twenty-three*. And as far as I know, and not that it *matters*," Walter went on icily, "She is as much of a maiden as Princess Arilin." Patricia felt the blood rushing back into her face, "That woman is what she is for two reasons, first that she's the old Field Marshal's daughter and second because she's actually very good at her job. *You* never could have turned the Fourteenth from a punchline into a combat unit." Walter growled, "Now get the hell out of my office."

Patricia had heard enough. Backing away from the grate, she collapsed into one of the kitchen chairs and felt the world spin around her. She distantly felt Vanessa put a hand on her shoulder and say something, ask a question. If she was feeling alright she supposed. Arilin hurried over and bent down, a concerned look on her face.

This was no time for weakness. Closing her eyes for a moment, Patricia pinched the bridge of her nose and took a couple deep breaths. Gradually the fog cleared. She heard her aide, "...am? Ma'am? Are you okay?" Vanessa asked Arilin, "Milady, what did you hear that, well...?"

Patricia reached up and squeezed her aide's hand, "I'm perfectly alright, Vanessa. Thank you, though." The two girls relaxed and stepped back a little as she went on, "I was just a little overwhelmed for a moment, I'm sorry. When you're both older I'm sure you'll understand." She smiled at the princess, "Would you like to tell her, or should I?"

Arilin beamed, "So, the Fourteenth is coming to join us here."

"Oh!" Vanessa brightened instantly, "That's great!"

"And..." Arilin went on slyly, "Patricia's getting command of the brigade. Well, the *division* now."

"Oh..." Vanessa trailed off and gave Patricia a questioning look, "That's wonderful news... but you don't look that happy, ma'am."

She shook her head, "I just felt five thousand troopers' worth of responsibility land on my shoulders." She laughed sadly and looked up at the two girls, "I thought I was ready for it, but, well... it's still a lot to take on out of the blue." She looked at Arilin and went on, "I was getting pretty used to our pleasant life, milady."

The princess nodded and said, "Thank you for everything, milady."

Snorting, Patricia shook her head and stood. Patting the girl on the shoulder, she said, "Oh, I'm not nearly through with you yet, milady. Up to now I've been teaching you theory. Now I can teach you *practice*." She chuckled, "At least until your father stops me."

"Really?" Arilin bowed her head graciously, "I look forward to it."

Turning to her aide, Patricia said, "Now, Vanessa. So far you've worked for me when I've been doing rather... sedate jobs. My routine is about to get much more hectic, and with it yours. I will be relying on you more than ever from now on."

Vanessa bowed her head, "My pleasure, milady. I will do my best."

Patricia nodded, "See that your best is good enough." She thought for a moment, then went on, "Now, I need my service uniform prepared immediately and our horses saddled. *We*," she looked around at her two companions, "Are riding out of here in half an hour to take charge of the division. I'll make the final arrangements with General Haas."

Vanessa nodded and rushed off, and Arilin looked down at her dress and observed, "I suppose I will need to change clothes."

Laughing, Patricia ruffled the girl's hair, "You suppose right, milady. They'll be angry enough about this without you showing up dressed for tea. Now run along and change."

The girl turned and disappeared into the hallway, calling for Becky. In the brief moment she had, before she went to go see Walter and get ready to take on the biggest challenge of her life, Patricia stretched her arms over her head and absently looked at the white-painted ceiling.

Patricia MacMahon, Commanding General, she thought. She liked it.

Chapter 23

Masked Intentions

"Commanding general!" Chairs dragged on the carpeting as their occupants pushed them back and stood. Arilin wouldn't call what the dozen or so colonels in the room were doing as standing at attention, but they were on their feet at least. She smiled unconsciously as she saw Eric in the back, and he smiled and gave her a gentle nod. He looked genuinely happy at this turn of events.

Vanessa, who had walked in ahead of them and made the announcement, pulled out a chair at the head of the table for Patricia. The lady general sat, pushed herself in and folded her hands on the table in front of her. Looking at the standing men in front of her, she said, "Good afternoon, gentlemen. Please take your seats."

Arilin slid into a convenient seat along the wall as the officers slowly sat down, most of them with wary looks at Patricia. It was as though they expected her to pull out a pistol and start shooting, something which now that Arilin thought about it wasn't too far out of the question. Near the head of the table one thin, intense-looking colonel in particular gave Patricia a hateful glare. The men were still sliding their chairs back in when he spat, "I don't suppose that you would care to tell us the meaning of this, *milady*?"

Patricia gave him a flat look back and replied, "Certainly. What do you do around here, Colonel, ah... Schrader?"

The man looked down at his double-breasted lancer's jacket quizzically before he raised an eyebrow and replied, "Command the Twentieth Lancer Regiment?"

Patricia leaned back in her chair and steepled her fingers in front of her chest before she said, "And I don't suppose you would know when your regiment was supposed to arrive here in Wolf Rock, Schrader?" The man drew back a little and started to say something, and she cut him off, "*Five days ago.* You only arrived last night. If I'd pulled a stunt like that in the last war, colonel, General Kellerman would probably have had me *shot.*"

Schrader gave her a steely look, "There's not much I can do about the train schedule, milady." He smiled thinly and looked around the room, "I'd think that's the Rail Service's problem, not ours." There were a few nervous laughs. The tension in the room dissipated a little as men leaned forward in their seats. Arilin supposed that they must have thought

Schrader had gotten in a telling blow.

Patricia snorted contemptuously and replied, "Oh, colonel, but it is *your* problem. Or how do you intend to explain the fact that your second squadron made a train wait on a siding at Gyrburg for twelve hours before they could be bothered to show up?" She pulled a notebook out of a pocket, looked through it for a moment and went on, "Or that your third squadron outright *missed movement* the next day and the Rail Service had to reroute everything and move them on two days late on a train that should have been carrying somebody else?"

The colonel growled back at her, "Milady, we never got orders from *corps* until too late."

Narrowing her eyes, Patricia replied, "No, you never got orders from *brigade*, who lied to you about it afterwards. And that is why *you* are still in command and Chapman is not." She swept an icy gaze around the room, "I don't suppose anyone else wants to know the *meaning* of all this?"

Schrader deflated a little and leaned back in his seat with a scowl as the atmosphere in the room darkened, and Arilin felt a chill work its way up the back of her neck. She had never seen Patricia like this, so cold and merciless. She hardly seemed to be the same warm, friendly woman she'd come to know so well over the last couple months. Arilin looked around the room, at the angry men lined up against Patricia, and the realization hit her. No wonder the news she was taking command had hit her like that. Patricia must have known she was walking into an ugly situation.

Arilin realized she'd been thinking about the whole thing all wrong. She'd thought that Walter had been doing Patricia, his old friend and maybe new love interest a favor by helping her out with her stalled career. And maybe he had. It had all seemed very romantic to her. But there was another layer to it, now that she thought about it probably a more important layer. *General Haas* had sent *General MacMahon* down to fix a broken unit, get it ready for combat and lead it onto the battlefield in a matter of days. Arilin felt her stomach ball up at the thought. Put that way, it wasn't much of a favor.

Patricia smiled coldly, "Good. Now, let's begin properly." She paused, crossed her legs and seemed to soften a little before she went on, "As we just discussed, General Haas saw fit today to relieve General Chapman and send me down to take over. I don't recall having served with any of you besides Eric back there before," She nodded at him and he smiled and nodded back, "So our previous conversation *aside* I do not have any preconceived notions about any of you."

She went on, "To introduce myself, I am Patricia MacMahon. I was commissioned into the Army in 1904 and I've seen combat at Dragon's Jaw Fortress, during the Marchlands War, the Jihadist War and Red December. I commanded First Squadron of the Third Hussars against the jihadists and then the Fourteenth Hussars against the communists." She chuckled a little humorlessly, "And I'd love to spend an hour we don't have telling you all about my command philosophy, but we have a war to fight. I will be conducting inspections of your squadrons throughout the afternoon, starting at..." She looked at her watch, "Fifteen hundred. I trust that will be enough time to get your troopers in order."

Watches were produced and eyebrows raised. A murmur went around the room. Patricia snorted and said, "Please. I'm not expecting some stage-managed inspection where you show me how perfect your unit is. I've been around real cavalry troops before and I know what they look like." She smiled and went on, "I also have some good news, I suppose. The Fourteenth Regiment is going to join us here shortly, and the brigade is being upgraded to a division. With that I expect nothing but the most gallant conduct from your men."

The other full colonel at the table, a rotund, mustachioed man whose name tag read, 'Morris', finally spoke up, "Of course, my lady. I would consider anything else a stain on the honor of the regiment."

She nodded, "Thank you, colonel." Patricia swung her gaze further down the table, to where Arilin could see a group of officers that weren't wearing the distinctive uniforms of the lancers or the cuirassiers. She supposed that was probably the brigade staff, at least the senior officers on it. "Gentlemen of the staff, many of General Chapman's... shortcomings could be seen as being actually your fault. I don't personally see it that way. For the time being you have my full confidence." Someone audibly sighed in relief as she went on, "General Haas has told me he will be sending down someone to take over as chief of staff today, given that we are a division now. I trust that he will have your full cooperation."

Smiling, Patricia leaned back in her chair, "Any questions, gentlemen?" Murmurs and shaken heads went around the room, and she nodded and said, "Very well. Dismissed."

The assembled men stood and saluted. Patricia stood, saluted back, and the group quickly filed out of the room. Eric exchanged nods with her and Arilin, but even he seemed to be in a rush to get out. As the last of the men filed out Arilin stood and walked over to where the general stood at the head of the table, saying, "Wow. I... I've never seen you like that, milady."

Patricia sighed, pinched the bridge of her nose and gave the princess a sidelong look, "You think I pulled it off?"

"Yes, absolutely!" Arilin exclaimed, "You were so, ah..."

"Commanding?" Patricia finished for her. She snorted and went on, "You don't call me 'milady' that much, so I know it worked on *you*."

Arilin felt herself blush, "Ah, yes, I was just surprised, milady." Catching sight of Vanessa, white as a sheet and clearly trying to disappear into the back wall, she laughed nervously and went on, "And I don't think *she* has either."

Turning quickly, Patricia saw her aide and raised her eyebrows in surprise. After a moment she smiled warmly and said, "It's okay, Vanessa. I'm not angry at *you*. In fact I'm not really angry at *them*." She chuckled, "Maybe Schrader a little. But," She paused, "That wasn't a crowd that was going to respond to compassionate leadership, if you get my meaning."

Vanessa nodded and said, "Y-yes, milady, I understand."

Checking her watch, Patricia said, "We have a little time before fifteen hundred rolls around. Would you like to get some lunch, milady?"

Arilin smiled, "Of course!" She thought for a moment and said, "Lady Kunst was telling me about the Red Table Café earlier, I think it's around here somewhere."

"I think I saw it on the ride over here." Patricia asked, "Shall we walk over, milady?"

Arilin chuckled, "I thought riding horses over here was a little dramatic in the first place."

Patricia smiled, "You only get one chance to make a first impression. Now let's go."

As the three women walked down the long flight of steps in front of the Fifth Cavalry Brigade's headquarters, which the Ninth Brigade had taken over lately, Arilin ventured, "Milady, I'd been meaning to ask you... what is the extra jacket for?"

Patricia looked down at herself and snorted. She and Vanessa were both wearing what Arilin gathered was the Fourteenth Regiment's service uniform, a close-fitting, dove-gray shell jacket with a standing collar showing their ranks over the regimental pink and white, dark red riding breeches and black cavalry boots. And despite the heat they both had a second jacket slung over their left shoulders on a broad strap that ran across their chests.

Patricia pulled at hers and asked, "The pelisse?" Arilin nodded and she went on, smiling, "For when it gets cold, of course!"

Vanessa chimed in, "Isn't it supposed to protect your left arm against sword strikes, milady?"

The lady general shook her head, "Not against a dragoon it won't." She chuckled, "Really, I think it's just because it looks good."

Arilin thought that it did look rather dashing. The trio walked out the headquarters' front gate and turned onto the sidewalk, and Arilin was about to make another comment when she spied two figures on horseback coming down the tree-lined street from the direction of the central fortress. One of them was clearly wearing a pelisse. The two figures turned to each other for a moment in conversation before the hussar kicked her horse and started to canter down the street at them.

Patricia gave her aide a sidelong look, "You don't suppose...?"

Vanessa nervously straightened her uniform jacket, "Yes, milady, I think that's the colonel."

The hussar pulled her horse up next to them with a clatter of hooves on the cobblestones, leapt off and saluted. Arilin saw she was a little shorter than Patricia, with chestnut hair and an open, friendly face. Smiling broadly, she said, "Milady! Colonel Bennett with the Fourteenth Hussars, reporting for duty!"

Patricia gave her a wry smile and saluted back, "Good to see you, Mina."

They both dropped their salutes and Mina sprang forward to embrace her, saying, "It's so good to see you again, milady! You should come by more often, we really all miss you."

Patricia chuckled and patted her on the back, "Sorry, sorry, I've been remiss. Also, ah, there's someone here I'd like to introduce to you." Mina looked over at Arilin and her eyes widened as Patricia went on drily, "Although she really needs no introduction."

"Oh my!" Untangling herself from Patricia, Mina turned to Arilin and said, "Ah, Princess, how thoughtless of me. You've grown since I saw you last!"

"A little." Arilin felt herself redden as Mina stepped forward and wrapped her arms around her, "Thanks, ah, I guess..."

Mina pulled away and beamed at her, "I'm sure your father is *very* proud of you. And I know Prince Adrian brags about you to anyone who will listen." She chuckled, "He told me you almost beat him with a sword before he headed out."

Arilin felt her face get very hot as she stammered, "Ah... he... he was going easy on me."

"Not the way he told it, milady!" Turning to the last of their group, she coughed, seemed to mentally straighten herself out and said, "Vanessa, I trust you've been taking good care of General MacMahon?"

The lieutenant nodded, "Yes, ma'am."

Patricia added, "Lieutenant Gable has been doing an excellent job, Mina. I'm honestly dreading the day I have to send her back to the regiment."

"Oh? I'm happy to hear it." Mina reached out and lightly patted Vanessa on the shoulder, "Good work, lieutenant."

The younger woman stiffened a little at the contact, but she quickly relaxed and said, "Ah, thank you, ma'am." Thinking about it, Arilin realized she had never seen Patricia actually touch her aide. She'd seen the other way around when Vanessa was helping her with her clothing, but that was different. *Maybe she doesn't like being touched? No wonder she had problems at the regiment,* Arilin thought.

Her thoughts were interrupted by a clatter of hooves as Mina's companion rode up. As he dismounted Arilin saw that he was a tall, middle-aged colonel wearing the uniform of an artilleryman. She'd seen him around headquarters a few times late at night. Giving them a wry smile under his impressive moustache, he saluted and said, "General MacMahon, I presume? I can see you've already met my companion."

Patricia saluted back, "Colonel Frost? I can see Walter was serious about sending me somebody."

"Thank you, milady. I'll do what I can." Frost chuckled, "Although hearing you call him 'Walter' is a little unusual for me. Truth be told we've all been dreading you leaving, he's been *so* much easier to work with these last couple months."

"Oh, really?" Arilin could swear she saw Patricia blush. The woman quickly composed herself and went on, "We're going to lunch, if you two would care to join us?"

Mina nodded enthusiastically, "Of course, milady!"

Frost shook his head, "I hope it won't hurt you if I decline, milady. General Reinhardt was telling me tales about the staff here and I feel I have my work cut out for me."

Patricia nodded, "Of course. Thank you, ah...?"

Frost bowed his head slightly, "Joseph, milady. Good day." Giving Arilin a shallow bow, collected the horses' reins and walked past them to the brigade headquarters, handing the animals off to a pair of soldiers that came out to greet him.

The four of them turned and walked to find the Red Table Café, Mina excitedly catching up with Patricia as they went. Patricia warmed quickly, and as they sat down to eat they were talking like old friends. Looking between the two of them, Arilin leaned over to Vanessa and asked quietly, "What's the story between those two?"

Vanessa whispered back, "Lady MacMahon was a senior to Bennett at the Academy, milady."

"Oh?" *That explains a few things*, Arilin thought as she replied, "I can see that."

The Red Table had excellent food, and they quickly finished off lunch. Mina said her goodbyes and left to attend to her regiment, which was due to start arriving at Wolf Rock within the hour. Patricia leaned back in her seat, stretched her arms over her head and remarked, "That was very good." Looking at Arilin, she asked, "So, milady, who do you think we should inspect first?"

The princess thought for a moment, "Hm. Do you think Eric would get angry if we...?"

"Oh?" Patricia raised an eyebrow, "I like the way you think, Arilin. Let's get going."

Wolf Rock Fortress was laid out in two concentric rings. The old Inner Fortress, bounded by massive walls studded with gun emplacements, contained the fortress town itself and V Corps' headquarters and administrative facilities. As the range and deadliness of artillery had increased the Royal Engineers had built a ring of satellite forts around the central bastion, known as the Outer Fortress, to prevent the fortress from being easily contained by threatening Imperial troops. Most of the Outer Fortress had originally been open farmland, but as the Royal Army required ever more space to meet the demands of training and preparing for modern war and the front line with the Empire had receded far to the east the fortress' military facilities had expanded to fill the area and the fortress town had overflowed the walls with them.

It was about a fifteen-minute ride through a patchwork of scenic suburbs before they came upon the Eighth Cuirassiers' billets. Someone had hung a painted board over the sign for whatever V Corps' cavalry unit occupied the place in peacetime proclaiming the new unit in occupation. The cuirassiers had moved into a sprawling complex of barracks blocks, stables and parade fields, all clearly purpose-built to house a cavalry regiment.

One of the troopers on guard duty mounted his horse and galloped off into the complex as they rode up, and Patricia and Arilin made small talk with the sergeant of the guard for a few minutes until Colonel Morris cantered up. A big man on a bigger horse, he looked down on the three of them, saluted and said, "Your ladyships! Pleased to see you this afternoon."

Arilin bowed her head as Patricia saluted him back and said, "You as well, colonel! Are your men ready?"

Morris guffawed and said, "As ready as they're going to be with this much time! Who do you want to see first, milady?"

"Well," Patricia said, ticking off on her fingers, "I'd like to see your Second Squadron's stables, your First Squadron's barracks, your Third Squadron's supply storehouse and your Horse Artillery battery's guns. In that order." She smiled warmly, "Can you do that for me?"

"Oh ho!" Morris exclaimed, "I think we can make that happen, milady. Let's go."

The stables were mostly deserted as they rode up. Arilin saw a few troopers in white fatigues moving around purposefully, and someone she pegged as an officer ducked inside as they approached. Eric appeared on horseback from the direction of his squadron's barracks block, which they could see was swarming with activity. He greeted them cheerily, dismounted with them and led them inside.

Arilin smelled horses and fresh straw as they walked into the dim building. It actually smelled very pleasant. Smiling, she turned to Eric and remarked, "I can see you've cleaned recently."

He chuckled, "Twice a day, and we went through it just before you arrived, milady."

Patricia asked, "Any problems with the horses in the last week?"

Eric sighed, "We had a case of laminitis coming off the train. Doc is working on it. He's over there, actually."

The officer that had been walking through the stables ahead of them heard himself being mentioned and came over. Eric introduced him as the squadron veterinarian, and after Patricia posed the question again he replied, "Well, milady, we've got one horse with laminitis that we should keep off of train cars for a while, so he's out of the fight. And that moron Alto put a foot through his stall this morning and cut himself to hell. I've got it bandaged and I'm hoping he'll heal adequately."

Eric raised an eyebrow, "Isn't this the third time that horse has beat himself up?"

The vet chuckled, "Fourth actually. At least he seems like a tough horse. He's been alright so far."

Patricia asked, "How are you doing on manning? Have enough mounts for your troopers?"

Eric shrugged, "So far, yes, barely. We're actually low on horses, but we're also low on troopers so it worked out for us."

Raising an eyebrow, Patricia asked, "How are you standing on manning?"

"About eighty pecent." Eric said, "We're at three hundred thirty-two sabers last I checked."

Patricia snorted, "I've taken worse to war. You two know the Fourteenth is *supposed* to have three squadrons, right?"

The cavalry soldiers chuckled. Arilin leaned over to Vanessa and asked, "Did I miss something?"

Vanessa explained, "We never have enough people, milady, so we only bother manning two squadrons."

"Oh." Arilin said. *Kind of a grim joke,* she thought. They walked through the stables for a few more minutes before Patricia was satisfied, then they mounted up and, saying their goodbyes to Eric, rode over to First Squadron's barracks.

Arilin immediately noticed something as they approached. It didn't seem *wrong* so much as it seemed *different*, which was practically the same thing when it came to the military. Eric's troopers had been milling around their barracks in their dark gray service jackets and the few that she'd seen in armor had camouflaged their breastplates with dull field covers. The troopers here were all in white jackets and steel armor, glinting in the sunlight as they went about getting ready for inspection.

Turning to her companion, Arilin asked, "Why are they all in dress uniforms?" She paused and went on, "It's like we were back in the Capital."

Patricia laughed, "My thoughts exactly, milady." Turning to Colonel Morris, she went on, "I don't suppose you could fill us in on that, colonel?"

The man harrumphed and said, "Indeed I can, milady. In fact I had words with young Janssen just before you arrived. He was quite insistent that you would want to see his men prepared for combat." Morris shrugged, "All I know, milady, is that if General Chapman was in your place he would be extremely displeased with him."

"I can imagine." Patricia went on, "Eric used to work for me and he has a very good idea of what I like. We should not prepare for the victory parade before we've won the war."

"Certainly, milady," Morris replied noncommittally.

Patricia sighed and shook her head. Arilin saw her dispirited expression and felt the pieces of the situation lock into place in her head, like gears meshing together. Chapman wouldn't have been able to lead the brigade unless he'd had a *constituency*. And Colonel Morris had deliberately kept doing things Chapman's way despite having been told otherwise. Arilin grit her teeth. She'd been taken in by Morris' polite manner and Patricia had clearly been as well. The man must have thought he had more to gain by undermining his new commander than by helping her. It was almost as though he expected her to be gone soon and his work to undermine her would be rewarded by the new regime.

But why would Patricia be gone soon? The King himself had signed the orders. Arilin's eyes narrowed as another gear locked into place in her mind. *The King himself had signed the orders.* Did Field Marshal White even *know* about this? He had shuffled Patricia off into obscurity in the first place, there was no way he would have supported giving her a command. And yet her father was perfectly okay with it for some reason. Arilin felt her head spin as she looked at her companions, Patricia stony-faced, Morris inscrutable, Vanessa blank as usual.

Her father, the King, was in a power struggle with Field Marshal White. And she felt her heart warm knowing that Walter and Patricia were on her father's side – on *her* side – she felt an icy hand clench around it a moment later. Walter had really stuck his neck out for Patricia, and she was trying to deal with a rebellious unit and subordinates she couldn't necessarily trust. She must have felt like she was drowning. And the King was a long way away. Maybe far enough away for White to have his revenge without interference.

Not to mention this would harm the division. Inhaling sharply, Arilin steeled her nerves and said, "Colonel Morris, sir, I have a question for you."

He looked over at her, surprised, "Oh? Please, milady."

They arrived outside the barracks, cuirassiers running forward to take their horses. Dismounting, Arilin looked up at the big colonel and said, "If Eric told you that Pa-, er, General MacMahon," She nodded at her respectfully, "Would want things a certain way, *why did you ignore him?*"

Morris looked nonplussed, "Milady, Janssen has been in charge of a squadron in this regiment for a couple of months. I saw no reason to adopt his suggestion."

"*No reason?*" Patricia looked over at her, shock spreading over her face at her tone, "I would think there would be a great deal of *reason* to do so, given Eric has served with her before and you have not."

Morris snorted contemptuously and looked over at Patricia, saying, "The princess seems quite... *agitated*, milady. Could you calm her, perhaps?"

Patricia gave her a hard look. Arilin glared back, and gradually realization spread over Patricia's face. Smiling slyly, she turned back to Morris and said, "I see no reason to. I'm curious myself. Milady," She held up a hand to stop the approaching squadron staff out of earshot and nodded politely to Arilin, "Please continue."

Arilin gave Morris a vicious look, "I will have you know that General MacMahon enjoys the King's, and General Haas', full confidence. My father will *not* be pleased if he learns there is some faction in the Army that believes his orders can be *avoided*."

Morris gave her a very level look in return, "Certainly, milady. I understand."

"Very well," Arilin's face suddenly brightened as she smiled sweetly, "I don't suppose there's any practice swords around here? If neither of you mind," She bowed her head respectfully, "I'd like to see a little of your soldiers' swordsmanship."

Patricia covered her mouth, shaking with barely-contained laughter, "Oh, milady, I'm sure we can find something." She smiled and looked across at Morris, "Make sure your men have their pads on. Milady is really quite dangerous."

Morris narrowed his eyes and grunted, "I'll say." Gesturing to the barracks, he went on, "Ladies first."

About an hour later Arilin pulled off her fencing mask and collapsed onto a stool some helpful cuirassier had set out for her. Her next opponent was already taking a few warm-up swings with his sword. She thought, *My God, is there no end to these guys?* Looking around at the circle of spectators, she smiled grimly, *There is, but I'm going to be done by the time I reach it.*

Someone helpfully handed her a damp towel, and she sighed as she wiped the sweat from her face. The cold cloth revived her a little, and she looked up to see her savior. Patricia smiled down at her, a rather irritable-looking Colonel Morris beside her. The lady general asked, "So, milady, what do you think of the regiment's swordsmanship?"

Arilin shook her head dazedly, "I'm at fifteen wins and five losses so far. They're pretty good."

"Oh?" Patricia asked, "Who's beaten you?"

Arilin tried to think for a moment, "Eric, Lieutenant Galen, Major Levine, Sergeant Costanzo and, uh... Private Burbank, I think?"

Morris grunted, "That's four of my best swordsmen. I'll need to look into this Burbank fellow."

Arilin gestured to her practice sword, a light thrusting weapon, "He used one of these. Maybe he's got experience as a duelist?"

Morris opined, "Hardly the first time someone joined the Army to get away from their past. In any event, ma'am, I now have a great deal of work to do."

Patricia nodded graciously, "Of course, colonel. We'll be on our way."

They extricated themselves from the regiment without further incident. Vanessa, who had disappeared from Patricia's side during all this, galloped up from the direction of the fortress as they rode out the front gate with a bundle under her arm. Sitting on her horse in her sweat-soaked clothes, Arilin was delighted as Vanessa revealed that she'd ridden all the way back to the Kunst house and gotten her some clean clothing.

As they were riding to the lancers' billets Patricia unexpectedly said, "Thank you, milady."

Arilin looked over at her, "For what?" She thought for a second and went on, "Helping you out with Colonel Morris?"

The lady general chuckled, "Yes, actually. I was trying to figure out how I was going to deal with him, and you just shut him down completely. He was like a different person afterwards." She looked over at her and smiled, "It seems I've underestimated you *and* your father, milady."

Arilin raised an eyebrow, "How so?"

"Well." Patricia paused for a moment, then went on, "Remember when you first came to my office and asked to accompany the Army?" It seemed like a lifetime ago now that she thought about it. Arilin nodded and Patricia went on, "I went and spoke to the King later that night. At the time I didn't quite believe he'd been serious with you in the first place. Him telling you to go find someone, well..." She snorted, "I thought he might have been trying to tell you 'no' and being nice about it. In all honesty I expected him to reject me out of hand. I sounded crazy to *myself*."

The princess laughed, "I know *I* sounded crazy asking you."

"He heard me out, thought about it for about a minute and told me to go ahead. I asked him why he was alright with it and he told me something that I only really understood just now." She paused, thought for a moment and went on, "He said he wanted to have more of a Royal presence forward, but that as things stood he felt he was obligated to the Field Marshal to not openly interfere with his command of the Army."

"Openly?" Arilin wondered, "That explains why he's been willing to go behind White's back. But why would he feel obligated? Now that I think about it he *should* be out here."

Patricia sighed, "I think those two have some kind of deal from the Coup. White was in command of the Guards Corps at the time and your father wouldn't have been able to move against *his* father without White's support. Next thing you know he was a Field Marshal, Daddy was retiring and he stepped right into his place."

"Daddy?" Arilin asked sardonically.

Patricia reddened, "Forget I said that. But, ah, I think the King has started to lose confidence in White recently. At the time he told me that Prince Adrian was going to be busy with his regiment and under White's thumb anyways, but you would have a lower profile and could still represent him." She shook her head, "I didn't really understand him at the time, but there you were just now making sure one of my subordinates knows who *actually* owns the Army. I don't think he would have done it better himself."

Arilin blushed, "Thank you."

Patricia asked, "Feel it, milady?"

Raising her eyebrows questioningly, Arilin replied, "What do you mean?"

Smiling slyly, Patricia said, "All that responsibility."

Something heavy and oppressive settled onto her, hanging on the back of her shoulders like a cold weight. Shivering despite the warmth, Arilin said, "Yes... I think I do."

Patricia nodded, "Good. Now let's go see how the lancers are doing. And we'll need to go check on the Fourteenth after them and see how they're settling in." She thought, then exclaimed, "Oh! And Walter's having a council of war tonight. Apparently the Empire's retreating from Grenville and we need to work out our plans going forward." She looked over at Arilin, "It's going to be a late night, milady. I trust you'll make it through it?"

Arilin nodded and smiled, "I'll do my best, ma'am."

"See that it's good enough, milady." Patricia spurred her horse and galloped ahead, and Arilin kicked hers after her.

Chapter 24

An Eventful Patrol

Sophia dropped her pack and gratefully sank down next to it in the long grass, leaning back against the rough canvas. Her bruised feet throbbed painfully against the tight leather of her boots as the weight came off. Her heels felt like someone was driving spikes into them. Her knees were jelly and her thighs were a mass of knotted pain. Her shoulders seared as she moved them experimentally where her pack's straps had left bloody bruises over the weeks of marching.

Had it really been weeks? Sophia shook her head gingerly and tried to think. They had marched out of Lorenvale ten, no... eleven days ago. So not weeks then. The endless days of walking down dusty Eastern roads under a heavy pack had all blurred together into a tangled mass in her mind, and she struggled for a moment to remember the details.

At first they had expected dragoons to be waiting for them in every village and stand of trees and they had advanced cautiously, sending soldiers out to clear every ambush site. It was exhausting work for nothing. Sophia saw a few riders on distant hills, but that was as close as the Imperials seemed to want to get. After the first couple days of marching a hussar troop had cantered past and taken over clearing the road for them, and the pace had increased. Since then they would sometimes hear gunshots in the distance or have to help a wounded trooper coming back down the road, but that was it. For the last few days all the distant horsemen she'd seen had been wearing gray jackets.

The countryside got rougher the farther they marched as the white spires of the Dragonspine Mountains rose to the south, sending ridges out to plow up the eastern plains. For the last couple of days they had been marching down, over and up endlessly, crossing from one valley full of tiny farming villages to the next by dirt tracks over wooded ridges. More than once they had been forced off the road by shepherds herding their sheep out of hidden pastures high in the mountains now that the Empire had passed on.

The sheep were about the only animals left in the country. Aside from a few broken-down horses every stable and pasture Sophia had seen was empty. The Imperial Army was one huge system of reserves, and from what the few talkative locals had said a lot of dragoons seemed to be cowboys in civilian life. They had no problem rustling cattle and stealing horses. Sometimes an Imperial officer would dignify the process with worthless Marchlands army scrip. One farmer had waved what looked like a couple of thousand marks at her and sarcastically asked if she wanted any.

The Imperials were digging in up ahead, at least according to Lieutenant Thorn. He'd told the platoon the night before that they were preparing to defend a particularly large spur coming off the mountains called Fire Ridge. He'd pointed it out on the map while he did it, and she could see why they would want to hold onto it. Fire Ridge was almost a mountain range to itself, a sweeping offshoot of the Dragonspine Mountains that jutted a hundred kilometers to the north. Beyond it lay the Moon River, the Marchlands and the Empire itself.

Sophia had been looking into the distance for Fire Ridge all day, but the low clouds and misting rain had made the exercise pointless. From where the company was sitting now, halfway down yet another ridge, she could barely see the valley floor in front of them through the trees. The overcast sky was growing darker by the minute as night fell, and she thought that soon she'd be lucky to see the hand in front of her face.

Speaking of hands in front of faces, she had a job to do. Sophia shook her head, gripped her rifle and wearily climbed to her feet, ignoring the twinges of pain as her muscles protested. Tony looked up at her tiredly as she walked over, sighed and said, "You're about to tell me to face out and pull security, right?"

Sophia would have chuckled if she'd had more energy. She snorted instead, "Yeah, I am."

Tony groaned, rolled over and made a show of propping his rifle across his pack. Turning his head to look at her, he said, "There. Happy now?"

Sophia snorted again, "Yeah. I am. Just don't fall asleep," she added.

Tony chuckled, "I'm good. Tell me when the food's coming."

"Sure thing." Sophia gave him a weak smile and went to go find Edward, who had flopped down somewhere on the other side of the road. The lanky man was half-asleep when she found him lying behind his pack, and she gently prodded him on the shoulder.

Edward jerked when she touched him, rolled to his knees and violently shook himself. Looking over at her quickly, he said, "I was out there, wasn't I?" He shook his head sheepishly, "And I thought the ferry was bad. Thanks, Rose. I'll stay awake. Er..." He paused and looked at her for a moment.

Sophia cracked a half smile, "I'll tell you when they bring the food up. I'm starving myself." She furrowed her eyebrows for a second as she thought of something, "Speaking of, have you seen Corporal Slaughter recently?"

Their new squad leader had started out in the morning with an obvious limp and now that she thought about it Sophia hadn't seen him for hours. Edward cocked his head and replied, "I think he said something about going to see the medics a while ago. He didn't tell you?"

Sophia shook her head, "No, he didn't." She thought for a moment as a ball of ice congealed in her stomach, "But if he fell out, ah... who's in charge of the squad now?"

Edward snickered, "Good question. I think *you* probably are."

The ball of ice sank, "That... that was what I was worried about."

"I guess Mulligan could try to claim seniority, but you'd have to wake him up first." He looked up at her and smiled, "Which you should probably go do, Acting Provisional Candidate Corporal Rose."

Sophia rolled her eyes, "Shut up, Ed. And stay awake yourself."

"Will do." Edward rolled onto his stomach and gave her a sarcastic wave as she turned to go find the rest of the squad and get them into some semblance of order. The two men in what was left of the 'B' rifle team, which Slaughter had been leading along with the rest of the squad since Lorenvale, didn't give her a whole lot of new information beyond confirming that he had disappeared to go see the medics around noon.

Of the two, Jeremy Higgins was only a couple years older than she was. She'd seen him around her school a few times in years past, although she supposed he had graduated recently. He greeted the news that she was taking over the squad with a shrug and went back to watching for the enemy, casting a nervous look at his partner while he was at it. Robert Hargrave had kids nearly as old as she was. She wasn't quite sure how the old man had kept up with the march so far or what had caused him to join the Reserves at his age, but she was pretty sure he was the reason Jeremy was awake and alert instead of sleeping like everyone else. Hargrave chuckled, lit his pipe and started winding up for what she suspected was a long winded story, so she quickly excused herself and went to find the machine gunners.

Sophia saw a standing figure through the trees a little way off and her heart sank a little as she recognized Lieutenant Thorn. He seemed to be looking down at someone, and by the set of his shoulders he was not pleased. She was pretty sure she knew what he was angry about as she approached and he turned to face her.

"Rose," he started, "You're Mulligan's friend. I don't suppose you could tell me *how* exactly he is capable of doing this?" He gestured angrily at the two soldiers sprawled on the ground at his feet.

Sophia walked closer to see Jack and his assistant gunner fast asleep, their machine gun neatly set between them. Jack was even snoring softly. Crouching, she looked up at Thorn and ventured, "I really don't know, sir." She smiled mischievously, "But watch this."

Sophia poked Jack, hard. No response. She shook his shoulder. He may as well have been dead. Then she reached over to touch his machine gun and Jack suddenly rolled over, snapped his eyes open and glared at her, "No way, Sophie." He looked past her to see Thorn, "Oh, hi, sir."

"Hi," Thorn said, turning to her, "Now, Rose, get this gun set up at the head of the column." He looked at his watch nervously and went on, "Caldwell wants to see all the officers in five minutes and he'll *kill* me if I'm late."

The lieutenant turned to leave and Sophia asked quickly, "Sir, am I in charge of the squad now?"

Thorn shrugged, "Until Slaughter fixes himself or I find someone else to fill the slot, yes."

Jack, standing, looked between the two of them in shock, "Sir, really?" He puffed his chest out, "You know I'm senior, sir."

Thorn rolled his eyes, "And yet I have never found Miss Rose asleep on duty. Now excuse me."

He walked away shaking his head, and Sophia smirked at Jack, "You heard the man."

Jack glared at her for a moment before sighing, prodding his companion and saying, "Come on, Kelly, boss lady says we need to move." Sophia rolled her eyes and left them to it.

The two men lugged the machine gun over to near where Sophia had set her pack down, unfolded the heavy tripod and quickly had the weapon loaded and sighted in down the road. As the evening darkened into night Sergeant Cross came around and told her to start sending people back for food. She sent Jack and his companion to go eat first, setting herself behind the machine gun as they left, then Bravo team before she finally grabbed Tony and Edward and made the trek back down the forest road towards the smell of cooking stew.

She was sitting on her pack and trying not to fall asleep halfway through eating her bowl of mediocre Army stew and chunk of excellent Charlie Company bread when she heard something rustle through the brush behind her. She turned to see a couple dim shapes coming through the trees. She recognized Captain Caldwell as he asked his companion softly, "Are they up here, Thorn?"

She faintly saw the lieutenant shrug, "I think so, sir... God, it's hard to see tonight. They're around here somewhere."

Sophia whistled and the two men turned towards her. Picking his way forward, Caldwell worked his way forward until he was close enough to touch and asked, "Is that you, Rose?"

"Yes, sir." Sophia replied, "What can I do for you?"

The commander chuckled, "I've got a mission for you tonight."

"Sir?" *Please don't let it be a patrol*, Sophia thought.

Caldwell said, "I need your squad to do a patrol."

Damn it. Sophia took a deep breath and replied, "Yes, sir." She grit her teeth, "Where to?"

"Go get your squad and come with me, I'll show you." The commander turned to Thorn, "Adjust your perimeter to fill the gap after they pull out."

Thorn nodded tiredly and walked off into the darkness as Sophia collected her pack and started rousting her troops. She finished her stew on the walk back to the command post. Caldwell gave her a couple funny looks as she ate but said nothing. Leaving the rest of the squad outside, the commander pulled open the tent's blackout flap and ushered her in.

Compared to the night's inky darkness even the dim light from the field lantern they had set up inside the tent hurt her eyes for a moment. Inside were a couple of field desks, a folding table with a map spread across it and a pack and cot she supposed belonged to the commander. The soldier on duty, who she recognized as one of the company's runners, looked up at them for a moment before going back to his game of Solitaire.

Caldwell led her over to the table, where Sophia noticed a couple sheets of paper covered in handwriting sitting on top of the map. The writing was sloppy and uneven, but she could make out enough of the header to realize that these were orders from battalion. A messenger must have come not long after they'd stopped for the night. The commander gestured at the sheets and confirmed her suspicions, "We got orders about an hour ago." He grit his teeth and glared at her, "Usually battalion doesn't mess with us like this, so this is probably coming down from higher. Keep that in mind while you're out there, Rose."

Sophia swallowed hard, "Uh, yes, sir." She ventured, "What do you want us to, ah, do tonight, sir?"

"Well." Caldwell said, "We're here." He pointed out their position, marked by a pin stuck into the map's damp paper. "There's an estate down in the valley below us, about four kilometers to the southeast. Your squad is to head out and secure it." Sophia made to say something and he shook his head, "No, I don't know *why* either."

She laughed nervously and said, "Yes, sir. Do you know if the enemy is there?"

He shrugged and shook his head, "No, but honestly I doubt it. Everything I've seen has them up on Fire Ridge by now. Maybe a couple scouts are this far forward." He gave her a serious look, "If you run into more than you think you can handle, Rose, pull back and I'll get the whole company over there tomorrow. Whoever it is that's pushing this can wait that long before I get soldiers killed." He paused for a moment, then remembered something and went on, "Someone will be by in the morning to relieve you. After you're relieved link back up with us. The battalion's assembling at Sharp's Mill tomorrow, find us there." He pointed to a small town just off the main road they had been marching along.

"Yes sir." She thought about the mission for a moment. She could hear a misty rain starting to sift down outside the tent. She was so tired her brain felt like it was melting and about to dribble out of her ears. The whole squad – *her* whole squad, now that she thought about it – was probably worse off than she was. And if they didn't want to get shot by those Imperial scouts they were going to have to walk for a couple hours down a steep ridge through a pitch-black, rain-slickened forest so they could come in behind the estate. It was going to be a bad night.

Sophia hesitated for a moment, then asked, "Sir, ah... why did you pick us for this?" Caldwell raised an eyebrow and she went on, "I mean, one of the other squads must have more... experienced people."

He chuckled, "Yes, Miss Rose, that's very much true. But you kids are the only squad I have that isn't half-dead right now."

She snorted, "I wish you could tell that to my legs, sir."

"You may laugh, Miss Rose," Caldwell gave her a stern look, "But after we stopped today and I made my rounds I saw the half of the company that hasn't fallen out *yet* concerned with two things, rest and food. In that order. Nobody even *cared* about the enemy. And then your lieutenant comes along and tells me we're secure up front because Private Rose figured out her leader was down, and without being told took charge and got her squad ready to fight."

Sophia would have blushed if she hadn't been so tired. She replied, "Ah, thank you, sir."

The commander chuckled, "Don't thank me. In the Army hard work gets you more hard work. I'm the guy sending you out on patrol tonight, remember?" He went on, "Now, do you need anything before you head out?"

She thought for a moment and replied, "I need a map, sir. And... do you mind if I bring my guys in here to brief them?" The pattering on the tent roof got louder as though to make her point, "I don't think I'm going to have much success in this rain."

Caldwell snorted, "Ordinarily I'd say no, but I'll make an exception tonight. Just don't expect this again.'

About half an hour later Sophia and her squad emerged into the wet darkness. Finding her way back to the road, she carefully made her way back to the front of the column with the others in tow. A silhouette that looked like Sergeant Cross appeared out of the darkness a few feet in front of her and asked, "Heading out, Rose? I've been waiting for you."

"Thanks, Sergeant. Yeah, we're ready to go." Sophia asked, "Is this the front line?"

"No, it's up here. Follow me." Cross led them forward for a ways, then stopped next to a couple of shapes on the ground she recognized as a machine-gun team. He said, "This is it. Are you ready?"

Sophia nodded, "Yeah."

"Alright." He patted her on the shoulder, "One." Tony was right behind her, "Two." Then Edward, Jack and Kelly. Three, four and five. Behind them, six and seven, were Mr. Hargrave and Jeremy bringing up the rear. Sophia walked forward and the forest closed around them, rain sifting down and wrapping around them like a cold, wet cocoon. After a hundred meters or so she held up a hand to stop the squad. Kneeling, she took off her hat and set it on the ground in front of her as she heard her squad crouching behind her. Tony shifted forward as though to say something, then back as he thought better of it.

Sophia breathed in and out, slowly, calmly. She smelled earth, dead leaves and the wet wool of her uniform. Wet wood, mold and the water itself, perfuming the air as it dripped through the leaves overhead. The pattering rain surrounded them, muffling everything in a blanket of soft noise. As she listened a gust of wind shook the trees, filling the air with the sound of shaking branches and showering them with cold water. An owl hooted softly in the distance. She thought she heard someone from the company moving through the brush far behind them.

Alright. Time to get moving. Pulling out her compass, she took a look at the glowing dial and carefully lined it up in the correct direction.

The forest was so dark the luminous dial, faint on a normal night, blazed brightly. Sophia picked her hat up, settled it back on her head, stood and started walking. Behind her she heard her squad rise to follow her, equipment creaking and rattling softly in the darkness. Her feet sank into the deep loam as she went, shapes looming out of darkness in front of her and resolving into trees almost close enough to touch.

Sixty-four paces to a hundred meters. As the ground descended and Sophia felt her way through tree roots and pushed aside dead branches that clawed at her face she adjusted it to seventy. Creeping through the trees it seemed to take an eternity to make those first seventy paces. Her legs protested under the weight of her pack as she waded along through the forest floor, following the glowing dial of her compass like a guiding star.

They walked. And walked. And walked. As she carefully felt her way over a fallen log in the darkness, Sophia counted to seventy for the tenth time and checked her watch. In the darkness she could barely see the glint of the glass face, and she held it next to her compass to get enough light. She grimaced as she saw they had taken almost an hour to get this far. It would be close to midnight by the time they got to the manor at this rate.

Sophia pressed forward a little to get the rest of the squad over the tree before raising a hand for a halt. The squad slowly bumped to a halt behind her and she realized they were following the sound of her moving. Tony probably couldn't even see her. Putting her hand down sheepishly, Sophia turned around and felt for him. After walking a couple paces back she put her hand out at something that looked less like a tree than most of what she'd seen for the last hour and felt Tony's jacket.

Tony grasped her hand and asked softly, "What's wrong, Sophie?"

"We're at a kilometer." Sophia whispered, "We'll probably be there around midnight."

He sighed heavily and shook his head tiredly, "Sure. Thanks."

"Do we still have everyone?" Sophia asked.

She felt him twist around and try to look before he turned back around and said, "I hope so. I can't see *anything.*"

"Heh." She patted him on the shoulder, "Stay here, I'll check."

Walking carefully back down the line, Sophia felt for her friends in the darkness. After a couple minutes of feeling and more than a few tree trunks she found the other five. When she reached him Jack asked, whispering, "How much farther? I can't see my hand in front of my face in this forest."

Sophia chuckled softly, "About three kilometers."

Jack groaned, "We're never going to make it at this rate." The shape of his head changed a little as he looked at her, "What was Caldwell thinking? This *really* couldn't wait until morning?"

She shook her head although she doubted he could see it, "I don't know." She patted him on the shoulder encouragingly, "Just think about us having a house to sleep in after we're done."

"If we don't die out here." Jack groused, "If we're not lost."

Sophia snorted, "Trust me. Now come on."

Picking her way back to the front of the line, Sophia snapped her fingers twice to get the squad's attention and set off. The noise wouldn't carry far in the rain and wind, and she soon heard them moving behind her. They trekked on, the hillside gradually flattening out into the valley floor as they went. After another kilometer Sophia saw a lightening in the wall of darkness in front of her, tree trunks starting to stand out against the background. Holding up a hand to halt the squad and hoping they saw it, she pressed forward cautiously and saw a gravel road cutting through the dense forest.

There was supposed to be a road between them and the estate. She felt a little weight come off her shoulders, and Sophia quickly backtracked to the squad and brought them up to the edge of the forest. Jack didn't need to be told to set up his machine gun, and Jeremy and Hargrave knelt behind convenient trees to cover the road to each side. Putting away her compass for a moment, Sophia tapped Tony on the shoulder and whispered, "Let's go. Follow me."

Hefting their rifles, Sophia and Tony darted across the road. She felt cold rain on her face for a couple seconds before they plunged into the wet brush on the far side and were swallowed by the dark forest. The two of them spread out and found nothing but wet trees and shadow. Leaving Tony in the woods, Sophia circled back and waved the others across. When they were all assembled on the far side she pulled her compass back out and led them onwards. They splashed through a stream and clambered up and over the ruins of a few ancient farm walls as the ground sloped back uphill slightly towards the estate. Gradually the forest thinned to the point they could barely make out each other's silhouettes.

Sophia started to feel the rain on her face as she saw the forest lighten abruptly a little ways in front of them. Her eyes widened as a light flickered for a moment in the distance beyond the trees, and she waved for the squad to spread out. Crouching low, they crept to the edge of the forest. Sophia found a gap in the bushes and peered through.

The wind had died down and a mist was rising, shrouding the soaked ground before them in a dark, waist-high blanket. Against the ashen sky, Sophia saw the hard angles of a roofline jutting from the black forest on the far side of the clearing. She worked her eye around a little and slowly made out the scene from the slightest contrasts in the black night. The ground rose out of the blanket of fog before them, with a bulky manor house set on top of the low rise. Behind it she saw another dark shape that she supposed was a barn. Although in a classy place like this she thought a better term would be stables.

As she watched and her eyes adjusted a little to the scenery, Sophia saw a couple faint flickers of light from the house's walls. Noticing a faint plume of smoke rising from the house's chimneys, Sophia realized that the house wasn't vacant at all. Whoever was inside had drawn blackout curtains over the windows. Her blood ran cold at the thought. Although she supposed that Imperial scouts wouldn't be sitting around inside a lit building with curtains over the windows.

Still, that was no guarantee there weren't Imperials in the upper floors or around the grounds somewhere. Backing off from the woodline, Sophia snapped her fingers to get the squad's attention. They rose and followed her as she set off around the grounds, sticking inside the forest. It took them another hour of careful creeping around the manor's perimeter, skulking across riding trails and moving back and forth from the edge of the woods, before Sophia had a good idea of what she was facing.

On the far, eastern side of the manor they found a groundskeeper's house set into the woodline. Sophia sighed and figured she may as well start there. Tapping Jack on the shoulder and setting him and his machine gun to cover the manor house and stables, she pointed Hargrave into position overlooking the house's front door. He was about to move out with his partner when she remembered something and tapped him on the shoulder.

Reaching back on her belt, Sophia grasped her bayonet and drew it. The blade made a soft noise as it scraped across the steel scabbard mouth. Fitting it to her rifle's bayonet lug, she pulled the catch back with her finger and slowly released it as she pressed it home, locking it to her rifle silently. Getting the idea, Hargrave, Jeremy, Edward and Tony all copied her. The older man crept off towards the side of the house with his partner, and Sophia silently set her pack on the ground and darted towards the back door. Tony and Edward weren't far behind her.

The house's windows were dark and nothing stirred inside as they waited beside the side door, listening to the soft sound of the other team getting into position. When Hargrave stopped moving, Sophia crouched under the window set into the door itself, drew her rifle back to get the long weapon into position, reached out and slowly tested the doorknob. It turned, and she slowly cracked the door and then pushed it the rest of the way open with the side of her bayonet, rotating herself into the entrance as she did.

The hinges creaked a little and Sophia felt her skin crawl as she stepped into the small kitchen. Nothing else moved. Her eyes, already adjusted to pitch darkness, quickly made out the details of the room and the one beyond. The kitchen was bare, stripped of anything of use. Stepping cautiously into the living room she saw that most of the furniture was intact, if worse for wear. Caked dirt scraped on the wooden floor as she stepped inside. The Imperials must have tracked it in, she supposed.

Imperials who were long gone. Nothing lunged out of the shadows at her. They carefully checked the single, spartan bedroom and the bathroom, with its large tub. Again, nothing. Seeing the facilities made her skin itch for a bath, and she tiredly shook off the thought. She doubted the cabin's stove and nonexistent water and firewood would support it even if they had the time.

Sophia quietly came out the same way she'd gone in, circled around to Hargrave's team and patted him on the shoulder. The man turned to look at her and she whispered, "Nothing. We're clearing the stables next. See anything?"

He shook his head tiredly, "Nothing, Miss Rose."

Jeremy piped up, "I thought I saw a light over in the main house. Just for a second."

Sophia replied, "They must have blackout curtains." She grimaced, "Hopefully it's civilians and not the Empire."

Hargrave mused, "You know how we can tell that, Miss Rose?"

She raised an eyebrow, "No, do you have an idea?"

"Check the stables for horses. The Masks haven't been leaving many." He chuckled, "Kids these days."

Sophia snorted, "Makes sense, old man. Let's go."

The five of them stole across the grounds, crouched low under the rising fog. The mist hid them from the house as they approached the stables, but it also made seeing anything impossible. After half-crawling for a ways they started going uphill and rose from the fog a short distance away from the building's large rear doors. Sophia again waved Hargrave and Jeremy forward to cover the front side, and they dropped to their bellies and started crawling forward as she rolled under the picturesque split-rail fence and into the muddy exercise yard.

Cold mud clung to her uniform as she stood, careful to keep her rifle out of the mess. Stealing up to the rear door, she noticed the latch was undone and the wide door, large enough to drive a carriage out of, swung free on its hinges. And she heard nothing from inside, not so much as a snort from a sleeping horse. Cracking the door carefully, she rotated herself inside bayonet-first.

The stables were a deserted mess, smelling of straw and manure. The Imperials hadn't bothered to clean the place before they left. Sophia and her two companions poked their bayonets into every stall and even climbed the wooden stairs to the hayloft to find it utterly bare. Coming back down, they quietly searched the attached garage for the estate's carriages. They found one that the Empire had clearly passed over and a couple obviously civilian riding saddles. What they didn't find was any trace of the Imperial Army.

As Hargrave had said, Imperial scouts would be dragoons. Dragoons would have horses, and they would probably keep them in the stables, although, Sophia thought wryly, that was no guarantee they weren't around. Even so, it looked like the Empire was long gone. Quickly backtracking out of the barn, Sophia rolled back under the fence with her two friends and crept back up next to the other rifle team.

Hargrave was carefully watching the manor house's back door from around the corner of the barn when she came up behind him and patted him on the shoulder. He turned and she whispered, "You were right. No horses."

Hargrave chuckled softly and said, "Civilians then. At least we hope so."

"Let's go find out." Sophia replied, "Can you get around and cover the far side?"

The older man nodded and said, "Yes. I just hope they don't have dogs." He thought for a moment and went on, "Although if they did I suppose we'd know by now."

Sophia whispered, "Thank God for small favors. Maybe the Empire took them too."

"Doubt it." Hargrave said, "Even the Masks aren't that low."

"Yeah." Sophia gestured towards the far corner of the house, "Alright, go. We'll cover you from here. If anyone runs, don't shoot them unless you *know* they're Imperials."

Hargrave scowled, turned to Jeremy and muttered, "Come on, kid. Let's go." The two men dropped into a low crouch and half-ran, half-crawled around the house as Sophia trained her rifle on the house's upper-floor windows. Tony dropped to his belly and crawled sideways crablike to get a better angle on the house's side door, and she heard Edward turn to cover the forest behind them. Hargrave's team quickly made it to the far side and after a moment she saw him raise his hand and wave her forward.

"Alright." Sophia swallowed, "Follow me."

Tony snorted softly and remarked, "Let's do this."

They darted out into the open, across the overgrown lawn and towards the manor house's side door. *Probably a servants' entrance*, Sophia thought. They quickly reached the wall and crouched beside the door. Sophia waited for a few seconds, listening intently. The rain pattered on the grass, ran through her soaked hair and down the back of her neck. The water moved in a cool, slimy wave down her back under her jacket, and Sophia shuddered involuntarily. She could feel the grit and dirt moving with it.

Sophia heard a voice, faint from inside, "Milady? It's almost one. More than time for you to go to bed." A voice replied, too faint for her to make out. The first voice went on, "Yes, I'm scared too, but it's not like sitting up will do you any good. Now come on."

Civilians. Sophia thought about her options for a moment. The Empire had been here. Whoever was inside was obviously scared and, from the sound of it, not exactly dangerous. Sophia reached out and tested the door knob. Scared enough to keep the back door locked. And probably scared enough to have whatever weapons they could scrape together immediately to hand, and it's not as though they knew it was the Royal Army outside. For all they knew the Empire was back. Or thieves taking advantage of the war.

So Sophia figured she had three choices. They could kick the door down, storm in, overpower the residents and explain things later. Better safe than sorry. However, she *really* didn't want to explain to her father why she'd given Lady Such-and-Such a heart attack and buttstroked a maid. They could break in quietly, which would mean waiting another hour until Lady Such-and-Such and her servant (servants?) went to bed, trying not to wake them climbing through a window and then probably *still* giving her a heart attack and buttstroking her maid. As though to make a point the rain started coming down harder.

Sophia shivered. That left option three. She turned around and whispered to her two companions, "Tony, you watch the window." She jerked her head at the window they were crouching under, "Edward, watch behind us."

Tony whispered back, "Sophie, what are you doing?"

Sophia sighed, gathered herself for a moment and replied, "Something stupid." Then she reached out and knocked on the door.

The first voice from inside said, "Milady, did you hear that?" There was a pause, then it came back, "It sounded like someone at the back door."

Sophia heard Milady reply, "Well, go see if someone's out there. And don't open the door. I'll go wake Sean." Milady had a high-pitched, bossy voice. She sounded like a little kid, actually.

This was a great idea, Sophie, she thought sarcastically. She heard footsteps approach the door and a voice hesitantly call out, "Is someone out there?"

Sophia shook her head quickly, cleared her throat and said, loudly enough to carry through the door but hopefully quietly enough that the dragoons she swore she could feel staring down a machine-gun's sight at her wouldn't hear, "Yes. Royal Army."

The maid harrumphed indignantly, "That's what the last group said, and they were lying."

Figures. Sophia rolled her eyes and said, "I'm with Charlie Company, Second Battalion, Twenty-Fourth Infantry Regiment." She added, "By Fire and Steel. Now open up, I've got my orders."

"Not many women in the Royal Army, Miss Dragoon." The maid replied snidely.

Should have thought of that one. Sophia sighed and said, "There are some of us. Now are you going to open the door or am I kicking it down?"

"Ah... wait a minute. Sorry. Milady!" The maid hurried off down the hallway and Sophia heard her quietly conferring with Milady and a third person, a man with a scratchy voice. She supposed that was Sean.

Tony remarked, "I think we should kick the door down."

Sophia sighed, "Just give me a minute, okay?"

Tony said, "Sure thing. I just *really* hope nobody ends up shooting at us."

She snickered, "You and me both, Tony."

Heavy, male footsteps approached the door. The man inside said, "Alright, if you're Royal Army, when is Princess Arilin's birthday celebrated?"

Sophia replied tiredly, "December twenty-third, but she was actually born on Christmas."

"Well, you're not a Mask. Hrm..." The man said something quietly inside. Sophia heard Milady reply, and he shot back, "Who's your corps commander?"

It was one in the morning and she was being rained on. This was ridiculous. She supposed she couldn't fault them for being scared, but it wasn't like they really needed to be let in. Who was in command of V Corps anyways? Who was even in charge of the division? She had no idea. Sophia was about to snap back at the man when Tony beat her to it, "We don't know?" He added helpfully, "We're in Fifth Corps."

The man inside chuckled, "Good answer."

She heard him mutter something about cards to the girl, and Milady giggled and said, "Open the door, Sean. I think they're actually Royal Army."

Sean grunted and she heard something heavy being moved, then the sound of the deadbolt sliding back. Maybe kicking the door down wouldn't have been the best idea. Light flooded out as the door cracked open. It was dim, but on a night this dark it half-blinded her as the weathered face of an older man appeared in the doorway above her, peering into the darkness. The man looked right past them for a few seconds before he asked, "Where the hell are you?"

Sophia stood quickly. She was all of a foot away from him as she said, "Right here."

The man jerked backwards in surprise as Sophia stuck her foot in the door and pushed it open with her leg. Stepping into the entrance, she saw him stagger backwards against a cupboard to her right. He had what looked like a shotgun in his hand, but he didn't make to raise it. Looking to the other side she saw a woman in a maid's uniform step protectively in front of a younger girl. She supposed that was Milady.

The man looked her up and down, then shook his head and said, "Damn infantry. You scared me half to death." He chuckled, "You look like you've had a fun night."

Sophia smiled tiredly, "Like you wouldn't believe." She narrowed her eyes, "Are there any Imperials still around here? Our orders are to secure this estate." She gestured with her head, "I've got guys outside."

"No, the last of them left this morning. Headed off towards town, although we've seen Masks heading east on the main road for days." The man looked like he wanted to spit, but being indoors he refrained and went on, "I figure they followed them. I would have noticed if they left anyone hanging around, I checked the grounds after they went."

Sophia felt like a weight had lifted from her shoulders. She suddenly realized how incredibly tired she was. She was almost dizzy with fatigue. Noticing the girl step out from around her maid, she asked, "Milady, do you... eh..." She yawned and went on, "Mind if I bring my guys in here?" She shook her head to clear it a little, "They're all worse off than I am. In fact my machine-gun team's probably asleep by now, rain or not."

Even at one in the morning Milady was very pretty, a short girl with golden curls, blue eyes and an imperious manner. She couldn't have been more than twelve or thirteen, but she was clearly the lady of the house. Looking her up and down, Milady replied, "*Your* men? I don't suppose you have an *officer* I could speak to, Private...?"

Sophia snorted, "Private First Class Rose, Milady. And the nearest person who outranks me around here is four kilometers *that* way." She jerked her thumb in the general direction they had come from. She went on, "So, do you mind?"

Milady looked her up and down again, then softened, "Certainly, please. Just try not to track mud all over everything, the Imperials were terrible about that." Milady snickered, "Although maybe we should just get you out of your uniform. What did you do, roll in the pasture?"

Sophia replied sheepishly, "Yeah, actually, I did." She looked at her hostess. Milady was clean. Really, really clean. She *smelled* nice. Taking her hat off, Sophia ran her hand through her hair and felt grime and greasy dirt come off on her fingers. The thought of bathing made her skin crawl in anticipation. Hesitantly, she asked, "You wouldn't happen to have a shower, would you, Milady?"

Milady smiled, "Oh, that's mandatory for you unless you want to sleep in the stables."

Sophia turned to see that Tony and Edward had crowded into the door behind her. Smiling, she said, "Can you two go get the other teams?" She added gleefully, "We're getting a *shower* tonight!"

Her friends grinned and disappeared into the darkness. Sophia closed the door and turned to Milady, "Do you mind if I look around the second floor, milady? We're supposed to hold this place, and I'd like to do it from *inside*."

Milady nodded and said, "Of course. Sean, please help Miss Rose."

She turned to her maid and said, "Alice, I realize it is *extremely* late, but can you please see to making our guests comfortable?" She looked back at Sophia, "You have... how many men with you?"

Sophia replied, "Seven, including me."

Alice laughed, "That's nothing, Milady. Leave it to me."

Milady giggled, "I've never been happier to have guests."

Sophia smiled, "I'm just sorry we couldn't get here sooner, Milady."

Half an hour later, Sophia was standing in the shower feeling blisteringly hot water flowing through her hair. Grimy water puddled around her legs and flowed into the drain, leaving a streak of dirt on the bottom of the tub. They'd probably have to clean it later. Sophia chortled. She'd never been so happy to think about cleaning a bathroom.

When I get home, I'm going to do this for an hour or two, Sophia thought. Then she had a better idea, *When I get home, I'm taking a bath. In fact, when I get home, I'm taking a bath every day for the rest of my life.* She chuckled. Then she laughed. It was such a good feeling, thinking about home. Thinking about the future. Thinking about her mother, waiting for her daughter and her husband to come marching back from war. Sophia felt something hot well up under her eyes and realized she was crying.

Sophia shook her head, wiped her eyes quickly and turned off the shower. The guys had generously told her to go first and she couldn't hog all the hot water. Drying herself with a towel, she realized why her uniform had been hanging off of her recently. The long days of marching had melted the fat from her body. Her breasts had shrunken and she could just about count her ribs in the mirror, while her legs bulged with muscle. Painful red welts covered her shoulders, waist and back where her equipment had rubbed and chafed.

Sophia finally looked at her face in the mirror. She'd seen herself gaunt and tired after field exercises, but not like this. Her eyes were dark and sunken with fatigue, and even in her own reflection her gaze was a little unsettling. And now that she thought about it all of her friends looked worse than she did. For a moment she felt sorry for Milady and her servants, having to contend with a bunch of ghastly-looking soldiers stumbling out of the rain just as the Empire had finally left them alone. Chuckling grimly, she wrapped her towel around herself, opened the door and walked out.

Tony was sitting on the floor outside in his underwear, dozing with their rifles across his lap. Sophia prodded him with a toe and, when he stirred, said, "Shower's all yours."

He looked up at her groggily, "Leave me any hot water?"

"Yeah, actually." Sophia went on, "Where are you sleeping tonight?"

Tony yawned, "Couch downstairs." He teased her, "Lucky girl, getting a bed."

She replied, "Take it up with Milady. I was *fine* with you and Ed sleeping with me."

He looked her up and down, then chuckled tiredly, "I can see where she's coming from, though."

Sophia looked back at him for a moment, then snorted. Here she was, wearing a towel, having a conversation with Tony in his underwear and all either of them could think about was sleep. Milady's concern for the morals of her guests was so misplaced it was actually funny. Chuckling, Sophia said, "Alright, I'll see you at five. Goodnight."

After making a final round of the upper floor to check on the guards and finding Mr. Hargrave punching Jeremy in the ribs to keep him awake, Sophia made her way to the guest bedroom, pulled back the covers, turned out the lights, wedged her rifle between the mattress and the headboard, climbed into the most comfortable bed in the kingdom and sank into a black abyss.

Chapter 25

A Chance Encounter

Sophia yawned and stretched her arms overhead. She could have slept for days in that bed. As it was Jack had woken her after four too-short hours for her guard shift and she'd put on a fresh uniform to step outside and watch the rain fall under the verandah's shelter. The world gradually brightened as she stood watch, rain sheeting down and beating at the trees under a lead sky. She felt sorry for the rest of the company, probably huddling in whatever shelter they could find right now.

Whoever was supposed to relieve them had yet to show up, and Sophia hoped they gave her a few hours. The last thing she wanted to do was go try to hunt down the company in this weather. With any luck the rain would break soon and they could at least be on their way in dry clothing. As though to emphasize her thoughts thunder rumbled in the distance. At least she hoped it was thunder. She hadn't heard artillery in days and she felt her stomach clench at the thought.

Sophia turned as the door opened behind her and Tony stuck his head out. He was still a little gaunt, but nothing compared to the mud-streaked zombie of last night. In a clean uniform he actually looked kind of dashing. Cheerfully, he said, "Hey, Sophie. Alice is making breakfast."

Right on cue Sophia smelled the familiar scent of fresh bread as it wafted out the door. It was a little bland and overdone. She supposed the Imperials probably hadn't left a whole lot of supplies. Smiling, Sophia checked her watch and said, "Yeah, it's time to change shift anyways. Can you spell me here while I go wake Hargrave?"

Tony shrugged, "Sure." He stepped outside onto the damp stone of the verandah, looked at her and smiled nervously, "You, ah... look amazing, Sophie."

Surprised, Sophia looked down at herself, then back at him. Sleep, a shower and fresh clothing had probably done wonders for her too. Feeling herself blushing a little, she replied, "Ah... thanks, Tony." She smoothed the front of her jacket and went on, "You... look fine yourself. Much better than last night."

She noticed Tony reddening as he replied, "You too." Sophia glared at him for a moment and he backtracked quickly, "Ah... not like you weren't okay earlier."

Sophia tried to keep glaring and failed as she burst out laughing. Tony looked at her with a weird expression on his face for a few seconds before she calmed down. Her face was hot, but her anxiety disappeared as she replied, "You're a bad liar, Tony Gravesend."

Tony stepped aside a little awkwardly, made a motion to wave her through the door and said, smiling, "I'd rather lie than be rude to you."

Sophia smiled and walked past him into the house, saying, "Thanks, Tony."

She quickly found Hargrave and Jeremy sprawled on the parlor's carpet. The older man woke quickly when she shook his shoulder, but Jeremy may as well have been dead. Seeing her efforts at waking him gently having no effect, Hargrave motioned her aside as he got up, rolled his companion over on his back and dragged his knuckles down Jeremy's sternum.

The younger man winced and jerked awake suddenly, glaring at Hargrave, "Hey! That hurts!"

Hargrave chuckled grimly, "A lot less than what Sophia here was getting ready to do to you, I suspect. Now get up. Time for our shift."

Grumbling, Jeremy rolled upright and stretched tiredly as Sophia said, "Thanks, Mr. Hargrave."

The older man chuckled, "Please, Sophia. No need for that at this point. Just call me Bob." His eyes twinkled as he went on, "And have someone bring out some food to us while we're out, that smells good."

Sophia laughed and replied, "Okay, thanks, Bob. I will."

Making her way back to the kitchen, Sophia passed by a large, elaborate sitting-room that she supposed was the *real* parlor before she walked in on Alice slicing vegetables. Alone in the large room, the maid was a lonely figure. A single pot was steaming on the gigantic stove and she smelled bouillon over the bland bread as she came in. The woman glanced at her as she came in and Sophia asked, "Making soup?"

Alice sighed tiredly and replied, "Yeah. It's about all we've got ingredients for right now." Setting her knife down, she turned towards her and Sophia saw the dark circles under her eyes as she said angrily, "The Masks ate us out of damn house and home. And *you* all have kept me up all night washing your disgusting clothes. So *please* let me cook in peace, because maybe Milady will let me get some rest after breakfast." She sighed and rolled her eyes, "Maybe."

Sophia set her rifle down against the wall and said, "Can I do anything to help?"

"I don't know." Alice looked her up and down, "Can you cook?"

Sophia smirked, "My family owns a bakery, and your bread needs some salt."

Alice sighed, "I'm trying to stretch what we have." She pointed her thumb behind her at a door on the other side of the kitchen, "There's a spare apron in the pantry and we've got some salt pork left. Not a lot, but I guess we should celebrate. Can you cook that up?"

Sophia nodded, "Yeah, sure." Alice turned back to her chopping block and she washed her hands and made her way past her to open the pantry door. The maid hadn't been kidding. The pantry was almost stripped clean, and Sophia wondered if they had enough supplies to last through dinner. Taking an apron off a peg on the wall, Sophia tied it on and spied a barrel in the darkness in the back of the room. Going over she saw it was marked in large inked letters, 'PRESERVED SALTED PORK BELLIES – 40 KG – TWO SOLDIER LIFT – IMPERIAL ARMY PROPERTY, RESALE PROHIBITED BY LAW' Crouching, Sophia saw some smaller, less official-looking lettering near the bottom ,'Fuller&Sons Meat Packing Company. 22 Corvus Avenue, Blade Lake, Lower Sylvania.'

Sophia thought for a minute and realized she had no idea where Lower Sylvania was. In fact, now that she thought about it she barely knew anything about the Empire. She knew what she'd been taught in school – The Faceless King, Lady Vai and so on. They had been the Kingdom's enemy for literally a thousand years. And from what she'd seen so far their soldiers fought terrifyingly well, but they were as human as she was underneath their steel masks. In a way that only made them scarier.

She chuckled. Some high-up Imperial quartermaster had been worried about soldiers throwing their backs out while illegally selling government rations on the side and had probably given this random meat-packing company very specific directions on how their product was to be marked in hopes of discouraging them. Some things really were universal, and in a way it made the Imperial Army seem less like a literally faceless killing machine and a little more like her own army. Cold, tired, marching long miles on sore feet and waiting for their next meal.

And speaking of their next meal, she had a job to do. Pulling the top off the barrel, Sophia looked inside and realized why the Imperials hadn't bothered taking it with them. There was barely any left. She scraped out what cold, gritty pork she could with her hands and carried it back out to the kitchen. After washing off the extra salt she asked Alice, "Do you have an extra cutting board around here somewhere?"

The maid jerked her head in the general direction of the cupboards under the counter she was standing at and said, "I hope you're not planning on using your bayonet. Knives are on the right."

"Thanks." Sophia quickly started cutting the slabs of pork into manageable slices as she ventured, "By the way, ah... what's Milady's *name?*"

Alice stopped chopping and looked at her blankly for a couple seconds. Then she chuckled tiredly and said, "Charlotte Espinay." She snorted, "Everyone calls her Milady, though. Even the Imperials did."

"What about her parents?" Sophia asked.

"I've heard the colonel use it a few times." Alice sighed, "I wish we even knew where they were. Do you know where the 26th Division is these days?"

That was a change of subject. Sophia furrowed her brow and thought for a moment, then shook her head, "Infantry unit? Never heard of them. Why do you ask?"

"Milady's father is in it. On the staff. Sorry." Alice turned back to her work and went on, "He was called up right after the war started. Left in a big hurry. About a month later we got a letter from him telling us things were going badly and we needed to take a vacation in the Capital."

Sophia took a frying pan off a peg on the wall and set it on the stove. Alice handed her a box of matches and she struck one. The acrid smell floated through the room for a moment as she lit the stove and replied, "I'm guessing that didn't work out for you?"

Alice shook her head sadly, "Not for us it didn't. Milady's mother left right away with most of the staff. She stuck around for a couple days to take care of affairs in town and, well... we *thought* we were safe." Sophia saw Alice clench her teeth, "The front was *supposed* to be at Fire Ridge. For God's sake, there were Royal troops in town."

Sophia paused for a moment from laying strips of pork into the frying pan and raised her eyebrows, "What happened?"

"They knocked on the door, said they were hussars and they had a wounded man. Of course we opened up." Alice deflated a little as she went on, "They weren't wearing their masks, and at the time I actually didn't know what Imperial uniforms looked like. I thought they were Royals until I took their lieutenant to meet Milady."

Sophia tried to keep from laughing, "How'd that go?"

Alice made a pained expression, "She... may have fainted." Sophia chortled and she rolled her eyes, "Go ahead, it's not like I haven't heard it before. That Mask was laughing harder than I've ever seen anyone in my *life*. God-damn pretty boy."

Sophia's laugh died as a chill shot up her spine, "Pretty boy? Did he have really long hair?"

"Yeah, past his *incredible* butt." Alice raised an eyebrow, "You know him? Kill him hopefully?"

"We've met." Sophia shivered. There had been blood on the *ceiling*. "He's scary. He... well, I hope we don't run into him again."

Alice sighed, "You and me both. Nice guy, but there was something underneath it that I didn't care for." Her eyes shifted to look behind Sophia as she went on, "You may want to mind the stove there." Sophia quickly turned around to tend to the now-crackling pork, and Alice said, "Sorry. Shouldn't have distracted you."

Sophia shook her head, "No problem." Alice got back to cooking, and soon enough they had prepared a serviceable meal. As they admired their work Sophia asked, "You want me to go gather everyone?"

Alice nodded, "Yeah, I'll finish up here. Milady's bedroom is upstairs at the end of the hall on the left."

"You want me to wake her up?" Sophia asked.

"Yeah." Alice added, "She'll complain, but I'm *not* cooking twice."

Sophia chuckled, "Sure, I'll go get her. And my guys."

As she took off her apron and turned to leave Alice said, "Hey, Sophia... thanks for helping me out."

Sophia ran a hand through her hair tiredly and replied, "Least I can do after you took care of us."

Alice smiled, "You've got what it takes. Ever thought about going into service?"

Sophia snorted, "Me? I can't see myself as a maid. And anyways, I've got a bakery to run."

"Well if it ever goes under, give it a thought." The maid turned to start digging plates out of cupboards and went on, "It's not a bad job."

"Sure, thanks." Sophia turned and left, waking people up as she went. Soon all of her soldiers and old Sean were shuffling tiredly downstairs. Finally she stopped in front of Charlotte's bedroom and knocked softly, "Milady? I'm coming in."

There was no response. Sophia gently opened the door and stuck her head inside. The room was dominated by an enormous four-poster bed wreathed in heavy curtains. The sound of the drumming rain outside filtered in gently through the half-open windows arrayed across the whole outer wall, bathing the room in soft gray light. *So this is how the other half lives,* Sophia thought as she crept inside, *if I had a room like this I'd never get up in the morning.* Spotting a collection of dolls in elaborate outfits perched on top of the girl's bookshelf, Sophia smiled as she made her way to the bedside.

She drew the curtains back to find Charlotte sleeping deeply, head wreathed in golden curls. She patted the girl's shoulder through the blankets and she stirred and slowly opened her eyes. As Charlotte gave her a sleepy look Sophia said, "Breakfast's ready downstairs, milady."

The girl yawned and sat up, "Alice sent you up here?" Stretching her arms over her head, she went on, "Something smells good. Tell her I will be right down."

"Of course, milady." Sophia hesitated for a moment, then added, "She's hoping she can get some rest after this, milady. She's been up all night."

Alice looked at her and slowly cocked her head to the side, "I had not thought of that." She pursed her lips in thought for a moment, then added, "Send her to bed immediately."

"Can do, milady." Sophia smiled, retreated and headed back to the dining room downstairs. Entering, she saw her friends sitting around the table, Alice bringing a plate in. Tony quickly stood and pulled out a chair for her to the right of the head of the table. The place of honor. She was probably the most common person who'd ever occupied it. Sophia snorted at the thought and said, "Thanks, Tony." Looking at Alice, she went on, "Milady says you can go to bed, Alice."

The maid set her plate down and yawned, "Thanks." Sliding out a chair and sitting down at the table she went on, "I'll eat first, though. No sense going to sleep hungry."

Robert remarked, "Spoken like a true soldier, Miss Alice."

Alice chuckled, "Thanks, I guess." She looked back at Sophia and asked, "Any idea when Milady is coming down? I feel rude to start eating without her."

"No worries, then." The young lady appeared in the doorway, still bleary-eyed from sleep and wearing a heavy woolen robe over her nightgown. She looked over at her maid and gave her a half smile, "I wouldn't blame you anyways, Alice."

Alice nodded in thanks as Charlotte worked her way to the head of the table. Sophia quickly got up and pulled her seat out for her, and as the girl sat she looked over at her groundskeeper and asked, "Sean, I don't suppose you could say grace for us? This is an auspicious occasion, after all."

Sophia saw the old man smile through his beard as he replied, "Of course, milady. Friends, let us pray." She quickly crossed herself and clasped her hands before her as he said, "Heavenly Father, today we thank you for our deliverance from the Empire of Masks. May they be driven from this land forever more. Please bless the Royal Army, in particular the young soldiers with us here today, as well as Lord Colonel Espinay wherever he may be at this time. We pray for their victory." He paused and went on, "I ask that you bless this meal and those with us here today. God save the king. Amen."

"Amen." Sophia unclasped her hands and set to eating. The food tasted about like she had thought it would turn out. The bread was bad, the soup was bland and the pork was, well, military salt pork. She'd had better meals since they'd gotten on that train in Wolf Rock. But she was having this one under a real roof, in a real chair, with the nicest silverware she'd ever handled and in fine company, so that had to count for something. Speaking of fine company, she turned to her hostess, who was politely dipping through her soup with a spoon and remarked, "Milady, that's the first time I've heard a prayer said at breakfast. I was surprised when you asked for it."

Charlotte raised an eyebrow and replied, "I suppose you're not very religious?"

Sophia gave her a look and replied, "I go to church on Sundays."

The girl chuckled and said, "No need to get defensive. I'm sorry if that came out wrong." She smiled and went on, "Sean prays a great deal. While the Imperials were here I suppose it... got into me. It was *terrifying* having them stomping all through the house constantly. And those masks..." Charlotte clasped her hands together suddenly, Sophia supposed to keep them from shaking as she went on, "They didn't exactly let us out much. I had to do *something*."

Sophia replied soothingly, "Please, milady. There's nothing wrong with that."

Charlotte looked back at her and for an instant Sophia saw fear deep in her eyes. Then the girl set her jaw and it was gone. "Thanks," she replied. Sophia turned back to her food and soon the meal was finished. Alice quickly excused herself and went off to bed, and Charlotte made a comment about reading a book and disappeared into her father's office. Head still fuzzy from lack of sleep, Sophia took her boots off, lay down on the couch in the parlor and closed her eyes, listening to the soft drumming of the rain outside.

"-one's coming, get up!" Sophia groaned and started coming awake as she heard someone shouting close by, "Cavalry!" At that word Sophia leapt upright, had her boots on and was halfway to the front door with rifle in hand before she had time to think that maybe they weren't dragoons. It was better not to take chances, though, as she flung herself down behind the open front door. Tony and Edward tumbled down the stairs a moment later and she shouted at them to get into position behind the front windows where they had a good field of fire.

She absently noted that the rain had cleared up and bright morning sunlight was streaming down outside. The wet forest and grass sparkled with light as she stared down the sights of her rifle at the road outside where it bent off into the forest. After a moment the thundering of her heart in her ears cleared. For a few seconds she saw nothing, but just as she was about to say something to her companions she *heard* it.

A low sound, like distant thunder. Birds took flight above the trees in the distance, startled into flight by the oncoming monster. Sophia listened for a few moments before the realization struck her, searing into her mind like lightning. It was cavalry. Hundreds of riders thundering towards them, shaking the earth with their hooves. Sophia felt ice run down her back again as she thought of an entire dragoon regiment thundering down the road towards them, green-jacketed horsemen about to charge into view any moment.

Wait, she thought, *when have we ever seen more than one or two dragoons at once? This isn't how they fight. They'd* never *do this.* Picking her head up, Sophia looked to her left and right. Tony and Edward were both breathing hard, fingers on their rifles' triggers. Tony was trembling as he squinted down his rifle's sights at the bend in the road where the cavalry was going to emerge any moment. *God in heaven,* she realized, *we're about to fire on our own cavalry.*

Sophia rolled upright, shouting, "*Hold fire!* They're friendly!" Her two friends snapped out of the spell of fear and gave her doubting looks as she rushed for the stairs, shouting for the machine-gunners upstairs to hold fire. Jack had only started raising his gun's barrel when she reached his shoulder, and she heard him say something angry to her. She barely registered it. Jack must have seen the look on her face, because he shut up abruptly and followed her gaze out the window.

A torrent of dark-jacketed horsemen were rushing out of the forest on gleaming white steeds, plumed helmets streaming behind them. Sophia saw something bright fluttering high through the trees and she gasped as it came into view. The twin sunbursts of the Kingdom's flag on white, not blue. The Royal standard. The blue flag flying beside it bearing the griffon and crossed swords of the Cuirassier Guards was almost an after-thought. And just before the colors rode a figure that stood out even in that sea of big men on huge horses. He was dressed no differently than the others, but all she could think of was a knight on his charger. She saw the dark helmet tip up slightly and Prince Adrian looked her dead in the eyes.

Sophia felt her back straighten automatically. She absently noticed Jack gawking with his mouth open as she turned and marched back downstairs. The cavalry was starting to flood around the house by the time she got back to the front door, and a group of riders broke off with the colors and pulled their horses to a halt in front of the porch. Not entirely believing her own eyes, Sophia saw the prince dismount with a few of his officers and walk up the front steps.

Prince Adrian walked through the door as Sophia snapped her rifle upright in a salute and shouted, "Squad, attention!" Tony and Edward stopped gawking and quickly snapped to as Adrian pulled his helmet off and looked around at them, blonde hair falling over his shoulders. His gaze passed over her two friends quickly and settled on Sophia. His eyes were the deepest, brightest red as they bored into her soul.

Almost conversationally, Adrian said, "At ease." Sophia relaxed auto-matically, lowering her rifle as Adrian stepped closer and looked down at her. Sophia was tall, but she found herself craning her neck to meet his gaze as he approached. He smiled warmly and said, "Fancy meeting you again, Miss Rose."

He was wearing that same cologne. It smelled even better now. *And he remembered her name.* Feeling herself blushing deeper than she ever had in her life, Sophia bashfully dropped her gaze and said, "Y-yes, mi-lord." He was wearing an armored breastplate now, covered with gray cloth the same shade as his dark jacket. Sophia absently supposed it must be heavy.

She saw Adrian reach up to stroke his chin, "I don't suppose the res-idents are in?" He added, "I'd like to meet them at least before I go and make their house into my headquarters."

"Oh, yes, milord, they are." Sophia rushed, "Lady Charlotte was in the office last I saw her." Adrian started turning to go find her and Sophia quickly stepped to the side and added, "Maybe I should go get her first, milord? I think she's kind of a fainter."

Adrian stepped aside, gestured with his arm and smiled, "After you then, Miss Rose."

A member of his entourage remarked, "Must be nice having to worry about ladies fainting at your sight, Adrian."

He chuckled and replied, "You're one to speak, Francis."

The other cuirassiers laughed, and Sophia looked over at the original speaker to see that Francis was tall, slender and dashingly handsome.
He'd probably gotten a few swoons himself, and he gave a catty smile and
shot back, "Oh, you *know* it, my lord."

The prince frowned abruptly, glanced at Sophia and her companions
and jerked his head. Francis and the rest of the prince's retinue seemed to
notice them for the first time, and they all coughed and started straightening their equipment. Adrian looked back to her and said, "If you would,
Miss Rose. I'd like to meet this Lady Charlotte."

Sophia nodded and said, "Of course, milord." She led him deeper into
the house, thinking, *what was that? Did I miss something?* Arriving at
the office door, she knocked and called out, "Milady? You've got a caller!
And please sit down when I bring him in!"

She heard a few movements inside and imagined Charlotte climbing
out from under her father's desk. After a few moments the girl replied, a
little quizzically, "Uh, sure! Please bring him in."

Sophia opened the door, stepped inside, ushered the prince in and
fought to keep from laughing as the color drained out of Charlotte's face.
Adrian gave the girl a short bow and remarked, "I'll forgive you for not
rising, my lady. To whom do I owe the pleasure?"

Just as quickly Charlotte flushed red and stammered, "C-C-Charlotte
Espinay, my lord!"

"Well, I'm afraid I'm going to be imposing on your hospitality for a
little while." Adrian said, "I presume you don't have a problem with that,
milady?"

"Of course not!" Charlotte squeaked.

"Thank you, milady." Smiling, Adrian turned to her, nodded and said,
"And, Miss Rose, thank you for clearing the place out for us." Sophia felt
herself blushing again, and was about to reply when he went on, "You can
consider yourself relieved. Take your men and go rejoin your regiment.
Please give them my regards."

Sophia snapped to, saluted and said, "Yes, sir!" Turning, she walked
out the office door and quickly collected her squad, led them past the
prince's retinue as they waited for his return and out the front door. The
cuirassiers were beginning to disperse around the estate as they walked
down the drive, and they got a few dismissive looks as they went. Mostly
the cavalrymen ignored them as they marched past. Sophia supposed

most of them thought of infantry as targets to be slashed down.

After a few minutes, and with the estate disappearing into the trees behind them, Tony caught up to her and needled, smiling slyly, "I think you've got a crush, Sophie."

She felt herself redden a little as she replied, "There's nothing wrong with liking the prince!"

"Yeah," Tony shot back, "Except he knows your name."

Sophia snorted and gave him a look, "Well," she smiled and added softly, "He's not the *only* person I like."

Tony blushed and smiled a little. The rest of the walk back to town and the company was pleasant and blessedly uneventful. The sun shone, the birds sang, and just for a while all was right in the world.

Chapter 26

Point of No Return

The morning sun filtered through the trees lining the Wolf Rock promenade, casting dappled shadows on the pavement below. Birds sang happily as a warm wind rustled the leaves overhead, the earthy smell of the fortress' lawns and gardens mixing with brewing coffee from the cafes set along the path getting ready for the rush of soldiers walking to work. It brought back memories of another promenade a long way away that, long ago, he had always taken his morning run around. It made him feel like a younger man. Walter snorted softly. His companion for the morning probably had more to do with it.

Patricia gave him a sidelong glance, covered her mouth and chuckled. Dropping her hand, she smiled and remarked, "I'm guessing this reminds you of something?"

Walter looked back at her and gave her a half-smile, "Yes, actually. The one good memory I have from the Black Citadel."

"Oh." The younger woman thought for a moment and replied, "I was thinking the Harem Gardens in Dar al-Suleiman."

"I can see that," Walter grunted and replied, "Although I wish our circumstances were closer."

Patricia asked, "Having won the war already?"

Walter chuckled, "Yes."

She gave him that wide smile again, "We've really been through a lot, haven't we?"

"More than I'd wish on anyone. Although," He gave her a sidelong look and teased her, "I've got a few more wars under my belt than you, young lady."

She huffed, "Oh, come *on*, Walter." It was remarkably cute.

Walter said, "You know, I almost didn't believe you last night when you told me why Arilin wasn't coming." He went on, "But I've had three people ask me this morning if I'd heard about what she did yesterday."

"What, fight all challengers in three cavalry regiments?" She asked, laughing, "That poor girl was *done*. She's probably still sleeping."

"I can imagine." Walter chuckled again, "Just as well. I don't think she would have enjoyed the meeting. *I* didn't."

Patricia replied, "Glad to hear you weren't the only one." She hesitated for a second, then asked, "Do you really think it's going to happen? That way, I mean."

He snorted, "Unless Slade Anjanou is as dumb as White thinks he is."

She rolled her eyes, "Yeah, he isn't. But, well..." She went on after a moment, "What are we going to do about it?"

He grunted. That was the problem. After a moment he replied, "White isn't giving me a lot of flexibility. I'll have to go behind his back."

Patricia's eyes grew grim, "You? *We'll* have to go behind his back."

"Thanks for your support," Walter said drily.

She thought for a moment, then asked, "But, wait. How do you know White isn't going to change the battle plan?" She furrowed her eyebrows angrily, "I saw the same analysis you did last night. It's solid. It's a lot better than what his staff keeps sending us."

"Because I've already asked him, several times. I've been sending him telegrams ever since the Empire pulled out of Grenville." Walter sighed, "I sent another one after we got out last night. With the full report. You should have *seen* his reply."

Patricia grimaced, "Not good?"

He shook his head, "No. One sentence, 'Your defeatism has been noted.'"

"Wow." Patricia remarked, "And I thought he was a jerk to *me*."

"Try working for him someday." Walter replied.

She nodded, "Well, then I guess it's up to us."

Walter gave her a look and said, "You realize if we do this – if – we're going to lose the battle anyways. And White will blame *us* for it."

Patricia sighed and looked at the pavement for a second, "Yes, now that you mention it." She grit her teeth and looked back up at him defiantly, "But I joined the Army to protect the Kingdom. White can go to hell."

He reached over and put a hand on her shoulder reassuringly. He could feel her trembling through the heavy cloth of her uniform. She looked back at him, surprised, and he said, "Don't worry. I'll take full responsibility, whatever happens."

The younger woman deflated, "Thanks."

Walter asked, "You think you can get Arilin to bring the King onboard with this? He might be willing to overrule White."

She nodded, "Yeah. We'll need to talk to her first though. It's not like she's my private link with the King."

"Bring her by my office after lunch." Walter replied, "I need to work out your part of the plan anyways. I'll brief you then." He went on, "In the meantime start getting your division ready to move. We may be leaving as early as tomorrow."

Patricia smiled, "Yes, sir."

He chuckled and breathed in the warm summer air. Weather like this was wasted on battles. Smiling, he changed the subject, "Now how about I get you a coffee, milady?"

* * *

Someone timidly knocked on her office door, or rather the side of her doorway given that the door was open. She'd already had to remind the secretary to not close it on her when she was in. She clearly wasn't used to the new leadership yet. Looking up, she saw the girl peeking timidly around the corner at her. She smiled and said, "Yes, what is it?"

"M-Milady, there's a visitor for you. He says Colonel Schrader sent him." She said nervously.

She raised an eyebrow, "What does he want?"

The girl replied, "Some papers signed. A range approval request."

"Oh? Send him in." Patricia put down the order she was reading and leaned back in her chair, steepling her fingers in front of her chest. Whoever had occupied this office earlier had exquisite taste. Her massive leather-upholstered swivel chair was more comfortable than some beds she'd slept in. The secretary disappeared and she heard her tell someone to go in. Shortly afterwards a nondescript major in a lancer's uniform walked in and stood to attention in front of her desk.

Patricia chuckled and said, "You can relax. Please, sit down. And let me take a look at what you have there."

The major nervously sat down in one of the chairs she'd pulled over in front of her desk earlier that morning. Apparently Chapman had preferred to keep his visitors standing. Leaning forward, he handed her a folder with what felt like a few papers inside. She opened it to see a printed form with quite a lot of information filled in on it and a number of signatures towards the bottom. Apparently the 20th Lancers' 1st Squadron wanted to zero their carbines at Range 33 tomorrow morning. No wonder they'd had someone walk this in. Patricia thumbed through rest of the papers in the folder. An ammunition request, an order for the range, the medical evacuation plan... everything seemed to be in order.

She got out her pen and was about to sign off on it when something twinged in the back of her head. She set the folder down abruptly and asked the major, "Why am I signing this?"

He raised an eyebrow questioningly, "Ah... because the brigade commander approves all ranges? At least that's how General Chapman did things. Ma'am."

"Well, we're a division now, for one. Wait a minute." She pulled out her notebook and quickly flipped through the pages. Finding Siegfried's phone number, she pulled her telephone off its heavy brass hooks and quickly spun the dial to the correct numbers. After a couple rings a familiar voice answered, "General Reinhardt, Chief of Staff."

She replied, "General MacMahon."

"Trixie!" He shot back, "Enjoying the new office?"

"Oh, absolutely." She replied, "Sorry, got a visitor. I just had a question."

He said, "Go ahead."

She asked, "Does V Corps have a policy on rank for approval of live fire ranges?"

"Whoever owns it, I guess." He paused for a minute, "Don't tell me Chapman..."

"Yeah." She said, "He did. Him, personally."

She could hear Siegfried rolling his eyes, "That explains *so many things*. Is that all? Sorry, the idiots in the Rail Service just decided it would be a *great* idea to shunt the entire siege train in front of us."

"Yeah, that's it." She finished, "Have fun up there."

"Tootles." Siegfried hung up and she turned back to her visitor.

She signed his papers, handed them back to him and said, "So, I'll sign these for you today, but in the future you're not going to have to ask me about this kind of thing. Sound good?"

"Yes, ma'am." He stood, rubbed at the back of his neck for a moment and said, "Ah, thanks, ma'am. Doing this every time we want to go shoot is a pain."

"I can imagine." He nodded and left quickly. She saw him do a double-take as he walked out and quickly step to the side and out of view as Arilin and Vanessa walked by into her office. She smiled, "Ah, milady! I've been waiting for you."

The princess looked like she could have used a few more hours in bed, but she replied gamely, "Pleased to see you too, Patricia. Although," She gave Vanessa a look, "She wouldn't tell me why I had to go get my measurements taken on the way over here."

Good girl. She smiled, "I told her to keep it a secret. I'll surprise you later."

"Oh?" Arilin laughed tiredly, "I'll look forward to it then."

Patricia checked her pocketwatch, "Oh, my. We'll be late if we don't leave soon."

The princess perked up a little, "Late? What for?"

"Walter's going to get us up to speed on the battle plan. And we have a favor to ask of you." She thought for a moment, then went on, "But I'll, ah... save that for when we get there. It needs to be explained properly."

The princess narrowed her eyes, "You want me to send something direct to my father, I'm assuming?"

Patricia sighed, "Yeah, basically. You'll understand why after we talk to Walter."

Arilin shrugged, "Okay."

"Before we go, sorry..." She turned to her aide, "Vanessa, I need you to go talk to Colonel Frost. Tell him that from now on if the regiments want to schedule training areas they will go through the operations staff, not me personally. And have him take a look at whatever other standing procedures Chapman had in place." She snorted, "I get the feeling if we turn this place upside down and shake it that *skeletons* will come falling out."

"Yes, ma'am!" Vanessa turned and rushed out of the room. Patricia was about to turn back to Arilin when she stuck her head back in the door and asked, "Ma'am, by the way, do you want me to get your tea set from your baggage? I figured that you have a new office now..."

Patricia cocked her head and asked, "You *brought* it?"

"Yes, ma'am." Vanessa added, "It's in the trunk marked 'fragile.'"

Which I have never opened. This girl thinks of everything. Seeing Arilin struggling to keep from laughing, Patricia regained her composure and said, "Ah, of course. Thank you, Vanessa."

"My pleasure, ma'am." Vanessa vanished noiselessly into the outer office.

Patricia smiled warmly and told Arilin, "Well, milady, let's get going." Her soldiers brought their horses around front and they were soon on their way back into the fortress. The soldiers milling through the streets hastened to make way for them, and they were soon riding down the promenade.

Arilin had been unusually silent for much of the ride, but as the imposing headquarters building loomed ahead she ventured, "What was the meeting about last night?" She smiled, a little sheepishly, "I'm sorry I didn't make it."

"Don't be, it was boring and depressing." Patricia replied darkly, "You would have either been scared or put to sleep anyways." Arilin gave her a look and she went on, "Ah, well... milady, General Haas asked the staff to look at the campaign from the Imperial perspective a couple weeks ago. They presented their work last night."

"And?" Arilin raised an eyebrow questioningly.

"Well, milady, it was... remarkable." She chuckled nervously, "I'm hoping it was just them going down a very dark hole, but I've fought the Empire enough to know their *real* plan is probably even worse."

The princess furrowed her eyebrows, "So it didn't look good for us?"

"No." They reached the long stone pathway branching off the promenade to the front of the headquarters and turned off onto it. The horses' shod hooves clattered on the pavement as they approached and two soldiers ran out to take their horses. Patricia dismounted and went on, "But Walter can explain it better than I can. Half of it's positioning."

"I think I understand." Hopping down from her sidesaddle, Arilin smoothed her dress and went on, "Let's go see him then." They walked in, climbed around the grand staircase circling the lobby to the third floor and were met by a nondescript captain who quickly took them back towards Walter's office. As they went Arilin leaned over and whispered to her, "Who is that guy? I see him around here all the time."

She replied softly, "He's Walter's aide... I think." She would have went on, but the man led them into a very nice wood-paneled reception area past a secretary typing away at something, pulled open a heavy door and ushered them into Walter's office. The door swung closed behind them noiselessly, and Walter looked up from his papers and rose to meet them. She smiled and nodded, "Afternoon, sir."

He chuckled, "I wish I could say this was a *good* afternoon." He looked over at Arilin, "Milady."

The princess bobbed her head graciously, "General. Patricia here has been telling me for the last hour that you're going to explain something to me, but," she gave her a look, "She's been very vague about what exactly *it* is. Something to do with the war plan?"

Walter grunted. Patricia got the feeling he would have laughed if he'd been in a better mood as he replied, "Yes, milady. I want you to take a look at this." He looked at her, "You too, Patricia." He pointed to a large map of the Western Marches pinned to the wall behind them. They turned as he came out from behind the massive desk and walked up beside her.

Arilin stepped forward and studied the map intently. Patricia didn't need to. It was the same thing she'd seen the last night, and she almost didn't want to look at it. The two of them watched silently as the princess walked back and forth in front of the huge map, peering at arrows and cryptic unit symbols and growing more agitated by the second. Finally she turned to Walter and demanded, "Is this *serious?*"

He nodded, "Yes, unfortunately. In fact, it's not even the worst-case scenario." He gave her a serious look, "And that is where I need your help, milady."

Arilin's eyes widened, "Why? What can I... do for you?" She went on hesitantly, "Have you... I mean, I'm assuming you've told White about this already?"

He chuckled, "Yes, for all the good it's done me."

Patricia chimed in, "Remember what I told you about Field Marshal White earlier, milady?"

The princess cocked her head and thought for a moment, "He thinks the Empire will fall over after one hit?"

Walter grunted, "A little more than that, milady. He thinks they're already defeated and running after his one good hit at Grenville, and his staff is unfortunately playing right along. All we have to do is push a little harder and we'll be in Lady Vai City before the leaves fall." He smiled grimly, "But let me explain this all to you properly."

Arilin nodded, "Of course." She smoothed her skirt nervously and gestured to the map, "Please go ahead, sir."

Walter strode in front of them, picked up a pointer he had set against the wall for the occasion and started, "Now, milady, this is Fire Ridge." He pointed to a long spur jutting north from the foothills of the Dragonspine mountains, "The Moon River and the Marchlands here to the east and Grenville to the west." He chuckled grimly and waved the pointer off to the left side of the map, "Wolf Rock is over here."

Arilin nodded, "I understand."

"Now the Field Marshal thinks there is an Imperial corps dug in on Fire Ridge itself *here*." He tapped an enemy corps on the map, "And another one *here* that will delay us and gradually fall back to the Moon River to give the Empire time to prepare defenses on that line." He tapped another corps farther to the north and went on, "Thus far I agree with his assessment."

Arilin pointed to the gigantic, imposing enemy symbol further to the north of the ridge, "I'm guessing you disagree about *that?*"

Walter nodded, "Yes, milady. White's worst-case scenario has the Western Area Army digging in behind the Moon River to fight it out in the Marchlands." He snorted, "I disagree."

Arilin's eyebrows narrowed, "Why?"

"It's *exactly* what they did in the last war." Walter gave her a stern look back, "And it plays to our strengths and against theirs."

Patricia added, "If the Empire lets us deploy and mass on the Moon River, we'll blast our way through eventually. We have the troops and the firepower. And," She added grimly, "White's more than willing to pay the price."

The princess looked at the map and ventured, "So, if White thinks the Imperial forces on Fire Ridge are weak, it looks like he's going to try a flanking maneuver?" She gestured to the arrows drawn across the map showing several Royal corps marching north through the flatlands beyond the ridge and swinging back beyond it.

Walter nodded, "Yes, milady. V Corps will pin the enemy in place on the upper ridge, VI Corps will try to break through on the lower ridge, and VII, VIII, XII and XIV with," He squinted at the map trying to decipher the mass of symbols, "II, III and IV Corps behind them will swing to the north, break through whatever defenses are in the flatlands and sweep down to the Moon River. The enemy on the ridge will be surrounded and destroyed and we'll be postured to continue the attack." Walter took out his monocle to polish it for a moment and added, "Of course, this is assuming General Anjanou plays along nicely."

Arilin cocked her head and asked, "So... what is the Empire going to do? I mean, I can see that if they're positioned that way our attack is going to miss their main army." She continued, "But wouldn't we be able to adjust anyways? Our cavalry should find them out before we commit."

Walter sighed, popped his monocle back in and gestured to Patricia, "All due respect to the hussars, Patricia, but..."

She finished his sentence, "We haven't been very successful at actually *finding* the Empire's main units thus far. From everything I've heard their dragoons are better than ever and every cavalry unit that has really pushed against them has gotten shot to pieces." She gave Arilin a mirthless smile, "I think I can change that, but, well, *my* division hasn't even deployed yet."

"What about the Airship Corps?" Arilin asked, eyes widening, "Or reconnaissance aircraft? A force this size should be *obvious* from the air."

"You'd think so, milady." The generals chuckled together humorlessly, and Patricia went on, "Truth be told, an airship made a run down the Night River the day before they attacked Raven Wing and didn't see a thing. The Imperials are *good* at hiding from aircraft, and with the amount of time they've had to infiltrate in we're not going to find them unless we actually shake the bushes or they all start moving at once."

"And by that point it will be too late. White is going to push forward into a situation where he has dragoons on his left flank." Walter added, tapping the map for emphasis, "He'll hit Imperial infantry and they'll start retreating east towards the river, pulling him in. He'll have *no reason* to think those dragoons are anything but a weak screen to be brushed aside while he goes for the kill."

Arilin observed, "Rather than hiding the main Imperial force to the north, past the ridge?"

Walter said, "Yes. And then..."

Patricia finished, "The bear trap slams shut and we lose half a million men and the Marchlands forever." She snorted, "Most likely scenario, right? Just wait, milady, this gets *better*."

The princess paled a little, but she said, "Okay, go on, please."

"Yes, as Patricia said, this is what I believe is the *conservative* scenario. Here the Empire only goes after the flanking force." Walter went on coldly, "If Slade really gets aggressive, he will do a broader encircling maneuver like *this*." He gestured in a broad circle with the pointer around the entire ridge, "And the Army of Drakenburg will die on Fire Ridge. Milady," His eyes pierced into Arilin's soul, "If the Empire pulls that off, this Christmas we will be fighting them in *the Capital*."

Arilin paled. Patricia remembered what she had told her after they had visited the hospital in Drakenburg, seemingly so long ago. *The Empire of Masks will not be safe until the High City burns.* That young dragoon, so sure of victory. And here it was. If the Empire pulled this off it would roll the clock back four hundred years, to the days when the Faceless King's army was battering down the walls of the Capital itself. She'd seen all this the night before and she still felt a chill up her spine seeing it all laid out so plainly. She couldn't imagine what the princess was thinking.

The girl looked a little shaky, so Patricia helpfully grabbed a chair and set it behind her, "Maybe you should sit down, milady. You look pale."

"Oh... thank you." Arilin sank into it gratefully and closed her eyes for a moment, visibly composing herself. Finally she opened them and asked, "What can I do?"

Walter replied, "I need you to send this analysis directly to your father. I'm assuming you can get it to him?" The princess nodded and he went on, "I need you to ask him to order White to halt and mass the Army at Fire Ridge before proceeding. Hopefully White will obey."

"And if he doesn't?" Arilin asked.

Walter said, "Then your father needs to relieve him of command and take over himself."

The princess thought hard for a moment, then said, "But this is all based on *analysis*. You said yourself White has a different view of this... couldn't he be right?" She finished, "My father will want *proof*."

Walter shook his head slowly, "I'll give you what I have, but like you said. It's all analysis. Very detailed, but still analysis. Unfortunately I'm not in a position to tell VI Corps to send their cavalry north and get hard proof. Maybe your father could dictate that, but I sure can't."

Arilin thought for a moment, then nodded slowly, "I'll do it. It's the least I can do for you, really."

He gave her a short bow, "Thank you, milady." Straightening up, he looked at Patricia, "Speaking of proof, I have a mission for you, Patricia."

His words snapped her out of a haze, and she straightened up as she replied, "Yes? Sir?"

He snapped his pointer against the map at a certain point on the railroad, "The earliest we'll be able to verify the Empire is even executing this is during the worst-case scenario, and they'll be most of the way through the envelopment by then." He grunted, "Knowing White he may not have even caught on by that point, so I'll need warning to reorient the corps."

Patricia laughed darkly and replied, "I think I see where this is going. You want us to deploy early facing north and try to find the Empire's lead units."

Walter gave her a satisfied nod, "Exactly. We'll make it look like you got shunted somewhere wrong by the Rail Service. They do that all the time, after all," He chuckled and went on, "If all you hit are dragoons, and you may very well hit them in divisional strength even if the Empire is doing their conservative plan, then we have some time. If you see infantry or heavy guns..."

"Then we're in for the fight of our lives." Patricia finished, "Sure thing. Send the orders over and we'll get right to work on it at the division." She thought for a moment and smiled, "Just like old times, huh?"

Walter snorted and remarked, "Yes, actually. Go see what's on the other side of that hill so I can figure out what to do. And try to not get killed while you're at it."

"They haven't gotten me yet." She glanced at Arilin for a moment. She was brightening a little at their banter. And she supposed she had played a pretty big role getting her to this point. Feeling her smile broaden, she finished, "Walter."

He smiled back and bowed his head, "Trixie."

Arilin was still giggling about that one halfway back to the division.

Chapter 27

The Day of Battle

A bird sang happily off to his side in the tree as the warm summer wind teased at the long braid that hung down his back. June smiled a little beneath his mask. The storm clouds from earlier were disappearing far to the west as bright sunlight soaked down on Fire Ridge, the recent rain giving the valley spread in front of him a jeweled sheen. He couldn't think of a nicer day. And, he thought as he raised his binoculars back to his eyes, the Royal Army had picked a fine day for a battle.

"Do you think they'll attack today, sir?" Anastasia Lai was sitting on the limb below him with the field telephone. He kept scanning the far side of the valley as she went on, "I... really hope they don't."

June replied, "Yes, I do." He glanced down at her for a moment, then back into his binoculars. She was hunched over into herself, clearly afraid. He couldn't blame her after what they'd gone through so far. He went on, "And honestly, I hope they do. Today. The sooner they attack, the better."

He could hear her move as she gave him a scared look, "Why... why would you s-say that, sir?"

"Officer business." That wasn't much of an answer, so he went on, "We all had a talk with Colonel Vann a couple days ago and she explained the battle plan to us. It will be better for the army if the Kingdom attacks us here, now."

Anastasia sounded doubtful, "That's not very reassuring, sir."

"No, it's not." June chuckled grimly, "And just between you and me, Lai, I'm terrified."

She laughed and said, "Thanks, sir." She paused, then ventured, "Do you think the old Black Knights felt this way? Before battle?"

"I'm sure Lady Vai herself..." June trailed off. He'd looked off to the right and seen something, tiny, dark figures emerging from a woodline off to the north. Holding out his hand, he said, "Give me the phone. Looks like the Royal Army just answered your question." After a couple seconds of fumbling beneath him he felt the hard plastic receiver in his hand, and before he raised it to his head he ordered, "Watch the valley in front of us for me. I'm going to observe off to the right for a while."

Anastasia swallowed and said, "Yes, sir." He heard her bring her own set of binoculars up to her eyes.

"Thanks," June keyed the receiver and said, "Knight Relay, this is Aegis

One Six. I've got a fire mission out of sector. Need to talk to Bronze."

The field telephone buzzed, "Roger, patching. Wait."

The line popped and crackled for a few seconds before a bored voice answered, "Bronze Control."

June licked his lips, "Bronze Control, this is Aegis One Six. I've got a fire mission."

The woman on the other end of the line audibly perked up, "Oh, really? Send it and I'll tell you if we can shoot it."

June looked down at the map he had shoved into the top of his thigh-length dragoon gaiters and replied, "Alright. Grid hotel victor seven three one, nine five one. Infantry moving in the open, I've seen a platoon so far." June looked back up into his binoculars to see more black figures coming out of the woodline. He corrected himself, "More like a company, actually. They're coming out of the forest."

The woman asked, "Speed and direction of travel? And do you need an adjustment?"

June replied, "They're moving east, walking pace." He thought for a second and went on, "No adjustment. They'll scatter."

He heard the fire direction officer smile predatorily, "I like you, Aegis One-Six. Light regiment, four rounds impact and time centered on predicted location. Stand by to observe, firing in four minutes."

June looked at his watch, "Roger, standing by for shot. Will update as needed."

The woman chuckled, "Thanks. Keep the line open."

June heard a few thumps off to the north towards Imperial lines, followed by dull rumbling off to the west. Probably Royal artillery. Anastasia said, "Do you think..." She trailed off, and June heard her steady her binoculars and peer off to their front. She went on, "Sir, I've got people on the far side of the valley."

June looked down at his watch. Three minutes before the artillery would fire. He had time. Swinging his binoculars back to their front, June looked across the line of fields and scattered houses far below them. Spotting a distinctive blue-painted house, he asked, "Where are they in relation to that blue house?"

His companion figured it out and replied, "There's a stand of trees two hundred to the left. You can see a few there. I'm looking for more."

June looked at the small group of trees for a moment and saw movement. A figure in light clothing walked between two trees on their side of the grove and knelt. June noticed a rifle in his hands and saw his head change shape a little as he talked to someone else. June quickly scanned around the grove, then back under the trees in the forest beyond it. No horses. Royal cavalry dismounted sometimes, but they'd been tangling with hussars for a hundred kilometers and they were never too far from their horses. And they had distinctive red breeches. This was different.

June looked down at his watch reflexively. Thirty seconds. He put the field telephone back to his ear and swung back to his right as he said, "Keep watching them. We'll call it up after this mission goes in." He keyed the telephone and said, "Bronze Control, this is Aegis One Six. Standing by. We may have additional targets after this mission."

The woman purred, "Lovely. Firing in three, two..." She dropped off the line for a second, then came back, "Shot. It's going to be east of your target location. Two hundred and sixteen rounds." June waited a few seconds, then saw dirt kick up in the fields to the north. Dark figures, dots at this range, disappeared as the valley suddenly filled with smoke and dust. As the woman said, "Rounds complete," June heard a few soft pops ring through the valley. They built to a thudding roar before dying off just as suddenly.

In the distance a few Royal soldiers ran back into the woodline, some of them moving slowly in clumps of two or three. June swallowed hard. They were dragging back the wounded. June keyed the telephone and said, "Rounds effective. They're pulling back... no." He couldn't believe his eyes. More Royal infantry were pouring out of the woods, and he saw a few figures emerge from the clearing smoke and press grimly forward. A flash of light caught his eye as an officer urged his men on with a drawn sword. June said, "Incorrect. They're still advancing and there are more troops coming out of the woodline. Maybe twenty or thirty casualties. Can you saturate the area?" He glanced back towards his front. He had his own battle to fight, "And I need to deal with my own situation, I'm way out of sector for this mission. Do you have another observer available?"

"Stubborn, aren't they?" The fire direction officer purred, "Sure, we'll pass it north. I'm sure *somebody* saw it. Call again, One Six. You sound cute. Out."

June glanced down at Anastasia and remarked, "Bronze Control thinks I sound cute."

"Really?" She said, "I mean, ah, it's not like you don't really, but aren't we kind of in a *battle* here?"

He snickered, "Hey, some people are into that kind of thing. Can you get me the company?"

"Sure." He heard her rearrange the field telephone's switches and the whirr as she cranked it, "Try it now, sir."

June swung his binoculars back onto the copse of trees and spoke into the telephone, "Six, this is one six. We've got Royal infantry in the valley."

After a moment a voice buzzed back at him, "Six tango." The commander's operator. "Roger, where?"

June thought about how they had planned the battle earlier and replied, "The stand of trees between target reference points five and six. Should be about eight hundred meters from you." June paused, then went on, "Gray uniforms, probably jaegers. I've seen two or three."

June imagined the operator getting the commander's attention. Sure enough, after a moment Captain Marsten's voice sounded over the line, "Infantry scouts? I don't see anything right now. Are you sure, one six?"

He squinted through his binoculars for a moment. He didn't either, but they were probably down in cover. June replied, "Yes sir. Saw them myself about three minutes ago. Want me to hit them with mortars?"

"You're sure they're jaegers?" Marsten asked.

June nodded and immediately felt stupid. He was talking on the telephone. Finally he said, "Sir, we've been fighting Royal cavalry for a while. These guys aren't them. No red pants and no horses."

His commander sighed, "Alright, go ahead. Let's poke this hornet's nest."

When Marsten had briefed June and the other lieutenants yesterday he'd told them they were just going to let any Royal cavalry ride by towards Fire Ridge unless they absolutely had to fight them. They were going to stay in position until the enemy's infantry, their main force, came into the valley. And infantry scouts meant the line infantry wasn't far behind. As June thought another rumbling roar shook the air and he glanced to the side to see smoke rising from the forest to the north. No, they weren't far. June imagined lines of blue-jacketed soldiers crouching on the far side of the valley, waiting for their officers to wave them forward.

Well, he'd see if that was the case or not soon. Looking back into his binoculars, June spoke into the handset, "Will do, sir." Pulling it away from his mouth for a moment he said, "Anastasia, get me the mortars." She obligingly made the connection and cranked the telephone to life, and he said, "Catapult, this is one six. I've got a fire mission."

"Send it, one six." Sergeant Jameson's no-nonsense voice came back at him.

"Need adjusting rounds," June started, "Grid hotel victor seven five five, eight nine eight. Infantry in a stand of trees." He thought for a moment, "Do you have white phosphorous?"

Jameson replied, "Yeah, six rounds shake and bake once you get zeroed. Stand by for adjusting round." June steadied his binoculars one-handed and wished he had an extra pair of arms to hold onto the tree, the telephone and them at the same time. After the better part of a minute he heard a mortar crack behind him and the telephone buzzed, "Shot."

"Heard it." June replied sarcastically.

June waited. And waited, peering intently through his binoculars. He was about to call the mortars back when he spotted a puff of dirt rising on the far side of the stand of trees. Close enough to work with. He called an adjustment into the radio and a mortar cracked behind him again, sending a round down on the near side. Satisfied, he spoke into the telephone, "That will do it. Add one hundred and fire for effect." A couple figures in gray suddenly stood in the grove and June added, "And make it quick, they're about to run for it."

The mortars started thudding behind him as more figures appeared and disappeared in the grove. June saw a couple jaegers run out into the open, throw themselves down and disappear as black and white puffs blanketed the trees. A few seconds later he heard the popping sound of the shells, and June spoke into the telephone, "Rounds effective. There's a lot of smoke... two or three casualties, I guess."

Jameson replied, "Good enough. Want another salvo?"

June thought for a moment and replied, "No. We'll see what..." He trailed off as he heard faint popping below him, then said, "Looks like they're angry. I've got machine guns in the valley. Stand by for more missions."

Below him, Anastasia said, "Sir, I've got the commander on the line."

"Put him on," June replied, then spoke into the telephone, "Sir? One six."

"Someone's shooting at us." Captain Marsten didn't sound too worried, "It's not well-aimed, I don't think they know where we are. See anything from your perch?"

"Wait a minute." June scanned the valley and saw something flash faintly from a farmhouse left of the trees. He looked closer and a few seconds later it flashed again. Smoke puffed faintly, and he saw what he thought was the muzzle of a Royal machine gun perched in an upstairs window. "Yep, got something. They're upstairs in TRP three."

"Well ain't that something." Marsten remarked, "I'll call a fire mission on it, you keep looking."

"Will do." June put his binoculars back to his eyes and went back to scanning the valley. After a couple minutes the mortars erupted behind him again and he looked back to see the house covered in a pall of gleaming white phosphorous smoke. Nasty stuff. June shivered and swung his binoculars back towards the copse of trees, now smoking as the wet vegetation reluctantly burned. He might have seen movement there, but it was hard to make out in the smoke. He looked harder as another string of deep bangs, a sound he recognized as a Royal machine gun, drifted out of the valley. Nothing... *no, wait,* he thought. *There.* Off to the side and a little forward of the trees a telltale plume of dust rose as the gunner fired another burst. He keyed the field telephone again, "I've got another gun by the grove, the one I hit originally. About fifty meters to the right and forward a little."

"Roger. We'll hit it again." Marsten replied, "See anything on our flanks? We can handle the guys in front of us just fine. You watch and see if they're trying to work their way around."

June thought for a moment. Two machine guns meant two squads, which meant there was at least a Royal platoon down there. A platoon with half of its heavy weapons unaccounted-for. Or a company feeling them out. He asked, "You think we're looking at a company, sir?"

Marsten came back on the line after a little while, "I hope not... I've got to deal with this fight. Call me if you see anything. Six out."

The mortars fired again and again over the next few minutes, little black smoke puffs chasing fleeting gray figures as Royal gunfire echoed through the valley. June saw a clump of jaegers heading back towards the woodline off to the left, probably a stretcher party. June moved his binoculars out in front of them and saw a tree-lined road emerge from the forest. *Logical place for an aid station,* June thought as he swung his binoculars left, farther down the road towards him and... June inhaled sharply as he saw them. About as far left as he could see, more than halfway across the valley, shapes were rushing through the ditch under the trees.

June picked up the telephone again and said, "Six, one six. I've found that flanking movement. They're in the ditch on the far side of the shaded road past TRP seven, moving east. At least a squad-" *And possibly many more.* June swallowed and went on, "Want me to bring my platoon around?"

His commander thought for a moment, then replied, "Yeah. We haven't been shooting, but I think whoever's in charge over there made a good guess about our position." He paused for a moment and then said, in the formal tones of someone ordering men to their deaths, "One six, move around on our left and defeat the flanking movement, then fall back on my position. We have extra foxholes."

"Acknowledged." June repeated back, "I'll come around on your left and take out whatever they're sending forward on that flank, then fall back into the position."

"You've got it." Marsten replied curtly, "Six out."

June handed his companion the handset back and said, "We've got a new mission. Pack up, we're heading back to the platoon."

Anastasia quickly climbed down the tree, June following a moment behind her. They hurried back through the forest over the top of the hill, Anastasia lagging behind to roll up the telephone wire. After a couple hundred meters June spotted one of his sentries waving him in, and he walked past the man to see Sergeant Khan winding her way through the position towards him. Carefully avoiding falling into a couple of foxholes, she made her way up to him and asked, "What's happening, sir?" She gestured to the dragoons spread out behind the hilltop, masked faces curiously looking at them out of foxholes, "The mortars told me there's a fight going on... are we going forward?"

June nodded, "Yes. The enemy's got at least a squad and probably a lot more moving on the company's left." Khan nodded and he went on, "We're going to go down there and stop them. Get the squad leaders in, we need get moving *now*."

Khan said, "Yes, sir," and turned to gather up their subordinates as he sat down on a convenient rock to figure out what exactly they were going to do. After a couple minutes Anastasia made it back with a roll of wire over her shoulder and he told her to hurry down to the mortars and disconnect it from their junction box. She quickly headed downhill reeling in the wire, passing Khan and the other sergeants coming back up towards him.

"So, sir," His platoon sergeant started as the NCOs gathered around him, "What's the plan?"

June had cleared the leaves from the ground and drawn a crude map of the hill and road to the south in the dirt. Drawing his bayonet, he gestured with the point, "We're here, just behind the crest of the hill. The company's on the front side of the hill here, and the enemy is maneuvering down the road here to flank them." He drew another line parallel to the road, "I think they'll cut into the forest early and try to sweep north."

"And if they don't? What if they keep going along the road and try to attack us from behind?" Newly-promoted Sergeant Marin asked.

June smiled beneath his mask, "We'll be ready for them anyways." He drew a line from the hilltop down to the road, "We'll start in platoon column. Marin, when your squad hits the road signal me and we'll do a right face and sweep west on line." He looked at his machine gun section leader, "Corporal Carsten, you'll go with Marin's squad in the lead. If they come down the road, set down and stop them."

The stocky gunner nodded wordlessly and June went on, "If we're lucky and they're in the forest, we'll flank them. If they're still on the road, well... it's not exactly going to be an L-shaped ambush, but it'll be close." He looked around the gathered dragoons, "Any questions?"

Khan asked, "How close do you want to engage, sir?"

"Grenade range. *Swords* if you can." June went on, "The closer the better. Don't even let them set their machine guns down. If it turns out there's a whole company down there I want to be running over them before they even know we're there."

Grim chuckles went around the circle. They were all remembering the charge in the fog at Grenville. June finished, "If that's all, get back to your squads and get them moving. We step off in three minutes. And," He gestured with the knife in his hand, "Fix bayonets."

Anastasia got back from recovering the telephone wire and found him talking quietly with Sergeant Ghaznavi, whose squad they'd be going with in the middle of the formation. Sensing what was going on, she drew her bayonet and attached it to her rifle as dragoons milled into position around them. June waved her into her position a little ways behind him and checked his watch, hanging from the straps of his load-carrying harness. One minute to step off. As the second hand swept around he heard a new, higher-pitched cracking float up out of the valley. The company's machine guns had finally opened up. They were needed.

The machine-gun section rushed by on the left carrying their heavy weapons and tripods. Just a few seconds later dragoons to his front started waving their hands forward, repeating Marin's signal. They quickly headed downhill, the platoon spreading out on the rocky, forested slope. June inwardly sighed with relief as he saw the machine gun crews make their way forward and disappear towards the head of the column.

After a few minutes they had worked their way downhill, June repeatedly waving for the platoon to spread out as they went. As he was beginning to worry that maybe the road was further down than he'd thought he saw a dragoon far ahead in the first squad raise his hand for a halt and then gesture to the west. Turning to Ghaznavi, June murmured, "That's it. Swing on line and advance on my signal."

The dragoons reoriented themselves, feet swishing through the carpet of wet leaves on the slope as June raised his hand. He looked to his left, then to his right. His soldiers were all looking to him, steel masks deceptively blank. He dropped his hand and the platoon began to stalk forward as one, winding their way around trees and rocks as they negotiated their way around the side of the hill. All around him he heard the soft crunch of boots on leaves, punctuated by the nearby cracking of the company's machine guns.

Occasionally something would hiss through the air and thud into a tree overhead. Ricochets. June didn't even bother ducking. As they moved further forward and the forest darkened June heard a shrieking whine off to the right, then a loud thud that shook the trees. Wings flapped overhead as birds took flight in terror. June found himself flat on his chest behind a convenient rock and, rolling to a knee and brushing himself off, raised his hand to wave the platoon forward again.

Just a ranging sho... June's hand clenched into a fist instinctively as something moved in the trees in front of them. He pulled his hand back and dropped it low to the ground, praying the rest of the platoon saw his signal as he eased himself back down into the tiny depression behind the rock, maneuvering his rifle in front of himself.

"-on, get up!" Someone was talking up ahead faintly. They must have thought the shelling and gunfire made it impossible to hear them, "Keep moving, we're close now." More movement in the trees up ahead, gray uniforms in the dappled sunlight from a light patch in the forest. A group of Royal soldiers climbed to their feet, maybe fifty meters away. Beyond them June saw what looked like another small group of jaegers. A platoon in column, flanking their enemy? June snorted under his breath at the irony.

A jaeger officer with a sword, map case and binoculars in the forward group impatiently waved his men forward and they started moving towards them again. June was pretty sure he was the man who had spoken earlier. He barely dared to breathe as the Royal soldiers got closer and closer. Forty meters. Thirty. Their formation spread out a little as the men adjusted off of each other. Twenty. He could see the officer's face clearly as he turned and muttered something to the machine-gunner beside him. Fifteen. June flicked his rifle's safety off. Ten meters, and the lead jaeger suddenly looked from side to side, face creased in worry as he turned and said, "Sir, something does-"

June hurled himself up onto his knee, raised his rifle to his shoulder and dropped his sights square onto the officer's chest. The man's eyes widened, looking at him in shock as he pulled the trigger. His rifle cracked and for an instant, as he let go of the trigger and pressed his hand down to work the weapon's lever, as the officer's eyes flickered down at the hole in his chest incredulously, the shot echoed through the trees.

And then the forest exploded into a shrieking hell. Bullets chewed the trees to sawdust in front of his eyes, machine guns tearing men to pieces before they could even fall. June slapped his rifle's lever back and forth, fired again into the seething carnage and shouted, "Attack! Attack! *Forward!*"

June's first rush took him clean over the dying Royal officer. He dodged behind a thick tree and fired a couple more times at gray shapes boiling through the trees in the distance until he heard Anastasia plunge to the ground behind him. She fired once and he got up and lunged forward into the midst of a group of Royal soldiers crouching and lying on the ground. June spotted one of them rolling upright away from a machine gun on the ground, hand reaching for a pistol. He dropped his sights onto the man's chest and pulled the trigger as figures rose to either side of him.

June reacted instantly, stepping backwards as a rifle butt slashed at air where his head had been a moment earlier. Twisting his hips, he slammed his rifle's butt into the side of the man's head and lunged forward, burying his bayonet in the other jaeger's ribs. The man jerked and dragged June forward as he fell, the knife stuck in his body. Someone screamed behind him and June finally yanked his bayonet free to turn and see Anastasia pulling her bayonet from the other man's back as he crumpled to the ground.

Suddenly they were surrounded by dragoons, people screaming and shrieking all around them, someone begging for mercy. Just as June turned to order someone to deal with any prisoners the guttering bang of a Royal machine gun tore through the forest, too close. He found himself on the ground as new voices screamed out and it seemed like every machine gun his platoon had roared back, silencing the weapon instantly.

June rolled to his feet, shouted for the platoon to advance and rushed forward again, only to see another group of gray-jacketed soldiers huddled on the ground. The trees around them had been chewed to pieces by his guns' retaliatory burst. The machine-gun team in the middle of the jaeger squad had been shot dozens of times, their bodies scarcely recognizable and clumped around their mangled weapon. Rounding on the nearest jaeger huddled on the ground, June kicked him viciously in the ribs and demanded, "*Surrender! Now, or you die!*"

The man rolled onto his back away from his discarded rifle, shaking as he raised his hands and begged, "Mercy! Mercy! P-please don't kill us!"

"You're lucky I don't!" June spat, "Now on your feet, all of you!" He looked around, his soldiers swinging past his field of view in slow motion in the adrenaline haze. Where the hell was Sergeant Ghaznavi? He saw a couple dragoons corralling some prisoners and attending to the wounded a little way behind them. Well, in a pinch that would do. He laid eyes on a familiar person a few steps away and ordered, "Corporal Tarai!" She turned towards him and he went on, "Take charge of the prisoners and get them and the wounded back to the horses."

The slender woman nodded and June looked to his left and right again. Dragoons were still rushing into position up and down the slope. Anastasia was, as ever, right behind him. He even heard Sergeant Khan bellowing at the machine gunners further down the slope, telling them to move up. Raising his voice over the chaos, he shouted, "Forward! Forward! Keep pushing!"

The platoon bounded forward again, climbing a shallow spur coming off the side of the hill. For the first few rushes he saw nothing, but as he climbed close to the top something gray popped over the top of the rise and a Royal rifle boomed loudly as he dove behind a tangle of roots. He popped up and fired at the darting gray shapes, maybe ten paces away on top of the rise. More rifle shots cracked, splinters raining down on him as they dug into his protection. A Royal machine gun banged to life so close he could almost feel the muzzle blast, then another further down. Then another. There was a whole new platoon here, on line and ready for them.

June's eyes widened as he peeked over his cover and saw light glinting off a Royal bayonet. Looking to his sides he saw his platoon crouching in whatever cover they could find as Royal bullets tore at the forest around them. It was only a matter of time until they charged and finished them off with bayonets. June felt for his sword instinctively and as his fingers touched the hilt it hit him like a lightning bolt. There was another solution to this problem. Pulling open a pouch on his web gear with frantic fingers, June screamed, "*Assault! Grenades!*"

All around him dragoons reached into the same small pouches on their harnesses and pulled out grenades. With him, they clamped their fingers around the arming spoons, yanked the pins free and hurled the bombs over the top of the hill as the evil hiss of burning fuses filled the air. Jaegers screamed. June tucked himself back into his nest of tree roots and the whole forest exploded around him.

Rolling forward, June threw his rifle over his head, felt it fall across his back on its sling and drew his sword as he rose and darted up the rise. He was greeted by a scene out of hell. Jaegers, gray jackets darkening with blood, screamed and moaned amid the smoke and stench of the grenades. A couple men, seemingly unhurt, raised their hands as he looked at them. Behind him he could hear the entire platoon appearing atop the rise, demons in their masks and bloody uniforms.

A little ways back he saw a cluster of men around the familiar shape of a field telephone. None of them seemed hurt, but they stood and raised their hands anyways as he approached. An officer was among them, a captain by his collar patches, and he dropped his hands to his belt as June drew nearer. He flexed his legs to lunge forward and strike when he realized what the man was doing.

The officer unclipped his sword from his belt and offered it to June as he stopped in front of him, saying in a shocked voice, "W-we have been d-defeated. Please accept our surrender."

Taking a deep breath, June reached out and took the man's sword with his free hand. It was a thin, straight Royal Army infantry sword, and June couldn't help but feel a twinge of contempt comparing it to his own blade. June nodded and replied, "I do, thank you." A realization hit him and he quickly added, "Sir."

The man cocked his head to the side in puzzlement, and looked him up and down before replying, "Oh. Please, lieutenant, ah, take me to your commander. I thought you were, well..."

"These are all my soldiers." June replied matter-of-factly, "My commander's nowhere near here."

"Oh." The man looked genuinely shocked. June supposed he must have thought he'd run into an entire enemy battalion.

June looked down at their field telephone and changed the subject, "Tell me, sir, does that work?"

"Yes, why...?" The man asked, trailing off.

June heard a couple dragoons walk up behind him. Deciding he wasn't at risk of being fallen upon suddenly, he sheathed his sword and knelt in the midst of the group of jaegers to pick up the receiver. A voice came through the earpiece, "Stag six, this is Magic three-three. Come in. What is your situation, over?" *Magic?* June thought back to the intelligence briefings. That was the Royal Army's Eighth Infantry Division. He supposed Stag was the jaegers' callsign.

June replied, "Magic three-tree, this is Aegis one six. You're going to have to do better than that if you want to get up Fire Ridge." June snickered and added, "Long live the Emperor."

There was silence on the line for a long time. Then, as June was about to hang up a deep voice growled over the line, "Aegis one six, this is Magic six." Hair stood up on the back of June's neck as the enemy general snarled, "*Watch us.*"

June was talking to Captain Marsten about an hour later when an entire Royal infantry regiment charged out of the trees on the far side of the valley.

Chapter 28

The Burning Ridge

The dragoons had ran for it. Faced with the whole regiment and with artillery pouring down on their hillside position the Imperials had fired a few machine-gun bursts and pulled out before the Royal infantry got too close. Enemy artillery had peppered the regiment as it advanced, but it was inaccurate and barely slowed them as they swept over and around the hill. The whole fight had barely taken half an hour.

Standing in the middle of what used to be their fortifications, Sophia supposed she didn't blame the dragoons for running. It didn't look like there had been more than forty or fifty of them here in the first place against... what, two or three thousand soldiers? She chuckled to herself as she realized she didn't actually know how large the regiment was. Her father had complained to her a few times that with people falling out on the march and re-joining the unit later Charlie Company had a different number of soldiers every day. Maybe the regiment's higher-ups had the same problem.

Sophia crouched at the edge of one of the Imperial foxholes and examined it. It was different than how the Royal Army would have done it. Whenever the company had dug in she and Tony, and lately Edward as well, had dug a large foxhole together and shared it. These were tiny, barely large enough for a singly dragoon to crouch in, and so well-camouflaged they'd only found them by noticing the gleaming shell casings scattered on the forest floor. She filed the idea away in the back of her mind and stood as she heard footsteps rustle on the forest floor behind her.

She turned to see Tony looking as though he'd seen a ghost. Raising her eyebrows, she asked, "Tony, what's wrong?" He'd gone off earlier to relieve himself. She half-joked, "Did you find a body or something?"

"Y-yeah." He swallowed, "I... found the jaegers. Ten or fifteen of them. It's bad."

Sophia remembered wild dogs snarling and snapping as they pulled dead soldiers from shallow graves in the ghostly moonlight. An icy finger traced its way up her spine. Shaking her head, she narrowed her eyes and demanded, "Where?"

He pointed off behind him, to the north side of the hill, "Off that way, a couple hundred meters."

"Go get Edward and meet me back here. And tell Slaughter where we're going." The medics had put the corporal's feet back together by the time they'd returned to the unit the day before. He wasn't even limping that bad now. She went on, "I'll find Thorn. He'll probably want to see this."

She found the lieutenant a little ways downhill, having a discussion with Captain Caldwell. The commander saw her as she approached and remarked, "Ah, Miss Rose. You look like you have news."

"Yes, sir." She replied, "Tony told me just now he found ten or fifteen bodies on the north side of the hill." She pointed for emphasis, "Jaegers."

Caldwell raised an eyebrow, "Tony?"

Lieutenant Thorn added helpfully, "Private Gravesend, sir."

The commander rolled his eyes, "Right. You reservists and your first names." He sighed and went on, "I've been wondering what happened to them." He nodded at Sophia, "Lead on, Miss Rose. Let's go take a look."

"Yes, sir." They quickly rejoined her two friends and Tony retraced his steps off to the north. As they walked down the south side of the hill Sophia spotted a dark shape crumpled on the ground and said, "Hey, Tony, I see something right there."

She pointed and he peered through the greenery for a few seconds before his eyes widened and he stepped back instinctively, "Yeah... yeah, that's one of them. God, Sophia... I didn't notice them earlier until I almost tripped over them."

Caldwell raised his eyebrows and remarked, "Good eyes, Miss Rose. Let's go see what we can."

They walked forward and into a ghastly scene. All along a small rise in the ground jaegers were sprawled in death, gray coats black with blood. As they drew closer Sophia saw the ground around them was churned up by what looked like explosives and the trees scarred by shrapnel. Thorn swore softly. The commander coughed and ordered, "Search the area. There may be survivors."

Sophia walked down the line of dead soldiers, her stomach churning. Pushing her queasiness to the back of her mind, she noticed a few things. A riddled and broken machine gun lay on its side among the bodies, but beyond that Sophia didn't see a single weapon. Not many shell casings either. The Imperials had carried off everything that worked, and it hadn't been a long fight. She grit her teeth and looked over the bodies, all of them shredded and torn by shrapnel. It had been a short fight, the enemy had thrown grenades and... then what?

The Imperials used small-caliber bullets that tumbled and broke apart in the body, leaving awful exit wounds. She didn't see any jaegers that looked like they'd been shot. And she knew too well what bayonet wounds looked like, let alone the body-cleaving slashes of Imperial swords. She looked behind herself, off to the rear of the line of jaegers. The commander was examining something on the ground intently off that way, but there weren't any more gray-jacketed bodies. That meant... Sophia shook her head, looked at Thorn and said, "Sir... I think they surrendered."

Thorn looked a little pale as he gestured at the bodies in front of them angrily, "Well, clearly these ones didn't." He went on, "Why would you think that?"

"It doesn't look like they were overrun, sir." She replied, "No bayonet wounds. No sword wounds."

The lieutenant looked at the line of the dead again for a few moments, then back at her. He didn't look happy about it, but he said, "Yeah... now that you mention it, I think you're right, Rose. After they got hit by grenades the survivors must have surrendered on the spot."

Sophia imagined the scene, half against herself. Jaegers throwing themselves down, firing frantically at a too-close enemy. A flurry of grenades hissing and popping as they sailed through the air. Blasts tearing men apart and an instant later demons in steel masks leaping over the rise. The long-haired dragoon charging out of the smoke, sword flaming in the dappled sunlight. June Anjanou, death himself. This was probably his doing. She shivered at the thought. No wonder they'd given up.

Caldwell, off a little ways to the rear by himself, had overheard them and chimed in, "I think you two are right. I found their field telephone wire back here." He snorted, "I guess the rumor was true then."

Thorn raised his eyebrows, "What's that, sir?"

The captain replied, "So I was told by a very good source, someone called Division on the jaegers' line and taunted them. Apparently General Jorgenson went *nuts*." He grunted, "Explains why we attacked on such short notice."

"Hey! Over here!" Tony was shouting further down the hill. They rushed over to find him and Edward standing over a couple of shapes tucked into a small hollow and covered with blankets. As Caldwell knelt to look under the blankets, Sophia felt something small and round underfoot and reached down to pick up a small, empty glass vial. Morphine. She looked up to see the commander pull back the other blanket to reveal a young man's face, eyes staring and glassy in death. Caldwell reached out and gently closed his eyes before drawing the blanket back over his face.

Sophia looked back at the ground to see several more discarded vials laying in the forest litter. "Sir," she started, holding up the one she had picked up, "There's morphine vials all over the place. Why would they...?" She let the question trail off. She had a feeling she wouldn't like the answer.

Thorn ventured, "Expectant casualties, sir?"

The commander stood and gave the four of them a grim look, "Yes. Don't look under those blankets." He had a flat, unreadable expression on his face as he looked at Thorn, "We need to get these men recovered. Lieutenant, keep searching the area. I'll get the rest of the company down here."

Thorn swallowed and was about to reply when Caldwell spun and stalked off back the way they had come. Sophia gave him a questioning look and asked, "Expectant, sir?"

The lieutenant sighed, "When medics do triage they separate out the worst cases, the ones that are still alive but which definitely won't make it. They get pulled off somewhere out of sight of the rest of the casualties so they don't spread panic."

Sophia felt herself going pale, "So all the morphine...?"

"Yeah." Thorn nodded grimly, "The Imperials drugged them up and left them to die."

Tony interjected angrily, "God-damn Masks. They'll pay for this."

The lieutenant gave him a look, "We do the same thing, Gravesend. In fact, it was probably *Royal* medics looking after these two." Tony subsided and Thorn shook his head and went on, "Come on, let's keep searching. For all we know this wasn't the only fight around here."

It wasn't. There were three more squads worth of dead jaegers a little ways to the east, all of them shot, stabbed and beaten to death with rifle butts. They even found tracks in the forest floor where the dragoons had come down from above, skidding on the steep slope to get into position to flank them. Thorn thought the whole fight had probably only taken a couple of minutes and involved at most twenty dragoons. Sophia felt her whole body go cold thinking how easily the dragoons had butchered a force of jaegers – *jaegers*, the Royal infantry's elite scouts – four times their size.

Their grim task completed, the four of them shakily sat down to wait for the rest of the company to come up. They didn't wait long. Soon blue-jacketed soldiers started coming through the forest, among them a very familiar tall silhouette. Sophia's father stopped in front of them and looked down at the lieutenant, saying, "Sir, the commander's looking for you. I'd go fill him in if I were you."

Thorn nodded, got up and hurried off back uphill. Sophia started to stand to follow him, but her father waved her back down, "Relax, Sophie. You look like hell." Embarrassed, she sank back to the ground as he looked over her two remaining companions, "And you two look worse. The rest of the company can handle this." He chuckled, "You three have had enough trauma for one day."

"Thanks, Dad." Sophia managed. Her friends nodded. Her father smiled, turned and strode off towards the Charlie Company soldiers milling through the trees before them. A few moments later they heard him barking orders. As she sat there trying to make sense of what had happened and fight the icy feeling in her chest, she heard the leaves rustle beside her and looked to see Tony and Edward laying on the ground, fast asleep already.

Sophia sighed. It wasn't like she didn't need the sleep, but with her stomach twisting like it was she knew it would be impossible. As she thought about it a popping machine gun off to their front reminded her that the enemy wasn't *that* far off. The jaegers, confident in victory, had been taken by surprise. She looked behind herself at the soldiers beginning to gather up the dead. It wouldn't happen to her company, her friends. Not on her watch.

She reached out and shook the two men awake, "Hey, guys. Wake up."

Tony groaned and opened his eyes, "C'mon, Sophie. Your dad said we could relax."

Sophia glared at him, "He didn't say we could *rack out*." As if to prove her point the machine gun in the distance fired another, longer burst, "The enemy's close. For all we know there's still some of them around here." She pointed at a convenient fallen log that would provide some cover, "Now get over there and keep watch."

Tony sighed and rolled his eyes, but he obligingly stood up, moved over and took up position. Looking over at Edward, Sophia said, "Ed, you stay put here."

"Sure thing." Edward replied, as he rolled behind a nearby rock and set his rifle within easy reach.

Sophia found a tree that looked solid enough to stop bullets and laid behind it. A few minutes passed uneventfully as birds chirped overhead and the breeze stirred the forest, shifting the pattern of light on the ground into dazzling life. The afternoon heat soaked into her body, and

Sophia was feeling her eyelids start to droop when she heard footsteps in the undergrowth behind her.

She turned to see Lieutenant Thorn with a field telephone slung over his shoulder and a roll of wire in hand. He looked down at her and smiled, "And here I thought you'd all be asleep." Sophia snorted and he went on, "Get up. We've got a new mission."

Sophia rolled over and sat up. "What're we doing?" She asked.

Thorn jerked his head behind him, "Caldwell wants us to put in an observation post. We'll get up on top of the hill and see if we can see anything from there."

"Shouldn't be too hard," Sophia said. *Better than falling asleep out here,* she added in thought. Grabbing her rifle, she climbed to her feet and said loudly, "Hey, Tony, Ed! We're heading out."

Her friends shook themselves and got up, and the four of them headed uphill. As they climbed the sound of battle from the east intensified, machine gun bursts chattering out below them punctuated by the steady popping of rifles. Further off they could faintly hear the high-pitched cracking of Imperial weapons. Sophia wondered for a moment why there hadn't been any ricochets around them before she realized the Imperials were firing downhill from the ridge itself. She was just thinking they were relatively safe on top of the hill when she heard a shrieking whistle and hammering blasts tore through the valley below them.

Sophia flung herself down as the forest shook. After a minute that felt like an eternity the wave of explosions below subsided and she climbed back to her feet with the others. Thorn gave them a look and said, "Come on, we need to keep going. There's got to be somewhere up here we can get a view from."

Sophia looked around. The forest was clearing a little as they got on top of the hill, but it wasn't like there were any clearings around they could get a good view from. She thought for a moment as they crept farther uphill. The Imperials had been shelling them all morning. How had *they* done it? She looked to her left, off towards the west. It wasn't like there was a view that way either. Then, as the hilltop flattened out and they passed a particularly sturdy-looking tree, it hit her and she laughed out loud.

Thorn turned around and raised an eyebrow, "Did I miss something?"

"Yes, sir, I guess." Sophia got herself under control and pointed at the tree that had inspired her, "We're in a forest. They climbed a tree."

"Oh." He looked from her to the tree, craning his head to see up into its branches. Then his eyes widened. Looking back down he chuckled nervously and said, "And, actually... they climbed *this* tree."

They all looked up. Sophia saw it instantly, two ropes dangling from sturdy limbs higher up. After a few seconds of squinting Tony and Edward both noticed it too. Tony snorted and said, "Well, that's spooky."

The lieutenant shrugged, "Our benefit. I bet there's a fine view from up there." He looked between the three of them, "Gravesend, Bellamy, you two run wire back to the company. Report to the commander when you get back where we are, then get back to you squad." He handed her the field telephone, "Miss Rose, take this. We're going up."

"Yes, sir," They chorused. Sophia took the free end of the wire as her friends took off downhill, spooling the line out behind them. Plugging it into the field telephone, Sophia slung her rifle across one shoulder, the phone across the other and started climbing. Clambering from limb to limb, Sophia made it up easily and tied herself off to the lower limb.

The view was amazing. She could see the whole of Fire Ridge rising to the east, forest gleaming in the afternoon light. A few roads cut small gaps through the trees on its steep lower slopes, and farther up the forest was patched with fields and a couple villages. Off to the right the ridge climbed steeply off into the snow-capped Dragonspine Mountains, while to her left it gently sloped away until it disappeared into the afternoon haze. As she watched she heard shells whistle overhead and dirt sprayed from the ridge's lower slopes, vengeance for the earlier Imperial fire. Looking behind herself she could see the whole valley they had just come through. No wonder the Imperials had been shelling them earlier.

A couple minutes passed as Thorn cautiously climbed past her and set himself on the upper limb. She looked up and teased him, "Not afraid of heights, sir?"

He rolled his eyes and replied, "I don't exactly do a lot of tree climbing at the bank." He chuckled, "Makes me wish I was still in high school."

Ouch. She replied sheepishly, "Fair enough, sir."

Above her she heard him take out his binoculars and start studying the ridge. After a while and a couple more artillery volleys he asked, "Notice anything yourself, Rose? Sometimes it seems like your eyes are better than my binoculars."

She squinted into the haze of dust that was building over the battlefield, "Not really, sir. Maybe try farther up the ridge? I'd think they'd have their artillery up there."

Thorn replied, "Their light guns at least. The heavy stuff is probably on the far side. Let me see..." As if to prove her point a cracking drumroll of Imperial artillery unfurled across the valley in front of them. As the shellfire quieted down he asked, "See anything that time?"

She had, in fact. It was faint, but she thought she'd seen a few faint puffs of smoke up in the upper reaches of the ridge while the enemy shells were falling. She replied, "Yeah, actually." She thought for a moment, trying to figure out how to talk him on, "See the second village from the bottom of the ridge, sir? There's a farm with what looks like a big red barn a little ways off to the left of it."

He looked for a minute, then replied, "It looks like there's a house on the left side and a shed or something to the right?"

It was really far in the distance, but it sounded right to her. She replied, "That's it, sir. It came from the fields just a bit left of there."

He snorted, "You've got good eyes, Miss Rose. Try the phone, maybe they've got it hooked up by now."

Sophia cranked the field phone and listened. After a moment a scratchy voice came through, "Charlie Six Tango. That you, Sophie?"

"Hey, Neil." Neil Ferguson had graduated her school the year before and gotten a job with the telegraph office. It was only natural he was manning the company switchboard. She went on, "We're set up here and I think I just saw an Imperial gun position."

"Great, we just got hooked up with Regiment again." Neil went on, "Got the coordinates?"

Sophia looked up at Thorn, "Sir, Company's asking for a location."

Thorn sighed and said, "I'm trying to figure that out now. Uh... try hotel victor six zero five, nine zero five. Probably a battery."

Sophia passed along the coordinates and added, "We think an artillery battery."

The operator cracked back, "Best report I've gotten all day. We'll pass it up, maybe they'll put some shells into it. Thanks, Sophie, six tango out."

"They're passing it up, sir." She paused for a moment, then asked, "Uh, sir... what's our callsign?"

"Clearly 'hey Sophie'." Thorn replied sarcastically, "It's Charlie One Six, try to use it please."

They sat for a while in silence, observing the ridge keenly as the battle developed below them, waves of machine-gun fire rolling back and forth across the base of the ridge. Eventually they heard heavy thudding close behind them accompanied by spraying dirt on the lower slopes, which

Thorn identified as the Regiment's heavy mortars getting into the battle. Shortly afterwards the farm she'd identified earlier disappeared in a cloud of dust and smoke, and the better part of a minute later a low, rumbling thunderclap rolled over the valley.

The battle ground on as the afternoon died, the sinking sun setting the ridge and the smoky cloud hanging above it ablaze with bloody light. As the darkness deepened they saw the red glow of fires burning across the ridge, machine guns and rifles flashing occasionally in the murk below. The Royal gunfire was noticeably fainter than it had been when they had first climbed the hill as the sky darkened to inky blackness and the stars burned to life overhead. Looking up, Sophia saw the two smallest moons, Truth and Wisdom, shining like icy jewels in the sky.

They didn't do much to break the darkness that had descended across the battlefield. As she looked back down to earth it seemed like the only light on the battlefield was from the fires on the ridge itself, red as demonic eyes through the smoke. Every now and then a flare shell popped over the battlefield, shining unearthly light over the lower ridge as the crackling machine guns slowly subsided. The front line wasn't that distinct through the forest, but given where the artillery was concentrating Thorn thought the Regiment's other two battalions had pushed forward about a kilometer or so from their positions earlier in the day.

Speaking of the Regiment, Sophia looked up at the lieutenant and asked, "Sir, when are we going to head back?" She yawned involuntarily, "I... I could use some sleep. Especially if we're going into that crap tomorrow."

She heard him shrug, "Good question. Call the company and ask if they're planning on relieving us."

She did exactly that, and Neil told her, "I was just about to call you, actually. You two sit tight up there, we've got some people coming up to meet you. After you talk to them you're clear to head back." He went on, "We're on the south side of the hill by the road. And good news, our packs caught back up to us."

That was good news, they'd left them at the assembly area when they'd attacked in the morning. But 'people'? That was pretty vague. She asked, "Any idea who these people are?"

Neil chuckled, "Not that I can say on a line with a ground return circuit. Y'know you can listen in on these if you do it right. You two have fun up there."

"Sure, thanks. One six out." Sophia looked up at Tony, "Sir, I think there's VIPs coming up. We can go back after we talk to them."

The lieutenant yawned, "Good. I hope they don't get lost and take all night getting up here. I can use some sleep myself."

About fifteen minutes later, as Sophia was trying to figure out if she would stay balanced on the limb if she went to sleep on it or fall off, she heard heavy footsteps coming up through the undergrowth. After a moment she made out a deep voice faintly, "...say he's lost it, but he's been fighting the Masks for a long time."

Another gruff voice replied, "So you think Haas is right?" Sophia cocked her head to the side. Who was that?

"There's a *chance* he's right, but there's damn all I can do about it even if I wanted to." The first man continued, "We have our orders. Get up this damn ridge. Now where the *hell* is this OP?"

Sophia whistled, and the second man said, "Hear that, sir? Sounded like it was up ahead."

Thorn muttered darkly, "Could those two make *any* more noise?"

Looking back through the murky forest, Sophia saw five or six dark shapes walking through the gloom beneath them. A tall, stocky figure stopped under their tree and looked from side to side, saying, "It sounded like it was around here... damn if I know how they're seeing anything with all these trees."

The second man, a thinner figure in the darkness, ventured, "Might have been a bird, sir."

Barely suppressing a giggle, Sophia quietly snapped off a small branch and dropped it between them. The larger man looked at the ground, "Huh, a stick just fell." He looked up into the tree, his face a pale blotch against his dark uniform, "You see anything up there, Joe?"

The thinner man also looked up, "Not really. God, I can't see anything in this forest."

Sophia was considering throwing another branch at them when she heard Thorn dig into his pocket above her. Looking aside, she saw him wave his handkerchief slowly out of the corner of her eye. She looked back down below herself to hear the first man say, "Wait, do you see that? Something's waving up there. You don't think...?"

"Evening." Thorn said behind her sarcastically. The men jumped backwards, and he went on, "You think you can be a little quieter down there? We're trying to not get our throats cut by dragoons tonight. Uh, sir."

"Well, I'll be damned." The man said, a little lower, "That's quite the setup you have up there."

Thorn replied, "It wasn't our idea, sir. The Imperials used it before us."

The man guffawed, "Well, I can't say I'm surprised. Can you come down here, son?"

Sophia and Thorn looked at each other. She shrugged and he nodded and said, "No problem, sir." Unplugging her field telephone's wire and dropping it into the darkness, she untied herself from the tree and slowly picked her way down. Jumping down the last few feet, she rose to find the first man from before towering over her. A carefully-trimmed dark beard framed what she could make out of his pale face.

He looked her up and down in the gloom, then asked, "Could you report on the progress of the 24th's attack? I was planning on looking myself, but I don't think I'm up for tree-climbing at my age."

"Ah, yes, sir," She replied, "Although you probably want to talk to my lieutenant, actually." She looked upwards at Thorn, still slowly making his way down.

The man raised an eyebrow as she spoke. "A girl?" He chuckled, "You wouldn't happen to be a, ah..." He looked at his companion, who had come up beside him, "What was her name again?"

The second man spoke, "Private Rose, sir?" He was just as tall, but rail thin against the first man's massive bulk. He looked at her and sniffed, "Prince Adrian mentioned you earlier today when we spoke."

The first man replied, "Yes, that was it, Rose. I couldn't believe him." He went on, "My God, you'd think this was the Empire. *Reservists.*"

Who are these guys? Sophia thought as she felt a chill crawl up her neck. They were clearly important enough to have a casual conversation with the Crown Prince. About *her.* She felt herself reddening as her stomach twisted itself into a knot. Prince Adrian didn't just know her name, he was bringing her up in conversation. She didn't know how to feel about that. He was *so handsome...*

Sophia snapped back to reality as the second man said, "Well, young lady, I don't suppose you can fill us in while your *lieutenant* gets himself down?"

Thorn was still carefully picking his way down the tree. She supposed he was probably terrified of falling in the darkness. She cleared her throat and said, "Well, sir, ah, the regiment has advanced over the afternoon. I think they've taken about a kilometer?" She thought for a moment and went on, "There's been a lot of artillery fire down in the valley.

The big man grumbled, "Sounds about right. How are the Imperial positions laid out?"

Sophia shrugged and replied nervously, "Sir... I've seen maybe twenty Imperial soldiers all day and maybe some guns firing. They're well hidden."

"Superb. We know nothing of the enemy's strength or dispositions, beyond that he's given the 8th Division a beating this afternoon." Looking at his slender companion, the man said sarcastically, "Perhaps Haas is right after all."

Thorn finally jumped the last few feet to the ground and landed beside her with a grunt. Standing, he took a long look at the larger man, and even in the darkness Sophia saw his eyes widen. He stiffened to attention and said, "Ah, General Kunst... good evening, sir. I apologize for my rudeness earlier, sir. I..."

The commander of V Corps raised an eyebrow and remarked, "Didn't realize it was someone *that* important?"

"Well, uh, no, sir." Thorn stammered.

"A word of advice, *lieutenant*, think before you open your mouth. Sometimes generals do come up to the front." Sophia faintly made out General Kunst rolling his eyes, "Women and disrespect. I don't suppose an officer of the 24th Regiment is at least *observant?* Your lady friend here was telling me you haven't seen any Imperial troops all day. Is that true?"

Thorn replied nervously, "Well, no, sir, we've barely seen any Imperials. A couple groups high up on the ridge, that's it."

Kunst snorted contemptuously, "Yes, I'm sure I know what you two were looking at." Sophia looked at Thorn quickly. Did he seriously just imply...?

"Sir, I'm not sure what you're getting at." Thorn replied levelly, "But we drove some dragoons off this hill this morning. I saw someone *fall* into one of their foxholes because he couldn't see it in broad daylight. And," He added, "Miss Rose is my best soldier. She saved my *life* earlier, sir."

Kunst glared at him and replied, "Oh? *Is that so?*"

"Sir, she fought off a dragoon who was about to kill me. And that bastard killed five of my men and *maimed* three more in less time than it takes to say it." Thorn spat.

General Kunst replied icily, "Women, disrespect and *bad swordsmen.* I can see with the reserves here, we have the war in the bag." He raised a hand and made a shooing motion, "Run along, *lieutenant*, I'm finished wasting my time tonight."

Sophia remembered June Anjanou's sword shrieking through the darkness, the bodies piled on the floor. A spark of rage lit in her chest and flared white-hot. *Bastard. This God-damn bastard. How* dare *he stand there and-* Sophia's thoughts stopped suddenly as she felt a hand on her arm. Thorn had seized her arm and was pulling her back. Reluctantly, she submitted and turned away. They walked downhill aimlessly for a ways until she said, "Sir, I think the company's off on the north side of the hill. We need to go left."

"Oh." Thorn turned that direction, "Alright then."

"Uh, sir," She added, "You can let go of my arm now."

He stopped and looked at her for a moment before she felt his grip loosen. Stepping back from her, he said, "I'm sorry, I didn't realize I was still..."

Sophia shook her head, "No, sir, thanks... I was about to do something really stupid."

Thorn shook his head, "That guy, well, I almost regret stopping you. What an *ass*."

She shook her head again, "Come on, sir, let's go back. I want to get some sleep before he tells us to go die heroically."

"You and me both, sister," He replied.

They walked through the forest for a few more minutes when Sophia heard a low, crunching rumble coming through the trees. She held up her hand to stop Thorn and whispered, "Sir, do you hear that?"

He replied softly, "Yes, I think so... that crackling sound?"

She looked at him and asked, "What do you think it is?"

"Don't know." He replied, "But I think it's coming from the road. Let's go see."

As they approached the edge of the forest Sophia began seeing red lights floating ghostlike in the distance as the grinding sound grew louder and louder. They reached the edge of the woods and looked out into the valley beyond. For a moment Sophia saw only the red lights bobbing across the farmland in the inky night, strung out across the valley like processions of ghosts as the rhythmic grinding floated in the air. The hair was rising on the back of her neck when she finally saw it and it all made sense.

The valley was full of Royal soldiers, column after column of dark shapes snaking towards the ridge like horrible, many-legged beasts in the darkness. The crunch of their marching feet on the valley's gravel roads was the grinding gears of some terrible war machine and the red lights their leaders used to light their path were the ghostly lights she had seen in the night.

They skirted around the edge of the hill to find the company where they had left it, waiting for orders to move forward. As she began wrapping herself in her blanket to sleep the clear sky rumbled and a roar like never-ending thunder filled the air. Sophia looked to the east to see a fiery glow scorching at the night sky through the forest as the barking roar of hundreds of machine guns drifted over the booming artillery.

Sophia sighed, stuffed her rolled-up jacket under her head and closed her eyes. The gates of Hell could wait. She might not get another chance to sleep for a while.

Chapter 29

The Royal Oath

Walter had seen them off at the Wolf Rock station. Tall and stately in his blue service uniform, he had patted Arilin on the shoulder and told her that her father would be proud of her. And, he'd added, that she should look after herself. She was more important than she realized, he's said with a sort of dark finality. As she turned to leave she thought that their next meeting might be under drastically different circumstances.

Arilin had stepped into the carriage and turned back to see Patricia standing on her tiptoes through the window, kissing Walter on the cheek. It only lasted a moment, so briefly she doubted anyone else even noticed. Patricia quickly stepped back, spun and hurried onto the train. Arilin suppressed a snicker at her obvious blush and pretended she hadn't seen anything.

That had been two days ago. Now their train was speeding through the rolling forests and farmland west of Fire Ridge, going through one tiny town after another as the sun cracked the horizon, burned the mist from the ground and started climbing. Considering the Empire had been through here recently, Arilin had half-expected the entire region to be burned to the ground. As it stood the only real damage they'd seen had been around Grenville, where much of the eastern side of the city lay in ruins and the tracks had been hastily repaired where the Imperials had dug their siege-works through them.

It was eerie. Arilin had asked Patricia about it, and the lady general had agreed with her. If the Imperial Army had been *really* trying to slow them down they would have blown the bridges and torn up the railroad tracks behind them. Walter's warnings had been disturbing but abstract in Wolf Rock. Looking at the undisturbed countryside east of Grenville made the briefings and maps frighteningly real. This land belonged to the Empire. They were just letting them borrow it back for a little bit.

Arilin looked away from the scenery rolling by in the early-morning light as she heard a soft knock on the door. Unusually, Patricia had not joined her for breakfast and she hadn't rang for Rebecca. Wondering who it might be, Arilin rose, smoothed her nightdress and took the few steps across her private cabin to open the door. Patricia was on the other side, her usually cheerful face shadowed and stern. Behind her she saw Rebecca, carrying what looked like a suitcase and another long, thin box, the kind of thing rifles or swords were transported in.

The lady general gave her a solemn nod and said, "Good morning, milady. May I come in?"

The princess raised her eyebrows and replied, "Of course, milady." Stepping aside to let the two women into the room, she asked worriedly, "What's the occasion? Is... something wrong?"

Patricia sighed, "No, milady, something's right and I'm going to *make* it wrong." She looked to the princess' maid, "If you please, Rebecca. It won't do for milady to be sworn in wearing her pajamas."

"Of course, milady." Rebecca replied, setting the suitcase on the bed and popping the latches. She opened it and quickly started laying out clothing. A stiff, black leather cap trimmed with gray cloth. A pair of tall black riding boots that someone had obviously spent some time shining to perfection. A thick leather belt, also shined and gleaming in the morning light. Dark red riding breeches with black stripes running up the sides. Undergarments, and a short-sleeved shirt. And finally a matching pair of dove-gray jackets, one a little larger than the other, with a strap to hang it over her back. The collar patches showed the pink and white of the Valkyrie Knights, with the crossed sabers of the hussars and the single bar of a second lieutenant.

Arilin felt a bone-deep chill as she saw the name tags on the jackets. On the left, to be worn over the heart, in black embroidery on gray cloth was 'Royal Army'. Standard stuff. But the right-hand tag read, 'Wehrherz'. She looked back at Patricia. The uniform looked exactly the same as hers, only the lady general had two stars on her collar. The older woman smiled sadly and said, "I had hoped to avoid this, milady, but given our present circumstances I have no choice."

The princess narrowed her eyes and said, "Please explain."

"When I talked to the King about bringing you along on this campaign he told me to keep you out of harm's way." She said, "Or, failing that, which I am *clearly* doing right now," she added, "To commission you so you'd at least be subject to my orders and less likely to run off to try to win the war by yourself."

Arilin replied drily, "Well, now I know why you had all my measurements taken earlier."

Patricia said, "Of course, milady. I had hoped to wait a few years before putting it on you, but," She smiled and went on, "I think you'll look quite dashing in the regiment's uniform." She turned to the maid, "Please, Rebecca, help her dress."

Becky nodded wordlessly and moved to help Arilin with her clothing. After a few minutes of dressing Arilin settled her second jacket around her shoulders on its strap, ran her hands behind her neck and pulled her hair free in a smooth motion, feeling it drape over her shoulders and far down her back. Patricia snickered and remarked, "We really must braid your hair up, milady. I'd been hoping having you in uniform would make you blend in a little, but there's not much chance of that as you look now." She smiled, "Still, we can worry about that later. Take a look at yourself." The older woman led her in front of the cabin's vanity and tilted the mirror up so Arilin could get a good look.

Arilin saw herself in the mirror, the same girl who always looked back at her. Blazing red eyes and golden hair, with features that were sharpening into adulthood. And yet something was different this time. Maybe it was the masculine cut of her jacket, the sturdy garment concealing what most of her clothing emphasized. It wrapped her slight body like knightly armor, gallant and yet somehow still a little feminine. Or maybe it was the look in her eyes, set just a little stronger than before.

She remembered a similar moment before, once. Arilin had been all of seven years old when she had moved to the Palace with her mother and Beatrice, but even at her tender age she had put two and two together and figured out that her father, who came by often but never stayed, was the King. That he was married to another woman, and that *her* mother was his mistress. And that something horrible had happened that led to her mother sitting her down one day and explaining that she was an actual, not-a-fairy-tale, honest-before-God, princess and they were going to live with her father in the High City.

She'd found out about the sordid details of the Affair of the Hanged Queen later, from her new brother. At the time Arilin had sensed the mood and been appropriately subdued instead of jumping for joy like everyone expected. So Adrian had told her, it had made all the difference to him and to the Palace staff.

She had zoned out. Looking back to Patricia, she smiled and said, "I like it, milady."

"One more thing." The lady general said, as Rebecca presented her with the long, thin case, "An officer needs her sword." She popped the latches and opened it to reveal a hussar's saber nestled the box's felt lining. Picking it up gently, she examined it for a moment before ceremoniously turning and holding it out to the princess.

Arilin reached out and took it from her, the painted steel of the scabbard smooth and cold in her hands. Popping the blade free with her thumb against the pierced handguard, she drew it a few inches to see that the blade gleamed smooth and razor-sharp. No engraver had wasted his time adding useless decoration to a weapon meant for the battlefield.

"You like it, milady?" Arilin looked up as Patricia spoke to see her smiling broadly.

She nodded and grinned back, "Yes, *very* much."

"I'm glad." Arilin re-seated the sword in its scabbard and clipped it to her belt's hanging straps as Patricia went on, "Now for the important part."

She looked back up to see that the lady general's expression had become stern, and she asked, "You're going to swear me in?"

"Yes, milady." Patricia replied, raising her right hand ceremoniously, "Now raise your right hand and repeat after me." The princess raised her hand and she went on, "I, state your name, swear before God that I will bear true faith and allegiance to His Majesty, King William the Fourth and his lawful successors,"

Arilin took a deep breath and said, "I, Arilin Catherine Wehrherz, swear before God that I will bear true faith and allegiance to His Majesty, King William the Fourth and his lawful successors."

The lady general went on solemnly, "That I will defend the Crown and the Nation against all enemies and all treachery,"

The princess repeated, "That I will defend the Crown and the Nation against all enemies and all treachery."

Patricia replied, "That I swear this faithfully and true in heart, so help me God."

Arilin said, "That I swear this faithfully and true in heart." Taking another deep breath, she finished, "So help me God."

The older woman dropped her hand, smiled and held it out to the girl, "Welcome to the Army, milady. Feel any different?"

Arilin reached out and grasped her offered hand with both of her own, "A little light-headed, I guess?"

Patricia chuckled, "That's normal." She turned slightly and tugged her towards the door, "Now come on, we're disembarking soon and I want to show you off to the staff."

"Yes, milady!" Arilin replied happily.

A couple hours later the train squealed to a halt at the platform in a picturesque town west of Fire Ridge. Soldiers pulled the doors open and Arilin and Patricia stepped out into the noontime heat. Arilin noticed the platform's faded signboard proclaiming, 'Welcome to Clarksburg' before she heard a familiar voice say, "Good morning, ladies!"

She looked to the side to see Eric standing on the platform, imposing in his charcoal-gray jacket and breastplate. He saluted and Patricia and, a little awkwardly, Arilin returned the gesture. The general replied cheerily, "Good to see you, Eric. Is your squadron prepared to move out?"

"Of course, milady..." He took a closer look at the younger girl and his eyebrows rose, "And what do we have here?"

Patricia clapped Arilin on the shoulder, "The Army's newest lieutenant."

Eric chuckled and gave her a dubious look, "The Royal Family sure starts young... I'm guessing this wasn't your idea, milady?"

"Of course not," Patricia snorted, "Orders from the King."

He shrugged, "Nothing we can do then." He changed the subject, "The lancers moved out on schedule at dawn. We've been in communications with them and the Fourteenth all day."

Gesturing for him to follow them, Patricia started walking off the increasingly-crowded platform and asked, "By radio? How far out have they pushed?"

He replied, "The Fourteenth is already twenty kilometers north of here, the lancers maybe ten behind them. They should align by nightfall." He chuckled, "Thank God for radio. If this was the old days I'd just put a question mark on the map north of here and leave it at that."

"I feel sorry for Mina." Patricia remarked, "Whenever old Kellerman wanted to talk to me he had to send someone to *find* me first."

Arilin imagined the gray-bearded general raging at his disappearing hussars, smiled and asked, "Did he ever succeed?"

"No, but I'd always send someone around eventually to tell him where the enemy was so he didn't *stay* that angry at me." They laughed as they stepped off the shaded platform into bright sunlight. Patricia went on, "I assume Colonel Frost has set up his operation around here somewhere?" Arilin had been wondering where Patricia's doughty chief of staff had disappeared to over the last few days, and she realized that she must have sent him ahead to supervise the movement.

Eric replied, "Yes, milady, I'll take you there immediately." They followed Eric through the town's cobbled streets, now swarming with soldiers on horseback and on foot, and eventually came to the town's small hotel. Arilin felt a surge of satisfaction as she noticed the radio antenna strung between two trees out front of the building. Two cuirassiers standing guard outside came to attention and saluted as they walked in.

"Commanding general!" Someone shouted as they entered to find the hotel's lobby converted into a command post. Patricia told the group to carry on, and Arilin quickly spotted Frost approaching from the map table.

They exchanged greetings and the lady general got right to the point, "Any contact with the enemy so far?"

Surprisingly, the grizzled colonel nodded, "Yes, actually. The Fourteenth just reported that they engaged a dragoon patrol. About..." He checked his watch, "Thirty minutes ago. No casualties, us or them." He gave Arilin a look and added, "Congratulations, milady."

"Thanks... uh, sir." Arilin ventured.

Patricia ignored the exchange and, narrowing her eyes, said, "Lead elements?"

Frost shrugged, "Or stragglers. Might not have even been dragoons. I'm not going to draw grand conclusions at this point." He went on, "When are you heading out, milady?"

She checked her watch, "As soon as the headquarters is ready to move. Maybe an hour?"

The colonel replied, "You should eat then." He gestured to a door off the lobby, "This hotel actually has a decent restaurant." He chuckled, "You two shouldn't worry yourselves, go ahead and eat and I'll go get the staff ready to move out."

Patricia snorted, "Come on, Joseph, I don't need the executive treatment and I'm sure you have more important things to do."

Frost chuckled and winked, "I'm not worried about *you*, ma'am, but I'll tell you *she's* hungry right now." He pointed at Arilin, "Right, milady?"

She felt herself blush as she replied, "Ah... yes, a little."

Before Patricia could protest Frost went on, "So there we have it. You two take a break and let me do my job." He looked at the ceiling for a moment, "The last thing we need right now is old Blood and Death Haas cursing out the whole corps staff again for not moving fast enough."

Patricia sighed, "Alright, you win. Come on, milady. Let's see if this place can make a decent sandwich."

Arilin followed as she headed towards the dining room and commented, "Maybe they have gelato?"

She got what she guessed was supposed to be a reproachful look back,

"That's enough of that, young lady."

A few minutes later, as they were working their way through some reasonably good soup, Patricia looked up and said, "Actually, milady, there is something I wanted to discuss with you. It slipped my mind earlier, I apologize."

"Oh?" Arilin raised her eyebrows questioningly.

"You're not expecting Rebecca to go forward with us, are you?" Patricia asked.

She shook her head, "No, of course not."

"She asked me recently if she could help at the field hospital until you return." Patricia added, "You know she used to be an Army nurse. I assume you don't have a problem with that?"

The princess shook her head again, "No, of course not. She couldn't be doing anything better."

"Very good then. I'll tell them to write some orders to activate her. Although," Patricia smirked, "She'll outrank you. You know she's a captain on the reserve list."

"Oh?" Arilin blushed, "That's... awkward."

Laughing, Patricia said, "It comes with the job. You know Walter called me 'Lieutenant' the other day?"

Feeling herself smile, Arilin asked, "By accident I hope?"

The lady general leaned forward conspiratorially and said, "You and I both. So this is what happened..."

Chapter 30

Fix Bayonets

Sophia got another chance to sleep. The battle on the ridge had ground on for all of the last day, the popping machine-guns and rifles gradually moving away up the ridge when she could make them out amid the unending thunderstorm of the artillery. Late in the day the guns had started moving forward into the valley itself and the company had gotten word to move up and get out of their way. A little uneasy at leaving the cover of the hill, they had packed up and marched out as the sun sank in the west.

The ridge before them was shrouded with smoke, towering into the dark eastern sky like the back of a great monster. Sophia supposed the name of the Dragonspine Mountains had never been more appropriate as a string of burning flashes unrolled across the lower slopes, white smoke billowing through the trees in the golden light of the sunset. Phosphorous shells. The Empire had been trying to set the ridge on fire for the last two days, and by the amount of smoke hanging over the ridge they were beginning to succeed. Sophia thanked God for the rain earlier and pressed on.

A couple of soldiers from the third battalion met them on the road and guided them in to their new positions just inside the forest, which looked like they'd been dug by the Empire and then blown up by the rest of the Regiment during the attack. Sophia was just happy they didn't have to dig in the darkness. Her father had cautioned everyone to check for booby-traps – maybe there was a reason nobody had set up camp here – before they piled into the convenient holes. Tony found one and she'd never seen him go that pale. They pulled a branch across the tripwire from a safe distance and got a laugh out of it before they set up camp.

Charlie Company did what they could to repair the positions, ate and went to sleep as the battle raged on above them. A few Imperials shells slapped down close enough during the night to wake her, and once she heard screaming and shouting for medics in the distance after a particularly heavy salvo shook the ground. She, Tony and Edward had sat up, looked at each other and laid back down. Whoever had been hit, they weren't from the company.

A very tired-looking Jack had come over to wake them for the last guard shift. With the great bulk of the ridge looming above them to the east dawn didn't really break. The sky overhead gradually lightened enough for Sophia to see through the shadowy forest, and as she looked around she spotted a shape she knew well moving through the gloom. Her father exchanged words with Slaughter as he passed the foxhole he was sharing with Hargrave and Jeremy, rolled his eyes at seeing Jack and Kelly asleep as usual in their hole, decided against waking them and walked over to take a seat on the rim of theirs.

"Morning, First Sergeant," her friends said.

"Morning, Dad," she said.

"You too. I guess it doesn't qualify as 'good'?" He remarked.

She snorted and replied, "No, not really. I'd rather be home."

"Oh, come on, Sophie." He chuckled, "I know you're happy you get to sleep in."

It was true. After growing up in a bakery, Army mornings were easy days. Laughing, she replied, "Not as much shelling back in Jade Falls, Dad."

Right on cue a shell whistled in and cracked a ways upslope. Her father didn't even bother to jump down in the foxhole with them. He gave them a grim smile and said, "This isn't shelling. Right now the Empire's just reminding us they're still out there." He grimaced for a moment, "I think this was about as good as it ever got in the Marchlands."

"Any word on when we're moving up, First Sergeant?" Edward asked.

Her father checked his watch, "Hopefully after our ammunition gets up to us. How're you all doing on that, by the way?"

They all patted themselves down. Sophia replied, "We're all full on ammo." She raised her eyebrows, "We're getting more?"

"Yeah." He pointed at the load-bearing belt wrapped around her hips, "How many grenades do you have there, Sophie?"

Instinctively feeling for the smooth, cylindrical heads of her stick grenades, she cocked her head and replied, "Uh, two?"

He replied, "You all need at least ten each." He swept his gaze across them, "Maybe more. And hang some on your backs so you can get at each other's. Those two grenades you've got, Sophia, are going to last about two minutes once we get into it."

She had seen pictures of soldiers in the last war with the Empire going into battle with grenades slung all across their bodies. They had been an ideal weapon in a war that had been fought half-underground, where soldiers wouldn't see each other most of the time until they were almost face to face. Sometimes a bomb that could be thrown into the next trench traverse was a lot more useful than a rifle. And in this war of bunkers, foxholes and burning underbrush she supposed it would probably still hold true. Nodding, she said, "Will do. We'll load up."

Her father nodded, said his goodbyes and moved on down the line. Sure enough after another hour she heard heavy footsteps and cursing further back in the company's perimeter, and the sound of heavy boxes being set down on the forest floor. A short while later Sergeant Cross came around to tell them to head back, drop their packs and get extra ammunition for the attack. He added, almost as an afterthought, for them to keep their blankets and ponchos. God only knew when they'd see their rucksacks again.

As they walked over Sophia saw the company's supply clerks had cracked open the heavy wooden ammo boxes and were handing out ammunition next to a growing pile of rucksacks. They dropped their own packs and she pulled her blanket and poncho off, rolled them together and asked Tony to strap them down across the rear of her harness. The rest of the squad looked at what they were doing for a moment, then did it themselves.

"Hold out your arms, Rose. Here you go. Watch out, they're explosive." One of the clerks handed her a bundle of stick grenades and a heavy bandolier loaded with ammunition. "Alright, next in line. You there..." he said to Tony as she took the awkward load and stepped aside. Each grenade had a carrying clip and she quickly arranged six of them around her hips and draped the bandolier across her chest as Tony stepped beside her with his own load.

"Can you put these on my back?" She asked Tony, offering him the last four grenades.

"If you'll do me." Tony replied as he looked at her for a moment, then started hanging his grenades off his belt exactly as she had.

"Sure," Sophia replied. Edward snickered loudly and she froze, feeling her face reddening.

Tony looked between them blankly, then burst out laughing. Getting himself somewhat under control, he chortled, "Oh, God, sorry, Sophie, you walked right into that one."

She rolled her eyes, "Go to hell, both of you."

"It was pretty funny, though." Edward remarked as Tony took her grenades, stepped behind her and started hanging them off the back of her suspenders, between her shoulders.

She glared at him and huffed, "Well, you two will just have to *do each other* then."

Edward smirked, "You want to watch?"

"*No!*" Sophia turned and stalked off. *Boys.* The duo caught up to her a minute after she got back to their foxhole. They were still snickering when they got the word they were about to get moving a couple hours later. Lieutenant Thorn came around shortly afterwards followed by a soldier she didn't recognize. From the regimental numbers on his collar he wasn't even from the division.

Sophia looked between her companions, then looked at her lieutenant and said, "We're ready to go when you are, sir." She nodded at the stranger, "Who's that?"

Thorn replied, "Our guide. He'll take us to a rally point where they'll direct us forward."

"Any word on the mission, sir?" She asked.

He shook his head, "No. I've heard there have been a lot of losses up front, so maybe we'll go into the line tonight." He looked at the man, "You don't know anything, do you?"

The stranger shrugged, "Sir, I'm just here to take you up to Division. What they do with you there is beyond me." As he spoke a long, *long* string of cracking thuds unrolled across the ridge above them, followed by a wave of machine-gun fire. Something zinged overhead and pocked into a tree nearby. The man remarked, "Although I bet it involves fighting the Masks, sir."

Thorn rolled his eyes, "Tell me something I don't know." He looked around at the company sticking their heads out of their foxholes around him. Sophia spotted Captain Caldwell off to the rear waving them forward. Sighing, the lieutenant said, "Lead on. Sophie, follow him."

Sophie nodded, "Yes, sir," and climbed out of her safe hole as the man started heading up the ridge through the forest. Thorn followed a short distance behind her as Tony and Edward fanned out to either side. Looking behind her, she saw the whole company rising and falling into column behind them as they went along. Here and there she saw signs of battle as they climbed, piles of shell casings and shrapnel-scarred trees. After they had gone a few hundred meters up the slope she saw another set of dark scars in the ground surrounded by shredded trees and strange shell casings. Another Imperial position, blown apart as the attacking troops advanced.

Their guide paused for a moment and looked around uncertainly. Sophia glanced over and asked, "What are you looking for?"

"There should be some engineer tape around here to mark the trail up." He shook his head, "We might not be high enough up yet. I came down on the road, so I'm not really sure where it starts."

It figured they were lost already. Fighting the urge to roll her eyes, Sophia replied, "Well, let's keep moving. It's not like we're going to miss the enemy." As if to make her point another volley of artillery boomed through the forest, seeming to bang on and on endlessly on the upper slopes as they all instinctively cowered. Even at a distance it sounded hellish.

Finally the artillery died down and Sophia gave their guide a pointed look. He sighed and started moving again. A kilometer and the better part of an hour later the slope leveled out and cleared into a broad patch of farmland. The far side of the clearing bustled with activity, horse-drawn ambulances careening out of the forest and clustering around a nondescript farmhouse swarming with dark-jacketed soldiers. Even at a distance Sophia could see that many of them were wearing Red Cross armbands.

Their guide visibly relaxed at the sight of the field hospital, turned to Thorn and said, "We're here, sir. Thought we were lost for a while. I'll be taking your commander now, ah, where is he?"

Thorn jerked his head back down the column, doing a bad job concealing his annoyance, "He'll be with the next platoon. Where are you taking him, again?"

"Division command post, sir. It's in the woods a little way uphill." The man bobbed his head and hurried back downhill. Thorn waved for the platoon to spread out, and Sophia plopped down behind a nearby tree. After a few minutes the guard returned with Captain Caldwell in tow. The two of them made their way across the clearing and into the far woodline. Sophia noticed the guide choose between one of several white tapes tied to trees on the far side to follow up. A short while later she noticed more parties emerging from their side of the woods and she recognized most of the rest of the regiment's leadership as they made their way across.

They scraped out shallow foxholes and waited for them to come back. The morning dragged on. Around noon the sound of battle on the upper slopes built again, the occasional thud of artillery rising to a pounding, shrieking roar overhead. Underneath it was the near-continuous chatter of machine guns. They were close enough Sophia could make out a high-pitched Imperial one occasionally. She exchanged looks with Thorn. It didn't sound like a particularly easy fight. She had the sinking feeling a lot of people back in Jade Falls were going to be wearing black in a couple days. She just hoped her mother wasn't going to be one of them.

Shells whistled too low overhead and crashed down a little ways off to their right. Sophia buried herself in the shaking earth until they stopped coming down, finally raising her head to see a cloud of dirt and smoke rising through the forest canopy. Thorn, picking himself up, remarked, "It's a good thing we decided against taking the road."

The road was over that way. As the blasts stopped echoing through the valley Sophia thought she heard screaming from off in that direction. Some of it was freakish, high-pitched and feral. After a minute she heard gunshots and the awful screams stopped. Sophia felt her blood chill as she looked at Thorn and said, "Horses?"

"Yeah, must have been." He sighed, "That's the other reason we went through the forest. They're using the road for wagons."

"Damn." More artillery whistled overhead and crashed down, a little farther away. They didn't bother to duck this time. Sophia snorted and said, "You know, sir, I hope they don't blow up this command post."

The lieutenant laughed grimly, "Yeah. We'd be screwed. Although worse things have happened." He added darkly, "I've heard some regiments in the last war lost *all* of their officers in a few hours."

Tony commented, "Sir, aren't you supposed to be motivating us?"

Thorn chuckled, "I think we're well past that point by now, Gravesend. We'll be all right."

"I'll take your word for it, sir," Edward remarked from her other side. They all chuckled.

A few minutes later they spotted Captain Caldwell as he hurried out of the far woodline and past the field hospital. Thorn waved his handkerchief and he headed towards them. Stepping into the woods, he nodded to Sophia, told Thorn to come with him and headed back downhill. Looking back, Sophia saw him huddling over a map with her father, Thorn, Lieutenant Stahl and the company's senior sergeants. Thorn and Sergeant Cross came back a few minutes later and called the platoon together.

Cross started up, "Alright, everyone, listen up. We've got a mission and we don't have a lot of time to get going." He looked at Thorn, "Sir, they're all yours."

"Thank you, sergeant." Thorn said as he unfurled his map, "Now gather in close." They crowded in and he pointed to a spot on the map, about a quarter up the ridge, "We're here. First Battalion is to the north on our right and Third Battalion is south of us, on our left. The front line is up here, about four kilometers up." Thorn looked around them, "Right now the 50th Regiment is attacking directly to our front. They've made good progress, but they're beginning to run out of steam. Five hundred angry Imperials will do that to you." They chuckled and he tapped a circle drawn on his map as the sound of battle rose above them, "We're going to move up and relieve them after they hit their next objective. That should be shortly. As you can hear, they're on the move."

"What then, sir?" Sergeant Slaughter asked. Sophia got the feeling he wasn't in the mood for much more walking.

"I was just getting to that." Their lieutenant went on, "We're going to keep attacking. They think there's one more Imperial defense line on the upper ridge and maybe another one on the reverse slope after we get over the top. We get through those..." He tapped his finger on the expanse of farmland marked on the map that descended slowly to the east, "And the cavalry comes through us and mops up."

"Maybe you can see your *boyfriend*, Sophie." Edward ribbed her, not quietly enough.

She gave him a venomous glare, "Shut up, Ed."

A good-natured chuckle rolled around the platoon. Lieutenant Thorn looked around for a moment for emphasis and went on, "In all seriousness, Prince Adrian's cuirassiers may be that cavalry. Make sure you do your work well. We wouldn't want to let His Grace down." The soldiers murmured, and Thorn gestured for quiet and went on, "The battalion's climbing up behind us. We'll spread out on line once we get closer. Bravo Company will come on line on our right and Alpha will be behind us. A company from Third Battalion will be to our left, but don't assume anyone you see on our flanks is friendly. You've all seen how the Imperials fight."

Another, darker murmur went through them. Thorn looked at her and went on, "Miss Rose, we shouldn't need your pathfinding skills today. They've been stringing lines behind them as they've advanced. We can follow them straight up. However," He went on, "I need you to keep a sharp watch out. It goes without saying we're not going to attack every Imperial position head on. If we can't go through we'll go around." The lieutenant added, "The 50th are regulars, but they're not *that* stupid. They're doing the same thing. We might run into the enemy sooner than we think."

Sophia nodded and replied, "Yes, sir. Will do."

Thorn looked at his watch and said, "Alright. We move out in ten minutes. Final checks, everyone."

The platoon dispersed back to their original positions. Sophia looked her friends up and down for a minute, made Tony get the ammunition in his bandolier out of its boxes and get it ready to use, and settled down to wait. The minutes dragged by like hours as the artillery seethed overhead like a never-ending thunderstorm. Finally she heard movement behind her and Thorn said, "Let's go."

Sophia picked up her rifle, climbed out of her hole and started walking. The early afternoon sun beat down on her as she crossed the field, avoided the stares of the walking wounded sitting outside the field hospital, found one of the white tapes tied up behind the building and followed it into the forest. The gloom under the canopy deepened as they went along, the ground rising steadily under their feet.

They walked through the forest for what seemed like forever, Sophia following the dim white line of the engineer tape up the ridge as the artillery grew louder and louder above. Here and there abandoned Imperial positions lay like black scars in the undergrowth, brass shell casings gleaming dully in the half-darkness. Trees lay toppled across their path where artillery had felled them, pillars of blinding light piercing the forest through the new holes in the canopy. The smell of green wood and sap filled the air, sickly sweet as the darkness clogged with smoke. Whole sections of the forest smoldered as they climbed, stinging her eyes, and more than once she felt Thorn grab the back of her harness to keep from losing her in the murk.

Imperial shells swept across the ridge again and again, forcing them to the ground as they crashed down. Twice they found the company. Trees shattered and smoking gobs of phosphorous rained from the sky as she heard familiar voices scream in pain. Sophia rolled over to see medics rushing over and soldiers falling out of the column to carry the wounded back down. Both times the shelling lifted as quickly as it had come and Thorn had gestured for her to get moving again.

They passed a few groups of soldiers coming back down, empty pack frames over their backs. They told them they were on the right track, but none of them knew how the battle was going. Mostly the men just seemed happy the regiment was being relieved. As the hammering artillery got closer and closer overhead, Sophia got the strong feeling the 50th had gotten more than they bargained for from the Empire.

Soon even the hammering rifles and machine-guns up ahead seemed terrifyingly close. Worse still, Sophia could make out the high cracks of Imperial weapons, and they almost seemed louder than the Royal ones. Glancing back over her shoulder at Thorn, she said, "Sir, it almost seems like they're mixed together up there."

The lieutenant gave her a nervous look, "We should have run into their headquarters, a rear position, *something* by now..." They were coming up a rise and the ground seemed to level out beyond it. She was about to go over when something small hissed overhead. Sophia threw herself to the ground as it thwacked into a tree behind them. An instant later she heard the sharp chatter of an Imperial machine-gun on the far side of the rise, still a little ways off.

Sophia rolled over and looked at Thorn, feeling herself grimacing, "Not one of ours, sir."

The lieutenant chuckled nervously as he crouched below the crest of the rise, "No, not at all." He paused as a new, smaller blast went off to their front. A few seconds later another one went off, a little different-sounding.

They waited a few more seconds, looking at each other nervously as a whole string of them ripped through the woods. Sophia said, "Grenades, I think?"

Thorn nodded and waved for the platoon to spread out, "Yeah... ours or theirs?"

Soldiers started fanning out along the cover of the rise as Sophia replied, "Both, I think." She gave him a sour look, "Probably mostly theirs."

"What's going on here?" They looked back to see Captain Caldwell, breathing heavily from rushing upslope.

Thorn swallowed and replied, "There's a battle going on up front, sir." A few bullets hissed overhead and they all instinctively ducked a little, "We've heard grenades. Lots of them."

The commander rolled his eyes, "*Tell* me next time, lieutenant." Turning downhill, he yelled, "Second platoon! Come up on the right and get on line! Third, follow behind!"

Thorn asked, "Want the machine guns here, sir?"

Caldwell shook his head, "No." Another wave of grenade blasts rolled through the forest, followed by staccato gunshots. Sophia thought she heard screams. He went on, "They're still a little ways off. With all these damn trees we'll never see anything to shoot from here. Keep your guns with your squads." He looked at Thorn, "Push on my command. I'll be with Third Platoon. If you and Stahl hit too many Masks to run over we'll come up and flank them. Got it?"

Thorn nodded, and Caldwell uncharacteristically turned to her, "Stay alive, Miss Rose. I do *not* want to have to tell your dad you got yourself killed."

Sophia felt a chill of dread in her heart, but she replied grimly, "Will do, sir."

"Very well." Captain Caldwell heaved himself up and scrambled back downhill. The rest of the company quickly moved up around them, soldiers falling into position just under the protective rise. Looking to her side Sophia saw Jack, stony-faced, haul back on his machine gun's charging handle and cock the weapon for action. He gave her a nod and turned back to Sergeant Slaughter, who was giving him some last-minute directions.

Sophia and Thorn peeked over the rise as they waited. The ground sloped down a little ways, the dense forest opening up and light streaming down from above. Off in the distance, almost swallowed by the trees, Sophia could see the pale stones of what she thought was a riverbank. The cracking Imperial gunfire seemed to have died down a little, but it also seemed to be getting closer. Here and there Sophia heard a deep Royal shot in return. Straining her eyes, she thought she might have seen dark shapes in the distance, almost lost in the trees and shifting darkness of the forest.

A shrill whistle cut through the air, followed an instant later by Caldwell's shouted, "Forward!"

Sophia looked at Thorn, and he nodded. She looked to her left and right. Tony and Edward were rolling back on their feet, picking up their rifles in anticipation. Picking up her own, she shouted, "Alright, guys! Follow me!"

Sophia leapt over the rise, hit the ground on the other side and rushed to the biggest tree she could see in front of her, throwing herself down in the protection of its roots. An instant later Tony and Edward were beside her, the rest of the squad throwing themselves down all around. A couple bullets whistled through the air overhead as Slaughter skidded in behind them and shouted, "Advance by teams! Stay on line!

Sophia got up and ran to the next piece of cover, and then the next and the one after that, her friends close behind her. Every time they moved they would throw themselves down and wait for Jack and Kelly to drop in beside them and bring their gun to bear before getting up to rush again. They covered ground quickly, rushing through the light-dappled undergrowth while Imperial bullets cracked and hissed overhead. Splashing across the stream, Sophia clambered up the far bank and threw herself down behind her rifle, peering into the darkness of the trees as they thickened to her front.

She blinked, and blinked again. The forest murk was moving in front of her eyes. And then something flashed in the darkness and one of the boiling shadows stumbled and fell. Royal soldiers, dozens of them, running for their lives. Behind them the forest was alive with flickering shadows and flashing gunfire, hissing bullets tearing at the air around them. Sophia felt her blood turn to ice as the fleeing soldiers ran for them, heedless of the bullets cutting them down as they fled the seething, devouring darkness.

And then a shout shook the forest, drowning out even the thunder of the artillery and the hammering gunfire. *"Charlie Company!"* Her father roared, louder than she had ever heard him, *"Stand your ground!"*

Sophia exhaled and felt her whole body flush hot as Lieutenant Thorn shouted behind her, "Hold fast! Let them pass through, then prepare to engage!"

She looked behind herself to see Tony and Edward leveling their rifles, Tony flicking his safety off with a shaking finger. As calmly as she could, she said, "Wait for it, guys..." She looked back to her front. The fleeing soldiers were almost upon them, rushing headlong through the underbrush. Raising her own rifle, she flipped her safety aside with a sweaty thumb and went on, "Hold, *hold*..." Behind them the forest was alive with gleaming bayonets and flashing gunfire, green-jacketed reapers in steel masks materializing from the murk like so many ghosts.

The defeated soldiers tumbled through the company's line and in the instant she brought her rifle to her shoulder and lined up the sights Sophia heard her father roar again, ordering the cowards to stand and fight. Then her sights aligned in the mass of boiling shapes and her finger tightened on the trigger. Her rifle bucked against her shoulder and the whole forest erupted around her as the company opened fire.

The forest in front of her seemed to wilt and shred apart, splinters filling the air as she worked her rifle's bolt and fired again and again. The leering ghosts in their green jackets and steel masks flew to the ground, flattening themselves into cover. The darkness flashed before them as they fired back, Sophia barely noticing as bullets stirred the air around her. Imperial bayonets glinted as the enemy rolled and rushed around, trying to escape the storm that engulfed them.

An Imperial machine-gun flared and Sophia felt earth shower down on her. As she worked her bolt and fired again, she abstractly realized it wasn't enough. If they sat there and fought it out the Imperials would recover from their shock and they would come at them again. The company, and probably the whole regiment, would be stopped cold. They *had* to attack.

With a force of will, Sophia let go of her rifle with her right hand and felt on her belt for her bayonet. Finding it, she popped the snap free with adrenaline-numbed fingers and drew the long blade, rolling back a little and raising her rifle to present the muzzle as it came free. She swung the blade up, aligned it and pushed it down over her bayonet lug. It locked into place with a solid click that she somehow heard even over the shrieking firefight.

Sophia looked around for Lieutenant Thorn, her vision blurring for a moment as she swung her head and saw him pulling back from the next tree to her right. Jack and Kelly had gone to ground in a depression a few feet in front of them, and he looked like he was about to scramble forward to them. Their eyes met, and she gestured with her rifle and its lethal blade as she shouted, "*Sir!*" She was about to say more, try to scream something over the shrieking machine-gun between them, but Thorn looked between her and her bayonet and she saw the realization hit him.

With a flash of steel Thorn freed his own bayonet and locked it to his rifle, screaming, "*Fix bayonets! Fix bayonets!*" Someone repeated it, then someone else, men's voices rising above the gunfire as they repeated the call. Looking behind her, Tony and Edward were drawing their own blades, and the next squad down the line gleamed and flashed in the forest's dappled light as they drew theirs. For a moment the company's rifles fell silent as a wave of sharp clicks rolled across the forest.

Thorn reared up into a crouch, waved his hand and shouted, "Forward! *Attack!*"

Sophia looked behind her. Tony and Edward were crouching there, rifles in hand and bayonets glinting as the sun washed over them. She met their eyes, and Tony nodded grimly. Turning away, Sophia lifted her rifle and shouted "*Let's go!*" as she darted out of cover, her bayonet a cold flame slicing through the forest gloom. She didn't need to look back to know the rest of the company was behind her.

Chapter 31

An Eye for the Battlefield

"Wow, they must be really going at it over there." Patricia remarked as a long, low growl murmured through the forest.

Arilin pulled absently at her uniform's high, stiff collar and asked, "What do you mean, that noise?" She looked at the lady general nervously, "Is that artillery?"

She replied, "Yes, milady." She gave the princess a wry smile, "They're firing so many guns you can't hear the individual bangs. And, really, I'm quite surprised we can hear them at all at this distance."

Reflexively sitting a little straighter on her horse, Arilin smoothed over a nervous feeling in her stomach and replied, "Must be quite a fight, then."

"I'll say." Patricia replied, "Last I heard before we left was they were halfway up the ridge and the envelopment was making progress. The whole operation's ahead of schedule." She grimaced, "For the Kingdom's sake, I hope we're wasting our time out here."

Arilin looked around, feeling her uniform's collar scratch at her neck. The great vault of the forest rang with hoofbeats as the division's staff rode through, a great column of horsemen filling the road. Just behind the two of them a pair of riders carried the division's blue and gold colors and the white Royal standard. Turning back to her front, Arilin caught a glimpse of Eric's squadron standard far to their front, the blue cuirassier colors flapping in a sudden breeze as the forest opened out. She imagined Maximilian's knights must have rode to war in much the same way, flags flying and armor shining in the sun. She winked at Patricia and replied, "Well, milady, if there's nothing out here then I can't think of a nicer day for a ride."

The lady general laughed, "I've had a few of those." She confided, "When I was at the Dragon's Jaw the Imperials only ever came at us when the weather was bad. On a day like this I could take the guys, go ride twenty miles around the fortress and nothing would happen." She chuckled, "Had a guy give me flowers once."

"How sweet of him." Arilin commented.

Patricia gave her a mischievous look and replied, "I found out later he was a dragoon that did it on a dare."

The princess laughed, "Sounds like you were quite popular." Jerking her head at the standard-bearers riding behind them, she said, "Speaking of popularity, is the Royal flag *really* necessary? It's..." She struggled to find the words for a moment, "I don't want to create trouble for you."

"Hardly, milady." Patricia said, "I don't think you appreciate the effect you've had on this division. We're all riding a little straighter in the saddle today just knowing that flag is flying. And, well..." She trailed off as they emerged from the forest, sunlight stinging their eyes for a moment as the landscape unfolded before them. Coming off the rise they could see endless farms, pastures and patches of forest stretching as far as the eye could see. And somewhere out there, maybe, was the Imperial Army. She went on, "Right now we can use all the help we can get."

"I guess so..." Arilin trailed off, casting a glance at Patricia. The older woman was looking across the landscape, brow furrowed in concentration. She asked, "Do you see something?"

Patricia turned and gave her a sly smile, "Two different ways to get across that river up ahead, milady. And I think where we're having dinner tonight."

Arilin looked back out at the landscape before her. The patchwork of fields and woods seemed to roll on forever below them, broken by villages nestled among the trees. The road snaked through what looked like a larger town far ahead where she supposed they might stop later. Looking back at the general, she said hesitantly, "I'm... not sure what you mean. You mean that town up there?"

Patricia shifted her gaze down a little, "Oh, that? Of course not, milady. We'll be through there in an hour." She pointed, "We're stopping for dinner *there*."

Arilin let her eye rise farther towards the horizon. Shimmering through the distant heat haze she saw what looked like church steeples rising above the forest. She had looked right past it earlier. Swallowing nervously, she asked, "And what about the river?"

The lady general gestured across the landscape with her outstretched finger, "You can see it there, in the trees. They're taller near it, and you can see a little bit of a gap." The narrow, swift mountain river almost popped out at Arilin now that she looked for it. Patricia went on, failing to keep a smug note out of her voice, "There'll be a bridge in the town up ahead. But do you see that track there?"

Following her finger, Arilin saw a muddy, anonymous rut emerge from the trees some distance away from the town, meander across the fields and eventually merge into the main road. A cattle path. Raising her eyebrows questioningly, Arilin said, "I do now. What about it, milady?"

Smiling, Patricia asked, "Do you really think the townspeople would be happy about five hundred cows going through their town and across their bridge? There's a ford there." Arilin looked back at her, feeling new respect building in her heart. It was exactly the kind of thing cavalry would need to get an edge in battle and Patricia had picked it out of the landscape in an instant. She had been looking at the landscape like a painting, as something to be appreciated for the sum of its parts. Patricia had seen a battlefield and found with a glance where her hussars could dart through and cut down the enemy.

Arilin sighed and looked down at her horse's mane. She noticed her gloved hands, holding the reins perfectly as though she was riding dressage. It was very different from how the soldiers around her carried themselves, relaxed yet upright in their saddles. Even Patricia, as elegant as she was on horseback, seemed ready to draw her sword and charge in an instant. There was so much she had yet to learn, and she had never felt so childish.

A familiar hand patted her warmly on the shoulder, and Arilin looked over to see Patricia's kind smile, "Don't get yourself down, milady. Reading the terrain is a skill." She added, "It's really much like reading your opponent in a sword-fight, and you're much better at *that* than I am."

"Really?" Arilin perked up, "If it's not too much trouble while we're riding, can you teach me?"

"I'd love to, milady. Although," Patricia chuckled, "We may be interrupted by the Empire."

"The story of my life." The princess remarked.

Laughing, Patricia said, "So true for us all." She cleared her throat and went on, "Now, milady, as I've told you before, you must pay attention to the smallest details..."

* * *

People turned out to gawk as they trotted through the first town half an hour later, the horses' hooves clattering on the cobblestones and echoing through the streets. Shouts went up and people came running at the sight of the Royal standard, and Arilin waved to the crowd good-naturedly. They were riding through the town square and the princess was having a polite conversation with the local mayor, who had appeared on horseback, when a messenger galloped up from the rear of the column and handed Patricia a note.

Eyebrows furrowed in concentration, she read it and asked the man, "Is this all? Nothing more?"

The messenger shook his head, "No, milady."

"Not much of a report." Patricia commented, "Very well. Send a message back, tell them to remain vigilant and keep moving north according to plan."

The man wheeled his horse and galloped back down the column towards the radio truck, and Arilin looked over and asked, "What was that, milady?"

"Some of the lancers just got into a fight with three or four dragoons. They escaped and we lost a man." Patricia sighed unhappily, "Same as this morning. Probably pathfinders."

The princess raised an eyebrow, "Pathfinders? What's that?"

The mayor, who had watched the exchange silently until then, interjected nervously, "Yes, milady, what are *they* doing around here? I thought the Empire had retreated, thank God."

Patricia looked at the man. He had the easy grace on horseback of a cavalryman, albeit one long past his prime. She guessed he'd gotten out of the Army after the last war with the Empire. Looking back to Arilin, she explained, "Something that doesn't exist, milady, at least according to Intelligence. Of course nobody seems to have told the Empire that." She went on, "When the Empire moves one of their field armies they send special troops to infiltrate ahead of even the dragoons. They move in very small groups, they don't wear masks or anything else like an Imperial uniform and they are very good at avoiding notice."

"You don't think they're stragglers?" Arilin asked.

Patricia smiled and said, "It's possible, milady, but lost men on blown horses don't outride lancers."

The mayor, now very pale, cut in, "Do... do you mean to say the Empire is moving south through here, milady?"

"That's what we're here to find out." Patricia gave the man a hard look and said, "If I were you I'd start preparing to evacuate. Half the Imperial Army could be bearing down on this place right now."

He objected, "But the battle is at Fire ridge right now."

"That's the problem." Arilin remarked.

The light came on in the man's head, "Oh. I'll see right to it, milady."

The mayor spun his horse around and rode off before they could even say their goodbyes, and Arilin asked her, "How are you so sure they're pathfinders?"

Patricia shrugged, "I'm not. One gunfight is an angry farmer and now two is a coincidence. If there's another I'll know it's the Empire." She smiled grimly, "But you recall what I was telling you earlier about reading the battlefield?"

The princess raised her eyebrows, "Yes?"

"Well it isn't just a visual thing." The lady general chuckled, "The days when you could just come upon the whole enemy army marching along are long gone. Now you have to piece together reports that come in, as bad as they always are, and figure out what the enemy is doing."

"And even a little information can mean a lot." Arilin observed.

Patricia nodded, "Exactly, milady. Now let's see what happens next."

Within the hour the 14th Hussars radioed in to report they had seen a suspicious group of horsemen who had fled when approached. As they discussed it with the staff another report came in from the 14th's other squadron. Two horsemen shot and killed. Old-style rifles and civilian clothes with black scarves, carrying Imperial military maps. Patricia grimaced and told them to send a message back to Corps: Imperial scouts confirmed moving south. The division would press on.

They rode north as the sun sank in the west and shadows lengthened across the road. Off to the east the artillery built to a low, constant rumble in the distance. Patricia felt a growing knot in her stomach as the guns ground on, hour after hour. It sounded like the biggest thunderstorm in the world just over the horizon and she wanted nothing more than to find someplace warm and safe to ride out the coming downpour.

The lancers reported contact with another small group of riders as they gradually moved up on the left of the hussars, and then they heard nothing more. The division rode north as the afternoon passed, the lancers and hussars sweeping a line twenty kilometers across for an enemy that stubbornly refused to appear. The sky turned gold in the west and the air began cooling with the dusk, and Arilin noticed Patricia chewing her thumbnail and asked, "What's wrong, milady?"

"This is always the worst part." Patricia self-consciously dropped her hand back to her lap and turned to Arilin. The girl looked a little saddle-sore, and she chuckled and went on, "Even when you *know* they're out there, you never find them when you think you will."

"I was going to ask," Arilin said, "Why we haven't run into any more pathfinders. It's been hours now."

Patricia replied, "We've probably ridden past all of them, or at least the lead regiments have. And they're not going to show themselves around us here." She grimaced and pointed at the plume of dust from Eric's squadron up the road from them, "Although I'm sure they know exactly where we are. You can see *that* for miles."

"So now what?" Arilin asked.

"Any minute now we should run into dragoons, milady." The lady general added cynically, "That's *if* there's anything out here at all. I've been on goose chases before." She sighed, "And then the real battle will begin. We have to stop them."

The princess raised her eyebrows questioningly, "Why's that? I thought we already know the Empire is moving south in force." She went on, "Unless you don't think the pathfinders are enough?"

"Unfortunately, milady, they're not." Patricia looked up at the sky for a moment. The moons were out, floating serenely across the darkening sky like a string of pearls. It didn't seem like a battlefield. It never did. She looked back at her companion and explained, "If we confirm the main Imperial force is marching south at us, milady, General Haas will stop his corps' movement, face north and move to meet them. He'll cut off the *entire* flow of reinforcements and supplies to Fire Ridge while he's at it to build up enough forces to delay the Empire."

"We'll lose the battle at the ridge." Arilin observed, "If it turns out White's right and you and Haas are wrong, well..." The thought was best left unsaid.

Patricia nodded, "Exactly, milady. That's why we're out here looking. Let me ask you a question." She went on, making quotations in the air with her fingers, "Worst case, what do these 'pathfinders' we've run into represent? What would White think of them?"

Arilin thought for a moment, "Stragglers?"

"Yes." She replied, "And what if we ran into dragoons? Lots of them."

The princess shrugged, "A raiding party?"

Patricia nodded again, "Yes. So, milady, what would *confirm* that the whole Western Area Army is out here?"

Arilin thought for a minute, swaying with her horse as it walked along under her. Finally she ventured, "Captured orders?"

"One in a million with the Empire, Milady." Patricia chuckled, "The only time I've ever seen captured Imperial orders was when they *wanted* us to have them. Try again. Think about what the Imperial Army will actually look like on the ground."

"Hm..." Arilin furrowed her eyebrows in thought before she suddenly perked up and exclaimed, "Infantry!"

"Or really heavy artillery, milady, but you're right." Nodding, she went on, "Yes. We're out here looking for Imperial infantry."

Arilin cocked her head, "So we have to get past their dragoons?"

Patricia laughed, "Not a lot of hope of that, milady." She looked around at the cavalrymen riding around them in the gathering darkness, "We're pretty good, milady, but realistically we're not going to just ride over them and find the enemy's main force. They know we're coming and a dragoon division has so many more heavy weapons than this one does it's scary."

The princess raised an eyebrow, "So... how are we going to do it?"

"Easy. We're probably not going to beat them outright, but we can sure *stop* them." Patricia smiled, "What happens then?"

"They... commit their infantry to move us?" Arilin ventured.

The lady general nodded, "Exactly, milady. *That's* when I call Walter and tell him to wheel north." She shrugged, "Until then, we're just taking a ride in the countryside."

"I see..." The princess trailed off. She changed the subject, perking up a little, "By the way, ah, when are we going to stop tonight?"

Patricia pointed at a dim glow ahead of the column, "Up there, milady. No sense wearing ourselves out this early in the battle. We'll start off again in the morning."

Soon a small town began to rise around them, gas streetlights bathing the streets in soft light. Eric's cuirassiers had moved ahead and prepared the town for occupation, and the local hotel had been cleaned out to serve as a command post. The staff dismounted outside and moved in to set up for the night. Arilin stretched herself happily before she walked up the front steps with Patricia.

"Attention!" Someone called as they walked in the front door into a broad, low-ceilinged room swarming with cavalrymen. The occupants stopped suddenly and stood to attention, the room suddenly falling silent.

Patricia waved her hand dismissively, "Please, carry on. We have a war to fight." The soldiers went back to their work and the two of them turned to see the hotel's owner, a balding, visibly nervous man. She smiled and said, "Good evening. I hope we won't inconvenience you for too long."

The man shook his head, "No, no, it is an honor to host the Royal family." He bowed deeply to the princess, "What, ah, what can we do for your ladyships?"

Arilin piped up, "Dinner would be nice. We haven't eaten since," She thought for a moment, "Noon, I guess?"

"Certainly, milady." The man made to turn and leave.

Patricia stopped him, "Wait." He turned back and she asked, "Before you go, has the Empire been through here recently?"

The man sighed, "Well, yes, milady." He looked around nervously, "They were moving through all last week. I thought we'd never see the end of them." He grit his teeth, "Damn Masks... speaking of, you all are the first Royal troops we've seen through here. Are there more of you coming?"

She replied noncommittally, "Maybe. Thanks for your assistance."

The man turned and left, and Arilin remarked, "Sounds like we're on the right track."

"Maybe." Patricia said darkly, "I'll believe that when we actually *find* them. They could be halfway back to the Empire right now for all we know."

They ate dinner and emerged from the dining room to see the command post had been completed in the hotel's hastily-rearranged common room. Patricia was talking to one of the operations officers about their objectives for the next day when Arilin suddenly exclaimed, "Quiet! Quiet! Everyone, please be quiet!"

The murmur of conversation died off quickly, and Patricia gave the girl a questioning look, "Milady, what's going on?"

"Wait a minute.... I thought I heard something." Arilin muttered.

Patricia said, "Let's go outside. Come on."

They quickly walked out the back door into the calm, still night. The distant roar of the artillery at Fire Ridge was still echoing through the air. Off to the southeast she could see a couple of flare shells in the far distance, floating over the ridge like ghosts. She looked over at the girl. Arilin's eyes were closed and her features set in concentration as she listened intently.

And then Patricia heard it. One faint thud, then another and another, off to the north. *Artillery*. The princess's eyes flew open and they looked at each other in alarm. They were turning to rush back inside when the door opened and Vanessa appeared.

"Milady!" Her aide said, "The Fourteenth just reported in. They're under attack, dismounts with artillery support."

"Dragoons?" She asked.

"I don't know, milady." Vanessa answered as Patricia walked past her into the hotel, "That's all we've gotten from them."

"Wonderful." The staff was looking at her expectantly, and Patricia ordered, "Tell the cuirassiers to move up and prepare to reinforce the forward regiments. Their second squadron will remain here in reserve. Otherwise the plan remains in force. The Fourteenth and Twentieth will hold in place and take measures to avoid being outflanked. Ensure they have coordinated with each other to prevent penetration at the regimental boundary." She finished, "We will let the situation develop overnight. Maybe the Empire will show their hand."

The staff set to work, and Arilin asked, "I'm guessing none of us are going to get a lot of sleep tonight?"

Patricia gave the girl a look. She was probably exhausted after riding all day. Patting the girl on the shoulder, she replied, "None of *us*, milady. *You* can go to bed if you'd like. We'll wake you up if the Empire attacks, I promise."

Arilin shook her head, "I'm fine. I can stay up."

Patricia chuckled, "Get some rest while you can, milady. Battles these days aren't decided in one charge. This is going to take *hours*."

The princess sighed, "Alright, I'll try to sleep."

She called for Vanessa to take care of Arilin and her aide led the girl upstairs. As Patricia turned back to her staff and the battle she heard another string of booms in the distance, louder and closer than the Imperial shells from earlier. She smiled. Her own horse artillery was firing back.

Chapter 32

By Fire and Steel

The forest before her filled with muzzle flashes. The air seethed with bullets and filled with splintered wood. For an instant Sophia's blurred vision cleared and she saw an Imperial soldier slam his rifle's lever closed as he lined up his sights on her, rifle clamped tightly to his featureless war mask. She could almost see his finger tighten on the trigger.

And then she dove behind a tree, a bullet cracking low overhead as she thrust her rifle forward, seated it against her shoulder, lined up the sights and fired. She worked the bolt automatically and fired again, and again as she saw Lieutenant Thorn slide into cover beside her out of the corner of her eye. She felt Tony thud down beside her, wiggle into the tree's cover and bring his rifle around to fire from the other side. Behind them Jack fired a long burst from his machine gun, the heavy bullets thundering overhead and tearing at the Imperials. Time to go.

Rolling to her feet, Sophia lunged forward through the hissing, cracking air. She threw herself down behind a large rock jutting from the mildly sloping ground, again maneuvered her rifle with its long bayonet into position and fired. Her friends rushed up behind her, Tony crouching over her awkwardly as he fired over the top of the rock. An Imperial machine gun shrieked nearby and shards of stone rained on them both as Tony fell on top of her.

She rolled halfway over and looked at him. He didn't seem to have any new bullet holes. Shouting over the gunfire, she asked, "You okay?"

Tony had covered his face instinctively when he fell. Pulling his hands away, he looked at her and nodded shakily as he said, "Yeah, I think so."

"Alright. I'm going, cover me!" She replied, and Tony visibly steadied himself and rolled over to fire from the other side of the rock. The machine gun fired again, showering them with dirt as Tony fired back. She thought she heard someone scream as she pushed herself up and darted forward, threw herself down and fired. And then she did it again. And again, her gleaming bayonet slicing through darkness under the trees until she was so close she could hear the Imperials shouting orders. Hold the line. Get grenades ready. The Imperials weren't running, and Sophia felt her blood turn to ice at the thought.

Sophia fired again, worked her bolt and tried to push it forward. The bolt stuck and she pushed at it for a second before she realized her rifle was empty. Dropping back behind her covering log, she fumbled with her ammo pouch and after an eternity managed to get a clip out. An enemy machine gun shrieked almost on top of her as she fitted it to her rifle and viciously jammed the rounds down into her magazine. Someone screamed. It sounded like Edward.

Sophia rolled over to look for her friend and saw Tony scrambling for her. As he slid into cover beside her she saw a blue-jacketed shape thrashing on the ground behind him, hands pressed to a face bright with blood. The machine gun fired again and bullets danced around Edward as he instinctively flatted himself to the ground. She felt her blood run cold. He wouldn't survive another burst.

Heaving herself back over, Sophia saw Tony rise on her other side and swing his rifle down to fire over the log. His rifle barked and the row of grenades across the back of his harness swung with the recoil. Sophia realized how she could save Edward. As the Imperial machine-gun fired again and bullets tore overhead she reached over and grabbed two of Tony's grenades as he dropped back into cover. He gave her a questioning look as she tore off the safety caps on the handles. She jerked her head at Edward and shouted over the gunfire, "I'm getting Edward! Cover me!"

Tony looked at the grenades in her hands and pulled a couple of his own off of his belt as he said, "I've got you! Go!"

Sophia yanked the igniter on her first grenade, wound up and hurled it over the log at the enemy. Someone shouted, "*Grenade! Get down!*" An instant later she ignited her second one and threw it as well. Rolling to her knees, she lunged for Edward as the bombs shattered the forest, one, two blasts tearing at the enemy as she scurried for him on hands and knees, grabbed the back of his harness and started dragging him to safety. Her feet dug into the soft forest floor as he half-rose and pushed with her. A bullet cracked inches away as another blast, then another shredded the forest and they tumbled into the log's protection.

Edward's hands were still clenched to his face, bright red blood seeping through his fingers as he curled into himself beside her. She looked between him and Tony, pale-faced and wide-eyed with fear beside her as enemy bullets sawed into the protection of their log. Edward was safe. He could wait. They needed to win the fight.

As if to punctuate her thoughts Sophia heard, somehow very clear over the banging chaos of the battle, something small and heavy thunk into the far side of their log. Tony was rising to fire again, and she grabbed the back of his harness and yanked him back down over her as the Imperial grenade went off. Their world went dark for a moment as earth showered on them and the log shuddered with the force of the explosion.

Pushing Tony off of her, Sophia rolled back to crouch behind her cover and felt for her own grenades. Beyond him she could see Jeremy and Hargrave readying their own grenades, and Lieutenant Thorn gesturing frantically for someone to move up.

Sophia popped the safety cap on her grenade, wound up and threw. It seemed like most of Charlie Company threw with her, and for an instant she saw the forest air fill with whirling, long-handled Royal grenades. More than a few egg-shaped Imperial ones came back at them. Someone on the other side screamed a curse, and Tony and Sophia flattened themselves behind their sturdy log as the forest erupted around them.

Day turned to night. Earth and splintered wood rained on them as Sophia's ears rang. She reared back over the log, fired, worked her bolt and was about to leap over it and at the enemy when something flashed in the smoke and darkness in front of her. She dropped back down as Imperial bullets cracked around her. They were still there. Somehow, the enemy was still there. God in heaven, how could they survive that and still be able to fight? Sophia was gritting her teeth in frustration and reaching for another grenade when she saw a familiar shape throw himself down next to Thorn at the next tree over and throw a long weapon forward on its bipod. An instant later Kelly threw himself down next to Jack and the lieutenant. Sophia saw Jack's finger tighten on the gun's trigger and the forest shattered again.

Their machine gun's roar drowned out everything else, even the shrieking Imperial guns so close nearby. Then, impossibly, Sophia heard another gun erupt as the next squad over got theirs into action. And another. And another, until it seemed like all of the company's guns were hammering away, tearing apart the enemy at point-blank range. This wasn't how machine guns were supposed to be used. They were supposed to hang back and support the advance from a safe distance. So much for doctrine.

Sophia pulled the igniter on another grenade and hurled it through smoke and flying dirt. The whole company threw with her, grenades raining onto the Imperial position as their machine guns scythed through the forest. None came back this time. For the last time Sophia ducked behind her log as a long, *long* string of blasts shattered the forest. Rearing up, she hefted her rifle and leapt over the log, screaming, *"Come on!"*

A low, dark shape shifted in the swirling smoke before her and time seemed to slow to a crawl as Sophia saw it swing the long barrel of an Imperial machine gun down and around, onto her. Her rifle's sights appeared in her field of view as she raised the weapon and fired. Something sparked in the darkness and the shape twisted away as her rifle thudded into her shoulder, her hand working the bolt automatically as she advanced.

Another shape reared up next to the first, a rifle coming up to its shoulder. Sophia lunged, knocked its rifle aside and buried her bayonet under its war-mask with one movement. Yanking her weapon free, she saw movement out of the corner of her eye and pivoted, bringing her bayonet around as the Imperial machine-gunner rolled over. She saw a pistol in his hand and she stabbed, once, twice, three times, pinning him to the ground. He died with a sick gargle and she yanked her weapon free and looked around.

Dark-jacketed Royal soldiers were swarming over the Imperial line and she could see a few of the enemy crumpled at their feet. A couple Imperial machine guns lay abandoned, their long, top-mounted magazines lying at wrong angles. Sophia looked behind her to see Tony nervously covering the dead Imperial rifleman as though he expected the man to leap back to life any instant. She gave him a nasty look and said, "Come on, let's go. We're sitting ducks standing here."

The words cut through the haze of adrenaline and suddenly she could hear people talking again, Lieutenant Thorn shouting at them to push forward and finish the assault. Sophia lifted her rifle, absently noticed the blood dripping down the stock and pushed forward with Tony another twenty meters. There weren't any Imperial troops farther out. If any had fled they had been fast and they hadn't stopped running.

Jeremy and Mr. Hargrave came up with them, and after a minute or so an angry-looking Jack hauled his machine-gun up by himself and flopped down between the two teams. Sophia asked him, "Where's Kelly?"

Jack jerked his head behind them and spat, "Taking care of *your* guy."

Edward. Damn. They'd left him back at the fallen log when they'd attacked. Gritting her teeth at Jack's tone, she replied levelly, "Very nice of him." She looked around. Where the hell was the corporal? She went on, "Seen Slaughter?"

Jack rolled his eyes at her, "Nope."

"He's dead." Sophia turned to see Sergeant Cross grimacing a few feet behind them. The man sighed and went on, "I saw him get hit. Took five or six rounds. Doc just looked at him and, well... it was fast."

Everyone looked at her expectantly. Damn. Sophia had never been close to the man. To be honest, she hadn't thought much of him as a leader. She'd had to do his job for him half the time. But he was still just... gone. If she were back in Jade Falls she would have found somewhere private to go cry over it. But she wasn't in Jade Falls, she and what was left of the company were halfway up a *God-damn* ridge that was literally on *God-damn* fire and crawling with *God-damn* Imperials who were trying to *God-damn* murder them and the *God-damn* people they were supposed to be relieving had decided to run for their *God-damn* lives and now she had to be the *God-damn* squad leader again. She was seventeen. She was supposed to be enjoying her summer. Swimming in the river. Flirting with Tony. Getting into stupid arguments with her parents. But *no*, this year the *God-damn* Emperor had decided he wanted to kill another million people for no *God-damn* reason.

God damn the Empire. Sophia took a deep breath, grit her teeth and got to her feet. Looking back at Cross, she asked, "What are we going to do about him?"

The sergeant raised an eyebrow, "Slaughter? We'll collect him and the others," He looked back significantly at the dead Imperials, "And leave them to be picked up."

"And the wounded?" She asked.

He shook his head, "Don't know. I think your dad and the boss are trying to figure that out right now."

She could see her father talking to Captain Caldwell some ways back and a weight she didn't know had been there lifted off her heart. He was fine. She sighed, looked around and said, "You guys stay here. I'm going to go get Ed and Kelly."

"Am I in charge?" Jack asked sarcastically.

"No." She smirked and pointed at Hargrave, "He is."

Her friends chuckled as she walked away. Edward and Kelly were where they had left them, sitting against the log they had taken cover behind. The fallen tree was half-torn apart, shredded wood spilling onto the ground as she came up to it, and her eyes widened as she saw the damage. Jesus. The enemy hadn't been screwing around. How many bullets had it stopped?

Hauling herself over the destroyed tree, Sophia found Kelly wrapping a bandage tightly around Edward's head. Her friend's face and the neck of his uniform were dark with blood, but he looked over and she saw him recognize her as she approached. Kneeling, she asked, "How're you doing, Ed?"

He grimaced and replied, "Been worse. How's everyone else?"

Sophia shook her head slowly, "Slaughter didn't make it. Cross saw him get hit." She looked around, "I'm... not actually sure where he is."

"Damn." Edward winced as Kelly tugged on the bandage and started to tie it, "Anyone else?"

She gave him a crooked smile, "Just you." She looked at Kelly, "How is it?"

The machine gunner shrugged, "It'll scar."

Sophia turned back to Edward and asked, "Think you can get back with the squad?"

He shrugged, shook his head, winced and felt at his bandaged head. Finally, he said, "I don't think I'm supposed to be running around after I just got *shot in the head*, Sophie."

She snorted, "I don't think we've got much of a choice, unless you want to hang out with the dead until someone comes for them."

"You've got a point, Sophie." Edward unsteadily climbed to his feet and picked up his rifle, "Lead on."

Sophia took the two of them back forward and set them in position. For a few minutes they sat there listening to the commotion behind them as the medics did their work and her father harangued the soldiers who had fled the Imperials earlier to carry the wounded north to the road, where hopefully they would be able to get onto wagons going back down-hill. She heard him calling out one of their squads afterward to go with them and make sure they got back to the 50th Regiment to be dealt with.

Speaking of the 50th Regiment, after Sophia's ears stopped ringing she could hear an awful lot of shooting going on off to the side and a little ways to their front upslope. It sounded like mostly Royal weapons. Lieutenant Thorn came around to check on the squad as the wounded started to move off and she asked him about it.

Thorn replied, "First Battalion's apparently in a fight. Major Clark was just up here and he told us he thought the 50th's command post is off that way." He looked around at the battle-scarred forest for emphasis, "We probably showed up just in time to keep them from getting overrun."

"Sounds like we're winning." Sophia observed.

The lieutenant smiled grimly, "That it does. Ready to get moving, Miss Rose?"

She nodded, "Yes, sir."

"Good. Let's go." Thorn waved his arm dramatically and shouted, "First platoon! Continue the advance! Platoon column!" She supposed there was no point in trying to be quiet any more. They'd lit off about a hundred grenades in the last twenty minutes after all.

Charlie Company collectively got up and climbed out, squads falling in behind her own. After a minute she spied the white engineer tape snaking uphill and continued following it up. As they climbed and the firefight to their side quieted down the line ran out, ending in a half-finished spool of tape sitting on the forest floor. Sophia sighed and walked on, following the line's general direction uphill. Behind her she heard Captain Caldwell tell someone to pick up the tape and keep stringing it.

As they went she noticed more and more of the unmistakable signs of battle scarring the forest. She saw bullet holes in the far sides of trees and distinctive furrows in the forest floor from gunfire. Imperial fire. She saw a couple Royal soldiers crumpled dead on the ground as they advanced, cut down as they had fled earlier. The forest started to thin out as the firefight, now behind them, finally died down. Sophia pushed through some brush and emerged into dappled sunlight as the dense, low forest opened up, massive trees soaring to a canopy far overhead. Feet sinking deep into the ancient forest's loam, Sophia walked forward cautiously.

And then she saw it. Glittering in the distance, cutting into trees and half-sunk into the mossy ground as it stretched across the forest in coils like a great, spined snake. Barbed wire. Sophia waved to her squad to take cover and sprinted into the protection of one of the great trees. Behind her and around her she could hear the rest of the company rush into cover as they obeyed her signal.

The footsteps and squeak of bouncing equipment died out quickly and the forest returned to stillness. If it hadn't been for the dull, ever-present rumble of the artillery she knew it would have been a dead, eerie silence under the trees. Soft footsteps broke the quiet and she half-turned to see Lieutenant Thorn easing up behind her. He asked, "See something, Sophie?"

"Yeah." She replied quietly, "Wire. Lots of it. And..." She trailed off. Now that she'd had a chance to get a good look at the Imperial wire belt in front of them she'd noticed the dark shapes staining the ground in front of it. On it. She could see where the belt had been cut and pulled back, how the breaches were littered with those too-familiar, blue-jacketed shapes.

Thorn lifted his binoculars to his eyes and swore softly. He went on grimly, "Guess we know where the 50th Regiment is. You think the Imperials re-occupied their positions?"

"They'd be stupid not to." Sophia said.

"If they had the troops to do it." Thorn replied.

She snorted grimly, "Only one way to find out, sir."

He said, "I have an idea. Hold here."

Sophia heard Thorn pad off and have a low conversation with Captain Caldwell. After a little while she heard soldiers moving around as the company pushed forward a little, forming a firing line. Thorn came up again and knelt behind her. She felt him set something down and looked over to see him cranking up a field telephone. Raising an eyebrow, she asked, "We've got comms, sir?"

He smirked, "If this phone works, yes." He spoke into it softly, "Vengeance Six, this is Charlie One-Six." Sophia heard a muffled reply and Thorn nodded and replied, "Roger. Can I get an orienting round?" He looked at his notebook and reeled off a string of coordinates. Sophia didn't need to be told to tuck herself into cover.

About a minute later Sophia heard an evil whistle overhead and a shell went off in the canopy, almost over her head. Branches and bits of wood rained down all of fifty meters in front of them and she rolled over and glared at Thorn angrily. The lieutenant gave her a sheepish look, picked up his field telephone and said nervously, "Ah, good round, Vengeance. Lay on these coordinates and stand by for a fire mission." He gave the Vengeance a set of coordinates that was a good three hundred meters further east. Looking back at her still glaring at him, he explained, "Hey, I've been dead reckoning here."

"Yes, sir." She replied bitingly, "We're lucky it wasn't *behind* us."

"Cram it, private." The lieutenant snorted, rolled over and gave a thumps-up to someone off to the side.

Sophia followed his gaze and saw Captain Caldwell make the same gesture back and raise a set of binoculars to his eyes. Voice breaking the forest stillness, the commander shouted, "Company! Enemy front, two hundred meters, five rounds rapid! Fire at will!"

Oh. *That's* what they were doing. Shoot at someone and they'll generally shoot back. Flicking her rifle off safe, Sophia leveled the sights on the most hostile-looking pile of brush on the other side of the barbed wire and pulled the trigger as the company opened fire around her. She was pulling back the bolt after her third round when the forest in front of them came alive with muzzle flashes and Imperial bullets started cracking by low overhead. She heard Thorn yelling into the field telephone for Vengeance to open fire moments before he was blotted out by Jack opening up with his machine gun.

They traded fire with the Imperials for about a minute before fire and dirty smoke washed over the enemy positions. The cracking thunder of their shells reached them a moment later over even the hammering gunfire, explosions shaking the forest as round after round burst among the trees along their front. The enemy gunfire died off as Sophia heard Caldwell blowing his whistle to signal the advance.

Once again, Sophia got up and charged. Once again, the company rushed forward after her. This time most of the bullets cracking around them were going the right direction. Sophia thought she saw a few dark shapes moving in the murk of smoke, dirt and seething shrapnel in front of them as she moved up, dashing from tree to tree with her friends close behind.

As they rushed closer to the barbed wire and shell fragments began hissing overhead they started passing blue-jacketed bodies crumpled on the ground. The deep forest moss had been churned and shredded by bullets and the great old trees torn around their bases and roots as though by some monster with a thousand teeth. Running to the cover of a tangle of roots, Sophia jumped one body and skidded to a halt beside another, slumped to the side where he had collapsed over his rifle. There was a hole the size of her fist blown out the back of his head.

Sophia looked away after a stomach-churning moment, waved her team forward and popped up over the protective cover of the roots. Another round flashed in front of her, terrifyingly close, and she quickly ducked back down as fragments whistled overhead. A few things that sounded more like bullets flew after it, and she eased herself back up and fired back in their general direction. An instant later she heard Tony and Edward skid into position around her along with someone else a little less familiar. She turned to see Lieutenant Thorn awkwardly kneeling over the body to her side as he cautiously peered over the tangle of roots at the barbed wire that now seemed almost close enough to touch.

Thorn ducked his head back down and looked at her. She saw his mouth move, "...to go?"

"Sir?" She asked. She could barely hear herself over the gunfire. On the next tree over behind Thorn she saw Jack and Kelly slide into position with their machine gun. She hoped Thorn said what he had to say before they deafened them all again.

The lieutenant repeated himself, louder, "You ready to go?"

Sophia snuck her head back over the tangle of roots and took a quick look at the barbed wire as their machine gun thundered to life. *God* was that thing loud. She wondered how those two dealt with it. Just in front of them the coiled wire had been cut apart and pulled back, forming a breach. The 50th Regiment had paid dearly to do it, and then they had paid double to get through it. Dead soldiers were hanging on the wire.

They covered the ground in front of the breach. Through the breach, to a second long coil of wire she'd only just noticed. And, finally, spraying out from the second belt like so much spilled blue paint. She could see the long tracks in the ground, crisscrossing where the Imperials had caught them in a crossfire.

She imagined the chaos and the sheer helpless vulnerability of the soldiers as they had forced their way into the killing field, Imperial fire raking in from all sides. The do-or-die rush that had carried them through, the desperate fight in the Imperial positions and the fear that had seized their hearts when the Empire counterattacked. Steel-masked demons appearing out of the swirling smoke of battle, guns roaring and swords slashing. No wonder they'd run for it. She wondered if she would have done the same in their position.

Sophia pulled her head back down and thought for a moment. The breach was all very convenient for them. She guessed the Empire hadn't had time or soldiers to do the work to repair it. Maybe it had been a closer fight than it seemed. But if they couldn't repair it, what would they do instead? Looking back at Thorn, Sophia shouted over the gunfire, "One thing first, sir!"

Thorn gave her a funny look back as she pulled one of her grenades off her webbing, yanked the igniter and hurled it into the middle of the breach. He ducked down with her as it roared to life, the shockwave pulling at them. Thorn made to get back up and look and Sophia pulled him back down as more explosions ripped through the forest. One, two, too many went off as the breach disappeared in a volcano of dirt and hissing shrapnel. *Damn,* Sophia thought, *how many grenades did they boo-by-trap it with?*

Sophia had just stuck her head up again when she saw Tony and Edward's grenades flying into the breach. She and Thorn ducked back down as five or six more bombs went off. Clearly the answer to her question was, *way too many.* Hopefully that was the last of them. Her ears were ringing and she thought she tasted blood. Looking at Thorn as he cautiously rolled back upright, she gave him a thumbs-up, pushed back from the tree and darted around him.

She saw movement out of the corner of her eye as she rushed around the lieutenant. Tony and Edward, coming around the other side of the tree. In front of her, sprinting into the breach, bayonets burning through the smoke. Well, that wouldn't do. Sophia sped up as bullets cracked around her. She wasn't sure if they were theirs or the enemy's. She wasn't sure if she cared.

Time seemed to congeal as she rushed through the breach, running over the backs of the men who had come before her and died to make the way. To pave the way. She followed the twin flames of her friends' bayonets as they bobbed through the darkness, and an eternity-long instant later they cleared the barbed wire and burst out of the stinking smoke, skidding into cover behind the protective roots of another gigantic tree.

"Hey!" Sophia shouted at them, "I didn't tell you to go!"

Tony rolled over and actually winked at her as he shot back, "I read your mind!"

"Whatever!" She yelled at him, "We're moving up! Cover me!"

Tony and Edward rolled onto their stomachs and started firing in the general direction of the Imperial gunners as she got up and rushed to the next piece of cover. And the next and the next, as they traded fire back and forth with the Imperials. Fortunately for them their artillery barrage shifted east, keeping in front of them as they advanced. Soon the whole company made it through, platoons and squads coming on line as they pushed forward relentlessly, shaking the forest with their machine guns as they swept into the attack.

It was too much for the Imperials. Sophia saw them popping up and down in the distance as they fell back, chased by the storm of their fire. Now and then one of their machine gunners would fire off a long burst and send them diving to the ground, but they mostly seemed to be interested in escaping. After a few minutes, as the forest closed in around them again and the last of the Imperials disappeared into the gathering gloom, Sophia heard Captain Caldwell blow his whistle for their attention. She looked back to see him holding up his hand to halt the advance, and she obligingly yelled at her squad to stop. Sophia arranged her troops into a rough defensive position, walked over to Tony and Edward and dropped to one knee.

And then the adrenaline started wearing off. Sophia realized how ragged her breathing was, how her sweat-soaked uniform hung from her body. Her vision blurred. Thirst burned at her throat, and she fumbled for one of canteens and drained half of it with one long gulp. Some got up her nose. Coughing, she lowered the bottle and shook her head slowly. This was awful. For a moment she wondered how the rest of her squad was holding up, and she chuckled to herself. She was their leader now. It was her job to find out.

Tony was shaking like a leaf. Edward's head wound was bleeding again. Jack's attitude was worse than ever. Kelly was low on ammunition for the machine gun and she gave him the extra belt she'd been carrying since they'd started climbing the ridge. Mr. Hargrave was smoking his pipe fixatedly and barely answered when she talked to him. And Jeremy was single-mindedly cleaning his bayonet with a bloody handkerchief. They were doing all right then.

Sophia turned to look back downhill at where the commander had planted himself, only to see Lieutenant Thorn sitting there puzzling over a map and her father walking uphill towards them. She walked back down to meet him partway.

He seemed a little grimier than usual, but otherwise perfectly normal. She supposed she looked like a complete disaster. He smiled to see her anyways, "Sophie! How're you doing?"

"Okay, I guess." She could only reply. She half-joked, "No new holes."

He actually laughed. Getting himself back together quickly, he shot back, "That's good to hear. Wish I could say the same for a lot of other people around here." He gave her a serious look, "I'm sorry about Corporal Slaughter."

Sophia sighed, "I didn't even see it. Cross told me..." She trailed off as an icy finger stroked at her heart, "Where is *he*, anyways?"

"Cross?" Her father raised an eyebrow, "He told me he was going to go check on the wounded a minute ago. He'll be around." He gestured back downslope as he went on, "I just came from there. We're lucky there aren't more."

Sophia fell in beside him as he walked uphill towards her squad's position, "So what's the plan?"

"For now?" Her father asked, "We hold here until the commander comes back with orders. He's off meeting with battalion." A long wave of gunfire rolled off to their left, and he went on, "From what I gathered they want us to wait here while they go help out First Battalion, and he wants to keep pushing."

She looked at him, "What do you want to do?"

"No sense dressing the line in all this. Might as well advance while we can." He gave her a half-smile back, "You feel up to keep going, Sophie?"

She thought for a moment. Finally, she sighed and replied, "Yeah. I'll be fine." They had arrived back at her squad's line and she corrected herself, "*We'll* be fine."

Her father nodded and patted her on the shoulder, "Good to hear, Sophie." Pulling her around to face him, he told her grimly, "Keep yourself alive. And take care of your soldiers."

His eyes were boring into hers. Sophia swallowed and managed, "Will do."

Her father replied, "Thank you." He grimaced and turned away to walk down further down the line, muttering, "Now for the rest of the company."

Captain Caldwell got back a few minutes later, visibly breathing hard from rushing back upslope. He had a short conversation with Lieutenant Thorn, her father and a couple sergeants from the other platoons, the group glancing significantly uphill and the commander making a few gestures in the air as he gave his orders. Sophia was starting to wonder where Lieutenant Stahl had gotten off to when the group broke up and Thorn came uphill towards her.

The lieutenant waved to call his subordinates in and she walked over to him. He looked over the small group and got right down to business, "The commander's convinced battalion to let us keep going. We step off in ten minutes. Platoon column. Second and Third will be behind us in a wedge."

"What's the rest of battalion doing, sir?" Sergeant Cross asked.

Thorn chuckled tiredly, "They're going to go bail out First Battalion. Apparently they ran into a bad fight over on the left. Delta is going to follow us up, but hang back in reserve." The lieutenant went on, "Our objective is the top of the ridge if we can make it by nightfall. Otherwise we dig in once it gets dark and hang on."

"No night attack, sir?" Sophia ventured. The forest was already darkening around them as the sun sank. It wouldn't be long before it was pitch-black under the trees.

Cross snorted and replied, "The Empire's still a long way away, Rose. We're not going to win this war with one more push."

Sophia looked around the group. Now that she thought about it, with his half-glazed eyes and vacant expression Thorn looked like he was about to collapse any minute. The others weren't far behind him. And with the adrenaline long worn off Sophia could feel the long fingers of fatigue plucking at her own body. She nodded slowly and said, "Alright. We could all use some rest."

Cross grimaced, "Just don't let your guard down, Rose. There are a *lot* of Masks out here."

She looked back at him levelly, "I won't, sergeant. I'm not *that* tired."

The man snorted again, "That's one of us." He looked back at Thorn, "Got anything else, sir?"

The lieutenant shook his head and they all dispersed back to their squads. Sophia got her friends up to speed on the plan and waited for the minutes to tick down. Soon she stepped off, the platoon silently falling into a ragged column behind her. There was none of the nervous stalking of the morning as they walked slowly uphill. None of them had the energy left to jump and wince at every sound as they climbed through the growing darkness, picking their way over rocks and tree roots that seemed to grab at their ankles with every step. A cool wind drifted through the forest as the light died, shifting the trees into a rustling dance.

Even the gunfire and shelling seemed to fade below them as they climbed through the forest. Finally, as they found their way by sifting moonlight an eternity after the sun had died in the west, Sophia heard something soft and light whistle through the air and pop softly into the ground beside her. A pine cone. She turned to faintly see Lieutenant Thorn holding up his hand for the halt. Sophia gratefully sank to a knee and gestured for her squad to spread out.

Thorn and Cross came around after a minute of adjusting the other squads to check their positions, and the sergeant gave her a nod and told her to start digging. They got out their entrenching tools and scraped at the rocky ground for what seemed like far too long without a lot of success. Sophia had worked out a depression about large enough to lie down in when her father came around.

Sophia turned over from her work and sat down as she heard him approach. He looked like a ghost, barely a hint of a person in the darkness as he came closer. Crouching, her father asked, "Is that you, Sophie?"

"Yeah. Hi, Dad." Noticing someone a little farther back in the darkness she went on awkwardly, "And, uh, you too, sir."

Caldwell snickered, "Perceptive as ever, Miss Rose."

Sophie turned back to her father and asked hopefully, "Bedtime?"

Her father gave her scraped fighting hole what she knew was a critical look. After a while he looked back at her and nodded, satisfied, "For you, yes." He looked over his shoulder at the commander, "Better than anything in Third Platoon, sir."

Caldwell sniffed, "Acceptable given the circumstances." He looked at her and went on, "Eat and put your squad down, Miss Rose. Keep one man awake on your machine gun."

Despite everything she'd been through that day Sophia felt herself smile, "Yes, sir."

Her father patted her on the shoulder, "Good job, Sophie." Standing, he turned to Caldwell and remarked, "Next squad, sir?"

"*If* we can find them." The commander replied sarcastically.

They ate their assault rations cold and in silence. Unpalatable in the best of times, somehow mind-numbing exhaustion and fear turned the hard crackers and slimy meat into something edible. Hargrave got the first watch as always. They'd long since learned his older body was less likely to just shut down after a long day than the teenagers'.

As the man settled himself behind the gun, Sophia loosened her boots and pulled off her harness. Setting it aside, she laid her spear atop it to keep it off the ground, unrolled her blanket and wrapped herself in it. Curling around her still-bayoneted rifle, she folded an arm under her head and blinked.

She heard the harsh click of the machine gun's safety.

Chapter 33

The Knight and the Dragon

Princess Arilin was an extraordinary girl, but at the end of the day she was still just a kid. She protested that she wouldn't be able to sleep with the battle going on up until she lay down in bed and passed out as soon as her head touched the pillow. Vanessa tucked the exhausted girl in and went back downstairs, closing the door softly behind her as she went.

General MacMahon noticed her as she came down and straightened up from where she had been listening in on a radio call. Vanessa sensed that she was wanted and walked over, squeezing by a couple members of the staff in the crowded room. The lady general asked her, "How's Arilin?"

"Asleep, milady." Vanessa felt herself smiling.

"Passed right out?" The general snickered, not unkindly, "I'm guessing she complained the whole time?"

Vanessa replied, "I won't deny it." She hesitated for a moment, then ventured, "Ah, milady... well..."

"Oh?" MacMahon raised an elegant eyebrow, "Out with it, Vanessa."

Coughing nervously, Vanessa went on, "Milady, ah, I don't suppose you have... further need for me tonight?"

General MacMahon gave her a disarming smile, "You want to go to bed too?" She chuckled, "I can see why, you look almost as gone as her."

Vanessa fidgeted, "Well, yes, milady."

MacMahon sighed and looked at the floor for a moment. Then she looked back up, her face stern. Gesturing with her chin towards the back door, she said, "Let's talk, Vanessa." She looked around significantly at the staff bustling around the room, "It's too noisy in here."

"Of course, milady," Vanessa replied as she followed the lady general outside, feeling her stomach curdling. Had she done something wrong? She closed the door behind them and turned to see the lady general leaning on the back deck's railing, half hidden in darkness as she looked out into the night. Vanessa inwardly sighed with relief. Her boss didn't seem angry. Stepping next to her, Vanessa nervously rested her elbows on the smooth wood and asked, "So, ah, milady...?"

MacMahon replied, "Vanessa, there are two kinds of lieutenants. The kind that would have gone to bed without telling me and the kind that would have stayed up until after I decided to turn in." She looked at her watch and chuckled, "Which at this rate is never." She gave her a sidelong look, "But you *asked*. Why?"

Vanessa swallowed hard, thought for a moment and replied, "It's... my job to be your aide, milady. I didn't see any reason to just stay up, but maybe you had something for me."

"I'm sure you noticed the game room in the back." MacMahon went on, "When I was a lieutenant I would have been asleep on one of the couches in there two hours ago." She snorted, "And Walter would have woken me up and cussed me out for it now that I think about it."

General Haas? She thought. It was always strange when she used his first name. Vanessa said nothing and the lady general continued, "Vanessa, I'm sure you've noticed this by now, but your thought process is a little *different.*"

Vanessa raised her eyebrows, "I take my job seriously, milady. And if other people don't, well... that's not my problem."

"And I'm not saying that you don't." MacMahon looked over at her apologetically, "Have you ever heard of the saying, 'the nail that sticks up gets hammered down'?"

"Of course, milady." *Where is she going with this?* Vanessa thought.

"When you showed up at the Regiment you raised a *lot* of red flags. I hate to break it to you, Vanessa, but you know there really *are* some lieutenants out there who don't deserve their commissions. And captains... majors, colonels, a few generals I know." She laughed, "Mina actually called me for advice about *you* in particular."

"Oh?" Vanessa's eyebrows rose again, this time in surprise. She hadn't realized things had gone that far.

Lady MacMahon went on, "I told her that some people are just a little off, and if she was still so worried about you that I needed an aide." She smiled at her, "It's not like being my aide was going to hurt your career."

Vanessa felt herself reddening, "Uh, thanks, milady."

MacMahon snorted, "Please. The pleasure's all mine. You've done a great job. Thank *you*. But." Vanessa heard her push herself back from the railing and turned to see the lady general stretching her arms over her head as though she wanted to get something out of her system. Relaxing, MacMahon went on as Vanessa turned towards her, "Unfortunately, or maybe fortunately for you, all good things must come to an end."

Vanessa felt her eyes widen, "What do you mean, milady?"

"The Regiment has been taking casualties. A lot more than I would prefer." General MacMahon scowled, "And right now Mina needs platoon leaders a lot more than I need an aide. She's expecting you at the front."

"Ah..." Vanessa felt an electric charge slither down her spine. She was going to the front. Suddenly the rumbling artillery was amplified, terrifyingly loud, pressing in from all sides. A fearful ride in the darkness to find her unit, leading unfamiliar soldiers against the enemy as they came on, wave after wave of faceless killers materializing from the darkness as though they were spawned from it. She swallowed hard and shook her head, and the vision was gone. She had a mission. Looking across at MacMahon levelly, she finished, "Yes, milady. I'll go forward immediately."

"Exactly what I thought you'd say." She smiled at her sadly, "Let me at least give you a map first."

* * *

Vanessa finished tightening her horse's girth strap, took her reins and led her out of the pitch-dark stables into the cool, moonlit night. By the Army's standards she was prepared and then some. She had a fast horse and saddlebags loaded with food, water and equipment. She had her saber, pistol and short cavalry carbine. Inside her jacket she had tucked the map General MacMahon had given her, with the 14th Regiment's command post marked on it. She had told her she'd get her final assignment from Colonel Bennett when she got there. *If* she got there.

Vanessa's blood turned to ice at the thought of the ride ahead of her. The division had spread out over the day as it had advanced, combing the countryside for the enemy. By nightfall the teeth of the comb, the lead cavalry troops, were kilometers apart and only in the most tenuous contact with their own superiors. What they absolutely *were* in contact with was the enemy. The regiments were radioing in constantly, an attack here, shelling there. Casualties. And Vanessa had fifteen kilometers to ride in the darkness just to get to her regiment and find out how much farther she had to go.

With a sigh, Vanessa boosted herself up into her saddle, swinging her leg over and settling into her seat. Her horse snorted at her, unhappy at having been woken and saddled up again in the middle of the night after a long day's ride. Vanessa patted the animal's neck apologetically and nudged it forward. She spared a look back at the inn's dark second-floor windows as her horse walked out on the road. Princess Arilin was sleeping up there. It pained her not being able to say goodbye to the girl.

It had seemed so wrong to Vanessa to take a girl of her age along on campaign, but Arilin had shouldered the burdens of the war and grown on everyone. The whole division, in fact the whole of IX Corps she suspected, was standing straighter knowing she was with them. And anyways, Vanessa thought as she turned her head back to the road ahead, it wasn't like this was the last she'd see of the princess. She was willing to bet a month's salary she'd run into a fire-breathing Lieutenant Arilin Wehrherz again in a few years. It was a good thought. Shrugging into her overcoat and buttoning it against the chill of the night and the wind of the ride ahead of her, Vanessa put spurs to her horse and cantered out of town into the darkness.

Getting to the 14th Regiment was easier than she had feared. There were plenty of ambulances on the roads bringing wounded soldiers to the division's field hospital, which had set up just north of town. She looked for drivers with female patients and they were more than happy to give her directions. Every time she felt herself getting nervous as the road twisted and turned in the moonlight she ran into someone, an ambulance driver, a supply column loaded with shells for the horse artillery, a dispatch rider, who directed her onwards.

After an hour Vanessa rode into the 8th Cuirassiers' encampment where they had pushed forward earlier to be ready to reinforce the forward regiments. The sergeant of the guard took her to their headquarters, where she learned Imperial troops had begun infiltrating through the porous front line and the roads north weren't safe for a girl like her riding alone. Fortunately the cuirassiers were sending out patrols to keep the roads open and she quickly found herself riding along with a dozen hulking cavalrymen.

Given how they treated her on the way she may as well have been riding sidesaddle with a parasol in hand, but they dropped her off in front of the 14th Regiment's command tent without incident. She supposed she could live with being patronized a little for that. Vanessa waved goodbye to the sergeant leading the patrol as he wheeled his men about to head back, handed her horse off to the sentry outside and walked in.

Lit only by a few oil lanterns, the tent was still bright enough to hurt her eyes after the long ride in the moonlight. Vanessa blinked a few times as they adjusted. The command post was quiet and only a few soldiers were still up and working. She supposed it was late enough even the most over-worked staff officers had gone to bed. Off to the front of the tent a sergeant was looking over the shoulder of one of the radio operators as she copied down a message, and a dark-haired captain had her feet up on a table and was boredly leafing through a stack of papers off to the side of the room. Another tired-looking captain straightened up from the map in the middle of the room and turned towards her as she let the tent flap fall closed behind her.

The woman, a redhead a little taller than her, raised her eyebrows in surprise. "Lieutenant Gable?" She ventured, "We weren't expecting you this early. I can see Lady MacMahon wasn't kidding."

Vanessa took off her hat and ran a hand through her hair to straighten it. Her neck muscles thanked her at being rid of the heavy leather shako. She gave the woman a half-smile and replied, "I guess not. Ah..." She went on awkwardly, "Lieutenant Vanessa Gable, reporting for duty, ma'am."

The red-headed captain gave her a surprised look, then laughed. It didn't seem to be mean-spirited, and she quickly calmed down and said, "So formal, Vanessa. You can calm down. It's night shift." She walked over and held out a hand, "Alyssa Helbrecht."

Vanessa reached out to take it, "Uh, pleased to mee-"

Captain Helbrecht seized her hand and swept her up into a one-armed hug. Suddenly *way* too close, Vanessa stiffened the woman's arm reached around her back. Sensing something was wrong, she looked down at her and said, "Oh... you don't like being touched?"

Vanessa looked up at her for a second. Captain Helbrecht had vivid green eyes, set in a concerned expression. Blushing, she looked down and muttered, "No, ma'am, not really..."

"Oh? I'm sorry." Helbrecht released her and stepped back quickly. Leaning back forward a little, she smiled and remarked, "Wow, you're really red. Really, I'm sorry, I didn't know about that."

"Stop harassing the new girl, Aly." The other captain looked up from her papers disapprovingly, "Don't worry, lieutenant, she's like that with everyone."

"I said I was sorry!" Captain Helbrecht shot back, before turning back to her and going on, "Come on, Vanessa, let's go figure out where you're going."

Vanessa felt like she wanted to melt into the floor, but she managed a, "yes, ma'am," and followed the woman over to the map. Some enterprising soul had covered it with little unit symbols cut out of card stock, and her stomach sunk further as she saw how many diamond-shaped Imperial dragoon symbols had been scattered over the map with question marks next to them.

Helbrecht leaned over the map table and tapped at one of the forward-most hussar troops. Looking over at her dark-haired companion, she asked, "Isn't Bravo Troop in First Squadron hurting right now? I think Ramsey was with them."

The other captain replied without looking up from her papers, "Yep, she was." She softened a tiny bit and added bitterly, "Poor girl." Now that Vanessa had a good look at her she noticed that her name tag read 'Schrader'. She wondered for a moment if she was related to the lancers' hard-bitten colonel.

Captain Helbrecht looked over at the sergeant, who had turned to listen to them, "Get First on the line. Thank God we're still up on wire with them."

One of the signal troopers cranked up a field telephone and was soon talking to someone on the other end. Helbrecht walked over and had a short exchange with whoever was on the other end of the line. Hanging up and coming back over, she said, "They'll take you. In fact, you wouldn't believe how happy they are to hear you're coming up." She chuckled, "Usually they're pissed when we call. Here, let me get you on your way."

The red-headed captain pointed out First Squadron's command post on her map and woke up one of the dispatch riders who had been dozing against the back wall of the tent to go forward with her. The girl ducked out the entryway to prepare her horse, and Vanessa was about to follow her when she felt Helbrecht's hand on her shoulder. She looked back at her and the woman said, "I should have talked to you about this earlier, but... you understand our mission out here tonight, right, Vee?"

Vee? She thought, *That's new.* Turning around, she replied levelly, "Yes, ma'am, we're looking for signs the Empire is moving south in corps strength. Infantry or heavy guns."

"Good." Helbrecht sighed and rubbed the back of her neck with a hand, "Sorry, it's been a long day. I don't want you going out there cold."

"Does she know the pyro codes?" Schrader interjected without looking up from her reports.

"Pyro... codes?" Vanessa asked. She very much did not.

Helbrecht explained, "We borrowed it from the Empire. They're always communicating with flares." She went on, "When you get down to your platoon they should have a flare pistol and a code card, but there's really two big ones to remember right now."

"Yes, ma'am?" Vanessa asked.

"Red-white-red means you're in trouble and need help." She smiled and went on, "Three blue flares means mission accomplished."

"Confirmed Imperial infantry?" Vanessa replied.

"Yep." Helbrecht nodded, "Now off you go, Vee. Good luck out there."

Vanessa smiled a little as she turned to leave, "Thanks, ma'am."

The messenger was already mounted and waiting for her outside. Climbing onto her own horse, Vanessa followed the girl as she spurred her horse up the deserted road north. They easily had another five or six kilometers to ride, and she deliberately avoided looking at her watch. She didn't want to know how late it was.

As they rode north Vanessa noticed mist rising off the low fields, lit an eerie silver by the moons overhead. Looking at the sky, she noticed a long, low band of clouds blotting out the stars to the north. Her stomach sunk. It hadn't been too difficult to navigate by the bright moonlight. In the darkness of fog and overcast it was going to get a lot worse. Still, they rode on as the path gently descended and the mist gathered around them.

Vanessa told her companion to hold up when they came over a rise and looked down to see a sea of fog below them. The girl pulled up her horse and said, "I was afraid about finding the place *before* we ran into this fog, ma'am." She went on nervously, "Do you have any ideas?"

Vanessa pulled out her map and looked at it in the fading moonlight. They were still a couple kilometers away and she didn't have their position fixed exactly. She could get off her horse, take some bearings with her compass, pull a poncho over her head, light up her flashlight and figure out exactly where she was and the distance and direction she'd need to go to get to the squadron's headquarters. It would take a while, though, and going kilometers through fog on horseback was no sure thing.

Or... *there*. Something flashed in the misty sea and a couple seconds later they heard the boom of an artillery piece. A few moments later a bright light flared under the clouds to the north. The horse artillery was firing star shells to light up the front line. Vanessa had been hearing them firing occasionally for the whole ride north. A few moments later she heard the faint chatter of a machine gun and a couple violet tracers bounced up to the north, off where the flare was burning. As they watched a few green tracers also ricocheted into the air, closer and brighter. She swallowed reflexively. That was the Empire shooting back.

"Ma'am?" The messenger's voice brought her back to earth.

Vanessa nodded in the direction of the artillery battery, "Those gunners know where they are, and they're probably wired into the squadron. They should be able to walk us in."

The girl's eyebrows rose, "Oh... I didn't think of that."

Vanessa replied drily, "I've spent a lot of time around artillerymen recently. Let's go."

They spurred their horses and plunged into the fog and darkness below. Cutting off road, they ploughed a path through the wheat fields, navigated treacherous drainage ditches and found a gate in a fence. After a couple minutes the gun fired again, then again, close, guiding them into the position in the murk.

It wasn't like they were bothering to be quiet at this point. Vanessa rode a little farther forward and shouted, "Hello! Royal Army! Hello!"

After a few moments a voice floated out of the mist. It sounded really close, "Reaper!"

The challenge and password. Vanessa replied, "Sunrise!"

Her companion added nervously, "Please don't shoot us!"

She gave the girl a dirty look as someone laughed in the darkness, "Come on in. How many of you are there?"

Vanessa nudged her horse forward and replied, "Two." She looked around, trying to pierce through the murk and find the man, "Where *are* you? I can barely see in this."

A dark shape seemed to detach itself from the darkness in front of her, "Right here, miss." He couldn't have been more than twenty feet away.

Vanessa dismounted and led her horse up to the man. She could barely see in the thick fog, but as she got closer she made out a burly artilleryman carrying a carbine. The voices of artillerymen going through a firing drill floated out of the murk faintly, and she thought she recognized a boxy ammunition caisson just behind him. She introduced herself, "Lieutenant Gable, Fourteenth Hussars. I'm trying to get to First Squadron's command post." She added, "I've been told the artillery's never lost."

The man chuckled, "I like you, ma'am." He gestured over his shoulder into the darkness, "Battery command's down the line that way. You should be able to follow the wire from there straight in. We've been firing for them all night."

Vanessa smiled as she felt a weight come off her back, "Thanks." They led their horses past him, groped their way down the line of guns in the murk and eventually found the battery's small command tent. They explained themselves to the very tired-looking commander and he told them to wait until they finished their fire mission before they went past the gun line. A few minutes and several adjusting rounds later the gun line lit the fog with a couple volleys and the man told them to get going.

Leading their horses, they followed the thin copper wire through the darkness for what seemed like an eternity. Finally, they crossed a road and saw trees looming in front of them as the fog cleared a little. And tucked back against the trees was the dark shape of a tent. Vanessa thought she saw the faint shapes of a few wagons pulled into the woodline. She suspected the horses were even further back in the trees.

A voice floated out of the darkness, "Reaper!"

Vanessa raised a hand and called back, "Sunrise! Two coming in!"

She faintly saw a sentry rise to her knees out of a shallow foxhole in front of them and wave them forward. The woman looked at them suspiciously, carbine ready, until they got close enough she could tell they really weren't dragoons. Satisfied, she laid back down in the long grass as they passed by. Vanessa faintly made out another woman sleeping beside her in the narrow scrape.

They lifted a blanket hung in front of the tent's entrance to keep light from leaking out, pushed through the tent flap itself and into the bright interior. It looked a lot like the regimental command post, but smaller. A few women were huddled around the radio and field telephones on the far side of the tent, but Vanessa's eyes were drawn to a tall, tired-looking woman who stood as they entered. The captain looked over her for a moment and asked, "Lieutenant Gable?"

Vanessa took off her hat again, the air of the tent cool against her sweaty brow as she replied, "Yes, ma'am. Reporting for duty."

The woman nodded, "Good. I'm your commander." She went on, "Karen Masters. You can call me 'ma'am'. You look like you've had quite an adventure getting here."

"Ah... yes, ma'am." Vanessa replied. She probably looked like hell now that she thought about it.

"Well, young lady, I don't know what you got used to up at Division, but don't expect any rest tonight." Masters turned to the group up at the front of the tent and said, "I've got her. Tell the colonel I've taken her down to the troop. I'll take her back to meet her if we get a chance."

One of the women in the group waved in acknowledgement, and Masters turned back to her and said, "Let's go, Miss Gable." She cast a glance at the messenger and went on, "Good job getting my new lieutenant here in one piece, private. Take your direction from the staff here."

Captain Masters swept out the door, and Vanessa gave her companion an awkward glance and followed her. A soldier quickly came around with her horse as Vanessa mounted her own, and soon the two of them were riding down the road and around the forest. Masters seemed to know where she was going almost instinctively, but Vanessa was soon hopelessly lost as the swirling fog closed around them. They rode in silence for a minute before her commander said, "You took me away from my troop in the middle of a battle and the middle of the night to go *get* you, Miss Gable. You had better perform." Vanessa looked over at her nervously as she went on, "Lieutenant Ramsey was my best, and now she's dead. You are going to take over her platoon. You will *not* come whining to me that you cannot handle your responsibilities." Masters looked over at her icily, "Is that clear, young lady?"

Vanessa swallowed. What had she ever done to deserve *this?* Still, she stammered out, "Y-yes, ma'am."

Her commander rolled her eyes, "We'll see."

Another burst of machine gun fire rolled through the woods, quite close now. A few seconds later she heard another gun chatter in the distance, much fainter and a little higher-pitched. A shiver went up her spine as she realized it was an *Imperial* gun. The Royal gun roared again in response, a little off to their right. Vanessa realized it probably wasn't more than a couple hundred meters away through the woods, maybe a little uphill from where the road seemed to wind through a shallow valley.

Vanessa made out the dim shape of a house in the fog and darkness as they turned off the road and up a long drive. A moment later a voice floated out of the murk, "Reaper!"

Captain Masters replied angrily, "I'm your damn commander."

"Uh... yes, ma'am, come on through!" The sentry shouted back.

"How about you stop shouting so much when the enemy is *right over there*." Masters growled back.

"Oh, sorry, ma'am." The soldier replied, much quieter.

Masters rolled her eyes, "Soldiers." Looking over at Vanessa, she jerked her head towards the house and said, "There's your platoon. Daily meeting at the company's at..." She snickered, "Zero eight, unless we get orders first. Make sure you watch your telephone."

Vanessa let herself glance at her watch. It was five-thirty. She realized the fog was already starting to lighten. Shaking off the cobwebs that wrapped around her thoughts, she looked back at Masters and said, "Yes, ma'am. I'll be there."

"So you know words besides 'yes' and 'ma'am'." Masters replied sarcastically, "I was getting worried."

Vanessa inclined her head and said, "Yes, ma'am."

The woman laughed, "Oh, you're a funny one. I see now." Wheeling her horse, Masters trotted off into the fog and left her. Through her haze of fatigue, Vanessa realized she had no idea where the troop command post even *was* as she heard the hooves of the woman's horse fade into the distance. Hoping someone in her platoon did, she nudged her horse closer to the house. Dismounting at the foot of the front steps, she wrapped her reins around the railing and climbed to the porch, the boards squeaking underfoot.

The machine gun fired again as she was about to open the door, startling her. It was *close*. Taking a moment to compose herself, Vanessa pushed through the door into the house. It was pitch-dark inside, and she gave her eyes a moment to adjust. Feeling her way out of the mudroom, the graying fog outside cast enough light through the large windows for her to barely make out her surroundings.

A dark, slanted mass to her right seemed to be stairs to the second floor, and she could make out a soldier slumped over what she supposed was the dining room table on her other side. A couple tiny, colored lights burned on a boxy arrangement set up on the table, and she recognized the field telephone they were supposed to be watching. She hoped absently that the volume was turned up high enough to wake the operator if they got a call and turned to the dark shapes sprawled out on the floor and couches to her right. If the enemy was so close her platoon didn't seem to be feeling it, although she supposed they did have sentries out.

As Vanessa stood there, fighting back her exhaustion and trying to figure out what to do, she heard the chatter of an Imperial machine gun in the distance. A moment later their machine gun fired a long burst back, loud and close. Had they been doing that all night? It was a waste of ammunition at best, and it wasn't like they were going to hit anything in the fog. Maybe they were trying to keep Imperial troops from moving around in front of them? It didn't seem smart. She would have to straighten them out the first chance she got.

Pushing her doubts about the machine gun aside, she shook the soldier manning the field telephone awake. Sitting up, the girl gave her what she supposed was a blank look in the darkness and asked, "Who... what do you need?"

"You to wake up. I need you to watch that phone." Vanessa said.

"Oh... sorry." The girl shook her head, "I, well, it's so dark in here."

"Just stay awake." Vanessa went on, "Where's the platoon sergeant? I need to talk to her." She remembered what the two women back at Regiment had told her and asked, "And where are the flares?"

The girl pushed a couple bulky packages across the table at her, "Here's the flare gun. Sarge is over at the OP. And, uh..." She hesitated for a moment, then asked, "Who are you, by the way?"

"Vanessa Gable. I'm your new lieutenant." She replied.

"Oh!" The girl sat up straighter, "Sorry, ma'am."

"Don't be. It's dark in here." Vanessa reached out and picked up the packages the soldier had pushed towards her earlier. She felt a flare gun in a belt holster and an envelope-shaped ammunition pouch stuffed with what felt like shotgun shells. Opening it, she chanced a look with her flashlight and saw red, white and blue shells neatly separated out on loops sewn into the inside of the pouch. She supposed Ramsey had at least been organized. The thought of the dead lieutenant sent a fatigue-dulled chill up her spine. Turning back to the soldier, she asked, "Can you help me with these?"

"Sure thing, ma'am." The girl helped her attach the flare pistol and ammunition pouch to her harness. Just as they were finishing they heard another exchange of gunfire, the Imperial gun faint in the distance and their own gun roaring back a moment later.

Vanessa raised an eyebrow, "I'm assuming that's the OP?"

The girl nodded, "Yes, ma'am." She sighed, "They've been shooting back and forth with the Imperials all night."

All night? Vanessa thought, *The Empire doesn't fight like that. At least they shouldn't... wait. This isn't right.* She pulled out the other chair at the table, shook her head and sat down for a moment. She needed to think.

"Ma'am, are you all right?" Her soldier asked. In the graying light Vanessa could see concern written over her features.

"I'm fine... just thinking." Vanessa closed her eyes and bent over, resting her face in her hands. She just wanted some sleep. If she'd been fresh this would have been obvious. She'd been up all night, straggling through hill and dale, through fog so thick she couldn't see her hand in front of her face, asking artillery units for directions because their guns firing were the only things she could pick out in the murk... wait. Finding her way by gunfire. And their OP was mechanically shooting back every time the Empire poked at it from a distance. Vanessa looked up to see gray, early-morning light flooding through the windows. *God in heaven,* she thought as an icy hand clenched around her heart, *they're attacking at dawn and we just walked them in.*

Springing to her feet, Vanessa shouted, "*Get up! Get up! All of you, on your feet!*"

The hussars sprawled around the living room came to life, women groaning and reaching for weapons. One of the quicker ones opened her eyes blearily and looked at her, asking, "What's going on... ma'am?"

"We're about to be attacked." Vanessa replied sharply, "Now who's in charge here?"

A woman a little older than her wearing corporal's stripes climbed to her feet and looked her over. Clearing her throat, she said, "I am. Who are you? Ma'am."

Vanessa glared at her, "Your new platoon leader. Now get your squad together. We're going to go pull the OP back in and then get out of here." She added grimly, "If the Empire hasn't killed us all by then."

The corporal gave her a look, but she eventually shrugged and turned to her squad, "You heard the boss. Strap up, girls."

The hussars quickly pulled their equipment on and piled out the house's side door, tramping loudly across a deck and down a short flight of stairs to the soaking, overgrown lawn. The corporal barked orders for them to spread out and get into formation as they hurried forward into the forest. Vanessa found herself walking in the middle of the group next to the corporal and a couple strong-looking girls managing the squad's machine gun.

They plunged into the trees and started up towards the observation post, the ground rising gently below their feet as they pushed through the wet leaves. As they climbed the fog cleared until Vanessa could clearly see the crest of the rise a short way away, the sky brightening through the trees. For an instant she saw a hussar silhouetted against the sky ahead of them, round helmet like a black paper cutout as she moved back towards the outpost on the far side of the rise. Vanessa blushed a little at the thought of relieving herself in the woods.

Wait. Vanessa looked around at her companions. They all had on their stiff, leather, *flat-topped* hussar shakos. *Oh my God-*, her thoughts cut off as explosions ripped through the forest, four or five all at once beyond the rise. Vanessa found herself flat on her face as gunfire rang out, high-pitched gunshots hammering through the trees. She heard one, two loud bangs from hussar carbines through the hail of Imperial fire and screaming voices.

Vanessa looked over to see the corporal getting to her knees and waving for the squad to get on line. She was about to get up herself when the forest in front of them danced with light and the back of the woman's jacket ripped open, five or six holes punching through the fabric from her stomach up to her shoulders. The corporal pitched over backwards, her head rolling to stare at her with glazing eyes. The woman's mouth moved, slightly, mumbling something to her.

Dirt showered down on Vanessa and brought her back to the shrieking chaos of reality. The forest in front of them burned with muzzle flashes, Imperial soldiers boiling out of the darkness to fire and disappear again. The air seethed with bullets as the forest shredded around her, splinters raining down from the fury of the enemy's assault. Looking aside, Vanessa saw a large tree and rolled into its protection as her own machine gun roared to life.

Vanessa peeked out from around her tree to see her two brave gunners silhouetted in their weapon's light, shell casings burning like meteors as they walked their fire over the Imperials. For an instant she thought they could do this, she could bring the rear team up, get them on line and they could run over the enemy. And then the forest flared and her machine-gunners disappeared in a cloud of flying dirt. She counted *five* machine guns flaming in the darkness. For an instant they lit an enemy soldier rushing forward. She saw his war-mask, the featureless symbol of the Emperor's hatred. She saw his bayoneted rifle with its sickle-shaped magazine. She saw his load-bearing harness, saw that he had no sword or pistol. And as he leapt a fallen log Vanessa saw that his leggings only came to his knees.

Infantry. They were fighting Imperial infantry. Vanessa instinctively felt for the flare pistol on the back of her belt, looked up to see if she could fire a signal out of the forest. Thick canopy loomed overhead as bullets cracked around her hiding place. Her flares would never make it out. Only one choice then. Vanessa hefted her carbine, flicked the safety off and fired into the seething darkness. Bullets swarmed back like a swarm of maddened bees as carbines started barking behind her. The squad's rear team hadn't been caught in the storm of fire. They were alive and they were fighting.

"*Fall back!*" Vanessa screamed over the gunfire, "*Back to the house!*" The cracking bullets lifted for a second and she heaved herself to her knees, turned and lunged for the biggest tree she could pick out behind her. A couple hour-long seconds later she skidded into the protection of its roots, rolled over and fired again. As she worked her carbine's bolt she saw movement in the corner of her eye. She looked over to see one of her hussars heave herself up and dart back towards the house, green tracers chasing her like evil fireflies. A couple seconds later the girl's carbine boomed behind her and Vanessa threw herself backwards again.

And on they went, Vanessa and the girl bounding backwards past each other. They would each only stop for a moment, long enough to fire a couple rounds and give the other a chance to sprint for the next piece of cover as the enemy fire snapped at their heels. She heard the booms of the rest of the team's carbines a few times but soon it was just her and her companion, firing and moving as they fell back. Imperial fire chased them the whole way.

Hearing a carbine bark behind her again, Vanessa turned, plunged through some bushes and stumbled onto the open lawn around the house. The girl was lying in the overgrown grass, stubbornly pumping rounds into the forest as Imperial bullets plowed furrows into the grass around her. She was going to die if she stayed there. A flaming green tracer cracked by inches from her face and Vanessa corrected the thought. They were both going to die if they stayed there. Scrambling over to the girl, Vanessa fired one last round, grabbed the back of her harness and pulled her up.

They shared a glance for a moment. Vanessa didn't have to say a word. They turned and ran for it, sprinting across the grass as bullets snapped at them like striking vipers. A machine gun thundered to life above them on the second floor as they vaulted the steps to the deck and someone inside yanked open the door for them to tumble through. Vanessa skidded to a halt to see the same girl she had run into earlier on the field telephone and realized she hadn't come along with them to relieve the observation post.

"Ma'am!" The commo girl said, "What's happening?"

"Imperial infantry. We made it out. The others..." Vanessa trailed off as bullets started pocking into the house's bricks like hail. The machine gun upstairs fired another long burst into the forest as she went on, louder, "Does the telephone still work?"

"Yes, ma'am, it should!" The girl replied.

Vanessa pointed at it for emphasis, "Good! Get me troop headquarters!" A window shattered and something dug a furrow into the ceiling, and she added, "And stay low!"

Grabbing the soldier she had come back with, Vanessa set her down by one of the large windows fronting onto the forest and sat down beside the next one over under the cover of the house's brick wall. The girl smashed out one of the window panes with her carbine's muzzle and quickly started firing into the forest outside. Vanessa pulled her own weapon's bolt open to feed another round and join her. The bolt stuck as she tried to push it forward and she looked down to realize she was empty.

Opening one of her ammunition pouches with clumsy fingers, Vanessa pulled out a clip full of ammunition and tried to fit it to her carbine's magazine guide as the enemy fire built outside. Her window shattered, glass shards tumbling into the room as she finally aligned the clip and jammed the rounds into her carbine's magazine. Slamming the bolt forward, she kicked most of the broken glass out of where she was going to crouch to fire and rolled up to her knees.

The woodline flamed with muzzle flashes as she looked out, a flood of green tracers flashing overhead to eat at their second-floor machine gun position. One burst swept lower, cracking over her head as she fired. Vanessa quickly dropped back into the protection of the house's walls, worked her bolt and came back up as their machine gun fired another defiant burst. For an instant, as she pulled her carbine into her shoulder and started looking down the sights, Vanessa felt a twinge of hope. They were holding. If she could get someone on the line she could get reinforcements and fire support. She could win, or at least escape.

Then Vanessa heard a low pop, almost inaudible over the hammering racket of the firefight. Something small and dark sailed out of the woods, clearly silhouetted against the gray sky as it arced towards the house. She had the presence of mind to scream, "*Get down!*" and throw herself to the floor as the grenade hit the deck outside, blowing what was left of the windows back into the house. Plaster rained from the ceiling as another bomb hit the house itself. Somehow their machine gun fired another burst, one long roar that died as a third explosion ripped through the house just over her head. Ears ringing from the blasts, Vanessa still thought she heard someone screaming from upstairs.

Another grenade slammed into the house as she lay there, buckling the wall and sending bricks flying. A few landed painfully on her back. Vanessa shook her head groggily and rolled up onto an elbow to look around. The girl on the field telephone was lying curled around the set, frantically cranking it and yelling into the handset. It didn't look like she was having a lot of luck. She looked over at her soldier under the other window as a tracer snapped into the room. Her eyes were wide and glazed with fear in the sickly green light.

The house shuddered again under another bomb. Vanessa looked up at the windows gaping wide above them. If one of those grenades came through they were all going to die. And it was only a matter of time before one did. Pushing herself up on her hands and knees she scrambled over to the other window, grabbed the girl by the collar and shouted, "*Get upstairs! Now!*"

Understanding flashed in her eyes as she pushed her towards the stairs, and Vanessa crawled over to her soldier still struggling with the field telephone. The girl looked over as she came and said, "Ma'am, it's no good! I can't reach anyone!"

Vanessa shook her head, "Don't worry!" She patted her flare pistol, "I have a plan. I just need you to hold them off. Come on!"

They could hear voices outside as they got up and ran. Imperial boots thundered on the deck as they rushed upstairs, Vanessa turning to fire a round through the door as she reached the top. Someone swore loudly outside and shouted, "On me! Breach the door!"

Vanessa backed into the upstairs hallway and out of view of the door as something boomed outside. Splintered wood crunched as the Imperials kicked the door open, boots drumming on the floor as they poured inside. Someone shouldered past her in the hallway suddenly and she looked over to see one of her soldiers pulling the igniter on a hand grenade. Vanessa turned and ran through an open door at the end of the hall as the girl threw her grenade down the stairs.

For all the good it would do her, she threw herself to the floor as someone screamed, "*Grenade!*" downstairs. The bomb went off a moment later, shaking the house and sending a plume of smoke into the hallway. Vanessa rolled upright and took stock of the situation. She found herself in a bedroom with a large, comfortable-looking four-poster bed to her left and, thank God, windows to her right. She hefted her carbine and smashed out one of the panes as her soldier rushed back into the room, the girl drawing her pistol as she spun around the door and took cover beside it. Her other soldier was already crouching on the other side of the door.

The Imperials didn't keep them waiting. As Vanessa drew her flare pistol, broke it open and fed the first shell into the breech she heard a small, hard object thud off the wall out in the hallway. Nothing to be done for it. Lying flat on her back, she raised her flare gun to the window and squeezed the trigger as the grenade went off, filling the air with smoke and hissing metal. One of her soldiers cried out in pain, but she heard two pistols firing as Imperial boots thudded up the stairs. Jamming another flare into the pistol, she raised it and fired again as screaming automatic gunfire filled the hallway outside. Bullets riddled the house's thin interior walls and her soldier, the brave girl she'd fought side-by-side with, slumped over on the floor.

Vanessa slid the third blue flare into her pistol, raised it to the window and pulled the trigger as masked soldiers burst into the room. The flare burned into the sky as she sprang to her feet and drew her saber. She saw her field telephone operator flat on her back, raising her hands as an Imperial soldier lifted a bayoneted rifle over her, and then she was fighting for her life as two of them came at her.

She knocked the first soldier's bayonet thrust aside, parried the second's and slashed down at the first as he came at her again. The Imperial raised his rifle to block her at the last moment and she leapt backwards away from his companion's stab. The bedroom wall hit her from behind like a freight train. Stars danced in front of her eyes as Vanessa staggered into the corner of the room, her sword held protectively out in front of her. The enemy soldiers flexed their legs to lunge. Vanessa realized she was about to die. Huh. She'd thought it would be more dramatic.

"Wait." Another Imperial had walked into the room after the assault team. Her attackers hesitated and Vanessa rocked forward a little out of the corner, sword up. He was wearing a sword himself. An officer? Did *he* want to fight her?

The man gave her what she knew was an exasperated look even through his mask. "How about you surrender." It wasn't a question. He went on sarcastically, "I don't think you've got anything left to prove, miss."

Vanessa cocked her head to the side. She hadn't even *thought* of surrendering. And given that the Empire wasn't in the business of cutting their prisoners' heads off any more, she supposed it was a better option than being bayoneted and pinned to the wall like a butterfly in an insect collection. She didn't like it on principle but considering the circumstances it wasn't like she really had a choice.

Sighing heavily, she lowered her sword and said, "Fine. I'm done." The enemy soldiers relaxed a little, and she looked at the man and asked, "I presume you're in command here?"

"Yes," he replied.

With heavy hands Vanessa sheathed her saber, disconnected it from her belt and held it out to him, "Uh... here you go."

"Thanks." He said drily as he took it. He looked at it cursorily before gesturing at her telephone operator, still frozen beneath an Imperial soldier who was clearly looking for a reason to bayonet her, "Marco, take that one downstairs with the others." He looked at the other hussar, who was twitching and gasping in a growing pool of blood, "And send the medic up here *now*."

His cold eyes, barely visible behind his mask, fell back on her. "Lis, search Miss..." He looked at her name tag for a moment, "Gable and tie her up." Another Imperial, one of the ones she'd fought earlier, stepped towards her. Looking at the masked soldier up close, Vanessa realized that Lis was a woman. An *extremely* strong woman, she thought, as she stripped off her harness and wrenched her arms behind her back.

The Imperial officer didn't waste any time. Once his soldier had tied her hands tightly and started giving her what she realized was going to be an extraordinarily thorough pat-down, the man drew a vicious-looking combat dagger and used the tip to prod at the black, braided cord strung across the right side of her chest. Vanessa felt her face reddening as he asked, quite conversationally, "So. Miss Gable. What is a *general's aide* doing all the way out here?"

She knew she'd forgotten something before she rode out. Like taking all the unnecessary decorations off her uniform. Or getting a new notebook that didn't have General MacMahon's tastes in gelato and Princess Arilin's *three sizes* written down in it. This was going to be awful.

And it was. But thirty seconds later an Imperial medic rushed upstairs, threw her equipment out on the floor and saved her soldier's life. And that wasn't awful at all.

Chapter 34

By Deeds Alone

Click. It was just a little metallic sound in the forest. Just a little sound that meant someone had taken a machine gun off safe nearby. Sophia shuddered like a corpse coming back to life, grabbed her rifle and forced her gritty eyes open as the gun fired, painting the forest with its hellish muzzle flash. Tracers bounced and burned in the darkness as the gun hammered away. The gunner finally let up on the trigger as Sophia got her rifle up on the rim of her scraped foxhole. Her ears rang and the darkness boiled with the enemy.

They were illusions. The Imperials weren't ghosts and they weren't stupid. They would have taken cover after that. Sophia looked over at her machine gun position and shouted, "What do you have?"

A voice floated back over the ringing in her ears, "Movement! Maybe one hundred meters, straight ahead!" It sounded like Jeremy. Second shift. Sophia got the feeling she wouldn't be getting a lot of sleep that night.

Another machine gun fired out on the perimeter. People were yelling as the company came awake in the darkness. Someone fired a rifle off on their other side, then another and another. Sophia tightened her rifle to her shoulder as Jeremy fired another long burst into the darkness, the jackhammering gun beating the last bits of fog from her mind. She was thankful she'd left her bayonet fixed. Any second now Imperial grenades would fly out of the darkness as the masked soldiers tightened their grip around Charlie Company.

The fire was starting to roll around their perimeter as more guns erupted into the darkness. Tracers lit the undergrowth all around with a sick violet light. Any second now green Imperial ones were going to flood back as the enemy gunners brought their weapons to bear. Any second now. *Any second now.* Sophia cast her glance across the flaming darkness in front of her, looking for the first sparking flame of an Imperial gun.

Jeremy fired again, a third long burst that filled the forest in front of her with tracers and eerie light. Where was the Empire? Why weren't they attacking? *Movement at one hundred meters,* she thought. How much movement? One person? God in heaven, they could be firing at a *deer.* Sophia reared up to her knees and shouted at him, *"Cease fire! Cease fire! No contact!"*

Just a few meters away, Jeremy looked up from his sights to give her what she knew was a confused look through the gloom. He shouted back, "Really?"

Sophia was about to say something when she saw Hargrave, a shadow on his other side, slap him on the back of the head and say something that was lost in the unholy racket of the firefight. A moment later she heard the old man shouting to cease fire further down the line. Sophia turned and shouted at the next squad down to cease fire, and their machine gun fired one last burst and fell silent. In the darkness around the perimeter she heard soldiers yelling to cease fire as the gunfire started to taper off.

She felt a hand pull on her thigh and Tony sat up next to her in the foxhole. He gave her a blank look, "W-what's going on?"

"Good morning." Sophia replied sarcastically, "I think we just killed a deer."

Tony sighed as he propped his rifle up on the lip of the foxhole, "Great. I was worried about getting too much sleep tonight."

"Haven't you heard?" Edward joined in. She saw his silhouette as he sat back in his own foxhole on Tony's other side, "According to the Army you only need thirty minutes."

Sophia chuckled along with them and replied, "Hey, look on the bright side."

Tony gave her what she knew was a foul look, "*What* bright side?"

She smiled in the darkness, "We're not being shelled."

Edward groaned, "Sophie, I swear, if they *do* shell us tonight I'm blaming you."

Footsteps crunched in the leaves behind them and Sophia turned to see a silhouette loom out of the darkness. After a moment she recognized it as Lieutenant Thorn. He called out, "Miss Rose! Are you around here?"

Sophia waved and he looked down at them, stepping back a little as he realized how close he'd come to falling into their foxhole. "Oh, there you are." He said, kneeling beside them, "Was that your gun that fired first?"

"Yes sir," Sophia replied, "Jeremy heard movement. Maybe a hundred meters straight uphill."

"A patrol?" He asked.

"Or a deer." She replied, "Do you want us to go check it out?"

Thorn hefted his rifle, "Yes, actually. And I'm going with you."

"Feel free, sir." Sophia sighed and looked over at Tony and Edward,

"Alright, guys, you heard him." She looked over her other shoulder at Jeremy and Hargrave's foxhole, "You two cover us."

"Sure thing, Sophie." Hargrave's gruff voice floated back. Light flared over in their foxhole for a moment as the older man lit a match and touched it to his pipe. Sophia scowled for a moment, but she supposed after they'd just shot a couple hundred rounds in all directions one guy smoking wasn't going to make much of a difference. If there were any Imperials around they already knew where they were.

The three of them got ready to move out. Sophia tied her boots, buckled her harness back around her waist and finished untangling herself from her blanket. For all his complaining Edward was a little faster than Tony, but soon enough they had climbed out of their foxholes and were kneeling on either side of her. Sophia got up and stalked into the darkness, and she heard them get up behind her and follow.

The forest was beyond dark. Sophia felt like she was walking into the abyss. She mentally counted her steps as she padded forward, the loam crackling slightly under her feet. Hopefully whatever Imperials had been out in front of their lines had fled and not gone to ground. She could almost feel the enemy lining up their rifle sights on her, the little glowing beads hovering over her chest.

Sixty paces for a hundred meters. Sixty-six in the dark and night. And, Sophia supposed, closer to eighty given how she was creeping along. It was the longest eighty paces she'd ever taken in her life. The forest was just a jumble of black shapes in a black night, silent and still around them. Sophia heard her father yelling at someone back in the perimeter. Gritting her teeth, she pulled her attention back to the task at hand. If there were Imperials out there she was going to find them before they found *her*.

There. Eighty paces. Sophia looked around at the forest and tried to figure out where she would take cover if the enemy suddenly started shooting at her. After the firing earlier her eyes had re-adjusted and she could see a little better in the darkness. A little. She waved for her companions to spread out and start looking.

"See anything, Rose?" Thorn had come up behind her.

Sophia took a couple steps forward and looked around again as she replied, "Not yet... wait." She knelt by a large tree and touched the churned earth next to it, "Take a look at this, sir."

Lieutenant Thorn crouched next to her. She was pretty sure he was squinting through the darkness, "Is that dug up there?"

Sophia said, "Looks like it." She looked around to see where the other two were, "Guys, I think I have something here. Any luck?"

Edward replied, his voice barely audible, "Nope."

Tony called from a little farther out, "Hey, come over here." He was crouching over something on the ground. They came over and he held up what looked like a piece of white paper, "Look at this."

Lieutenant Thorn took it from him, "Looks like a... field dressing wrapper?"

Sophia looked around for a moment and saw a pale shape on the ground in the murk. Bending over, she picked it up and examined it. It was a little packet made out of sturdy white paper that had been ripped open and had its contents removed. There was something printed on the front, but the lighting was too poor for her to make it out. Turning to the others, she said, "Hey, I found another one."

Edward touched his bandaged head and said, "Entry and exit wounds?"

"Maybe." Thorn replied.

A chill ran up Sophia's spine. They hadn't been shooting very long, and you did not just bandage someone up in a few seconds. If those dressings were fresh the Imperials might be *looking* at them. Not to mention whoever they had been shooting at had been stone-cold enough to not cry out when they were hit.

She looked over at the others and said, "They're close. Spread out." Tony and Edward self-consciously moved to either side and crouched behind solid-looking trees, almost disappearing in the darkness. Kneeling herself, Sophia went on quietly, "Sir, do you want us to keep pushing? They can't have made it far."

The lieutenant crouched next to her and thought for a moment before replying, "No. Not without more people." He went on, "I'm not going out farther without the whole platoon."

Sophia sighed with relief, "Thanks, sir." She turned to the others, "We're heading back. Come on."

They turned and retraced their steps back to the perimeter, following the little red ember of Hargrave's pipe as he puffed at it in the darkness. They made it back incredibly quickly considering what it had felt like walking out. Climbing back into her foxhole, Sophia was about to say something when Thorn beat her to it, "Hey, old man. Kill the pipe. You're lighting up the whole position."

Hargrave shrugged and replied, "Yes, sir." Taking one last draw, he dumped the embers out into his foxhole. Thorn walked off downhill and he commented to no one in particular, "A man can't smoke in peace these days."

Sophia said, "You *were* pretty bright. We could see you from all the way out there."

Tony cut in angrily, "Oh, come on, Sophie. You're as bad as they are sometimes."

She gave him a look, "Who's *they?*"

He avoided the question, "You don't have to be a wet blanket *all the time.*"

"Lay off her, Tony." Hargrave chuckled, "She's just trying to keep us all alive. No worries, Sophie."

Tony sighed and looked at her, "Yeah, uh... look, I'm sorry." He went on apologetically, "It's *really* late and we've been getting shot at all day, and-"

She stopped him, "It's fine, Tony." He was *so* cute when he was like this. Smiling, she went on, "I understand. We're all scared."

Tony rubbed the back of his neck, "Yeah... thanks, Sophie."

Edward chimed in, "Get a room, you two."

She shot him a poisonous glare, "You're welcome for saving your li-" She cut off suddenly as Tony grabbed her and roughly yanked her down into their foxhole. Spitting dirt out of her mouth, she was about to protest when the first Imperial shell went off. Wood creaked and splintered and a tree crashed to the ground nearby a moment later as more shells started raining down. Sophia wrapped her arms around him and hung on for dear life as the bombardment seethed across the slope, blasts tugging at their clothing as shrapnel hissed through the air above.

As suddenly as they had come the shells started crashing down further down the slope to their rear, and Sophia awkwardly untangled herself from Tony and rose up into the smoking, thundering night. Moonlight flooded through new gaps in the canopy overhead, and she smelled the reek of phosphorous and burning wood as she squinted into the darkness in front of them. A minute passed as a couple voices called for medics out in the perimeter. No masked soldiers lunged out of the night. Maybe they weren't in position yet. Maybe they were just harassing them and wouldn't attack at all. The one thing she wasn't unsure of at all was that the Imperials *were* out there somewhere. Her heart clenched at the idea.

Sophia called out into the darkness, "You guys all right?" Hargrave and Edward called back that they were okay. Something tickled in the back of her mind, and after a moment she furrowed her brow and said, "Jack? Kelly? Has anyone seen *them* recently?"

She gave Hargrave an angry look in the dim moonlight. The old man shrugged and nudged Jeremy, and the younger man climbed out of their foxhole and crawled over to the next one down the line. Sophia saw him drop down inside, and a moment later his voice floated back over the banging shells down the slope, "They're out. Want me to wake them?"

Had those two slept through the *whole thing?* Although, knowing them they had probably woken up for the gunfight and went right back to sleep afterward without telling anyone. Sophia sighed. Idiots. Shaking her head, she called back, "No, wait for their shift." She looked at the little glowing beads of her watch and changed her mind, "It's in ten minutes. Might as well."

"Alright." Sophia heard Jeremy go on, "Hey, you two! Wake up! We're under attack here!"

She heard Kelly's voice faintly, "No we're not."

Jack added angrily, "Go to hell."

Jeremy changed tactics, "Also, it's time for your shift."

"Oh," Jack replied, "*Fine.* Give us our gun back then."

A shell flashed a little way upslope of them, sending shrapnel pocking into the trees overhead. Sophia flattened herself back into her hole with Tony as another one slammed in nearby. Bits of wood and earth rained on her and she suddenly felt very naked in the shallow pit they had scraped out earlier, barely deep enough to get their bodies down into. Feeling for her entrenching tool, Sophia rolled over and called out, "While we're all up, let's make these holes a little deeper!"

She looked over at Tony. He was already digging.

It was a bad night. The enemy shells washed across the ridge again and again, and after every barrage that slammed into the company's line of deepening foxholes they would rise up and point their rifles into the ragged, smoking darkness for an Imperial assault that never came. More than once, though, Sophia heard voices calling for a medic as a shell found its mark. She and Tony dug as far down as they could and huddled in the roots and dirt at the bottom of their foxhole, praying one wouldn't find them.

After a while clouds rolled in and smothered the ridge under a blanket of fog so thick Sophia couldn't even see to the next foxhole over in the gloom. The temperature plummeted and she shivered under her rough blanket in the sudden damp. She could feel Tony shaking under his own blanket next to her, and she had an idea. She wouldn't have done it ordinarily, but this was not an ordinary time.

"Hey, Tony." She said, "You awake?"

"Yeah?" He replied. He sounded miserable.

"Wanna cuddle?" She asked.

Tony opened an eye and looked at her, "Yeah." Before she could reply he reached out and pulled her tight against him. After a moment they rearranged their blankets around themselves, and his warm presence made the night a little less awful. Sophia was just closing her eyes again when he went on, "I've got an idea."

She opened an eye and looked back at him, "Oh yeah?"

Tony chuckled and said, "Let's get Edward over here."

It was a *great* idea. Covered with blankets and sandwiched between her two friends, Sophia actually got a little sleep before Jack shook the three of them awake for their shift on guard.

The Imperial shells had tapered down to an occasional boom well downhill of them, and the three of them spent the next hour or so elbowing each other awake as they stared into the murk in front of their position. Sophia hallucinated a few masks in the darkness, but they evaporated into branches and shadow when she looked closer.

Eventually she realized she could start to make out the outlines of trees again, and she looked at her watch. It was almost dawn. Time for stand-to. Sighing, Sophia lifted herself out of the cramped foxhole and crept down the line, waking the rest of the squad. Jeremy and Mr. Hargrave got up right away. Jack and Kelly weren't nearly as enthusiastic, but they brightened up a little when Sophia told them they could get their machine gun back.

The world brightened from black to charcoal to a muddy, dim gray. Sergeant Cross came by after a while to check on them, nodded and walked off into the mist. Down below them Sophia heard her father curse someone out for not having his soldiers up and standing to. After a while he let the man go and the whole perimeter fell silent. The fog drifted slowly out in the wet forest, stirred by the faintest of breezes. Sophia almost felt like she was floating as she sat there, waiting for the Imperials to come screaming out of the fog.

The forest brightened slowly as they sat there, straining their eyes into the fog. After half an hour crept by Sophia heard footsteps crunching in the bed of leaves behind them and turned to see Cross, her father and Corporal Stennis from the second squad appear out of the mist. She raised a hand in a small wave and her father's grim expression creased into a smile.

"Sophia," He crouched by her foxhole, "Good to see you and your men are alright."

She cracked a smile back, "Rough night."

He chuckled, "I can see. At least you were actually shooting at *something*." He went on, "I hear you got one of them?"

"We found some bandages." She grimaced, "Whoever it was out there was *cold*. We didn't hear any yelling afterwards, and they were pretty close."

"I doubt you could have with that racket." He snorted, "Your gun opened up and the whole rest of the company thought half the Imperial Army was charging us." Sophia laughed and he went on, "Good shooting by the way. Who was that?"

She pointed at the next foxhole down, "Jeremy was on the gun." The man turned at the sound of his name and gallantly tipped his cap in their direction. She heard Hargrave snickering beside him at the gesture.

Sergeant Cross crouched down next to her father, "Anyways, Miss Rose. Have your men eat. You're coming with me." He went on, "Lieutenant Thorn is working out the plan for the day with the boss. As soon as he gets back he'll brief us."

"Sure thing, sergeant." Sophia pulled herself out of her foxhole and turned to her squad, "You heard the man. Breakfast time."

The rest of them waved in acknowledgement and she followed Cross and the others off across the slope. After they talked to Third Squad her father went off down the line to check on the next platoon and the rest of them retreated to a little hollow she supposed passed for Lieutenant Thorn's command post and broke out field rations while they waited. After a few minutes he walked out of the mist and sat down with them.

Seeing them eating, he reached for his own haversack and pulled one of his own out, saying, "Well, that's a good idea."

"Gotta eat, sir." Sophia remarked, although given how awful cold canned beef and hardtack were she wasn't entirely sure how true that was. She patted the much lighter haversack at her hip, "By the way, sir, when are we getting resupplied? If this keeps up through tonight we'll run out of food."

Sergeant Cross gave her a dirty look and added, "And ammo, sir. Any word?"

The lieutenant shrugged and replied, "Tonight, probably. We were supposed to get some stuff last night, but between the shelling and the fog I don't think they ever made it up." He went on, "Speaking of tonight, this is what we have going on."

Thorn pulled his map out and showed it to them. They were actually most of the way up the ridge, and after the fighting yesterday the regiment had broken through what headquarters was calling the second Imperial defensive line. The higher-ups thought that what was left of the Imperial defenders had fallen back to a third line of defenses located on the upper reaches of the ridge, although they couldn't say whether it was on the front or rear side.

By this point the rest of their division, the 8th, was being thrown back into the fight to keep V Corps' attack going and the 25th and 77th Regiments were to follow them up and either reinforce them or flank around if they got hung up. Their regiment was going to push forward in a sort of L-shape, with Third Battalion attacking on their right and First Battalion trailing directly behind them. Apparently the regimental brass wanted to keep it out of the immediate fight after the beating it took yesterday.

And as for Charlie Company of the Second Battalion of the 24th Infantry Regiment, they were leading the attack again, straight uphill into whatever the Empire had in store for them. She would be walking point as usual. Thorn must have realized it, because he finished up and looked at her, saying, "So, Sophia, how's it feel to be leading the corps into combat?"

She thought for a moment and remarked, "I bet General Kunst would be *pissed* if he found out."

They all laughed. Thorn said, "I bet he would be. I'll tell the boss to send it up tonight, maybe it'll get to him." He looked at his watch, then around the group, "Alright, we step off in fifteen minutes. Get going."

Sophia hurried back to her squad and filled them in on the operation. Lieutenant Thorn came up after a bit to walk with them on the attack, and after their fifteen minutes were up she looked back at him, pointed to her watch and gave him a thumbs-up. He nodded and they climbed out of their foxholes and started forward.

After a couple hundred meters of climbing through the white-shrouded forest the fog suddenly cleared around her and Sophia looked up to see blue sky shining through the canopy far overhead. Looking behind her she saw the forest wrapped in clouds, the company's soldiers emerging from the mist one by one as they climbed. It was the most scenic thing she'd seen in the whole war, and for a moment she wished she had a camera handy. Sighing, Sophia turned around and kept walking. If they were out of the clouds that meant the Imperials would be able to see them easily. She had no time to admire the scenery.

The slope flattened out to a gentle grade and morning sunlight shone brightly through the trees ahead of her, a sure sign they were about to come to the end of the forest. Sophia motioned her squad to crouch and spread out, and they stole forward stealthily from tree to tree as glimpses of spreading farmland started showing through the trees. Finally they dropped to all fours and crawled the last bit of the way, and Sophia cautiously stuck her head out from behind a hefty tree trunk and looked over the scenery.

Sweeping hay fields spread out before her, broken up by a couple rustic farmhouses and barns as they rose towards the crest of Fire Ridge, a sharp line against the blue sky maybe a kilometer away. Off to the right she could see a row of trees marking the road to their south, and as the ridge dipped and rose again to their north she saw the tops of a line of trees along what she supposed was a stream or road and another farmstead on the rise beyond that.

Sophia felt a twinge of confusion as she looked over the scenery – Lieutenant Thorn had told her there would be farms up here, but she hadn't expected it to be so open. In fact, she hadn't seen this part of the ridge at all when they had gone out and looked over the ridge, what, three nights ago? After a moment of wracking her fatigue-dulled brain she realized what they had taken for the top of the ridge back then was actually a false summit, and they had been too close to see the true summit hidden behind the curvature of the hill. They were a *long* way up. Her legs ached at the thought.

Lieutenant Thorn crouched beside her and studied the farms through his binoculars, "Seems clear enough..." he said, trailing off uncertainly.

Sophia felt chills running up and down her back just looking at the fields ahead of them. She was starting to be able to recognize a killing ground when she saw one, and given the wide open fields of fire this looked like just the kind of place where five or six machine guns could hold off an army. Furrowing her brow, she asked him, "See any wire, sir?"

"No, but that doesn't mean it's not there." She could hear the grimace in his voice, "That hay hasn't been harvested. It must be waist-high by now. Plenty of room to hide things."

"Think it could hide us, sir?" She asked.

He thought for a moment, "Maybe if we waited until nightfall." He chuckled grimly, "Not sure how much I want to crawl, what, half a kilometer?"

Sophia squinted at the farm buildings and the few small stands of trees rising out of the fields before them. Ideal places to set up machine guns, with good fields of fire. Although, Sophia thought, that didn't mean the enemy would shoot at them from directly in front of them. She pointed off at where the ridge rose again to the south, "Sir, take a look over there. I bet they'll hit us from that way if we push in."

Thorn swung his binoculars over, "A crossfire? Makes sense." He bit his lip, "Got any good ideas, Miss Rose?"

She shrugged, "If we can wait until nightfall we can crawl it, sir."

Thorn snorted, "Not much of an option, I'm afraid. Although..." He dropped down and pointed at a section of the field, "Does that look like a drainage ditch to you?"

Sophia squinted at the waves of hay in front of them, and then she saw the long grass dip out of sight and rise up again a little ways off to the far side. It was much too large to be a ditch. She guessed, "Looks like the field dips there, sir. You think that'll give us cover from the flank?"

"Yeah." He said. They heard footsteps in the wet leaves behind them and turned to see three people making their way up towards them. Her father, Captain Caldwell and a major she barely recognized came up and crouched down next to them. She noticed his name tag read 'Clark'. The new battalion commander? If he was up here this *had* to be important.

"Well, I can tell what they *want* us to do." Her father said. Sophia thought she heard sarcasm.

"Charge out on line with the colors flying?" Major Clark snorted, "We'd make it to the barbed wire. I still can't believe the 50th made it through that line downhill the way they went at it."

"Worse fields of fire in all those trees, sir." Caldwell said, "We'll need to do better."

Thorn pointed between the two farms, separated by the grove in the small valley between them, "I bet these are mutually supporting positions." He pointed at the depression leading up into the one in front of them, "If we get into *that* we'll have some cover from the flank. Your daughter thinks so anyways."

Her father peered at the landscape and raised his eyebrows, "Good eyes. That's shallow though. We'll need to keep low."

"Better than nothing." Sophia said.

"Alright." Major Clark sounded like he'd made his decision, "Gerald, your company will seize this farm and push on to gain a foothold on the ridgeline. Delta will come up and support you from here." Sophia wondered who Gerald was for a moment before she realized it was Caldwell's first name, "The other two companies will take that farm over there and push to the ridge on that side. We'll drop smoke on both positions so they can't support each other." He pointed at the road off to their right, "Our boundary is the road. First Battalion is attacking on the other side." The battalion commander looked at his watch, "Zero hour is... nine exactly."

Sophia looked at her own watch. That gave them about forty minutes to get ready. "Smoke at eight fifty-five?" Caldwell asked.

Clark nodded, "Works for me. Get your men ready and pass the word to Delta, I've got to go get the other companies into position." He got up to leave, then paused and turned back to them, "Just so you know, once we break through there's a cavalry regiment waiting to be committed. It's the Crown Prince's. We should ensure they get their ride."

Even through the haze of fatigue weighing down on her, the thought of seeing Prince Adrian again brought a glow to her heart. Smiling, Sophia replied, "Yes, sir!"

Caldwell chuckled sourly, "I can see that motivated some of us more than others."

Her father raised an eyebrow and remarked, "I can hardly blame her, sir."

"I suppose I can't." Caldwell replied as the major departed down the hill, the added quietly, "But I hope this attack isn't for *his* sake."

Her father shrugged, "Wouldn't be the first one, sir." He gave the commander a look, "And I doubt he'd want it that way either."

Caldwell scowled, "I hope so." He turned to Thorn, "Get your platoon into position to get into that defile, lieutenant. I'm putting the machine gun platoon here." He checked his watch theatrically, "And we have thirty-nine minutes before we attack. Get moving."

Thorn got the platoon up and moved over to where the depression ran into the woods some ways off to their left and put the squads down on line before disappearing to talk to the commander again. Off to their right Sophia could hear the soft sounds of the heavy machine gunners moving into position, mechanical clicking and the occasional muffled curse as they set up the old, water-cooled guns. As he left she saw men carrying the company's spindly infantry-support cannons upslope on their stretcher-like mounts, and the tension in her chest dissipated a little. The enemy could have fortified the houses against rifles and machine guns, but the heavy shells from those guns would tear through sandbags or even steel plates.

Her father had come with them, and he sat down next to her as they waited. Patting her on the knee, he asked, "How're you holding up, Sophie?"

She sighed. Her body ached, she was more tired than she'd ever been before in her life and people she'd never met before had been trying to murder her for the last few days. She forced a half-smile, "I'm alright, I suppose. Wish I was back home with Mom."

"So do I, trust me." He chuckled, "Now for the more important question. How are your guys?"

Sophia looked around to make sure they were all there. That they were. Tony had crawled out to the very edge of the forest to keep an eye on the fields surrounding them. Edward was fingering the bandage around his head where blood had seeped through from his wound. She'd have to have the medics look at him again after this was over. Hargrave had lit his pipe up again and was puffing away stoically while Jeremy was tightening his load-bearing harness around his waist. Jack and Kelley had their machine gun pulled open and were squeezing oil into its internal parts.

Sophia looked back at her father and shook her head, "We're doing alright. Ed needs his head looked at again, he's still bleeding a little." She snorted and went on, "We could all use about twenty hours of sleep."

Her father laughed softly, "Only twenty?" He gave her a fatherly look, "Come complain to me when you need a hundred, young lady."

Confused, Sophia looked back at him for a moment. He was still giving her that very particular stern look, the exact same one he'd use if he'd caught her coming back home too late at night. She burst out laughing. Holding a hand over her mouth to keep from making too much noise, she slapped weakly at his shoulder as her body rocked with suppressed laughter. Finally, she managed, "Oh, come on, Dad, really?"

He snorted and dropped the stern façade, "No, no, I'm kidding. I had you there, though." Checking his watch, he stood, "Alright, I need to get moving. Not all of the squad leaders around here need as little help as you." He winked and walked off down the line.

Lieutenant Thorn came back after a few minutes, called the squad leaders in and filled them in on the plan of attack. Unfortunately the artillery did not have enough smoke shells available to support both this attack and all the fighting they were expecting to happen on the back side of the ridge. They would have to make do with normal, explosive shells. Beyond that it was a simple plan. The artillery, mortars and guns would unload on anything that looked remotely like an Imperial bunker, the company would crawl as far upslope as possible through the irrigation ditch before deploying to attack and they would fight from there.

Sophia headed back to her squad, crouched low to avoid being seen in the thicket of vegetation, and filled them in on the plan. After she finished Jack gave her a sour look and weighed in, "Y'know, Sophia, this is the kind of plan we get right before we all die."

She glared back at him, "You've got a better one?"

Jack looked around at the rest of the squad. They looked back at him expectantly. Finally, he sighed, "No, I don't." He gave her a look she hadn't seen out of him before. She thought he almost looked afraid as he went on, "Just try not to get us killed, Sophia. I... don't have a good feeling about this."

Her friends turned back to her, and she saw it in their eyes. Their faith in her to lead them. The hope that she'd lead them well. She even saw it in Jack, a tiny spark somewhere in those dark, resentful, bad-boy eyes of his. Was this how she looked at her father? No, it wasn't, she thought. She didn't have to hope with him. For a moment her vision blurred and her breath caught in her throat.

Hargrave came to her rescue, "I'm not too worried, Jack. You do your thing with that gun of yours and let Miss Rose do hers." He gestured with his watch, "It's not long now that we'll be stepping off, better get ready."

The squad nodded in acknowledgement and quickly started getting into position, flattening themselves down at the very edge of the forest. Hargrave lingered for a moment and Sophia said softly, "Thanks, ah, Mr. Hargrave."

The older man chuckled, "You're way too young to have those kids looking at you like that. I couldn't have handled it at your age." He hefted his rifle, "Now let's go kill some Masks, eh?"

Sophia snorted and picked up her own rifle, "Yeah. *Let's.*"

Three minutes later the artillery shrieked overhead and their machine guns roared to life. Gritting her teeth and pushing forward on her hands and knees, Sophia brushed aside a tangle of thorns and branches at the edge of the forest and plunged into the field. What she had taken as a drainage ditch wasn't much more than a shallow depression cutting through the fields, a broad, shallow trough that she would have bet the farmer never even thought twice about, the bottom soggy from the recent rains.

Mud quickly coated the front of her uniform as she crawled along, overgrown hay rising all around her like a cage as the thick stalks bit into her palms. She quickly lost track of how far they had come as the seconds stretched into gunfire-filled eternities, and her heart sank as she twisted around to look back at the forest. Tony, right behind her, propped himself up a little and gave her a questioning look with his head framed by the trees still close behind them. He was opening his mouth to say something when an Imperial bullet clipped a piece out of his cap.

Tony flattened himself to the ground as more bullets snapped overhead, and Sophia turned around and kept crawling. Talking wouldn't get them any closer to the enemy. Fortunately for them all she seemed to have chosen their path of advance well. Imperial bullets cracked low over her head as she slithered forward, more than a few of them popping into the wet earth that rose on either side of her, but nothing hissed into the shallow ditch itself.

The thundering explosions of their shells grew closer and closer as she crawled along, until the ground shook underneath her with every round and she could see plumes of earth flying high into the sky above the thicket of hay all around her. Smoke started to fill the air, and she smelled wet, burning grass and the sour reek of phosphorous. Sophia was about to roll over and call for Lieutenant Thorn to come up and start spreading the company out to attack when she made one last push forward and saw the Imperial barbed wire, a coil of it nestled in the overgrown hay six inches from her face.

Sophia smirked. And then, despite the bullets snapping overhead and the deafening crash of the artillery nearby, she laughed. It was a little hysterical, but it still felt good. *Of course* the Empire would hide their barbed wire in the overgrowth and wait for them to charge bravely into it, trip, fall flat on their faces slapstick-style and get machine-gunned while they thrashed around helplessly. There were probably three or four more coils stretched out behind this one for good measure. And they'd *seen right through it*. Imperials stopped being so scary once you figured out how they thought. How they just had to be so *clever*.

Sophia rolled over and looked at Tony, who raised his head reluctantly to look at her. She jerked her head at the tangle of wire and shouted over the thundering shells, "Help me cut through this!"

Tony nodded and quickly crawled up next to her. Hoping the wire wasn't booby-trapped, Sophia pulled out her wire cutters and got to work. A few snips later and she was through the coil. Tony had fixed his bayonet to his rifle while she worked and thrust it out past her, hooked the coil with the bayonet's guard and yanked it back, creating an opening for her to slither through. She crawled a few feet further and put her hand into the next coil of wire before she realized it was there. Out came the wire cutters again, the work made more awkward by her having to bring her knees up and lie on her side to give Tony enough space to finish widening the breach in the last line.

Again, Tony came up next to her and pulled the wire aside as she finished. Sophia crawled forward, thrusting her rifle out in front of her to hopefully trigger any booby-traps before she did. It tangled and hooked on something stiff, and Sophia pulled herself up to see a single strand of wire, strung taut about six inches off the ground. She cut through it and the five strands behind it, cursing as she went. Whoever had laid out this wire was a *psycho*.

With a final effort, Sophia crawled past the tanglefoot trap and cut apart a final coil of barbed wire behind it. Edward had crawled up to help them, and he and Tony hooked the wire and pulled it open for her to push through into the tall grass beyond. She crawled for ten feet, twenty, as another volley of artillery shrieked down and pebbles and clods of earth rained down around her from the blasts. Nothing. Flipping over onto her back, she saw Lieutenant Thorn crawling up close behind her.

"Sir!" She shouted, "I think we're through!"

"Good!" He shouted back at her, "Come on! Get your squad on line!" He rolled over and waved for the platoon to start moving up. Sophia saw Jack and Kelly grimly pulling their machine gun through the wire behind him, dirt puffing up on either side as Imperial bullets whipped down. Behind those two she got a glimpse of Hargrave, pushing on Kelly's boots to hurry him up.

Sophia rolled over as another burst of enemy gunfire cracked overhead, the machine gun loud and close, much closer than their own guns back in the woodline. Where were they, anyways? Close to the farm? Close to some bunker they hadn't seen earlier? There was only one way to find out. Sophia swallowed nervously, worked her rifle up to get a firing grip on it and looked behind her. Tony and Edward looked back at her from right behind her, and she could see Jack getting his machine gun back in front of him behind them. The others would be right behind.

Shouting over the gunfire, Sophia ordered, "On my signal, get on line and attack *that way*." She pointed towards the sound of the nearest enemy gun, "Jack, suppress them! Everyone else, forward on me!" They all nodded, and she raised her hand, rose up onto her haunches and waved them forward, "Go!"

They all lunged forward, scrambled through the long hay up the shallow embankment and over the top. The farmhouse rose out of the field barely a hundred meters away and almost directly off to their side, half-demolished and smoking from the shelling, and Sophia saw the Imperial machine gunner on the second floor notice them rise up out of the field. His first burst walked up the field straight towards her, bullets whipping around her for a moment as she leveled her sights on him and pulled the trigger.

Her bullet took a chunk out of the windowsill he was firing over. He was aiming back down on her for another burst when Jack opened fire, jackhammer loud and terrifyingly close. The masked soldier vanished for a moment in a sea of splinters and sparking metal, and Sophia saw him topple to the floor as Jack let off. Adjusting his aim, Jack fired again, working his fire across the house's first floor. Sophia saw shapes diving for cover inside.

Time to go. "Come on!" Sophia shouted, got up and sprinted forward. Bullets seethed through the air around her, seeming to come from every direction. She threw herself down after a moment, fired, yanked her bolt back and forth and fired again as the rest of the squad dove into the long grass around her. Jack, behind them now, let off another long burst with his machine gun and splinters sprayed from the house as his bullets ripped the walls apart.

They kept moving, bound by bound, as Jack laid into the house from his original position by the breach. Sophia threw herself down for the fourth time and heard another machine gun erupt behind her, a little fainter, and she realized the second squad had come through the breach and started attacking to the left and away from them. That probably explained why she'd thought some of the bullets were coming from *behind* her.

Sophia fired again, felt Tony hurl himself down next to her and looked over at him. She pointed at the house and shouted, "*Grenade!*" She turned her head the other way to Edward, picking himself up on his elbows to fire on her other side, "*We'll cover him!*" They both fired a few rounds as Tony pulled a grenade off his harness, reared up to his knees, yanked the igniter and hurled it into one of the shot-out windows. Sophia realized absently it was actually a pretty good throw from that distance.

A green shape darted out of the side of the house an instant before it flashed with fire, smoke pouring from the windows. Sophia twisted to fire when two shots rang out, Hargrave and Jeremy firing from off to her left. The shape stumbled and fell into the long grass, and those two fired again and again at where it had landed. *Damn,* she thought. Mentally shaking herself, she reared up and called out, "*Keep moving! Come on!*"

Sophia lunged forward again, hurtled up the front steps and kicked the door in, bringing her rifle down into her shoulder as she rushed inside. She heard Tony a step behind her as she pivoted and scanned the room through a fog of stinking smoke. Somebody moaned in pain deeper into the house. The Imperial soldiers in the front room they had charged into were a long way beyond pain. She counted six of them crumpled on the floor, dead. They had piled sandbags up against the walls for protection, but their heavy guns had torn their protection apart and the machine guns had done the rest. She could see bright daylight and the woodline through what had to be thousands of bullet holes in the right-hand wall.

Sophia heard Edward, then Hargrave and Jeremy, file into the house behind them. Pointing at the staircase off to the side, she said, "Hargrave, you two take upstairs. We'll clear down here." She heard that moan again, and Sophia grit her teeth. If someone was wounded around here there might be someone *un*-wounded with them. Creeping softly, the three of them carefully cleared the rest of the downstairs, leading with their bayonets into every room.

They found the wounded Imperials in the back, laid out on the floor. The woman was barely twitching, the front of her steel mask smashed in a way that told Sophia she was well beyond help. The other one rolled his head over at them as they walked in, his breath rattling in his throat. Someone had pulled his jacket and shirt off and taped plastic seals all over his bloody chest. Sophia lowered her rifle and knelt as she realized he was trying to say something.

The eyes behind that steel mask were dark and glazed as he whispered, "Casey? Is... that you?" He tried to breathe in and only made it a quarter of the way, blood frothing from needles someone had stuck in his chest to keep the pressure off his lungs. He went on, "Did... did we stop them?"

Her heart felt like it was about to seize up in her chest. What was she even supposed to do? Finally she grit her teeth, reached out and patted him on the forehead. The metal of his mask was cool and smooth under her fingers, "Yeah. We beat them." She beat her lower lip for a moment, then added, "Killed them all."

She could *tell* that he smiled under that mask of his as he whispered back, almost too soft to hear, "Liar." Then he closed his eyes, gasped a little and just stopped breathing.

God-damn it. Sophia quickly rubbed at her eyes and stood, turning to see Tony and Edward looking at her, wide-eyed. She jerked her head to the side angrily, "Come... come on, let's go. We need to get back with the platoon."

"Sure thing." Tony said quickly.

Edward added, slower, "Yeah... yeah."

They came back outside to see the rest of the company coming through the breach, her father standing upright beside it and waving the last few soldiers through. Across the little valley to their north she could see the dark uniforms of the other company spreading across the fields. A few bullets hissed by high overhead, but nothing like earlier. Sophia waved for Jack and Kelly to come up and went to go find Lieutenant Thorn.

Half an hour later, with artillery seething over her head and white smoke billowing up against the sky, Sophia put her spear together, pulled the scabbard off the lethal blade and unrolled the flag she had wrapped up so long ago. Rising up out of the long grass, she strode forward the last few feet and planted Charlie Company's flag on top of Fire Ridge.

Chapter 35

The Message and the Messenger

"Wake up, milady." Someone was shaking her shoulder gently. Arilin rolled over and opened her eyes to see Patricia looking down at her in the gray morning light, "We're leaving soon." She gave her a strained smile, "How did you sleep?"

Arilin shook her head groggily and propped herself up on her elbows. She didn't even remember Vanessa turning out the lights last night. She must have passed out instantly and slept like the dead. Rubbing the sand from her eyes, she yawned and replied, "Just fine. Better than I thought I would, I guess." She raised an eyebrow, "Did you get any?"

Patricia sat down on the bed. From the look in her eyes it was painfully obvious she wanted to lie down next to her, "A couple hours. After a while I got the feeling the Empire wasn't going to try anything until the morning, and I wasn't accomplishing anything staying up." She chuckled, "Looks like I was right. The Fourteenth just reported Imperial infantry moving south. Lots of them."

Running a hand through her hair to straighten it, Arilin asked, "Where's Vanessa?" Patricia raised her eyebrows at the question, and Arilin went on, "I'm just surprised you're waking me up yourself. Ma'am."

"Well, milady." Patricia looked down at her lap, "I sent her forward to the regiment last night after she put you to bed. I... haven't heard anything since." She sighed, "I hope she's all right. From the sound of things the Fourteenth is in for quite the fight."

Sitting up, Arilin reached out and grabbed the older woman's hand, "I'm sure she'll be fine."

Surprised, Patricia looked back at her. She smiled after a moment and said, "Thanks." She snorted and went on, "Vanessa's tougher than she looks anyways. I shouldn't be so worried. Anyways," She gave the princess a look, "You need to get dressed, milady. We've got breakfast downstairs. I'll see you in a bit."

Patricia got up and left, closing the door softly behind her. Some kind soul, probably Vanessa, had laid out a fresh uniform for her on a chair beside the bed, and Arilin climbed out of bed and quickly dressed. Buckling on her sword belt, she headed downstairs to find the staff bustling around the headquarters purposefully. They barely noticed her as she came down.

The smell of fresh bread wafted out of a side room, and Arilin ducked in to see the hotel's staff had laid out a breakfast buffet for them. Before she could even get a good look at it, though, a slightly terrified-looking maid pounced on her and ushered her to a seat. A little amused, Arilin made her order and an instant later was digging into breakfast. She supposed this place hadn't seen many visits from royalty before.

Arilin was about to finish off her coffee and get up when a familiar shadow fell across the table. She looked up to see Patricia standing beside her. The lady general was paler than she'd ever seen her before. Frowning worriedly, Arilin asked, "Patricia... what's wrong? You don't look well."

The lady general sighed heavily and slumped into the chair next to her, "I suppose I must not." She gave her a bleary look, "And... I don't want the staff to see me like this."

Arilin raised her eyebrows, "What happened?"

"You know how I told you the Fourteenth had eyes on Imperial infantry right now?" Patricia went on, "It's a little more *complicated* than that. One of their outposts was attacked and got a signal out before they were overrun. Because of that the rest of the regiment had time to pull out before they could be attacked." She pinched the bridge of her nose and sighed. Arilin felt the bottom drop out of her stomach as she went on, "Vanessa was at that outpost. She, and that whole platoon, are missing."

Arilin swallowed hard, "Oh my God..." She went on, "I'm sorry."

The lady general gave her a piercing look, "Why are you apologizing? It's *my* fault. *I* sent her forward. Now..." She sighed and looked at the table, "God, I hope she's all right. Poor girl."

Arilin reached out and patted her on the shoulder, "I'm sure she's fine." It was a lie and they both knew it, but what else was she supposed to say?

Patricia grabbed her hand and snorted, "I hope so." She shook her head, "One more life on my conscience. One among many." Pushing the girl's hand off her shoulder, she looked up again. Arilin saw the old, confident lady general descend over Patricia's face like a mask as she stood and said, "Thanks, milady."

The princess stood as well, "Think nothing of it. Vanessa is my friend too."

Patricia smiled sadly, "This isn't an easy job, milady. Now come on, we have things to do."

Walking out into the headquarters floor set up in the hotel's large common room, Patricia quickly spotted Colonel Frost over by the central map table and walked over to him. He turned as they approached and greeted them, "Ladies! Good to see you." He gave Patricia a sympathetic look, "I'm sorry to hear about Lieutenant Gable. Poor kid."

Patricia sighed, "Thanks. So am I." She gave him a look and went on, "But we've got a battle to fight. Anything new since I left?"

"Yes, milady." Frost replied, "The lancers just reported that they're in contact with Imperial infantry. Lots of them."

"Where?" Patricia asked.

The colonel pointed at the map, on the far side of the division's front line from where they had marked the Fourteenth Regiment's ongoing fight with the Imperials. It was more than thirty kilometers away. Patricia raised an eyebrow, "Damn." She looked over at her chief of staff, "Are you thinking what I'm thinking, Joe?"

Frost chuckled grimly, "Probably, milady, but Princess Arilin is the junior officer here. We should hear her opinion first."

The older officers turned and looked at her. Arilin swallowed hard. What would Patricia really be interested in from this information? What did two enemy infantry attacks thirty kilometers apart mean? What did this say about how the Imperials were advancing? After thinking for a minute she ventured, "These are two separate enemy divisions?"

Colonel Frost nodded and stroked his beard, "I'm sure they are." He grunted, "What I'm not so sure about is whether these divisions belong to the same *corps*. In fact they probably don't." He looked at Patricia, "Milady, I think we might be trying to fight a field army here. At least."

The lady general nodded, "I agree. And God knows what we're looking at to the side." She gestured to either side of the division's long front line, "I haven't heard anything about dragoons recently, and that's never a good thing. They've probably found our flanks."

Frost gave her a worried look, "Milady, at this point extricating ourselves from this situation is going to be... difficult."

"Trust me, I know." Patricia smiled grimly, "I think we need to send out a patrol to clear our line of retreat first thing. How soon can the Eighth get a platoon ready?"

Frost looked at his watch reflexively, "Half an hour easily."

She nodded, "Have them standing by here and ready to ride in half an hour. They're going to take a messenger with them." Patricia went on, "Have the staff put together an updated map and a full set of reports for the Corps. And... give me a few minutes, please. I need to write up something of my own."

He nodded, "Of course, milady. I'll have them get right on it."

"One more thing." Patricia turned to Arilin and smiled, "Now, milady, I have a mission for you. I need *you* to carry this message to General
Haas." She went on, "I shouldn't need to tell you how important this is."

Arilin felt her heart flutter. It was a huge responsibility. She'd be out
by herself, carrying a critical message on the situation to General Haas
to allow him to deploy IX Corps to face the threat and save the day. And
she'd also be surrounded by a platoon of cuirassiers and headed away
from danger as fast as her horse could carry her. She felt her heart sinking
as she replied, "Yes, but... you aren't just trying to get rid of me, milady?"

Frost and Patricia laughed, and she replied, "Not *just*, milady. But
if you weren't here I'd have to send someone else." She added, "If Walter
isn't quick on his feet *none* of us may get out of this at this point. I'm not
letting that happen to you."

The princess sighed and looked at the floor, "Sure."

Walter patted her on the shoulder, "Don't look so down, dear." He added, "Trust me, you're going to be in *plenty* of danger riding back. Don't
feel guilty for our sake."

That just made it worse. Tears started welling up in her eyes unbid-
den. Hurriedly rubbing at them, Arilin turned and managed, "I'll... go
get my horse ready." She could *feel* those two exchange a look behind her
back as she turned and walked out.

Arilin stormed out the front door, probably giving the soldiers standing guard a shock, and had her hand on the stable door to yank it open
when she stopped. She looked down at her hand, poised on the latch.
She was *shaking*, anger clawing and seething in the back of her mind.
How *dare* they just send her away like that, as soon as things got even a
little dangerous? She might as well have stayed in the Capital. Patricia
was sure showing a lot of gratitude to her for *fixing her dead-end career*.
But *no*, as soon as it looked like they were going to get into a real battle,
you know, *the thing she was out here to see*, it was suddenly *too dangerous*. Here's your parasol, your grace, now head to safety like a good little
princess. We're giving you *thirty bodyguards*. She was lucky they weren't
sending the whole squadron. And of course Patricia had a perfectly good,
sound, military justification for all of this and she didn't have a single leg
to stand on to complain. She was a soldier now. She'd sworn an oath.
And she was bound to follow orders whether she liked them or not. Even
if they made her want to scream.

Which brought her to back to the present, standing at the door to the
stables. There was *no way* she was going to go saddle up her horse seething like that. Horses are smart. They pick up their rider's mood. And as

fast as she was, Midnight was a nervous, screwy horse. The last thing she needed was for her to be running away from her for forty kilometers.

Closing her eyes, Arilin took a deep breath and concentrated for a moment. The anger was shrieking in the back of her mind, a seething mass of fangs and teeth and spikes. She reached a hand into that mess, took hold of it and choked it until it stopped struggling and lay still for a while. Objectively speaking, she couldn't blame Patricia. The lady general had a duty to her father after all, and she'd probably pushed things as far as she could. That was a good thought. Arilin held onto it, exhaled and pulled open the stable door.

A little while later she had Midnight saddled and prepared for a long ride, and she led her back out in front of the hotel to see a whole mass of cuirassiers had arrived with their horses. Their platoon leader, a very tall young lieutenant with a cute little moustache, called them to attention and saluted as they approached, "Good morning, milady! I've been told we're taking you back."

He was head and shoulders taller than her. In fact, most of them were. Arilin felt positively tiny in comparison. Forcing a smile, she returned his salute and replied, "I feel safer already." She looked for his name tag and realized his armor breastplate was covering it, "What's your name, sir?"

The man gave her a short bow, "Gabriel Bettancourt, milady."

Arilin raised her eyebrows, "Can I call you Gabe?"

He smiled, "Of course." That moustache really was adorable. She wondered if it was intentional or if he was trying to make himself look older and failing.

"Thanks, Gabe." She looked over at the closed front door to the headquarters, "Now, if you'll give me a second I should have some reports to pick up..."

Arilin trailed off as the front door opened and Patricia stepped out with a bulging satchel in hand. She cast her eye over the assembled cuirassiers for a moment until her gaze landed on the two of them standing a little off to the side, and she quickly walked over. Thrusting the bag at the princess, she said, "Here you go, milady." Patricia took her shoulder and pulled her aside as Arilin reluctantly took it, saying softly, "Look, milady, I... shouldn't have sprung this on you like that. If Walter had decided I was needed in the rear as soon as things started getting hot around Dragon's Jaw I would have pitched a fit, and I was twice your age at the time." She gave her a sympathetic look, "Right now your brother's on the wrong side of Fire Ridge, and there's a limit to how irresponsible the Army can be with your family's lives. I'm sorry."

Arilin sighed. Now *she* felt awful. Patricia had been operating on a whole separate level, as usual. They had just confirmed it. There were hundreds of thousands of Imperial soldiers wheeling into position as they spoke, like the fangs of a giant monster that was going to tear the Army of Drakenburg apart if they didn't stop it, do *something* to hold the jaws open to help the army escape. The Ninth Cavalry Division was soon going to be fighting to survive, and objectively speaking there was nothing to gain and everything to lose by her staying. The thought of her brother in combat up on Fire Ridge made her stomach clench with fear. The thought of what would happen if *she* died as well was too much to contemplate.

None of that made it any easier. Her eyes blurred as she looked back at Patricia, "I-I understand." She stepped forward and hugged the older woman, sobbing, "Thanks... thanks for everything."

Patricia patted her back reassuringly, "I'll see you soon, I'm sure of it." She chuckled on as Arilin let go of her and stepped back, "I've been in worse trouble before. Some of it with Walter." She winked, then unbuttoned the top few buttons of her jacket and reached inside. Producing a letter, she held it out to the princess, "Speaking of him, I want you to give this to him when you get the chance."

Arilin raised an eyebrow, "Your personal report, milady?"

Patricia snorted, "You could say that." The lady general gave her a stern look, "This is secret information, milady. It's for him, and him *only*. Understand?"

Arilin smiled, "Of course."

The lady general nodded, "Alright then. Off you go, milady. Take care."

"Will do." Arilin replied, and Patricia turned and walked back inside. Walking back to her escorts, Arilin swung herself up onto Midnight and turned to Lieutenant Bettancourt, "Ready to go, Gabe?"

The man nodded, "Of course, milady." He shouted for his soldiers to mount up, and they were quickly trotting south. Arilin chanced a look back at the hotel as they headed down the road, but the hulking cavalrymen spread around her blocked out any view she had. Sighing, she turned back to her front and gave the bag of reports over her shoulder a reassuring pat. She wasn't planning on losing them, or the letter she had tucked inside her jacket for that matter.

Soon the village disappeared far behind them as they rode south, the terrain gently rising towards the Dragonspine foothills they had come down from the day before, now invisible in the low clouds. Far off to her left Arilin could hear what sounded like an endless, low growl of artillery as the Royal Army fought its way forward around Fire Ridge. It chilled her blood to think of the enemy guns that *weren't* firing, yet, and she turned down a couple of early offers of rest from Gabriel.

As if to make her point, after a couple hours they heard chains of blasts much closer behind them. Arilin had by this point learned to recognize them as individual artillery fire missions, and Gabriel opined that they sounded a lot larger than anything the division had. Arilin prayed that the village wasn't being shelled and urged Midnight onwards.

After a couple hours the lieutenant ordered a halt anyways. No matter how urgent the situation, men and horses could not keep going without water and a little rest every once in a while. Arilin was snugging up Midnight's girth straps when Gabriel said to her, "You're a fine rider, milady. Where'd you learn?"

She turned and looked at him. He was rubbing at his lower back absently under his armor breastplate, and Arilin realized he hadn't called the halt for *her* sake. The lightest cuirassier had to be twice her weight with armor and weapons on top of that. While she felt fine and she was sure Midnight could go on for miles, the same probably wasn't true of her escorts or their horses. Arilin put the realization aside for the moment and replied, "From my brother, a little. Otherwise I have instructors." She snickered, "They're not as good."

"That makes sense." He smiled, "You ride like a cavalryman, milady." He thought of something and went on, "Actually, you *don't*. We need to teach you some bad habits."

Arilin laughed, "Thank you!"

Gabriel bent backwards and looked up at the sky for a moment. Satisfied, he straightened up and said, "I think we've rested long enough, milady. Let's get going." He looked around at the cuirassiers milling around them and called, "Mount up! We're moving out!"

The cavalrymen quickly mounted their horses and they were on their way, riding up the long, gentle slope as the forest began to close around them again. Soon they heard wheels creaking ahead of them as they overtook a medical column heading back to the train station. Arilin exchanged pleasantries with some of the more lucid patients while Gabriel asked the harried-looking convoy commander if he'd seen any Imperials or unfamiliar horsemen. The man denied it, but Arilin's ears perked up and she looked over as he asked who she was.

Gabriel snorted, "She's a hussar lieutenant with red eyes. Read my mind."

The man raised an eyebrow, "I think I have. Taking her to safety? You're a lucky man."

Her escort chuckled, "Very."

"Still." The man grunted, "When you see the Royals heading the other way it must be getting serious. What's the latest?"

"Hey," Gabriel ignored the question, "She's *thirteen*, for God's sake. It's not like she asked for this. Give her a few years and she'll be leading the charge."

"Guess so." He replied, as the cuirassier motioned for his platoon to move on ahead of the wagon convoy, "You all take care. Shoot a Mask for me."

Gabriel laughed, "Will do." He looked back at her, "Come on, milady, we need to get moving."

"Sure thing." She replied, nudging her horse onwards. She felt the convoy commander give her a sour look behind her back. Grimacing, she caught up to Gabriel and asked, "What was his problem?"

The lieutenant chose his words carefully, "I am a Royalist and a Legitimist, milady, but it shouldn't be news to you that not everyone is." He gave her a look, "Please forgive him. This operation has everyone on edge right now."

Arilin shrugged, "I can hardly blame him."

They rode on for a ways in silence, the cuirassiers' jackets and breastplates forming a gray wall around her as the fields and villages turned to pastures and the forest closed in around them. They were crossing a wide expanse of grassland when Gabriel ventured, "You know, I meant what I said, milady."

She looked over at him and raised an eyebrow, "What do you mean?"

He grinned, "The Fourteenth is getting quite the deal with you, milady. I heard about your little stunt back at Wolf Rock." He went on, "After that I don't think there's a regiment in the Army that would turn you down if you asked."

She laughed, "What, fighting all comers?" Arilin patted the saber hanging at her side, "My brother taught me how to fight, too, you know."

Gabriel didn't reply. He was looking very intently off to the side, towards the forest as it rose again at the edge of the clearing, a few hundred meters off. Arilin followed his gaze and for an instant didn't see anything. She rose up out of the saddle to get a better look, and *then* she saw it. Two tiny shapes, almost lost in the gathering mist at the far end of the clearing. Riders in dark uniforms.

Arilin sat down quickly and asked, as calmly as she could, "Do you have binoculars, Gabe?"

"Oh, right." The man popped open a case on his belt and retrieved his binoculars. Holding them to his eyes, he looked for a moment before cursing and lowering them, "They ducked back into the woods."

He looked around at the rest of the platoon, "Did anyone else get a good look at them?" Murmurs went around. A few soldiers on that side of the formation said they had, but they hadn't been able to identify them. Gabriel went on, "That's what I was thinking. Spread out!" He pointed at the front of the formation, "First squad, take advance guard. Two hundred meters separation. And we're speeding up, double time. Go!"

The cavalrymen quickly spread out and kicked their horses into a trot, the first squad galloping forward to scout ahead. Arilin looked over at the lieutenant and asked, "Dragoons?"

He grunted over the clatter of hooves, "I don't know any of our guys who would be skulking in the woods like that." He looked down at Arilin's sword, "You might have to use that, milady, and soon."

Arilin looked down at the saber riding at her left hip and felt her breath catch in her throat. She'd been training for a long time, it was true. But she'd always thought any sword fight she was going to get into was going to be more... dramatic. A gallant charge at the head of the Valkyrie Knights. If those were dragoons out there, she could be fighting for her life in a dirty little cavalry skirmish. Hardly the stuff of legends. More like the stuff of ignominious deaths. Gritting her teeth, she replied, "I'll be ready."

They plunged into the forest, looking nervously to the sides for signs of an ambush as the trees rushed past. After a couple minutes Arilin heard a bugle faintly through the woods. The call was unfamiliar, and she looked over at Gabriel uneasily, "What's that?"

"Assembly." He said grimly, "And they have a bugler."

Arilin exchanged a look with the lieutenant and ventured, "At least a troop?"

"Looks like it." He replied. Raising his voice, he shouted to the platoon, "Enemy right! Troop strength! Triple time! Prepare to charge as soon as we clear the woods!" A murmur went through the soldiers as they kicked their horses into a canter, stringing out into a line along the right side of the road. Gabriel slapped his sword confidently and added, "Remember! We're protecting *Princess Arilin* here!"

"What we joined the Army for, sir!" Someone up front shouted.

"That's right!" Gabriel shot back, *"To the brave!"*

Arilin nudged Midnight into a canter as the rest of them shouted back, *"To the brave!"* Ahead of them the she saw the advance guard ride out of the forest and wheel off the trail to the right. Drawn swords flashed through the trees. A gunshot rang out, close and high-pitched. Arilin ducked in the saddle instinctively.

"Milady!" Gabriel shouted over the rushing wind and thundering hooves, "We'll hold them off! When we get clear, ride like hell and *don't look back!*" She looked over at him as he pointed at two cuirassiers nearby, "You and you! Go with her!"

"Yes, sir!" They chorused as they pulled their horses over to her. More gunfire rang out, even closer. Something small and fast snapped overhead as the forest opened around them. Something *clanked* as the head of the column broke into the open and a cuirassier toppled and crashed to the ground ahead of her. He bounced and rolled like a rag doll, came to rest and stared blankly up at her as she darted past and into the light. Arilin tore her eyes away, looked up and felt her blood freeze.

Gabriel was already pulling his horse around and shouting for the charge, his sword burning against the gray sky. But beyond him and the line of wheeling cuirassiers the fields boiled with green-jacketed horsemen, flashing and smoking as they fired from the saddle. She only counted five or six riders still up from the first squad, charging bravely into the enemy's midst. As she watched one went down, then another as the bugler played a call she *did* recognize. The line of dragoons *shimmered*, growing shining fangs as the enemy drew their swords and charged. Arilin fought back the fear as it clawed at her, kicked at Midnight and held on as the horse exploded under her.

Someone shouted something behind her that she didn't quite make out. It sounded like a warning. Arilin looked over and saw a group of dragoons far out in the fields, ahead of them and off to the right. They were already wheeling around to cut them off, their leader gesturing with his sword towards the road. Mentally apologizing to Gabriel, Arilin chanced a look back to see her two remaining escorts falling well behind her, one of them frantically waving for her to slow down. Beyond them the dragoons and cuirassiers crashed together in a tangle of horses, steel and blood.

Arilin swung her head forward to look at the group of dragoons heading them off, then back at her fading escorts and the seething, hacking melee behind them. They wanted to cut a path through the dragoons for her. She looked back at the dragoons as they galloped for the road, swords drawn. If she kept going, maybe sped up a little, she thought she could *barely* make it past them. The enemy leader must have realized it at the same time as she did. He waved his sword and two dragoons gave their horses rein and surged forward, out of the line towards her.

Ignoring the faint cries from behind her, Arilin kicked Midnight again and felt her *accelerate*. The two dragoons rushed on, angling away from their comrades to intercept her. They were so close she could see the glaring eyes behind their steel masks, could tell she was facing a man and a woman. Light danced and flared on their swords as they rushed at her, raising them to strike her down.

Fear screamed in the back of her mind, clouding her vision. Every muscle in her body trembled and shook, her breath seizing in her throat as it demanded she give up, surrender, beg for mercy. Of course they wouldn't kill her. She was a princess. She would be valuable to the Empire as a prisoner.

Arilin saw her fear as it shrieked in her face. She understood it, deep down to its core. She was a little girl, after all. What chance did she have of defeating two of the Empire's black knights? But. She was also an *officer of the Royal Army* and a member of the *Wehrherz family*. She'd been training for this for years. Princess Arilin grit her teeth, narrowed her eyes and swatted her fear aside as she reached down and seized her saber's hilt. Her vision cleared and her body loosened as she drew her sword, the blade coming free in a bright arc of steel. Arilin looked the first dragoon dead in the eyes as he thundered down on her, and she saw *fear*.

Then he was upon her, his first slash crashing down like a thunderbolt, almost smashing her sword out of her hand as she raised her sword's hilt and deflected it down. Arilin whipped her sword around her head in a circular counterstroke, reaching out for him as she hauled on Midnight's reins to dodge out of the way of his charge. He blocked her attack as he raised his sword for another strike, twisting around in the saddle as he pulled his horse back to fall in beside her. His sword came down again as Arilin pulled her sword back, hilt beside her jaw, parrying the blow aside as her blade came on line. She felt her hat come loose and her golden hair unfurl across her back like a battle flag, the man's eyes widening behind his mask as she lunged in the saddle and stabbed him through the chest.

The man jerked backwards, yanking on his reins instinctively. His horse dropped back instantly and Arilin tightened her grip on her saber to pull it free. It might as well have been set in concrete. For a terrifying instant she felt herself being dragged off Midnight's back by her own sword. Letting go, she desperately got a grip on her saddle with her other hand and hauled herself back upright as Midnight bolted. She looked back for an instant to see the man, still quite upright in his saddle, pulling his horse to a stop with her sword sticking clear through him.

"It's the princess! After her!" The dragoon's companion charged past him, sword high and screaming in pursuit. Some distance behind her she could see green jackets boiling through the trees. Now defenseless, Arilin brought her head back around, crouched low on Midnight's back and kicked her forward savagely. The horse gave her a shuddering snort and shot down the road like a bullet.

Wind whipped at her face, streaming through her hair as the trees turned to a dark blur all around her. Arilin pulled herself forward in the saddle, crouching low as Midnight exploded underneath her. Fighting to keep her seat, Arilin didn't dare look back at the pursuing dragoons. It didn't matter. Either they'd catch her or she'd outride them. Looking back wasn't going to help her at this point. Gritting her teeth, Arilin silently apologized to Midnight and pulled her riding crop free from her boot. She didn't have to use it. The horse got the message and somehow *sped up.*

They charged on and on as the road wound through fields and forests, Arilin quickly losing track of where they were as the scenery shot by and the clouds darkened overhead. Cold rain swept over them suddenly, quickly soaking her and steaming off Midnight's neck as she ran onwards, screaming for breath as her hooves slipped and clattered in the muddy road. Arilin finally pulled back on the reins and Midnight skidded to a shambling, swaying walk, heaving underneath her as she fought for breath. For a moment she feared she was going to collapse underneath her.

Arilin wiped water from her stinging eyes and chanced a look back down the road. Nothing, just a winding road that curved back into the trees and disappeared behind them, the dirt quickly turning to mud in the downpour. Through the wind and the rain she could barely hear Midnight's hoofbeats, let alone those of their pursuers. Maybe they'd given up. Then she thought of the dragoon charging past her injured comrade, shrieking for her blood. They hadn't given up. They were probably still whipping their horses after her. Arilin shuddered and nudged Midnight. The horse twisted her head back and gave her the dirtiest look she had ever gotten in her life, but she somehow sped up into a stiff trot.

As they rode along Arilin thought she heard voices over the hissing rain and Midnight's clopping, splashing hoofbeats on the muddy road. She took a ragged, fearful breath as she peered through the trees as they slid by. The cold rain chilled her spirit, seeming to seep into her soul as it soaked her to the skin, rivulets running down her back like icy, slick fingers. Who was she even kidding? She was riding a blown horse and armed with a riding crop. If there were dragoons in front of her she was done for.

Arilin guided Midnight around a curve and almost bowled over a gray-uniformed soldier. The man leapt out of the way and Midnight skidded to a halt and reared as she hauled on the reins. Arilin fought to hang on and somehow kept her seat as the horse landed and made to rear again. A sharp tug on the reins kept Midnight's front end on the ground, but the horse backed up skittishly as more gray-jacketed men emerged from the bushes all around them.

The princess looked around nervously. They were surrounded. Panic flared in her heart before she saw the faces under their brimmed infantry caps. Faces, not masks. This was the Royal Army. She was safe, and relief lifted the weight from her heart like angel wings. Midnight noticed her relax and she stopped prancing long enough for the leader of these jaegers, the man she'd almost run over earlier, to approach.

"Miss!" He must have noticed her horse was near collapse, "Are you being pursued?"

"Yes! At least a squad of dragoons!" She replied, "And I guarantee they're still after me!" She tossed her wet hair and looked the man in the eyes to explain.

The man's eyes widened, "God in heaven. My lady." He looked around at the gawking jaegers angrily, "Well, don't just stand around, there's dragoons on their way! Fix bayonets! Get the road covered! *Move!*"

The men quickly spun into action, plunging back into the forest to take up positions. Arilin felt tension bleed out of her shoulders as two machine gun crews rushed past them to the bend and set up to cover the road as it descended. Grateful, Arilin said, "Thank you... sir," The man was a captain, "Please, tell your men to be careful. I had some cuirassiers with me when we were attacked... they were trying to hold them off. There were at least a troop of dragoons."

"I will. A troop, huh?" He replied, then raised an eyebrow, "What happened to your sword, milady?"

Arilin looked down at the empty scabbard hanging uselessly by her side, "I... ran a dragoon through and, uh... couldn't pull it out afterwards." She shivered at the thought of the fight, how her sword had just *stuck* in the man's body, "Ugh, God..."

The man nodded, "Good job, milady. We'll handle it from here." He looked around and spotted one of his lieutenants, "Hey! Ackerman! Got a job for you!"

The young man hurried out of the forest and up to them, giving her a curious look before he turned to his commander and asked, "Sir, what do you need?"

The captain pointed at her, "I need you to take a squad and escort Princess Arilin back to the station. Division should be set up there by now. They'll figure out what to do with her from there." Arilin gave an obvious shiver in the cold rain, and he noticed and went on, "And give her a blanket or something, she's freezing."

Arilin ventured, "Do you know where I can find General Haas?" She patted the side of her coat where she had slipped Patricia's letter into an internal pocket, "I have a message from General MacMahon for him personally."

Both of the men raised their eyebrows in surprise. The lieutenant ventured, "He was waiting for us at the station, actually." The man chuckled, "He yelled at us to hurry up and get moving. I guess I understand why now."

The commander jerked his head at her, "Speaking of, lieutenant, get a move on." He gave a significant look down the road, "Those dragoons could be here any minute, and the last thing we need is the princess in the middle of a gunfight."

"Oh, right, sir." Lieutenant Ackerman quickly called out one of his squads, and Arilin set off down the road surrounded by a protective ring of infantrymen. Midnight was a little unsteady of her feet as they set off, so Arilin dismounted and led her. The horse seemed grateful for it, and Arilin had barely touched down when one of the soldiers wrapped a heavy, mostly dry greatcoat around her. She was grateful for *that*.

They had barely been walking a couple minutes when gunfire erupted behind them. It sounded like the whole jaeger company was firing every weapon they owned. They had barely ducked off the road, Midnight following Arilin into the trees, when it died as suddenly as it had begun. The lieutenant looked at her and snickered, "There goes your dragoon problem, milady."

Shaken, Arilin replied, "Yeah... right."

They quickly got back on the road and started heading back to the station. It was only five kilometers, and even on foot Arilin kept up with the infantrymen easily enough. They passed two companies of line infantry and an artillery battery heading north on the road. The men cheered and tried to crowd around as they recognized her, but their officers quickly got them moving again. As the artillery went by Arilin recognized the heavy, long-range cannons of the Corps Artillery, weapons that made the cavalry's mobile pieces look like toys. General Haas was clearly not taking half-measures.

Soon enough they were back in sight of the station, a plume of black smoke crawling over the town's rooftops as a train slowed and stopped. It and the surrounding town were crawling with soldiers, men assembling to march out while officers rushed about bringing order to the chaos. Another battery of those massive guns headed out past them as they entered the town, the crash of hundreds of hooves on the cobblestones echoing from the buildings around them as hulking draft horses hauled their loads north.

They found General Haas standing outside the town hall, deep in conversation with a two-star general that Arilin recognized as the 30th Division's commander. Lieutenant Albrecht gave her a look as they recognized them from some distance away and said, "I'm not interrupting them, milady, but if you want to... well, you're the princess." He trailed off.

Arilin gave him a smile, "No, I understand. Thank you, sir."

The lieutenant turned red, "No, my honor, milady."

Arilin replied, "Thank you regardless, then." Pulling off the heavy infantryman's overcoat, she handed it back to the man who had leant it to her, took a deep breath and walked up to the two generals, leading Midnight behind her.

The two generals looked over as she approached, and Haas' eyebrows rose in surprise, "Princess!" He looked at his watch, then at the jaegers behind her, "That was a *fast* ride. We weren't expecting you for another hour... and what happened to your escort?"

Smiling nervously, Arilin tried to think of a way to explain what had just happened without giving him a heart attack, "Ah..."

General Haas looked her over and narrowed his eyes, "Young lady, where *exactly* is your sword?"

Arilin swallowed and said, "Uh, well, it's stuck through a dragoon's chest. Unless they've pulled it out by now, sir. I... well, it was stuck." She went on quickly, "We were attacked and I outrode the rest of them." She sighed, "I don't know what happened to Lieutenant Bettancourt or his platoon. They stayed behind to hold them off."

Haas and his companion gave her a look for a long moment, then glanced at each other significantly. Looking back at her, he snorted and reached out to ruffle her hair. Ordinarily she would have protested, but his rough, heavy hand felt amazingly reassuring as he said, "Looks like you've had quite the adventure, milady." He let her go and went on, "Can you write me a letter about Lieutenant Bettancourt? It sounds to me like that man deserves a Hero's Medal."

She smiled and nodded, "Yes, sir." The mention of a letter jogged her memory, and she unbuttoned her jacket and pulled out Patricia's letter. It was a little damp but otherwise had come through her ride in good shape, and she offered it to Walter, "Lady MacMahon told me to give this to you personally."

Walter took it from her, popped the wax seal on the envelope and read through it quickly. Then he read through it again, more slowly. Arilin thought she saw him turning red. Finally, with a strange, thoughtful grunt, he carefully re-folded the letter and tucked it into his jacket. Deliberately buttoning his jacket back up, he gave Princess Arilin a look she'd never gotten before. The old general was somehow both furious and extremely pleased at the same time as he said, "This is your doing. And Siegfried's." He rolled his eyes, "That girl is going to be the *death* of me."

The other general remarked, "Now I'm curious."

Walter snorted and told him, "You'll find out soon enough." He went on, "Have your people send the 9th Division a radio message, 'Acknowledge receipt of secret dispatch from original messenger. Command wishes to discuss it when time permits. Be advised dragoons have infiltrated into your rear area.'"

The man nodded, "I'll get right to it, sir." He turned and walked back inside, and Arilin was left alone with Walter.

She was about to say something when she heard a screeching roar coming from the train station, loud enough she could hear it clearly even from the few blocks that separated them from it. Then another, and another, and more rattling, howling roars joined it. It sounded like a pack of lions made of rusty iron and badly in need of oiling as the sound echoed through town. Which, she supposed, wasn't a bad analogy. Arilin raised her eyebrows and asked, "Is that what I think it is, sir?"

Walter smirked, "Yes, it is. And speaking of that train, you need to hurry up and get on it. We'll have you take it to Corps." He nodded at her satchel, "You need to deliver the rest of that to Siegfried." He thought for a moment, "I'll get someone to escort you. Come with me."

He took her inside. Half an hour later, after a change into her spare uniform and an introduction to a starstruck young lieutenant on the Division staff who could herself be spared during the battle, she was walking down the street from the 30th Division's headquarters to her waiting train. Despite the smoke and the hellish noise, Arilin smiled as they passed the column of tanks clawing their way down the middle of the road.

Chapter 36

The Kingdom's Spear

The Imperials saw her flag, and they were *not* happy about it. Bullets started whipping past as she stood there, and Sophia quickly ducked back behind the crest of the ridge and laid down with her squad a few paces back. They were all smiles despite the rounds hissing by overhead. Tony high-fived her and said, "Yeah! Sounds like they're *pissed!*"

On her other side, Mr. Hargrave added drily, "Sounds like a lot of them." He chuckled, "You sure we want this fight, Sophie?"

She snorted, "Not sure if we have a choice about it." Noticing Lieutenant Thorn approaching up the shallow slope, Sophia called out, "Hey, sir! Are we still on plan?"

He gave her a thumbs-up, "We are! First Battalion's moving up now, they'll be swinging around on our left." Crouching down next to them, he went on, "Dig in so you can fire over the crest. We'll be supporting the attack from here." He gave Jack and Kelly a look, "You two still have your tripod?"

Kelly wordlessly jerked his thumb at the heavy, narrow canvas bag he'd slung over his back and carried all the way up the ridge. Sophia laughed, "Really, sir? You shouldn't have to ask us that."

He gave her an exasperated look, "You'd be surprised, Miss Rose." An enemy shell shrieked overhead and exploded some ways behind them. It didn't sound that big, and Thorn quickly rolled back up to his knees and went on, "Now get digging."

Sophia threw him a salute from flat on her back, rolled over and yelled to the squad, "You heard the man!" Thorn started cautiously crawling up the slope as she pulled out her entrenching tool, and she called after him, "Sir! What are you doing?"

The lieutenant turned and pulled his binoculars out of a belt case, and she noticed he had a field telephone trailing a thin wire slung over his shoulder, "Observing. The other battalions will need some time to get into position." He jerked his head towards the other side of the ridge, "Might as well use it."

She nodded and crawled a little ways up after him to find a good spot to dig in. If they were going to fire over the crest they'd need to be almost on top of it. And to determine exactly where that was, she'd need to know exactly where they were firing *at.* Lieutenant Thorn gave her a surprised look as she flopped down next to him on the crest and asked, "Found the enemy yet, sir?"

Thorn put his eyes back to his binoculars and remarked sourly, "No thanks to you, yes." He went on, "Looks like two rows of trenches. Standard stuff." He handed her the binoculars, "Here, take a look."

Putting the binoculars to her eyes, Sophia scanned the enemy position. The smoke from earlier had begun to clear, and after the near-invisible spider holes and bunkers they'd been dealing with it was almost a relief to see actual trenches scrawled across the landscape. She could make out a patchy line of earthworks near the base of the shallow slope they were looking down and a second, clearer line farther into the valley as the slope flattened and rose again into a low, forested line of hills. The trenches snaked over rising ground to both of their flanks, creating a shallow valley to their front the Imperials could easily saturate with fire. Another ridge, a spur sweeping to the east of the main bulk of Fire Ridge as it tumbled towards the Marchlands, rose a ways over the trees. Looking closer, Sophia saw sheaves of barbed wire jutted menacingly from the cleared fields in front of and between the trench lines, and as she looked at the entanglements something gnawed in the back of her head for a moment.

She looked over at Thorn, already asking for a first round on his field telephone. He finished up and she handed him the binoculars back. As he took them she said, "Sir, I don't see any communications trenches."

He took the binoculars back from her and took a quick look, then turned back to her and said, surprised, "You're right. I don't know how I could have missed that... they must be covered or something."

A shell hissed in and exploded some ways down the slope. Sophia asked, "Sir, was that yours?"

Thorn grunted, "No. That was Imperial." He thought for a moment, "But... we might have just been bracketed." He gave her a worried look, "You all might want to start digging, *now*."

Sophia chuckled and shouted for the squad to come up and start digging in. When a ragged volley of Imperial shells hissed down across the top of the ridge a few minutes later they had all sunk into shallow scrapes in the soft earth and the shrapnel seethed overhead harmlessly. Lieutenant Thorn got up out of the scrape they'd dug for him, barked some orders into his field telephone, and a couple minutes later the sky was splitting with Royal shells coming down well beyond the enemy lines, back into the second valley in front of them. Thorn had clearly worked out that the enemy batteries were firing from there.

She heard shouts from farther down the slope. Clearly not everyone had been as lucky as they had. Flipping over to her back, Sophia saw someone familiar being hoisted onto a stretcher. *Dad?* She thought, a spear of ice piercing her heart at the thought. It melted as she noticed him hurrying uphill towards them, bent low to throw himself on the ground again if he needed to. And if that wasn't her father being carted away downhill now, then who was it?

Sophia thought she knew when she saw the pained look on his face. Crouching down next to her, her father looked at Lieutenant Thorn, still fixated on his binoculars and the shells coming down on the far side of the ridge, and said gravely, "Sir."

Thorn pushed himself back and rolled over. His eyebrows rose in surprise on seeing her father, and he asked nervously, "What is it?"

"Caldwell... the commander's been hit. It's bad." The first sergeant gave Thorn an unreadable look, "Sir, it's your company."

Thorn grit his teeth and exhaled slowly. After a long pause he asked, "How bad?"

Her father shook his head, "Shrapnel through the chest. A *lot* of it. I've seen men survive worse, but..." He trailed off significantly.

"God damn it." Thorn swore, and went on, "*Now* of all times."

"Nothing we can do for it now, sir." He replied, "We've come this far. We have to keep going."

The lieutenant sighed and looked at the ground, "You're right." Looking back up, he asked, "When can we expect that ammunition to come up?" He waved in Sophia's general direction, "Your daughter's doing a great job, First Sergeant, but even she can't fight without ammo."

Her father smiled grimly, "It's already coming up with Delta. They should be here any minute." Suddenly seeming to realize her presence, he looked over at her an added, "You know how much you need, Sophie?"

Snapping out of her shock at hearing about the commander, Sophia swallowed hard and sputtered, "Ah, er... as much as they'll give us?"

Her father snorted and Thorn chuckled grimly. The lieutenant replied, "Sounds about right." Handing his binoculars to her, he said a few words into the field telephone, then slid down a little and got up, "Looks like you've got observation, Miss Rose. I've got a company to command."

Still a little dazed, Sophia asked, "Sir?"

Thorn gave her a half-smile, "Drop rounds on the enemy, Miss Rose. You know the calls." Her father got up to go with him and he finished, "Be seeing you."

And then they were gone and Sophia was left holding his binoculars with her whole squad looking at her. Clearing her throat awkwardly, she looked around and said, "Keep digging! One man down's enough!" They quickly got back to work, and she slid into Thorn's former spot next to the field telephone. Picking up the handset, she tried, "Vengeance Six, this is Charlie One-One, replacing Charlie One as observer."

Whoever was on the other end gave a low laugh, "This isn't Vengeance, missy. You're speaking to Tyrant Eight." He went on, "You sound pretty. I could get used to this."

Sophia felt her skin crawl a little as she replied, "You're not my type. When's your next round?"

"So cold." He gave her that creepy laugh again and went on, "Splash in... ten. One round, one thousand meters and about eighty-five degrees from you." Sophia looked up to see a flash and a huge fountain of dirt erupt from the second enemy line. A couple seconds later a distinct *thud* floated over the general hammering of artillery.

That round was *gigantic*. Who the hell was she talking to? She got back on the telephone, "Tyrant Eight, round on target. Be advised we're hitting a trench line running north to south. Fire for effect, over."

He came back, "Roger that, babe. Regiment, three volleys. Be advised we need to hold *something* back for the main attack." He went off the line for a couple minutes, then came back on, "Firing... now. Splash in sixty."

"Understood," She replied. About a minute later she heard a sound like a dozen freight trains plowing through the sky and the whole Imperial second line disappeared in a volcano of fire and earth. Sophia swallowed hard as the rounds kept raining down. Clearly Tyrant was nobody to be trifled with. As the smoke cleared, Sophia saw the enemy trench was still more-or-less intact and got back on the telephone, "Rounds on target, but we need more. Got any white phosphorus?"

Tyrant purred unpleasantly, like a tiger about to snap a deer's neck, "You're *my* type, Charlie One-One. Stand by for the good stuff. Two volleys."

And on they went, for the next hour as D Company came up with their ammunition and started digging in beside them. With Tyrant's help she was able to batter the Imperial defensive lines and shred the barbed wire strung throughout the position. After the other company's position started to take shape a couple of their officers took over from her and Sophia was able to go back to her squad. As she arrived she noticed a couple soldiers coming up with a much larger flag to replace hers on top of the ridge. Quickly making her way over and pulling her spear out of the ground, she got a good look at its replacement and realized they had come up with the regimental colors. Sophia smiled all the way back to her squad.

Lieutenant Thorn came back by eventually and filled her in on the current plan, straight from Major Clark. First and Third Battalions would push on the high ground to their flanks first and seize any enemy positions that could fire into the valley to their front. This would leave the Imperial position there isolated, and they would attack and break through. Once that was done Prince Adrian's regiment would pass through them and finally get their ride.

It sounded great, she supposed. One more push and they were done. Sophia felt a dull throb of doubt. Her father had told her all of his war stories he was proud of, and since she'd joined the Army a few of the ones that he wasn't. This was how it had been in the Marchlands. The Empire was on its last legs, he'd been told. Their regulars had been destroyed in the Salient and there was *nothing* behind them. One more attack and they'd collapse. After the fifth time it had started sounding hollow. Eventually the Empire had retreated across the Night River, but not before most of his friends were dead.

Looking at her ragged squad hastily digging their foxholes, Sophia sighed. She'd done a fine job so far of keeping her friends alive. She just hoped her luck would hold.

Lieutenant Thorn snapped her out of it, "...right, Miss Rose?" He sounded concerned.

She looked at him blankly for a moment before she realized he'd been asking if she was alright. Shaking her head slowly, she rubbed at her eyes with her fingers and replied, "I'm... okay." Dropping her hand, she looked up at him, "God, sir, I just realized I'd forgotten how many fights we've been in over the last couple days. I... I don't think we've got much left."

The new commander chuckled, "Your father said the same thing. He told me this was getting pretty bad." He leaned back on the slope and looked at the sky overhead meditatively as a couple Imperial rounds zinged over. By this point it was almost scenic. Thorn went on, "I saw that look you gave me earlier, Miss Rose. I don't think the Empire's done here either."

If Sophia hadn't been so tired she would have blushed. As it was she said, "Thanks, sir." She shook her head to clear out the cobwebs, "We'll manage." The lieutenant made to get up, but Sophia stopped him, "Sir, can you do me a favor?"

Thorn gave her as much of a smile as he could manage, "Depends,

Miss Rose."

"Can you... just call me Sophia?" She sighed, "You're so stiff with us all the time. It bothers me." She added, "Sir.'"

"I'll think about it." Thorn snorted, "I can hear Caldwell screaming from here." They both laughed and he went on as he got up to leave, "Well, I *am* the commander now. You take care of your men, Sophia. We've got... ten minutes to the attack."

"Yes, sir!" She chirped as he turned and left.

Tony remarked as soon as Thorn was out of earshot, imitating her, *"Just call me Sophia."*

She rolled her eyes, "I think we're there by now, Tony. No need to get *jealous*." He reddened a little and she looked around and went on, "Now keep digging! You heard the man, we need to be ready in ten."

The squad set to, and Sophia picked up her entrenching tool and joined them. A few minutes later their positions just behind the crest of the ridge were as complete as they were going to get, and Jack and Kelly were finishing up mounting their machine gun to its tripod. Jack tightened the last clamp and gave her a thumbs-up. Sophia looked over at Lieutenant Thorn, kneeling a little behind their company's line of positions on the ridge, and gave him a thumbs-up in turn. He nodded and flashed three fingers at her. Three minutes.

Sophia settled down to wait. The seconds crawled by as occasional Imperial rounds cracked by overhead. A couple enemy shells splashed down a little ways behind them, shrapnel pattering down harmlessly nearby. She looked at her watch. Two minutes. One minute. Thirty seconds. She shared significant glances with her friends on either side of her. Tony still looked pissed. Edward snickered and remarked, "You should give Tony a kiss, Sophie. I wouldn't want him to die angry."

She snorted, "Go to hell, Ed."

"You're still smiling." He winked at her, "Hey, Tony! You've got this, brother!"

Oh my God. Boys. Sophia thought. She was about to say something when she heard Lieutenant Thorn blowing his whistle over the shriek of shells ripping the sky overhead. Getting her hands under her, she remarked, "Kissing later, guys." Rolling up to a knee, Sophia shouldered her rifle and shouted, *"Open fire!"*

Her finger tightened on the trigger and her rifle bucked as the Imperial lines in front of them disappeared in clouds of earth and fire. Their machine gun hammered to life next to them as the sound of the bombardment washed overhead, an endless string of thunderclaps beating at their ears. They pounded away for maybe a minute, the artillery shredding at the valley and the hills to either side before the Imperials realized they were serious this time and bullets started cracking overhead. Shells started raining down on their ridgetop position, heavy ones that shook the earth and sent dirt raining down on them as they crouched there firing.

Sophia thought she heard screaming and shouting farther down the line. It sounded like D Company had been hit, not them. Laying back down to reload, Sophia rolled onto her back and jammed another clip into her rifle. Rolling back upright, she slammed the bolt closed and took aim at the smoking, flaming battlefield in front of her again. She was about to fire again when she noticed it and felt her hair stand on end.

Their artillery and mortars were tearing at the enemy's first and second lines. But between the walls of smoke and fire, where their artillery *wasn't* hitting, Sophia saw smoke starting to waft up out of the ground. It was almost as though the Empire had machine guns set up in those covered communications trenches strung between their lines, angled to fire to their flanks. She looked to either side, at the blue-jacketed soldiers starting to surge forward on the high ground beside them. They were barely more than dots in the distance, speckling the heights as they moved into the open. Perfect targets.

A couple Imperial shells smashed down just on the far side of the crest, sending volcanoes of dirt into the air as they ducked into cover. Jack and Kelly were up and firing again instantly as the dirt started raining back down. Brushing a particularly big clod off her back, Sophia pushed herself back from the rim of their foxhole and said, "Keep firing! I've got to go talk to the observers!"

Tony gave her a surprised look, "In this? It's dangerous!"

She looked back at him and shook her head, "I've got to! They're hitting the wrong area!" She jerked her head towards Jack and Kelly, as they fired off another long burst, "Get those two shooting into the area *between* the lines. Look for the smoke!"

He looked confused, "Why?"

"It's where the enemy is!" Pushing herself up, Sophia rolled out of their foxhole and was sprinting towards their observation post before Tony could say another word. She thought she heard him yelling to watch out.

A few terrifying seconds later she skidded into the observers' dugout and rolled inside. The two men inside looked over at her in surprise, and she quickly explained herself to the officer holding the binoculars, "Sir! You're hitting the wrong area!"

The lieutenant raised an eyebrow, "Oh?" He snorted and went on, "Then where should we be firing, missy?"

Sophia told him, "They've got..." She struggled for words for a moment. Explaining things clearly in the middle of a gun battle was *not* easy, "Ah, covered trenches between their lines. There's smoke coming out of the ground there if you look closely."

The man shrugged, "Makes sense. We haven't seen any of the bastards yet." He put his binoculars back to his eyes and searched for a moment before saying, "You're right, missy. I just saw muzzle blast." Looking over at his telephone operator, he said, "Have Tyrant drop three hundred and start firing a range spread. Maybe we can dig them out."

Sophia smiled with relief, "Thanks, sir."

"No problem." The man put his binoculars back to his face and said dismissively, "Got anything else, missy?"

"Nope," Sophia replied as she hauled herself out of the foxhole. Sprinting back towards her squad, she jumped back in between Tony and Edward just as another volley of enemy shells slapped down, sending shrapnel seething overhead. A jagged chunk the size of her fist bounced into their foxhole and dug a chunk out of the wall between her and Tony.

Her friend ducked instinctively, "God, this is getting bad!"

Sophia got her head and her rifle back up, "It's worse down there. Keep shooting!"

A string of shells crashed down between the Imperial lines, Tyrant's handiwork. Most of them hit dirt. A couple punched through the ground and for an instant Sophia saw the enemy's traverses fill with death, fire and smoke bursting from every firing slit as their camouflaged covering heaved. An instant later something *big* exploded out in the valley where the rounds had come down, earth and splinters rocketing into the air as a jagged roar filled the air over the hammering battle.

They ducked instinctively as Edward ventured, "Ammo dump?" Sophia could barely hear him over the ungodly hammering of the battle.

"Sounds like it!" She shouted.

She was about to tell them to get back up when she realized Tony was already there, shouting sarcastically, "Get up and fire, yeah, yeah!"

Sophia saw something bright in the corner of her eye as she got up and looked to see a blue flare burning over the high ground to their north.

First Battalion had a foothold in the trench system. They kept on firing, Tyrant steadily tearing apart the enemy's concealed positions, and a few minutes later another flare burned into the sky to their south as Third Battalion got into the trenches themselves. The Imperial fire cracking over their heads slackened off quickly as the battalions on their flanks started firing down into the valley from their new positions, and Sophia swallowed nervously as she realized what was coming up.

Sure enough, about a minute later white flares burned into the sky to their north and south. Supporting positions established. Time for Second Battalion to attack. A moment later Sophia faintly heard Lieutenant Thorn blowing his whistle to cease fire. She shouted, "*Cease fire! Cease fire!*" She thought for a moment and added, "*Fix bayonets!*"

Surprisingly Jack and Kelly actually heard them, and she saw them pull their machine gun off its tripod and quickly start making it ready for mobile use again as she drew her bayonet and locked it to her rifle, a little awkwardly given the barrel was too hot to touch. Sophia quickly patted herself down, making sure all of the ammunition pouches hanging across her load-bearing harness were still full, as though she hadn't checked exactly that an hour ago. They'd been fighting so far using clips from a pile of ammunition bandoliers in their foxhole courtesy of D Company and their ammunition resupply, and they hadn't had cause to even dip into their own ammo load yet.

Sophia, Tony and Edward were quickly hanging the remaining bandoliers across their chests when she heard Thorn blowing his whistle again. Long, repeated blasts. Looking over, Sophia saw him raising his arm. He held it there for a moment as he noticed her looking at him, and he smiled and nodded at her as he swung his hand forward for the attack.

"Come on!" Sophia hefted her rifle and scrambled out of her foxhole. Tony and Edward were a moment behind her, and she heard Hargrave shouting for Jeremy to hurry up as she sprinted forward. She got maybe twenty yards before she threw herself down in the field's cut-down stubble, rolled to put her rifle to her shoulder and fired as Imperial rounds started whipping down again. One kicked up dirt not far in front of her. She'd never felt so naked and exposed as she lay there in the full view of the enemy.

After a few much-too-long seconds Jack and Kelly ran past and flopped down a little ways in front of her with their machine gun. Jack lit off a long burst as Sophia climbed to her feet and rushed forward again. She wasn't sure how much good he was really doing. Tyrant, on the other hand, dropped a salvo square across the first line of enemy trenches as she was running and the enemy's fire immediately died off. They took advantage of the lull to push forward and quickly reached the first line of Imperial barbed wire a couple hundred meters out from the summit. Chopped to pieces from the bombardment earlier, they dove through it almost without stopping.

Rounds shrieked overhead, pounding into the enemy trenches before them. Sprint, dive, roll, fire, get up and do it again. And again, as Sophia covered the longest two hundred meters of her life in bound after agonizing bound. She felt like she was falling into a pool of fire and smoke, as the ground shook beneath her feet and the air filled with flying metal. By that point she wasn't sure if it was Imperial bullets or splinters from their guns.

The second belt of barbed wire was a mere hundred meters from the enemy trenches, wreathed in blinding smoke from the bombardment. High-pitched rifles barked out of the murk, bullets snapping by overhead as Sophia skidded into a shell crater hacked into the entanglement itself. She looked back for a moment from the scant cover and saw, miraculously, every one of her friends plow through the smoke and throw themselves down into the field of craters and churned earth.

They didn't need to cut the wire open. The ground was so torn up that Sophia could worm her way into and through the entanglement without too much trouble, half-feeling her way through the thorny hell of barbed wire as enemy rounds sliced overhead and their artillery crashed down, pattering them with earth with every round. Barbs clawed at her skin and tangled in her uniform a few times, but she was able to carefully untangle herself and keep pushing herself forward every time. The other riflemen followed her, Jack and Kelly firing long bursts back at every enemy gun that barked at them. All around her she could hear the rest of Charlie Company doing the same thing.

Sophia got out of the wire, slithered into a wet shell crater that nonetheless was perfect for keeping the bullets off, and rolled over to check on her troops. Tony was easy, he flopped in on top of her. Pushing him off, she noticed Edward throwing himself into a crater nearby and Jeremy hitting the ground off to the side. Mr. Hargrave was nowhere to be found. Heaving herself up a little, Sophia shouted, "Jeremy! Where's Hargrave!"

"What?" Jeremy shouted back.

God damn it, Sophia thought. Fortunately Tony and Edward were already up and firing as quickly as they could work their rifles' bolts, and Sophia was able to heave herself up and rush over to Jeremy's crater. Sliding in next to him, she shouted over the battle, "*Where is Hargrave?*"

Jeremy shouted back, "He got tangled up and I had to pull him out!

Then Kelly got hit and he went back to help him!"

She *had* heard someone call for a medic just a minute ago. Sophia's stomach congealed as she asked, "How bad?"

Jeremy shook his head, "Don't know! But he's got him, we need to keep going!"

They needed their machine gun for that, though. Sophia propped herself up on her elbows, barely enough to look back at the tangle of barbed wire they'd just come through. She didn't see anyone, Jack, Kelly or Hargrave. Feeling fear clutching at her heart, she shouted, "*Jack!* We need you over here! Where are you?"

In the middle of the unholy roar of the battle Sophia heard Jack's voice faintly, "In the middle of this *damn* wire with this *damn* gun! Give me a minute!"

She shared a glance with Jeremy, and then they both got up and started shooting. Another artillery salvo crashed down on the trenches nearby, terrifyingly close and skull-cracking loud. Finally, Sophia saw Jack crawl by out of the corner of her eye, disappear into a shell furrow, come back up machine-gun first and start firing.

The next volley of artillery rumbled overhead and thudded into the far trenches, another few hundred meters away. A seething storm of Royal bullets replaced the heavy shells overhead, and as the smoke cleared Sophia could see their fire chewing at the enemy earthworks like a great beast, the final line of barbed wire lying shredded and impotent before it. She supposed Lieutenant Thorn was probably blowing his whistle for the assault. She sure couldn't hear it as she rolled to her knees and screamed, "*Let's go!*"

They covered the last hundred meters in a few terrifying bounds, leapt what was left of the final strands of barbed wire and threw grenades, seemingly the whole company at once. Royal grenades rained into the enemy lines and filled every traverse with fire and shrapnel. Sophia leapt into the trench a second afterwards, her boots punching into something soft as she parried a bayonet thrust from a shape lunging from a dugout in the trench wall. She lunged forward and pinned her attacker to the trench wall with her bayonet as another masked soldier rounded the corner in front of her. Yanking her bayonet free, Sophia was flexing her knees to lunge at him when Tony put his rifle over her shoulder and fired. The muzzle blast beat at her face as the man toppled backwards.

The trench quickly filled with Royal soldiers. There were some gunshots and screams up and down the line, then a silence broken only by the occasional crack of Imperial rounds over the trench. They sounded different, and a lot louder, than in the open. It was a little eerie. Sophia noticed a blue flare burning overhead and hoped that Lieutenant Thorn had survived to fire it. Jack skidded in after a moment and Sophia took advantage of the lull to ask him, "How's Kelly?"

Jack, looking a little white, shook his head, "He got hit in the shoulder. Hargrave... told me to take the gun and keep going." He went on, "He was working on him when I left."

Sophia grit her teeth and took a long, deep breath. Finally she looked at Jack. It was more of a glare than the sympathetic look she was going for, and he looked a little taken aback as she managed, "We need to keep going." She added with a certainty she didn't feel, "He'll be fine. Kelly's tough."

Jack nodded slowly, "Yeah... yeah, he'll be fine. Let's go."

If Sophia remembered correctly the entrance to one of the covered enemy trenches was close to where they had gone in. Thorn had been very clear about this when he'd briefed them the plan. Once they got into the trench network they would *stay* in it. Better to claw their way forward with bayonets and grenades in the trenches than get machine-gunned fighting in the open. They'd save *that* for the regulars.

She heard Sergeant Cross shouting from further up ahead, and Sophia headed that way with her squad in tow, pushing their way past Charlie Company soldiers still getting their bearings. After going around a few corners she found him standing by a very dark hole in the side of the trench towards the enemy's second line. It looked like another branch of entrenchments that had been roofed over and camouflaged. It was exactly what they were looking for. Lieutenant Thorn and her father were standing on the far side of the opening, having what passed for a quiet discussion amid the clattering gunfire and popping bullets.

Her father brightened at seeing her, "Sophia! Good to see you!"

Despite everything she smiled, "You too, Dad." Opening her rifle's action, she started topping off the magazine with some loose rounds she had in a pocket as she added, "Kelly's hit and Hargrave's taking care of him. Have you seen them?"

Her father grimaced, "Yeah. I pointed Hargrave towards the medics. Kelly looked... bad, but he was walking."

Sophia sighed with something like relief, "I'll take that." Finishing with her rifle's magazine, she pushed the bolt forward and gestured at the dark opening, "Want to come with, Dad?"

Her father chuckled maliciously. It was a sound she'd never heard him make before in her life, and it made her skin crawl. Sophia had always known, in the back of her head, that her father had killed a *lot* of people. Looking into his icy eyes it really sank in. Although, looking at her bloody bayonet, she was far from an innocent girl herself by now.

Hefting his bayoneted rifle, her father purred, "I thought you'd never ask, Sophie." He gave her a hard-eyed look, "Are your guys ready?"

Sophia looked behind her. Tony, Edward and Jeremy were all finishing topping off their rifles, and Jack was tucking his pistol back into its holster. She supposed he'd just racked a round into it. It was strange, actually, that this was the first time she'd ever seen him with it out. That machine gun of his wasn't the best weapon for what they were about to go into although, she thought, they could probably find a use for it.

Sophia gave her father a steely look of her own, "Yeah. We're ready."

"Alright," he replied, "You all follow *me*."

Sophia's father turned and vanished into the darkness like a hunting panther. Sophia took a deep breath, steadied her hands on her rifle and plunged in after him.

Chapter 37

The Last Trench

June Anjanou stared at the flag flying atop Fire Ridge and gritted his teeth. At this distance all he could see was a tiny white speck and the glint of a spearhead just above it in the morning sunlight, but it told him enough to make his blood boil. The Royal Army was, *somehow*, on top of Fire Ridge. The defensive lines on the forward slope should have held them up for weeks and they had smashed through in *three days*. As June stared the Royal smokescreen from the valley below billowed higher and slowly blotted it from view.

"I bet they feel special." Sergeant Khan remarked sourly.

June looked over at his platoon sergeant lying next to him on the crest of the hill, "I bet they do." He chuckled bitterly, "I would in their shoes."

She grunted, "Looks like we'll have to dash their hopes then."

"Speaking of," June rolled over and looked downhill at where Anastasia Lai was crouching with their field telephone, "Anastasia, get me the company."

The girl cranked the telephone, spoke a few words into it, nodded and handed the handset to him, "They're on, sir."

June rolled back onto his belly and raised his binoculars as he brought the handset up to his head. The smoke had started to clear, and with the magnification he could barely make out the crossed rifles on the flag flapping in the wind coming off the mountain. More concerning, there were an awful lot of blue-jacketed figures popping up and down around it on the crest of the hill. Collecting his thoughts, June spoke into the handset, "Six, this is one-six. A Royal infantry guidon just went up on top of Fire Ridge immediately west of my position." He went on, "From the gunfire we've been hearing it looks like they own about a kilometer of the ridgeline."

There was no reply. June was about to repeat himself when Captain Marsten's voice buzzed out of the handset, "Are you sure, one-six?"

"It's white and they don't seem to be surrendering, six." June went on, "I've seen Royal troops skylined all up and down the ridge from here. They look like they're digging in." He went on, "Estimate at least a hundred on the crest itself. No idea about what's behind it."

His commander chuckled over the line and asked, "What do you think their intentions are?"

June replied, "They've come this far and it's still morning. I think they're setting up a support by fire position to keep up the attack." He concluded, "They wouldn't be digging in on the crest if they wanted to defend anything."

Marsten sighed, "I think you're right, one-six. I'll pass it up." He went on, "This meets conditions. The division reserve is probably going to move through your position to counterattack. Be ready to orient them if it comes to that."

"Acknowledged," June said, then added, "Is the regiment going to support them?"

"Maybe. It's above my pay grade. Makes sense, though." His commander finished, "I'll keep you up to speed. Make sure your platoon is ready for action. Six out."

Setting down the handset, June looked over at Sergeant Khan, "They're going to send infantry up to counterattack. Probably. We might have to get involved ourselves."

Khan's mask shifted a little on her face as she raised an eyebrow, "Involved *how*, sir?"

"I think they're going to mass the regiment here and support the counterattack." June said, "The Kingdom isn't anywhere near breaking through anywhere else." He looked back to Anastasia and went on, "Can you get me Bronze? We need some fire on that ridge."

"Yes, sir." The girl quickly rearranged the connections on the field telephone and cranked it before looking back to him, "Should be good now, sir."

"Bronze Control, this is Aegis one-six," June started, "I've got a fire mission for you."

"One-six, Control. Send it." The woman on the other side of the line sounded dead tired.

"Roger. I've got an infantry company digging in on top of Fire Ridge." June rattled off the coordinates.

Bronze Control sighed audibly and asked, "Need an adjustment?"

June thought for a moment before replying, "Yeah."

"Roger, wait a few here." Control went on, "Hopefully we've got a battery that can still shoot this."

June chuckled, "Bad last few days, Control?"

That got a tired laugh out of her, "Tell me about it. Stand by." About a minute later June saw a flash downhill from him and the phone buzzed again, "Shot, one-six."

Quickly raising his binoculars, June scanned the ridgeline. After a too-long wait he thought he saw a faint plume of dust rising over the far side of the ridge. He spoke into the phone, "Control, this is one-six. Round was over the ridgeline. Drop two hundred."

"Drop two hundred, got it." A short while later the cannon flashed again and June saw dirt spray from the forward slope. Looking back at the ridge he noticed the dark figures had vanished from the skyline, and he snorted with frustration. These troops were smart and they *knew* they'd been bracketed. They were probably all huddled in whatever cover they could find by now.

Time to finish this, "Add one hundred and fire for effect, Control."

"Roger. Light battalion, three volleys. Seventy-two rounds. Wait one." Control dropped off the line for a few minutes, then came back, "Stand by... shot."

The battery in the valley in front of him erupted as June heard Imperial shells whistle overhead and for a few moments dirty black explosions and flying earth sprayed across the ridgeline. June hissed through his mask in annoyance. The light shells weren't very effective at the best of times. They'd need a *lot* more than that to stop this attack.

Picking up the phone, he was midway through asking Control for a repeated attack when something, a *lot* of things, screamed through the air overhead. An instant later the valley in front of him filled with fire and smoke, explosions hammering at his ears as he flattened himself in the long grass. A sputtering roar rose out of the boiling chaos for a moment and June lifted his head a little to see a fireball rising from the valley floor like an evil flower. His stomach sank as he realized it was square in the middle of the battery from earlier. Getting back on the phone, June changed tack, "Bronze, your battery west of me just got hit. I saw secondary explosions."

Control cursed on the line and came back, "Roger, wait one." She dropped off the line for a minute, then came back, "No can do on that repeat mission, one-six. We'd just be wasting ammo. Let me know if you see anything better."

June grit his teeth and replied, "Sure thing." Handing the phone back to Anastasia, he turned to Sergeant Khan and remarked, "Well, Bronze is out."

"Great. What next?" Khan shot back.

A huge fountain of earth erupted in the middle of the Imperial lines in front of them and a few seconds later the powerful thud of the heavy cannon's shell beat at their ears. June snorted and replied, "You just *had* to ask." June could feel Khan roll her eyes behind his back, but she said nothing and he went on, "At this rate we'll have to join in soon. Go make sure the platoon's ready to fight."

"They are, sir." Khan replied curtly.

June raised an eyebrow, "When was the last time you checked them *yourself*, Sergeant?"

The woman snorted, "That's what squad leaders are for, *sir*." By her tone, 'sir' actually meant 'idiot'.

"Most of whom are *replacements* at this point." June shot back, "Or are you expecting *me* to teach them their jobs?"

Khan gave him a long, hard look. He glared back. Finally, she shook her head and said, "Fine. Suit yourself." Sliding back down from the crest of the hill, she stood and started heading back downhill to the rest of the platoon.

Hell of a relationship I'm building, June thought, scowling under his mask. Turning back to Anastasia, he said, "Give me the phone." She handed him the plastic handset and he added bitterly, "Might as well report on something while I'm up here." Noticing movement in the valley beneath him, June smiled a little as he saw what was left of the battery limbering up their guns to pull out of the position. It looked like they still had three of them.

The Royal Army didn't disappoint. Over the next hour hundreds of heavy shells rained onto their defensive lines and started methodically cutting a path through the barbed wire strung through the position. June didn't envy the soldiers on the front line sitting under that bombardment, the massive shells cratering the trenches into rubble and filling the air with shrapnel and flying earth. While the rounds crashed down he noticed someone pull down the Royal flag on top of the ridge, and his smile turned to a hiss of displeasure as it was immediately replaced by a much larger one. Probably the regimental colors. It wasn't a good sign for the Empire.

At least, he noted, they didn't seem to have clued into the concealed trenches running between the lines yet. No good defensive system had soldiers facing the enemy head-on, so to speak. In many cases bunkers wouldn't even be built to allow for fire to their own front. Instead they would fire to their sides, laying a devastating crossfire onto assaulting troops as they struggled through the wire obstacles. A position was thus defended by positions to its flanks. And in this case, if the Royals tried to seize the spurs coming off the ridge on either side of him they would be shot apart from the concealed trenches in the low ground to his front.

Finally, as June started to wonder if there was any end to the Royal Army's supply of shells he saw dark shapes pour over the ridge, Royal troops pressing forward down both of the spurs. For a minute the whole distant battlefield seemed as though it was caught in a storm, dirt spraying everywhere as bullets churned the afternoon air and volleys of shells built into a screaming barrage. And for that minute it seemed like their defensive plan was working. June saw Royal troops, ones and twos and then entire clumps of them, fall on the spurs. Many of them didn't get back up. Bronze opened up behind him and wreathed the attacking Royal troops with fire and shrapnel, and he *saw* the attack stall as they dove for cover.

June was picking up the phone to call Bronze Control back and drive them back over the ridge with shellfire when another volley of those massive shells strung itself between the first and second trenches with a crunching roar. More shells rumbled overhead and crunched down behind him. They sounded awfully close to where their guns had been firing earlier. The Imperial shellfire immediately slackened off, just a few shells slapping down on the spurs as the dark shapes started pressing forward again.

June held out his hand and Anastasia slid the telephone handset into it. He heard her crank the set as he held the handset to his ear and asked grimly, "Bronze, this is Aegis One-Six. What's your status?"

Control came back on. Her voice was flat and unreadable, "We're displacing. This whole area's getting shot to hell." As though to prove her point another volley of big Royal shells thundered overhead, "Give us... twenty, maybe thirty minutes."

The little dark shapes in the distance were crawling through the masses of shredded wire in front of the Imperial trenches. As June watched a blue flare burned into the sky on the spur to his left, and another string of massive shells crashed into the lateral trenches in the valley. June snarled back into the handset as the blasts washed over him, "Bronze, they are *in the trenches*. We need fire *now*."

"We're no good *dead*, one-six." Control sighed over the net, "Sorry. We'll be up for the counterattack. See you later."

The line went dead and June cursed. Giving Anastasia a glare she didn't deserve, he ordered, "Get me the company." The girl obediently switched some connections around and cranked the phone, and a moment later June spoke into the handset, "Six, this is one-six. There are

Royal troops getting into the first trench line and Bronze just decided to pack up and move."

June heard a shell come down close on the other end of the line, and the telephone operator indistinctly shouting for Captain Marsten. A few moments and a muffled exchange later his commander came on the line, "Understand all, one-six. We'll have to deal with it."

June asked, "What's the status on the counterattack?"

Marsten's voice buzzed over the line, "Three-Twelve Infantry is en route. Callsign is Fang." The 3rd Battalion, 12th Infantry Regiment, June thought. The name was vaguely familiar, "They should be at your position in thirty minutes."

June replied, "Understood. What about the regiment?"

He heard Marsten's smile as the man replied, "They're coming too, with some more artillery. Should be an hour at least." He went on, "The boss wanted me to tell you to keep up the good work."

"Thanks," June went on, "Tell her to hurry. We're going to need all the help we can get."

"Sure thing, one-six." Marsten finished, "Keep reporting. Six out."

June handed the phone back to Anastasia and said, "Looks like we're in for a fight."

The girl crawled up next to him and was looking over to say something when a light caught both of their eyes. They turned back to the battlefield to see another blue flare rising to their right as Royal soldiers leapt down into the first line of trenches on the spur. A few moments later June saw Royal machine guns blazing away from the captured positions, shredding into the Imperial trenches in the valley. White flares rose from both spurs and a wave of dark-jacketed infantry surged over Fire Ridge and into the valley. Sunlight gleamed off bayonets as they charged, leapt into the cover of the cratered ground, popped up and rushed forward again and again.

The Royal wave was unstoppable. In a couple minutes they had slithered through the barbed wire and June could see grenades raining into the first trench line. The first Royal soldier followed bayonet-first and a few moments later the wave of Royal troops poured into the trench and vanished, a blue flare rising overhead to mark their victory.

June scowled beneath his mask and turned to Anastasia, "Call up Six and tell him the Kingdom just took the first trenchline." Pushing himself back downhill he stood, a little unsteady after the hours he had spent motionless on the observation post.

Anastasia asked, a note of worry in her voice, "And you, sir?"

June grunted and patted his sword reflexively, "I'm going to go check on the platoon. At this rate we're going to be fighting soon. Not to mention we need to walk the infantry in." Raising an eyebrow, he looked at her and went on, "Are you going to be alright, Miss Lai?"

Her mask's jaw piece moved a little in what June recognized as a smile, "Yes, sir. I'll keep the commander up to speed." She gave him a thumbs-up and turned back to the battlefield, her own binoculars raised to her eyes.

"Thanks, Lai." June started heading downhill towards the rest of his platoon. Now, if only the rest of his subordinates were as cooperative as Anastasia Lai. They had enough of a battle on their hands with the Royal Army already.

Chapter 38

The Reaper's Scythe

Arilin looked out the window pensively as the gray, rain-soaked countryside sped by. Water beaded on the glass and flowed down, leaving clear streaks in its wake. The hiss of the train's wheels and the creak of the heavy steel carriage drowned out the distant thunder of the guns, but she felt like she could still hear them at the edge of her consciousness. It was like a sharp gray rock lodged deep in her chest.

"Milady!" Arilin glanced over to see her escort looking at her worriedly. The girl was well-meaning, but she was clearly very nervous dealing with a member of the Royal Family. She stammered on, "A-Are you alright?"

The princess sighed and pinched the bridge of her nose like she'd seen Patricia do so many times. It just felt uncomfortable. Maybe when she finished growing up it would be relaxing. Finally she replied, "Yes, yes, I'm fine."

In truth she *really* wasn't, but Arilin wasn't about to give her escort a heart attack. She couldn't stop thinking about how her saber had just *stuck* in that dragoon's chest. It was as though it had been set in cement. And the man hadn't even seemed that inconvenienced by it. That wasn't supposed to happen. She had thought that the instant someone was stabbed they would fall over and die instantly. Although, thinking about it logically that made absolutely no sense. People were *shot* all the time and recovered. A sword wound wouldn't be that much different. Arilin shivered at the thought.

Her escort noticed and ventured, "Are you cold, milady?"

No, she wasn't, but it was an opportunity to get the girl out of her hair for a moment. Smiling a little, Arilin replied, "Yes, a little. I'm sorry... with everything that's happened I didn't even notice."

"I don't blame you, milady, I'll go fetch a blanket for you." Her escort rose and quickly left.

"Get one for yourself!" Arilin called after the girl. She wasn't sure if she heard her. Sighing, the princess went back to looking out the window at the forests and wet farmland speeding past. The carriage lurched a little as the train started climbing, the distant roar of the locomotive growing a bit as the engineer increased power. It honestly looked pretty bad out there, unseasonably cold rain sheeting down on what should have been a warm summer day as they climbed into the foothills of the Dragonspine Mountains.

Arilin's thoughts drifted to her brother, out there on the front lines with his cuirassiers. Just like Lieutenant Bettancourt and his men. Her stomach clenched at the thought of the outnumbered cavalrymen charging into certain death for her sake. The whole fight hadn't even taken very long. Maybe a couple of minutes? All those men dead. For the princess. For her. Christ, she felt guilty. That could have been Adrian just as easily. He would have done it for her. And he and his men could end up dying just as easily. Bullets didn't care about royalty. Neither did swords, not really. God, she could have ended up with a sword through *her* chest just as easily. And a blow from one of those Imperial swords would have cut her clean in two.

"Milady?" Her escort had come back in. She hadn't noticed. The girl unfolded a blanket and gently tucked it around her shoulders. Finishing, the lieutenant pulled back a little and went on, "Milady, you're *clearly* not all right." Sitting down next to her, she reached under the blanket to take her hand and said, "You can let it out, you know... God, *I'm* scared to death right now."

"I... don't think I should," Arilin replied, "I'd start crying."

The lieutenant gave her hand a reassuring squeeze, "Just us girls in here, milady." She winked, "I won't tell on you."

With a whimper, Arilin buried her face in the girl's chest and cried. She had *no* idea how the soldiers around her kept it together as well as they did. After a while her eyes dried and she raised her head, feeling her cheeks redden with embarrassment. The lieutenant laughed kindly, produced a handkerchief and gently wiped her eyes and running nose for her. Arilin realized she'd misjudged the girl. She hadn't been nervous because she was a princess, she'd been nervous because Arilin had been so obviously about to break down on her. For the first time Arilin bothered to read her name tag. Remarque.

The rest of the journey passed uneventfully, and Arilin and Lieutenant Remarque disembarked a little more than an hour later at the little town of Sharp's Mill. Getting off at the station, they were quickly spotted by a Royal Navy officer who seemed quite out of place on the platform crawling with soldiers. Arilin smiled as he approached and bowed, and she started, "Steiner! What brings you out here?"

Commander Steiner chuckled and replied, "There's not much use for a sailor around headquarters right now, milady. General Reinhardt figured I could best be spared to get you." He gestured at a car idling by the station steps, "I hope it suits you. I've never been much for horses, and I figured you've probably had enough riding for one day."

Arilin laughed a little as they walked down and climbed in, "You guessed right, sir." She settled into the upholstery and their driver put the car in gear and pulled out a moment later, bouncing across the town's cobblestone streets. After a couple minutes the buildings thinned out and the road turned to muddy dirt as they sped off into the forest to the south. Leaning forward to speak to the commander, Arilin asked, "Where are we going?"

The man turned to reply, "There's an estate a little way south of town we're using. The residents cleared out a few days ago and we've had the place to ourselves ever since." He added, "Apparently it's owned by some colonel in V Corps." He chuckled, "Actually, he had a daughter about your age. Everyone's been too embarrassed to use her room, so you should have it to yourself."

Arilin brightened, "I like that."

They pulled off the main road, drove for a few minutes through the forest, came around a final bend and the estate emerged before them. A modest manor house stood at the top of a long lawn, ragged-looking from grazing horses, with what looked like stables and a carriage-house behind. The car ground its way around the long gravel drive and dropped them off in front of the manor house at the foot of a spreading porch. The commander handed Arilin out and they climbed the steps and walked in.

General Reinhardt had clearly been told of their arrival, and he walked into the entryway as they came in. He looked haggard and his narrow features were shadowed with stubble, but he brightened and smiled as he saw the two girls. "Milady! Good to see you," He greeted them, "You too, lieutenant."

"You as well, sir." Arilin replied. She offered him her bag of dispatches, "I've got these for you, straight from General MacMahon."

Siegfried took them from her and hefted the bag critically. Chuckling, he said, "Well, she's getting better at this. I was expecting one page of stick figures." He sniffed at it and added sarcastically, "Doesn't *smell* like crayons. I guess we'll see when we open it up."

Arilin burst out laughing, and the lieutenant joined her a moment later as she realized the general had been making a joke. When she calmed down a little the princess managed to ask, "How're things going? They can't be *that* bad if you've still got jokes."

Siegfried gravened quickly, "They really are, milady, but you have to keep it together somehow." He gave Lieutenant Remarque a look, "But before that, Maria, the communications chief is expecting you urgently. They're set up at the end of the hall on the right."

"Thank you, sir." The lieutenant turned to give her a warm look, "Milady."

"Thank you, Maria." Arilin replied and the girl turned, stepped by Siegfried and vanished into the house. Turning back to the general she went on, "So, about the war?"

"Come with me, milady," Siegfried turned and led her back into the house. They walked through what had been a plush waiting room before soldiers had spent months sleeping there and down a hallway. They paused at an archway cut into the hall's left side and looked down onto a large parlor, now converted to a command center. At the center of the room was a huge map of the area west of the Moon River, with Fire Ridge jutting to the north prominently. Even where she stood Arilin could see the friendly and enemy unit markers, and it didn't look pretty.

They descended into the room and Siegfried took her up to the map. A captain quickly finished putting a new unit marker on the map and stepped away to give them some room as they approached. Siegfried pointed at an area thirty or so kilometers west of the ridge itself, tucked up to into the folds of the Dragonspine foothills. She faintly made out the small dark block of Sharp's Mill on the map as he said, "We're here, milady." He pointed at the symbols for the three divisions of IX Corps, now an arrowhead pointing north, 30th Division some thirty kilometers directly north of them, the 15th Division ten kilometers farther south and to the west and the 19th forming the other prong on the arrowhead to the east. Siegfried pointed to the symbols of their cavalry regiments, still a good thirty kilometers north of the 30th Division, "Patricia's pulling her troops back as fast as she can, but it's looking dicey for them. They're getting hit hard, and by this time tomorrow the 30th will be in it with them."

The map north of the cavalry regiments was bleeding with red Imperial Army symbols. Arilin looked to the east on the map and instantly saw how bad things were. The 30th Division had deployed on line with VI Corps, sketched out on the map as most of the way up the ridge, its divisions still attacking on line to the east. There was a forty-kilometer gap, the better part of two days' march between the 30th Division's infantry marching north to meet the onrushing Imperial horde and the soldiers of VI Corps locked in combat a mile up on the ridge. Arilin did the math in her head and realized VI Corps was almost inevitably going to be encircled. And if their cavalry had already identified two enemy corps spearheading the attack, God only knew how many more were behind them.

North of VI Corps, as the ridge petered out on its long sweep down towards the northern sea the Army of Drakenburg was hanging in thin air. VII Corps had already pushed past the crest of the northern ridge and the rest of the army's main force was arrayed even farther to the north and east, a full seven corps starting to swing south in an irresistible phalanx to trap the Imperial defenders fixed high on Fire Ridge. It was a textbook maneuver, executed by Field Marshal White with parade-field efficiency. And he and the better part of a million Royal soldiers were completely surrounded, attacking in the wrong direction and hadn't realized it yet. Arilin pointed at the Imperial field army north of the 30th Division and said, more calmly than she felt, "Sir, how did *this* happen?"

Siegfried rubbed the back of his neck tiredly, "Milady, as near as we can tell right now the Empire's been planning this battle since they crossed the ridge in May." He went on, "I think they did two things. First, milady, how many Imperial troops do you think actually advanced past the ridge and were eventually stopped at Grenville?"

Arilin raised an eyebrow, "At the time we thought several corps' worth. I'm assuming we were mistaken?"

The general grunted, "It probably wasn't more than two. Army intelligence, White's people, did an assessment of what they supposed to be the maximum number of Imperial troops that could be sustained that far forward in the Kingdom and *assumed* that was what we were facing." He went on, "We supposedly met them with close to an equal force dug in at Grenville and, having been stopped cold at the end of a stretched supply line with a lot more Royal troops on the way, they logically retreated."

Arilin cut in, "But if they only attacked with a couple corps past the ridge... of course they would have retreated immediately as soon as we stood and fought. They never planned to win at Grenville... they wanted to fight *here*. I think I see where you're going with this."

"Yes, milady," Siegfried said, pointing at the massive block of Imperial troops to their north, "And with their logistics freed from having to push troops that far west they could build up a *massive* force here. Our intelligence people are telling me we are probably outnumbered considerably." He grunted, "And that brings us to the second part of General Anjanou's plan."

The princess replied, "Go on."

"For maximum effect, he wanted to maneuver us into a position in which he could surround us. This would be *much* easier if we attacked on a narrow front." Siegfried pointed at the southern side of the map, close to the Dragonspine Mountains, "Which the Field Marshal, military genius that he is, obligingly did in his haste to get to grips with the supposedly fleeing enemy. There are four east-west railways in this part of the country, milady. The Empire badly damaged the northern two as they retreated. The southern ones, not so much. We *assumed* it was because they retreated to the south themselves."

Arilin snorted, "And we've come this whole way hugging the mountains to follow the railroads. The last thing he wanted, I suppose, would have been for us to attack on a broad front."

"Exactly, milady. There goes his encirclement battle. He probably had his troops massed well off the north side of the ridge, arrayed south with just a corps or so on the ridge itself." Siegfried chuckled, "White, of course, saw exactly what he was supposed to see. A fleeing enemy with a corps or two delaying us at Fire Ridge so they could defend in force at the Moon River to hold on to the Marchlands."

"And White marched right past the enemy's main force." Arilin said, feeling her head spinning a little, "God, why would the Empire fight for the Marchlands? It's not like there's a lot there. But destroy the whole Army of Drakenburg and..." She trailed off.

Siegfried finished the thought for her, "Milady, this time next year we'd be fighting them in the Capital." He added sadly, "As it stands we're going to lose half the army. Really, we should be retreating *now*. We're not going to last long with our backs to the mountains like this."

Arilin's eyes narrowed, "Why aren't we?" Her heart clenched in her chest and she went on, "Where... where is my brother right now?"

General Reinhardt grimly pointed at the 8th Infantry Division, proudly sitting on top of Fire Ridge, "Milady, last we heard from General Kunst is that V Corps is close to breakthrough on top of the ridge. Prince Adrian's regiment will be committed as soon as the infantry have cleared the way. Victory is at hand." He finished sarcastically.

The bottom dropped out of Arilin's world. For a couple seconds that felt like hours she felt like she was floating. No, she felt like she was falling. The harsh truth of reality came up from below and slammed into her like a sledgehammer as she fell back into her own body. Arilin felt her knees buckle and quickly grabbed the table to steady herself as she gasped.

There was a hand on her elbow. Siegfried was looking at her worriedly, "Are you alright, milady?"

Arilin swallowed hard and looked up him, "No, I'm... really not."

"I think it's best if you sit down, milady. You've had a rough day." Hand on her arm, Siegfried guided her out and into a small sitting room set off to the side of the parlor. A few staff officers who had been taking a break there jumped up as the general and the princess entered and quickly escaped behind him as he walked Arilin over to a fainting couch by the window and sat her down. A note of concern in his voice, he asked, "Milady, when did you eat last?"

"I had breakfast." Arilin replied, a little surprised, "I'm not really that hungry right now..."

Siegfried harrumphed, "Then you clearly need some rest. I'll have someone take you upstairs."

"Look, sir, I appreciate the offer, and I'll take you up on it, but please just answer me this." Arilin went on, "Surely you've gotten the word to General Kunst about what's happening. Why is he still attacking? My brother *needs* to get out of there. Those *soldiers* need to get out of there. They still can, if they go now!"

The general sighed heavily, "Milady, General Kunst has his orders from the Field Marshal and the enemy in front of him. And the Field Marshal has been extremely clear about his view of the situation." He pulled a folded sheet of paper from his pocket and held it up, "We contacted Army headquarters as soon as Patricia confirmed Imperial infantry were in their rear in force. By radio, because the wire was *somehow* out. I wonder who cut it. Anyways, we gave them our full plan of action." Siegfried went on, "Our friend White sent this back. We are hallucinating Imperials where there are none. Walter Haas was relieved of command four hours ago, and we received orders in no uncertain terms to proceed per our original plan of action and reinforce V Corps on the ridge."

Arilin remarked, "We don't seem to be doing that."

"Strictly speaking, milady, we're in mutiny right now." Siegfried chuckled sadly, "White's been screaming over the radio all morning for the other corps to disregard anything Walter's sent them lately and proceed per his orders. The people *behind* us are more in tune with Walter's view of the situation, and they're stopping movement to wait and see what develops. But Kunst's in a fight right now and, without any way to tell who's right, he's going to keep following his orders until he gets something official otherwise."

The princess narrowed her eyes, "What about my father? Has he been informed?" She almost spat, "Even the Field Marshal doesn't outrank *him*."

"He has received our message." Siegfried said, "Beyond that, milady, we haven't heard anything from the palace." He gave her a look, "I don't suppose he has any secret codes he shared with you, anything like that? We might be able to make more sense of what the Palace is sending back to us."

Arilin shook her head, "No, nothing like that."

The man grunted, "Well, it was a thought." A colonel appeared beside him in the doorway and the two had a short, hushed conversation. Finally, Siegfried nodded and the man disappeared back into the parlor. He turned back to the princess and said grimly, "We just lost wire contact with VI Corps."

"Enemy cavalry?" Arilin asked.

Siegfried nodded again, "Probably. And if there's dragoons there..."

She finished the thought, "They're going to keep heading south until they hit our troops or the mountains. It's not like there's a lot stopping them right now." She asked hopefully, "Ah... sir, can the 19th extend their line?"

"To keep open a line of retreat for V Corps?" Siegfried asked, "Of course, although they're not going to be able to hold out for long like that."

"They'll stop dragoons, though." Arilin replied, "And we need to get them out. With my brother." She grit her teeth, "If my father did in fact get that message, he'll do *something*."

"Faith in your father, milady?" Siegfried asked gently.

Arilin smiled a little, "Dad is the King for a reason. He'll come through." She added quietly, "He *has* to."

"For all our sakes, milady, I hope you're right. I'll have the 19th extend east and tell them to hold like hell." Siegfried smiled, "Now, milady, I have a war to fight and there's a very nice bed upstairs waiting for you."

Arilin said dubiously, "I'm not sure I can sleep right now with everything going on..."

Siegfried chuckled, "You're lying, but I'll have the doctor give you something anyways. Now, young lady, you are going to go upstairs, clean yourself up, take whatever the doctor gives you and get some rest. I need you hovering around bothering my staff right now like I need a hole in my head." He added sternly, "Those are orders, lady lieutenant."

Arilin sighed and bowed her head for a moment. Standing, she gave him the best smile she could manage and said, "Yes, sir. And... thanks."

Siegfried smiled, patted her on the shoulder, turned and strode back into the bustle of the command post. Arilin sighed and turned to go upstairs. It wasn't often, she supposed, that a soldier could help win a battle by getting some sleep.

Chapter 39

The Bloody Roses

The darkness quickly swallowed Sophia as she followed her father into the tunnel, a narrow slash in the ground roofed over with rough-cut boards and so thick with dust from the bombardment she could taste it. Sophia felt dirt sprinkling down over her head as shells crashed down overhead, the sound muted to a dull thudding that seemed to come out of the walls. Duckboards creaked underfoot as they padded through the traverse, the only light in the murk streaming in from a few firing slits high on the tunnel walls.

Sophia's eyes slowly adjusted to the darkness, to the point she could make out her father's shape a few steps ahead of her. He'd been moving quickly. She sped up to get close behind him again and caught up as he paused at a bend in the tunnel. The boards creaked behind her as her friends closed up on them. Crouching at the corner, her father reached behind himself and patted her on the leg. Sophia flipped off her rifle's safety, counted to two and rotated herself around the corner just as her father leaned out himself, two bayonets jutting into the darkness beyond.

For an instant all she saw was swirling darkness. Then something moved in the shadows, a long, thin shape narrowing in the murk down near the floor at the next bend, a black rifle against a black shoulder in a black trench with a black mask behind it, swinging up onto her chest. Her rifle's sights swam out of the darkness and lined up as Sophia's finger tightened on the trigger.

Flash and blast tore through the trench as time seemed to stand still, the enemy soldier at the end of the traverse transfixed for an instant, slumping aside as Sophia's round tore through his helmet. Another shape moved as the darkness slammed back down and another gunshot beat at her from below as her father fired, catching an Imperial coming around the corner. Sophia slammed her rifle's bolt home and fired again as the soldier staggered. There was a wet thud in the darkness as the soldier fell, her father shouting, "*Tony! Frag them!*"

Sophia felt her friend yank a grenade off the back of her harness, heard him crack the safety cap off and yank the igniter. A moment later he stepped outside of her and whipped it down at the end of the corridor. He grabbed her as he backpedaled, and Sophia had the presence of mind to grab her father by the back of his harness as Tony dragged them both back into cover. A moment later the grenade's blast slapped at them in the confined space, shrapnel showering off the far wall into them as the trench filled with smoke. Her father slapped her leg and disappeared into the fog down the traverse, and Sophia followed.

Sophia came up short and flattened herself against the wall as she heard the too-familiar pop of a safety cap coming off a grenade. A moment later she saw her father's shape blur in the smoke as he threw the bomb down the next traverse. An unfamiliar voice shrieked out of the murk a moment later, "*Grenade! Get back!*" She heard boots, lots of them on the duckboards ahead as the Imperials backpedaled. Someone fell with a crash and a high-pitched scream. Her father's hand gripped her shoulder hard, and without him speaking a word Sophia understood what they were going to do.

The grenade went off, filling the trench with fire and death for an instant. Sophia saw the two Imperial soldiers they had killed lying on the corner in the sudden flash of bloody light, mangled lumps in dark uniforms. The second one, the one her father had shot, stared at her out of the black pools beneath the eye-holes of her mask, head lolling to the side where she had fallen at a grotesque angle. Then her father lunged around the corner, a lithe predator in the tunnel. Sophia darted after him and left the dead woman behind.

They rushed down the traverse to the next corner and plunged through the grenade's stinking smoke. Her father pivoted into the turn, crouched and *charged*, Sophia an instant behind him as he ran over a dark shape that crunched over his boots and put his bayonet into an inky mass that separated from the wall in front of him. She rushed past him and saw shapes in the trench, leering masks recoiling from her in the dim light of a firing slit. Sophia brought her bayonet up and leapt at them.

Her bayonet caught the first Imperial in the throat and she wrenched it out and lunged past him, hammering him to the side with her shoulder as he gargled and died. Sophia dropped low and stabbed up, picking the next man in the tunnel up on her bayonet and driving him onto his comrades behind him. In an instant she pulled her bayonet free, lunged and spit the next Imperial through the neck as he staggered back. A shape fled through the darkness in front of her as her father's rifle barrel loomed out of the darkness beside her head. A gunshot painted the trench with fire and the shape pitched forward, dead.

There was a gunshot in the tunnel behind them, and Sophia and her father turned to see the rest of her squad emerging into the traverse. Tony took a step back and bumped into Jack and Edward as he saw the carnage. She could see the whites of his eyes even in the dim light as her father demanded, "What was that shot?"

Tony swallowed hard and replied after a moment, "There... there was one of them on the floor back there."

Sophia's father nodded, "Good. We left him for you. Now keep up." He gave her a look and jerked his chin at the bodies carpeting the trench, "*This* was their counterattack. If we hurry we'll catch them off guard."

Her father turned, and Sophia chanced a look at the ground before she followed him. There were seven or eight shapes sprawled there, shuddering and gargling as they died. She felt her head spin a little as she thought of how *fast* her father had been. How little of a chance they'd had against him. Against *them*. All the better. Sophia grit her teeth, turned and rushed after the man.

They hurried through the suddenly-quiet tunnels, the silence broken only by the pounding of their boots on the board floor and the shells beating through the earth around them. Here and there lucky shells had punched through the ceiling and clawed craters into the earth. More than once they had to squeeze their way past fallen roofing timbers, sunlight burning at their eyes as the full sound of the battle flooded in around them for a moment. Her father forbade them from putting their heads up to get their bearings, and they were soon safely back in the murk of the trenches.

After a couple minutes and what Sophia reckoned was three or four hundred meters of trench without running into a single Imperial, Sophia's father suddenly stopped in front of her and raised a hand for a halt, then gestured for them to get back against the wall. The four of them quickly pressed themselves against the rough boards as her father knelt and listened intently. Sophia heard it too after a moment. Automatic gunfire echoing down the tunnels, somehow close and muffled at the same time. A machine gun nest was up there somewhere firing at their comrades back in the first trench.

He slapped her leg as a signal to come along and swung himself out into the next traverse a moment later. She followed close behind as the hammering gunfire grew louder. Rounding another corner, they saw the tunnel branched ahead of them in the dim light. Voices floated faintly down the tunnel from up ahead. Sophia's ears were ringing to the point she couldn't make out words. Her father gestured for her to cover the right traverse while he checked the left-hand one, and she crept up on her father's left as he advanced. Reaching the branch, they rotated towards each other, their rifles crossing in the intersection of the tunnels as they covered their opposite sides. Sophia saw another blank traverse in the dim light, and her father scowled beside her as he found nothing on his end. At this point, however, it was obvious that the gunfire was coming from their left.

Sophia ventured, "I think there's a strongpoint on the left." She guessed it was firing at the rest of their company in the first trench, "Should we go in?"

Her father thought for a moment, "It's probably where the ones from earlier came from... but, no. We'll let the company mop it up." He went on, "Make sure your guys are watching our backs. And mark it before we move on."

"Sure," Sophia replied, fishing in a pouch for one of the wolf tails they had made earlier. It was simply a strip of white engineering ribbon with a piece of heavy-duty tape folded over itself on one end. Sophia pulled the tape apart and stuck it to a ceiling beam to hang down over right-hand branch. Friendlies went this way. Her father had told them one too many stories of Royal troops getting lost in trench-mazes during the March-lands War and they had not been keen to repeat the experience. Looking back at Edward's shape behind her, Sophia went on, "Ed, take rear. We might have Imperials coming up behind us from now on."

Edward nodded, "Sure thing."

They pushed forward around another few traverses and passed another branch that seemed to have half-collapsed earlier. Sophia recalled the huge explosion in the middle of the Imperial defenses earlier and realized they were passing close by it. Probably a mortar ammunition dump that had been hit and blown up. Knowing more-or-less where they were, Sophia smiled grimly and pressed after her father as the sound of machine-gun fire built in front of them, seemingly filtering in from all around through the firing slits.

They were huddling against another wall, which Sophia guessed was very close to the end of the tunnel when deep, booming gunfire echoed from behind them. Royal rifles, punctuated by the dull thuds of grenades exploding. Sophia's father snorted softly, "Looks like we missed out."

Sophia was about to reply when a wave of shells thundered down so close the wall buckled, punching her in the back and throwing her to the floor. She rolled to her knees with the rest of the group as dirt poured from the ceiling, spikes of pain from her kidneys shooting through her body. Tony groaned and clutched at his back. Looked like he'd gotten hit worse than she had. The shells kept pounding down around them as they huddled there, wall boards cracking around them gunshot-loud and the floor heaving like a ship in a storm. This was probably Tyrant's doing, she thought. Any second she expected one of their own shells to punch through the roof and kill them all.

After a couple too-long minutes the storm subsided and Sophia ventured, "Dad, I think we're close. *Real* close." She went on, "Do you have a signal? If we get out of here with *that* coming down we're dead."

Her father hefted a flare pistol and smiled, "Way ahead of you. Cover me while I launch this." He climbed up to the nearest firing slit before he paused and said, "When I fire this, they're going to *know* we're here. We'll need to rush the exit." He looked at her, "When we get out of the tunnel, Sophie, we'll need a team to hold the exit and we'll need an assault team to start clearing the trench."

She nodded at Tony and looked back at her father, "We'll go with you." She looked back at her friend, "Tony, grenade every dugout and branch trench we run past." She hefted her bayoneted rifle, "We'll take anyone in front."

Her father nodded, "Good. We'll start clearing to the left."

Tony nodded, "Got it, First Sergeant."

Jack hefted his machine gun and asked, "What about us?"

Sophia's father smiled grimly, "Hold in place and keep the tunnel exit open. I'll need you to direct reinforcements as they come out. First group out gets the right side. After that get your machine gun set up oriented east. We're *going* to get counterattacked." He snorted and added, "Don't spare your grenades. We brought them for a reason."

Jack grinned, "Will do, First Sergeant."

Popping the flare gun open, her father loaded a shell, held it to the firing slit angled as high as he could and pulled the trigger. Quickly loading another shell, he fired again and hopped down to their level. Hefting his bayoneted rifle, he looked at Sophia, "Ready?"

She snorted and felt one side of her mouth twist into a smile, "Yeah. Let's do this."

"Alright," Her father shouted, "*Follow me!*" In an instant he was gone, sprinting down the traverse. Sophia charged after him, feeling the wind catch at her hair as she rounded a turn, then almost ran over her father as she came around another bend and saw daylight spilling around the next corner, illuminating a wall of sandbags with a firing port cut out of them. Dark, jagged strands slashed across the front of the Imperial bunker, a barbed-wire mantrap laid in the middle of the trench to keep people and grenades out.

Sophia skidded to a halt and dove back into cover as machine-gun fire tore at the wall beside her. She was still climbing to her feet when she felt her father yank a grenade off the back of her harness and pitch it down the traverse. She heard her friends coming up short behind them and her father yelling something at Jack, and then the grenade went off. The blast beat at them in the narrow trench and Sophia felt shrapnel bouncing off the wall beside her and pocking into her body as her father helped himself to another one of her grenades, his solid form a shadow over her head as he threw it down the trench after the first.

She instinctively huddled against the near wall as the second grenade erupted, seemingly a bit farther away than the first. A moment later a dark form with the distinctive silhouette of a machine-gun threw himself down in the corridor, tucked the heavy weapon into his shoulder and fired. For a few long, *long* seconds the trench turned into a hell of fire and ricocheting brass as Jack put an entire belt of ammunition into the bunker's firing port. Sophia's father pulled her to her feet as the gun roared, and as the gun fell silent and the last shell glinted in the dim light they rounded the corner and charged.

The barbed wire was shredded by their grenades and they plunged through it without slowing down, Sophia barely noticing the sharp thorns tearing at her clothing. Her father dropped to a knee and skidded to a halt in front of the bunker, rifle spitting flame into the firing port. She heard someone scream inside as a shape loomed out of the light pouring in through the opening beside the bunker. Sophia pivoted, knocked the masked soldier's bayonet aside and stabbed him through the chest in one motion, hurling him back outside. Her bayonet came free and she lunged into daylight.

An Imperial rushed her immediately, leaping over his fallen comrade as his bayonet reached for her chest. Sophia quickly twisted and knocked his thrust aside with her rifle's butt. The man staggered past her and she heard him scream as her father skewered him. Sophia, half twisted-around, tried to bring her rifle back on line as a hulking Imperial seized her and slammed her against the trench wall. Stars dancing in front of her eyes, Sophia tangled his first knife-thrust up with her rifle. Roaring like a lion, steel mask inches from her face, he drew back for another brutal stab and suddenly went limp.

Her father pulled his bayonet out of the man's side and he crumpled at her feet. Looking at her, he shouted, "*Come on!*" Behind him she saw her friends piling out of the tunnel, Tony, Edward and a very pale-looking Jack. Turning, she rushed down the trench after her father. They rounded a corner, her father shooting a surprised Imperial halfway down the next traverse as a grenade went off behind her, Tony at work. She jumped the woman's body and plunged around the next corner, straight into an Imperial officer. Taken by surprise, his sword was down and she had her bayonet through his neck before he could bring it up.

Behind him, Sophia saw a group of Imperial soldiers quickly backpedaling around the next curve. High-pitched rifles barked in front of her and bullets tore at the trench walls, and Sophia threw herself backwards. Feeling a hand on her shoulder, she heard her father yell, "*On my signal, charge them!*"

Sophia was about to ask him what the signal was going to be when he leapt over the top of the trench and disappeared. For a few seconds she and Tony were alone, with bullets cracking into the boards of the far wall and grenades going off behind them. *Lots* of them. Maybe that *hadn't* been Tony earlier. And they didn't all sound like Royal grenades. She heard Jack's machine-gun light off as another volley of grenades shook the air behind them, and she felt her stomach twist as she realized Jack and Edward were fighting on their side.

Then a Royal grenade cracked in front of her and the shooting suddenly died. Sophia gave Tony a quick look before she threw herself out into the traverse, feeling him running hot on her heels. God, did he look scared, but his presence behind her was incredibly reassuring as she rounded the corner. Amid the carnage and scattered bodies an Imperial was climbing the firing step on the far side of the bay and swinging his rifle down at a target in the open behind the trench. Her father.

Sophia and Tony fired simultaneously and the man staggered and fell. A moment later her father leapt back into the trench, waving them up to cover the next traverse. As they hurried up Sophia remarked, "Dad, I thought you wanted us to stay *in* the trench."

Looking over her shoulder at his bloody handiwork, he grimaced and looked down at her, "There's always exceptions." Now that she had a good look at him, Sophia realized his blue uniform was several shades darker than when they had gone into the tunnel and his face and hair were matted with dark, thick liquid. She looked down at herself. Her jacket and pants were clammy against her skin and stained *black*. Her skin crawled like it wanted to jump off her body at the realization.

Jesus. They were both *covered in blood*. Like they'd taken a *bath* in it. Seeing the look on her face, her father snorted and clapped a hand on her shoulder, "I know, Sophie. War is... ugly." He jerked his head at the next traverse behind him, "Now you and Tony hold here. By the sound of things the company's through the tunnel, and I need to go direct traffic. I'll send those two over in a moment."

Her father's matter-of-fact orders brought Sophia back down to reality and she replied, "Will do." It sounded like her father had been right about the rest of the company. As he jogged off back the way they had come she heard dozens of heavy, booming rifle shots and Royal grenades working their way farther and farther away on the other side of the trench. A couple minutes later they heard footsteps behind them and Sophia turned to see Corporal Stennis leading his squad up behind them.

The wiry man stopped beside her and took a cautious peek around the curve in the trench, asking, "Enemy territory from here, Sophia?"

"Yeah," she replied, "All yours."

She expected the man to chuckle. He instead replied sadly, "It's a shame about Mulligan. Good man."

Sophia's eyes widened as she looked over at him, "What about Jack?"

He gave her an unreadable look, "He's... not looking good. Not when I passed him. The doc's working on him now." Stennis jerked his head back down the trench, "We've got it from here. It's best you go see him yourself."

Sophia replied, "Thanks. Come on, Tony." Without a look back they turned and ran back down the trench to the tunnel's exit, shouldering their way past Charlie Company soldiers now pouring into the trench. Over the parapet they could even see a few blue-jacketed soldiers popping up in the open as they raced to secure the trench. A couple high-pitched Imperial shots rang out as they made their way back, every one met with a chorus of booming Royal gunfire and a volley of grenades. It seemed the battle was almost over.

And Jack... hadn't made it. Sophia rounded the last bend in the trench to see a huddle of figures standing around a shape laid out on the trench's firing step. She recognized quickly recognized her father, clearly gritting his teeth as Edward bent over the shape's head, saying something she couldn't make out. The medic was drawing a blanket over the shape, tucking it in around its shoulders. Jack's shoulders. As Sophia rushed up she reached for the blanket, meaning to pull it back and get a look at his wounds. The medic laid a hand on her arm as she reached out and shook his head significantly, and Sophia drew her hand back.

"Jack. Jack!" Edward was saying, "Come on, man, stay with us!"

Jack's glazed eyes swung slowly from Edward to Sophia and he coughed weakly and mumbled something indistinct, a ribbon of frothy blood running down his cheek. Sophia quickly knelt and put her ear by his mouth. Jack gave a shallow, rattling breath and whispered, "Mom... it's da... dangerous..."

Sophia sat up suddenly, her eyes blurring. She tasted bile in the back of her throat. Her world spun. She wanted to scream, vomit and break down into a sobbing wreck, all at once. Jack, the jerk she'd known for years, who'd only joined the Army so girls would talk to him. Who'd treated his machine gun better than any girlfriend he'd ever had. Who'd been senior to her and had resented her endlessly for bossing him around after she'd been put over him. And he'd died mistaking her for his own *mother*, after eating what had sounded like four or five grenades following orders *she* had given him, using her *father's* plan.

Sophia looked back at her father through tear-streaked eyes. A little while ago it had really sunk in to her just *how many* people he'd killed. She realized then, looking at the unreadable expression on his face, that not all of those people had been his enemies. Too many of them had been friends he had failed or subordinates sent to die under his orders. God in heaven, it was an awful feeling.

Setting her rifle down, Sophia climbed to her feet unsteadily and wrapped her arms around her father. He patted her on the back gently and murmured, "I'm sorry, Sophie."

She buried her face in his shoulder and replied, "It was as much my fault as yours, Dad."

He snorted mirthlessly, "Blame the Empire. I always have." She stepped back a little and he gave her a stern look, "Now, Sophie, Jack was a good man but he's in the Lord's hands now. *We* still have a battle to win."

Sophia stepped back and wiped her eyes quickly, "I understand. What do you need us to do?"

Her father cast a sour look around, "Right now, just get your men ready and hang tight. I think we'll keep you three in reserve with the headquarters for a moment..." He continued, half to himself, "Now, where the *hell* is Thorn? Most of the damn company is already over here."

Sophia turned and picked up her rifle. As she stood the medic caught her eye, gave a very significant glance at Jack and shook his head. Sighing heavily, Sophia knelt next to her friend's lifeless body, closed his eyes and pulled the blanket over his face. Edward and Tony both gave her shocked looks and she grit her teeth as she glanced between them, "Look, there's nothing we can do for Jack right now. But we owe it to everyone *else* here to keep it together." She narrowed her eyes with a sternness she didn't feel, "Understand?"

Edward, a pained look on his face, only nodded. Tony spat, "Yeah. This attack *better* have been worth it." He glared at her, "We still don't know if Kelly made it either. I'm *done* with losing friends."

"We all are, Tony, but we still have a job to do." Sophia shot back. It came out harsher than she intended.

Tony snorted angrily, "Yeah, yeah." He looked at Edward, "Is the machine gun still working?"

"Yeah, I think so." Edward pointed off at a familiar shape laid out on the far side of the trench, "It's over there."

"Well, you've got it for now. Get it set up facing that way." Sophia said, pointing at the western side of the trench, "We're going to hold here until Dad or Lieutenant Thorn say otherwise." She noticed a familiar shape coming out of the tunnel, "Speaking of the..."

Sophia trailed off as she saw the huge man following Thorn out of the tunnel straighten up into the daylight, long blonde hair falling to his shoulders as he adjusted his helmet. Demon-red eyes swept across the trench and landed on her as Prince Adrian remarked, "Well, well. Miss Rose. Why am I not surprised to see you here?"

That probably explained why the commander had been taking his time. Sophia swallowed nervously and replied, "Good to see you, milord." It was strange. Now that she'd actually talked to him a couple times the absolute terror of speaking to a member of the Royal Family had worn off. Feeling a little bold, she ventured, "I hope we've met your expectations."

The prince chuckled, "Oh, you've exceeded them. I thought this would take all day." Stepping close to her, he reached out and ran a gloved finger down her shoulder. Sophia felt the blood-stained fabric press back into her skin and release cloyingly as he pulled his hand away. Inspecting his fingertip, Prince Adrian raised an eyebrow and went on, "And I can see you weren't joking about your bayonet skills. Well done."

"Ah... thanks, milord." Sophia replied.

Adrian gave her a nod and turned back to Lieutenant Thorn, saying, "Now, lieutenant, call in the smokescreen immediately. As soon as those rounds land I need your men," He snorted and corrected himself, "Ahem, people to clear the wire in front of this position. Major Clark already understands, he's taking care of the wire on the near side." The prince finished, "As soon as we have lanes clear, we ride. Understand?"

"Yes, milord," Thorn replied. Gesturing at a signalman who had followed them out, he took a field telephone from the man and started talking. Sophia heard him say 'Tyrant' a couple times during the conversation. The next couple minutes were a blur of activity as Thorn readied Second and Third Platoons to spring out of the trench and start clearing obstacles as soon as smoke rounds started falling, which meant he had to send her and Tony to go *find* Second Platoon and tell them the plan. Sophia had no sooner finished describing what was needed to Sergeant Brockman, who she recalled had been a squad leader in that platoon a couple days ago when smoke rounds started popping nearby. Looking over the trench parapet, Sophia saw smoke billowing out of the sparse trees crowning the next low rise to the west.

Brockman got his platoon in motion quickly and they returned to find Mr. Hargrave standing by Jack's body, hat in his hands. He turned as they approached and started, "Sophia! I... I'm sorry. I wish I could have been here." He went on, "Poor boy."

Sophia sighed and shook her head, patting Hargrave on the shoulder, "Not your fault, old man. How's Kelly?"

Hargrave smiled a little, "He'll make it, thank God. Took a couple rounds in the arm, but they went through clean." He went on, "I was able to get him to the medics pretty quickly after you all took the first trench. My Lord was he screaming. You would have thought it was blown clean off."

Sophia snorted grimly, "Good to hear." Climbing up on the firing step beside Edward, she chanced another look around. Their whole front to the west was a solid wall of thick smoke, stirring a little as the wind started to pick up. Every now and then she heard a pop as another smoke shell burst and fresh, white smoke billowed from another patch of the forest. A few small Imperial shells had also started to fall across the line, but they weren't close and Sophia didn't bother to pull her head back down.

Looking back, Sophia's felt her eyebrows rise at the sight playing out before her eyes. Out in the space between the trenches she saw the two platoons hard at work, barely fazed by the incoming shells as they cut the wire apart and pulled it aside to make two large breaches wide enough to drive wagons through. She spotted the familiar silhouettes of Lieutenant Thorn and Prince Adrian directing the work, the prince pacing back and forth in the breaches and even lending a hand as the soldiers pulled out a particularly stubborn wire picket.

Beyond them, up on the sunlit crest of Fire Ridge, two flags caught her eye. The white and gold Royal standard and the blue and gold of the 1st Cuirassier Guards Regiment, carried by horsemen on the very crest of the ridge. They paused for a moment before spurring their horses forward and down the slope. Behind them the rest of the regiment mounted the hill, a carpet of men, horses and steel studded with battle flags unfurling down the slope. Blue-jacketed infantrymen working on the wire sprang aside as they approached, flowed through the first set of breaches, jumped the first trench and cantered onwards to where Prince Adrian was walking out to meet them.

The Crown Prince met the color party in front of the second breach and leapt onto a horse they had brought out for him. She saw Lieutenant Thorn standing by the breach and saluting as Adrian wheeled his horse and led his regiment through. Adrian put spurs to his horse and galloped straight for them, and Sophia and Edward quickly scrambled off the parapet, Edward having the presence of mind to pull down the machine gun as the cuirassiers thundered towards them.

Why the hell not, Sophia thought, *Thorn did it*. Bringing her hand to her cap, Sophia saluted Prince Adrian as he leapt his horse over the trench. He couldn't have been more than ten feet away, and she could have sworn he gave her a look out of the corner of his eye and a nod before his horse landed with a clatter of hooves and he was gone. An instant later Sophia ducked as the rest of the regiment leapt the trench, a seemingly-endless wave of horsemen thundering directly overhead with a roar of hooves loud as an endless thunderclap.

After minutes that felt like hours, finally the last cuirassier leapt the trench and cantered into the west. Sophia cautiously stuck her head up to see the first wave of horsemen riding into the trees and the swiftly-dissipating smoke, the colors ducking beneath low branches. She saw Prince Adrian at the head of the regiment, cresting the rise and disappearing behind it with the tidal wave of horsemen behind him. A few seconds later Sophia heard high-pitched gunshots ring out and then, faintly, the bugle call for the charge. The regiment accelerated, spreading out on line as the gunfire crackled, and then they were gone over the rise. Sophia thought she could hear the regiment's battle cry in the wind, a thousand men screaming as they charged down the enemy.

The distant gunfire built to a staccato, popping roar over about a minute, then started dying off. It sounded mostly like rifles, although Sophia heard a few Imperial machine guns start cracking away before they died off just as quickly. After another minute it had died down to occasional, sporadic bursts drifting over the rise. Feeling her father at her shoulder, Sophia turned and asked, "What... what do you think's going on, Dad?"

He chuckled, "I think the Crown Prince just ran over the Imperial counterattack." He gave her an understanding look and went on, "Don't worry, dear. It takes a *lot* more than that to stop a cavalry charge."

She barely heard him. On the second, more distant rise, out past where Prince Adrian and his regiment were fighting, she saw a lone horseman on the ridge. The wind gusted and, though he was barely more than a dot at that distance, she saw long hair billowing out beside him. The late afternoon sun caught the dragoon's sword as he drew it, and it burned in the golden light as he raised it overhead.

The long-haired dragoon. *June Anjanou.*

Sophia's blood ran cold.

Chapter 40

The Black Knights

God in heaven, June thought, *this is bad.*

June had ridden out onto the infantry's approach route, spotted the green-jacketed soldiers marching south along the farm trails behind Fire Ridge and found their commander, a gruff colonel who had taken him at his word and ridden back to his observation post with him to plan out his approach. They had arrived to find Anastasia, Corporal Tarai, the rest of Second Squad and the machine gunners strung out along the ridgeline. They didn't look happy and he quickly found out why.

The second trenchline, the last Imperial trench between Fire Ridge and the Moon River, was swarming with Royal soldiers. The lateral trenches hadn't just been neutralized by the Royal artillery, they had given the enemy infantry a highway straight into the second line. Apparently they had poured out of the ground a couple minutes after he left. Who the hell *were* these people? They must have charged into the tunnels bayonet-first as soon as they had gained a foothold in the first line. The colonel had remarked that he wouldn't have expected that out of his own troops.

The infantry commander had quickly taken the lay of the battlefield and galloped off back to his troops as more shells popped over the thin forest on the near side of the second trench. June saw the tiny dark shapes of smoke grenades rain into the trees and soon the trenches vanished behind a billowing white wall. Five, ten, fifteen minutes passed as shadows moved through the veil of shifting smoke and the knot in June's stomach grew tighter and tighter.

Finally the infantry arrived, the approach columns fanning out on line as they reached the base of the slope and started the climb. June thought their masks looked a little grimmer than usual as they unslung rifles and hefted machine guns, the wave of soldiers coming on in deathly silence. He felt his heart lighten a little as the green-jacketed infantry poured through his position on top of the rise, the colonel, now on foot, giving him a nod as he walked past. The man gestured for his communications team to jack a wire into June's switchbox and was gone downhill just as quickly.

The infantry was about halfway to the trees, spreading out to attack the whole length of the Royal breach when June realized the shelling had stopped. For a minute the battlefield was silent as his stomach took the opportunity to start clawing at his insides again. June felt a sudden gust of wind pull at him, whipping his hair around as it rippled across the fields, shook the trees and stirred the thinning smokescreen. And then June saw it. Shadows in the churning mist. Phantoms that solidified into solid black shapes, bursting into clarity like ink slashed across a page.

Royal cavalry erupted from the forest, forming on line at the gallop as the infantry threw themselves down and opened fire. Somehow the horsemen *accelerated* into the storm of bullets, the afternoon light dancing over a sea of swords as they hurtled forward, every gap in their lines filled instantly even as machine guns screamed to life against them. June faintly heard the bugle sound the charge as a knot of horsemen galloped out of the trees, color bearers letting their flags fly. June recognized the white and gold of the Royal standard just as the first wave of the 1st Cuirassier Guards Regiment, Maximilian's Knights led by Prince Adrian himself, smashed into the infantry.

Cuirassiers plowed over footsoldiers like the half-ton, steel-tipped missiles they were, swords working like the jaws of a murderous beast. In an instant the infantry battalion was submerged in a tide of horsemen, cuirassiers wheeling about to charge back at those lucky few who hadn't been killed instantly by the first rush. June finished his thought and looked over at Corporal Tarai, who was staring slack-jawed at the massacre. "Corporal!" He said, breaking her out of her reverie. Her mask's jaw-piece snapped up as she shut her mouth hard and he went on, "Give me the phone! Local circuit!"

Anastasia quickly rearranged the connections and June half-shouted down the line, "This is one-six. I need one-seven, *now!*"

"One second..." June looked downhill at where the rest of his platoon had taken cover a couple hundred meters away. He could see the operator gesturing hurriedly to someone that looked like Sergeant Khan. The woman hurried over and came up on the line. June heard some bitterness in her voice, "Well, one-six, I checked and they're ready for combat. Got something?"

"Yeah." June went on, "I need everyone up here with me, *now.*" He glanced at the carnage playing out in front of him, cuirassiers now swarming and charging down the last few knots of resistance. The Royal Standard and the blue-and-gold regimental colors flew gloriously above the slaughter, and June felt a desperate idea tickle at the back of his mind. Swallowing hard, he went on, "With horses. Understand? *With horses.* I'll explain when you get here."

Something in his tone must have gotten through. Khan replied curtly, "Got it." Looking downhill, he saw her stand up from the phone and start gesturing. An instant later the rest of the platoon was in motion, troopers rushing to their horses.

"Sir..." June looked over to see Coproral Tarai. Worry shone in the eyes behind her mask, "What's your plan?" She gestured at the two machine-gunners behind her, already cocking their weapons, "We can engage with machine guns from *here*."

"And then what?" June asked, gesturing at the battlefield, "You saw how much good it did the infantry." He went on, "Fire doesn't stop charges. *Obstacles* do, and right now we have *nothing*."

Tarai's mask shifted slightly as she raised an eyebrow, "So we're running away, sir?"

June looked at her for a moment, then snorted with laughter. Getting himself under control quickly, he replied, "No, we're not *running away*." She drew back a little in confusion as June went on, "Give me a minute. I'll explain." He looked back at Anastasia, "Get me the commander." By the time June finished his short conversation with Captain Marsten, nodded and handed the phone back Tarai was staring at him wide-eyed. Poor Anastasia was shaking so badly she almost dropped the receiver.

Drumming hooves announced the rest of the platoon and June held up his hand, gesturing for the troopers to stop short and dismount. Sergeant Khan jumped down quickly and hurried up, saying, "Sir, what's going..." She trailed off as she got a look at the battlefield, "God-damn. Is that the Royal Standard?"

"Yes, it is," he replied. She gave him an unreadable look as he walked downhill a little and went on, "Everyone, gather around! We do *not* have a lot of time!"

His soldiers quickly gathered in front of him with their horses. Sergeant Marin handed him Lucky's reins and asked, "Sir, what are we doing?"

June jerked his thumb at the hillside behind him, "Our infantry just got run over by enemy cavalry. They're flying the Royal Standard. You know what that means." Prince Adrian's cuirassiers. The Royal Army's elite cavalry, the tip of the King's lance and the closest thing they could face on the modern battlefield to the knights of old. June saw eyes widen behind masks, soldiers stepping back reflexively at the thought. Feeling his hair starting to stand on end, he went on, "Right now they're scattered all over the valley riding down what's left of the infantry. If they reform and keep going they'll go straight through the rest of the regiment, the artillery and they'll have a free ride all the way to the river." June looked around his troops, his eyes narrowing as he pointed at the ground, "We have to stop them *here*, and we have to do it *now*."

Sergeant Khan gave him a skeptical look, "That's great sir, but we're a platoon against a *regiment* right now. I'm assuming you're getting to that?"

"Yes, thank you, sergeant." June replied sarcastically. He went on, "Right now our regiment is massing to counterattack. They *need* more time, and if they're going to win we need the enemy to be in *chaos*." Royal cuirassiers were hulking, armored men on big horses. Fighting them on horseback without some kind of an edge was suicide. June chuckled and smiled like a hunting panther, "We have an opportunity right now. *We're taking their colors*."

June saw his words sink in, saw his soldiers turning them over in their heads. A daring charge into the midst of the enemy, a desperate fight with their fiercest soldiers, probably with Prince Adrian himself. Seizing their battle flags, the sacred symbols of the regiment. Fighting for their lives as a thousand cuirassiers wheeled on them, screaming with rage. Finally Khan spoke, "Sir, this is suicide." She went on, "We should retreat. *Now*." She glared at him, "I'm not dying for-"

For your glory. June cut her off icily, "I intend to win this battle, sergeant." He looked around at his soldiers. Twenty masks looked back at him, the officer who had led them through hell and back, always in the middle of the hardest fighting. Waiting for his command. Khan must have sensed the mood. He saw her jaw drop as he ordered, "Now mount up!"

His dragoons quickly climbed into their saddles, June quickly tightening Lucky's girth strap before swinging himself up with an easy motion. The horse gave him a sour look over his shoulder and June patted his shoulder apologetically, saying, "Now there, boy, you'll be thanking me in a minute."

June felt a horse pull close alongside his and Khan's familiar voice cut in, muttering to keep out of the troopers' hearing, "Sir, if I die on this charge you'd *better* apologize to my husband."

He raised an eyebrow, "I wasn't aware you were married, sergeant."

The woman shifted her head so he couldn't see her roll her eyes under her mask, replying, "I have two kids, you *ass*."

June chuckled grimly, "I'll keep that in mind." Now that he thought about it he barely knew most of his soldiers. He had gotten his commission with the rest of his class on the parade field of the Imperial Army Academy the day after Raven Wing Fortress fell, had caught up with the 5th Dragoons shortly before they crossed the Moon River out of the Marchlands and had been fighting or riding ever since. There had simply been no time for small talk, least of all with his standoffish platoon sergeant. The only one of them he felt like he knew well at all was Anastasia, and that was because she handled his communications and was around constantly.

No matter. He would have to work on that later. They were willing to ride with him now, which was what was important. June glanced over his shoulder, saw they were all mounted and ordered, "Wedge formation, on me! Remember, we are *taking* their colors! Do *not* let yourselves get bogged down!"

"Yes, sir!" Voices chorused back, the dragoons nodding their understanding.

Turning back to his front, June took a deep breath and nudged Lucky forward, the battlefield unfolding before him as they crested the rise. The artillery-scarred trenches, the forest shrouded in the dying wisps of the smokescreen and the fields over which they would fight, now swarming with cuirassiers and spread with misshapen green lumps. Imperial infantry, their bodies hacked apart and twisted in death. June heard a few gunshots and saw a couple figures on foot running, all that was left of the battalion that had swept through a few minutes before. And in the middle of it all were the enemy's twin flags, the white standard of the Wehrherz monarchy and the blue and gold colors of the Cuirassier Guards. June made out a man on horseback right next to the twin flags. Prince Adrian towered a good head over the small knot of horsemen around him as he shouted and waved his sword, calling for his men to reform and press on.

June paused for a moment atop the hill as what felt like an electric charge crept through his body. He took a deep breath and ceremoniously reached for his sword, the braided silk of the hilt wrapping biting into his gloves as he popped the blade loose in its scabbard and drew it free. Raising the gleaming weapon overhead, he raised it overhead for a moment before slicing it down, kicking Lucky forward as he shouted, "On me! *Charge!*"

The horse flew downhill as though he had grown wings, an arrow loosed straight for Prince Adrian and the enemy's colors. June reined him in slightly as he heard his soldiers shouting voices recede behind him, and after a few hair-raising moments he heard their hoofbeats catch up. Kicking Lucky forward again, June looked for a way through as cuirassiers started to notice them and turned, swords flickering in the sunlight as men gestured and spurred their horses towards them. June could almost hear the shouted warnings as a group of riders angled in from the side to intercept them, probably a platoon just like his.

June twisted to shout over his shoulder, "Cut at their arms! Pass through and *keep going!*"

His troopers had spread out behind him, bare swords burning in the sunlight. One man, it looked like Sergeant Marin, had his pistol out instead. Someone sounding like him shouted back sarcastically, "We *understand*, sir!"

June snorted, turned back and locked eyes with the enemy's lead rider as the man cut across his path a hundred meters ahead, hauling his horse around to head straight at him as his platoon swung around a second behind. The big horse dug in, struggling to swing around under its rider's weight as Lucky, sensing his rider's wishes, dug in and accelerated even before June's kick landed. The cuirassier raised his sword as his horse lumbered forward, bringing it down as June flew at him. June dodged inside the clumsy blow and cut down, his sword biting steel and popping free an instant later.

Gunfire pounded behind him as June's slash brought his blood-streaked sword across his body. Lucky surged forward, hooves hammering as another cuirassier loomed in front of him. June saw the man's eyes widening with sudden fear as he slashed down at him. June dodged to his other side, cut back across his body and beat the man's blow aside with one of his own. He felt a tug on his blade as he finished and knew by the next cuirassier's wide-eyed horror that his aim had been dead on.

That man, a straggler from the main group, hauled on his reins and veered out of his path. June heard an angry shout and a crash behind him and then they were clear. Twisting in the saddle to look behind himself, June counted his troopers quickly. The formation looked a little smaller. Maybe he was missing one or two? The cuirassiers milled in confusion as they receded behind them, riderless horses galloping away in all directions. An enemy rider crumpled from his saddle and fell to the ground limply as he watched.

June waved for his troopers to close up and turned back to his front, casting his eyes over the battlefield as he moved. Cuirassiers were reining their horses around towards them across the field as they galloped deeper into the enemy's formation. The horizon roiled with dark horses and shining swords, the enemy's battle flags burning against the trees ahead of them like twin suns. In front of those flags June saw a massive horseman wave his sword, signaling his personal guard to charge with him against the intruders.

Prince Adrian. June felt a live-wire charge course through his body from his boots to his mask, crackling like lightning just behind his eyes as his lips skinned back from his teeth in a vicious snarl. He cast his eyes from side to side quickly. Other groups of horsemen were closing in from the sides, men kicking their horses forward desperately, but they were falling behind faster than they could close the distance. For the moment at least the only thing between June Anjanou and the Crown Prince's colors was Prince Adrian himself. And the colors barely moved as the Crown Prince and his men separated and accelerated towards them. Kicking Lucky ever faster, June shouted over his shoulder, "They've left the colors behind! *Pass through them! Follow me!*"

Any reply was lost in rushing wind and thundering hooves as Prince Adrian and his guards loomed before them, swords gleaming like a monster's fangs, the Crown Prince's red eyes flaming demonically at their forefront. June locked eyes with him and kicked Lucky savagely, the horse digging in and accelerating as the lines swept together. At the last second June angled Lucky slightly to the right, Adrian adjusting his murderous strike across his body into a brutal horizontal slash as June slipped to his weak side. June flattened himself to Lucky's mane as Adrian's sword screamed through the air for him, letting his sword's tip fall over his shoulder as he angled it back.

With a crack of steel biting steel the sledgehammer blow beat into June's blade, sparks spraying across his face as Adrian's attack deflected up and away. All around him in that instant the air filled with crashing steel, screaming men and shrieking horses, crunching thuds as riders and mounts slammed to the ground. Then Lucky lunged forward again and June was clear, the twin colors almost close enough to touch as their bearers turned and *fled.*

Hoofbeats rose over the blood rushing in his ears, and June looked to his sides to see that he still had dragoons with him. Definitely not as many as earlier, but enough to win regardless. The flags bobbed in front of them, the white Royal Standard quickly falling behind the regimental colors as the faster horse pulled away. June pointed with his sword at slower rider and cried, "Take that one!" Snarling, he jabbed his sword at the faster cuirassier and the blue standard of the Cuirassier Guards, *"He's mine!"*

The two riders split apart, June's quarry making straight for the forest while the other rider pulled in his reins and dodged left. A few seconds later June galloped behind him and looked over to see the man twisting in the saddle, raising his sword to meet the onrushing dragoons. A moment later he was swamped by masked horsemen, one of June's troopers wrenching the Royal Standard from his hand as the others slashed all about him. The cuirassier, wounded a dozen times, was falling from his saddle when June swung his eyes back to his own foe and kicked Lucky onwards.

The tired horse gave June another burst of speed as the trees loomed before him, inexorably closing the distance with the fleeing cuirassier and the Regimental colors. Twenty meters. Ten. Eight. *Five*. The man looked over his shoulder as June raised his sword, panic in his wide eyes as he viciously kicked his horse faster. The cuirassier's fresh horse accelerated, starting to pull away as Lucky heaved with exhaustion. *So close. So close*, June screamed inwardly as his enemy started to escape, the man turning back forward and kicking yet more speed out of his horse.

Gritting his teeth as he lowered his sword, June shifted it to his left hand as his right fell to his belt and closed around the grip of his pistol. Pulling the weapon free from its deep cavalry holster, June cocked the hammer against his thigh, raised it and aligned the sights. The safety clicked down under his thumb and June pulled the trigger. Once, twice, again and again as he emptied the magazine into the man's back.

For an instant after June's slide locked back empty and he stabbed the weapon back into its holster the cuirassier galloped on as though he was unhurt. Then the man slowly turned in the saddle to look at him, blood frothing from his mouth as his horse slowed. Lucky surged and June's hand closed on the staff of the 1st Cuirassier Guards Regiment's battle flag, tightened like a steel vise as the dying man weakly tried to keep his grasp. The man gasped wetly as his grip weakened. June looked him dead in the eyes and snarled, "*Mine*," as he wrenched the colors from his grasp. The man toppled backwards as June held the captured flag aloft in triumph.

June heard a sound like a thousand howls as he reined Lucky to a panting halt at the edge of the woods, turned and saw an entire regiment of the enemy's most elite cavalry charging for him, men screaming with rage at the dishonor he had just inflicted on their ancient regiment. Maximilian's Own, the senior regiment in the Royal Army, the knights who boasted of their ancestors' charges against the Faceless King and Lady Vai, had just suffered the ultimate disgrace. It had *lost its colors*. June chuckled grimly. As a Black Knight he could practically feel his forebears' approval.

His remaining troopers galloped up, Corporal Tarai proudly holding the Royal Standard aloft. Looking between them, June saw Sergeant Marin calmly jacking another magazine into his pistol. Anastasia swayed in her saddle, blood soaking the neck of her green uniform a slick black. The girl had lost her sword at some point.

Khan was... June looked once, twice. Gone. He felt his stomach sink as he counted his soldiers. Sagara was missing too, and eight other troopers with him. He had ten troopers, and with every second the enemy horde bore down on them. June looked around to see the horizon dark with charging enemies as his soldiers swung in beside him, grimly gripping their swords.

June was searching for words when Tarai beat him to it, "Sir, it's been an honor riding with you."

The soldiers murmured their approval, and June blinked sudden tears from his eyes and replied, "You too. *All* of you. Thanks." Chuckling, he pointed his sword at the onrushing cuirassiers and said, "Now how about we cut out way *out* of this?"

Marin actually laughed, "Sounds good, sir."

"Alright then," June said, kicking Lucky forward, "*Follow me! Cut through!*"

The horse had barely started moving when something shrieked and popped behind them, immediately building to a rolling roar across the valley. And below it, ever so faint in the distance, June heard a bugle. He couldn't make out the notes, but he knew what it was commanding as flags appeared over the far hill, the one he had just come down so shortly ago. *Charge.*

An instant later the first ranks of the 5th Dragoon Regiment crested the hill and charged into the valley, the slope blackening under an endless wave of Imperial cavalry. Rank upon rank, knee to knee, swords burning in the sunlight, the dragoons hurled themselves into battle like the Black Knights of old. June made out the black and red of the Imperial flag streaming in the first rank, the regiment's black and gold colors next to it. The howl of the cuirassiers strangled and died. June looked from side to side at his companions, smiled predatorily and spurred Lucky into the battle.

The cuirassiers roiled, the regiment disintegrating into absolute chaos as men fought to turn to meet this new threat in the seconds they had. June heard a thunderous voice rise above the storm, calling for his soldiers to come about and charge. An instant later the dragoons plowed into the seething Royal cavalry with an indescribable crash and the great mass of Royal horsemen in front of June *shuddered.* Then June saw it, as shrieking Imperial war cries filled the air and the cuirassiers were physically thrown back by the force of the charge.

One man, a cuirassier in the back ranks, close enough for June to look him in his terror-stricken eyes, wheeled his horse about and spurred it for the woods. Then another and another, a stream that almost instant-ly built to a torrent, a flood of fleeing enemies as the Cuirassier Guards disintegrated. June ignored them, angled his horse for the largest intact knot of cuirassiers and dove into the melee.

They were easy prey. June's sword shrieked back and forth, leaving a trail of death in his wake as he fought his way forward. He barely spared a glance for the men he killed as he drove Lucky forward towards the man who rode head and shoulders above the storm of Imperial blades sur-rounding him, roaring like a lion, helmet gone and blonde hair flying as he mowed down dragoons with every sweep of his sword.

June cut down the last cuirassier still blocking his way and had start-ed shoving his way through the scrum of dragoons around Prince Adrian when he saw it. A flash of steel as the prince raised his weapon to slash down another Imperial. A sword buried under his arm and wrenched out as he twisted in the saddle, his killer backing away as the press of dragoons suddenly loosened and a circle opened around the prince. June nudged Lucky to the front as Adrian swayed in the saddle. The big man's horse, wide-eyed and snorting, shifted under him and he slipped from the saddle. Prince Adrian landed with a thud, his sword's hilt flying from nerveless fingers and bouncing away.

If the conditions were better, if artillery hadn't been rumbling over-head and men screaming and dying close by, if the world had helped with the moment, June thought that he could have heard a pin drop. The dra-goons stared impassively, a ring of steel-faced statues as Adrian struggled to sit up, gasping blood as bright as his eyes. His lips moved. Seconds dragged by. Finally as Adrian weakly tried to sit up again June wordlessly handed his captured colors to Sergeant Marin, who had appeared beside him and dismounted. His steps felt like he was floating as he approached the fallen prince and knelt by his side.

Adrian was pale as a sheet, the only color in his face the startlingly red blood flecked around his mouth and his half-glazed red eyes. Fixing June with a look, Adrian weakly reached up to his left shoulder where a large pink bow had been pinned, an incongruity on the prince's charcoal-col-ored uniform. His lips moved as he tugged on it, "...sister's." His breath rattled as he went on, "Promised... return it."

June swallowed hard. Slowly reaching down, he found the safety pin on the back of the ribbon, unsnapped it and pulled it free from Prince Adrian's uniform. Pulling the bow apart, June rolled the heavy silk ribbon around his hand and tucked it inside his jacket. Looking the dying prince in the eyes, he said, "I'll get it back to her."

Prince Adrian looked back at him for a moment. Then his head rolled back against the ground, his breath rattling wetly in his throat. He didn't draw another.

June reached out, closed the man's eyes and stood heavily. Princess Arilin's ribbon weighed in his pocket like a brick. Sighing, he turned to get back on Lucky. The battle would go on, and he needed to see to his soldiers. Those that were left.

Chapter 41

The Long-Haired Dragoon

The last of the small group of dragoons, twenty or so by her count, disappeared below the trees. Sophia turned to her father and remarked, "That's not very many of them." She sighed with relief, "Thank God. I was worried we were in real trouble."

Her father gave her a hard look back, "I'm not so sure we're *not*, Sophie. Imperials aren't stupid." He grunted and went on, "That looked to me like someone with a plan."

Sophia shivered. That wasn't just *someone* leading the charge. She was certain she'd seen June Anjanou's long hair as he stood atop the hill for a moment. After a long moment she replied, "So what are we going to do about it?"

Her father gave her a grim smile and started to say something in reply when she heard something in the distance, faint and high-pitched. Springing forward, she grabbed him by his load-bearing harness and pulled him to the ground as she shouted, "Watch out!"

An instant later the first shell crashed down just beyond the trench rim, buckling the wall above them and showering them with dirt. More followed across the trench a moment later as the barrage unrolled above them. Her father was already climbing to his feet as she brushed the dirt from her eyes. Extending a hand to help her up, he said, "Thanks, Sophie. Now get to cover." He pulled her back to her feet and added, "I don't think the Empire's done today."

She looked down the trench to see Tony diving into a dugout cut into the wall. Turning back to her father she saw him disappearing around the corner and into the next traverse. A moment later someone off that way called faintly for a medic. Wondering how her father had known someone was wounded even before hearing the call, Sophia rushed over to the dugout and ducked inside as another wave of shells crashed down.

Tony, Edward and Mr. Hargrave looked back at her in the sudden darkness of the dugout along with a few other soldiers she vaguely recognized. Tony pushed the men on his side farther back along the wall to make a space for her to sit down and she gratefully sank onto the hard wooden bench next to him. Patting her leg, he asked, "Where's First Sergeant?"

She looked over at him and replied, "Someone was hit farther down the trench. He was heading that way last I saw."

Tony scowled at the news and grumbled, "*His Highness* is off having his ride and we're still getting shelled. If he's so great he needs to hurry up a little." His fingers tightened on her thigh, digging in painfully. Sophia yelped and he quickly let go, apologizing, "Sorry, I'm just... so angry. We paid too much to get here."

The scene of Jack lying there dying as she sat helplessly flashed through her mind. Sophia pushed it away quickly. They were still fighting and she had to keep it together. Looking up, she saw Edward and Hargrave grimacing uncomfortably. They were probably thinking the same thing she was. Gritting her teeth, she tried to change the subject, "Look, we need to keep going. They're not going to stop themselves." A shell crashed down nearby and sent dirt sifting onto them, making her point. She took Tony's hand and squeezed it reassuringly, "I'm sure the Prince will take those guns out in no time."

Tony gave her a pained look. It floated through her mind, absurdly, that he might be jealous. Or not so absurdly. Prince Adrian *had* been mentioning her to people. It wasn't like Tony could exactly compete. Finally, he looked at the floor and replied, "Yeah. I hope so."

Something had been nagging at the back of Sophia's head ever since she had ducked into the dugout. It bloomed into realization as heavy boots sounded on the trench's boarded floor outside and Lieutenant Thorn knelt to stick his head in. They all straightened up a little as he asked, "Who's in here?"

Sophia answered, "My team, sir. And, uh..." She gestured at the other occupants.

One of them spoke up, "Commo section, sir."

Thorn sighed with relief, "Thank God. I've been looking for you." He hefted a field telephone he had slung over his shoulder, "Wire's out again. Fix it."

The man groaned and pointed at one of his companions, "You, come with me." Quickly getting up, they squeezed past the rest of them and disappeared into the light outside.

The lieutenant looked back at her and went on, "And as for you, Miss Rose, get someone out on watch." He ducked a little as another shell slapped down nearby, then went on grimly, "We can't let the Empire just walk up on us."

Sophia sighed, "Yes, sir. I'd... actually just thought of that."

"Sure you did." Thorn chuckled and went on, "Seen your father recently?"

Sophia pointed, "Last I saw he was heading that way. Someone got hit when the shelling started."

"Right, thanks." Thorn stood back up and she heard him rush off further down the trench.

More shells thrummed down overhead as Sophia looked around her friends. None of them seemed particularly eager to leave the safety of the dugout. Tony muttered, "You think he could keep watch himself, he's out there already."

Hargrave growled at him, "Enough of that, Tony. The man has better things to do." He sighed and looked at her, "I'll go, I guess."

Sophia smiled and shook her head, "No, don't worry. I've got it. I'll come get one of you in..." She looked at her watch, "An hour, I guess."

Edward sighed heavily and said, "Thanks, Sophie."

Picking up her rifle, Sophia ducked back out into the sunlight and stood up in the trench. A few shells slapped down nearby and sent fragments hissing overhead, but the shelling seemed to have dropped off a little from earlier. Thanking God for small favors, Sophia found a sheltered gouge one of the earlier shells had taken out of the trench wall and climbed up into it. Taking her distinctive blue hat off, she carefully raised her head over the crater lip and felt her blood turn to freezing, jagged shards of ice at the sight.

The hill in the distance rippled like green cloth in the wind and danced with light, the afternoon sun flashing from the enemy's swords as wave after wave of dragoons poured over the crest. She could almost hear the bugle blowing the charge in the distance. For a few moments she sat there, slack-jawed, until the last of what was clearly an entire dragoon regiment kicked their horses downhill and another wave of shells slapped down on their trench. The blasts brought her to her senses and she quickly scrambled down out of her crater and rushed back to the dugout.

Surprised, her friends looked over at her as she stuck her head in and said, "Guys! Get ready!" Tony opened his mouth to ask what was going on and she kept going, "We could be fighting dragoons *real* soon."

Hargrave raised an eyebrow and hefted his rifle, "How many?"

Sophia took a deep breath to calm down and replied, "More than I've ever seen. Maybe a whole regiment. They just charged over the far ridge."

"There's the counterattack." The older man snorted, "Well, they'll have to get through the Prince's men first. Do you need us out now?"

Sophia thought for a moment. More shells rained down outside, a fragment thudding loudly into the trench wall behind her as she stood there. Finally she shook her head, "No... no need to stand to now." The occupants of the dugout visibly deflated with relief and she went on, "I need someone to spell me though. I need to go find Thorn."

Hargrave was gathering himself to stand up when Tony raised a hand and said, "Hold on, old man. I've got this." The man chuckled and sank back into his seat as Tony rose. He looked at her and smiled grimly, "Lead on, Sophie."

Sophia smiled back and replied, "Let's go." Backing out of the low dugout with Tony in tow, she showed him the shell scrape she had been using earlier. As he slithered up to carefully peer over the edge, she reminded him, "Take your hat off when you're up there, Tony. You'll be less visible."

He paused, halfway up into the crater as it sank in. Quickly taking his hat off, he rolled over onto his back and gave her a sheepish look as he said, "Thanks, Sophie. Wasn't even thinking about it."

"No problem. See you." She gave him a half-wave and hurried off down the trench in search of the commander. She found him a couple traverses down, having a hushed conversation with her father a couple steps inside the tunnel they had originally come through. Her chest tightened as she saw Jack's body lying on the firing step, an indistinct lump under a blue army blanket. Forcing herself to look away, Sophia ducked into the tunnel.

Her father noticed her entering and raised an eyebrow, "Here about that dragoon regiment, Sophie?"

Lieutenant Thorn turned to look at her and nodded, "I saw them myself. Thanks for coming in to report, though." He turned back to her father and asked, "So, do you think we should be worried?"

Her father gave him a sour look, "I'd like to say no."

Thorn raised an eyebrow, "That doesn't sound like a vote of confidence to me."

"That's because it isn't." Her father went on sourly, "We're being shelled right now because the Imperials don't want us moving forward to help." Grunting, he looked back at her, "What do you think, Sophie? I'm assuming you don't have anything else to report besides the dragoons?"

"Yeah, just them." Sophia rubbed the back of her neck nervously. It was awkward being asked for her opinion on tactics. She had to think for a moment before she replied, "Well... we've been fighting those same dragoons the whole way here. They're veterans. *This*," She gestured at the trench around them as a couple more shells smacked down nearby and sent a little dirt drifting down onto them, "Is normal for them. Prince Adrian's men haven't seen combat until now."

Her father gestured at her and gave the lieutenant a look, "There you go, sir."

Thorn shrugged, "It's not like we have much a choice right now. We're just going to have to find out." He was turning to dismiss her when he saw that she had closed her eyes, her brow narrowed in concentration, and he asked, "What's go-"

Sophia held up a hand to cut him off as she listened intently. *Something* was clopping around outside, over the way the cuirassiers had gone. More than one something. Finally she opened her eyes and replied, "Sir, I hear horses."

Thorn and her father exchanged glances. The first sergeant beat him to it, "Let's go take a look."

The lieutenant nodded and they all hurried outside, heedless as more shells whistled in. One smacked down close behind them, close enough they all ducked involuntarily as dirt showered down into the trench. A little gingerly, Sophia mounted the trench's rear firing step and peered over the edge. Her breath caught in her throat as she saw horses galloping around in an aimless panic in the open ground between the trench and the forest. She recognized the heavy cuirassier saddles instantly. More were galloping out of the woods by the second only to pull up short as they saw the shells exploding over their line of escape.

Then she saw the first rider. A cuirassier charged out of the woods, spurring his horse viciously for the trenches. Even at the distance Sophia could see his eyes wide with fear, and an instant later she noticed he had lost his sword. More shells whistled in and Sophia ducked as blasts ripped across the trench and shrapnel tore the air. As she stuck her head back up she saw the man kick his horse forward to jump the trench. The poor animal took a couple staggering steps forward as blood poured from its flanks, swayed and toppled into the trench on top of its rider. She heard the man scream from a couple traverses down.

Sophia's father growled the vilest curse she had heard in her life and took off down the trench, calling for the medics. On his other side she saw Lieutenant Thorn looking back into the forest with a horrified expression and she turned back to see more cuirassiers, dozens of them pouring from the forest as though monsters were snapping at their heels. As more shells smashed down most of them pulled up short and joined the mass of riderless horses milling in the field between the trench and the forest. She heard officers screaming for the men to reform as more riders fled out of the trees.

Then she saw it, tiny in the distance but unmistakable. Sophia's heart soared for a moment as she saw the white and blue flags climb the far ridge. Prince Adrian's men hadn't been defeated after all. They must have swept the dragoons before them and were even now chasing them down. The men and horses milling around in the field in front of her must have fled from the initial shock of the enemy's attack while the rest of the Prince's regiment had stood their ground. Then, almost unwillingly, her eyes fell on the soldiers carrying those colors. Green-jacketed roughriders, each of them leading a dozen mismatched horses. She blinked and looked again, as the riders crested the hill and the battle flags were for an instant silhouetted against the darkening eastern sky. The soldiers holding them were still Imperial dragoons, calmly leading the rest of their regiment's horses back into cover. The 1st Cuirassier Guards Regiment had just *lost their colors*, and they were probably about to be attacked by a thousand dismounted dragoons. And she didn't see Prince Adrian out on the field in front of her. He wouldn't have run. He would have fought to the end. *To the end.*

Sophia had overheard her superiors discussing 'morale' more than once, usually when they thought the company was unhappy for some reason. Nobody in their right mind would actually *want* to march hundreds of miles while having a running gun battle with dragoons, so Charlie Company had not been the happiest unit in the Royal Army for the last few weeks. That being said, they had a mission and they were damned well going to finish it. War wasn't fun and nobody had been expecting a vacation. Sophia had privately dismissed the concept of 'morale', the almost sacred measure of the troops' willingness to fight, as a load of garbage. They were soldiers and they were going to fight regardless.

She was wrong. Morale was *real*, and as she watched the Cuirassier Guards' colors disappear over the hill she felt hers drain out of her body. It bled out of the bottom of her feet, pooled in her boots, spilled across the duckboards and poured into the earth, leaving her standing there weak-kneed and gasping. Unsteady, she looked over at Lieutenant Thorn and asked, "Sir, did you just see that?"

He gave her a haunted look, "Yeah. I did."

Swallowing hard, she tried to collect herself and ventured, "They... they've dismounted."

"The dragoons?" She nodded and he thought for a second, then went on, "Damn. We need to stand to... *now.*" Sophia stared at him for a second until he put a hand on her shoulder and pushed her away, "Go. Now.

Stand to!"

Reacting automatically, Sophia turned and rushed back down the trench, calling for the company to stand to and prepare to fight. She heard Thorn going the opposite direction yelling the same things. By the time she got back to her team's dugout Hargrave and Edward were already out of the bunker and getting the machine gun ready for action. She pointed them back towards Tony's shell scrape, told the other soldiers reluctantly piling out of the dugout to carry the message further down the line and hurried to rejoin her friends.

Tony slid out of the scrape looking like he'd seen a ghost, and Sophia quickly waved Edward and Hargrave up with their machine gun before he could fill them in. After a few seconds she heard the reassuring click-clack of Hargrave racking the gun's bolt back and riding the bolt handle back forward, and a moment later the old man rolled over and gave her a significant look. Sighing, Sophia filled them in, "Guys, uh... the cavalry just lost their colors."

Hargrave and Edward both cursed. Tony looked at her blankly. Edward asked bitterly, "Got any more good news, Sophie?"

She sighed and looked back at him, "Yeah. An entire dragoon regiment just dismounted on the other side of those woods."

Edward blinked. A corner of his mouth turned up slowly, then the other as he snorted. The snort turned into a strangled chortle before Edward's head rolled skyward as hysterical laughter ripped through his body, the man holding his ribs as though to keep them from bursting as he rocked back and forth. Tony gave him a funny look for a second almost as though he didn't understand the joke before he snorted and joined in. Even Hargrave was chuckling grimly. And now that she thought about it, their situation *was* pretty funny. They'd gone to all this effort to break through and make a breach for the cuirassiers and not ten minutes later the Royal Army's best cavalry had *lost their colors* and Charlie Company was about to be swimming in dragoons. The Empire was not making this easy for them, Sophia thought as she felt her mouth curve into a leering smile. The fear and anger of battle melted into each other as she doubled over with laughter, tears turning her world into a bubbling fog.

After a few seconds Sophia reached down inside her heart, found her self-control and straightened up. Half a smile hung from her face as she gestured for the others to quiet down. They quickly got control of themselves as she remarked, "Yeah, we have the *best* luck in the Army." Hefting her rifle, she climbed onto the firing step and laid it across the parapet, "Just get ready. We've got this."

Out in the field to their front the cuirassiers were at last milling into some semblance of order. Sophia heard a couple voices shouting for the men to get back on line, and as riderless horses galloped off to the sides to escape the shelling the cavalrymen were able to wheel back into a semblance of a formation. Men fought with rearing horses as shells slapped down close behind them and she saw a couple riders go down as shrapnel hissed across the battlefield, but slowly, ever so slowly, the cuirassiers reformed. She supposed the Imperial barrage had ironically forced the fleeing cavalry to stand and fight, and her heart lightened a little as she saw someone, clearly an officer, galloping back and forth and screaming at the men to get back into the fight.

He was close enough for her to make out a little of what he was saying as the bombardment lifted, the thudding Imperial shells suddenly moving off behind them. Wheeling his horse about in front of the forming ranks, he thundered, *"...on, you cowards! Are you men or not? Prince Adrian is in there, and he's fighting! He needs us, now!"* A few men shouted their agreement, swords gleaming above the line of cavalry as it shifted forward, soldiers eager to attack again. With a theatrical flourish the officer reared his horse, sword burning above the rest of the line as he screamed, *"On me! C-"*

The man toppled off his horse backwards, his body bouncing in the dirt as a sharp crack echoed across the battlefield. Between the legs of the milling horses before her Sophia saw a green-jacketed figure standing in the woodline, not even *bothering* to take cover as he racked his rifle's lever forward. The shell casing flashed beside his head as he slammed it back home. In the instant before he fired again Sophia saw the forest was alive with dragoons, dozens of them, golden afternoon sunlight painting them like bronze statues as their weapons swung onto the line of cuirassiers.

The forest erupted with shrieking Imperial gunfire, dragoons firing as fast as they could at a target they couldn't miss. Machine guns, a dozen or more, screamed like banshees and filled the air with death. The cuirassiers lurched forward and *died*. Horses staggered and collapsed, dead men flopping in the saddle like rag dolls as the Imperials fired. And fired. And fired, until what was left of Prince Adrian's proud regiment lay dead in the dirt.

Sophia sat there in shock for... seconds? Minutes? Time just seemed to stop. A harsh gunshot nearby brought her out of her stupor and she looked over to see Hargrave mechanically working his rifle's bolt. Numbly, she looked over at Tony and Edward. They were giving him the same glazed look she was sure she had. Shaking her head viciously to clear the cobwebs out, Sophia tightened her rifle to her shoulder and shouted, "It's us next! *Open fire!*"

Sophia's finger tightened on the trigger and her rifle bucked in her hands. An instant later Charlie Company's whole line came alive with gunfire and the Masks dove for cover. They fought it out as the sun sank in the west below the crest of Fire Ridge, bathing the battlefield in shadow as green and blue tracers snapped through the air like evil fireflies. Imperial grenade launchers popped between volleys of gunfire and the little bombs whistled in around them in the darkness. Their own mortars pounded back, filling the forest with fire and smashing trees down atop the dragoons. Star shells popped overhead and canisters whistled to earth, Royal and Imperial flares bathing the battlefield in unearthly light as the False Sun set behind the true one and the night sank into blackness.

Time and again the enemy fire built to a whipping crescendo and Sophia's heart froze in her chest, fearing what she'd see when she next climbed back out into the storm of bullets. If the Masks *really* meant to kill them they would charge into the open first, throwing themselves down behind the rapidly-disintegrating windrow of dead men and horses in the field for cover. Machine guns and grenade launchers would turn the trench into a burning hell as the dragoons launched their final assault. Sophia could practically hear the Lieutenant Thorn's whistle blasting for the machine guns to pivot and fire down the length of their line, a last desperate measure as grenades fell like hail and steel-masked demons poured into their trench.

The assault never came. Charlie Company's guns roared back every time, Sophia firing clip after clip into the darkness until her shoulder ached from the recoil. The dragoons never dared to leave the shelter of the trees. After *far* too long the Imperial fire died off to the occasional crack of a rifle and Sophia gratefully let herself slip back down the side of the trench. Sitting down on the firing step, she trembled as she gingerly set her searing-hot rifle aside in the cool night air. The shaking died down a little as she took a couple ragged breaths and called out in the darkness, "Guys? Get down... are you all okay?"

Her three companions slipped back into the trench wordlessly. Tony shook as he sat next to her, his breath hissing through clenched teeth. She didn't need to ask him his opinion of what had just happened. Hargrave grunted, produced his pipe, struck a match and started smoking automatically. Finally, Edward rubbed theatrically at the bandage wrapped around his forehead and said, "Well, I've only been shot in the head once today."

Sophia gave him a half-chuckle, "Good to hear it, Ed." Sighing, she looked around the little group and said, "Look, this is going to get worse before it gets better. How're you all on ammo?"

Her own bandoliers were empty and she was down to what she carried on her harness. Hargrave wordlessly lifted his bandoliers and they flopped emptily. Edward looked back up at where they had left the machine gun on the parapet and said, "We've got two or three belts left. Not a lot." He tugged at his harness and added, "I've got plenty for my rifle... guess we need to cross-load?"

Great, Sophia thought sarcastically at the prospect of loading machine gun belts in the dark. Looking over at Tony, she noticed his bandoliers sagged off his body heavily. It stood to reason, she supposed. He'd been helping Edward with the gun. His head was turned down, his face hidden by the brim of his cap as he hunched over into himself, hands curled into fists between his knees. Tony's shoulders shook with every heaving breath he took, and Sophia gingerly reached out to rest a hand on his thigh, "Tony... are you all right?"

Her friend jerked his head up to look at her, his eyes gleaming wetly. "No! I..." He looked between the three of them quickly, then buried his face in his hands, "What are we even *doing* here?"

What did Jack die for, Sophia finished the thought. To watch Prince Adrian's regiment get massacred in front of them after they'd fought for miles to break through? She was wondering herself. Everyone was, she was sure, even her father. He was probably angriest of all of them right now. And there wasn't a damn thing any of them could do about it.

Sophia leaned forward and wrapped her arms around Tony, pulling him into her as she said, "We've got this. We're going to get through this together. Alright?"

Edward sat down on Tony's other side and wrapped an arm around him affectionately, "Sophie's right. Who needs the cavalry? We've been fine so far." He gave her a look and cracked a half-smile.

Hargrave stepped over and rested a hand on Tony's shoulder reassuringly. Looking up at him, she was pretty sure she wouldn't be getting a lot out of him for the rest of the night. Tony sighed heavily and relaxed in her arms. After a long pause he said, "Thanks... thanks, guys. It was just too much for a minute there."

Sophia felt herself smile a little. She was about to reluctantly untangle herself from Tony when she heard a familiar voice behind her, "Group hug, huh? Somehow I'm not surprised." Lieutenant Thorn remarked as they hastily pulled apart, "Can I get one when you're finished?"

Edward shot back sarcastically before she could manage an answer,

"Rough day, sir?"

"Oh, it's getting worse." Thorn sat down next to her heavily and kicked his feet out in front of him on the duckboards, "I just got off the phone with battalion, and they're going crazy right now. Apparently higher," He waved his finger in the air tiredly in the universal sign for echelons above reality, "Is losing their minds over some Imperial troops in our rear. *Way* in our rear. Like all the way back down the ridge."

Sophia raised an eyebrow, "How's that our problem?"

The commander rolled his eyes, "That's what I tried to tell them. Caldwell even jumped in on the call with me." He shook his head, "We bypassed a lot of Imperials getting up here. They're probably all still there. How this is news to anyone is *beyond* me. You know they actually pulled the artillery over this?"

"Really, sir?" Sophia said, "I was wondering where Tyrant was just now."

"Really." Thorn confirmed tiredly, "They're all firing on some Imperials off to the north. Anyways," Climbing heavily to his feet, he gave her a weak smile, "We might be staying here for a minute while headquarters sorts themselves out." He jerked his chin at their machine gun nest, "Keep someone on watch. I don't think they're going to try anything more tonight, but we'll have to see."

"Sure thing, sir." Standing, Sophia climbed up on the firing step and carefully looked out across the field as the lieutenant turned to leave. Something caught her eye under the shadows of the trees on the far side. She blinked, rubbed at her eyes and looked harder. *There.* She saw it again, a pale little shape darting in a quick arc under the trees. Not taking her eyes off it, she said, "Sir, something's moving out there."

Thorn turned back around and climbed up next to her, carefully propping his binoculars on the rim of the trench as he asked, "What do you see?"

"Something small and light." She replied, "It almost looked like a little bird or something." The shape darted under the trees again and she nudged him, "There! See that?"

"Yeah..." Thorn said, adjusting himself a little on his elbows, "What in the world... oh."

The lieutenant swallowed heavily and said nothing. After a few seconds of silence Sophia looked over at him and asked, "What, sir?"

"That's..." Thorn trailed off, shook his head and tried again, "That's a guy hiding behind a tree waving a handkerchief in the air so we can see it."

She gave him a look, "Well, I doubt they're trying to surrender."

Thorn growled, "They could be making a pretext to scout us out." He gave her a look back, "If they figure out we're in the shape we are right now, this could get bad in a hurry."

Sophia chuckled grimly, "Sounds like a good idea, sir. Not every day we get to see the Masks up close."

"I like the way you think." Fishing a white handkerchief out of his back pocket, Thorn waved it over the trench parapet, shouting, "*Hold your fire! Hold your fire! Truce party coming out!*" The shout to hold fire quickly traveled down Charlie Company's line. Satisfied, the commander gave her a look, "Feeling brave, Miss Rose?"

Sophia swallowed heavily and replied, "Yeah. Let's do this." Looking over her shoulder, she said, "Hargrave, you've got it until I get back."

The old man nodded and motioned for Tony and Edward to stand up as he said, "We'll cover you."

"Thanks," She replied, turning back to Thorn, "Let's go, sir."

Slinging their rifles over their backs, Sophia and Thorn carefully pulled themselves up out of the trench and stood on the parapet. Sophia felt icy needles crawling up and down her spine like the legs of some monstrous centipede as dozens of gunsights lined up on her body. They stood there for a couple seconds, frozen, waiting. The gunshots didn't come. Finally, Thorn grit his teeth and started forward, saying, "Come on."

Sophia forced herself to walk forward. She felt naked out in the open, so exposed she felt like she was part of something obscene. Her boots plowed through the field's shredded grass behind Thorn, the ground clawed raw and wet by thousands of bullets. After a few steps she saw a shape move against the darkness under the trees. A dragoon walking into the open. She looked at the dragoon as they walked forward, its dark shape resolving into a tall, slender form as her breath caught in her throat and her blood turned to ice. *Oh, God,* Sophia thought as the wind rustled across the battlefield and the figure's long hair stirred, *it's him.*

She barely even saw the line of dead horses and fallen cuirassiers in front of her, bodies shredded and unrecognizable from the gunfight. Her feet seemed to float over ground slick with blood and worse. Sophia's eyes fixed on one thing and one thing only. June Anjanou, walking out of the field towards them like a storybook monster given life by the Faceless King himself. It would have been easier if he'd been some ten-foot tall ogre, bellowing with rage and brandishing a steel club, a slow, stupid monster for her to kill. No, he was actually only a little taller than she was.

A steel-masked reaper staring back at her, dark golden eyes burning in the moonlight as they bored into her soul.

They stopped a few feet away from each other. After a long moment Sophia felt June's basilisk glare lift off her, almost leaving a wake through the air as it settled on Lieutenant Thorn. She heard him swallow as they stood there in silence for a moment. Finally Sophia saw June's mask shift, the lower plate that protected his jaw rising slightly on one side. She realized in the back of her mind that his mouth had curled into a humorless half-smile.

"Well, well," June Anjanou said, his voice cutting through the silence like a sword-blow, "The lucky lieutenant and his quick little friend. I can see you haven't bothered getting a new sword."

Lieutenant Thorn growled, "June Anjanou." He jerked his chin in her direction, "It's what I've got her for."

"Good thing," June said coldly, "You're a lousy swordsman."

Sophia cut in, glaring at him, "Go to hell."

His petrifying glare swept back onto her, the corner of his mask tilting up again as he replied, "Go to hell, *sir*."

She snorted and shot back, "Go to hell, you *ass*."

June actually chuckled, "How cute." His gaze swung back to Lieutenant Thorn, "But you seem to have me at a disadvantage. Your names?"

After a long pause Thorn said, "Lieutenant Joshua Thorn." He gestured at her, "This is Sophia Rose. I'm in command of this forward line here."

"Pleased to meet you." June said sarcastically, "Now, *Josh*, do you hear that? In the distance?"

They listened for a moment. All Sophia heard was the rumbling of artillery, far away on the other side of the ridge. Raising an eyebrow, she asked, "The artillery?"

Looking at her again, June chuckled and replied, "Yes, *Sophia*, the artillery." Hearing him say her name made her skin crawl, "*Your* artillery. Notice how it's not landing anywhere around here?"

Thorn replied uncomfortably, "And that has... what to do with anything?"

"Well, Josh," She saw June's mask tilt into a cruel smirk, "Who do you suppose they're shooting at?" Thorn looked at him uncomfortably for a couple seconds and June chuckled maliciously and went on, "Oh, you've already gotten the word? Imperial troops in your rear? Your higher's got to be going *crazy* right now. I bet you're just *so* confused."

"What are you getting at?" Lieutenant Thorn spat.

"Half of the Imperial Army is *behind* you right now." June growled, "If you're not surrounded already, you will be by sunrise." Those molten-gold eyes swept across them as he went on, words landing like sledgehammers, "I watched Prince Adrian *die* today, and I'm getting *tired* of killing you people. *Surrender. Now. End this.*"

For a second they stood there in shock as his words washed over them. Adrian, dead? Sophia had thought she was prepared for the awful news, but that had just been grim uncertainty. The tiny candle of hope she'd had for his survival died in her heart and she felt her fighting spirit drain from her body again, here, in front of an enemy demanding her surrender. She shook her head and looked over to see Lieutenant Thorn standing there, white as a sheet in the moonlight.

It would be *so easy* to just give up. They were probably screwed anyways. How many more of her friends would have to die on this ridge? She didn't want *anyone* to die. *She* didn't want to die. But then, as Lieutenant Thorn started to look over at her and the gloom of defeat rose around her soul, Sophia remembered an old story her father had told her. The breakout from the Dragon's Jaw. Her father and his comrades had fought for a hundred miles through half the Imperial Army to claw their way free of another trap in the last war. And her mother had walked the whole way with them, carrying her in her arms. Like *hell* were they going to surrender over some pretty dragoon's *bluff*.

Thorn must have seen the fire in her eyes. The color returned to his face as he looked at her, and he nodded and turned back to the dragoon. Snorting sarcastically, he said, "I appreciate the offer, but I'm going to have to turn you down. Even if you're telling the truth, we got up this ridge," He smiled grimly, "And we'll get back down it."

June glared at him icily, "Go ahead and *try*. None of you will get off Fire Ridge alive."

Sophia shot back, "Try and stop us, you *long-haired bastard*."

June gave her a long glare. She glared back, gritting her teeth. Finally June rolled his eyes, spun and stalked back toward the forest. Sophia and Thorn both let the breath they'd been holding out, turned and started making their way back to the trench.

They were most of the way back when Thorn ventured, "Long-haired bastard? Really?"

"Yeah," Sophia replied, stretching her arms over her head, "*Man*, did that feel good."

Chapter 42

Heir to the Throne

Princess Arilin swam out of black, dreamless sleep, opened her eyes and saw nothing but darkness. Shifting groggily in the unfamiliar bed that smelled like a girl she didn't know, she felt at her face for a blindfold and found nothing. It was just *that* dark. Laying there in the blackness, listening to the murmur of voices below and the low rumble of thunder that wasn't thunder outside, she let the memories of the last day flow through her mind.

Vanessa putting her to bed, gone when she woke up in the morning. She still didn't know if the quiet lieutenant, her friend for the last couple months, was alive. Her goodbye with Patricia and the now-obvious love letter she'd given her. She hoped the lady general was still alive herself. The ride south, the fight, the chase. Lieutenant Bettancourt wheeling his men into battle against an overwhelming enemy. She hoped he'd made it. More likely she'd be putting flowers on his grave. Her meeting with General Haas, the old man amused more than anything at his sudden romantic entanglement as the battle built around him.

She'd taken the train back south and gotten a look at the unfolding disaster with General Reinhardt. The Royal Army would be talking about the Battle of Fire Ridge in hushed tones for a hundred years. And then he had sent her to bed. Enough adventures for one day, and she was only going to bother the staff trying to extricate the Army from the worst disaster in its history. A couple polite but very firm soldiers had taken her upstairs to this girl's bedroom and made sure she'd washed herself and changed. The staff doctor had given her some pills and tucked her deep into the massive four-poster bed. She didn't remember him closing the curtains.

Whoever had slept in that room before had *clearly* not been afraid of the dark. Feeling her way in the darkness, Arilin found the edge of the bed, drew aside a layer of delicate lace and felt a second, heavy curtain behind it. This girl had set her bed up like a birdcage with a sheet thrown over it. Pulling the heavy fabric aside, she slipped her legs out of bed and sat for a few seconds, trying to make shapes out as the noise from below instantly became much louder without the deadening curtain. No luck. There were blackout curtains over the windows and she was certain it was pitch black outside. Standing to feel for the light switch, Arilin sardonically wondered if this girl was a vampire.

After a couple minutes fumbling around in the darkness Arilin eventually found the light switch and flicked it on. A couple table lamps blazed to life and she winced at the sudden light. Slowly opening her eyes, Arilin saw that someone had cleaned her uniform and folded it up for her on the vanity. Pulling off her pajamas, Arilin got dressed, noting sourly that they had neglected to replace her sword. She found her boots standing freshly shined by the bedroom door, and wondered absently as she slipped into them just how many people had been walking around the room while she'd been sleeping. Those pills must have knocked her out cold.

Arilin took a couple minutes to brush her hair, thinking the whole time that it was ridiculous that she was bothering in the middle of a battle. Still, she could almost hear Patricia in the back of her head lecturing her about the importance of her appearance, and it wasn't like she *really* had anything better to do. It was a couple minutes more when she didn't have to find out how much worse things had gotten while she had slept. Finally, when she was satisfied that she looked acceptable and couldn't justify putting it off to herself any longer, Arilin walked to the door and reluctantly pulled it open.

The dull roar from downstairs resolved into recognizable voices as she made her way towards the pool of light spilling up the stairs at the end of the hall. She recognized Siegfried as he said, "...believe they got out at eighty percent. I was worried we'd just sent Lady MacMahon on a suicide mission." A few people chuckled tiredly and Siegfried went on, his tone growing grim, "Speaking of. What's the latest from the Nineteenth?"

A voice she vaguely recognized, one of the staff officers, answered, "Last report was fifteen minutes ago, sir. They can *hear* the Twenty-First, but they're swimming in Masks." Arilin felt a chill creep up her neck. It sounded like her suggestion for the 19th Division had gotten them into a fight for their lives.

Another voice spoke up as she crept down the stairs. She couldn't name the person, but she'd been around headquarters for long enough to recognize the barely-suppressed condescension in an intelligence officer's tone as he explained the obvious for the millionth time, "We assess the Empire has motorized at least a division to account for the amount of infantry we've seen this far south this early in the battle."

"Thank you," She could practically hear Siegfried rolling his eyes, "Maybe we should try that ourselves. It seems to be working *wonders* for them." The chief of staff paused for a moment, then asked, "Do you have anything, sir?"

Arilin's ears perked up. A moment later she heard a familiar grunt and Walter Haas said, "Yes. Get Fifth Corps on the radio. Tell Kunst if he hasn't broken through by dawn I'm pulling the Nineteenth out." The old general went on coldly, "There are *always* too many Imperials. The Twenty-First needs to stop *dancing* and use their damn bayonets."

The first voice replied, "Will do, sir."

"Good. That concludes the update." Siegfried went on as she stepped into the parlor's open door, "Now get back to work... milady!"

The room *froze*. Everyone in the room turned to look at her, and they all looked *guilty*. Everyone except one. Walter Haas was sitting with his back towards her. His shoulders rose and fell as he sighed heavily, and she saw him raise a hand to his face to pull off his monocle. Depositing the eyepiece in a pocket, the old general stood and turned to face her. His face was hardened into a grim mask as he said, "Milady, we need to talk." He shared a glance with Siegfried before striding over to her, "Come with me."

Arilin felt her stomach twist itself into a knot as she stood there looking up at Walter. Bile burned in the back of her throat for a moment. Swallowing heavily, she nodded and stepped aside. Slipping past her, he headed down the hall towards the front of the house and she followed. A couple drowsy soldiers on duty in the front room did double-takes as they appeared and made to stand, but he waved them back down and pulled the front door open for her.

The guards on the front porch leapt to attention as she emerged. A step behind her Walter growled, "The princess and I have something important to discuss. Move your post."

"Yes, sir!" One of the soldiers yelped. He whistled and waved his arm, and an instant later they were alone on the porch.

Walter sat heavily in one of the wooden chairs scattered on the porch and gestured at the one next to it, "Please, sit down, milady."

Arilin sat gingerly, her stomach doing its utmost to turn itself inside out as she perched on the hard wooden seat. She had a horrible feeling that she knew *exactly* what this was about, and she ventured, "Is this... about my brother?"

Walter reflexively pulled a cigar from his jacket. Seeming to examine it closely, he replied, "Yes. It is." He paused for a long moment, and as Arilin was opening her mouth to demand what it was he knew he looked over at her and the words died in her throat. Even in the darkness she could see the look in his eyes, somehow hard and deep at the same time. It reminded Arilin of the cold blue ice on the bottom of a glacier she had seen in the Shield Mountains once, on a hiking trip a lifetime and a world away. Finally he continued, "I'm sorry, milady. He's dead."

The general had not tried to talk around it, to disguise it in soft euphemism. Adrian was not fallen. He had not passed on, or left them, or gone on to a better place. Her brother was *dead*, and the word landed like the great bell in Heaven was tolling the end of the world. It was funny. She had been sure she would faint. She felt like she almost owed it to him to pass out dramatically at the news. And yet there she was, sitting there staring at her hands. Exhaling, Arilin leaned back against the chair's hard wooden back and closed her burning eyes. After a few sobs she felt a heavy hand on her shoulder and looked up to see Walter leaning over her, offering his handkerchief. Taking it, she wiped her eyes and managed, "Please... tell me more."

Walter grunted and settled back into his chair. Pulling the cigar out again, he gave it a hard look and sighed. Arilin got the feeling he very badly wanted to have a smoke as he started, "Late this afternoon the Twenty-Fourth Regiment broke through the last Imperial line on the far side of Fire Ridge. Adrian's regiment was committed to exploit the breach." He paused before going on, "We... don't have a lot on what happened afterwards. There must have been one *hell* of a counterattack. They were wiped out, almost to the last man. They lost their colors."

Arilin didn't know what to say. Seeing the look on her face, Walter grimaced and plowed ahead, "We got confirmation from the Red Cross about an hour ago. I asked them to delay releasing the news to the public, but realistically we've maybe got a few hours."

Release the news? What was he even talking about? *Why does he want to delay... oh.* Arilin's thoughts came to a sudden stop, black dread boiling up within the red, raw grief tearing through her mind. A few weeks that felt like a lifetime ago her father had mentioned in one of his letters that his brother, Alphonse, had returned to the High City. She remembered meeting him once, shortly after she had first arrived at the Palace. Her uncle had given her a look that chilled her to the bone, even as a child. She hadn't seen him since. From the little her father mentioned him, he seemed to be content to split his time between the Dominion and Royal estates far from the capital and them.

Arilin grabbed hold of the thought and followed it. Why had Alphonse withdrawn into self-imposed exile? She had never devoted a lot of thought to it before, but it struck her that he was probably outraged over the Legitimation. He had good reason to be, after all. She and Beatrice had bumped him from third in line to the throne to fifth. With Adrian stubbornly unmarried he had stood a good chance of being King someday. Of course he would be furious.

But there was more to it than that, Arilin realized as the dread poured down onto her, black and sticky as pitch. *The Legitimation.* People were reluctant to talk, but she had picked up enough over the years to know what had led up to it. How the old Queen, Amelia, had tried to turn Adrian against his father. How she had failed. How she had died. Her father had married his longtime mistress and brought her two bastard children to the Palace mere days after the servants cut her down from the chandelier in her chambers. And then just to spit on her grave the King had decreed that those two girls were his legitimate children and *dared* anyone to object.

The family curse had no objection. Arilin remembered watching her father sign the decree. For a couple seconds she had felt a mild itching behind her eyes. An instant later the Faceless King was stabbing red-hot pokers into her eye sockets, shrieking with maniacal glee in the back of her skull. After a couple minutes of screaming she'd mercifully fainted. She and Beatrice had cried blood for a week, and when they took the bandages off afterwards their eyes were red as rubies.

The Stigmata shut the anti-Legitimists up for about a month. Even so, their disdain had always had a sort of hypothetical tone to it. Amelia had been icy, distant and widely hated. The High City quickly warmed to the warm, interesting new Queen Catherine and her two cute daughters, at least in polite society. And the *actual* heir to the throne was... *had been* completely legitimate. No more.

Arilin felt the weight settling onto her shoulders, darker and heavier than the shadow of her grief. It built and built and built, crushing her, forcing the breath from her lungs. It was the mere idea of the weight of the Kingdom, every brick and every soul. She was Crown Princess now. One day she would be *Queen.* And standing right in front of her was Prince Alphonse, who would have the full support of every anti-Legitimist, every person who hated her father or sneered at her. She could almost see the ambition in his blood-red eyes. The *hate.*

She felt a heavy hand on her shoulder, "Milady, are you all right?" Walter sounded worried.

The princess shook her head slowly and gave him a sheepish look, "Yes... well, no... not really, I guess." She sighed, "Sorry I drifted off there."

"Milady... you may not believe me, but I know what you're going through." Walter went on, "It's worse at your age. If you'd like, milady, I can have the doctor give you something to help you rest." He chuckled sadly, "Something real this time, anyways. Nobody here is going to blame you for it."

An embarrassing suspicion tickled in the back of her mind. It was a relief to think about something mundane as Arilin asked, "Wait, were those...?"

The old general gave her a look. She thought she could see the slightest twinkle in his eye as he replied, "I told the doctor to give you some sugar pills earlier. He said it was like he'd clubbed you over the back of the head."

Arilin felt her cheeks redden, "That's... embarassing."

Water snorted, "You're in good company. I used that trick on my own commander once." He went on, "In any event, milady, when this news gets out we need someone responsible from the Royal Family in the Capital, and I am almost certain that is not the case right now."

Arilin warily raised an eyebrow, "What do you mean?"

"A few hours ago we got an encrypted message from the War Ministry, telling us to get an airship landing field ready and to be prepared to receive an important visitor." Walter went on, "It should be coming in about two hours from now." He gave her a significant look, "The number of people, milady, who have the authority to use an airship as their personal taxi is *extremely small*."

Arilin turned quickly and looked over at him, eyes wide, "You mean... my father's coming *here?*"

Walter nodded once, "I'm almost certain. And you're going to be on that thing heading back to the Capital as fast as it can fly."

She was going home. Back to the Palace, back to her family and friends and normal life. Sitting there in the darkness listening to the unending rumble of artillery in the distance, Arilin felt relief mixed with shame well up in her heart. Then her thoughts turned back to Alphonse and icy dread wrapped around her again. After a long pause, she said, "Thanks... especially if my father's coming here, I *really* need to go back."

The general grunted and raised a craggy eyebrow, "I was expecting you to throw a fit, milady."

Arilin sighed, "Did I ever tell you my uncle's back in town?"

"I recall you mentioning it..." Walter trailed off as he thought for a moment. She could see him mentally connecting the same dots she just had. Finally, he snorted, "I *was* concerned about your safety, milady. I hope I'm not sending you back into danger."

"I hope so too." Arilin remarked, "But either Dad or I will have to deal with him, and Dad's needed here."

Walter was silent for a long time. Finally, he said, "Arilin..." She looked over at him in surprise as he went on. She couldn't recall him ever using her name, "Whatever happens, you have my support and, I am sure, most of this army's." He gave her a stern look, "Just remember, milady, this will not be a *schoolgirl intrigue* you're going into."

"Walter... I..." Arilin looked at him, vision blurring as tears flooded her eyes. Finally, she got up and dove into his arms, saying, "Thanks... thanks."

The old general stiffened for a second as she cried into his chest. Then she felt his arms wrap around her supportively as he muttered, "There, there, milady." Patting her gently on the back, he said, "Come on, let's get you cleaned up. Your father isn't going to want you to be a mess."

* * *

Bonfires blazed across the field, a great ring of them studding the darkness with smudges of orange light. The group stood near the cluster of fires on the windward side of the landing field, the uncomfortable heat in the warm night forcing them to stand a little ways away in the wet grass. Looking nervously at the few shafts of moonlight streaming through the blanket of clouds overhead, Becky remarked, "It's been almost an hour now... I hope they're still coming."

Her maid had showed up half an hour before they were to leave, still in a blood-spattered white nurse's dress. She had quickly changed into a more presentable uniform she had brought with her, but it had still been a little shocking for Arilin to see her so disheveled. On her other side, Walter grunted, "Give them time. They're fighting the wind coming in here." He looked at his own watch, "Although it *will* be sunrise soon. I do *not* want you anywhere near here in an airship in daylight, milady."

She raised an eyebrow and asked, "Why's that? I think it would be safer to land, at least."

"Fighters." Walter growled, "We got some reports of enemy aircraft north of here yesterday afternoon. Once day breaks they'll see an airship fifty miles out and they'd be stupid not to come after it." He went on, "Not much we can do right now, either. Most of ours were pulled north with the Field Marshal."

"For all the good..." Arilin trailed off. The others looked at her quizzically, and she finally said, "Does anyone else hear that?"

After a few seconds Becky spoke up, "Yes... I think I do." They shared a glance as she went on, "Sounds like an airship, milady!"

Walter chuckled, "I'm afraid you two have me at a disadvantage. Too much artillery. I'm half-deaf." He signaled to one of the soldiers standing nearby and the man raised a heavy Airship Corps flare rifle skywards. An instant later a bright blue flare burned skywards over the landing field, bathing them in its faint light for a few seconds as it arced away.

Arilin scanned the sky for a few seconds before she heard Walter remark, "Well, *there* it is." She glanced over at him, then followed his gaze. Off in the distance she saw a small blue star falling from the clouds. Another flare popped into the sky behind her, white this time, and a moment later she saw a white flare burn to life just below the cloud layer in the distance. Walter went on, "Looks like they're landing."

A few minutes later the airship's engines had built to a steady drone overhead and it slipped out of the layer of clouds off to their southwest, downwind at the far end of the landing field. It looked like nothing so much as a dark hole against the charcoal clouds as its engines grew steadily louder, sinking into the breeze as it came nearer. Then it was on top of them, mooring lines falling from the sky and dozens of soldiers rushing forward to seize them as it filled the sky overhead. It was almost unreal watching the airship's battleship-sized bulk settle to earth like a feather amid the shouting soldiers and the roar of engines against the wind.

As the soldiers secured the final mooring lines Walter turned to the two of them and spoke over the humming engines, "Come on, let's go." They made their way forward to the gondola at the chin of the great machine, the enormous gas envelope blotting out the sky as they approached. Figures moved in the darkness inside, lit only by red blackout lights.

A door swung open in the side of the gondola and shadowy figures inside swung a set of stairs down to the wet grass. A couple figures moved past the red-lit doorway to make way as a very familiar silhouette appeared at the top of the stairs. Walter saluted as the man descended. Becky curtsied deeply. And Arilin ran to embrace her father.

King William swept her up in his arms, spun her around and set her back down, a little dizzy, next to Walter. Smiling broadly, he said, "Arilin! My God, I've missed you..." He trailed off, growing suddenly grave as he looked between her and Walter, "*Today* especially."

The general dropped his salute and ventured, "My lord, have you been... informed about your son?"

Her father took a deep, hissing breath, his features hardening into an unreadable mask, "Yes. I heard when we stopped at Wolf Rock." He went on flatly, "Are the reports correct?"

Walter sighed, "Yes, my lord, as far as we can tell. I'm sorry."

"What are you apologizing for?" The King snapped, "You didn't sign his commission." Her father softened a little as he glanced at her, then back at the general, "In any event, General Haas, you seem to have read my mind. I was going to have you send for Arilin here. She needs to leave on this airship, *immediately*."

Arilin looked up at him and asked, "Is this to do with Uncle Alphonse, Dad?"

Her father swung his stern gaze back at her, "Yes." He patted her on the shoulder and went on, "Look, dear, I *like* my brother. That doesn't mean I completely *trust* him right now." He gave her the most serious look he'd ever given her. It was the kind of look he'd give to an adult, "I need you back in the High City to remind the court that *you* are the Crown Princess now. You might have to do some things that *I* normally do." He chuckled sadly, "Ceremonies and meetings, mostly. Do you think you can?"

Arilin wanted to break down crying. She smiled anyways and replied, "Of course!"

He gave her a sad smile back, "That's my girl." Taking a step beside her, her father clapped her on the back, pushing her gently towards the airship as he said, "Go on, Arilin. Time is precious right now."

Arilin hesitantly looked between her father and Walter for a second. Smiling a little himself, the old general bowed slightly and said, "Take care, milady. It has been a pleasure having you with the Army."

Arilin nodded back at him, "It's been an honor, sir." Turning back to her father, she went on, "I love you, Dad. I'll see you."

Her father stepped forward and swept her into another hug, muttering, "I love you too, dear. More than you know. Take care of your mother for me."

"Will do." Arilin replied. They pulled apart reluctantly, and the princess turned and walked up the stairs into the airship. Becky fell in behind her, and she heard her father thank her as she went by. Becky's reply was lost in the roar as the airship's engines began throttling up out of their rumbling idle. The maid stepped into the ship's red-lit belly behind her and an instant later the crew pulled up the boarding stairs and heaved the hatch shut, blotting out her view of the two men as they strode away, already deep in discussion.

The airship's captain was already calling out headings and altitudes as she walked forward and emerged onto the ship's forward bridge. A couple short minutes later the deck pitched under her feet as the airship lifted off, engines howling behind them as the enormous machine came about and the ring of signal fires fell away below them. A little while after that they broke through the clouds and into moonlight so bright it was almost blinding.

Blinking her eyes to let them adjust, Arilin let her breath out and felt herself relax into the deeply cushioned seat the captain had kindly made available for her. Becky's voice beside her brought her out of her thoughts, "Happy to be going home, milady?"

Arilin sighed, "I hope it's still home when we get there."

Chapter 43

The Rattlesnake Regiment

Sophia felt a hand on her shoulder and startled awake. It was pitch black where she sat inside the dugout and she could only make out the murkiest outline of a figure in the dark. Rubbing at her eyes, she asked, "What's... what's going on?"

Sergeant Cross' voice floated out of the darkness, "Get your men up, Rose." His voice was gritty with fatigue and... something else. Grief, almost, she thought as he went on, "We're pulling out. *Now.*"

Shaking her head to clear out the cobwebs, Sophia grabbed at his hand and he pulled her upright and out of the rough shelter. Putting out a hand to steady herself as she emerged, she felt the rough boards of the trench walls dripping with water. It was barely any brighter out of the dugout as Sophia took a breath of the cold, wet air. The whole world seemed to have a blanket thrown over it. Even her sharp senses couldn't make out more than Hargrave's fitful snoring back in the hole and the soft shuffle as Cross stepped back a little to give her space. Fog, thick as a smokescreen, must have rolled in over the fields as she slept.

Looking back at the sergeant's dim silhouette, Sophia asked, "What's the plan? Where are we going?"

Cross replied softly, "They're pulling the other platoons out ahead of us. We're last." He grunted, "We're pulling out through Third Battalion's area to the south once we get back to the first trench. That's all I've got."

Sophia sighed and smiled, "It's enough for now. Thanks."

A rifle boomed down the line, a little muffled in the murk. Sophia glanced over at it instinctively. Noticing, her sergeant said, "We're going to put on a little show for the Masks on the way out. Just enough to keep them from getting too curious." He went on, "Anyways. Keep your squad around here and take a few shots while you're waiting. I'll come back to get you."

"Sure thing, sergeant." Sophia replied, turning to duck back into the dugout. She heard Cross' footsteps recede down the trench behind her as she started prodding her friends awake. Hargrave and Edward soon emerged, stretching stiffly in the darkness and complaining under their breath. The signalmen piled out after them and she sent them off towards the tunnel. Lieutenant Thorn or her father were probably around there and could put them to work. Finally, Sophia turned and walked the short distance down the trench to the shell-gouge they'd pushed their machine gun up into.

One of Tony's boots jutted from the jagged gash in the trench wall, for a second reminding Sophia of a particularly grisly story her father had told her from the last war. Pushing the thought away with a grimace, she tapped at his boot and was rewarded with a "Yeah?" from the darkness above. She raised an eyebrow. If he had been asleep he was at least getting better at hiding it.

She pulled herself up next to him and said quietly, "We're pulling out in a few minutes."

Tony gave her a sour look before settling back behind the gun, muttering, "Figures this was all for nothing."

Edward chimed in from behind them, "Look on the bright side, Tony. We're not surrendering."

Tony spat back, "Go to hell, Ed."

"Tony. Calm down." Sophia said, laying a hand on his shoulder reassuringly, "I need you to take a few shots at the enemy while we're waiting. We don't want them to know we're leaving."

She felt Tony sigh heavily. Finally he shook himself and replied, "Yeah. I've got it."

"Thanks. I'll come get you when it's time." Sophia pushed herself back out of the scrape. Her feet had barely touched the duckboards when Tony fired off a long burst into the darkness, the gun's muzzle flash searing through the blanket of fog for a moment. A couple rifles popped back from the forest, Imperial bullets cracking low overhead.

Edward turned to her and asked, "Now what do we do?"

"We wait." Sophia replied. After a couple minutes a group of Charlie Company soldiers hurried past them in the trench, forcing them up on the firing step to get out of the way. She recognized Sergeant Brockman at their head. Second Platoon, then. Tony fired off a couple more bursts as the minutes stretched out in the darkness.

Sophia had just stood up to go find Sergeant Cross and make sure they hadn't been left behind when he appeared. He nodded and gestured them after him, and she waved Edward and Hargrave on down the trench. Reaching into the shell scrape, she found Tony's leg amidst the mud and shell casings and gave it a tug. A moment later she heard him quietly pull down the machine gun and slither out of the gash feet-first. Hefting the heavy weapon, he audibly sighed and headed off down the trench. Cross gestured for her to go on and she pushed past him after Tony, feeling him close behind her as she went.

Her father was waiting by the tunnel, rifle in hand. He counted her friends off as they ducked inside. Edward, seventy-four. Mr. Hargrave, seventy-five. Tony, seventy-six. He looked at her as she passed by and said, "Sophie, good to see you. Seventy-seven." Turning to Cross, he asked, "Is that all of yours?"

She heard her sergeant reply as she ducked into the tunnel, "Yes. That's everyone."

"Alright," her father replied behind her, "Seventy-eight and seventy-nine. Let's go."

They hurried down the seemingly-endless tunnel, Sophia feeling her way forward by the rough wall boards in total darkness. After a while she bumped into Tony and grabbed hold of the back of his harness instead. After a few minutes of walking through the tunnel's endless twists and turns the air seemed to brighten around them and she realized she could make out Tony's silhouette again. They emerged into the cold night air a moment later. Sophia let go of Tony and looked around to get her bearings, stepping back a little as she realized the whole right side of the trench was full of soldiers.

A vaguely familiar silhouette leaned forward. She recognized Lieutenant Curtiss' voice as he asked, "Are you two the last from Charlie?" Alpha Company's commander added, a hint of annoyance in his voice, "We're waiting for you guys to clear."

Sophia smiled a little despite everything. She hadn't seen him since Lorenvale. "No, sir," she replied as her father and Cross' footsteps sounded out of the tunnel, "They are."

The man nodded, "Alright. You two get going."

Sophia and Tony turned and hurried down the trench, quickly catching up to the other two. She heard her father and Curtiss exchange words faintly behind her as she went. The trench snaked uphill in the wet, inky darkness, the fog growing brighter and brighter overhead as they climbed. Sophia actually winced as she broke free of the fog and emerged above the cloudscape, gleaming white all around her from the five moons flaming overhead. It was nearly bright as day, and looking up she could clearly see dark figures spilling out of the trench further uphill and running for the cover of the forest, which here stretched over the ridge's crest. She shivered a little at the thought. It was a good thing the fog had rolled in. If they'd had to do that in full view of the Imperials it would have been bad.

Now they could see their way forward they quickly sped up and reached the top of the spur. Sophia looked behind her for a moment to see her father and Sergeant Cross coming around the traverse behind them, and she heard the thrum of Alpha Company's boots behind them. "Alright," Looking around her friends, she said, "Follow me."

Climbing onto the firing step, Sophia scrambled up the trench wall into the open and ran for the trees. The sea of fog behind them stayed silent as they rushed through the fields and, after a heart-stopping minute of running through cut-apart barbed wire and vaulting shell craters, they plunged into the dark safety of the forest. Lieutenant Thorn's voice came out of the darkness, "Sophia, is that you?"

She skidded to a stop beside where he was crouching behind a tree, breathing a little hard as she replied, "Yeah... where to, sir?"

"Stay with me." Thorn replied, "We're leading the company out of this." Cross and her father made it into the forest behind them and he turned and went on, "First Sergeant! Is that everyone?"

Her father replied, "Yes, sir. Seventy-nine, all told."

Thorn sighed, and Sophia didn't need to be told why. They'd marched out of Jade Falls with almost twice that and she knew almost everyone in the company. Even though most of them weren't *dead*, the town would be draped in black by now. It wasn't a pleasant thought. Finally the lieutenant said, "Okay. Cross, come with us. We'll move out as soon as we close up with First Platoon."

Her father read Thorn's mind before he could go on, "I'll get Second and Third moving, sir." He jerked his head back at the field behind them, "Alpha's going to want to use this area in a couple minutes."

Thorn nodded and the five of them rushed off after him, her father peeling off to get the other platoons moving. They soon came upon familiar soldiers crouched among the trees, and Thorn took them forward as Cross broke off to check on the other squads. As they moved forward of the others Edward, Hargrave and Tony fanned out behind them, and the lieutenant pointed off into the darkness in front of them. "Head southwest and down the ridge diagonally." He started, "We need to put as much distance between us and *whatever* is it the Empire has coming down the back of the ridge as we can."

Sophia looked over at him and raised her eyebrows, "It's that bad, sir?"

"Infantry, heavy artillery, *armored cars*..." Thorn trailed off, "Yeah, it's that bad. You still have your S bullets, right?"

Sophia instinctively patted at the ammunition pouch that was furthest-left on her webbing, the one she never used because it was so difficult to get to. Everyone in the company had gotten a clip of armor-piercing ammunition at Wolf Rock. Suddenly she hoped they all still had them as she replied, "Yeah."

"Good." Thorn replied, gesturing into the darkness, "Let's go."

Sophia pulled out her compass, spun the bezel ring with its glowing mark around to line up with the similar glowing line of the north-facing arrow as it pointed off behind and to her right and started walking. As long as she kept the two lines together she was heading in more or less the correct direction. As she went she heard the soft noise of Thorn's footsteps behind her, then the muffled shuffling and grunting of the rest of the company as they climbed to their feet and headed out.

The ground rose gently under her feet as she made her way through the forest's dense undergrowth, hoping the rest of the company was keeping up with them. Looking around she was having a hard enough time keeping track of Thorn and her squad as they pushed through the vegetation and snaked through dense thickets of trees. The lieutenant didn't seem concerned enough to stop her, so she kept going as the ground leveled off below her feet and then, ever so slowly, began to descend. Sighing, Sophia took one last look over her shoulder as she began the walk down. There was nothing there but darkness, trees and Thorn's murky silhouette.

By some trick of the ridge they had barely been able to hear the battle being fought behind them from their trenches. No more. Fire Ridge *thundered* below them, the thuds and cracks of the artillery, popping mortars and the faint rasp of gunfire echoing from the hills below. It sounded like hell. More importantly most of it didn't sound *Royal*. The ground grew steeper beneath her feet and the forest opened up around her, and with a shiver Sophia quickened her pace.

The trees opened up ahead of her, and Sophia pushed forward towards what she thought was a clearing. At the last minute she jumped back and quickly held up a hand to stop the company as the ground disappeared in front of her feet. Looking down carefully, she saw a steep scree slope stretching away below her where the side of the ridge had given way long ago, loose gray gravel shining in the bright moonlight as it dropped into shining white clouds. Trees reassuringly poked their heads out of the mist a little way off.

"What's going... oh." Thorn remarked as he came up beside her. Examining the slope, he added, "We're going to have to go around. It looks like it ends over to the left."

Sophia barely heard him. Even with the battle going on below the gleaming-white cloudscape before her, with the moons hanging in the starry sky and the great, dark mass of the Dragonspines looming above, had an unearthly beauty. But what had caught her eye was a tiny silver speck as it emerged from the clouds far in the distance and gradually rose into the night. Pointing, she asked Thorn, "Hey, sir. Do you see that?"

Thorn squinted, then said, "Barely." Pulling out his binoculars, he looked for a moment and went on, "It's an airship. Huh." He gave her a look, "I'm surprised they'd bring one in that low with the battle going on. Must be important."

Sophia chuckled, "Maybe it's the King."

The lieutenant snorted, "Wish he'd give us a ride then. Come on," He gestured off to the left, where they could see trees sloping down past the rocky slope, "We've still got to walk."

"Yes, sir." Sophia turned and made her way along the cliff to where the ground leveled out and, checking her compass again, kept descending into the clouds. The cold, wet darkness quickly surrounded them, Sophia feeling her way forward through the black-on-dark outlines of trees by the faint glow of her compass. After a few more minutes of walking she turned to Thorn and murmured, "Sir, where's the rest of the battalion? I haven't heard *anyone* ahead of us."

He whispered back, "They should be a ways up ahead. They had a head start on us." She was about to reply when a sharp Imperial gunshot drifted out of the forest below. Sophia instinctively ducked into the cover of the nearest tree as a couple deep Royal gunshots boomed through the woods, followed an instant later by the shrill hammering of an enemy machine gun. More and more gunfire unfolded in the distance in front of them like an unrolling carpet as the firefight built, and Sophia caught her breath as she heard a grenade go off. It sounded Imperial.

Edward chimed in sarcastically from the darkness, "Found 'em."

Sophia shot a dirty look in his general direction, then looked back at the commander, "What's the plan, sir? Go around?"

"Yeah." Thorn replied, "Aim well past the left flank of the fighting. We'll either attack to break through and open a route or roll them up from the flank."

"Yes sir." Sophia thought for a moment, then snorted and drew her bayonet, locking it to her rifle with a sharp click. A moment later she heard Edward and Hargrave fix their own bayonets, then, faintly, Second Squad behind them.

Thorn said as she finished, "Good idea, Miss Rose." He went on, "If we hit the enemy, bayonets *first*. Rush through. It's so dark shooting will just draw fire and slow us down."

"Got it, sir." She heard Sergeant Cross's voice faintly, a little further back, "Cameron, go tell that to Second and Third."

She heard the man from Second get up behind them and start moving back through the forest. Lieutenant Thorn said, "Thanks, sergeant." He turned back to her, "Move out, Miss Rose."

Pocketing her compass, Sophia got up and stalked downhill, bayoneted rifle cutting the darkness ahead of her as she aimed well off to the side of the unfurling battle below. Soon it sounded like dozens of Royal and Imperial machine guns were hammering away at each other below, grenades thundering through the trees every few seconds. Off to her right an Imperial grenade thudded and an instant later a whole new arc of Royal gunfire unrolled through the trees to their side. Imperial weapons chattered back a moment later. Thorn commented softly, "There's First Battalion."

Sophia pressed on wordlessly as the gunfire spread across the ridge to their front, forcing her to bear farther and farther left. After a little while the air seemed to clear and she made out green tracers dancing deep in the forest before her like evil fireflies. They were below the clouds. A little more confident in her footing, Sophia hefted her rifle and sped up.

They had just gotten even with the left edge of the battle, maybe three or four hundred meters back when Sophia heard a too-familiar sharp cracking sound far behind her. Gritting her teeth, she glanced over at Lieutenant Thorn as the dragoon rifles fired away behind them, steadily, as though they were looking for a response. Looking for someone to *shoot back*. She heard him mutter, "Come on, come on..." A Royal machine gun roared back upslope and he cursed as another curtain of enemy gunfire unrolled upslope of them. Thorn gave her a hard look that told her everything she needed. She turned back to the forest in front of her, the one open side of the Imperial net that was rapidly closing around the 24th Infantry Regiment, and dove into the darkness. She wasn't going to be giving that long-haired Imperial bastard the satisfaction. Not tonight. He was probably waving his dragoons down the ridge after them at that very moment.

Green tracers snapped through the trees overhead as they rushed forward, bullets cracking into the trees and bits of wood and branches raining down around them. As they got past the edge of the battle Sophia turned downslope again, dodging around trees and leaping half-seen roots as she pushed forward. The battle drifted off to her right, blue and green tracers flashing through the trees to her side and the flashes of bursting grenades piercing through the murk under the trees. Giving her just enough light to see the Imperial soldier stalking through the trees not twenty feet in front of her.

Sophia hurled herself forward and slammed into him bayonet-first, hard enough she felt his feet leave the ground. He let out a gargling scream as she twisted, jerked her bayonet free as he flew backward and charged on as the forest around her came alive with shouts and the enemy boiled out of the shadows. A rifle cracked off to the side and in the harsh light of the muzzle flash she saw another Imperial ducking into cover behind a tree in front of her as she charged. Pivoting in the deep forest loam, she stabbed into the shadows and felt her bayonet bite.

Yanking it free, she made to dash forward again when an Imperial machine gun hammered to life just beside her, the muzzle flash backlighting the soldier beside the gunner as he spun and raised his rifle for her. Sophia had flexed her legs to throw herself aside when a Royal machine gun erupted too-close behind the man and he shuddered and pitched forward. A familiar silhouette emerged with a smoking machine gun at his hip as the Imperial gunner rolled over and raised a pistol for Tony. Sophia darted forward, reversed her grip on her rifle and stabbed once, twice, again until he stopped thrashing. Pulling her weapon out, she looked at Tony and said, "Come on."

Tony grunted, "Yeah," and they rushed into the darkness. By now the forest was alive with rushing shapes, men screaming and shouting as they fought. Here and there Imperial gunshots rang out, usually followed a moment later by the sick thud of a bayonet slamming home and a scream. They charged through the forest for what felt like an eternity more, blood pounding in Sophia's temples as the enemy seemed to loom out of every shadow only to dissolve before her bayonet, before the shrill blast of Lieutenant Thorn's whistle brought her back to reality. It couldn't have been longer than a minute, she realized as the long chain of short whistles rang through the trees. Halt attack and reorganize.

Sophia ducked behind a tree and shouted, "First squad! Edward, Hargrave, over here!" Waving Tony into cover, she added, "Tony, watch your fire."

Tony flopped down in a tangle of protective roots and said, "Imperials only, got it."

Her other two friends emerged from the darkness behind them. Hargrave sounded a little shaken as he said, "We're here. Where's Tony? Are you alright?"

"I'm here, *Dad*." Tony's voice drifted sarcastically out of the darkness.

Sophia snorted and shot back, "Shut up, Tony." She turned back to Hargrave, "We're fine, thanks. Somehow." Green tracers started snapping through the woods in their direction from the main firefight, and she added, "You'd better..."

Edward finished the thought from behind the next tree over, "Get to cover, yeah, we get it. Thanks, Sophie."

It would have been funnier if she hadn't just killed three people. Sophia hissed out something like a laugh as she heard her father calling for Lieutenant Thorn in the darkness behind her. Thorn's voice answered and she heard the commander's running footsteps going through the undergrowth away from her a moment later.

Figuring she might as well save the man the work, Sophia called out, "Sergeant Cross! First squad's good! We're over here!"

Dawn must have been breaking. She could just barely make out his silhouette a little ways off as he turned towards her and replied, "Thanks, got it! Second, where the *hell* are you?" Corporal Stennis' voice floated over faintly and Cross cursed and went on, "Get up and get over here! You're on Rose's right side, she's over there!"

The platoon had mostly reassembled when Sophia heard Lieutenant Thorn indistinctly shout something. She was about to ask Cross what was going on when her father roared, clear even over the nearby battle, "*Charlie Company! On line towards the enemy to our three o' clock! Support by fire! We will cover the regiment as they withdraw around us! Bugler, signal!*"

A moment later Sophia heard the company bugler butchering 'Assembly', and she realized she hadn't heard the man play since they'd marched into Southbend. He tried again, better this time, and again as the company picked up, fell in on line behind the sturdiest-looking trees and rocks and opened fire in the graying darkness. More bugles sounded amid the hammering gunfire, acknowledging the command as the Imperial line before them slowly bent backwards under the weight of their fire and Royal soldiers poured through the forest behind them. Off to their right Alpha Company seemed to be firing every weapon they owned uphill, somehow keeping the dragoons above them at bay as the murk brightened into a sullen, gray dawn. Imperial artillery began shrieking in across the ridge and Sophia heard screams behind her as trees exploded above the retreating soldiers.

Finally, *finally*, as Alpha Company fell back against the right end of their line and the forest seemed to be alive with Imperials sniping at them, she heard Sergeant Cross shout, "*Alright!* First platoon, fall back! Southwest, same direction as before! Go!"

Sophia gratefully got up and ran off diagonally downslope, followed a moment later by her friends. After a short rush she dove back into cover, fired a round in the general direction of the enemy and repeated it again and again until the Imperial bullets were ricochets snapping harmlessly overhead instead of aimed shots at her. Gathering her squad back up, she made her way back to the front of the platoon and hurried down-hill. After a little while she heard Alpha Company obviously disengage behind them, every now and then turning to rake the forest with their machine guns. Imperial gunfire followed for a little while before tapering off. Clearly the enemy had enough of them for one day, at least.

They hurried down through the forest, Sophia following the few sol-diers she could see in front of her along a trail beaten through the un-dergrowth by the hundreds of feet ahead. The day gradually brightened to a dull gray as rain began to sift down onto the forest and patter cold-ly through the leaves, filling the trees with soft noise that drowned out their footsteps as they descended. Off to their right unnatural thunder boomed through the valley, and now and then the wind shifted and they could hear the soft crackle of gunfire in the distance. Most it sounded Imperial.

Sophia walked on for what felt like hours. What *were* hours, she re-alized. Every now and then they would stop to drink water and dress the formation, her father walking the company back and forth to make sure nobody had disappeared along the way. The soldiers in front of them moved up and were replaced by a group carrying stretchers, the wounded men stoically silent as their bearers jostled them down the hill on their awkward diagonal path. Finally, as the morning rain dried up and the sun began breaking through the clouds far overhead the ground began to level off beneath her feet.

The enemy shellfire lifted out of the valley and onto the slopes behind them as they walked through the gently sloping forest, and Sophia's skin crawled as she realized the reason why. Whatever Royal troops had been in the valley behind them had been defeated and the enemy was pivoting to sweep up the ridge. Anyone still off to the north along their original line of attack was going to be encircled and crushed. If they had retreated that way, even if they had managed to break through that first group of Imperials they would be facing God-knows how many more now. They wouldn't have had a chance.

The soft sound of flowing water reached her ears ahead and a small, swift-flowing creek soon emerged through the trees. Water seeks the lowest point in the land, and Sophia smiled involuntarily as she realized they had reached the bottom of Fire Ridge. She paused for a moment to refill her canteens before splashing across it, her legs protesting a little at the unfamiliar demands of climbing as she scrambled up the bank on the far side. The trees thinned ahead and Sophia caught her breath nervously as she saw what looked like a pasture through the trunks. Even at a distance she could see a few blue-jacketed soldiers milling around in the trees on the far side of the open space as it began to rise again, probably three or four hundred meters away.

Just inside the shelter of the trees ahead she saw a familiar figure gesturing to someone up at the head of the stretcher party. Sophia heard an indistinct command through the trees and the men broke off to the left, moving a little quicker now that they knew they could set their burdens down soon. Looking off in that direction she saw a few medics moving through the trees, their Red Cross armbands standing out brightly even at a distance. They walked closer to the figure directing traffic and Sophia recognized Major Matheson as he looked her over.

"Miss Rose," He commented hoarsely. She supposed he'd probably been up all night shouting at people, "Good to see you again. Charlie, Second Battalion, right? Who's in charge of you now?"

"I am." Lieutenant Thorn walked up from behind her before she had a chance to respond, "What's the plan, sir?"

Matheson snorted, "Good question. I'm working on it." He tiredly pointed up the ridge behind them, "How's the company? Alpha's behind you, right?"

The lieutenant nodded, "Yeah. They're last. We've got seventy-five effectives, two walkers and a stretcher case." He scowled and went on, "One man missing since we pulled out."

"You're doing better than most of this regiment." The major went on, "Is Clark with you?"

Thorn shook his head slowly, "I haven't seen him all morning, sir. I... don't think he made it."

The major sighed, "That's what I was afraid of. God *damn* it."

"Sir?" Thorn asked.

Major Matheson shook his head bitterly. It seemed as though a weight had descended onto his shoulders for a moment before he straightened up tiredly and said, "Looks like I'm in command now."

Matheson worked for the regimental staff, Sophia recalled. Her stomach curdled a little as she realized he probably wouldn't have put it that way if it had just been a matter of him taking over the *battalion*. Thorn echoed her thoughts, "Of the regiment? Where's Colonel Paget?"

"Missing." Matheson said bluntly, "He was down at Division when we got the order to pull out. Said he'd meet us." He shook his head again, "I haven't seen *him*, or anyone else senior to *me* all morning."

"Great." Thorn said sarcastically, "Alright, sir. Where do you want us?"

Matheson gestured off in the direction of the medics, "Set up over there. Your Bravo company is down that way about two hundred meters. Face up the ridge." He went on, "When you're done with that, get your First Sergeant and meet me over at the house." He pointed at a small herdsman's cottage sitting amid a stand of trees on the far end of the pasture, "We're having a council of war."

Thorn nodded, "Yes, sir." Turning around, he gestured off towards the medics and called, "Charlie! Move out!"

A little while later Sophia walked through the pasture's ragged grass behind her father and Lieutenant Thorn. Figuring they would be deciding on a route out of the valley they had decided to take her with them to save the time of explaining it to her later. Turning around and walking backwards for a moment, Sophia looked up at the green bulk of Fire Ridge looming overhead. They had come off the ridge *miles* south of where they had gone up, shielded from the enemy's eyes in the valley as it curved west a little and climbed behind the bulk of the ridge.

The ridge was earning its name now. Pillars of black smoke climbed skyward behind the ridge as it jutted north, pooling into an ugly haze slowly filling the valley. Every few seconds the thud of an exploding shell rolled through the valley, and whole volleys unrolled faintly over the smaller ridges to the west. Shivering despite the hot sun overhead, Sophia turned around and hurried after the two men. She didn't want to stay in that valley a second longer than necessary.

Major Matheson waved to them from under the shade of the trees around the cottage. The building itself was tiny, not nearly large enough for the thirty or so people converging on it. The major had spread a poncho on the wet grass to make a dry surface to lay a map down on. Sophia looked at the group as they gathered around. They had gone up the ridge a little ragged from battles fought and miles marched, but they had been a *regiment*. Sophia's stomach curdled as she realized the price they had all paid.

What was left of the Twenty-Fourth Infantry Regiment, the Rattlesnakes of the Serpent River, was led by a bunch of filthy, exhausted lieutenants. There were a few captains among the crowd. She recognized Delta Company's commander, probably in charge of all of Second Battalion now. Matheson was the only senior officer there. Among the NCOs,

Sophia didn't see *any* of their sergeant majors. Looking over at her father, she saw the muscles of his jaw bulging as he looked across the group himself. Noticing her glance, he softened for a moment and reached over to pat her on the back reassuringly. It was fake confidence but it felt good anyways.

Major Matheson stood up and looked around the group. The soft murmur of conversation died off quickly and he started, "Alright, gentlemen. I'm not going to mince words with you. We're all that's left." He paused for emphasis as artillery rolled across the ridge to the north, "We've picked up a few stragglers from further up the valley, and it's *bad*. We're lucky we're not swimming in Imperials already. We need to decide what our next move is going to be."

The commander looked around the group and went on, "The way I see it we have two options. One," He pointed over his shoulder with a thumb, "Is to keep pushing west from here and try to evade the Masks as they sweep south. We'd have to be ready to fight our way out. Two," He pointed up the valley, to where the pasture narrowed into a herd path climbing into the mountains, "Is to march south into the Dragonspines and make our way west from there."

"Sir," A lieutenant she didn't recognize said, "We don't have the supplies for a march like that. Most of my men are flat out of rations."

"I was about to get to that," Matheson said, "We aimed for this area coming off the ridge for a reason. There was a jaeger battalion based here earlier screening our right flank, and they left their supplies when they pulled out. We found their wagons back in the woods." He went on, "It's enough food for two or three days and enough ammunition for us to get into a fight with."

"I have ten or so stretcher cases that are *not* going to survive without surgery." Another captain wearing a Red Cross armband said, "I should be able to stabilize the rest of them."

Matheson grimaced, "Get a couple medics to volunteer to stay with them here, then. If they don't want to, pick two." He went on as the man nodded, "The Empire will be through here in hours, if that."

"Sir," Her father spoke up, "I walked out of the Dragon's Jaw." He gave her a look, chuckled grimly and went on, "So did Sophie here, strictly speaking. We have fewer soldiers, *no* artillery, a lot more Imperials in front of us and right now we don't even know how far we have to march." He looked around the group, "If we try to fight our way out of this, we're going to *die*. We need to disappear."

A murmur of agreement went around the group. Matheson replied,

"You make a good case, First Sergeant. Does anyone object?" A few people looked unhappy, but nobody spoke out. Nodding, the major went on, "It's decided then. We march south. If this map is correct, there are high passes and trails we can use to move west."

"One more thing before we move out." The commander said, looking around the group, "Right now we do not have a single sergeant major with us. I need an NCO. First Sergeants... which one of you is senior?"

Sophia noticed her father pointedly looking at his feet, muttering something under his breath as the non-commissioned officers in the group looked around at each other and then, one by one, looked at him. Silence descended under the trees. Finally he sighed heavily, looked up and said, "I think I am."

"Alright." Matheson nodded, "John, right?"

"Yes." Her father said flatly. It was a little strange hearing someone call her father by his first name.

The commander went on, "Looks like you're the new Regimental Sergeant Major."

Her father sighed again, then straightened up. Casting a steely glare around the group, he said, "This will *not* be an easy march. You *will* keep your soldiers going, no matter what. And," He went on icily, "Unlike the old bastard, I am not going to spend all my time pretending to inspect the field hospital while the rest of us are fighting. I have standards *off* the parade field. You will remember that."

Some of the sergeants visibly swallowed. Major Matheson chuckled and said, "Thank you, Sergeant Major. Now, gentlemen," He looked around as the ragged circle, "Move out."

Half an hour later Sophia Rose stepped forward onto the rocky path leading up into the jagged spires of the Dragonspine Moutains. The regiment followed behind her.

Chapter 44

Supreme Commander

Some armies die hard. Ravaged by unending combat, out of ammunition, their uniforms torn to rags. Every prisoner a desperately wounded man. If they believed in their friends and their leaders, if they had half of a glimmer of a chance, soldiers would fight beyond the limits of human endurance. He'd seen it again and again in a lifetime of battles.

Lord General Slade Anjanou felt himself smiling as they trotted past another column of dazed-looking prisoners, herded off the road by his dragoon bodyguards. The Army of Drakenburg had not died hard. It had been crushed in the blink of an eye, its corps shattered in as many hours as his trap slammed shut. Units had wheeled about and tried to fight only to be torn apart by a hurricane of fire and a tsunami of masked soldiers. Many had simply surrendered. This group had barely gotten their blue uniforms dirty.

"Looking forward to a swim in Sapphire Bay, sir?" The circumstances had made the young lieutenant in charge of his escorts talkative. The Lord General chuckled. When he was that age he never would have thought about making chit-chat with the five-star commanding general of the Western Area Army. On the other hand, the circumstances had been different after *that* battle.

He humored the kid, "Yes. However." Artillery rumbled ominously off to the southwest, beyond the forested bulk of Fire Ridge as it climbed into the mountains. The general went on, "This battle isn't over yet."

The lieutenant nodded in the general direction of the ridge, "You're worried about that, sir?"

"Yes." Slade replied sternly, "At least one of their corps deployed facing *north*. Fifth Army is having to fight."

"Oh." The man hesitated for a second, "Ah... sorry, sir. I didn't know."

Slade snorted and pointed at the church steeples jutting up from a small rise ahead of them, fingers of ugly black smoke reaching skywards around them in the morning light, "I believe that is Lindestadt. Hurry." He smiled cruelly, "I don't want to keep them waiting *too* long."

"Of course, sir." The lieutenant shouted to his men ahead, who had just finished cleared the tail of the column of prisoners off the road, "Up ahead! Triple time!"

The Lord General kicked his horse into a canter, the young lieutenant following a second behind as the dusty road twisted gently towards the town. Everywhere he looked was another sign of the Royal Army's disaster. Whole columns of wagons lay abandoned on the roadside piled with supplies and ammunition, perfectly secured like on peacetime maneuvers. Dragoons had already rustled whatever horses the King's soldiers hadn't fled with. Passing through a windrow of trees stretching across the fields, Slade looked out at a mass of dirty smoke in the distance and saw the lean shapes of Royal field guns beneath. It looked like a whole battalion drawn up facing north. Around the guns the ground had been plowed up crazily, black earth and golden wheat dotted with blue and brown lumps. Off behind them a few ammunition caissons still burned sullenly.

Slade reined his horse in as his dragoons turned another column of prisoners off the road. The last group had been shocked but they had clearly put up a fight. This one was *terrified*, men and a few women stumbling off the road to let them pass. Slade raised an eyebrow as he noticed most of them weren't even wearing the Royal Army's ubiquitous black puttees. Administrators then, a bunch of clerks on the Army of Drakenburg's staff. They must have expected to fight the war behind their typewriters. It had probably been quite the rude awakening for them. Slade chuckled darkly and rode on.

They came over the rise and Lindestadt unfurled before them as the dirt road turned to cobblestone beneath their horses' hooves. It was larger than it had seemed from below. In peace he was sure it was a beautiful provincial town, a picturesque stop on the long railroad from the Marchlands to the Great Pass and beyond. Country lovers had once strolled through its leafy streets, marveling at the snow-capped Dragonspine Mountains and the green bulk of Fire Ridge rising to the south.

Now it was crawling with Imperial troops and Royal prisoners. Black smoke curled above tiled roofs overhead as the horses picked their way through streets gouged by shells and here and there torn up in ugly slashes as though some great beast had raked at the ground. A group of masked infantrymen rushed past, most of them peeling off down an alleyway in search of fugitives. A couple stopped to salute and Slade quickly waved them off after their comrades. As they rode on he heard the familiar thud of a door being kicked in down the alley.

The dragoons up ahead shouted and jostled with their horses, herding another knot of blue-jacketed prisoners off onto the sidewalk to let them pass. The handful of soldiers guarding them did double-takes at his appearance obvious enough to notice through their masks and their sergeant instantly barked at them to get back to work and move their charges along. Slade rode on impassively.

As he looked back up Slade noticed the dragoons had stopped ahead and parted ranks, making way for a pair of riders. The Lord General squinted a little and made out the colonel's insignia on the lead soldier's collar alongside the rifle and bayonet of the infantry. Riding through the curtain of dragoons, the lithe woman and her orderly saluted as they pulled up before him. Her voice was hard and a little raspy from too much shouting as she said, "Sir. We've been expecting you."

Slade returned her salute and said, "Colonel Holloway. Good work here."

She dropped her salute and swung her horse in alongside him as he gestured for the dragoons to get going again, saying, "The regiment deserves the credit, sir." She snorted, "I just give the orders."

He chuckled, "They deserve it." Looking over at her, Slade felt a thin smile play across his lips, "Now where *are* they?"

The woman gestured to a gap in the buildings to the side of the road up ahead. Trees spread over the rooftops before them as the street opened up, fronting onto what had once been a scenic little park at the heart of the town. The trees had been torn by shellfire and the carefully-maintained grass churned up in ugly swathes by the same monsters that had clawed at the cobblestones earlier. Letting his eyes play over the scene, Slade saw a couple of the culprits sitting under the trees at the far end of the park. The Imperial tankers had popped open the access hatches on their war machines and most of them were busy working on their temperamental mounts. The rest of them were gawking at the knot of Royal soldiers standing in front of a particularly grand and fine-looking house fronting onto the park. A couple Imperial guards stood off to one side of the group awkwardly, and Slade smiled as he saw the reason why. It would be a strange experience indeed for any private soldier to stand guard on a bunch of enemy generals.

"There they are, sir. We've already marched off most of the lower-ranking prisoners." The hard-bitten woman snorted contemptuously and went on, "They'd moved into about half the town. I don't think I've ever seen so many colonels in my *life*, not even at IJHQ. How big of a staff did this guy think he needed?"

Slade replied darkly, "I'll just have to ask him myself."

Holloway rubbed at the back of her neck nervously, "About that, sir..." Slade looked over at her wordlessly, raising an eyebrow enough to make his mask shift. The woman went on quickly, a little flustered, "Well, it'll be... better if you see for yourself."

"I'm *tingling* with anticipation, colonel." Slade replied sarcastically, "I'm sure he knows what happened last time they tried to stand us up."

The Royal officers backed away a little as they rode up, the dragoons parting into a semicircle around the group as they approached. Slade rode his horse up within a couple paces of the assembled generals, feeling the pressure slowly build in his jaw as he played his glare across them. There were *nineteen* general officers shuffling nervously beneath him from every branch and service in the Royal military, even a rather forlorn-looking admiral. None of them would meet his gaze. Just to drag the moment out a bit longer Slade counted their stars. They had thirty-two between them.

When he judged they were thoroughly intimidated Slade Anjanou dismounted and strode up to their leader, a dazed-looking full general holding what he recognized, now that he got a closer look at it, as a Royal Field Marshal's baton. Slade glanced at his nametag for a moment. Fischer. The Army of Drakenburg's Chief of Staff. The man finally looked him in the eyes as he approached, and Slade's gaze held him transfixed as the others backed away nervously. The man's eyes went wide with fear as the Lord General wordlessly glowered at him.

The silence stretched out over a long moment. Realizing the masked general wasn't going to speak first, General Fischer nervously held out the baton and said, "Sir... from the Field Marshal."

Slade fought off the urge to backhand him. Taking a very slow, deep breath, he finally growled, "Where is *Lawrence White?*"

Fischer visibly swallowed. Colonel Holloway unexpectedly rescued the man, "That's what I was talking about, sir. You... just need to see this. If you'll please follow me."

Slade looked over at her for a long moment, then gestured for her to go ahead. The Royal generals parted quickly to let them pass and a soldier at the door instantly pulled it open as they approached. Slade returned the man's salute wordlessly and followed the colonel inside, the mansion's cool air a welcome respite from the heat. The house murmured with low, serious conversation, papers ruffling and floorboards creaking under heavy boots as military intelligence pored through a mountain of documents in the rooms off the grand foyer.

Colonel Holloway turned and started up the stairs set against the foyer wall and Slade followed. The second floor was quieter, rooms improvised into offices standing open and empty, papers chaotically strewn over desks where the infantry had pawed through them when they had first come through. A few had drifted into the hallway. Slade grimaced at the thought of the analysts having to waste time cleaning up the mess, but he supposed it couldn't be helped. The infantry smashed and grabbed for a reason.

They rounded a corner and Slade saw an Imperial soldier standing guard outside a particularly ornate door at the end of the hall. The man saluted with his bayoneted rifle as they approached, and they both returned it as they stopped before the door. Turning to Holloway, the Lord General said, "This is what you were talking about?"

The colonel nodded, "Yes, sir." Taking a deep breath, she stepped forward and pulled the door open for him.

Slade took a couple steps into the room, his eyes falling on the massive desk taking up the far end of Field Marshal White's office. For a long moment he was silent as the colonel slowly entered and stood beside him. Finally he snorted with contempt and gave the woman a look out the side of his mask, "You could have just told me."

"Sorry," She said, "It... didn't seem right, sir."

Field Marshal White lay crumpled over the desk in a pool of congealed blood, a pistol in his outstretched hand. As Slade approached he saw the small hole in the man's temple, ragged and burned from the weapon's blast. The elaborately patterned paper on the far wall was speckled with blood and bits of tissue. General Anjanou contemplated his enemy for a few moments, then shook his head slowly.

The woman looked at him and asked, "Sir?"

"Colonel, my son writes me pretty often." He looked up from the dead man and sighed, "June's always bragging about how many prisoners he's taken. Two or three hundred by now, if he's at all telling the truth." Slade went on, "I always want to write back and tell him he's supposed to be *killing* them." Holloway was silent and he snorted, "The war the kids are fighting these days... it's *civilized*."

The colonel replied, "I've never seen this many Royal prisoners, that's for sure."

"I have." Slade said darkly, gesturing at White's body, "But. That makes *this* unnecessary."

"It's a damn shame, sir." Holloway ventured, then asked, "What do you want us to do with him?"

Slade replied, "Lay him out and clean him up. I'll send a mortuary team to come get him today." He went on, "We'll give him a proper funeral."

"Yes, sir." Holloway nodded.

Slade's reply died in his throat as he noticed the corner of a sheet of paper sticking out beneath the Field Marshal's crumpled body. Reaching forward, he took hold of it and carefully pulled it out, leaving a red streak across the blotter where the paper had soaked with blood. The markings across the top said that it was a radio message received very early that morning and decoded a couple hours ago, probably as Imperial troops stormed into the town. It read:

> Field Marshal Lawrence White is relieved of command, effective immediately. Published succession of command in Army Order 004 is revoked, effective immediately. Headquarters, Army of Drakenburg shall exercise no command functions until further notice.

> Lieutenant General Walter Haas is hereby promoted to General and appointed as Commanding General, Army of Drakenburg, effective immediately. Headquarters, IX Corps will exercise functions as the Army Headquarters pending reorganization.

> All Royal troops engaged in the vicinity of Fire Ridge shall retreat to the west immediately, if necessary attacking to break out of encirclement. Any unit that is in extremity forced to surrender shall ensure cryptographic equipment, weapons, supplies and any other items that may be of use to the enemy are destroyed.

> Assume current codes have been captured by enemy forces at this time. New codebooks will be distributed by courier. Assume any radio messages sent in current codes are compromised. Be aware the enemy may have tapped field telephone networks vicinity Fire Ridge.

> ACKNOWLEDGE RECEIPT BY SECURE COMMUNICATIONS.

> BY ORDER OF THE KING.

General Anjanou grunted and set the paper back down on the desk. Giving him a look, Holloway asked, "What's that, sir?"

"Probably the reason White shot himself." Slade replied, pointing at the paper, "This is important. Make sure the analysts get this immediately. Now, colonel, excuse me." The general went on coldly as he turned and strode past her out the door, "I have to get back to headquarters. *Immediately.*"

"Yes, sir!" The woman replied, a little surprised. She followed him down the stairs and he heard her calling for the intelligence team as he walked out the front door.

The group of Royal generals recoiled a little as he walked down the front stairs and stopped in front of General Fischer. He fixed the man with his glare and held out a hand wordlessly. Fischer handed over the Field Marshal's baton like it was on fire and visibly exhaled as Slade took it. Not even bothering to look at it, Slade looked around the assembled group and said, "You will surrender your swords to Colonel Holloway." The colonel had appeared on the stairs behind him and he turned to her, "Contact my headquarters and have them send transportation for this group immediately, if they haven't done so already."

"Ah, sir?" One of the Airship Corps generals spoke up. Slade glared at him and he swallowed, then managed, "Can we keep our batmen?"

Slade thought about it for a moment. Then he rolled his eyes and said, "*One* military servant each."

"Thanks, sir." The man said, remarkably cheerfully.

Forestalling any more questions, Slade strode through the group and swung himself up onto his horse. The dragoons remounted around him, and his lieutenant turned to him and asked, "Where to, sir?"

Slade jerked his chin back the way they had come, "Back to headquarters." Stuffing the Field Marshal's baton into a saddlebag, he kicked his horse down the road out of town.

They were well out of town and trotting down the dusty road at a good pace when the lieutenant spoke up again, "You seem... concerned, sir. Is everything all right? I mean, we *did* just crush the Royal Army."

God in heaven this kid was talkative. Slade made a mental note to have him sent back to his regiment. But while he had the time he might as well teach him a little. He replied, "Let me tell you a story, kid."

"Sir?" The lieutenant looked at him questioningly. Somehow his mask had an annoying expression.

"I recall you went to the Academy." Slade started. The lieutenant nodded and he went on, "You remember the painting in the lobby of Nakamura Hall?"

The man nodded, "Yes, sir. The one of the Royal officer surrendering to General Nakamura after we took back the Black Citadel?" He thought for a moment, "I guess I never understood why that painting seems so *tense*, sir. Everyone in it besides the General looks like they want to kill that guy."

Slade gave him a stern look, "You didn't do well in Military History 301, did you?"

"Uh..." The lieutenant rubbed the back of his neck nervously, "It was either study for that or High Elven, sir."

"The most exalted tongue is not so difficult that you can neglect studies of a practical nature, young knight." Slade replied in Elven. Switching back, he went on, "They look that way because we *did* want to kill him. I'm sure you noticed the sword on the table in front of him?"

"Yes, sir." He could almost see the lightbulb go off in his head as he remembered, "It was from his commander, wasn't it?"

"Yes." Slade went on, "After we'd besieged the Black Citadel for a couple months the Royal commander, Major General Reiner, figured out help wasn't coming. At that point he had two options. One, break out. The major in charge of the fortress artillery advocated *very* strongly for that option. Or, two, try to negotiate terms of surrender better than immediate death." Slade paused for effect before going on, "He chose option two and decided to stick this unfortunate major with the job of negotiating."

"What Reiner didn't know was that we had our own problems. That whole campaign was successful because the enemy thought we had about five times more soldiers in the siege lines than we actually did and their relief force spent weeks marching in circles trying to outmaneuver our field army instead of actually *fighting* them." Slade chuckled, "If they'd tried to break out, *really* tried, they would have gotten out." The lieutenant nodded eagerly and he continued, "So we were much happier to give them terms than we let on at the time."

The general went on, "We eventually agreed they would destroy their arms, burn their own colors and receive safe passage back to their own lines. All we wanted on top of that was for General Reiner to present himself to General Nakamura and surrender the fortress in person, soldier to soldier." Slade snorted, "My commander was no *rebel gangster*, he was a soldier of the Emperor and he was going to be treated that way."

The lieutenant connected the dots, "And Reiner sent this major back with his sword?"

"Yes." Slade Anjanou went on, "The painting makes it look more dignified than it actually was. I was just a lieutenant like you at the time, and I *breathed fire*. I'd already drawn when the general held up his hand and told us to stop. This major apologized for his commander's conduct and offered his own sword as well, and Nakamura told him to keep it. He said that he respected his bravery. He was the one Royal officer to walk out of the Black Citadel with his sword."

"Didn't Reiner, ah..." The lieutenant trailed off awkwardly.

Slade replied, "We pulled him out of the column afterwards. The General asked me to do the honors."

"Damn." The man left it at that.

"It was different back then. You kids are lucky." Slade grunted and went on, "That major, Walter Haas, went on to command the Royal garrison at the Dragon's Jaw. And as of this morning he's in command of the Army of Drakenburg." He gave the kid a hard look, "He does *not* give up, and he has seen worse than this."

"Oh. So..." The dragoon looked back at him expectantly.

Slade chuckled grimly, "This war's just beginning, lieutenant."

Epilogue

Patricia MacMahon looked over at the dark-haired captain sitting on horseback beside her. The woman was stoically gazing out across the sea of fields and green, forested hills west of Fire Ridge. Off through the fields they could see a patrol moving out on horseback, blue-jacketed lancers disappearing one-by-one over a distant rise in search of the enemy. She sighed. She couldn't blame her for being nervous.

It had been a week since they had somehow broken free of the Imperial Army and retreated to the west. After she had sent Arilin away her division had taken a beating over a day of desperate fighting with the lead elements of what she had gradually realized, to her horror, was an entire enemy field army. The avalanche of masked soldiers would have swatted her division like a fly if she had tried to stand and fight. As it was she had managed to make its advance guard deploy for combat early just to kill her. This had probably delayed their advance by about twelve hours. It was enough time for Walter to push the enemy's motorized spearhead aside on their right flank, get what was left of V Corps off the ridge and pull his own IX Corps out before it could be swept away.

Field Marshal White had thrown almost half of the Army of Drakenburg into his left hook sweeping around the ridge, corps after corps and hundreds of thousands of men. Every last unit had simply disappeared as the jaws of the enemy's trap slammed shut. From the few, desperate radio calls they had gotten the survivors of the Imperial assault had fallen back onto the ridge to make their last stand. A couple days after they began their retreat the distant rumbling of artillery lashing the northern ridge faded to deathly silence.

The Empire had mostly left them alone since then, but Patricia didn't expect the quiet would last much longer. They would attack again, and when they did her cavalry would give Walter enough time to do, well, *something*. She didn't particularly enjoy thinking about the odds they were facing. Even with the King's reassuring presence and Walter in charge of the Army now, they were probably outnumbered three to one or more. There was only so much a general could do against that.

Speaking of reassuring presences, she *wasn't* being one. Patricia pushed her dark thoughts aside, looked back over at her companion and said, "By the way, Holly, congratulations on your command."

Holly Schrader looked down at her new lancer's uniform for a moment. The corner of her mouth turned up a little as she replied, "I think my father might have something to do with it, milady."

Patricia laughed, "The Army's a family business. Just between you and me," She winked at her, "I think my father might have helped me out a little too."

Holly looked at her blankly for a moment, then chuckled. It didn't seem to be something she did a lot. Growing serious again, the younger woman replied, "He even had *uniforms* ready for me." She thought for a moment and went on, "I'm just surprised Colonel Bennett let me go."

Patricia snorted derisively, "She didn't have much of an argument against it."

"That explains things." Holly raised an inky eyebrow, "She was white as a sheet after she spoke to you, you know."

"She should have been." Patricia replied sourly, "I did not give her Vanessa so she could get her *captured* four hours later. If I could spare my aide, she could spare a staff officer."

"Lieutenant Gable, milady?" Holly asked, "She's alive? I just knew she was missing."

"Somehow, yes." The lady general said, "We got word from the Red Cross this morning. Not a scratch on her."

The captain smiled a little, "That's a relief. I liked her."

Patricia chuckled, "You know, she was listed as 'Taken Prisoner' and not 'Surrendered'. For someone who hadn't been wounded, well... that's almost unheard-of, coming from the Empire."

"Huh," The younger woman asked, "You think she was overwhelmed?"

"Probably..." Patricia trailed off as something caught her eye off in the forest spreading out to their south. Looking intently off into the woods, she held up a hand and said, "Wait. Do you see that?"

"Milady?" Holly followed her gaze. A second later whatever it was in the forest flashed again, then again. Nudging her horse forward a little, the captain frowned, "Yes... I think it's a *signal*, milady."

The lady general chuckled and gave her a look, "You're the one with the troopers, Captain Schrader."

Holly looked back at her for a second before nodding, "Yes, ma'am." Turning to the handful of lancers standing a respectful distance behind them on the hill, she waved towards the forest and shouted, "You men! Mount up and go check out the woods down there! Someone's signaling!"

The men quickly jumped onto their horses and cantered off towards the forest, changing course a couple times as they zeroed in on the signal. Eventually they pulled up near the edge of the forest and dismounted, cautiously unslung their carbines and stalked into the trees. The one man left behind collected up the horses to wait for their return, and even from a distance they could see him shuffling back and forth anxiously as the minutes dragged by.

Patricia was starting to get a little nervous herself when the man in the distance suddenly straightened up. After a few seconds he made a thumbs-up towards the forest, turned and waved for them to come down to him. Looking over at her, Holly smiled a little and said, "Looks like good news, milady. Coming with?"

The lady general smiled back with relief, "Of course!"

Holly kicked her horse downhill and Patricia followed close behind. They quickly pulled up beside the lancer and his horses, and Patricia peered into the tangle of brush at the forest's edge as the captain asked, "What do you have?"

"Sir, ah, ma'am," the man started, flustered, "Well, they said there's a *lot* of them and you needed to get down here."

"That's... helpful." Holly replied, raising an eyebrow.

Patricia heard footsteps in the forest undergrowth behind the bushes, a lot more than the small group of lancers should have been able to make. Shadows moved behind the curtain of greenery and someone started pushing their way through as the man started, "Ah, they're coming out..."

He trailed off at the sight of the first soldier that pushed through into the daylight. Patricia didn't blame him. She had to stifle a gasp as the sight herself. She had served in the Royal Army for eighteen years, at the Dragon's Jaw, through the muddy hell of the Marchlands and the searing wastes of the Caliphate. She had led the Valkyrie Knights against the Red Brigades in the streets of the Capital itself. And she had rarely seen a more ragged soldier than the girl that came stumbling out of the forest and squinted up at her, raising a hand to shield her eyes from the midday sun.

The girl's shredded, sun-bleached uniform hung loose on her body, and Patricia saw where her fingertips had cracked and bled as the sunlight fell on her hands. Her deep blue eyes traveled unsteadily over them for a moment before landing on the stars on her collar. Jerking back a little, she straightened up and turned her upraised hand into a sketchy salute. Smiling a little, Patricia returned the gesture and remarked, "You look like you've seen better days, young lady. What's your unit?"

The girl dropped her salute and nervously hiked her slung rifle up on her shoulder. Patricia furrowed her eyebrows a little as she studied her.

Even though the girl was an obvious fugitive she still seemed to have all her equipment. Finally the girl replied, "Ah... yes, ma'am. Charlie, two two-four."

A couple more ragged soldiers had emerged from the forest behind the girl. As Patricia looked across them she noticed one of them was carrying a *machine gun*, a belt of ammunition loaded into the side and coiled into a hopper underneath, ready for combat. Soldiers running for their lives generally didn't take thirty-pound boat anchors and belts of ammunition with them. And they were from the Twenty-Fourth Infantry Regiment. Where had she heard that name before... *oh*. Her eyes widened as she asked, "You're part of *Eighth Division?* The last we heard you were on the far side of the ridge. How did you get out?"

The girl gestured over her shoulder tiredly at the snowcapped mass of the Dragonspines rising above the forest, "We, uh, hiked out. Through the mountains." She bit her lip nervously for a moment before plunging ahead, "Ma'am... do you guys... have any food? We haven't eaten for days."

Patricia didn't know if she wanted to laugh or cry. The Army of Drakenburg had been retreating as fast as their feet could carry them for the last week, and these soldiers had somehow *caught up* from the far side of Fire Ridge while marching through a mountain range. No wonder they looked like hell. No wonder they were starving. More and more soldiers had begun emerging from the forest all around them, and she smiled reassuringly and replied, "We'll get you some right away. How many of you are there?"

The girl thought for a moment, "About eight hundred." She paused for a moment and looked around as Holly audibly inhaled, "My dad would know more, he's around here somewhere..."

Eight hundred? That was a whole *battalion*. It made her head spin just thinking about it. Still, though, there were *some* limits to decorum in the Army. Raising an eyebrow archly, Patricia asked, "Your *dad?*"

"Uh... yes, ma'am." The girl swallowed and went on, "I mean, the Sergeant Major."

The lady general was in the middle of chuckling when one of the other soldiers, a young man who had a grimy bandage wrapped around his head in place of a hat, ribbed the girl, "Really, Sophie?"

Patricia felt like her heart had stopped. The girl was turning to glare at her companion when she felt the general's gaze bore into her and she turned back, eyes widening as Patricia asked, "Miss, *what's your name?*"

The girl answered, "Sophia Rose, ma'am."

Patricia blinked and started laughing, drawing confused stares from the growing crowd. Finally calming down, she wiped tears from her eyes, smiled broadly and replied, "Miss Rose. God, I haven't seen you for a while. How *is* your father these days?"

Sophia fidgeted nervously and was opening her mouth to answer when John Rose's familiar, gruff voice boomed out from the side, "I've been better, milady!" Patricia looked over to see the burly sergeant pushing his way towards her. He was older and gaunter than when she had seen him last and looked a little better than most of his soldiers, but not by much. Even his inexhaustible energy had clearly met its match in the Dragonspines, she thought as he went on, "Harassing my daughter, I see?"

"Oh yes," Patricia laughed, "She's as cute as ever. Took after you, I see."

Sergeant, well, apparently now Sergeant Major Rose chuckled, "Hardly. She's got her mother's brains." The man looked at his daughter, then around at the crowd of haggard soldiers still emerging from the forest, "Milady, we *are* hurting right now. Can we get some transport, or at least some rations?" He shook his head, "My men are dead on their feet, and I don't know how much farther we have to go."

Patricia smiled, "I'll get you both." Turning to Holly, she said, "Send a rider to my radio truck and have them get ahold of Corps. We need a transport company at the crossroads north of here immediately to take these guys back to Lorenvale." She chuckled, "Tell them we found an infantry battalion in the woods."

* * *

Two hours later, Sophia Rose climbed into the back of a truck as it sat idling on the dusty country road, one of the two dozen or so that had appeared to rescue them. Making out Tony's shape in the darkness under the thick canvas cover as he sat down against the sideboards, Sophia made her way over to him as more soldiers piled in behind her. Sitting down next to him, she set her rifle on the floor, put her head on his shoulder and instantly fell asleep.

Postscript

This book came together over the course of four years, at a rate of roughly one chapter per month from its beginnings in August 2014 to the conclusion of final edits in October 2018. Preparatory work and initial outlining (most of it quite different from what I actually wrote) took a year and a half before that. During this entire time I served as an officer in the United States Army, an organization I am sure any veteran can see reflected in these pages despite my own best efforts at worldbuilding. I wrote this book between three different duty stations, two stints at the National Training Center, huffing and puffing my way through Airborne School as a 30-year old and a deployment to Iraq for what I believe should be called the War of the False Caliph, but which is currently known blandly as Operation Inherent Resolve.

Many people have asked if I have written people I know into the story. I have not. Fact and fiction should not mix that way, especially for an author to butter up his friends or get petty revenge on his enemies. The world under the Five Moons has many similarities to our own, but a "coincidental" similarity of characters to my personal acquaintances is not one of them.

I would like to thank my first two fans, my father, Brian Weaver, and his old college roommate and fellow veteran of the Cold War Navy, "Doc" Batze. Both of them tore through my early manuscript and gave me valuable criticism, some of which I actually used to improve the story. My father holds the particular distinction of being my first *shipper*, although I don't think his preferred pairing of Sophia and Prince Adrian will have legs with the wider fandom. In his defense, when he first read through the manuscript it was ten chapters short of an ending.

I would also like to thank my mother, Heidi Schmitt-Weaver. She is a truly impressive woman and a real inspiration to me, and if my appreciation for horses comes across in the book it's entirely thanks to her. She also gave me some excellent advice on color coordination. Arilin's ball gown in Chapter 12 was originally a *peach and red* war crime against fashion.

Finally, I want to thank my comrades. Something too often overlooked in the modern day of an all-volunteer military, when memory of the great wars of the 20th century has faded, few make the choice to serve and those that do are hailed as heroes by the rest of society, is that service-members are ordinary people trying to meet the demands of an extraordinary job. I hope this came across in the book.

* * *

The above was written when I had finished writing *The Maiden's War*. Now that I am completing the process of *publishing* it I have a whole new group of people who deserve thanks and recognition. I decided to take the plunge and self-publish this novel after months of frustration with the traditional publishing process. After I launched my IndieGoGo campaign to publish the first edition a small group of people helped me to turn it into a success.

Edwin Boyette, a fellow veteran and promoter of independent comics, gave *The Maiden's War* an immense boost by getting it listed on indie-cron.com, featuring it many times on his YouTube show and even having me on as his guest. He suggested I produce a graphic novel set under the Five Moons in the future, and that's something that I may very well end up doing.

Many of my backers were fellow fans of YouTube supervillain and pop culture critic Overlord DVD. He was personally extremely supportive of my project and had no problem at all with my using his Discord as a platform to advertise and make sales. Hail, indeed!

I also want to thank another of my father's comrades from the Cold War Navy. Mike Zeiders provided an extremely generous dontation to my campaign and his words of encouragement as a fellow creator meant a great deal to me.

My artist, Bekarys Zhabagin, created an exciting and dynamic cover and was a joy to work with. As a writer it's amazing seeing your characters come to life and he pulled it off flawlessly. I'll never forget the feeling I had when I opened that first commissioned sketch and saw Sophia Rose looking back at me. His portfolio can be found at www.artstation.com/chelobek.

Finally I want to thank you, my readers. There are few better feelings than realizing that, as an author, people *want* to read your work and are willing to pay for it. I would not have been able to do this without your extremely generous support, and I hope the product in your hands has lived up to your expectations. You have helped me turn my dream into a reality, and I really can't thank you enough.

I hope that you've enjoyed *The Maiden's War*, and I hope you'll join me again as Sophia, Arilin and June's adventures continue in *Valkyrie Knight!*

www.ingramcontent.com/pod-product-compliance
Lightning Source LLC
Chambersburg PA
CBHW070928100726

47908CB00001B/135